The horsemen charged forward. Melli felt a sharp pain in her arm. She screamed with panic as she saw the arrow sticking out of her forearm . . .

Jack, seeing what had happened to her, lifted her to the top of the rise. She leaned on him for support, and to her amazement he turned and faced the horsemen.

His face was ashen with pain and anger. Arrows shot past them, Melli felt one graze her ear. She raised her arm to check for blood, and as she did so she felt a shifting of the air. Time seemed to slow down; the wind calmed for a fleeting moment; the mercenaries' horses reared in fear. The air shimmered and thickened and blasted into the horsemen, knocking them from their horses. Leaves took flight from the forest floor, tender saplings were uprooted, and branches snapped from trees.

The mercenaries were thrust back. One man's neck was broken as he was flung against a tree trunk, another man was impaled on his own spear. Melli looked on, as a horse fell on one man; the creature tried frantically to stand once more and in doing so kicked the man's skull in. She grabbed hold of Jack's arm for comfort: his flesh was cold and rigid.

The Baker's Boy

J.V. Jones

ORBIT

An *Orbit* Book

First published in the United States by Warner Books in 1995
First published in Great Britain by Orbit in 1996
Reprinted 1996 (twice), 1997 (three times)

Copyright © 1995 by J. V. Jones

The moral right of the author has been asserted

A CIP catalogue record for this book
is available from the British Library.

ISBN 1 85723 375 1

Printed in England by Clays Ltd, St Ives plc

Orbit
A Division of
Little, Brown and Company (UK)
Brettenham House
Lancaster Place
London WC2E 7EN

*This book is dedicated, with love,
to the memory of my father,
William Jones*

Prologue

"*T*he deed is done, master." Lusk barely had a second to notice the glint of the long-knife, and only a fraction of that second to realize what it meant.

Baralis sliced Lusk's body open with one forceful but elegant stroke, cleaving from the throat to the groin. Baralis shuddered as the body fell to the floor with a dull thud. He held his hand up to his face where he detected a sticky wetness: Lusk's blood. On impulse he drew his finger to his lips and tasted. It was like an old friend, coppery, salty and still warm.

He turned away from the now lifeless body and noticed his robes were covered in Lusk's blood; it was not a random spraying, the blood formed a scarlet arc against the gray. A crescent moon. Baralis smiled, it was a good omen—a crescent moon marked new beginnings, new births, new opportunities—the very currency he would deal in this night.

For now, though, he had some minor details to take care of. He must get changed for one thing; it would not be fitting to meet his beloved in bloodstained clothes, and there was the body to deal with. Lusk had been a faithful servant, unfortunately he had one tiny flaw—a tongue too prone to flap with indiscretion. No man with a fondness for ale and a tendency for drunken disclosure would jeopardize his carefully laid plans.

As he dragged the body onto a threadbare rug, his hands began to ache with the familiar, stabbing pain. He had taken a small amount of pain-relieving drug earlier to facilitate his use of the long-knife, but it had quickly worn off, as it did all too often these days, and he was reluctant to take more in case it interfered with his performance.

Baralis wielded the long-knife once more, marveling at the sharpness of blade and the way he, who had never been an expert in such matters, seemed to be endowed with a certain finesse when haft was in hand. He made the appropriate cuts and placed what were the better part of Lusk's features in a linen swath, which quickly soaked with blood. This really was most unpleasant. He had no liking for bloodshed, but would do what was expedient. He moved across the room and threw the swath onto the fire.

In the distance, a clock began to chime. Baralis counted eight tolls of the bell. It was time to get cleaned and changed. He would arrange to have the rest of Lusk's body taken away in the morning by the hulking dimwit Crope. Now *there* was a man who would tell no tales.

Less than an hour later, Baralis quietly left his apartments. His destination lay above him, but his route took him downward. Stealth was the greatest consideration; he could not risk being challenged by an over-zealous guard or engaged by a damn fool nobleman.

He made his way to the second cellar level. The candle he held was not usually necessary to him, but tonight was special; he would take no chances, tempt no fates.

Baralis crept to the innermost section of the second cellar. The dampness was already affecting the joints in his fingers and his hand trembled, but only partly from pain. The candle wavered and hot, liquid wax fell onto his hands. A sharp spasm coursed through his fingers. He dropped the candle and it went out, plunging Baralis into darkness. He hissed a curse; he had no flint to relight the flame and his hand was throbbing violently. He could not risk drawing light on this night. He would have to proceed in darkness.

He felt his way to the far wall and, using his hands like an insect's antennae, carefully felt for inconsistencies in the stone. He found them, manipulated them delicately with his fingertips, and stood aside while the wall moved backward. He stepped into the breach. Once inside, he repeated the same procedure on the wall of the passageway and the section fell back into place. Now he could begin to move upward.

Baralis smiled. Everything was going to plan: the lack of light was only a minor problem and, after all, what was a little darkness now compared with what was to come?

He felt his way through the passages with remarkable ease. He could not see openings and stairways, but he felt their approach and knew which ones were for him. He loved the dank underbelly of the castle; some knew it existed, but few knew how to enter it. Fewer still knew how to use it other than as a way to surprise a buxom lady's maid on her chamberpot. With the use of this network of passages, he could move around the castle undetected and find his way into many rooms. Rooms of both the lowly and the exalted. One should never underestimate the lowly, he mused. Some of his best information came from overhearing the casual gossip of a milkmaid or a cellar boy; who was plotting against whom, who was sleeping where they should not, and who had more gold than was good for them.

Tonight, however, he was not concerned with the lowly, tonight he would gain access to the most exalted room of all—the queen's bedroom.

He made his way upward, massaging his hand to ward off the cold. He was nervous, but then only a fool would be otherwise. Tonight he would enter the queen's chamber for the first time. He had spent many hours watching her, marking her routines, her womanly rhythms, recording every detail, every nuance. Recently, though, his cool observations had been enriched by the delight of expectation.

He approached her room and peered inside to check that she was asleep. The queen was lying fully clothed on the bed, her eyes closed. Baralis felt a tremor of anticipation run through his body. The queen had drunk the drugged wine: Lusk had done his job. With the utmost caution he entered the room. He decided to leave the gap in the wall open, in case of the need for quick escape. He immediately crossed over to the door of the chamber and drew the bolt. Nobody beside himself would enter this room tonight.

He approached the bed. The queen, normally so haughty and proud, looked impossibly vulnerable, and of course she was. Baralis shook her arm lightly, and then harder; she was out cold. He glanced over to the flagon of wine—it was empty, and so was the queen's golden cup. A ripple of anxiety showed on his brow. Surely the queen would never drink a whole flagon of wine? One of her ladies-in-waiting must have shared it. He was not unduly worried; the unfortunate girl would spend the night in an unusually deep sleep and wake slightly groggy in the morning. Still, it was a slipup, and he didn't like those. He made a mental note to check into it on the morrow.

Baralis regarded the queen with detachment for several minutes. Sleep suited her. It smoothed her brow and softened the set of her arrogant mouth. He put his hands beneath her, rolling her onto her stomach and then proceedeed to unlace her gown. This took some time, as his hands were stiff and the lacing intricate, but he endeavored, for he could not risk cutting the laces—that would arouse too much suspicion.

Eventually the ties were loosened and he rolled her onto her back. He pulled the front of her bodice down, revealing the pale curves of her breast. Although he had all but given up the pleasures of the flesh these past years, he could not help but respond to the sight. Poets and minstrels were forever harping on about the queen's beauty, but he had always remained unaffected by it—until now. Ironic, he thought, that she had to be out cold before he could find her desirable. He chuckled mirthlessly and lifted her skirts around her waist.

He loosened her undergarments and pulled them off, spreading her legs. Her thighs were soft and smooth, a little cool perhaps, but that was only to be expected, a side effect of the drug. Baralis found the coolness not unpleasant. He was, he realized with relief, sufficiently aroused. He had feared lack of performance; after all, the queen's fare was not to his normal taste. If he had any preference at all it was usually for the young, the very young. Her thighs might be soft, but she was no newly broken maiden and the mark of years could clearly be seen in the delicate blueness of her veins. She was beautiful, though, her legs long and slender, her rounded hips an enticement to any man. Unlike most women her age, her body had been spared the ravages of childbirth. Her breasts were still high and her belly flat as an altar-stone. He slipped down his leggings and entered the queen.

He was sure she was in her fertile span; he had spied on her often enough to know what time of the month she bled. He had heard of men in the past having the ability to sense which stage of her cycle a woman was in by just being in the room with her, feeling the ebb and flow of her menses as palpable force. Such illustrious accomplishments had eluded him, however, and he was forced to rely on more prosaic methods.

He had gleaned the knowledge he used this night from the wisewoman of the village he grew up in. Many young boys besides himself had been keen to know the best time to take a maiden without risk of begetting. He had been the only one to ask what time was best *for* begetting. The wisewoman had looked at Baralis with foreboding on her old, careworn face, but she had answered him anyway; it was not her habit to question motives.

Baralis had waited fourteen days from the onset of the queen's bleeding before making his move. But that was nothing—he had planned and waited years for this. Everything he had done in the past and would do in the future depended on this night. For years he had studied the portents, the signs, the stars, the philosophies: tonight was the time. He would be altering the course of the known world and securing his own destiny. The stars glittered brightly for him this night.

His attention returned to his task. He was nervous at first, but there was not a flicker from the queen, so he continued on more forcefully. He knew the quickening of desire and was surprised by its familiarity. As his excitement grew so did his abandon, and he pushed into her with all his strength. He had not expected to enjoy it and was surprised when he did. Eventually he reached his climax and his seed flowed deep within the queen.

As he withdrew from her, a trickle of blood escaped from the queen and ran lazily down her inner thigh; maybe he had been a little rough, but no matter. For the second time that evening he drew bloodied fingers up to his lips. He was not surprised to find the queen's blood tasted different: sweeter, richer. Quickly, he wiped the remains of the blood from her thigh. He pushed her legs together and pulled her skirts down.

Before he pulled up her bodice, Baralis traced his hand over the arc of her left breast, such pale perfection. On impulse he pinched it viciously, squeezing the delicate flesh cruelly between his fingers. He then arranged her body carefully and even placed a soft pillow beneath her head.

Now it was time for him to go away and wait. He would be back later to finish the job. He did not remove the lock on the door; he wanted no one disturbing the queen's peace while he was gone.

Bevlin looked into the deep, clear sky, searching. His eyes scanned the myriad of stars; he knew something was not right in the world this night. He felt the weight of it pressing his old bones and weakening his old bowels. When it came to sensing unease in the world his bowels were as sure as blossoms in springtime, if not as sweet smelling.

He sat, looking upward for almost an hour, and was beginning to blame the queasiness in his bowels on the greased duck he'd eaten earlier when it happened. A star in the far north grew suddenly brighter. Bevlin's bowels churned unpleasantly as the brightness lit up the northern sky. Only when it started to fall toward the horizon did he realize that it was not a complete star at all, but a portion of one: a meteor, racing toward the earth with a speed born of light. As he watched, it hit the atmosphere—but instead of burning up, the meteor split into two. The cleaving sent sparks and flames streaming into the air. When the light diminished, Bevlin could make out two separate pieces where one had been before. As they arced across the sky, trailing stardust in their wake, he saw that one shone with a white light and the other shone red as blood.

A single tear ran down Bevlin's cheek: he was surely too old for what was to come.

In all his years of looking at the stars and of reading the books, he had seen no reference, no prophecy of what he had just witnessed. Even now, as the two meteors raced toward oblivion on the far side of the horizon, he could hardly believe what had happened. He went inside quite sure there would be nothing else to see.

In a way it was quite a relief to him. He had waited for so long for a message in the sky, and now that it had happened, a subtle tension uncoiled within him. He did not know what it meant or what action, if any, should be taken. He *did* know his bowels had been right and that meant the greased duck was fine, which was just as well, as there is nothing like a great sign in the sky to make one hungry. Bevlin laughed merrily on his way to the kitchen, but his laughter had turned slightly hysterical by the time he got there.

Bevlin's kitchen also served as his study: the huge oak table was covered in books, scrolls and manuscripts. Having sliced himself a fair portion of duck and loaded an abundant helping of congealed fat on top, he settled amidst the cushions on his old stone bench and relieved the pressure in his bowels by farting loudly. Now it was time to get down to work.

Baralis returned to his chamber and was met by the pleasing smell of cooked meat. Puzzled but hungry, it took him a few seconds to realize where the odor came from. Resting amongst the glowing embers in the fireplace was what looked like an irregular, burnt, cut of meat. It was, Baralis recognized, what was left of Lusk's features.

"Too well done for me," he said, relishing the joke and the sound of his own voice. "By Borc! I'm hungry. Crope!" he shouted loudly, sticking his head out of the door. "Crope! You idle dimwit, bring me food and wine."

A few seconds later Crope appeared in the passageway, huge and wide, with a disproportionately small head. Crope managed to appear both menacing and stupid at the same time. "You called, my lord?" He spoke in a surprisingly gentle voice.

"Yes, I called, you fool. Who do you think called, Borc himself?" Crope looked suitably sheepish but not too worried, he could tell when his master was in a good mood.

"I know it's late, Crope, but I'm hungry. Bring me food!" Baralis considered for a moment. "Bring me red meat, rare, and some good red wine, not the rubbish you brought me yesterday. If those stinking louts in the kitchen try to palm you off with anything less than a fine vintage, tell them they will have to answer to me." Crope balefully nodded his consent and left.

Baralis knew Crope didn't like to perform any task that involved talking to people. He was shy and awkward around them, which was, as Baralis saw it, a definite advantage in a servant. Lusk had been too talkative for his own good. He glanced to the left of the door, where what remained of Lusk lay wrapped in a faded rug. Crope had not even noticed the unseemly bundle or, if he had, it would never occur to him to mention it: he was like an obedient dog—loyal and unquestioning. Baralis smiled at the vision of Crope appearing in the kitchen this late at night; he was sure to give the light-fingered kitchen staff quite a shock.

Before long, Crope returned with a jug of wine and a portion of meat so rare, pink juices oozed from the flesh and onto the platter. Baralis dismissed Crope and poured himself a cup of the rich and heady liquid. He held it up to the light and reveled in its dark, crimson color, then brought the goblet to his lips. The wine was warm and sweet, redolent of blood.

The events of tonight had given him a voracious hunger. He cut himself a thick slice of the fleshy meat. As he did so, the knife slipped in his hand and cut neatly into his thumb. Automatically, he raised his finger to his face and suckled the small wound closed. He shuddered suddenly, half remembering a fragment of an old rhyme, something about the taste of blood. He struggled for the memory and lost. Baralis shrugged. He would eat, then take a brief nap, until the better part of the night was over with.

* * *

Many hours later, just before the break of dawn, Baralis once more slipped into the queen's chamber. He had to be especially careful—many castle attendants were up and about, baking bread in the kitchens, milking cows in the dairy, starting fires. He was not too concerned, though, as this last task would not take too long.

He was a little worried when he saw the queen was in exactly the same position as when he had left her, but closer inspection revealed that she was breathing strongly. The memory of the previous evening was playing in his loins, and he had an urge to mount her again, but calculation mastered desire and he willed himself to do what must be done.

He dreaded performing a Searching. He had only done one once before, and the memory still haunted him to this day. He had been a young buck, arrogant in his abilities, way ahead of his peers. Great things were hoped for him—and hadn't they been proved right? He had a ravening thirst for knowledge and ability. He had been proud, yes, but then, were not all great men proud? Everything he read about he tried, desperate to accomplish and move on, move forward to greater achievements. He had the quickest mind in his class, outpacing and eventually outgrowing his teachers. He'd rushed forward with the speed of a charging boar, the pride of his masters and the envy of his friends.

One day when he was thirteen summers old, he came across a musty, old manuscript in the back of the library. Hands shaking with nervous excitement, he unraveled the fragile parchment. He was at first a little disappointed. It contained the usual instructions—drawing of light and fire, healing colds. Then at the end a ritual called a Searching was mentioned. A Searching, it explained, was a means to tell if a woman was with child.

He read it greedily. Searching had never been mentioned by his teachers; perhaps it was something they could not do, or even better, something they didn't know of. Eager to attain a skill which he supposed his masters not to have, he slid the manuscript up his sleeve and took it home with him.

Some days later he was ready to try his new ability, but

who to try it on? The women in the village would not let him lay his hands upon them. That left his mother, and it was certain *she* would not be with child. However, having no other choice, he resigned himself to using his mother as a guinea pig.

Early the following morning, he stole into his parents' bedroom, careful to ensure his father had left for the fields. It was a source of shame to him that his father was a common farmer, but he took solace in the fact that his mother was of better stock: she was a salt merchant's daughter. He loved his mother deeply and was proud of her obvious good breeding; she was respected in the village and was consulted by the elders on everything from matters of harvest to matchmaking.

Baralis' mother had awoken when her son came into the room. He turned to leave but she beckoned him in. "Come, Barsi, what do you want?" She wiped the sleep from her eyes and smiled with tender indulgence.

"I was about to try a new skill I learnt," he muttered guiltily.

His mother made the error of mistaking guilt for modesty. "Barsi, my sweet, this new trick, can you do it while I am awake?" Her face was a picture of love and trust. Baralis momentarily felt misgiving.

"Yes, Mother, but I think I might be better trying it on someone else."

"Copper pots! What nonsense. Try it on me now—as long as it doesn't turn my hair green, I don't mind." His mother settled herself comfortably amid the pillows and patted the bedside.

"It won't do you any harm, Mother, it's a Searching . . . to tell if you are well." Baralis found the lie easy. It was not the first time he had lied to his mother.

"Well," she laughed indulgently, "do your worst!"

Baralis laid his hands on his mother's stomach. He could feel the warmth of her body through the thin fabric of her nightgown. His fingers spread out and he concentrated on the search. The manuscript had warned that it was more a mental than physical exercise, so he focused the fullness of his thoughts on his mother's belly.

He felt the blood rushing through her veins and the forceful rhythm of her heart. He felt the discharge of juices in her stomach and the gentle push of her intestines. He adjusted his hands lower; he met his mother's eyes and she gave him a look of encouragement. He found the spot the manuscript spoke of: a fertile redness. Excitement building within him, he explored the muscled embrace that was his mother's womb.

He detected something: a delicate burgeoning. He was unsure; he searched deeper. His mother's face was beginning to look worried, but he paid her no mind. His abandon was growing; there was something there, something new and separate. It was wonderful and exhilarating. He wanted to touch the presence with his mind; he dug deeper and his mother let out a cry of pain.

"Barsi, stop!" Her beautiful face was contorted with agony.

He panicked and tried to withdraw as quickly as possible, but as he drew back, he dragged something out with him. He felt a shifting, a dislodging and then the tear of flesh. Terrified, he removed his hands. His mother was screaming hysterically and she doubled up in pain, clutching her stomach. Baralis noticed the quick flare of blood on the sheets. The screams! He could not bear her agonized screams! He didn't know what to do. He could not leave her alone to call for help. Spasms racked his mother's body and the blood flowed like a river, soaking the white sheets with its bright gaudiness.

"Mother, please stop, I'm sorry. I didn't mean to hurt you, please stop." Tears of panic coursed down his cheeks. "Mother. I'm sorry." He hugged her to him, heedless of the blood. "I'm sorry," he repeated, his voice a frightened whisper.

He held his mother as she bled to death. It took only minutes, but to Baralis it seemed like an eternity, as he felt the strength and life wane from her beloved body.

Baralis stirred himself from his recollection. That was then, many years ago, when he had been young and green. He was a master himself now. There would be no mistakes caused by inexperience. He now understood that to have tried such a mental task when only a boy was pure stupidity. He'd barely known what "being with child" meant, and had only the whisperings of adolescence as his guide to how children were conceived.

Baralis realized he was taking a risk performing a Searching on the queen, but he had to know—conception was at the best of times a chance event. He dared not think of what he would do if his seed had not found favor. Part of him was aware it might be far too early to tell, but the other part of him suspected that he would be able to discern a tiny change, and that would be enough.

He bent over the body of the queen and placed his hands on her stomach. He knew straight away that the fabric of her elaborate court gown was too heavy. He lifted her skirts once more and was surprised to see he had forgotten to replace her undergarments. It was just as well, really, he thought, as *they* were uncommonly bulky, too.

More experienced he may have been than when he was thirteen, but he wished his hands were still youthful. It was a strain to spread his fingers full-out upon her belly, and he bit his lip in pain; he could not allow his own discomfort to interfere with the endeavor. He found the right place straight away; he was no novice now.

He began the Searching. It was so familiar, the cloistered warmth of the organs, the pulsing redness of the blood vessels, the heat of the liver. He proceeded with filigree fineness, deep within the queen's body and deeper within her womb. He felt the intricate tanglings of muscle and tendon, felt the sensuous curve of the ovaries. And then he perceived something, barely discernible, hardly there, a gentle ripple on a pond, a pulsing other. A life minutely separate and distinguishable from that of the queen. Scarcely a life at all, more a glimmering suggestion . . . but it was there.

Elated, he made no quick move to withdraw—with infinite slowness and patience he removed himself. Drawing away with a surgeon's skill. Just as he left, he felt the other presence assert itself: a dark pressure.

Baralis withdrew. There had been something in that last instant of contact which gave him cause to be wary, but his misgivings were eaten up and forgotten by the joy of his success.

He removed his hands from the queen and straightened her dress. She moaned lightly, but he was not concerned—she would not wake for several hours. Time for him to leave. With a light tread he moved toward the door and unbolted it. One last pause to admire his handiwork and then he was off, back to his chambers, barely casting a shadow in the thin light of dawn.

One

"*N*o, you're wrong there, Bodger. Take it from me, young women ain't the best for tumblin'. Yes, they look good on the outside, all fair and smooth, but when it comes to a good rollickin', you can't beat an old nag." Grift swigged his ale and smiled merrily at his companion.

"Well, Grift, I can't say that you're right. I mean, I'd rather have a tumble any day with the buxom Karri than old widow Harpit."

"Personally, Bodger, I wouldn't say no to either of them!" Both men laughed loudly, banging their jugs of ale on the table as was the custom of the castle guards. "Hey there, you boy, what's your name? Come here and let me have a look at you." Jack stepped forward, and Grift made a show of looking him up and down. "Cat got your tongue, boy?"

"No, sir. My name is Jack."

"Now that is what I'd call an uncommon name!" Both men erupted once more into raucous laughter. "*Jack* boy, bring us more ale, and none of that watered-down pond filler."

Jack left the servants' hall and went in search of ale. It wasn't his job to serve guards with beer, but then neither was scrubbing the huge, tiled kitchen floor, and he did that, too. He didn't relish having to see the cellar steward, as Willock had cuffed him around the ears many a time. He hurried down the stone passageways. It was drawing late and he would be due in the kitchens soon.

Some minutes later, Jack returned with a quart of foaming ale. He had been pleasantly surprised to find that Willock was not in the beer cellar, and he had been seen to by his assistant. Pruner had informed him with a wink that Willock was off sowing his wild oats. Jack was not entirely sure what this meant, but imagined it was some part of the brewing process.

"It was definitely Lord Maybor," Bodger was saying as Jack entered the hall. "I saw him with my own eyes. Thick as thieves they were, he and Lord Baralis, talking fast and furious. Course when they saw me, you should have seen 'em scramble. Faster than women from the middens."

"Well, well, well," said Grift with a telling raise of his eyebrows. "Who would have guessed that? Everyone knows that Maybor and Baralis can't stand the sight of each other, why I never seen them exchange a civil word. Are you sure it was them?"

"I'm not blind, Grift. It was both of them, in the gardens behind the private hedges, as close as a pair of nuns on a pilgrimage."

"Well, I'll be a flummoxed ferret!"

"If the codpiece fits, Grift," chirped Bodger gleefully.

Grift noticed Jack's presence. "Talking of codpieces, here's a boy so young, he hasn't got anything to put in one!" This struck Bodger as so hilarious he fell off his chair with laughter.

Grift took this chance, while Bodger was recovering, to haul himself off his bench and pull Jack to one side. "What did you just hear of what me and Bodger were saying, boy?" The guard squeezed Jack's arm and fixed him with a watery gaze.

Jack was well versed in the intrigues of the castle and knew the safest thing to say. "Sir, I heard nothing save for some remark about a codpiece." Grift's fingers ground painfully into his flesh, his voice was low and threatening.

"For your sake, boy, I hope you're speaking the truth. If I was to find out you're lying to me, boy, I'd make you very sorry." Grift gave Jack's arm one final squeeze and twist and let it go. "Very sorry, indeed, boy. Now get you off."

Grift turned to his companion and carried on as if the nasty little scene had not occurred. "You see, Bodger, an older woman is like an overripe peach: bruised and wrinkled on the outside, but sweet and juicy within." Jack hastily gathered up the empty jug of ale and ran as fast as his legs could carry him to the kitchen.

Things were not going well for him today. Master baker Frallit was in the sort of black mood that made his normal demeanor seem almost pleasant by comparison. It should have been Tilly's job to scrub the large baking slabs clean, but Tilly had a way with Frallit, and one smile of her plump, wet lips ensured she would do no dirty work. Of all the things he had to do, Jack hated scrubbing the huge stone slabs the worst. They had to be scoured with a noxious mixture of soda and lye; the lye burnt into his hands causing blisters, and sometimes his skin peeled off. He then had to carry the unwieldy slabs, which were almost as heavy as he himself, into the kitchen yard to be washed off.

He dreaded carrying the huge stones, for they were brittle, and if dropped would shatter into a hundred pieces. The baking slabs were Frallit's pride and joy; he swore they baked him a superior loaf, claiming the dull and weighty stone prevented the bread from baking too fast. Jack had recently found out the penalty for shattering one of the master baker's precious cooking slabs.

Several weeks back, Frallit, who had been drinking heavily all day, had discovered one of his slabs missing. He'd wasted no time in confronting Jack, whom he found hiding amongst the pots and pans in the cook's side of the kitchen. "You feeble-witted moron," Frallit had cried, dragging him from his hiding place by his hair. "Do you know what you have done, boy? Do you?" It was obvious to Jack the master baker did not expect a reply. Frallit made to cuff him round the ears, but Jack dodged skillfully and the master baker was left slapping air. Looking back on the incident now, Jack realized the dodge had been a major mistake. Frallit would have probably given him a sound thrashing and left it at that, but what the master baker hated more than anything was being made to look a fool—and in front of the sly but succulent Tilly, no less. The man's rage was terrifying and culminated with him pulling a fistful of Jack's hair out.

It seemed to Jack that his hair was always a target. It was as if Frallit was determined to make all his apprentices as bald as himself. Jack had once woken to find that his head had been shorn like a sheep. Tilly threw the chestnut locks onto the fire and informed him that Frallit had ordered the chop because he suspected lice. Jack's hair got the only revenge it could: it grew back with irritating quickness.

In fact, growing in general was starting to become quite a problem. Not a week went by without some evidence of his alarming increase in height. His breeches caused him no end of embarrassment; four months ago they'd rested discreetly about his ankles, now they were threatening to expose his shins. And such horrifyingly white and skinny shins they were! He was convinced that everyone in the kitchens had noticed the pitiful expanse of flesh.

Being a practical boy, he'd decided to make himself another more flattering pair. Unfortunately needlework was a skill that required patience not desperation, and new breeches became an unattainable dream. So now he was reduced to the unauspicious step of wearing his current ones low. They hung limply around his hips, secured by a length of coarse twine. Jack had sent many a desperate prayer to Borc, begging that the twine in question didn't give way in the presence of anyone important—especially women.

His height was becoming more and more of a problem: for one thing, his growth upward bore no relation to his growth outward, and Jack had the strong suspicion he now possessed the physique of a broom handle. Of course, the worst thing was that he had started to outgrow his superiors. He was a head above Tilly and an ear above Frallit. The master baker had started to treat Jack's height as a personal affront, and could often be heard muttering words to the effect that a tall boy would never a decent baker make.

Jack's main duty as baker's boy was to ensure the fire under the huge baking oven did not go out. The oven was the size of a small room, and it was where all the bread for the hundreds of courtiers and servants who lived in the castle was baked early every morning.

Frallit prided himself on baking fresh each day, and to this end he had to wake at five each morning to supervise the baking. The massive stone oven had to be kept going through the night, every night, for if it was left to go out, the oven would take one full day to fire up to the temperature required for baking. So it was Jack's job to watch the oven at night.

Every hour Jack would open the stone grate at the bottom of the huge structure and feed the fire within. He didn't mind the chore at all. He became accustomed to grabbing his sleep in one-hour intervals, and during winter, when the kitchen was bitterly cold, he would fall asleep close to the oven, his thin body pressed against the warm stone.

Sometimes, in the delicious time between waking and sleeping, Jack could imagine his mother was still alive. In the last months of her illness, his mother's body had felt as hot as the baking oven. Deep within her breast there was a source of heat that destroyed her more surely than any flame. Jack remembered the feel of her body pressed against his— her bones were as light and brittle as stale bread. Such terrible frailty, he couldn't bear to think of it. And, for the most part, with a day full of hauling sacks of flour from the granary and buckets from the well, of scraping the oven free of cinders and keeping the yeast from turning bad, he managed to keep the ache of losing her at the back of his mind.

Jack found he had a talent for calculating the quantities of flour, yeast, and water required to make the different bread doughs required each day; he could even reckon faster than the master baker himself. He was wise enough to conceal his talents, though. Frallit was a man who guarded his expertise jealously.

Recently Frallit had allowed him the privilege of shaping the dough. "You must knead the dough like it were a virgin's breast," he would say. "Lightly at first, barely a caress, then firmer once it relents." The master baker could be almost lyrical after one cup of ale; it was the *second* cup that turned him sour.

Shaping the dough was a step up for Jack, it signaled that he would soon be accepted as an apprentice baker. Once he was a fully fledged apprentice, his future at the castle would be secured. Until then he was at the mercy of those who were above him, and in the competitive hierarchy of castle servants that meant everyone.

Somehow, from the time he left the servants' hall to the time upon his arrival in the kitchens, night had fallen. Time, Jack found, had a way of slipping from him, like thread from a newly made spindle. One minute he would be setting the dough to rise, the next Frallit would be cuffing him for leaving it so long that it had toughened and was attracting flies. It was just that there was so much to think about, and his imagination had a way of creeping up on him. He only had to look at a wooden table and he was off imagining that the tree it came from once gave shade to a long-dead hero.

"You're late," said Frallit. He was standing by the oven, arms folded, watching Jack's approach.

"Sorry, Master Frallit."

"*Sorry*," mimicked Frallit. "*Sorry*. You damn well should be sorry. I'm getting tired of your lateness. The heat in the oven has dropped perilously low, boy. Perilously low." The master baker took a step forward. "And who'll get into trouble if the fire goes out and there's no baking for a day? I will. That's who." Frallit grabbed his mixing paddle from the shelf and slammed it viciously against Jack's arm. "I'll teach you not to put my good reputation at risk." Finding a place that took the paddle nicely, he continued the beating until forced to stop due to an inconvenient shortness of breath.

Quite a crowd had gathered at the sound of shouting. "Leave the boy alone, Frallit," one wretched scullery maid risked saying. Willock, the cellar steward, silenced her with a quick slap to her face.

"Be quiet, you insolent girl. This is none of your business. The master baker has a perfect right to do whatever he pleases to any boy under him." Willock turned to face the rest of the servants. "And let it be a lesson to you all." The cellar steward then nodded pleasantly to Frallit before shooing the crowd away.

Jack was shaking, his arm was throbbing—the paddle had left deep imprints upon his flesh. Tears of pain and rage flared like kindling. He screwed up his eyes tightly, determined not to let them fall.

"And where were you this time?" The master baker didn't

wait for an answer. "Daydreaming, I bet. Head in the clouds, fancying you're something better than the likes of us." Frallit swept close, grabbing Jack's neck—the smell of ale was heavy on his breath. "Let me tell you, boy, your mother was a whore, and you're nothing but the son of a whore. You ask anyone in this castle, they'll tell you what she was. And what's more, they'll tell you she was a *foreign* whore at that."

Jack's head felt heavy with blood, spent air burnt in his lungs. There was one thought in his mind—the pain was nothing, the risk of ridicule wasn't important—he had to *know*. "Where did she come from?" he cried.

He'd spoken the one thing that mattered most in his life. It was a question about himself as much as his mother—for wherever she came from so did he. He had no father and accepted that as his fate, but his mother owed him something, something she had failed to give him—a sense of self. Everyone in the castle knew who they were and where they came from. Jack had watched them, he'd witnessed their unspoken confidence. Not for them a life of unanswered questions. No. They knew their place, their personal histories, their grandfathers and grandmothers. And armed with such knowledge, they knew themselves.

Jack was envious of such knowledge. He too wanted to join in conversations about family, to casually say, "Oh, yes, my mother's family came from Calfern, west of the River Ley," but he was denied the pleasure of self-assurance. He knew nothing about his mother, her birthplace, her family, or even her true name. They were all mysteries, and occasionally, when people taunted and called him a bastard, he hated her for them.

Frallit eased up on his hold. "How would I know where your mother came from?" he said. "I never had call for her services." The master baker gave Jack's neck one final squeeze and then let go. "Now get some wood in the oven before I change my mind and decide to throttle you all the way." He turned and left Jack to his work.

Bevlin was expecting a visitor. He didn't know who it

would be, but he felt the approach. Time to grease up another duck, he thought absently. Then he decided against it. After all, not everybody had a taste for his particular favorite. Better be safe and roast that haunch of beef. True, it was a few weeks old, but that hardly mattered—maggot-addled beef had never killed anyone, and it was said to be more tender and juicy than its fresher counterpart.

He hauled the meat up from the cellar, sprinkled it with salt and spices, wrapped it in large dock leaves, and buried it amongst the glowing embers of the huge fireplace. Roasting beef was a lot more trouble than greased duck. He hoped his guest appreciated it.

When the visitor finally arrived, it was dark outside. Bevlin's kitchen was warm and bright, and fragrant cooking smells filled the air. "Come in, friend," croaked Bevlin in response to the knock on the door. "It's open."

The man who entered was much younger than the wiseman had expected. He was tall and handsome; gold strands in his hair caught the firelight in defiance of the dirt from the road. His clothes, however, had little fight in them. They were an unremarkable gray; even the leathers that had once been black or tan bore testament to the persistence of the dirt. The only bright spot was a handkerchief tied about his neck. Bevlin fancied there was something touching about its faded scarlet glory.

The stranger looked a little saddle weary to the wiseman, but then that was to be expected; after all, Bevlin lived in a very remote spot—two days ride from the nearest village, and even then the village was no more than three farms and a middens.

"Welcome, stranger. I wish you joy of the night; come share my food and hearth." Bevlin smiled: the young man was surprised to find himself expected, but he covered it well.

"Thank you, sir. Is this the home of the wiseman Bevlin?" The stranger's voice was deep and pleasant, a trace of country accent went unconcealed.

"I am Bevlin, wiseman is not for me to say."

"I am Tawl, Knight of Valdis." He bowed with grace. Bevlin knew all about bowing; he had stayed at the greatest courts in the Known Lands, bowed to the greatest leaders. The young man's bow was an act of newly learned beauty.

"A knight of Valdis! I might have guessed it. But why have I been sent a mere novice? I expected someone older." Bevlin was well aware that he had insulted the young man, but he did so without malice, to test the temper and bearing of his visitor. He was not disappointed with the young man's reply:

"I expected someone *younger,* sir," he said, smiling gently, "but I will not hold your old age against you."

"Well spoken, young man. You must call me Bevlin— all this 'sir' nonsense makes me a little nervous. Come, let us feast first and talk later. Tell me, would you prefer salt-roasted beef or a nice greased duck?"

"I think I would prefer the beef, sir, er, Bevlin."

"Excellent," replied Bevlin, moving into the kitchen. "I think I'll have the duck myself!"

"Here, drink some of this lacus. It will calm the rage in your belly." The wiseman poured a silvery liquid into a cup, and offered it to his companion. They had eaten and supped in silence—the knight had resisted Bevlin's attempts to draw him into casual conversation. Bevlin was willing to overlook the young man's reticence, as it could conceivably be due to gut sickness. Looking decidedly pale and sickly, the knight tasted the proffered drink. He drank reluctantly at first, but as the liquid found favor on his tongue, he drained the cup empty. Like so many men, in so many ages, he held his cup out for more.

"What in creation is this stuff? It tastes like—like nothing I've ever had before."

"Oh, it's quite common in some parts of the world, I assure you. It's made by gently squeezing the lining of a goat's stomach." The visitor's face was a blank, and so Bevlin elaborated. "Surely you have heard of the nomads who roam the great plains?" Tawl nodded. "Well, the plains goats are the tribes' livelihood; they provide the nomads with milk and coarse wool, and when they are killed, they provide meat and this rather unusual liquid. It's a rare goat that favors the plain. A most useful creature to have around, don't you agree?" The young man nodded reluctantly, but Bevlin could see he was already beginning to feel much better.

"The most interesting thing about the lacus is that served cold it cures ailments of the belly and—how should I put it—the, er, private parts. When the lacus is warmed, however, it changes its nature and provides relief from pain of the joints and the head. I have even heard said that when condensed and applied as a paste to wounds, it can quicken healing and stave off infection."

Bevlin was feeling a little guilty. He realized the addled beef was responsible for his visitor's illness, and decided that before the young man left he would make amends by giving Tawl his last remaining skin of lacus.

"Is the lacus more than the sum of its ingredients?"

The knight had keen perception. Bevlin revised his opinion of him. "One might say there is an added element that owes nothing to the goat."

"Sorcery."

Bevlin smiled. "You are most forthright. All too often these days people are afraid of naming the unseen. Call it what you like, it makes no difference, it won't lessen its retreat."

"But there are still those who . . ."

"Yes, there are those who still practice." The wiseman stood up. "Most think it would be better if they didn't."

"What do you think?" asked the knight.

"I think that like many things—like the stars in the heavens, like the storms in the sky—it is misunderstood, and people usually fear what they can't comprehend." Bevlin felt he'd said enough. He had no desire to satisfy the youthful curiosity of the knight. If Tawl was to find anything out, let it be through experience—he was too old to play teacher. Guiding the conversation around to its former topic, the wiseman said, "I think maybe you should sleep for now. You are weak and need to rest. We will talk in the morning."

The knight recognized the dismissal and stood up. As he did so, Bevlin caught a glimpse of a mark on his forearm. A branding—two circles, one within the other. The inner circle had been newly branded: the skin was still raised and puckered. A knife wound of some sort ran through the center of both circles. There were stitches still holding it closed. It seemed an unusual place for an enemy's blade to fall.

Battle scars aside, the knight was young to have gained the middle circle. Bevlin had guessed him to be a novice. Perhaps he should have spoken further about that which made the lacus sing. The knight would have been keen to learn—the second circle marked scholarship, not just skill with a blade. Still, he was offering the knight a chance for glory—why should he offer him knowledge as well?

As soon as Melli entered the chambers of her father, Lord Maybor, she made a beeline for his bedroom, in which was to be found that most precious of objects: a looking glass. This was the only glass that Melli had access to, as they were considered too valuable for the use of children. Melli drew back the heavy red curtains and let the light shine into the luxuriant bedchamber.

Melli considered the chamber—all crimson and gold—to be a little gaudy for her taste, and resolved that when she had a chamber of her own one day, she would show greater discrimination in the choosing of furnishings. She knew well that the rug she walked on was priceless and that the looking glass she had come to use was supposed to be the most beautiful one in the kingdom, better even than the one possessed by the queen. Still, she was not greatly impressed by these trappings of her father's great wealth.

Melli moved directly in front of the mirror. She was disappointed by what she saw there: her chest was still flat as a board. She breathed in deeply, pushing her meager chest out, trying to imagine what it would be like to have womanly breasts. She was sure they would arrive anyday now, but whenever she stole into her father's rooms, her image remained unchanged.

Part of Melli longed to become a woman. Oh to be able to use her lady's name, Melliandra, instead of the rather short and decidedly unimpressive Melli. How she hated that name! Her older brothers would tease her mercilessly: *Melli, Melli, thin and smelly!* She'd heard that rhyme a thousand times. If only her blood would start to flow, for then she would be allowed to use her proper name . . . and then there was the court dress.

All young ladies were given a special court dress on reaching womanhood. Wearing them, they would be presented to the queen. Here Melli knew that she, as Lord Maybor's daughter, would have a definite advantage. He was one of the richest men in the Four Kingdoms and would certainly use the presentation of his daughter at court as an opportunity to show off his wealth.

She had already decided what her dress was to be made from: silver tissue—expensive and exquisitely beautiful, made from combining silk with threads of purest silver. The art of weaving such fabric had long been lost in the north, and it would have to be specially imported from the far south. Melli knew nothing would please her father more than spending his money on such a publicly displayable commodity.

Becoming a woman was not all good, though; at some point she would be forced to marry. Melli knew well she would have little say in the matter—as a daughter, she was considered the sole property of her father and would be used as such. When the time came, he would trade her for whatever he deemed suitable: land, prestige, titles, wealth, alliances . . . such was the worth of women in the Four Kingdoms.

She had no great liking for the pimply, simpering boys of the court. She'd even heard mention of a possible match between herself and Prince Kylock; after all, they were the same age. The very thought made her shiver; she disliked the cold and arrogant boy. He might well be rumored to be learned beyond his years and an expert in swordplay, but he rather scared her, and something in his handsome, dark face raised warnings in Melli's heart.

She was about to leave the bedchamber when she heard the sound of footsteps and then voices in the other room. Her father! He would be most annoyed to find her here and might even punish her. So, rather than make her presence known by leaving, she decided to stay put until her father and his companion left. She heard the deep, powerful voice of her father, and then another voice: rich and beguiling. There was something familiar about the second voice. She knew she'd heard it before. . . .

Lord Baralis! That was who it belonged to. Half the women at court found him fascinating, the other half were repulsed by him.

Melli was puzzled, for although she knew little of politics, she was aware that her father and Baralis hated each other. She moved closer to the door to hear what they would say. She was not an eavesdropper, she told herself, she was just curious. Lord Baralis was speaking, his tone coolly persuasive.

"It will be a disaster for our country if King Lesketh is allowed to make peace with the Halcus. Word will soon spread that the king has no backbone, and we will be overrun with enemies knocking at our door, snatching the very land from under our feet."

There was a pause and Melli heard the rustle of silk followed by the pouring of wine. Baralis spoke again. "We both know the Halcus won't be content with stealing our water— they will set their greedy eyes upon our land. How long do you think Halcus will keep this proposed peace?" There was a brief hush, and then Baralis answered his own question. "They will keep the peace just long enough for them to mass and train an army, and then, before we know it, they will be marching right into the heart of the Four Kingdoms."

"You need not tell *me* that peace at Horn Bridge would be a disaster, Baralis." Her father's voice was ripe with contempt. "For over two hundred years, well before any family of *yours* came to the Four Kingdoms, we had exclusive rights over the River Nestor. To give up those rights in a peace agreement is a serious miscalculation."

"Indeed, Maybor," Lord Baralis again, his tone calming, but not without irony, "the River Nestor is lifeblood to our farmers in the east, and, if I am not mistaken, it runs through much of *your* eastern holdings."

"You know well it does, Baralis!" Melli caught the familiar sound of anger in her father's voice. "You are well aware that if this peace goes through, it will be *my* lands, and the lands set aside for my sons, that will be affected the most. That is the only reason why you are here today." Maybor's voice dropped ominously low. "Mistake me not, Baralis. I will be drawn no further into your web of intrigue than I deem fitting."

There was silence for a moment and then Lord Baralis spoke, his manner changed from moments earlier. It was almost conciliatory: "You are not the only lord who will suffer from peace, Maybor. Many men with eastern holdings will support us."

There was a brief pause, and when Baralis continued, his voice was almost a whisper. "The most important thing to do now is to disable the king and prevent the planned meeting with the Halcus at Horn Bridge."

This was treason. Melli was beginning to regret listening in; her body had grown cold and she found herself trembling. She could not bring herself to move away from the door.

"It must be soon, Maybor," murmured Baralis, his beautiful voice edged with insistency.

"I know that, but must it be tomorrow?"

"Would you risk Lesketh making peace at Horn Bridge? He is set to do so and the meeting is only one month hence." Melli heard her father grunt in agreement. "Tomorrow is the best chance we have; the hunting party will be small, just the king and his favorites. You yourself can go along to avoid suspicion."

"I can only go ahead with this, Baralis, if I have your assurance that the king will recover from his injuries."

"How can you ask that, Maybor, when it will be your man who will aim and fire the arrow?"

"Don't play games with me, Baralis." The fury in her father's voice was unmistakable. "Only you know what foul concoction will be on the arrowhead."

"I assure you, Lord Maybor, that the foul concoction will do nothing more than give the king a mild fever for a few weeks and slow down the healing of the wound. In two months time, the king will appear to be back to normal." Melli could detect a faint ambiguity to Lord Baralis' words.

"Very well, I will send my man to you tonight," said her father. "Be ready with the arrow."

"One will be enough?"

"My man is a fine marksman, he will have need of no

more. Now, I must be gone. Be discreet when you depart, lest you be marked by prying eyes."

"Have no fear, Maybor, no one will see *me* leave. One more thing, though. I suggest that once the arrow is removed from the king's body, it should be destroyed."

"Very well, I will see to it." Her father's voice was grim. "I wish you good day, Baralis." Melli heard the door close and then the soft tinkle of glass as Baralis poured himself another cup of wine.

"You can come out now, pretty one," he called. She could not believe he was addressing her. She froze, not daring to take a breath. After half a minute, Baralis' voice called again: "Come now, little one, step into the room, or I will be forced to find you."

Melli was about to hide under the bed when Baralis entered the bedroom, casting a long shadow before him. "Oh, Melli, what big ears you have." He shook his head in mild reproof. "What a naughty girl you are." His voice had a hypnotic quality, and she found herself feeling sleepy.

"Now, Melli, if you are a good girl and promise not to tell what you heard, I will promise not to tell your father that you heard it." Baralis put down his goblet on a low table and turned toward her, fixing Melli with the full impact of his dark and glittering eyes. "Do we have an agreement, my pretty one?"

Melli's head felt so heavy she found she could barely remember what she was agreeing to. She nodded as Baralis sat on the bed. "That's a good girl. You are a good girl, aren't you?" Melli nodded again dreamily. "Come here and sit on my lap and show me just how good you can be." Melli felt her body move forward of its own accord. She settled herself on Baralis' lap and put her arms around his neck. She smelled his scent; it was as compelling as his voice: the sensuous fragrance of rare spices and sweat.

"That's a good girl," he said softly, his hands enclosing her waist. "Now tell me how much can you remember of what you heard." Melli found she couldn't speak, much less remember; her mind was a blank. Baralis seemed satisfied with her silence. "Such a very pretty girl." She felt him caress the stiff fabric of her dress. His hand moved lower, down her leg and under her skirt; she felt his cool touch upon her calf. She was dimly frightened, but she couldn't act, and his hand moved upward. Then, with his other hand, Baralis traced his fingers over her thin breast. She noticed for the first time how loathsome his hands were, scarred and swollen.

Repulsed by the sight of the ugly hands, something in Melli stirred, and with great effort she forced herself out of her lethargy. Her thoughts sharpened into focus and she pulled away from him. Quick as a flash she stood up and ran out of the chamber, the sound of Baralis' laughter echoing in her ears.

That little whippet will be no problem, thought Baralis, as he watched her flee. It was a shame that she had seen fit to leave so soon. The encounter had just begun to get interesting. Still, he had more pressing matters to attend to and desire was already thinning from his blood.

He exited Maybor's chambers by means of a hidden passage, making his way to his own suite. He must prepare the poison for the king's arrow: a delicate and time-consuming task. Also a dangerous one—the many scars and blisterings on his hands could attest to that. The poison that he would paint on the arrowhead would be of an especially pernicious kind, and he would not be surprised if, before the day was through, he had more welts and reddenings etched upon his tender palms.

Baralis had another task he was anxious to do: he needed to recruit a blind scribe. He'd just secured the loan of the entire libraries of Tavalisk—the events that he and Maybor had been discussing were in fact part payment for the loan. He smiled knowingly. He would have arranged the king's *accident* regardless of Tavalisk and his precious library, but it suited Baralis for the moment, to have Tavalisk believe that he was running the show.

Not that he'd ever make the mistake of underestimating Tavalisk. The man had a dangerous talent for trouble-making. One wave of his heavily jewelled fingers, and he could sanction the wiping out of entire villages. Whenever it suited the interests of his beloved Rorn, Tavalisk could be heard to cry loudly, *"Heretics."* Baralis had to admire the particularly potent power which the man's position afforded him.

It was, however, not too stable a position. In fact, that was part of the reason Tavalisk had agreed to loan his library. He needed Rorn to be prosperous; as long as the city was doing what it did best—making money by trade and banking—his place would be assured. Rorn, much like a surgeon in times of plague, always did best when others did badly. A spark of insurgency in the north would result in the cautious money moving south.

There was more, of course. With Tavalisk one always had to be careful—the man had knowledge of sorcery. How much was hard to judge, as rumor was never a reliable source. Baralis had met him once. It had proven difficult to take his measure—his obesity had proved an effective distraction, yet it was enough for each man to know what the other was. Yes, it was best to be wary of Tavalisk: an enemy was at his most dangerous when he had intimate knowledge of the weapons at his opponent's command. That one day Tavalisk would become his enemy was a fact Baralis never lost sight of.

But for the time being, the alliance served both men: Tavalisk was able to promote income-generating conflict within the Four Kingdoms, and in turn Baralis was given access to some of the rarest and most secret writings in the Known Lands.

He was no fool; he knew, even before the huge chests had arrived last week, that there would be volumes missing. Tavalisk would have kept back those writings which he considered too valuable or too dangerous for him to see.

There was still, however, a wealth of knowledge in what remained: brilliant, fantastic books, the likes of which he'd never imagined, bound in leather and skin and silk. Relating histories of people he'd never heard of, showing pictures of creatures he'd never seen, giving details of poisons he'd never made. Infinitely delicate manuscripts, made brittle by the passing of time, tied with fraying thread, providing insights into ancient conflicts, showing maps of the stars in the heavens, presenting listings of treasures long lost to the world . . . and much, much more. Baralis was made light-headed by the thought of so much knowledge.

One thing he had determined to do was have all of Tavalisk's library copied before it was returned. To this end, Baralis needed a blind scribe: someone who could copy exactly, sign for sign, what was written on a page but not understand a word of it. Baralis had no intention of sharing the rare and wondrous knowledge which the books contained.

He needed a boy with a dexterous hand and an eye for detail, a clever boy, but a boy who had never been taught to read. Crope was out of the question; he was a blithering, big-handed fool. The sons of nobles and squires were taught to read from an early age and so were of no use. Baralis would have to look elsewhere for a blind scribe.

Jack was woken up by Tilly. The pastry maid took great delight in shaking him much harder than was necessary. "What is it?" he asked, immediately worried that he'd overslept. The light filtering through the kitchens was pale and tenuous, a product of freshly broken dawn. Pain soared up his arm as he stood, and the memory of Frallit's words the night before raced after it.

Tilly put her finger to her lips, indicating that he should be quiet. She beckoned him to follow her, and she lead him to the storeroom where the flour for baking was kept. "Willock wants to see you." Tilly pushed one of the sacks of flour aside to reveal a hidden store of apples. She selected one, hesitated a moment, considering whether or not to offer Jack one, decided against it, and then pulled the flour sack back into place.

"Are you sure it's me he wants, Tilly?" Jack was genuinely surprised, as he had little dealing with the cellar steward. He cast his mind back a few weeks earlier when he'd secretly tapped a few flagons of ale on a dare from a stablehand. It suddenly seemed quite likely that Willock had discovered the missing ale; after all, the man was known for his scrutinous eye. Jack had a horrible suspicion that the famous and slightly bulging eye had turned its gaze his way.

"Of course I'm sure, pothead! You're to go straight to

the beer cellar. Now get a move on." Tilly's sharp teeth bit through the apple skin. She watched as Jack smoothed down his clothes and hair. "I wouldn't bother if I were you. No amount of grooming can make a stallion out of a packhorse." Tilly gave Jack a superior look and wiped the apple juice from her chin.

He hurried down to the beer cellar, wondering what form his punishment might take. Last year, when he'd been caught raiding the apple barrels in an attempt to brew his own cider, Willock had given him a sound thrashing. Jack sincerely hoped another sound thrashing would be called for. The alternative was much worse: being forced to leave the castle.

The kitchens of Castle Harvell had been his home for life; he had been born in the servants' hall. When his mother grew too sick to tend him, the scullery maids had fostered him; when he needed food to eat, the cooks had fed him; when he did something wrong, the master baker had scolded him. The kitchens were his haven and the great oven was his hearth. Life in the castle wasn't easy, but it was familiar, and to a boy without father and mother or anyone to call his own, familiarity was as close as he could get to belonging.

The beer cellar was a huge chamber filled with rows of copper vats in which various grades of ale were produced. When Jack's eyes became accustomed to the dim light, he was surprised to find Frallit was there, standing beside Willock, sipping on a cup of ale. Both men looked decidedly nervous to Jack. Willock spoke first. "Did anyone follow you down here?" His small eyes flicked to the door, checking if anyone was behind him.

"No, sir."

Willock hesitated for a moment, rubbing his clean-shaven chin. "My good friend the master baker has informed me that you are nimble with your hands. Is this true, boy?" The cellar steward's voice seemed strained, and Jack was beginning to feel more than a little worried. He brushed his hair back from his face in an attempt to appear nonchalant.

"Speak up, boy, now is not the time for false modesty. The master baker says you have a real feel for kneading the dough. He also tells me you like to carve and whittle wood. Is this true?"

"Yes, sir." Jack was confused. After last night's encounter with Frallit, he hardly expected praise.

"I can see you are a polite boy and that's good, but the master baker also tells me you can be quite a handful and need a good whippin' from time to time. Is this true?" Jack didn't know how to respond, and Willock continued. "A rare opportunity may be coming your way. You wouldn't want to miss a rare opportunity, would you, boy?"

The hair which Jack had pushed from his eyes was threatening to fall forward again. He was forced to hold his head at a slight angle to prevent its imminent downfall. "No, sir."

"Good." Willock glanced nervously in the direction of several huge brewing vats. A man stepped out from behind them. Jack could not see him clearly, as he was beyond the light, but he could tell the stranger was a nobleman from the soft rustle of his clothes.

The stranger spoke, his mellifluous tones oddly out of place in the beer cellar. "Jack, I want you to answer one question. You must give me a truthful reply and do not be mistaken, I will know if you lie." Jack had never heard a voice like the stranger's before, low and smooth but charged with power. He didn't question the man's ability to tell truth from lie and nodded obediently. At this sudden move of his head, Jack's hair fell over his eyes.

"I will answer you truthfully, sir."

"Good." Jack could make out the curve of thin lips. "Come forward a little so I may better see you." Jack moved a few steps nearer the stranger. The man stretched out a misshapen hand and brushed Jack's hair from his face. For the briefest of instances, the stranger's flesh touched his, and it took all of Jack's willpower not to recoil from the touch. "There is something about you, boy, that is familiar to me." The stranger's gaze lingered over him. Jack began to sweat despite the chillness of the cellar. The pain in his arm sharpened to a needlepoint. "No matter," continued the stranger, "on to the question." He shifted slightly and the candlelight fell directly onto his face. His eyes shone darkly. "Jack, have you ever been taught how to read?"

"No, sir." Jack was almost relieved by the question; the threat of being banished from the castle receded upon its asking.

The stranger held Jack enthralled with the force of his stare. "You speak the truth, boy. I am pleased with you." The man turned to where Willock and Frallit were standing. "Leave me and the boy alone." Jack had never seen either man move so fast, and he might have actually laughed if it hadn't been for the stranger's presence.

The man watched with cold eyes as the two scuttled away. He moved full into the light, his silken robes softly gleaming. "Do you know who I am, boy?" Jack shook his head. "I am Baralis, King's Chancellor." The man paused theatrically, giving Jack sufficient time to fully understand the importance of the person who was facing him. "I see by the look on your face that you have at least heard of me." He smiled. "You are probably a little curious as to what I want of you. Well, I will prolong your wait no longer. Have you heard of a blind scribe?"

"No, sir."

"A blind scribe is a contradiction in terms, for he is not blind, nor does he understand what he sees. I can tell I am confusing you. Let me put it simply. I require someone to spend several hours each day copying manuscripts word for word, sign for sign. Could you do this?"

"Sir, I have no skill with pen. I have never even held one."

"I would have it no other way." The man who now had a name drew back into the shadows. "Your job is merely to copy. The skill with pen is nothing. Frallit tells me you are a clever boy—you will pick that up in a matter of days." Jack did not know if he was more amazed at Baralis' offer or that Frallit had actually spoken well of him.

"So, Jack, are you willing to do this?" Baralis' voice was a honeyed spoon.

"Yes, sir."

"Excellent. You will start today. Be at my chambers at two hours past noon. I will require your presence for several hours every day. You will not give up your kitchen duties." Jack could no longer see Baralis; the shadows hooded the man's face. "One more thing, Jack, and then you may go. I require your complete discretion. I trust you will tell no one of what you do. The master baker will provide you with an alibi if you need one." Baralis slipped away into the darkness between the brewing vats. There was not a sound to be heard upon his departure.

Jack was shaking from head to foot. His knees were threatening a mutiny and his arm felt as if it had been keel-hauled. He sat down on the cellar floor, suddenly tired and weak. The stone was damp, but the unpleasantness went un-noticed as he wondered about what had happened. Why would the king's chancellor choose him?

Coming to the lofty conclusion that the world of grown men made little sense, Jack curled up into a ball and drifted off to sleep.

It was a perfect morning for a hunt. The first frost of winter hardened the ground underfoot and crisped the under-growth. The sun provided light but not warmth, and the air was still and clear.

King Lesketh felt the familiar knot of tension in his stomach that always accompanied the hunt. He welcomed the feeling; it would keep an edge to his judgment and a keenness to his eye. The small party had set off for the forest before dawn and now, as they approached their destination, the horses grew skittish and the hounds barked noisily, eager to begin. The king briefly looked over his companions. They were good men, and the fear of the hunt was a bond between them on this fine day: Lords Carvell, Travin, Rolack and Maybor, the houndsmen, and a handful of archers.

He did not miss the presence of his son. The king had felt relief when Kylock had failed to show at the predawn meet. The boy was turning out to be a brilliant sportsman, but his cruelty toward his prey troubled the king. Kylock would toy with his game, needlessly wounding and dismembering— trying to inflict as much pain as possible before death. More disturbing than that was the effect his son had on those around him. People were guarded and uneasy in the boy's presence. The hunt would be more joyous in his absence.

The party waited as the hounds were loosed. Minutes

passed as the dogs searched for quarry. The king's hounds had been specially trained to ignore smaller game such as rabbit and fox. They would only follow the bigger prize: the wild boar, the stag, and the bristled bear. The hunting party waited, tension written on every man's face, breath whitening in the cold air. Before too long, the baying of the hounds changed and became a savage beckoning. All eyes were on the king. He let out a fierce cry, "To the hunt!" and galloped deep into the forest, his men following him. Sound blasted the air: the thunder of hooves, the blare of horn, and the yelping of hounds.

The hunt was long and dangerous. It was difficult to maneuver horse around tree and over ditch. The hounds led the party on a twisting path into the heart of the wood. The trees became so dense that the party was often forced to slow down. The king hated to be slowed. The cry of the hounds urged him to go faster, to take risks, to pursue his game at any cost. Lord Rolack was at his flank and threatened to take the lead. Lesketh dug spur into horseflesh and pushed ahead. The men were gaining on the hounds. Over stream and fallen log they leapt, through glade and brush they charged. Then suddenly, unexpectedly, they caught a glimpse of a huge and fast-moving form.

"A boar!" cried the king exultantly. That single vision had sent a shiver of fear through him: the beast was massive, much larger than was usually found in these parts.

The horsemen closed in on hound and boar, and the archers loosed their first arrows. Most went wide as the boar dived once more into the bush. However, when the boar was spotted again, it was sporting two arrows: one on its neck, the other in its haunch. The king knew that the first hits would actually quicken the boar, filling it with a dangerous blind rage. He turned his horse quickly and pursued the game deeper into the bush.

The hounds smelled blood and were wild with excitement, their cries reaching a fever pitch. The men responded to the sound; blood had been drawn, the hunt had now truly begun.

The king had no time for thought. He survived on his reflexes and those of his horse, which seemed to know when to jump and turn without any prompting from its master. The

boar was sighted again. This time its escape route was cut off
by a deep gully. The archers fired once more and the boar
was hit a further three times. The beast let out a piercing
squeal. One of the arrows went astray, striking a hound and
puncturing its eye. In the confusion, the boar turned on the
party and blazed a path through them. The king was furious.
"Put that hound out of its misery!" he said through clenched
teeth. He spun his horse round, drawing blood with his spurs,
and charged after the game.

The boar did not slow down. Pursued by the hounds, it
fled into the depths of the forest, leaving a trail of blood in
its path.

Finally the boar was cornered by the hounds; it had run
toward a still pond and could go no further. The dogs kept it
from moving by forming a half-circle around it. The mighty
beast kicked at the earth, preparing to charge. The men readied their weapons. The king moved closer, his eyes never
leaving the beast. One wrong move, one hesitation could
lead to death. Lesketh knew he had only an instant before the
boar charged. He neared the beast, raising his spear and, with
all the force in his body, thrusting the weapon deep into the
boar's flank. The beast sounded a chilling death cry and hot
blood erupted from the wound.

One moment later, all the lords were upon the beast,
stabbing it countless times with their long spears. The boar's
blood flowed onto the ground and down to the pond. The
houndsmen called the dogs off; the party was jubilant.

"Let's have its balls off!" cried Carvell.

"Off with its balls," repeated Maybor. "Who will do the
honors?"

"You should, Maybor. It's rumored you're skilled in the
art of castration." Everyone laughed, relieving the tension of
the hunt.

Maybor took his dagger from its sheath and dismounted
his horse. "By Borc! I don't think I've ever seen such huge
balls."

"I thought you had a looking glass, Maybor!" quipped
Rolack. The lords guffawed loudly. With one quick slice,
Maybor relieved the dead beast of its testicles and held them
up for his companions to admire.

"On second thought," he said with mock seriousness, "I think mine *are* bigger!"

As the men chuckled in response, the king thought he heard a familiar whirring sound. The next instant, he was knocked off his horse by the force of something hitting his shoulder. As he fell he saw what it was . . . an arrow. The instant of recognition was followed by the forewarning of danger. It didn't feel right. He'd been hit by arrows before and knew well the sting of impact. The sting was there, but there was more—almost as if something was burrowing into his flesh. A thin but biting pain gripped his body and he passed out.

Bevlin awoke in a bad mood: he'd had a terrible night's rest. He'd slept in the kitchen amongst his books. He wondered where his good sense had been—here he was, as old as the hills, barely able to walk, and yet he'd offered his bed to the young and abundantly healthy knight. He himself had slept on the hard wood of the kitchen table. Of course he could have slept in the spare room, but the roof leaked above the bed, and he'd reached the age now where he'd rather be dry than comfortable.

His spirits picked up somewhat when he discovered his visitor was cooking breakfast. "How did you manage to do that without waking me?" he demanded testily.

"It was easy, Bevlin. You were fast asleep." Bevlin did not like the idea of this handsome young man seeing him asleep in such an undignified manner. He was willing to forgive him, though, as the food he was preparing smelled delicious.

"There was no need for you to do this. I would have cooked breakfast."

"I know," said Tawl. "That was what I was afraid of."

Bevlin decided to let the remark pass without comment. The young man had good cause to be wary of his cooking. "What are you making?"

"Hamhocks stuffed with mushrooms and spiced ale."

"Sounds good, but could you grease the ham up a little? It looks a smidgen dry to me." The wiseman had a liking for grease; it helped food slip down his rough old throat more easily. "So tell me, where does a fine man such as yourself pick up the skills of the hearth? Last time I heard they didn't teach *cooking* at Valdis."

Tawl's smile was sad. "My mother died in birthing while I was still a boy. She left me two young sisters and a babe in arms to care for." The knight hesitated, looking deep into the fire, his face an unreadable mask.

When he spoke again his tone had changed: it was bright with forced cheer. "So I learnt to cook." He shrugged. "It made me popular with my fellow knights at Valdis, and I earned more than a few coppers roasting up pig's liver in the early hours of the morning."

Bevlin wasn't a man who valued tact highly and curiosity always got the better of him. "So where are your family now?" he asked. "I suppose your father will be looking after your sisters."

"Suppose nothing about my family, wiseman."

Bevlin was shocked at the bitter fury in the knight's voice. He lifted his arm as a beginning to an apology, but was denied first say.

"Bevlin," said Tawl, his face turned back toward the fire, "forgive my anger. I . . ."

"Speak no more, my friend," interrupted the wiseman. "There is much in all of us that bears no questioning."

A candle length later, when the two men had finished eating and were sitting in the warm kitchen drinking mulled ale, Bevlin carefully opened a fat, dusty book. "This, Tawl," he said, gesturing the yellowing pages, "is my most precious possession. It is a copy of Marod's *Book of Words*. Not any old copy, mind you, but one faithfully transcribed by the great man's devoted servant, Galder. Before his master died, Galder made four exact copies of Marod's great lifework. This is one of those four copies."

Bevlin's old fingers traced the inscription on the sheep's-hide cover. "One can tell it's an original Galder copy if one looks very closely at the pages: Marod was so poor near the end that his servant couldn't afford to buy new parchment and was forced to reuse existing papers. Galder would wash the ink off the paper with a solution of rainwater and cow's urine, he would then leave the paper in the sun to dry. If you look carefully, you can still see the ghosts of some of those previous documents."

Tawl studied the page that Bevlin opened: the old man pointed out the merest whisper of words and letters lying beneath the text. "Of course, the unfortunate fact is that the very solution used to soak the pages clean eats away at the nature of them, making them brittle and delicate. I fear it won't be long before it is rendered unreadable and will only be good as a relic in a collection. That will be a very sad thing indeed, for Marod's book holds much of relevance for those who live today." The wiseman closed the book.

"But there must be thousands of copies of the *Book of Words* around. Every priest and scholar in the Known Lands must have one," Tawl said.

Bevlin shook his head sadly. "Unfortunately copies are often vastly different from the original. There is not one scribe who failed to alter Marod's words in some subtle way, changing ideas to suit their beliefs or those of their patrons, omitting sections they considered immoral or insignificant, altering verses they thought were miswritten or frivolous or just plain dull." Bevlin sighed heavily, the weariness of age marked clearly on his pale features. "Every translator's interpretation minutely altered the essence of Marod's words and prophesies. In consequence, through the course of centuries, his work has been irrevocably changed. The priests and scholars of which you speak may well have books of the same name, but they are not the same work.

"For all I know, the other three Galder copies are lost or destroyed: I may be the only person in possession of the true word of Marod." The wiseman finished the last of his ale and placed the empty goblet on the table. "It is a source of much sadness to me."

Bevlin looked thoughtfully into the face of his companion. Tawl was young, maybe too young to undertake what would be asked of him. The wiseman sighed heavily. He knew the immensity of the task at hand. This young man before him, strong and golden and self-assured, had his whole life in front of him, a life that could be blighted by a fruitless search. Bevlin extinguished the candles with his fingers. What could he do? *He* had no choice; no one had asked him if he wanted the responsibility for all that was to come. All that could be done was to give the young man a choice—he could at least do that.

The wiseman held his hands closely together to stop them from shaking and looked firmly into the blue eyes of the knight. "I expect you must be wondering what all this has to do with you coming here?"

"What you doin' here, boy? This ain't no place for the likes of you." The guard's voice echoed through the stone halls of the castle.

"I need to get to the nobles quarters," said Jack.

"The nobles quarters! The nobles quarters—what business could you have in the nobles quarters? Get going, you little snot."

Jack was late. He couldn't understand why he'd been so exhausted after meeting the king's chancellor earlier. It seemed as if the man had drained all the energy from him, much to his great misfortune: the morning loaves had been late to bake, and were, by the time they were ready, more precisely called afternoon loaves. Frallit's fury had been stoked to an inferno by that particular observation. Even more infuriating to the master baker was the realization that he couldn't beat Jack on the spot—he could hardly send a bruised and bloodied boy to the king's chancellor.

Jack almost felt sorry for Frallit, who was shown to be powerless in the face of genuine power. The master baker might be lord of the kitchens, but Baralis was lord of the castle. Still, Jack was sure Frallit would come up with some suitable punishment for sleeping when he should have been baking. Besides an armory of physical punishments, the master baker had a stockpile of humiliations at his flour-caked fingertips. For the second time this day, Jack found himself preferring the tried and tested sting of a sound thrashing to the blow of the unknown.

Jack contemplated the guard and realized that he wouldn't get far with chitchat. The man wasn't going to believe that he, a mere baker's boy, had an appointment with the king's chancellor. For some reason Jack felt like action—it would be good to be the one in control for once. A faded tapestry hanging against the wall caught his eye. He took a step forward and pulled hard on its corner. It fell to the floor in a cloud of dust. The guard's face had just time enough to register amazement and Jack was off, jumping over the tapestry, dodging around the guard and running down the corridor.

Dust was in his lungs, the guard was at his heels, stone raced beneath his feet. The chase was on.

In between wheezing breaths, Jack realized it hadn't been such a good idea—he didn't have the slightest notion in which direction Baralis' chambers lay. It was exhilarating to outrun the guard, though, to pit himself against another and grab the chance for success. After a short while the footsteps receded and his pursuer could be heard shouting obscenities from behind. Jack smiled triumphantly—a man reduced to shouting obscenities was a man with not enough breath to run.

Finding the chamber was not as difficult as Jack thought. Staircases and turnings presented themselves to him, and he knew instinctively which to take. It appeared that the very castle itself was beholden to the great man. Its most dark and vital passages seemed to lead to Baralis' door.

Jack paused on the threshold, trying to decide if a humble tap or a confident knock was called for. He'd just decided that humility was probably his best course when the door swung open.

"You are late." Lord Baralis stood there, tall and striking, dressed in black.

Jack tried to keep his voice level. "I'm sorry, sir."

"What, no excuse?"

"None, sir. The fault was entirely my own."

"My, my, we are an unusual boy. Most people would have a hundred excuses at their lips. I will forgive you this time, Jack, but do not be late again."

"Yes, sir."

"I noticed you were admiring my door." Jack nodded enthusiastically, pleased that the great man had misinterpreted his reason for dallying on the threshold.

Baralis ran his scarred fingers over the etchings on the door. "You do well to admire it, Jack, for it has several interesting properties." Jack expected him to expand further on the subject, but Baralis just smiled, a guarded curve of lip with no show of teeth.

Jack followed him through what seemed to be a sitting room and then into a large, well-lit chamber crammed from top to bottom with all manner of paraphernalia. "You will work here," said Baralis indicating a wooden bench. "You will find quill, ink, and paper on the desk. I suggest you spend today learning how to use them." Jack was about to speak but was cut short. "I have no time for mollycoddling, boy. Get to it." With that Baralis left him at the desk and busied himself at the far side of the room, sorting through papers.

Jack didn't have the slightest idea of what to do. He had never seen anyone use a pen before. Certainly no one in the kitchen could read or write; recipes for breads, beers and puddings were kept in the head. The cellarer was the only person who Jack knew could write. He was the one responsible for keeping account of all the kitchen supplies, but Jack had never actually *seen* him use a pen.

He picked up the quill and turned it in his hands, then readied a piece of paper and pressed the nib to it. Nothing. He realized he must be missing something. His eyes glanced around the desk. The ink. That was it. He poured a quantity of the liquid onto the page, where it quickly spread out. He then ran the quill through the ink, making crude marks. He felt he hadn't got it quite right so tried again on a fresh piece of paper, once more pouring the ink onto it. This time Jack managed to trace some lines and shapes in the ink.

"You fool." Jack looked up to see Baralis hovering over him. "You are not supposed to pour the ink on the page. The ink stays in the pot. You dip the pen *into* the ink. Here." Jack watched as Baralis demonstrated what he described. "There. Now you have a go." Baralis left him alone once more.

Several hours later, Jack was beginning to get the hang of it. He had mastered the exact dipping angle required to pick up maximum ink and could draw signs and shapes. To practice he drew what he knew of: the shapes of various loaves—the round, the platt, the long loaf. He also drew baking implements and various knives and weaponry.

After a while Jack's attention began to wander. He'd never been in a place of such wondrous luxury. Walls lined with books and boxes tempted him, bottles filled with dark liquids wooed him. He couldn't resist. He stole over to the wooded sill and took the stopper from a particularly seductive-looking jar. A smell sweet and earthy escaped. There was nothing to do but try it. He raised it to his lips.

"I wouldn't do that if I were you, Jack," came Baralis' mocking voice. "It's poison. For the rats."

Jack's face was hot with shame. He hadn't heard Baralis approach—did the man walk on air? Quickly replacing the stopper, he tried his best not to look like a person caught in the act. He was almost light-headed with relief when some-one else entered the room. Jack recognized the huge and badly disfigured man at once.

"Yes, Crope," said Baralis, "what is it?"

"The king."

"What about the king?"

"The king has been hit by an arrow while out hunting."

"Has he indeed." For the briefest instant, malice flashed across Baralis' face, but just as quickly, his expression changed to one of deep concern. "This is ill news." He looked sharply at Jack. "Boy, go back to the kitchens at once."

Jack raced out of the chambers and down to the kitchen, his mind awhirl with thoughts of the king. He would proba-bly be the first person downstairs with the news; he would be the center of attention and Frallit might even treat him to a cup of ale. The thought of ale wasn't as cheering as usual, and it took Jack a moment to realize why: he was afraid. The look that had so quickly flitted across Baralis' face had formed a memory too disturbing to ignore. Jack hurried on his way. Baralis' expression would be one detail he would leave out of his account to the kitchen staff—he was a smart boy and knew that such things were best not repeated.

"There are grave times ahead." Bevlin exhaled deeply and continued, his voice thin with age. "Just over twelve summers back I saw a terrible thing in the sky. A fragment of a star fell from the heavens. As it sped toward the earth a great cleaving occurred. The two pieces lit up the sky with equal brilliance before disappearing beyond the horizon in the east." The wiseman walked over to the fire and stirred the embers. He had need of more warmth.

"I need not tell you that such an event is a sign of great importance. At the time I had little idea what it meant, and I have spent the past years looking for answers. I read all the great books of prophecy, all the ancient scripts." Bevlin managed a wiry smile. "Such works are always filled with vague predictions of doom: dark clouds looming on the horizon, fatal curses upon the land—the stuff with which parents frighten their children into obedience. I found little of value in any of them; more often than not they are written with the reasoning that if one predicts doom long enough, one is bound to be proven right. Doom, I fear, is just as inevitable as leaves falling in autumn."

Bevlin placed a pot of ale upon the fire and spooned some honey into it. "Of course, one man's doom is often another man's triumph." He grated cinnamon into the pot, stirred it once and then spat in it for luck. He let it warm a little while and then ladled the mixture into two cups, handing one of them to Tawl.

"Marod's work is different. He is emboldened to specifics. He was not a man given to ambiguity like a cheap fortune-teller." The wiseman's hand settled on the thick book. "Marod was chiefly a philosopher and historian, but, thanks to the benevolence of the Gods, he had instances of foretelling. Unfortunately, although he was a specific man, he enjoyed making references to other, more obscure works known to him. Most of those works have failed to be passed down to our time. They have either been lost, or destroyed: burnt by overly fanatical clergy, eager to be rid of the works of heretics.

"I finally managed to track down one such book mentioned by Marod. I paid a heavy price for what was little more than a few pages with failed binding. However, in it I found what I was looking for—a mention of what I saw in the sky twelve years back.

"The pages tell that it was a sign of birth, dual births. Two babes were begot that night, two men whose destinies lie in shaping the world—for good, or bad, I do not know. Their lives are linked together by an invisible thread and their fates will pull against each other.

"There is a specific prophecy divined by Marod, which I believe is relevant to one of the two. You may be familiar with some of it—scholars have pondered its meaning for years—but this is the original. Possibly no one else besides you and I will ever know the true wording of the script:

> *"When men of honor lose sight of their cause*
> *When three bloods are savored in one day*
> *Two houses will meet in wedlock and wealth*
> *And what forms at the join is decay*
> *A man will come with neither father nor mother*
> *But sister as lover*
> *And stay the hand of the plague*
>
> *The stones will be sundered, the temple will fall*
> *The dark empire's expansion will end at his call*
> *And only the fool knows the truth."*

Bevlin warmed his hands against his cup and looked into the eyes of his companion. Tawl met his gaze and, with the fire crackling in the background, an unspoken communion passed between them.

"The world is ever changing," said Bevlin softly, breaking the silence. "And it is always greed that compels those changes. The archbishop of Rorn cares more for money than he does his God, the duke of Bren grows restless for more land, the city of Marls in its desperation for foreign trade has brought a plague upon itself. Even now, as we speak, King Lesketh in the Four Kingdoms seeks to avert war with Halcus . . . it is not for me to say if he will succeed."

Bevlin and Tawl remained silent for some time, both deep in thought. It was the young man who spoke first, just as the wiseman knew it would be. "Why was I sent here?" Bevlin suspected that the young man already knew the answer.

"There is one thing I believe you can do."

"Tyren expected you would set me a task. What is it?"

Tawl was so willing, so eager, the wiseman felt an unaccountable sadness.

"Your job will be to find a needle in a haystack."

"What do you mean?" Tawl was mouthing the appropriate words, but Bevlin realized that the knight knew the future was set, and all that was now being said was already understood and decided.

"I need you to find me a boy: a boy of about twelve summers."

"Where will I find this boy?"

"There are no easy answers to that question, I'm afraid."

"One of the two?" asked Tawl. The wiseman nodded.

"The one named in the prophecy." Bevlin resisted the urge to talk further about the prophecy—the knight would not be pleased with his reasons for believing it would soon come to pass. "I have little for you to go on. The only advice I can give you is use your instincts. Look for a boy who appears more than he seems, a boy set apart. You will know him when you find him."

"And if I find him?"

"Then you will receive your final circle. That's why they sent you here, wasn't it?" Bevlin regretted the words as soon as they were spoken. The young man before him had done nothing to deserve offense.

"Yes, that's why I came." The knight's voice was gentle. "These," he uncovered his circles, "are all that matter now."

Bevlin watched as he pulled down his sleeve. Tawl was somehow different than other knights he'd met. The commitment was the same, but it was tempered with something akin to vulnerability. Valdis specialized in breeding a particularly single-minded race of knights: unconditional obedience, no question of marriage, all income to be relinquished to the cause. And what was the cause? The knights had started out as a moral order, dedicated to helping the oppressed and the needy. Nowadays it was discussions on politics, not humanity, that could be heard most often filtering through the halls at Valdis.

Money was ever an interest, too. It was gold that had brought the knight here—though Bevlin was certain Tawl had no knowledge of the transaction. Tyren had probably told him there was a great deed to be done, a chance to bring honor to the knighthood. And there was, of course, but Valdis didn't know it. All *he* was to Tyren was a foolish old man with a dream of stopping a war that hadn't even started. Well, if his gold had spoken more seductively than his prophecies, so be it. The result was still the same. He got what he wanted: a strong young knight to help him search for the boy. And Tyren got what he wanted: more money to finance his political maneuverings.

It hadn't always been that way with the knights; they had been glorious once, famous for their chivalry and learning. They were counted on to keep the peace in times of unrest, famine, and plague. No city was powerful enough to intimidate them, no village too small to ask for their help. A whole legion of them had once ridden a hundred leagues with barrels on their backs to bring water to a town that was dry. A thousand songs were sung about them, generations of women swooned at the sight of them. And now they had stooped to intrigue.

Exactly what the knights hoped to achieve by their maneuverings was difficult for Bevlin to understand. Valdis was not as great a city as it once was; Rorn had long eclipsed it as the fiscal capital of the Known Lands, and Valdis was obviously envious of its rival's success. Tyren, perhaps in an attempt to regain a foothold in trade, was quietly buying up interests in salt pans and mines. If the knights gained control over the salt market, it would mean they could virtually hold cities for ransom, especially the ones dependent on the fishing trade in the south. But there was more than trade at stake: Tyren had only taken over the leadership a year ago, but he was already advocating a more zealous approach to their faith.

The major southern cities—Rorn, Marls, Toolay—all followed the same religion as Valdis, but they were more liberal in their interpretation of the creeds and dogmas. Hence Valdis was positioning itself as the moral leader in the south and had begun stirring up trouble in the name of religious reformation.

All in all, it added up to trouble. Bevlin foresaw conflict ahead. It was really quite ironic—the knights, who with their peculiar mix of greed and religious fervor could conceivably spark off a major war, had sent one of their number to find a boy who could conceivably end one! Indeed, by sending Tawl here, with gold not good deeds as their motive, they may well have put Marod's prophesy into motion: *When men of honor lose sight of their cause.*

Bevlin sighed deeply; there would be much suffering ahead. He turned and looked at Tawl. The young knight was sitting quietly, lost in thought. There was something about the way he sat, with his whole body enthralled by the fire, that affected the wiseman deeply. The knight was trying to deal with some inner torment; every muscle in his face, each breath from his lips, attested to it. Bevlin made a silent promise that he'd never be the one to tell Tawl the truth behind Valdis' reasons for sending him here. "Well, my friend," he said. "Have you made your decision? Will you help me find the boy?"

"There was never any question." Tawl looked up, his blue eyes deep with need. "I will do as you ask."

Baralis entered King Lesketh's chamber. All the members of the hunt were there, still wearing clothes soaked in boar's blood. The queen was at the king's bedside, her normally cool and haughty features stricken with worry. The surgeon was busy stripping the clothes away from the king's shoulder while murmuring the appropriate prayers of healing.

"What happened?" asked Baralis.

"The king was shot." Carvell looked down at the floor, as if he bore part of the blame.

"Who would dare do such a thing!" exclaimed Baralis, careful to keep a note of indignant surprise to his voice. "Where is the arrow? Did anyone get a good look at it?"

"Maybor removed it," answered Carvell.

Maybor moved forward. "Yes, it is true I did, but in my panic to withdraw it from the king, I threw the damned arrow away." His gaze met Baralis'.

"That was not a wise move, Maybor." Baralis turned to look at the other men present. "What if the arrow had been barbed? You might have caused the king worse damage by removing it." There were murmurs of agreement in the room. Baralis noted the quick flash of hatred in Maybor's eye.

"How do you know the arrow was *not* barbed?" asked Maybor coolly. The room grew quiet as they waited for Baralis' reply.

"I could tell the moment I saw the king's wound that a barbed arrow had not been used." The men reluctantly nodded their heads. Baralis promised himself that one day he would deal with Maybor; the man was altogether too unpredictable. Furthermore, he was beginning to suspect Maybor regretted entering into the conspiracy. *Well, I have one more card up my sleeve that you don't know about, Maybor,* thought Baralis, *and it is time I played it.*

"Did anyone else get a look at the arrow?" he asked, his voice pitched low to gain the attention of everyone in the room.

"I did, my lord." One of the houndsmen stepped forward. Maybor looked up, his face ashen.

"And who are you?" Baralis knew well who the man was—he had paid him ten gold pieces only days ago for his part in this little performance.

"I am Hist, King's Houndsman."

"Tell me, Hist, what exactly did you see?"

"Sir, I can't be exactly sure, but the shaft did seem to have a double notch." Maybor stepped forward, his hand raised in protest, about to speak. Baralis did not give him the chance.

"A double notch!" he exclaimed to the room. "We all know the Halcus arrows are double notched." The room erupted into an uproar:

"The Halcus, those treacherous bastards."

"The Halcus have shot our king."

"To hell with the peace at Horn Bridge," pitched in Baralis.

"We must avenge this deed."

"We must beat the Halcus senseless."

Baralis judged the time was right. "We must declare war!" he cried.

"Aye," cried the men in unison. "War!"

Two

"No, Bodger, there's only one way to tell if a woman has a passionate nature and it ain't the size of her orbs." Grift leant back against the wall, arms folded behind his head in the manner of one about to impart valuable knowledge.

"How can you tell, then, Grift?" Bodger drew closer in the manner of one about to accept such knowledge.

"Body hair, Bodger. The hairier the woman, the more passionate the nature. Take old widow Harpit. She's got arms as hairy as a goat's behind and you won't find a randier woman anywhere."

"Widow Harpit's not much to look at, though, Grift. She's got more hair on her upper lip than I have."

"Exactly, Bodger! A man would count himself lucky to bed her." Grift smiled mischievously and took a long draught of ale. "What about your Nelly, how hairy is she?"

"My Nelly has arms as smooth as freshly turned butter."

"You won't be getting much then, Bodger!"

Both men chuckled merrily. Grift filled their cups and they relaxed for a while, sipping their ale. They liked nothing better, after a cold morning patrolling the castle grounds, than to sit down with a cup of ale and bandy ribald remarks. There was usually a little gossip exchanged, too.

"Here, Grift, last night while I was relieving myself in

the ornamental gardens I heard Lord Maybor having a real go at his daughter. He even gave her a good slapping."

"Maybor ain't what he used to be. Ever since this damned war with the Halcus he's been getting nasty and hot tempered—you never know what he's gonna be doing next." Both men turned at the sound of footsteps.

"Here comes young Jack. Jack, lad, do you fancy a sup of ale?"

"I can't, Bodger, I haven't got time."

"If you're off wooing, Jack," said Grift, "you'd better brush the flour from your hair."

Jack smiled broadly. "It's there for a purpose, Grift. I want the girls to think I'm old enough to be gray—just like you!"

Jack didn't wait around to hear the guard's reply. He was on his way to Baralis' chambers and was late as usual. The king's chancellor had been making him work long hours recently, and he was often scribing into the early hours of the morning. Jack suspected that the library he was copying would soon be due back to its owner, and that Baralis was eager to have what was left copied down to the last page as quickly as possible. In consequence, Jack now spent his days baking and his nights scribing. There was little time left for rest, and he had been close to falling asleep at his copying desk on more than one occasion.

Jack found that scribing became easier with practice. At first he could barely copy a page a day, but over time he'd grown better at his job, managing to complete as many as ten pages in one session.

Jack now had a guilty secret. For the past few years he had been able to read every word that he copied. Five summers had passed since Baralis had first recruited him to be a blind scribe, only Jack was no longer blind.

It had begun after the passing of three moons. Jack had started to notice patterns in the words and symbols. His main breakthrough had taken place over a year later when Baralis had asked him to copy a book full of drawings of animals. Each drawing was meticulously labeled, and Jack recognized many of the creatures in the book: bats, bears, mice. He began to understand that the letters underneath the drawings corresponded to the animals' names, and gradually he became able to comprehend simple words: the names of birds or flowers or animals.

Eventually Jack had learnt other words—connecting words, describing words, words that made up the basis of language. Once he had started he raced ahead, eager for knowledge. He found a book in Baralis' collection that did nothing but list the meanings of words. Oh, how he would have loved to have taken that precious volume to the kitchens with him. Baralis was not a man to grant favors lightly and Jack had never dared ask.

Over the past years he had read whatever he copied, stories from far lands, tales of ancient peoples, lives of great heroes. Much of what he copied he couldn't understand, and nearly half of it was written in foreign languages or strange symbols that he could never hope to decipher. *All* that he could understand made him restless.

Reading about faraway places made Jack yearn to visit them. He dreamt of exploring the caverns of Isro, sailing down the great River Silbur, fighting in the streets of Bren. He dreamt so vividly he could smell the incense, feel the cool spray of water on his cheek, and see defeat in the eyes of his opponents. Some nights, when the sky was brilliant with stars and the world seemed impossibly large, Jack had to fight the urge to be off. Desire to leave the castle was so great that it became a physical sensation—a pressure within that demanded release.

Usually by morning the pressure had lost its push. But more and more these days, Jack's gaze would wander to the map pinned to the study wall. He scanned the length of the Known Lands and wondered where he'd visit first: should it be to the north, over the mountains and into the frozen waste; should it be to the south, through the plains and into territories exotic and forbidden; or should it be to the east, where the power lay? He needed a place to head for, and eyes following the contours of the map, he cursed not knowing where his mother had come from, for he surely would have headed there.

Why had she kept so much from him? What was there in her past that she needed to hide? When he was younger,

Jack had assumed it was shame that held her tongue. Now he suspected it was fear. He was nine when his mother had died, and one of his most enduring memories of her was how she would insist on watching the castle gates each morning to see all the visitors arrive. They would go together arm in arm, up to the battlements, where they would have a good view of everyone applying for entry into Castle Harvell. It was his favorite part of the day; he enjoyed being out in the fresh air and watching the hundreds of people who walked through the gates.

There were great envoys with huge retinues, lords and ladies on fine white horses, richly dressed tradesmen from Annis and Bren, and farmers and tinkers from nearby towns.

His mother would keep him amused by telling him who people were and why they were important. What struck him now was how keen a grasp she'd had on the affairs of Harvell and its northern rivals; she kept herself well informed and was always eager for news of politics and power plays. For many years after her death, Jack had thought it was curiosity that made her watch the gates. Yet curiosity wouldn't make a dying woman, who toward the end could barely walk, drag herself up to the battlements each day to search the faces of strangers.

It was fear that marked her features at such times. Oh, she tried to hide it. She had a hundred anecdotes at her lips to take his mind from the cold and from her true reasons for being there. She had nearly succeeded, as well. Even now, though, he could recall the pressure of her fingers as they rested upon his arm and feel the delicate strain of her fear.

What had caused this watchfulness? This fear of strangers? To discover that, he must first find where she came from. His mother had left nothing for him to go on. She had been ruthless in withholding all information about herself. He knew nothing, save that she wasn't from the Four Kingdoms and had been branded a whore. Through the long nights, when sleep refused to come, Jack dreamt of tracking down her origins like a knight on a quest, of finding out the truth behind her fear.

Dreams were one thing, the reality of life in the castle was quite another. If the night stirred his imagination, then the day stifled it. What was he but a baker's boy? He had no skills to speak of, no future to plan for, no money to call his own. Castle Harvell was all there was, and to leave it would be to leave everything. Jack had seen the way beggars were treated at the castle—they were spat upon and ridiculed. Anyone who didn't belong was considered lower than the lowest scullery maid. What if he left the kingdoms only to end up scorned and penniless in a foreign land? At least the castle offered protection from such failure; whilst in its walls he was guaranteed a warm bed, food to eat, and friends to laugh with.

As Jack climbed the stairs to Baralis' chamber, he couldn't help thinking that a warm bed and food to eat were beginning to sound like a coward's reasons to stay.

Baralis was well pleased with the events of the last five years. The country was still embroiled in a disabling war, a war that served only to sap the strength and resources of both Halcus and the Four Kingdoms. Many bloody battles had been fought and heavy casualties were incurred on both sides. Just as one party seemed to gain the advantage, the other party would suddenly receive some unexpected help; news of enemies' tactics would be whispered in an interested ear, details of supply routes would fall into improper hands, or sites of possible ambush were revealed to unfriendly eyes. Needless to say, Baralis had been responsible for every fatal betrayal.

Stalemate suited him nicely. With the attention of the country focused to the east, Baralis could hatch his own plots and follow his own agenda at court.

As he sipped on mulled holk to soothe the pain in his fingers, he reflected on the state of the king. Since Lesketh had taken the arrow to the shoulder, he had never been the same. The wound had healed after a few months, but the king had been badly weakened and could no longer mount a horse. The king's wits were also, sadly, not all they had been, not that the king had *ever* been a great thinker, thought Baralis spitefully. If anything, he may have gone a little easy on the poison the day of the hunt: after all, the king could still remember his name!

The king's affliction was never mentioned aloud at court. If people talked of it at all, it was in hushed voices in the privacy of their own chambers: it was not a subject to speak of lightly. The queen was known to view any such talk as treason. Queen Arinalda had unofficially taken the king's place as ruler, and Baralis grudgingly admitted that the woman was doing a better job than her dull, hunt-obsessed husband ever had.

She had performed a delicate balancing act; due to her efforts the kingdoms were not perceived as a weak country lacking a leader. She had kept up diplomatic ties with Bren and Highwall, and had even signed a historic trading agreement with Lanholt. The Halcus were seething at her success. But she had shown wisdom in her restraint as well as her strength, and had not given the Halcus too much cause to worry—else Halcus might be forced to go in search of allies and the war escalate beyond the control of the two countries.

Today Baralis would tie up a loose end, one that had been left dangling since the day the king was shot. Lord Maybor had been a thorn in his side for many years now. The man had been party to the events leading up to the shooting, but it had become evident that Maybor regretted his actions and Baralis feared the man might use the incident against him. There was potential for blackmail and other unpleasantness, and Baralis ill liked having reason to be wary of any man.

The portly lord was up to something else that gave him cause for concern. Maybor was trying to secure a betrothal between his daughter, Melliandra, and the queen's only son, Prince Kylock. Baralis was not about to let that proposal take place: he had his *own* plans for the king's heir.

"Crope!" he called, eager to be relieved of his problem.

"Yes, master." His huge servant loomed close, blocking all light in his path. He always carried a small painted box and was busy stuffing it out of sight into his tunic.

"Go down to the kitchens and get me some wine."

"There's wine here already. I'll fetch it for you." Crope started to reach for the wine jug.

"No, you repulsive simpleton, I need another type. Now listen carefully, for I know you're liable to forget." Baralis spoke slowly, pronouncing each word distinctly. "I need a flagon of lobanfern red. Have you got that?"

"Yes, master, but you always say lobanfern red tastes like whore's piss."

"This wine is not for me, you feckless imbecile. It's a gift." Baralis stood up, smoothing his black silk robes. He watched Crope leave the room and then added in a low voice, "I hear Lord Maybor has a fondness for lobanfern red."

Crope appeared some time later with a jug of wine. Baralis snatched it from him. "Go now, fool." Baralis uncorked the jug and smelled its contents. He grimaced; only a barbarian could like this sickly brew.

He took the wine and moved over to a tapestry hanging on the wall, lifted it up, and ran his finger over a particular stone and entered his private study. No one besides himself knew of its existence. It was where he did his most secret work, wrote his most confidential letters, and manufactured his most potent poisons.

Poison was now one of Baralis' specialities and, since gaining access to the libraries of Tavalisk—who was himself a poisoner of high repute—Baralis had honed his skills to a fine art. He now realized that the mixture he had used on the king's arrow was the crudest of potions.

Baralis could now make poisons that were infinitely more subtle, less detectable and more varied in their results. It was a foolish practitioner who thought a poison's only use was to kill or disable. No, poisons could be used for much more: they could be made to slowly debilitate a person over years, effectively mimicking the characteristics of specific diseases; they could corrupt a good mind and turn it rotten; they could weaken a heart to a point where it stopped of its own accord; they could paralyze a body but keep the mind sound.

Poison could rob a man of his virility, his memory, or even his youth. It could stunt the growth of a child or, in the case of the queen, prevent the conception of one. It was all a matter of the skill of the poisoner, and Baralis was now in command of such skill.

He moved toward his heavy wooden desk where an array of jars and vials were placed. Most poisons were better made fresh as needed—for poison, like men, lost potency over time. Baralis smiled inwardly: time to cook up a batch.

Tavalisk entered the small, damp cell. He held a scented handkerchief to his nose; the smell of these places was always most unpleasant. He had just eaten a fine meal of roasted pheasant stuffed with its own eggs, a truly remarkable dish, the flavors of which still played in his mouth, whetting his plump tongue. Unfortunately, as well as lingering on his tongue, a small portion of the tenacious bird seemed to be caught between his teeth. Tavalisk pulled forth a dainty silver toothpick from his robes and skillfully dislodged the offending piece of fowl.

He found that inflicting pain and food complemented each other perfectly: after eating a fine meal he liked nothing better than to dabble in a spot of torture.

He regarded the prisoner dispassionately. He was chained up by his hands to the wall, his feet barely touching the ground. Tavalisk had to admit that the young man did have an unusually high tolerance for pain. He had been kept in this dungeon for over a year now. It might have been enough to kill another man. This one, however, had proven to be most exceptional.

Tavalisk had personally supervised the program of torture. Torture was, he considered, a special skill of his. He had designed a specific schedule just for this one prisoner, but was his prisoner grateful? No. This prisoner didn't even have the decency to succumb to the torture. Burns to the feet had been useless, starvation had been useless, the strain on his arms and wrists had been useless. Even his personal favorite—hot needles in soft flesh—had proved useless. He had been careful not to cause too much damage, though, and had practiced great personal restraint, for Tavalisk had far worse punishments in his repertoire.

He didn't want to see this young man permanently disabled. He knew that the prisoner was a knight of Valdis, that much was evident from the mark upon his arm—two circles, one within the other, meaning the knight had attained the middle circle and was obviously young to have done so. Unfortunately, the young man had visibly aged since he had been under his care. No longer did the golden hair shine and the cheek run smooth.

But that was of little consequence to Tavalisk. What did matter was what the young man had been doing when he'd been picked up. The knight had been snooping around asking questions, wanting to find somebody, a boy he had said. When the spies had brought him, bound and gagged, to their master, he had refused to speak.

There was one thing which made Tavalisk suspect the knight was involved in something of importance: when he had been brought in, he had in his possession a lacus skin. That skin had Bevlin's mark upon it. Tavalisk was determined to find out what connection the knight had to the aging wiseman.

Bevlin was considered an old fool by most people, but Tavalisk preferred to give him the benefit of the doubt. Eighteen years ago there had been a momentous sight in the night sky. Tavalisk himself had even heard of it. Most people said it was a sign that the next five years would bring good harvest. And indeed Rorn hadn't had a bad year since—though gold not grain was harvested in this fair city. But that aside, Tavalisk had the uncanny feeling that the sign *had* meant more, and that Bevlin had somehow discovered what it was. The wiseman had ranted on about doom and its usual accompaniment, destruction. All but Tavalisk had ignored him: it never hurt to keep an eye on the doings of wisemen—like birds they always knew when a storm was coming. If this prisoner before him was sent on a mission by Bevlin, then Tavalisk was determined to find out the reason behind it.

Of late, he had grown frustrated by the prisoner's silence and had decided upon another way to discover who the knight was looking for and why. That was what brought him here today. He was going to let the knight go free. All *he* would have to do is watch and wait; the knight would lead him to the answers he sought.

"Guards," he called, moving the silken handkerchief from his face. "Free this man and see he gets some water." The guards hammered the metal stakes from the wrist irons and the prisoner fell heavily to the floor.

"He's out cold, Your Eminence."

"I can see that. Take his body and dump him somewhere in the city."

"Any special part of the city, Your Eminence?"

Tavalisk thought for a moment, a mischievous smile spreading across his full lips. "The whoring quarter will do nicely."

The city of Rorn boasted the largest whoring quarter in the known world. It was whispered that there was not a pleasure imaginable, no matter how illegal or bizarre, that could not be bought for the right price.

The quarter was a refuge for the miserable and the wretched: young girls barely eleven summers old walked the streets, beggars racked with disease could be found on every corner. Pickpockets and cutthroats waited in the shadows for a chance to relieve an unsuspecting passerby of his purse or his life. Weapons and poison and information could be purchased from the countless inns and taverns that jostled for business on the filth-ridden streets.

The streets themselves were so thick with human waste and rotting vegetation, it was said one could tell an outsider by the cloth he held to his nose. It was not a good idea to look like an outsider in the whoring quarter. Outsiders were an easy mark for con men and thieves; they were asking to be robbed or tricked out of their money. But still they came, drawn by the promise of illicit diversions and the thrill of danger. Young noblemen and honest tradesmen alike stole into the quarter as the day grew dim, looking for a game of chance, or a woman for the night . . . or both.

The sharp smell of excrement was the first thing he became aware of. The next was pain. It was unbearable, pulling every muscle into its knotted snarl. He tried to move through it, to come out where there was now light, but he was too weak. He spiraled downward to meet oblivion and found that it too was crafted from pain.

The dream tormented him once more. He was in a small room. There were children around the fire; two young girls, golden haired and rosy cheeked, smiled up at him, and there was a baby in his arms. The door opened and something glittered brightly on the threshold. Light from the vision eclipsed the glow of the fire, but not its warmth. As he reached toward the brightness, the baby fell from his arms. Stepping through the portal, the door closed behind him. The vision fled, receding to a pinpoint on the horizon, and he turned back to the door. Only the door wouldn't open. Try as he might, he couldn't get back to the room and the children around the fire. In desperation he flung himself against the door. His body met with stone.

He awoke with a start, sweat dripping into the corners of his mouth. Something had changed and unfamiliar air filled his lungs. It made him afraid. He was accustomed to his cell, and now even the comfort of familiarity was denied him.

When had he been released? He could barely recall when he'd last felt the cool brush of water upon his lips. One thing was fixed in his mind, though, and that was his name: he was Tawl. Tawl—but there had been more than that. Surely he had been Tawl of somewhere or something. The vaguest of stirrings rose in his breast; his mind tried to focus, but it was gone. He could not remember. He was just Tawl. He had been imprisoned and was now free.

He forced his mind to deal with the present and he began to take in some of his surroundings: he was in an alleyway between two large buildings, there was a chill in the air, and he was alone.

Tentatively, he raised an arm and pain coursed through his body. His arm was bare and he noticed the two-circled mark. It was familiar to him, it meant something, but he didn't know what. Tawl looked up as the sound of voices approached him.

"Hey, Megan, don't go near that man there. He looks as good as dead."

"Hush, Wenna. I'll go where I please."

"You're not liable to get a penny out of him. He doesn't look up to it."

Tawl watched as a young girl approached him—he was unable to do anything else. A moment later, her friend also drew close and he began to feel uncomfortable under their scrutiny.

"He smells really bad, like he ain't seen water for a year or more."

"Wenna, be quiet, he might hear you. Look, his eyes are open!" The one called Megan smiled gently. "He's not like the usual type down here."

"He's half dead, ain't he? To me that's the usual type."

"No, he's young and golden haired." The girl shrugged, as if to excuse her own folly. "There's something about him . . . look, Wenna, he's trying to say something." Tawl had not spoken for many months and could only manage a bare murmur.

"I think he's saying his name. It sounds like Tork or Tawl."

"Megan, come away before you land us in a pickle. You're right he ain't the usual type and that spells trouble." The one named Wenna pulled at her friend's arm, but she would not be budged.

"You go if you choose, Wenna, but I can't leave him here all alone. He'll surely die before the night is through."

"That, my girl, is not my problem. I'm off. I'm wasting precious time here when I need to be earning. If you've any sense in that pretty head of yours you'd do the same, too." With that, the older of the girls marched off, leaving him alone with the other.

Tawl tried to raise his arm again, and this time the girl took it. "Here, let me help you up." She noticed the mark. "Oh, that's strange. I've never seen a knight's circle with a scar running through it." Tawl let the girl help him to his feet and then promptly fell over again. He could not stand; his legs were not used to carrying any weight. "Oh, you poor thing. Here, try again. My little place ain't far from here. If you could just manage to walk." They tried again, this time

Tawl leaning on the girl for support. He was surprised that she could bear his weight for she was slightly built.

"Come on," she encouraged him. "There's not far to walk. We'll be there soon." Tawl struggled along by her side, learning to master his pain.

Baralis carefully allowed four drops of the pink-tinged poison to fall into the jug of wine. The poison rippled and then thinned, its deadly transparency soon lost to the eye. He was rather proud of his latest brew, as it was nearly without odor. He washed his hands thoroughly in a bowl of cold water. It wouldn't do to have any residue of the materials left on them; this was a particularly lethal mixture and he could already feel a burn upon his flesh.

His hands bore the marks of years spent working with deadly substances. Corrosive acids had gnawed the fat from his flesh, leaving his skin upon the bone. The skin itself was taut and red, and as it tightened he could feel it pull upon his fingers, drawing them inward toward his palms. Every day he rubbed warm oils into the straining flesh, hoping to retain what little mobility was left. His fingers, once long and elegant in youth, were now old beyond their years.

It was a price he paid for his expertise. It was high for one who valued manipulation and swiftness of hand as much as he did, but he would have it no other way. There was a cost to all things, and glory only came to those who were willing to pay the price.

It was time to place the jug of wine in Maybor's chambers. The lord was usually away from the castle in the afternoons, hunting or riding. This was a job he would have to do himself. He could not trust Crope with a task that required such stealth.

He needed to be very cautious. He would have preferred to enter Maybor's chamber at night, with darkness as his ally, but that did not suit his plans. Twilight was the best he could manage. He slipped into the labyrinth by way of the beer cellar—no one marked his passing. He had a talent for going unnoticed; it was his natural disposition to search out shadow and shade.

He made good time and was soon approaching Maybor's chamber. Baralis was surprised to hear the sound of voices and he moved close against the wall, putting his ear to a small crack in the stone. He was astounded to hear the voice of the queen. Arinalda in Maybor's chambers—what intrigue was this? The queen never visited private chambers, she always called people to *her*. Baralis concentrated on listening to the rise and fall of their voices.

"I am well pleased to hear that your daughter, Melliandra, is willing for the match, as I had harbored a thought that she may have been reluctant." The queen spoke with little warmth, her regal tones filtering through the breech in the stone.

"Your Highness, I can assure you my daughter wishes to marry your son more than anything else." Maybor spoke with exaggerated deference. Baralis' eyes narrowed with contempt.

"Very good," the queen was saying. "We will hold the betrothal ceremony ten days from now. I am sure you will agree that we should move quickly on this matter."

"I do, my queen. I also think, if you will pardon me for saying, Your Highness, that the betrothal should be kept a secret until it has taken place." There was a slight pause and then the queen spoke, her cold tones carrying straight to Baralis' ear.

"I agree. There are some at court who I would prefer kept in the dark about this matter. I will take my leave now, Lord Maybor. I wish you joy of the day." Baralis moved his eye to the crack and saw Maybor bow low to the queen. After the door closed, Maybor's expression of humility changed to one of triumph.

Baralis smiled coldly as the lord poured himself a glass of wine. "Enjoy your wine, Maybor," he murmured. "You might not relish your next cup as much." Baralis settled down to wait for Maybor to take his leave, the vial of poison warming in his hand.

Melli was in a turmoil. Her brother Kedrac had just left.

He had informed her the betrothal was agreed upon—the queen had set a date for the official announcement.

On hearing the news of her fate, decided upon without her consent, rebellion stirred within her breast. She would never in a million years marry the cold and arrogant Prince Kylock. She had no wish to be queen of the Four Kingdoms if Kylock would be her king. She couldn't exactly say why she disliked him so much—he was always polite to her when they met. But there was something about him that touched a nerve deep within her. Whenever she caught sight of him around the castle, she shuddered inwardly. And now her father had finalized the match.

Oh, she knew well what her father's plan was. With the king weak, every lord was grabbing for power, and her father was no different: when he was not at war, he was plotting and scheming. Now he had decided upon the ultimate move, to place his daughter in the role of future queen. Maybor cared not a jot for her; his only interests were his precious sons. One of the reasons the war with the Halcus had taken place was because he had wanted to secure land for her brothers.

The war had backfired on him, however, for his lands along the River Nestor were now a battlefield and the yields of the famous Nestor apple orchards were at an all-time low. Her father would be feeling the cruel pinch of war upon his pocket.

She hated him! But she was not sure if she meant her father or Kylock. Last night, when she had refused point-blank to ever marry the prince, her father had actually slapped her. In the gardens! Where anyone could have seen. She had noticed of late her father often held his meetings in the gardens. It appeared nowadays that he didn't even trust stone walls.

To Melli the past five years had been a great disappointment. She had longed to become a woman, but when her breasts swelled and her blood flowed, she found that she was still a young girl. Her presentation to the queen had not been the glorious triumph she had imagined. The country was at war and no one had much time for frivolous ceremonies, so there had been few to admire the beauty of her gown. That had not been her biggest disappointment, though.

She was most disillusioned with her life as a lady of the court. She'd come to realize that the very dresses and jewels she had once dreamed of now bored her. The young men at court were naive and pompous fools, and she wanted none of them. But what she most hated were the restrictions placed upon a woman of her rank. As a child she could race down the corridors, steal to the kitchens for an illicit treat, and laugh loudly at the top of her voice. Now, as a young lady she might as well not leave her rooms for all the freedom she was afforded elsewhere. It was always:

"Walk with your head up, Melliandra."

"Keep your voice low and pleasing, Melliandra."

"Never, ever contradict a man, Melliandra."

The rules for women were endless. She was expected to change clothes three times a day, she was not allowed in the gardens without a servant accompanying her, she could only ride sidesaddle, she must drink her wine watered and eat her food like a bird. To top it all off, she was forced to spend all of her days cooped up with old matrons, sewing and gossiping.

Her friends might love to dress up and flirt, but playing the role of dumb female was beneath her dignity, and she would never, ever pretend a man was right when he was wrong. She hated it so much, she even hated the sound of the very name she had so desired and now longed to be just plain Melli again.

She sat on the corner of her bed and wondered what she would do. She had no choice about the betrothal. Her father was insisting upon it and she dared not defy him. She'd heard chilling stories of daughters who defied their fathers, tales of floggings and starvations and worse—stories told with relish by her aging nurse.

She'd harbored the distant hope that the queen might object to the betrothal at the last minute, deciding she was not good enough, or pretty enough, or well bred enough for her son, but it appeared that the queen was as anxious for this match as her father.

Queen Arinalda was in a weak position and the country

was ripe for invasion. The duke of Bren's greed for land was making her nervous. The city of Bren was becoming too big to support itself and was starting to look elsewhere for food for its tables. The Four Kingdoms were a feast for the taking. The queen needed the country to appear strong in order to curb any thoughts of conquest the duke might be harboring. To this end she needed to ally herself with the most powerful lord in the kingdoms: Melli's father. Maybor would then be forced to defend the weak king from those who sought to challenge or invade. Whatever the reasons for the match, Melli was sure of one thing: she was just a pawn.

She had tried to reason with her father last night: she'd pleaded with him to give up the idea of the betrothal. He would not listen to her. He'd pointed out that he owned every scrap of fabric on her back, every ring on her finger and, although he didn't say it . . . every breath in her body. She was no more than a possession, and the time had come to bring her to market.

No, Melli thought, *I will not be traded like a sack of grain.*

She would run away. Kedrac's visit had been the final straw. Her brother had told her, in his condescending manner, that the betrothal was a great honor for their family, a great advancement, a chance to acquire more land and more prestige. Not one word about her. He'd just droned on about his future, his increased prospects, his expectations. She was nothing to him, merely a means to bring greater power and glory to himself. The same was true of her father. The very fact that he had sent Kedrac to break the news instead of coming himself showed how little he thought of her.

Melli took a deep breath. She was going to leave the castle. No longer would she be beholden to her father and brothers, no longer would she be a chattel, a pawn in their games of power. They had misjudged her if they thought she would quietly submit to their plans.

Pacing the room, she tried to hold onto her anger. It strengthened her, made her want to take charge of her own life. She moved to the window, wanting to look upon the outside world, a world that she would make herself part of. It was dark and quiet, a light rain was falling and the chill of night caressed her cheek. Instead of feeling exhilarated, she found herself afraid: the world outside beckoned . . . ambivalent and unfamiliar. Melli shuddered and pulled the heavy brocade curtains together.

She *would* go ahead with her plan. She would leave the castle tonight.

Her thoughts were interrupted by the entrance of her maid. The sly-eyed Lynni busied herself laying out a dress for the evening. "You'd better hurry, my lady, or you'll be late for dinner."

"I am not feeling well, Lynni. I will take a cold supper in my room."

"You look well enough to me. You must go down. There are visitors from Lanholt and your presence will be expected."

"Do as I say," said Melli sharply. The girl left the room, swinging her hips with studied insolence.

Melli began sorting through her things, deciding what she would take with her. She had no money of her own, but was allowed to keep a modest amount of jewelry in her room, and these she placed in a small cloth bag. She scanned her chamber. She now possessed a mirror of her own, and her reflection caught her eye; she looked small and frightened.

She caught hold of her straight, dark hair and pulled it back with a leather thong, thinking it suited her a lot better than some of the overelaborate court styles. Next Melli put on her plainest woollen dress, tied the cloth bag containing her jewels securely around her waist, and then selected her thickest riding cloak. All she had to do was wait for Lynni to return with her supper and she would be off, stealing out of the castle under the cover of darkness. Never for a moment did she consider leaving without her supper—that would be foolish.

Melli slipped beneath the bedclothes to wait, and thought of where she would go. Her mother, before she'd died, had spoken of relatives in Annis. She would head there.

Lord Maybor was having a very good day. The queen

had approved the match between Kylock and his daughter. He had supped well this night.

As he dined, he looked around the hall. The huge tapestries caught his eye. They showed the story of how the Four Kingdoms had been ripped asunder during the terrible Wars of Faith. They went on to depict the one man who, over a hundred years later, was responsible for reuniting the four glorious territories in defiance of the Church. The Four Kingdoms boasted the most fertile soil in the north. It was well placed for farm land and timber, its people were plump and prosperous, its armies well trained and well fed. Harvell the Fierce had been the driving force behind the Wars of Reunification. Thanks to him, the green and vibrant country was made whole once again.

Maybor fancied there was a little of Harvell's nature in himself, and certainly before the year was out he would form part of the great tradition that was the lineage of kings. He would be father to a queen! He could barely contain his excitement.

He noticed that many of the lords gathered around the great table were puzzled by his uncharacteristic good humor, and it pleased him greatly that they were ignorant of his impending elevation. Maybor felt an overflowing of goodwill. He called for more venison and ale, and even cheered the minstrels, who he normally enjoyed pelting with vegetables and chicken bones.

The king must be made to step down, he thought. He is an empty vessel and has no place on the throne of the Four Kingdoms. Fresh blood should flow into the leadership, the blood of his future son-in-law, Kylock. True, Kylock was young, but Maybor had plans to use that youth to his advantage, guiding Kylock's decisions, molding the new king. He, Maybor, would be the power behind the throne.

He paused in his delicious reverie for a moment and considered Prince Kylock. There was something about the lad that gave him the shivers, but no mind, he thought, *he will make a fine king with me to guide him*. Melliandra, his ungrateful rebel of a daughter, had actually said she would not marry him. Well, it was too late for her objections now.

He would personally beat the defiance out of her if necessary.

The first thing he would urge the new king to do would be to end the war with the Halcus once and for all. He was tired of his lands being used as campsites and battlefields. Once the war was over, he would claim the land to the east of the River Nestor for himself: it was fine land for growing cider apples.

Personal profit aside, there were other more pressing reasons why the war should be won quickly. Bren was up to no good. The duke had already started a program of annexation to the southeast, and it wouldn't be long before his eye turned west. Highwall and Annis were strong and well armed. The kingdoms, however, were so distracted by warring with Halcus that they were practically asking to be invaded. No matter they were a distance apart, the good duke's ancestors had once held land west of the Nestor, and a prior claim, no matter how tenuous, always served to incite the indignant passions of would-be invaders.

Maybor drained his cup. It was getting late, and he took his leave of his dinner companions, his feet a little unsteady from the large amount of ale he had drunk. As he returned to his chamber, the only thing he wanted to do was have a glass of lobanfern red to aid his digestion and then to bed for a deep sleep.

"Kelse, you idle lout," he shouted before entering his chamber. "Come and turn down my bed and stoke up my fire. There is a bite in the air tonight." Maybor was surprised not to hear the scurry of his servant's feet on the stone; Kelse was usually quick to respond. He might already be in the chamber, warming the sheets with hot bricks.

Maybor entered his room. It was cold; the fire had gone out. "Damn!" he muttered. "Kelse, where in Borc's name are you?" Maybor crossed to the table where he kept a jug of his favorite wine. He poured himself a generous cup and moved through to the bedchamber.

As he lifted the cup to his lips, he caught sight of a body on the floor near his bed. It was his servant Kelse. Puzzled, he put down the cup, moved toward the body and slapped Kelse hard on the cheek.

"Kelse, you drunken malingerer. Awaken this instant, or I swear I will have your innards on a platter." Kelse did not respond. Maybor grew alarmed; the man had not moved. "What treachery is this?" His eyes alighted on the upturned cup that lay beside Kelse's body. Maybor drew the cup to his nose and smelled it: lobanfern red. He felt his servant's lifeless body: it was cold. "Poison," he spoke.

Maybor felt the hairs on his neck bristle. He was in no doubt that the poison had been meant for him. The unfortunate Kelse had stolen a glass of the tainted wine and had paid for it with his life. Maybor smiled grimly. Kelse had unknowingly performed the greatest service a servant could do for his master: lay down his life. He trembled to think what might have happened if the drugged wine had passed his lips. He would be the one lying on the cold stone, dead. He knew who had done this.

"Baralis," he whispered under his breath. He had almost been expecting it. For many months now he had seen the look of hatred on Baralis' face. They both had scores to settle, and it seemed that the king's chancellor had made the first move to resolve them.

Poison was just the sort of cowardly method that Baralis favored. Maybor was a fighting man, a veteran of many campaigns, and had only contempt for such underhanded tactics. If *he* were to plan an assassination—and, after the events of tonight, it would seem likely he would have to, a man could hardly be expected to ignore an attempt on his life—*he* would resort to more conventional techniques. There was more beauty and certainty to be found in a knife to the throat than in a jug of poisoned wine.

"Your plans have gone wrong on this dark night," he murmured softly. "Sleep soundly in your bed, Baralis, lord and chancellor, for there may not be many nights left for you to dream in."

Jack was, as usual, up at four. He no longer had to keep the ovens fueled all night—that job had passed on to a younger boy. He was now in charge of supervising the first baking and, after the oven-boy left, he usually had the kitchen to himself for an hour before Master Frallit and the other bakers appeared.

He dressed quickly, the temperature in his room giving speed to his actions. His breeches were four months old and he was pleased to notice they fitted him now exactly as they did when newly made, which meant he'd finally stopped growing. About time, too. It wasn't much fun being the tallest person in the kitchens. He was always the one called upon to chase spiders from their webs and to shake the moths from slow-drying herbs.

Pulling on a light tunic, he noticed it smelled a little too strongly of sweat. He'd hoped to cross the path of the table-maid Findra later on in the day, and had recently found out that girls didn't appreciate too generous a smell. Of course the confusing thing was that Grift had informed him that no smell at all was worse than the most terrible stench: "Women choose a lover with their noses first, so a man's odor must declare his intentions," was a favorite saying of his. Deciding that he'd flour his tunic down later to create the delicate balance needed for wooing, Jack made his way to the kitchens.

The first thing he did was add fragrant woods to the furnace. Frallit maintained there were only two types of wood in the world: one for heating and one for cooking. Overnight the oven was fueled with plentiful woods such as oak and ash, but a day's baking called for more delicate fuel. Hawthorne, hazel, and chestnut were added before the bread was put to bake. The master baker swore by them: "They give a fragrance to the dough that becomes a flavor when the flame is high," he would say.

Once that was seen to, Jack brought the dough down from the shelf above the oven. The shelf benefited from the heat of the furnace and the dough rose well overnight. He removed the damp linen cloth from the tray and absently punched each individual portion of dough down and then kneaded them, his hands deft with experience. Quickly, he formed neat rows on the baking slabs and then opened the huge iron door of the oven, its blazing heat hitting Jack in a familiar wave. He had singed his hair on more than one occasion in the past. He loaded the slabs onto shelves and closed the door. Next, he threw a measure of water into the furnace; the steam produced would add extra vigor to the crust.

Jack then turned his attention to mixing the "noon loaves." These would be the third and fourth batches of the day. The population of Castle Harvell was so great that the oven had to be in use nearly every waking hour. The first batches of the morning were maslin loaves. Formed from rye and wheat, maslin loaves were the staple of lords and servants alike. What was cooked next often depended upon who was visiting the castle. When foreign noblemen and envoys were in attendance, the master baker usually honored them by baking their native loaves and delicacies. Later in the afternoon, when the sweet breads and fancies were still cooling, Frallit would indulge in what he called his "baker's privilege."

Harvell, like most towns, had several communal ovens where women brought their dough to be baked. A copper penny a loaf was the charge. Frallit had taken to renting out space in the castle oven for a similar rate. Being a canny businessman, the master baker offered the women one free loaf with a dozen, and now had rather a profitable sideline going. The head cellarer and the chief cook were given a silencing cut of the proceeds. Jack's inducement for keeping quiet was nothing more than the threat of a sound thrashing.

Once the noon loaves were mixed and the yeast set to proof, Jack was free to find himself something to eat. He usually spent the proofing time visiting the servants' hall for a measure of ale and a bowl of whatever was served the night before. This morning, however, Baralis had kept him up so late scribing, that all he wanted to do was sit down for a while and have a short rest.

He settled himself on the baker's bench and rested his head against the ledge. His eyes were heavy with lost sleep. He'd only managed to snatch about three hours rest last night and he was tired beyond measure. Before he knew it, he had drifted off into a light and dreamless sleep.

When he next opened his eyes, he saw the alarming sight of black smoke bellowing from the oven. "Copper pots!" he exclaimed, immediately realizing he had fallen asleep leaving bread baking in the oven. He rushed over to the oven, but his nose had already told him what his eyes could see: the loaves were burnt. All eight score of them. Jack grew cold with fear. Frallit would surely kill him for this. Half the morning's bread burnt to a cinder. Oh, if only he hadn't fallen asleep.

His mind was racing with panic as he stared at the charred loaves in the oven, desperately wishing they were not burnt. Master Frallit had whipped the hide off a boy once for burning the loaves. The boy had never been seen in the kitchens again. Just this week the master baker had warned Jack about sloppy work, threatening to send him away from the castle if he didn't improve. It was one thing to dream about leaving, but quite another to be thrown out.

What was he going to do? Master Frallit would be along any minute. If only he could change things, make the loaves dough again. His brow creased with desperation and he felt pain course through his head. He suddenly felt faint and light-headed, and stumbled to the floor, losing consciousness.

Baralis had not slept all night. His head was full of what he'd overheard outside of Maybor's chamber. The queen was obviously trying her hand at politicking, seeking to consolidate her position by marrying Kylock to Maybor's daughter. She would be a fool to think that the king would be made safe by an alliance with Maybor. The first thing Maybor would do would be to oust the old king and put Kylock in his place, thinking he could control the young and inexperienced boy.

Only now there would be no betrothal: with Maybor dead, the queen would find his charming daughter, Melliandra, to be less useful a bride for her son. Baralis smiled, his teeth glittering in the firelight. He had a more glorious match for Kylock in mind. He would see the prince married to one more exalted than the daughter of a mere lord. It was time that the kingdoms took up a more central position in the arena of the civilized world.

Baralis tossed and turned in the pale morning light,

imagining gleefully what the new day would bring. To finally have that scheming viper Maybor out of his way! He must be careful to rehearse Crope in his alibi: he and Crope were to have been out yesterday gathering special herbs for medicines, and indeed it was partly true—he had sent Crope to the woods and told him to pick some flowers. Flowers to place on Maybor's grave.

Suddenly, Baralis felt something, the unmistakable sensation that signaled the use of power. Someone was drawing raw, untrained power in the castle. Foreboding crept over him. The power being wielded was mighty indeed but strangely crude. Baralis' body was a razor edge of perception. He shot out his mental awareness, searching out the source of the drawing.

"Jack, Jack, wake up. What do you think you're doing falling asleep when there's loaves in the oven?" admonished Tilly. "It's a wonder they didn't burn, else you'd been in deep trouble with Frallit."

Jack sat up, startled. "But they did burn, Tilly, I—"

"Oh, hush, you big dimwit. You must have been dreaming. They're just browning off nicely now. Look."

Jack looked through the gap in the oven designed for monitoring the baking and was startled to find that Tilly was right—the loaves were not burnt. Someone must have replaced the burnt loaves with a new batch while he was unconscious. He stood up and felt a wave of nausea flood over his body.

He checked the trays of waiting dough. There was the same number as earlier—if a new batch were in the oven, they would be empty. He smelled the air. There was the faintest whiff of burning—he had not been dreaming. He rushed over to the waste bins, but no charred loaves had been thrown out.

Tilly was looking at him as if he was mad. He was sure he hadn't dreamed the incident: the loaves *had* been burnt. What had he done? He recalled the instant before he passed out there had been a sick feeling in his stomach and great pressure in his head.

Jack felt the turn of fate. Something had happened here, something that went against the laws of nature, something terrible—and he was responsible for it. He was trembling and his legs were threatening to give way beneath him. He needed to lie down, to sleep, to forget.

"Tilly, I don't feel too good. I need to have a rest."

Tilly, seeing something strange in the young boy's face, softened. "Very well, I'll cover for you with Frallit. Be off now."

Baralis perceived that the unleashing of power had come from below, and he became a hound on the scent. Quickly, he dressed and called for Crope. When the huge simpleton arrived, they both headed out of his chambers and down to the lower depths of the castle.

Baralis knew fear for the first time in many years. He hated the unknown. He was a great believer in careful planning and attention to detail. Nothing disturbed him more than the unexpected. Users of sorcery were few and far between—particularly in the north—indeed, that was why he had settled here in the first place. To be the only one at the court of the Four Kingdoms with the advantages of deviltry at his disposal.

For that is what the fools thought sorcery was: a gift from the devil. Let them think what they would; the ignorance of others had long proved to be one of his greatest allies. The people in the castle were afraid of him. They whispered that he was a demon, a sorcerer, a madman. It suited him nicely to let the whisperings persist: people were afraid of him, and he liked it that way.

The thought that someone in the castle had access to the same elusive source as he gave great haste to his step.

He drew nearer to where the power had been drawn, Crope lumbering behind him. The kitchens! The power had been drawn in the kitchens, he was sure of it. Baralis was oblivious to the servants and guards, who quickly stepped out of his way to let him pass.

Once he found himself in the huge castle kitchens, he could feel the aftermath prickling upon his skin. Without a word to the startled staff, he crossed from the cook's section to the baker's kitchen. This was it, every hair on his body confirmed it. He drew close to the huge oven, vestiges of the drawing lapping over his body in waves. It had happened here. Wildly he looked around, ignoring the master baker and Tilly. Next to the oven was a large wooden table on which scores of loaves were cooling. It was the loaves! The power had been drawn on the loaves.

It seemed like madness. Who would draw the power to eight score of loaves? Baralis rubbed his chin as he considered the situation. He looked to the master baker and to Tilly: it was certainly neither of those terrified wretches. He surprised Tilly by grabbing her arm and twisting it painfully behind her back.

"Now, my pretty little wench," he said, the gentleness of his voice belying his actions. "I see you are frightened by the sight of my man Crope." Another twist of the arm. "You do well to fear him, for Crope is a dangerous man, aren't you, Crope?" He turned to Crope, who nodded enthusiastically. "Now, answer my question. What happened here this morning?"

Tilly looked bewildered. "Nothing, sir." Tears welled in her eyes.

"Who was in the kitchen this morning?" Another twist of the arm.

"Why, no one, sir. Just me and Master Frallit and Jack."

"Are you sure there was no one else?"

"Well, sir, I've only been here a few minutes. You'd better ask Jack—he was here earlier."

"Where is Jack now?" Baralis' voice was as smooth and inviting as silk.

"He went to lie down. He said he wasn't feeling well."

Baralis let Tilly go, a notion beginning to form in his mind. "What do you mean he felt unwell? What was wrong with him?"

"Well, sir, it was quite queer really. When I came down, he was fast asleep on the floor, and he said something about the loaves being burnt, and of course they weren't . . . and then he said he didn't feel well."

"Where is his room?"

"On the south side of the servants' quarters, right at the top."

Baralis paused a moment, his eye on the oven. "All the loaves must be destroyed."

"But that's half a morning's baking—"

"*Do as I say!*" Baralis' gaze challenged the master baker to defy him. Satisfied he would be obeyed, he spun round and marched out of the kitchen, Crope in his wake.

Jack had decided not to go to his room, but to get some air instead. His head felt thick and heavy, like it did when he drank too much ale.

He sat down on the grass, his legs giving way beneath him. When he looked up, he saw in the distance the unmistakable figure of Baralis. He was followed by Crope, and they were heading across the grounds in the direction of the servants' quarters. They had come from the kitchens. There was something about the sight of Baralis' dark cloak shifting in the breeze that filled Jack with apprehension.

Although he was some distance away, Jack saw determination in the line of Baralis' brow and the sight of it made him shudder. Jack knew without a doubt they were looking for him.

He began to piece his thoughts together. He had done something terrible this morning; he'd transgressed some fundamental law. And now it seemed that Baralis, the one person in the castle who was rumored to have knowledge of such things, had discovered what he'd done. Baralis and Crope were looking for him, probably to punish him or worse. He'd changed the course of events, performed an aberration against nature . . . and people were stoned for such things in these parts.

Everyone knew there were forces in the world that couldn't be explained, but no one liked to speak of them. To mention sorcery was to mention the devil. Grift had told him so a hundred times, and everyone knew the dangers of naming the devil. What did that make him, then? He didn't feel evil. Sometimes he was slow about his work and didn't pay the respect he should to Master Frallit—but was he *evil*?

Clouds drifted across the path of the sun, casting Jack in the shade. There *was* something about him that was evil, one thought in his mind that *was* as good as a sin. He harbored a terrible hatred—the man who had fathered and then abandoned him, he would like to see dead. It was the first time that Jack had admitted the strength of his feelings. For too long he had tried to fool himself into believing he didn't care a jot about who his father was. Yet the events of this morning had somehow allowed him the freedom to admit the depth of his feelings. His mother was no saint, that was common knowledge, but she'd deserved better than to be forsaken—they both did.

Somehow it seemed that all things were connected: the loaves, his mother, his father. He tried to grasp at the common thread, but it eluded him, and then, after a moment, it was gone.

What did remain was the reality of this morning. He had a decision to make: should he stay in the castle and risk the wrath of Baralis and the condemnation of his friends, or should he leave and make a new way in the world?

Perhaps because the shade was akin to the night, Jack felt the urge to be off. If the sun had still been shining, maybe his life would have taken a different path.

With the decision made, Jack began to feel calm. Perhaps this morning was a blessing—it gave him reason to do what he'd only dreamt of before. Swiftly, not turning to look back, he made his way across the castle grounds and to the outer wall. With each step came strength of purpose, and by the time he passed the castle gates, he was sure he'd made the right choice.

Three

Lord Maybor awoke late and immediately felt a deep happiness. A man who has been saved from a certain death has reason to be happy. Maybor had yet another reason: his daughter would be queen.

Once he was king—no, he corrected himself, when his son-in-law was king—things would be very different around the court at Harvell. The Known Lands were in a state of unease—those damned knights of Valdis, with their high ideals and low tolerances, were busy making trouble. Having lost out on trade to Rorn in the south, they were trying to gain a foothold in the north. He wasn't going to have any of that. He heard the knights were ridiculously honest, and everyone knew honesty was a dangerous habit in a trading partner. Bren was another place that bore watching: he wouldn't be against the idea of forming a peaceful alliance with some of the other northern powers just to keep ideas of conquest out of the duke of Bren's ambitious head. Yes, there would be much for him to do behind the throne.

Maybor dressed quickly, careful not to step on his dead servant. He felt like wearing one of his more ostentatious robes on this fine morning, so chose a beautiful silk in deep red. One never knew when one might be called upon to entertain foreign dignitaries. On most days there was usually someone interesting or influential applying for entry at the castle gates.

Maybor was beginning to feel a little guilty for having slapped his daughter the other evening. Now that he knew the future was certain, he would be kinder to her; she would eventually come round. He would buy her a gift. That was it: buy her a beautiful and hugely expensive gift. He had recently heard tell of a rare and exquisite gemstone that came from beyond the Drylands—what was it called? *Isslt,* that was it. It was supposed to flicker with an inner light. He had been told it was a deep, sea blue—the color of Melliandra's eyes. Even better. He would spare no expense. She would have the biggest one he could find, big as a fist. He would make the arrangements for acquiring it this very day.

As he was admiring his portly figure in the mirror, there was a knock on his door.

"Come." He was surprised to see his daughter's maid Lynni enter the room. Then his spirits picked up; perhaps the young chit fancied a tumble.

"What is it, my pretty one?" The girl looked frightened. "Speak up, girl. There is no need to be shy, many women take a fancy to an older man." Lynni turned as red as Maybor's robe.

"Sir, it's not that." She hesitated, her eyes narrowing. "But you are an uncommonly handsome man, sir."

"Yes, the mirror tells me that every day. But come along, girl. Spit out what you have come to tell me, and maybe then we can take a quick tumble if you are willing."

"Well, sir, I'd be willing for a tumble myself, but I fear my news might wilt your swell."

"What is it? Hasn't Lady Melliandra got a clean dress to wear?" Maybor smiled indulgently. Such were the nature of women's problems: a lost comb, a broken locket, a shoe so tight it pinched.

The girl looked down at the floor. "Lady Melliandra has gone."

A cold dread stole over Maybor. "What do you mean, gone? Where has she gone?"

The girl could not meet his eye. She played nervously

with her fingers. "Well, sir, I came to her room this morning, same as usual, and she was not there."

"Could she have gone for a walk, or to see a friend?"

"She would have told me, sir."

Maybor felt the quick flare of anger. He took the girl's thin shoulders in his hands and shook her. "Does she have a lover?" he demanded.

"No, sir." The girl's voice trembled with fear.

"If you are lying to me, I will have your tongue pulled out."

"No, sir, she is a virgin. I'm positive."

Maybor changed his line of questioning, "Has her bed been slept in?"

"Well, sir, the covers were ruffled somewhat, but I have a feeling she had not slept there."

"Come with me." He grasped Lynni by the arm and marched her to Melli's bedchamber. Baralis! If that demon had a hand in this, he would be dead before the day was finished.

By the time they arrived at his daughter's chambers, Maybor had worked himself into a fury. There was no sign of his daughter. His eye alighted on the ivory box in which she was allowed to keep her less valuable jewels. It was empty!

"Find out if any of her clothes are missing . . . *now*!" he boomed loudly when the girl hesitated. As Maybor waited, he held the fragile box in his hands, shaking his head.

The girl ran from the dressing room. "One of her woollen dresses and her heavy riding cloak are missing."

Maybor was frantic—what had become of her? A thousand dangers could befall a young girl outside the castle walls. Melliandra had no idea of the real world, no idea at all. She was a lamb to the slaughter. "Damn." Maybor flung the box across the room, where it shattered against the wall. "She is only a *child*!" The rage left him as he looked upon his handiwork. Fragments of ivory lay scattered upon the floor. He spoke quietly, more to himself than the girl. "She has to be brought back. She cannot have gone far.

"You," he said, turning to Lynni, "had better hope she is found, for I will hold you responsible if she is not. You were supposed to watch her." Lynni was shaking from head to foot. "Do you know where she might be headed? Think hard, girl."

"No, sir, nowhere."

Maybor scrutinized the girl. She was too stupid to be hiding anything from him. As an afterthought he said: "Visit me in my chamber this night." He hurried from the room, not bothering to wait for her assent.

His daughter had run away! The willful, headstrong girl, more like himself than any of his sons, his most cherished possession and his greatest asset, had fled the castle. He would need to mount a search party. He would call his sons to him and they could head the search. After all, he thought, it is in their interest to find her. He stopped in his tracks. The queen! He could not let the queen find out Melliandra had fled. She was a proud woman and liable to call off the match if she thought his daughter wasn't willing. He would have to proceed carefully. He wouldn't call out the guards after all; he would use only his own men.

As he dashed down through the castle, he caught sight of Baralis' fool, Crope. Maybor bowed in mock politeness. "Be sure to give my regards to your master." If nothing else today, he would have the comfort of knowing his were not the only plans that had gone awry.

"Here, have a little mulled holk. It will make you feel better." Megan handed Tawl a cup of pungent, steaming liquid. As he drank the holk, he seemed to remember being given a drink in the past that promised to make him feel better. He tried to remember the name, it was on the tip of his tongue. "Lacus," he said out loud.

Megan gave him a querying look, and then asked, "Is that where you are from?" Tawl managed a smile and a weak laugh.

"No, the lacus was a drink I was given years back by a wise old man. He said it cured most ailments."

"It's a pity you haven't got any of that here." She smiled brightly, her green eyes twinkling. Tawl saw for the first time how pretty she was.

"Why did you help me last night? It would have been easier for you to have left me to die."

Megan shrugged. "Who can say? I'm not sure myself. Maybe it was your golden hair. You don't see much hair that color around here." The girl seemed a little embarrassed and Tawl let the matter drop.

The holk was easing the pain in his arms a little. With the pain letting up, he could begin to try and remember what had happened to him. "What city am I in?"

"Why, Rorn, of course. The greatest city in the east." Tawl smiled indulgently at her pride. *Rorn,* he thought. *What on earth am I doing in Rorn?*

When Megan had brought him to her meager room last night, she had bathed and hand-fed him with the tenderest of care. She rubbed curative oils into his sore flesh and wrapped him in warm blankets.

Tawl felt bare skin under the covers and discovered he was naked beneath them. Megan caught the action and smiled cheekily. "Come now, surely you are not modest." Tawl *was* in fact very modest, and he was about to say so when Megan continued, "Besides, in my line of work, you get to see that kind of thing all the time." She looked directly at him, challenging him to say something. When he was silent, she continued, "I can see you are shocked."

Tawl shook his head. "I'm more concerned than shocked."

"Well, I don't need your concern, thank you!" Megan's pretty lips tightened and she spoke with the bite of irony. "I'd be more *concerned* if I'd been left for dead down a dark alleyway." Her face softened into contrition. "I'm sorry, Tawl. I know you meant no offense." With that she pulled on her cloak. "I'm off out for a bit to pick up some food, and you'll need some new clothes. I threw your old ones out in the street. I'll be back before too long. Good day." One flick of her chestnut curls and she was gone.

Tawl sipped on his drink. The holk soothed his aching body and helped clear his head. He began to remember how he had come to be here. He was a knight of Valdis and had been sent to the wiseman Bevlin, who in turn had sent him to look for a boy. Memories flooded back. Five years spent searching for someone with no name and no face. All the cities he'd visited, all the people he'd talked to, all the years he'd spent pursuing the dream of an old man in a small cottage.

He recalled the night he was picked up. He had been drinking in a darkened tavern. Four men set upon him. They had dragged him outside and beaten him, and then, even before his blood was dry, they chained him up. He'd hated being chained at first, but once they began to torture him, he found himself longing to be strung up once more. Tawl shuddered. He had no desire to remember the torture. Through it all he'd been asked a question, one that was not within his power to answer: "Who is the boy you seek?" Countless times he'd been asked, countless times he had no answer.

He wondered how long he had been kept chained. He had no memory of the time leading up to his release. Why had they released him? He had not told them what they wanted to know; indeed, he could not. So why set him free now?

Tawl remembered a fleshy, overweight figure, a man who often lurked in the shadows while he was being tortured. The fat man had reeked of exotic fragrances and his voice was rich with privilege. He was the one who was in charge. It would have been his decision to let him go. How long had he been kept there? How much time had he lost?

There was something else to remember, something hidden deeper. He strained for the memory. It came to him with sickening clarity, bringing in its wake the familiar wave of despair. With its remembrance, Tawl felt complete. It was his burden, and he was so used to its weight that without it he felt insubstantial. It defined who he was and what he must be.

It had been a hot summer the year he'd turned thirteen. Mosquitoes rose from the marshes like smoke from a fire. The world hummed to their tune. The only time of day worth leaving the shade for was early morning. Tawl would make his way along the marsh tracks and down to the ever-shrinking fishing hole. Fixing his line in place by jamming the rod between two stones, he'd settle down for a couple of hours to give the fish chance to bite. Only today he couldn't rest. His thoughts, which normally dwelt on dreams of combat and glory, were taken up with pictures of the sickroom.

The birth wasn't going well. The midwife had halved the candles before lighting them, and Tawl, like everyone who came from the Great Marshes, knew what that meant. Not that he needed a ritual to tell him what his eyes could see: his mother was dying. The labor was too long. The house was too hot. Half the night he'd been awake, tossing and turning in sheets damp with sweat. His mother's breath drew the mosquitoes. The smell of urine drew the flies.

He was ashamed to feel relief when morning finally came, for it provided an excuse to be out of the house. The midwife had to be paid whatever the birthing might bring, and fish were the only currency they had to offer. Tawl shook off his sisters; they were too young to keep up with him, and he needed to be alone. The fish were slow to bite and it was mid-afternoon before he'd caught what was needed: three for the midwife, two for his mother, one for each of his sisters and himself, and one extra in case the baby had arrived. His father could see to his own.

The midwife met him at the door. "She's too weak to birth. Should I cut her open and at least save the child?"

Tawl beat his fist against the wall. The pain brought him back to the present. How could she do that! How could she put the decision to end his mother's life into his hands? He, a boy just past his twelfth year. No one of any age should have such a responsibility placed upon them. Tawl's pain crystallized into anger. Where had his father been? His useless, drunken father. With anger came release. Anger made everything bearable; it was how he coped. And, as long as he didn't think about what had happened later—much later—coping was enough.

Megan burst into the room, her brightness was a useful distraction. "Here we are. I wasn't too long, was I? I've got all sorts of goodies." Her arms were filled with packages. "Look, I've got some hot eel pie, and some jellied goose livers, and even some fresh figs!" She duly unpacked these items, holding them up for Tawl to admire. Tawl smiled, approving the purchases. He was glad of her presence. It kept his demons at bay.

"I think I'll have a few figs. I haven't the courage for eels." As soon as he spoke, he regretted it, for the look on Megan's face turned from joy to disappointment. He was quick to mend his error. "Maybe I could manage a few of the jellied livers, though."

Megan smiled brightly, "Oh, I am pleased. Tawl, I bought them specially for you. I'll have the eel pie myself. I nearly forgot! I bought you some clothes, as well." She unwrapped the largest of her bundles. "I'm sorry they're not new, but they're not bad. Look." She held up a canary yellow tunic and a pair of striped breeches. "Oh, and I bought you a cloak, too—real goat's wool. Here, feel it." She held it out. Tawl admired the quality to gratify her, the twinkle in her green eyes being more than worth the effort.

After they had eaten, Megan poured them both glasses of honey-colored cider. "Ever since the war in the northwest, this nestor cider is mighty difficult to come across. The price of it has tripled these past years." Tawl drank the golden liquid, appreciating its subtle, fruity flavor. He was beginning to feel a little light-headed.

"I think you should go out tomorrow and take a little fresh air." Megan smiled prettily. "Besides, tomorrow is the parade, and there will be great sights to see. There will be singing and dancing and jugglers from Isro." Tawl nodded, but he wasn't sure if he would feel up to it.

Megan looked at him thoughtfully and then moved across the room muttering something about getting changed. She undressed in a gloomy corner and Tawl tried to do what was expected of any knight: look away. Megan's skin glowed like summer peaches and he could not help but look.

"It's perfectly all right for you to look. I don't mind." Tawl blushed deeply.

"I am sorry, my lady." Megan's face grew grave as she came toward him: she was naked and her body was beautiful in the soft light.

She said gently, "I am no lady, Tawl, but I thank you for your courtesy." She knelt and kissed him on the lips.

"I don't think I'm in any condition to pleasure a lady this day."

"But you are in a condition to be pleasured *by* a lady." She smiled sweetly, pulling the blanket from his body and moving her head lower. Desire, long lost to Tawl, came to him with its welcome blankness. To love was to forget, and coupling with a stranger by a dimming fire was enough to ease the pain for a while.

Melli was beginning to wish she had never left the castle. The first few hours had been like an exciting adventure, stealing out in the dark of night with her hood drawn over her face, evading the guards. But it had been cold outside and she had begun to suspect that she was woefully unprepared. She had spent the night sleeping against the castle's outer wall. She had decided not to take a room at a tavern in the town, for she couldn't risk being recognized, and besides, she had no money.

She felt utterly miserable. She was hungry and cold, and although it had not rained, she had still somehow managed to get wet. She wanted nothing better than a hot meal and some mulled holk to soothe her aching bones. Sleeping outside on the hard ground, she discovered, was a most unpleasant experience. Hunger won over caution and she headed into Harvell.

Harvell was more a large town than a city. Most of the people made a living serving the needs of the hundreds of courtiers and thousands of servants and soldiers who lived in the castle or on its grounds. The town was just half a league to the west of the castle, a pleasant place with neatly timbered buildings.

Melli had visited it many times to buy ribbons or posies. *Buy!* she thought, she had never been allowed to buy anything. She would say to the storekeepers, "Lord Maybor will honor this," and they had let her take anything she wanted. Melli suddenly drew her hand to her face. That was it! Of course, why hadn't she thought of it sooner? She could go to the market, purchase anything she might need, and leave her father with the bill! It was perfect: her father would be financing her escape. She could not help but smile. Maybor would be furious when he received the charges.

Her step grew lighter as she made a mental list of things she would buy: she would need food, there was that little bake shop that served hot pastries and rolls, and she could buy a cup of cider and maybe even a custard tart.

Melli slowed down her pace. She was not on a pleasure-outing. This was no idle trip to market. She was running away from the only life she had ever known, heading to a city that lay far beyond the battlefields of the Halcus.

She breathed in the cold air of early morning, feeling alone and afraid. A shadow crossed her path and she looked up to see a gray swan in the sky. The noble bird was heading south for the winter. It was a sign. A gray swan formed part of her family's coat of arms. Determination hardened on her smooth brow: was she not Lord Maybor's daughter? *Bravery and Resolution* was her family motto; she would be the first woman to prove the maxim true. She walked into the village deciding that she would have a custard tart after all.

An hour later, Melli was well fed and in the process of buying some travel supplies. She carefully considered the wares. "My brother Kedrac assured me that you would be able to supply me with what he needs for his hunting expedition. He specifically said to ask for . . . Melli found she could not remember the name over the door.

"Master Trout, m'lady."

"Yes, Master Trout. What would my brother need?"

"Well, it depends on where he's going and how long for."

Melli struggled for a plausible lie. "He's going west."

"West, m'lady? There's no hunting to the west at this time of year."

Melli decided to change her tactics. "Look, Master Trout, I really couldn't care less about the hunting or lack of it in the west. I am purely here as a favor to my brother. If you feel you can not supply me with what he needs, then I will go elsewhere." She made as if to leave.

"M'lady, please don't be so hasty. I will find you what

you want. It's probably the fishing that he's going for. Does he have a good pole for a rod?"

"He has a rod, Master Trout. Now hurry, please!" She watched as he loaded a sack with all sorts of strange-looking dry food. He then went in the back and came out with an empty water flask and some miscellaneous cooking pots.

"Blankets?"

"Yes, and a good warm cloak." Melli had found the one she was wearing to be most inadequate.

"If I know Lord Kedrac, he'll be wanting some snatch. I'll throw a tin in should I?"

"If you please." She was beginning to get very impatient. This whole operation was taking longer than she had hoped. Finally the shopkeeper handed her the sack.

"It's a mite heavy for you, miss. Shall I have my boy carry it back to the castle?"

"That will not be necessary, Master Trout. I have my own boy outside. Lord Maybor will honor the bill."

"Of course, m'lady. I wish you joy of the day."

Melliandra carried the heavy sack outside and quickly donned the heavy cloak. She decided on impulse not to throw away her old cloak—it was not too heavy and the nights would be cold. She turned toward the inn. She dared not stretch her father's credit as far as a horse, so she would have to purchase one with her jewels.

She had waited outside the inn for several minutes when a boy approached leading a rather tired, old-looking horse. It was not what she was used to, but she was in a hurry.

"Boy! How much for the horse?"

The boy looked up slyly. "This horse is powerful fast and strong, miss."

"I didn't ask you that, boy. I said how much." Melli looked around nervously; the sun was growing higher and the morning was almost over.

"I couldn't take less than two gold pieces for it." Melli knew it was an outrageous price for such an old horse. She turned away from the boy and fished in her purse for her gold bracelet.

"Here, take this." She watched as his face grew ugly with greed.

"That will do right nice. Right nice indeed." He handed her the reins of the horse and watched cunningly as she led it away.

Melliandra stroked the horse's muzzle. "I never asked your name, did I, boy?" she said. "I'm going to need a saddle for you, too." For a brief moment she hugged the horse, placing her arms around its back and belly, resting her head on its flank. "What will become of you and me?" she whispered softly.

Baralis ignored Crope as he entered his chambers, but was forced to turn around when Crope loudly cleared his throat. "What is it, you great oaf? Is the boy found?"

"No, sir, but I know he's not in the castle."

"How do you know this?" demanded Baralis.

"One of the guards saw him leave early this morning— said he was heading for the woods."

"Ah, the woods." Baralis mused over this fact for a few minutes. "Go now, Crope, and tell the guards to search the woods. I must think a while on what to do."

Crope hovered uneasily, not making any move to leave. "There's one other thing, my lord," he said sheepishly.

Baralis looked up, annoyed. "Be gone, you imbecile."

"Very well, but I thought you might like to know Lord Maybor sent you his regards."

Baralis stood up. "He what!"

"He sent his regards. It was probably for the gift of wine you sent him last evening."

"You mean to tell me that you have seen Lord Maybor up and about in the castle this day?"

"Yes, sir, just a few hours back. He smiled most pleasantly."

"Leave me alone." Baralis' voice was coldly menacing and his servant wasted no time in doing what his master commanded.

Baralis was in a fury. He paced the length of his chamber, absently rubbing his pained hands. How could this have happened? How could Maybor have avoided the poison? He knew for a fact that the drunken lord took a glass of wine every night to help him sleep. He must have discovered the poison, yet the drug had been odorless and tasteless. Maybor had the luck of the devil!

Baralis calmed himself. He needed to think clearly; he now had several problems to solve. He could not allow the betrothal to go through. If he could not prevent it by murdering Maybor, he would have to set his sights upon the daughter—the sweet and lovely Melliandra. The girl would have to be disposed of. Maybe he would do it with own hand. He shivered with anticipation; it would indeed be a pleasure to steal the life from one so fair. He might even have a little fun with her first. Women, he found, were always more appealing with terror in their eyes.

Then there was the problem of the baker's boy. So Jack had headed into the woods, undoubtedly seeking cover amidst the dense trees. Well, the boy was a fool to think he could hide from him. There were methods by which a man could gain access to the deepness of the wood. Baralis lifted the tapestry and entered his study.

He handled the bird gently, trying not to damage any of its feathers. He had calmed it, and although it was restless in his hands, it made no move to escape. He stroked its small head and it cooed lightly. Baralis was about to change the nature of the bird.

He was determined to find Jack. The search would probably locate him, but it never hurt to make contingencies. He didn't place great trust in the castle guards—it would take them many days to scan the thick woodland that surrounded much of the castle, and even then the feckless fools might miss him. He had other matters to attend to and so would send something to do his work for him.

A dove. What better creature than a bird to sight someone in the depths of the forest?

To this end he would change the nature of the bird, superimposing his wishes over the natural inclinations of the dove. Baralis had done such drawings many times before in birds, in cats, in mice. It was a delicate operation requiring twinned animals. Creatures born from the same egg. Baralis, like other masters, had ways of cultivating such creatures and usually had an assortment of them at hand, identical to each other in every way.

He soothed the first bird into an uneasy sleep, then poured some fresh water into a bowl. Next, he made a careful incision into the second dove, straight down the center of its breast. The bird's blood ran into the bowl. Baralis took the still beating heart between his fingers and made an invocation as the life drained away from the bird. He raised the heart to his lips and swallowed it. The bond. He then took the first dove and immersed it in the bloody water, its gray-white feathers becoming pink with blood. Baralis then dried the bird with a soft cloth and commanded it to awaken. The bird's eyes opened and it was eager to be on its way.

He carried the bird out of his study and let it out of the window. It flew away quickly: it had no will of its own—it was Baralis' creature now.

He was pleased the messy business was over. He had no taste for warm dove hearts, but, he thought grimly, at least they were small.

It now was time to see what mischief Maybor was cooking up. He was bound to have some unpleasant revenge planned for the attempt on his life. *Let him try,* Baralis thought as he made his way down to the second cellar, *he will not catch me unawares.*

Before long Baralis was on the dark side of Maybor's chambers, listening with great interest to the conversation between father and son:

"She has been in the village this very morning, Father."

"Who saw her?" Maybor's voice was low and strained.

"Quite a few people, Father. She even bought some supplies."

"What supplies? She has no money to buy supplies."

"She never paid for them. The shopkeeper gave me the bill. She said you would honor the payment."

"Oh, she is a sly one. What did she buy?"

"Apparently she bought supplies for a fishing expedition."

"Fishing!" Baralis could hear the amazement in Maybor's voice.

"Yes, and she was seen heading east with a horse."

"Damn it! She must be found, Kedrac. Put your best men on it and swear them to secrecy. I want no one to know of this—especially the queen. Tell anyone who asks that Melliandra is abed with a fever."

Baralis' lips curved into a delicious smile. So his dove was not the only bird to have flown the coop. Melliandra had done his work for him. As long as she remained unfound, the betrothal could not take place. Furthermore, he thought with delight, if the queen were to be told of the disgraceful behavior of Maybor's daughter, she might well decide to call the match off altogether. He was almost glad Maybor was still alive. He would enjoy witnessing the unraveling of the great lord's plans.

Jack's confidence was dwindling fast. He was cold, he was wet, and he was lost. What was he but a baker's boy? He wasn't cut out for adventuring. Heroes never forgot to bring warm clothes with them, or if they did, they killed then skinned some wild beast and made a cloak from its hide. He didn't even have his knife.

Judging by the gray of the sky, it was mid-afternoon. Normally at this time he'd be mixing the dough for the fancies. The fancies were the special pastries that he and Frallit made for the noblewomen of the castle. The pastries were heavy with honey and syrup, rich with butter and brandy, or aromatic with fruit and spices. The mix depended upon two things: what ingredients were in season or store, and what the current fashions were in the south. What Rorn did one day, the kingdoms did the next.

Jack enjoyed making the fancies. Unlike the daily bread, there was never any rush to get them to oven, so he could spend time kneading and dreaming. And, if the ingredients weren't measured too carefully and the sweet breads didn't bake to plan, he could remove the threat of a beating by telling Frallit it was a new mix he was trying out. The master baker had received much acclaim by taking the credit for Jack's recipes.

At this time, two hours before dark, the kitchens would be warm and busy, there'd be ale losing its chill by the fire, and broth warming on the top of the stove. There'd be the yeast to wash and spread, and then he'd be done for the day. If he were lucky, Findra the table maid might have smiled his way and invited him to sit beside her later at supper.

It was all gone now. Everything he'd ever had. All the people he'd ever known. And for what? One moment's madness and eight score of loaves.

For the first time in his life he was truly alone. What had happened this morning had set him apart. If he traveled to another town and became a baker there, the same thing might happen. Only next time there might be people around and his condemnation complete. Yet what alternative did he have? He was a baker with a baker's skills. He would travel a while and settle where he could. Jack stepped up his pace and tried to find his way out of the woods.

Harvell Woods began sparsely at first, a mere sprinkling of bush and tree. The woods had a way of sneaking up on one, though, and before he knew it was he in the heart of the wood. Tree and bush crowded thick and close, and even with the dwindling foliage of winter, little light passed through their branches. With every step he took, he seemed to make an alarming amount of noise: twigs and bracken crackled harshly underfoot, breaking the guarded silence of the wood.

The smells of early winter assailed his senses: the ripe but cooling earth, the fragrant rot of leaf, the dampening bark and the suggestion of rain upon the breeze.

Jack was a little unnerved: the heady scents together with the denseness of the trees combined to make him confused. He was sure he'd only walked a league or so and couldn't remember the wood being so thick when he had collected berries in the past.

His leather sandals were soaked with dew and his clothes were too thin for warmth. He was afraid. The memory of the loaves haunted him. He recalled the sick feeling in his stomach, the feeling his skull would surely burst. It was sorcery, and every child knew sorcery was an evil used by heathens of old. Even Borc himself had condemned it. Jack sighed deeply. He didn't want to be stoned as a heretic or marked as an outcast.

The air of the forest stirred within his lungs, slipping

softly into his blood. He became calm, and out of calmness came determination.

He was already an outcast. At Castle Harvell he was known to be fatherless, his mother branded a whore. People were usually kind to him, but when his back was turned, or when he did something wrong, the whisperings would begin again. As long as he stayed, he would never be anything but a bastard. To leave Castle Harvell would be to leave his shame behind. There was hope. He could bake in another town and never have to bite his tongue or stay his hand at the sound of people whispering. He could begin a new life, where no one knew he had neither family nor history of his own. Finding his mother's origins was an impossible dream; he had nothing to go on. It was better to make a fresh start and put childish fantasies behind him.

With renewed optimism, Jack made his way through the trees. The wood presented a subtle path and he was content to go where it led.

After a while he heard the sound of someone crying out. "Help! Help!" came a woman's voice. Without hesitation, Jack headed toward the noise. He found himself on a cleared road. Ahead, he saw a woman being attacked by a young boy with a knife. He wasted no time in rushing to her aid. The boy was fast and sped off into the woods. Jack dashed after the lad, but he was already out of sight. He turned back to the woman and realized she was only a girl.

"Are you hurt, lady?" he asked gently, coming toward her.

"Please, leave me be. It is only a nick." Jack saw that she was referring to a cut on her wrist.

"Please, lady, let me help you. It looks more than a nick to me."

The girl regarded him coolly. "It is not the wound I am concerned with. My purse has been robbed."

Jack desperately searched for something intelligent to say. "Lady, you should return to town and inform the royal guard. They will catch the lad." The girl paid his words scant attention.

"At least he never stole his horse back, and I still have

my supplies." As she spoke, she dragged forward a large woven sack.

"Lady, you should return to Harvell at once and get the cut seen to."

The girl considered for a moment and then said, "I will never return to Harvell again." Her voice was strong and clear, and despite the coarseness of her cloak he could tell she was a noblewoman.

"Where are you headed?"

"You ask too many questions. It is no concern of yours. I must be on my way." With that she loaded the sack on the horse's back and faced east. Jack did not want to see her walk off.

"I am heading east, too," he said, thinking quickly and deciding that he would indeed head east.

"That is nothing to me. I will walk alone." The coldness of her voice made him wince, but he was not about to be put off that easily.

"Next time they may steal your horse."

The girl hesitated, her deep, blue eyes flickering over her horse and its burden. "Very well, you may accompany me a little way, until we are free of town and castle."

They walked in silence for a while, the girl sucking on her wrist to stop the bleeding. Then she surprised Jack by saying, "I think it would be better if we left the road." He'd been thinking just the same thing and wondered what *her* reason was for suggesting it. Her tone did not invite questions.

He led her into the woods and tried to strike a path parallel to but some distance from the road. As they walked, the lowering sun shone through the trees and illuminated the face of the girl. Jack had never seen such perfect milky skin or such large dark eyes. The image of Findra the table maid, who had long stood for female loveliness to Jack, now seemed less enchanting. Here at his side walked someone more exquisite, more regal, and therefore more unattainable than any woman he had ever met.

Jack was thrown into a turmoil of self-awareness. Never had his legs seemed so long and so beyond his control. Every step he took seemed fraught with the potential for embarrassment. What if he misstepped and tripped on a twig? What if his foot became stuck in a rabbit hole? His hair had lost all semblance of order and fell over his eyes every fourth step—he knew, he'd counted them. And to top it all off, he'd been robbed of the ability to speak. Not only were his lips refusing to move, but his mind had stopped playing its part in the whole process, as well, and kept coming up with ridiculous subjects to talk about. As if this girl with the perfect profile and cheeks as pale as just-kneaded dough would want to hear about Master Frallit's gout!

He stole a sideways glance—there was something about the expression on her face that struck a chord within him. Gradually he began to comprehend what he saw there: it was a reflection of his own emotions. She was scared and trying to hide it. He decided to risk speaking—if he made a fool of himself, so be it. "What's your name?" he asked softly.

"What is yours?" she replied quick as a flash. Jack could not help but smile.

"I am called Jack." The girl seemed reluctant to name herself, so impulsively he asked the name of her horse.

"He has no name. Or rather he has a name, but I don't know it." That she did not know the name of her own horse struck Jack as funny, and for the first time that day he laughed. It felt good to do so and his spirit was lightened. "I just bought it today," the girl explained, mollified by his laughter. "If you think it's so funny, come up with a name for him yourself."

Jack was pleased to be asked to do this and thought for a while. "How about Silver, after the flower. I just saw one earlier." It was the girl's turn to laugh now.

"He can't be called Silver—he's brown." Her voice was lightly mocking and Jack felt foolish: *Silver! where was his brain?* He quickly searched his mind for something clever to say in response. When nothing came to him, he settled for attempting to endow his silence with a knowing air.

They walked for a while more before the girl spoke up. "My name is Melli. I will tell you that, but I beg you, ask me no more questions." Jack nodded slowly. He knew she was a lady, and so that was not her full name. Ladies had long and beautiful names. He was pleased she had told him part of it, though, and for a time, the pleasure of sharing names with the girl by his side was enough to keep the morning in the past.

The sun gradually descended below the treeline and the sky turned to dusk. The woods, which already knew the still-ness of winter, embraced the greater quiet of the night. Jack and Melli both agreed they were hungry. The day was draw-ing to a close and so they decided to make camp for the night. They had stumbled upon a deer path which headed southeast, and they were now several leagues south of Harvell's east road.

Melli unceremoniously dumped the contents of the sack on the ground. There was a large amount of a very unappe-tizing dried meat and several packages containing drybreads. There were two tins, one of which was sealed closed with wax. Melli opened them: the first contained snatch, and the second, to her horror, contained live maggots.

"Ugh." She threw the tin away, which proved a disas-trous action, as the maggots spilled out all over the ground and onto the precious supplies. Jack quickly gathered the food, pots, and blankets, shaking them free of maggots. He then moved a few yards away, leaned against a tree and pro-ceeded to chew on a length of pork.

"How can you eat that after maggots have been on it?" Melli grimaced, annoyed at his casual manner.

"Easy," he replied, "there's nothing else to eat." This answer did not please Melli one bit. She was furious. What on earth had Master Trout been doing, giving her maggots?

"Were you planning to go fishing?" asked Jack. "You don't look like much of a fisherman."

"What on earth are you talking about?"

"Why, the bait of course. Come to think of it, you don't look like the type who would chew snatch, either." Melli knew Jack was angling for information, but she had no wish to confide in him. Still, she was glad that she was not alone; the incident with the boy had badly scared her.

For the first time she looked properly at her companion. He was tall, if a little thin, with brown hair that kept falling over his face. His hands were large and calloused—powerful hands, used to hard work. Yes, there was something attractive about him. He was certainly brave; he'd run to her aid with no thought for himself. Bands of robbers were notorious on the east road and most people walked away at the first sign of trouble. For all he knew, there were more men lurking in the bushes. It wouldn't have been the first time a child was used as bait in a trap.

She noticed that he was dressed very inadequately for the cold weather; he didn't even have a cloak. She decided on impulse to give him her lambswool riding cloak; she would keep the one she was wearing because it was a lot warmer.

"Here, take this." She offered him the gray cloak. He took it gratefully and she immediately felt a little guilty for keeping the warmer one for herself.

Melli forced herself to eat a little drybread, which unfortunately only served to make her thirsty. The water flask was, of course, empty. Jack offered to go off and find a stream, but she didn't like the thought of being alone. So they went off in search of water together, Melli guiding the horse.

Neither spoke as they walked through the trees, and Melli was glad of the silence. Her father would be searching for her by now, she almost felt sorry for him. It would shame him to admit to the queen that his daughter had run away. She loved her father. There was softness behind his bullish facade, and he'd always been indulgent with her, but now she had to consider herself first. No, she didn't regret running away. With her newfound ally at her side she wasn't even afraid.

She caught Jack's eye and he smiled gently. There was strength in his face—and kindness. She had to fight off the urge to touch him, to casually brush her hand against his. She told herself it was folly, brought on by the tensions of the day. What was he but a common laborer—and a smug one at that. He'd purposely made her feel foolish about the maggots. Indignation, combined with the fear that she might actually reach out and touch him, made Melli strike out ahead on her own.

She walked through the woods enjoying the night. The air was cold and soon to frost; the trees formed elegant silhouettes against the night, their branches reaching toward the heavens in patient anticipation of the spring. A flash of white caught her eye. High in the trees a bird settled to a branch. She stopped in her tracks, suddenly wanting Jack to draw level with her. When he came to her side, she pointed above and said, "I didn't think doves flew at night."

My, my, thought Baralis, *this is an interesting turn of events. My clever dove has located not one but two fugitives from the castle.* He was seeing through the eye of the bird—an unsettling view of form and movement. He watched as the two companions made their way to a shallow stream. It was almost dark and the moon glimmered softly upon the slow-moving water.

He had seen all he needed. The pair would go no further tonight. He would have them captured tomorrow. There was no need for haste, as his creature would track their movements. He let the dove sleep, and as he withdrew his perceptions from the bird he was aware that it was cold and had not eaten.

Four

*L*ord Maybor was in bed with his daughter's maid, Lynni. The enjoyments of the flesh had failed to lessen his distress. His carefully laid plans would be foiled if he could not find his daughter.

From an early age, Maybor's only goal was to accumulate land and power. He had been born the second son to a minor lord. His father had not subscribed to the view that the land should be shared equally between sons and had died leaving all his holdings to Maybor's older brother, Reskor.

Maybor had bided time, hiding his resentment beneath a veneer of fraternal duty, until one day an opportunity presented itself to him. There had been a deep spring snow and the two brothers were out helping locate lambs in the field. They were in a section of land that Maybor knew well and Reskor did not. Maybor suggested to his brother that there might be sheep still trapped in the distance beyond a low rise. Reskor galloped off. Not long after, the still air was filled with the horrifying sound of cracking ice. Maybor heard his brother's cries for help, heard the terrified squeal of his horse. He took no heed, riding off to the manor house, never once looking back.

After the spring thaw, Reskor's body and the body of his horse were found floating on a small lake. Snow had concealed its frozen surface, and it was concluded that Reskor had accidentally ridden to a cold oblivion. Maybor inherited his brother's land, but he soon coveted more.

His eyes looked to the east, where the crops were bountiful and the climate more temperate. He married the only child of a great eastern lord. There was no doubting his motives, for the girl was not sound of mind and had been born with only a stump for a right hand. It had been easy to convince her father that the troubled girl had one day taken it upon herself to jump from a high battlement. Both Maybor and the girl's father were glad to see her dead. Maybor's position as heir to the father's estates was solid, for the brief union had produced a son. Five years passed and his father-in-law died, and Maybor gained possession of the vast stretches of fertile land that lay west of the River Nestor.

Within a month of his father-in-law's death Maybor married again. Never one to let his heart choose his mate, he married a girl of little beauty and taste, but whose father owned land adjacent to his own. His new wife had a brother who was due to inherit her father's land. He was a sickly boy of eight summers. He soon caught a terrible chill while out riding with Maybor and died shortly afterward.

And so Maybor became the greatest landholder in the east. His second wife eventually died a natural death, having provided him with two more sons and a daughter. She had lived a miserable life, unloved and ignored by her husband.

Maybor then began an aggressive policy of buying up neighboring land: if the landowners would not sell, Maybor would force them. He would hire men to burn their crops and barns, set loose their animals, and build dams to stop their water. Eventually most landowners succumbed to the pressure, and Maybor picked up the land surrounding his for a very reasonable price.

He soon found that acquiring land was not enough. He wanted power and prestige. He yearned to be a man of importance, to have the ear of the highest in the land, and he succeeded—he bought and ambitioned his way into the king's favor. Now he aspired to his greatest accomplishment: father to a queen. He had to locate Melliandra; she held the throne room's only key.

He found he had no further appetite for the girl in his

bed and he commanded her to leave. She was a spirited wench, abundant in thigh and hip, and normally he would have enjoyed her once more, but his daughter's flight lay heavy upon his mind and worry blunted the edge of his desire.

He thought long on where his daughter might be headed, and he eventually recalled his second wife having relatives in Annis. He hoped with all his being that she was not headed there, for the way to Annis led through the battlefields and lands of the Halcus. The enemy would love to get their hands on his daughter: they would rape and then tear her limb from limb. Maybor couldn't bear thinking about it, and with shaking hands he poured himself a glass of red wine. Just before the liquid met his tongue, he did something he had not done for over thirty years: he sent a silent prayer to Borc, begging him to keep his daughter safe.

Tavalisk was enjoying his breakfast. He was eating lamb's kidneys, savoring their delicate flavor of blood and urine.

Today was to be an important day for the city of Rorn. The whole city had been given a holiday and all the people would be crowding the streets to watch the procession. It was on this day, nearly two thousand years ago, that the great hero Kesmont had founded the city. Legend told that Kesmont was being pursued by his enemies and had managed to evade them only by the swiftness of his mount. The unfortunate horse was ridden so fast and hard that it was said to have dropped dead under the great man. The hero was immediately filled with intense remorse and dug a deep grave for his beloved mare. With tears in his eyes, he vowed he would build a great city on the site of his mount's final resting place. That city he named Rorn after his horse.

Tavalisk had studied the life of Kesmont and thought him to be a rather foolish and sentimental man. He had been rumored to have founded another city, this one named after his mother. Lamentably, that city had been situated perilously close to the Great Marshes and eventually had succumbed to the inevitable pull of the slow mud, never to be heard of again. Yes, thought Tavalisk, Kesmont may have been a master with the sword, but he'd been sadly lacking in common sense.

Tavalisk expertly skewered another kidney and placed it between his full, wet lips. There was much to do today. Not only had he to dress for and take part in the procession, but he also had other matters to attend to. Last night he had received a very interesting piece of information.

Gamil, his aide, had placed a letter in his hands—a very interesting letter, indeed. Gamil informed him that the letter had been intercepted by his spies in Bren. The letter was from the upstart Baralis and was addressed to the duke of Bren. It spoke of a marriage between Catherine of Bren, the duke's daughter, and Prince Kylock. So: Baralis was seeking to ally the Four Kingdoms with Bren. This situation would definitely warrant careful monitoring. There was nothing Tavalisk disliked more than people making plans without his knowledge or consent.

He pulled the satin cord which hung conveniently close to hand, and a few moments later his aide appeared.

"Yes, Your Eminence."

Tavalisk made a point of making his aide wait while he finished his last morsel of kidney. "Gamil, I think we should keep an eye to what our cunning friend Lord Baralis is up to." After the velvety dryness of the kidneys, Tavalisk needed something to cleanse his palate. He poured honey into a bowl and proceeded to dip morsels of bread into the amber liquid. "Tell our spy in Castle Harvell to step up his vigilance."

"It will be done."

"If I'm not mistaken, Baralis should soon receive the note I sent him, regarding the return of my books. They were due back several months ago." Tavalisk drank deeply from his golden cup. "The letter's delivery will act as a timely reminder of my presence." Tavalisk smiled sweetly as he recalled selecting the books which had been sent. He had been careful to ensure that nothing of great significance had reached Baralis' greedy eye. It had been a small price to pay for the pleasure of stirring up trouble between the Four Kingdoms and Halcus. The fact that the war had gone on longer than he anticipated was an added bonus: interest was accruing most deliciously from war loans to the Halcus. In the spirit of neutrality, the archbishop had of course offered a similar loan to the Four Kingdoms. His offer had been declined: the kingdoms were too rich for their own good. Whenever they needed money, all they had to do was cut down another of their damned forests. Timber was a valuable commodity in the southeast, and the kingdoms had the greatest resource in the Known Lands. Annis, Helch, and Highwall had their share of timber, but it was mostly fir and pine. What carpenter would choose pine when he could have walnut, oak, and ash?

Tavalisk licked the honey from his finger; it was so much nicer than a spoon. "What has become of our knight?"

"He was picked up by a prostitute, Your Eminence."

This statement struck Tavalisk as amusing, and he laughed showing his small, white teeth. "Well, well. I thought it was the prostitute who was supposed to be picked up." He looked to his aide to appreciate his joke, but Gamil did not share it.

"What should we do next, Your Eminence?"

"Why, nothing of course. It is well that he has been picked up; it would have been unfortunate for one so young to die." Tavalisk poured himself a generous cup of wine. "Do nothing, Gamil . . . save watch him like a hawk." Tavalisk waved his arm in dismissal. "You may go now. I must dress for today's festivities. The people will be disappointed if I do not look my best."

"Very well, Your Eminence."

Tavalisk watched as Gamil walked across the room. The aide was about to open the door when he spoke. "Oh, by the way, Gamil, there's no need for you to bother dressing up. After last year's unfortunate incident with the horse dung, I feel it's best if you keep out of the public eye altogether." The archbishop smiled benignly and pretended not to notice the look of hatred on his aide's face as he left the room.

"You mean to tell me, Bodger, you ain't ever heard of the Glinff?" Grift had a roguish twinkle in his eye.

Bodger leaned forward and lowered his voice. "No, Grift, I can't say as I have."

"Oh, the Glinff are a mighty strange people, Bodger. They live deep in the forest and would rollick you as soon as look at you."

"You mean the women?"

"Aye, and the men, too. They're a powerful passionate race are the Glinff."

"I'll be a-walkin in the woods soon then, Grift."

"You wouldn't want to do that, Bodger. The Glinff might well give you a good rollickin', but when you're off your guard, it's *whoosh,* off with your plums."

"Off with my plums!"

"Aye, they eat 'em for breakfast. What do you think makes 'em so randy?" Bodger gave Grift a dubious look—he could never tell when Grift was pulling his leg. The two men downed more ale.

"Something mighty strange happened in the kitchens yesterday, Bodger."

"What makes you say that, Grift?"

"Lord Baralis himself came charging down. In a right state he was, ordered Frallit to destroy half a morning's baking."

"That does seem a bit odd, Grift."

"It's more than odd, Bodger. It's sorcery, if you ask me."

"Sorcery?"

"Aye, Bodger, the worst evil in the Known Lands."

"I thought there was no such thing, Grift."

"More fool you, then, Bodger. It's real all right, as real as Lady Helliarna's thighs are wide. It was rife in Borc's time. He put an end to most of it, though, slaughtered all he could find who used it."

"All of them, Grift?"

"No, more's the pity. His blade was sharp, but his wits grew soft."

"That's blasphemy, Grift."

"Call it what you will, Bodger. Borc failed us, and Lord Baralis running round the kitchens ordering the destruction of perfectly fine loaves serves to show us how badly."

"Maybe the loaves weren't to his taste, Grift."

"No one decent has a taste for sorcery, Bodger."

The nagging pain in his back finally awoke Jack. He shifted his position and realized that he had been sleeping most of the night on top of a collection of small rocks. He rubbed his bruises as he remembered the previous night.

He and Melli had eventually managed to find a small stream and had filled the flask with its clear, cold water. They had decided that they would walk no further that night and so they made a meager camp. Melli had agreed with Jack that they should not light a fire, for fear of attracting attention—neither person daring to say who they sought to avoid.

The night had been moonlit and cold, and they bedded down under the stars, Melli ostentatiously keeping a noticeable distance between Jack and herself. They had not thought to set guard against intruders or wild animals. The two companions merely bundled themselves up in the coarse blankets and fell asleep on the hard ground.

Weak, morning light filtered through the trees, and Jack felt the need to be up and stretch his legs. He also felt a more basic need and scanned around for a suitably dense bush behind which he could relieve himself.

Quietly, to avoid waking the sleeping form of Melli, Jack stole away from the campsite. He decided he would gather some wood and bracken for a fire; he would surprise Melli by making a warm porridge with the drybread and stream water.

He was some distance from the campsite when he first heard the distant thunder of hooves. Jack's heart began to beat quickly—he knew they came for him. He poised, motionless for the barest instant, deciding whether to return to the campsite and Melli, or whether to capitalize on what little head start he had and run alone into the heart of the wood.

Jack turned back toward the campsite and ran swiftly calling Melli's name.

Melli was awakened by a distant rumbling. She opened

her eyes and saw that Jack had gone. She glanced over to her horse and her sack of supplies. At least he had not robbed her. She became aware that the nagging sound was getting louder; it was familiar to her. It was the sound of horses. She knew they were for her. They were drawing closer and she had little time. With lightning speed, she gathered the blankets in her sack and tied it to the back of the mount. She untethered her horse and jumped on its back.

She had never before ridden a horse without a saddle and she had no time for lessons. She gripped its flank with her thighs and took up the reins, urging the creature into a brisk canter. The riders were approaching from the north so she would head south, into the depths of the forest.

As her horse broke into a run, she fancied she heard her name called, but the sound was lost under the noise of leaf and hoof, and she paid it no heed.

The men were gaining on her. She risked a glance backward and could see their shadowy forms looming close. Her old horse would go no faster, and so she decided to head for the thickening trees, where it would prove harder to maneuver a group of horses.

Her horse moved with surprising agility if not speed in the dense trees, as if it were well used to the wood. She listened to the approach of the riders as they crashed through the undergrowth, calling harsh cries to one another: there sounded to be many. She had no time for fear, only action, and she instinctively moved deeper into the heart of the wood.

Her plan appeared to be working, for the approach of the riders was slowed as they were forced to ride through ever thicker trees and bushes. Melli urged her reluctant horse onward, but the wood became so dense she was forced to slow down to a trot: the branches of trees were low and plentiful and could easily knock her from her horse.

Melli heard the riders bearing down upon her and she began to realize there was little hope for her escape. She glanced back: the head rider was visible behind her. She was surprised to see the man was not wearing her father's colors of red and silver. There was no time to ponder what it meant, though, as her horse had carried her to the banks of a fast-flowing stream.

"Come, boy," she urged. "It looks not too deep." The reluctant horse whinnied nervously. Melli leaned forward and stroked the beast's ears, fear rising in her breast. The men were upon her. If only her horse would move forward!

Baralis had neither the time nor the inclination to watch his men bring in the boy and girl. They were not blithering fools like the royal guard. They would do what he had paid them for. Baralis was well pleased with engaging the service of the mercenaries. A discreet trip into Harvell and eight golds apiece was all it had taken to purchase their expertise. It had been a most reassuring experience. One always knew where one stood with a mercenary: greed was so much simpler to deal with than loyalty.

For now, however, he had something much more important on his mind. He was about to have an audience with the queen.

He dressed with great care, donning his most splendid robe, jet black and edged with the finest fur. Baralis himself had little interest in finery, but such display was necessary when dealing with Arinalda—she was a woman who set great store by appearances.

Baralis absently smoothed the soft, black fur with his twisted hands as he contemplated his meeting. He knew he would have to proceed very carefully. He was well aware the queen had no liking for him. He did have an interesting gift for her, though, one she would be most anxious to receive.

He stepped into his study and took out a small glass vial. The fluid within rolled thickly like oil, catching the light in its unctuous core. Baralis turned the vial in his hands, a trace of a smile upon his pale lips. The contents of this bottle would greatly increase Her Highness' willingness to listen to what he would propose.

He made his way down to the queen's chamber. Once he arrived at the beautifully carved door, he knocked loudly. He was not a man to meekly tap. He waited for several seconds and was about to knock again when the queen's voice rang out coldly: "Enter."

Baralis stepped into the great room. The walls were hung with exquisite silken tapestries; chairs and benches were upholstered in the richest of fabrics, worked with gold and silver thread. The queen issued an unspoken insult by not turning to greet him as he entered. He was forced to address the back of her head: "I wish Your Highness great joy of the day."

She whirled around quickly. "I have no wish to exchange pleasantries with you, Lord Baralis. Say quickly what you will and then leave."

Baralis remained unruffled by the queen's venom. "I have a gift for Your Highness."

"I want no gift from you, Baralis, save your quick withdrawal." She was beautiful in her aloofness, her back straight and noble, her profile cool as marble.

"The gift is more for your husband, the king, than for yourself." Baralis watched with amusement as a flicker of interest crossed the queen's brow. She worked quickly to conceal it.

"What could you have that would be of interest to the king? You tire me, Lord Baralis. Please withdraw from my presence." The queen was indeed a fine actress. Baralis found himself admiring her.

"Your Highness, this gift of which we speak will do more than interest the king. It may very well help him."

"How will it help him, Lord Baralis?" The queen's voice was scathing. "The king is not so ill that he would need *your* help."

"Oh, Your Highness." Baralis shook his head with mock sympathy. "We both know the king is seriously ill and is only getting worse. These past five years since the unfortunate hunting incident, he has deteriorated visibly. All the court is deeply saddened by his decline."

"How dare you speak so of the king!" The queen drew close, and for a brief instant he thought she would strike him. Her blue eyes met his: he could smell her, the subtle fragrance stirring up memories in his breast. Unsettled by his nearness, she took a single step back. "I cannot bear your presence an instant longer. Be gone now!" She spoke the last words in a fury and Baralis obligingly withdrew.

As he walked the distance back to his chamber, there was a suggestion of a smile upon his thin lips. Things had gone very well. The queen had, of course, been most proud and indignant—he had expected no less. She had failed to hide her interest, though, and the bait had been taken. All that remained for him to do now was to wait for her inevitable summons. Proud she might well be, but she would regret her hasty words and would soon seek him out, demanding to know the nature of the gift.

It seemed that every person who lived in the huge city of Rorn was out on the streets. People were drinking and dancing and gathering in groups to exchange pleasantries and gossip. Buildings had been hung with brightly colored banners, and flowers were strewn amongst the filth on the streets.

Vendors cried their wares, proclaiming fresh apples or hot pies or cool ale. Children ran unchecked through the crowds, and old women found the shade. Young girls wore dresses cut so low that their breasts seemed ready to spill out. Indeed, some voluptuous curves did—to the great delight of the men, who watched lecherously as the unfortunate girls tucked their bounty back beneath their bodices.

It was the greatest day of the year for the city. The annual festival attracted scores of people from many leagues away. There would be a huge parade, exotic performers, great singers, and amazing fireworks displays. The city would feast and frolic for three days. These three days were the single biggest event of the pickpockets' year.

Thousands of people on the streets, money in their pockets, their minds dulled by drink. Why, the pickings were so rich and easy that the pickpockets almost bemoaned the loss of their art. It wasn't a skill to take a purse from a man who was pickled in ale—it was child's play. Still, there were proceedings to be followed even on these three idyllic days of plenty. It wouldn't do for a 'pocket to encroach upon another's turf. Not if he valued his life. For Rorn, like all other cities, was controlled by an established system of extortion and corruption.

'Pockets, cutthroats, thieves, prostitutes, con men, they all lived in fear of the men who ran the city. These men collected their dues, and they in turn answered to one man. The man who ran the crime in Rorn was without face or name. He was known simply as "the Old Man." Tales of the Old Man's power and influence abounded in the city. It was said that not a thing happened on the streets or in the taverns that he did not know about. If a whore was overcharging, he knew it; if a trader loaded his scales, he knew by how much; if a thief robbed a house, he knew the value of what was taken down to the last tin spoon. Rorn was said to be riddled with his spies and informants, and it was rumored that he had friends in the highest of places.

For today, at least, people forgot about the darker side of life in the city. The festival had begun and the people of Rorn were determined to celebrate.

Tawl was jostled and pushed by the heaving crowds. He had not liked the idea of coming out today, but Megan had been insistent that he stretch his legs and get some fresh air. He was pleasantly surprised by how his body responded. He had always been physically strong, but he hadn't expected his muscles to be so resilient. He was weak, yet already he could feel his blood pumping through his flesh, bringing new life to tissue and tendon.

After his months of confinement, he was alarmed by the size and noise of the crowds. He was sure he'd never seen so many people in his entire life.

Megan had given him six silver pieces with which to buy a knife. She had told him the saying that *in Rorn, a man without a weapon is a man without a future*. Tawl had disliked taking her money, and he suspected it was her last. But he needed a weapon of some sort before he risked leaving the city, so he had accepted, swearing one day to pay it back.

He was surprised to find his unusual attire seemed to fit right in with the mood of the festival. In fact, his clothes seemed modest in comparison to what some were wearing. The men of Rorn paraded like peacocks in bright leggings and tunics, and the women wore shawls in the colors of the rainbow. As he walked through the streets, he noticed the advance of a great parade. People on horse and foot were bedecked in fabulous costumes, and the crowd made way to let the parade pass.

He didn't take great interest in the parade at first; he had no love of jugglers and tumblers. Then, after a while, horns sounded and the crowd grew quiet as a huge man on a massive horse rode through their ranks. A noticeable hush fell upon the people as they looked in awe upon the august figure of the rider. The man was dressed all in white and was adorned in fabulous jewels: bracelets, rings and necklaces, all sparkling with harsh luster in the bright sunshine. He even wore a crown. There was something about the man's fleshy profile that was familiar to Tawl.

Instinctively he slipped deep within the crowds, searching out shadow as the rider passed. He watched from a distance as the man rode by. Tawl was certain that he was the same person who had supervised his torture. He turned to a young boy standing nearby and asked, "Who is the man in white?"

The boy gave Tawl a disgusted look and retorted, "Why that's the archbishop. Every fool knows that." He then gave Tawl a kinder look and added, "I suppose you're from out of town." Tawl nodded and moved on.

He headed toward the tavern which Megan had recommended for knife buying. He was feeling weak and his eyes were still not accustomed to the bright of day. As he neared his destination, he came upon yet another crowd of people. They were gathered around a handsome and brightly dressed young man. Tawl could tell from the red tassels on his hat that the man was a fortune-teller.

"Yes, madam," the man was saying with dramatic flourish, "I can see that your daughter longs for another child. Tell her to offer a prayer up to the goddess Huska and her wishes will be granted." The crowd moaned in approval. The fortune-teller moved on to the next person, taking his hand and looking enigmatically toward the heavens.

"Sir, you are a man in need of money." Tawl could not help but smile. *Show me a man who is not in need of money,* he thought. After a pause for theatrical effect, the fortune-teller continued, "You will find seven gold pieces under the floor of your house."

"Whereabouts?" asked the man.

"But two steps away from your door," said the fortune-teller, his voice gaining an edge of boredom, as if to say he was too important to be concerned with specific details. "You, madam," he called as a woman was about to leave the group. She came forward and he took her hand, once more looking to the sky. "I see a great future for you." He closed his eyes, as if receiving divine guidance. "I see that you will become dressmaker to a queen." The crowd applauded with admiration as the woman informed them that she did indeed do a little sewing on the side.

Tawl prepared to move on, but the fortune-teller stopped him. "You, sir!" Tawl had no intention of moving forward, so he shook his head and stepped away. The fortune-teller was too fast for him and caught his arm. The man squeezed his hand and looked to the heavens. "You sir, are searching for a boy." Tawl's face remained impassive. The fortune-teller continued. "You will not find him in this city. You need to visit the Seers of Larn—they will tell you where he is." Tawl's eyes met briefly with those of the fortune-teller and then the man was off.

"Madam, give me your hand. You are a widow in need of a husband. . . ."

Tawl walked away, rubbing his chin as he reflected upon what the fortune-teller had said. He'd never heard of Larn or its seers. He tried hard to dismiss the incident as mere fancy or trickery, but as he walked the tawdy streets, it weighed heavily on his mind and he decided he'd find out more about Larn.

He soon came upon the tavern Megan had named and slipped inside, glad to be free of the noise and the crowds. He settled himself in a dark corner and was relieved to take the weight off his still weak legs. A sour-faced girl approached him. "What d'you want?" she asked, making no show of welcome.

"I'll take a cup of ale." The girl was obviously affronted at being asked for such a meager service. She huffed away, returned much later with a cup of flat and watery ale. "Before you leave, could you tell me if Tucker is here?"

"Who's askin'?"

"A friend of Megan's." The girl withdrew to the back room. Several minutes passed and eventually a man emerged. He looked critically toward Tawl and then approached him.

He wasted no time with greetings. "What do you want?" The light from the window did the man no favors; it highlighted the depths of the pock marks on his cheeks.

"I need a knife."

"What sort?"

"A long-knife." Tawl was hoping he had enough money to make a purchase. He suspected the price of such goods in Rorn would be high.

"Cost you ten silvers."

"We won't be doing business, then." Tawl motioned to leave. His bluff paid off.

"Eight silvers," countered the man.

"Six."

"Done." The man headed to the back and returned minutes later with a long-knife, which he drew from within his coat. Tawl was surprised to see it was a remarkably fine knife. Undoubtedly contraband. The two men exchanged money and goods, and Tawl headed toward the door.

"By the way," he asked, "have you ever heard of Larn?" The man gave him a warning look and then shook his head.

Tawl got the distinct feeling the man knew something but would not say. He stepped out into the bright sunlight and headed back toward Megan's. The fortune-teller had planted a fertile seed, and Tawl was determined to find someone who could tell him about Larn and its seers.

Jack had watched as Melli sped not an arm's length away from him. She had neither seen nor heard him. He listened to the approach of the mounted men and quickly turned in the direction from which he had come. There was nothing he could do to help his companion now, but he took some comfort in the fact that she was at least on horseback.

To his untrained eye, Melli had appeared to be an expert horsewoman.

He ran as fast as his long legs would take him; over bracken and fallen log he raced, his breath coming fast and heavy. As he looked back to check on his pursuers, he misplaced a step and his ankle twisted painfully. He fell forward onto the damp floor of the forest. He struggled to his feet and attempted to put his weight on his leg, but the ankle could not bear it. "Damn!" he whispered, half in pain, half in anger. He knew he would have to hide now, for he had no chance of outrunning his pursuers with a twisted ankle.

He made a quick scan of the terrain and his eye spotted a low ditch. He hobbled as fast as he could and flung himself into the trench. It was not very pleasant; fungus clung grimly to the sides and at the bottom lay cold, foul-smelling water. He still felt he was too exposed and lay down in the icy wetness, covering himself in a blanket of wet, dead leaves. The water stole through his cloak and breeches, chilling him to the bone.

As he waited he couldn't help feeling a little ashamed— Melli was being chased by Baralis' men while he crouched in a ditch like a coward.

There was no doubt in Jack's mind that Baralis was behind the chase. If anyone in the castle knew anything of sorcery it was the king's chancellor. It was widely murmured that the man dabbled in the ancient arts; however, he was so powerful that no one dared mention it aloud, let alone challenge him about it. A breath of revelation passed through Jack—he'd *felt* it. Looking back on his time scribing, there had been instances when he'd felt sick and head sore. Up until now he'd dismissed it as a result of eyestrain and late nights, but the sensation was akin to what he'd felt yesterday morning. Baralis had practiced sorcery and somehow *he* had perceived its use. Jack recalled many instances of nausea, and whenever he'd seen Baralis the same day, the man usually looked pale and weak.

Excitement over his discovery quickly turned to worry: all it had done was confirm that he wasn't normal.

The thing Jack wanted most in life was to be normal, to be able to walk through the castle without someone calling him a bastard. He wanted a father like everyone else, and a mother who no one called a whore. He wanted to be on the same footing as legitimate offspring and have the same sense of belonging. Now, more than ever, it seemed impossible.

He could move to the east and become a baker's apprentice. But the best he could hope for would be to conceal his past. He wouldn't lie. No. When someone asked about his parents, and they surely would, it would be an insult to himself and his mother to make up stories about a life he'd never had.

Jack shivered violently, chilled to the bone. It seemed there would be no easy option for him. Wherever he went, he would be an outsider. The incident yesterday had merely sealed his fate. The sooner he accepted that and stopped dreaming about finding his mother's family and being welcomed with open arms as a long lost relative, the better. He had to deal in realities. The ditch was a reality, the loaves were a reality, and he would never be more than a bastard.

He settled down in the cold water and listened to the progress of the mounted men. Before long he felt the ground tremble as some of their number drew near to his hiding place. Judging from the sound of hooves, they were only few in number. He heard them slow down and then shout to each other. They spoke with accents unfamiliar to Jack's ears.

"You said the boy ran this way."

"He did. I'm sure of it."

"He can't have gone far. You head over there and we'll take this path. Go now and hurry." Jack heard one horse gallop off. The two remaining riders were quiet for some time. Jack imagined them to be listening very carefully. He lay as still as he could manage, hardly daring to breathe. Eventually the two riders were off. Only when they had run a fair distance did Jack feel safe to breathe again.

He decided not to risk moving, unpleasant though his circumstances were. His ankle was throbbing, but more distressing was the slow chill of the water upon his skin. He noticed a slight pressure under his left leg and tentatively felt for the cause of it. It was something furry. Jack could risk no further movement but was now sure that the foul smell in the ditch was due to the decomposing carcass of a small animal.

Jack hoped it wasn't a rat. He was afraid of rats. The one thing he'd hated most about his job with Frallit was going to the storeroom for the flour. As soon as he opened the door, he would hear the sound of rats scurrying. He always gave them a few moments to hide before bringing his lantern forward, not wanting to see their fleshy legs and tails. Even with the lantern ahead of him, there were always some rats who defied its light and carried on feeding. Those were the worst—their beady eyes cold with defiance. Jack had kicked one once, and its bones crunched against the wall. The next day when he entered the storeroom, there were a score of rats feeding upon the carcass. There had been something else, too dark to make out; its teeth glinted for an instant, then it was gone.

Master Frallit gave him a beating over the incident. "Live rats are bad enough," he said, "but dead ones attract the devil."

According to Frallit, there were no end of things that attracted the devil. Long hair and daydreaming were two of his favorites. Jack knew the master baker said such things just to bully him, but he wasn't about to take any chances over a dead rat.

He scrambled out of the ditch. His clothes were soaked in mud, and he shivered as the wind picked up. As he limped deeper into the wood, his thoughts were with Melli: he hoped she had not been caught instead of him.

"There's a good boy." Melli's horse reluctantly stepped into the flow. Her pursuers were only feet away. She ignored their approach as she coaxed her mount to cross the stream. The horse was now up to his fetlocks in icy water. "Good boy, good boy." She spoke more to comfort herself than the horse. The creature stumbled a little as he found his footing on the rocky streambed. "It's all right, boy," she whispered gently.

The guards came to a halt only a few yards from where she was. Two of their number moved forward to the stream.

One of them had his sword drawn. "Go no further, lady," he warned. As he spoke, he motioned to his men to surround her. Melli waited in the middle of the stream as she was encircled by seven men. All now had their swords drawn. She stroked her horse and tried to control the wild beating of her heart—she would not demean herself by showing fear.

"Take her down and bind her." Hands pulled cruelly at her legs and body, some lingering unnecessarily over her breasts and thighs. She was pulled down and carried to the bank, where she was thrown hard to the ground. The smell of dead leaves and earth assailed her nostrils.

"She's a pretty one," said the man who appeared to be in charge.

"Aye, and she's well filled out under that cloak," commented one of the others who had just handled her. Melli grew frightened. The men had sheathed their swords and were looking to their leader.

"I'm sure he wouldn't mind if we had a little fun with her," he said, grinning to his company and moving toward Melli. He knelt beside her and untied her cloak. She lashed out at him. "You bitch!" The leader slapped her cruelly on her face, the force of the blow sending her head reeling. The men cheered.

One of them shouted, "Give it her rough, Traff, and hurry up about it so we can all have a go."

The leader grabbed the bodice of Melli's dress and tore it from her. Her pale breasts were exposed to the men. She tried desperately to cover her chest, but the leader was pressing down on her, forcing his lips on hers and roughly handling her breasts. The man was fumbling with his belt buckle with one hand while pushing up her skirts with the other. Melli was screaming hysterically, trying to fight him off.

Suddenly, the pounding of hooves could be heard. The leader stood up quickly, worry creasing his brow. Melli used this opportunity to pull her dress together as best she could.

"To your mounts," cried the leader, flashing a look of contempt at Melli. "Draw your swords."

A group of horsemen were bearing down on them. Melli could tell from a distance they were her father's men— the silver and red was clearly visible. Relief flooded through her. She noticed the men were now paying her little attention as they waited tensely for the approach of the horsemen, and she slipped under the cover of some nearby bushes.

The two parties met. Her father's men had drawn their swords and the sound of clashing blades filled the air. The adversaries seemed to be evenly matched at first. They thrust mercilessly at each other, eager for blood.

To Melli, the fight she watched bore no resemblance to the dainty exchanges that were demonstrated at court. The swords were yielded with no finesse; the men sliced and hacked with savage frenzy, caring not if they injured man or horse. The fight grew long and bloody. The dull, heavy swords cut through leather and into flesh. Melli thought she spied her brother amongst her father's men, wielding his sword in the fray. She could watch the fighting no longer.

Unheeded, she crept silently away. On her hands and knees she crawled, the dry growth of winter brushing against her tender belly. As she went, she could hear the sounds of combat, the grunts and cries of the men, the squeal of frightened horses and the ringing of blades.

Melli headed downstream until she found a place that was easy to cross on foot. She waded into the stream, welcoming the sensation of cold water on her legs; it helped cleanse the stain of unwanted hands.

When she reached the other side, she found a small glade and fell to the ground. She was shaking, and tears soon followed. She wept for a long time. Leaving home, being robbed, the chase and the capture and finally the fight—it had all proven too much of a strain on her emotions. She cried quietly, hugging the remains of her dress close to her body. She didn't really care anymore if her father's men found her as long as the first men did not. Melli swore she would rather be killed than ever touched again.

After a while she grew calm. She could no longer hear the sound of fighting, but couldn't remember when it had ceased.

She pulled the cord from her hair and tied her dress together as best she could. She no longer had a cloak; she'd left it at the scene of the fight. She doubted that she could survive the night without it. Her head turned quickly as she heard the snapping of twigs and rustle of leaves that announced someone's approach. She would not run anymore. She stood up and held her head high, prepared to return to the castle.

It was her horse! He must have left the stream after she had been pulled from him. Running to the tired creature, she flung her arms around its neck. Melli kissed the old horse many times, and then her eye was caught by its back. Somehow it had managed to keep possession of her precious supplies! Quickly she untied the sack, letting it fall to the ground. She would use one of the blankets as a cloak. She drew a blanket around herself, beginning to feel much better: she was warm; she had her horse and her supplies.

She decided it was high time to eat. With relish she tucked into the dried pork and drybread—never had a meal tasted so good.

Lord Maybor was in a terrible rage, and his eldest son Kedrac was feeling the full strength of it. "You imbecile, how could you let her get away?" Maybor threw his cup across the chamber, where it hit his precious mirror, shattering the glass. "How could you let this happen?"

"It was the armed men, we had to fight them," retorted his son.

"What armed men? What fight?" Maybor raged. "What were you doing fighting armed men when you were supposed to be looking for your sister?"

"The men had her, that's how we found her. We heard her screaming."

"What men were these?"

"I'm not sure, father. They had no colors. I think they were mercenaries."

"By Borc! What is this?" Maybor felt the pressure of blood pumping in the veins of his neck. "What were mercenaries doing with my daughter?" His eyes scanned the room looking for something else to hurl: he felt the need for destruction.

"Father, they may have just come across her in the woods and decided to have a little fun with her."

"What do you mean?" Maybor's voice was as cold as ice.

Kedrac could not meet his father's eyes. "I think they tried to rape her. I can't be sure, but from the sound of her screams . . . and then later we found her cloak." He watched as his father's face became ashen.

"Did you capture any of these men?"

"No, Father. We killed two of them and wounded another three, but they escaped deep into the woods."

"And the bodies?"

"We searched the two that we killed, and the only thing we found of interest was that each man had eight gold pieces." Maybor thought for a moment, growing calmer.

"Eight gold pieces, eh? These men have been paid to do a job, and handsomely at that. Are you sure no one besides you and my men know that Melliandra is missing?"

"Father, we have been most discreet. I myself asked around the town about her and made as if it was a casual inquiry. As for your men, you know they are loyal to you."

Maybor nodded his head; what Kedrac was saying was the truth. Still, he had a feeling someone had paid the mercenaries to find his daughter. "Kedrac, you must go back into the forest tomorrow, take a tracker and the hounds. She must be found at all cost."

"Yes, Father." Kedrac took his leave.

When he had gone, Maybor went over and inspected the shattered mirror. He'd paid over one hundred gold pieces for it ten years back.

He was sure that the mercenaries were in the pay of Baralis. The king's chancellor had no men of his own, so that would fit. How had that scheming viper come to know of this? Maybor struck the shattered mirror with his fist. The sharp glass drew blood, but he didn't notice. Baralis had sent mercenaries to capture and rape his daughter.

Five

Jack was beginning to feel the first signs of a fever. He was soaked to the skin and his bones felt the chill of water and air. He had no food or dry clothing, and somewhere in the chase he had lost one of his shoes.

Jack had spent the rest of the day walking around the forest, hoping to catch sight of Melli. At one point he heard the clash of blades in the distance. He felt it would be unsafe to draw too close to the sound of fighting, so he veered off in another direction, his route taking him ever deeper into the heart of the wood.

His clothes were slow to dry in the frosty air, and he found himself shivering violently. His ankle was still tender and he walked with a limp. He tried to find berries or nuts to eat, but winter was drawing nigh and the forest had little bounty to offer.

Tired, hungry, and feeling the cold deeply, Jack had made a meager bed for the night. He curled up at the base of a great oak, hoping for some small protection from the wind. He covered himself with fallen branches and leaves and fell into a restless sleep.

Jack awoke the following morning to the smell of rain. His eyes looked up past the naked canopy of the oak and the sky confirmed his fears. It was gray and water laden. Rain would soon fall. He noticed his body was acting differently

from normal. All his muscles seemed to ache, his head felt
unsteady, and his limbs were slow to move. His skin was
clammy and drawn, and despite the obvious cold, he was
feeling hot and sweaty. Jack had caught fevers before and he
recognized what the symptoms meant. What he was unsure
of was what to do about it in a forest leagues from home.

In the castle now the first batch of loaves would be baking, the air would be heavy with the smell of yeast, there'd
be a bowl of pork broth for breakfast and an hour to waste by
the fire. Jack had to laugh. It was quite ridiculous: how could
he ever hope to be a hero when he'd only been away from
home for two days, had already managed to catch a fever,
and would have given the whole thing up for a hearty breakfast and a missing shoe?

Laughter made him feel stronger and he struggled to his
feet. Nausea swelled in his empty stomach. He stumbled and
was long regaining his balance. It occurred to Jack that if
Frallit were watching now, the master baker would think he
was drunk and ration his ale for a week. The idea of a week's
rationed ale seemed very appealing at this point—he would
have gladly suffered Frallit's scorn for as little as a cup of
soured water.

Jack labored on. He remembered drinking from a spring
the night before and headed toward it. His mind drifted from
subject to subject: Bodger and Grift warned of the dangers of
ditch water, and Findra the table maid mocked his bare foot.
He was becoming confused and disorientated: the people
from the castle seemed as real as the trees. He spent what he
could have sworn was an eternity making his way through
the woods only to end up at an oak tree that looked suspiciously like the one he'd slept under.

Every tree and bush began to look like the last one. He
was growing light-headed; he no longer even remembered
what he was supposed to be looking for. He desperately
needed to lie down, to stop the voices of reproof that were
spinning in his head. A tiny part of him was aware that lying
down was not a good idea. Jack ignored his own warning. He
had to stop his body from reeling. He had to sleep.

He collapsed by the foot of the tree. His last thoughts
before he dropped into unconsciousness were that the rain

had started to fall, and he was pleased. It felt cool and delicious on his hot skin.

Other eyes watched as the rain fell, just as they had
watched the boy wander in circles for most of the morning.
The man to whom they belonged paused as he considered
what to do. He knew the boy would die if left there for the
rain and cold to take their toll. Yet, he was not a man given
to acts of compassion. He lived in the heart of the forest and
did not trouble himself with the world of men. He knew the
beast and the tree, and had little interest in that which did not
concern him.

He was compelled to watch, though. He had seen much
in his time; he had seen men murdered, men robbed, men
hunting, and men hunted. He watched it all from his green
havens and had never once intervened.

The boy's plight had touched him. He was an innocent,
and that was a rare quality to find in the forest. But there was
more to it than that, for the man had seen people die many
times from cold or hunger. The boy struck a chord within the
man; he felt as if there was something more to this traveler.
The man imagined he saw the pale glow of destiny around
the lad. He shook his head, smiling at his own whimsy.

The man thought at great length as he watched the still
form of the boy. To act might threaten his own safety. It
might bring unwanted scrutiny upon himself, and he had
spent many years avoiding just such thing. Even as these
thoughts formed, he knew he would ignore them. He walked
forward from the deep trees and made his way toward the
boy.

Baralis met with his mercenaries outside of the castle
walls. It was a chill day and he drew his cloak close. He already knew that they had failed, but it suited him to act as if
he did not.

"So, are the boy and the girl in the said place?" he asked
Traff, the leader.

"No, lord, they are not. We had both the girl and the
boy, but Maybor's men descended upon us." Baralis knew

the man lied. They had never caught the boy; his dove had watched the chase. Baralis was not concerned about the lie—they were, after all, mercenaries not priests.

"How many of Maybor's men were there?" he asked slyly, knowing full well there had been less than ten of them.

"Two dozen," said the leader.

"More, I would say," interjected another. The rest of the men grunted in agreement.

"How many did you lose?" Baralis genuinely did not know this, as he had sent the dove to watch over the boy and had not been witness to the end of the exchange.

"We lost two, but we took out double that number of Maybor's."

"Hmm." Baralis was skeptical. "Go away now and conceal yourselves in the said place. I will call you to pick the fugitives up when I have better intelligence on them."

The leader made no move to withdraw. "My men were not engaged as fighters. You said we would just be picking up two young'uns. Two of my men are dead and the rest are not content."

"What is your point?" Baralis spoke coldly, knowing precisely what the leader was after.

"We want more money. Eight more golds apiece." Traff rested his hand upon his sword—a subtle threat.

Baralis was not so easily intimidated. With a sudden sweep he threw open his cloak. Once he was sure he had the full attention of the gathered men he spoke, his voice a harshly coiled whisper. "Do not be foolish enough to get greedy with me. With just one finger I could send you to an oblivion so deep your own families would forget you had ever existed." Baralis sought the eye of each mercenary, and not one of them could return his gaze. Satisfied, he modified the tone of his voice. "I will call you either later in the day, or on the morrow. Be sure to be ready. Now go!"

Baralis watched as the men mounted and rode away, the faintest of smiles on his grim face. He drew his cloak around him once more and headed back to the castle. He had much to think on. For his plans to succeed, Melliandra's pretty face must never be seen again at the court of the Four Kingdoms.

His mind travelled east to the dukedom of Bren—the

mightiest of the northern powers. The duke was getting greedy: he wanted more land, more timber, more grain. Baralis knew he would have to tread carefully to bring about what was planned between them. People in the Four Kingdoms were nervous of the ambitions of Bren, yet ironically, that very same nervousness might actually help seal the pact. It was always easier to neutralize, rather than eliminate, a threat.

Not that he would use that particular tactic with the lovely Melliandra. She was a threat which required swift elimination.

When he was finally back in his room, sipping on mulled holk to relieve the pain in his fingers, he considered what his dove had shown him. After leaving the queen yesterday, Baralis had returned to his chambers, deciding he would look upon the capture after all. The dove had seen his men descend on the fugitives. It had watched as the girl and boy were separated. Baralis looked on as the greatest number of mercenaries had followed the girl, sending only three of the number after the boy. He had willed the dove to follow the plight of the girl, who he felt might be easily lost on horseback. He had seen the approach of Maybor's men and had watched as both sides let the girl slip away.

His dove followed the girl and, satisfied that she would not go much further, he sent the bird to look for the boy. The boy was nowhere to be seen.

Baralis had remained calm; the baker's boy was merely a puzzle that needed solving, while Maybor's daughter was a hindrance to glory. He sent the reluctant bird back to watch the girl. Once she'd made camp for the night, Baralis let the dove sleep. The bird was cold and exhausted, and he feared it would not be long before the unfortunate creature died.

As the holk alleviated his pain a little, Baralis considered what to do next. In all likelihood, Maybor knew by now that the men out looking for Melliandra were in his pay. Maybor was sure to move against him—those damned fool mercenaries had tried to rape his only daughter! Maybor would bear watching closely: an indignant father could be a dangerous adversary.

*   *   *

"No, Bodger, the way to tell if a man's well hung ain't the size of his kneecaps."

"Old Master Pesk says it is, Grift."

"The reason why old Pesk says that is because he's got kneecaps the size of watermelons."

"They are unusually big, Grift. I can't argue with that."

"No, Bodger, the way to tell if a man is truly well hung is to look at the whites of his eyes."

"The whites of his eyes?"

"Aye, the whites of his eyes, Bodger. The whiter the eye, the bigger the pole. It's right every time."

The two men pondered this thought for a while, Bodger secretly planning to check out his own eyes at some point. They downed some more ale and then the talk moved to other matters.

"Here, Grift, something's going down at the moment, mercenaries in the castle grounds, fighting in the woods. Just this morning I saw a face I hadn't seen in a long time."

"Who was that, Bodger?"

"Remember Scarl?"

Grift took a sharp intake of breath. "Scarl. This bodes no good, Bodger. Scarl's one villainous fox. I wouldn't care to cross him."

"Too right, Grift. Last time Scarl was seen in the castle more than one man ended up with his throat slit."

"If I remember correctly, Bodger, last time he was here, Lord Glayvin met a sticky end."

"He was the one who refused to sell his pear orchards to Maybor, wasn't he?"

"Aye, Bodger. His widow had no such compunction, though. After her husband's death, she sold Maybor those orchards so fast you'd think they'd been riddled with brown worm."

Maybor decided that this meeting was best held out in the open, away from the listening ears of the court. He had been careful to choose a place in the castle grounds where he and his companion would be undisturbed. Downwind of the middens was just such a spot. Maybor covered his face with a handkerchief to prevent as much of the foul smell from entering his nose as possible. This action also had the added benefit of concealing the greater part of his features.

Maybor watched as the assassin approached. He was a slight man, not strong but rumored to be wiry and quick. No one, it was said, was craftier or more skilled with a blade.

"Well met, friend," said Maybor.

"I wish you joy of the day, Lord Maybor." The assassin scanned the area. "You have picked a foul spot in which to meet."

" 'Tis a foul deed that needs be done."

"Whose absence from the world do you seek this time, my lord?" The assassin constantly watched the surroundings, making sure no one approached.

Maybor had no love for mincing words. "I seek the death of Baralis, the king's chancellor." Their eyes met and held, it was the assassin who looked away first.

"Lord Maybor, I think you know just how powerful Baralis is. He is more than man; he is said to be a master."

Maybor didn't like to think on such things. He tried to convince himself that Baralis' powers were nothing more than hearsay, but he never quite quite succeeded—a smidgen of doubt always remained. He wasn't about to let the assassin know that, though—the man's price would double if he thought sorcery was involved. "Listen, Scarl, Baralis is not as powerful and all-seeing as everyone thinks. He has his weakness. A keen blade will slit his throat the same as it would any man's."

"His chambers will be warded against intruders."

"That is not my concern. You must evade *anyone* who blocks your path," said Maybor, deliberately misinterpreting Scarl's words. He was damned if the assassin was going to talk openly about sorcery! They both suspected the risks— why add weight to them by giving them air? "It is your job to find the time and place when he is most vulnerable. All I ask is that there be no trail leading back to me."

"Are you presuming to tell me how to do my job, Maybor?" The assassin spoke lightly, but there was a hint of reproach in his voice.

"No, no. I am anxious that the deed be done. Too long

has Baralis held power in the court." Maybor took a deep breath, forgetting where he was, and his lungs filled with the stench of human waste. He coughed violently, ridding himself of the foul air.

Scarl looked on, a hint of distaste showing upon his clever face. "I do not much like the sound of this commission. There is great risk."

"Name your price," uttered Maybor, impatient to be away.

"The price will be high." The assassin raised a querying eyebrow.

"It is of no matter. I will pay whatever you ask."

"I have no need of money, Maybor. Well you know I am paid a good price for my work. No, I seek a little something for my retirement."

"Yes, yes, name it."

"I want land, Maybor. I fancy growing apples when I'm older."

Maybor did not like the sound of this; nothing was more precious to him than his land. "I will give you two hundred gold pieces," he countered.

"No." The assassin moved away as he spoke. "No, Maybor, I would have land in payment, or I shall take my skills elsewhere."

Maybor relented. "Very well, I will give a stretch of land in the north. I have thirty acres outside Jesson that you can have."

"Apples grow better in the east," said the assassin.

"I cannot think why you would want land in the east with the war against the Halcus still raging."

"Wars of man come and go. Land endures."

Maybor relented. "So be it. I will give you twenty acres of orchards in the east."

"You would give me thirty in the north," replied the assassin, once again stepping away.

"Very well. I will give you your thirty acres. But you will not see a blade of grass until I have proof you have done your job."

The assassin nodded. "I think we have reached a fair agreement. I will take the commission."

"Good. Is there anything I can do to facilitate this undertaking?" Lord Maybor received the answer he hoped for.

"No. I must find my own way. A good murder can often be an act of great inspiration. I prefer to work alone." With that the assassin bowed neatly to Maybor and was off. Maybor forced himself to wait for the passing of a few minutes and then followed in the assassin's footsteps. He was eager to be free of the smell of decay.

Melli spotted the dove on her waking. It was high in a tree. It seemed to her to be a sign of hope, and she was glad of its presence.

She had spent a surprisingly comfortable night. She had found a peaceful glade and wrapped herself warmly in blankets. The mossy floor was soft and springy, and she woke refreshed and hungry. Her horse had found its own food and was slowly chewing at a patch of grass. She wished there was something different for her to eat than just pork and dry-bread.

She thought to monitor the direction of the sun, for she still intended to head east. The sun, however, was not on show. The sky was bleakly gray, and she realized she would soon need to find shelter, for the clouds held promise of rain. Melli had scant protection from the rain: the blanket that served as her cloak was not oiled and water could easily soak through. Suddenly she had an inspiration: she could use the heavy sack that contained her supplies as cover. The fabric was woven, but its coarse and prickly thread promised more protection than her woolen blanket.

Melli emptied the contents out of the sack. Then, taking the small but sharp fish-boning knife that Master Trout had so thoughtfully packed, she cut holes in the bottom and the sides of the sack. She secured her blanket around her chest and then slipped the sack over her head, sliding her arms through the side holes. It was a perfect fit, covering her body to below her knees. She burst into laughter—how silly she must look. What would Master Trout say if he saw what had become of his sack?

She reveled in the sound of her own laughter, skipping

gaily around the glade, making mock curtsies to imagined ladies of the court. "Yes, Lady Fiandrell, this is all the rage in Rorn. I had the materials brought in from beyond the dry-lands. But, if I do say so myself, the expense was well worth it." Melli had now succumbed to a wild fit of giggles as she imagined herself at court, dressed in a sack.

Her old horse looked up, attracted by the sound of her laughter. "What are you looking at?" she shouted. "I won't be the one who gets wet when it rains."

Melli took a guess at where she thought the sky looked a little lighter and headed off in that direction, munching on a piece of drybread. Her belongings she had made into a neat package with the help of the second blanket. As she walked, she considered names for her horse: he wouldn't suit a ro-mantic name like Goldarrow, nor a military name like War-rior. He needed a simple name like Pippin or Brownie. Only she didn't like either of those.

"I'm afraid you're destined to be the horse without a name," she said, patting the creature's back. One thing was certain: she had no intention of riding again without a saddle. The experience had proved to be most uncomfortable and her thighs chafed sorely as a reminder.

As she walked, her thoughts turned to her lost compan-ion, Jack. She fervently hoped that he had not encountered her pursuers. He may have abandoned her, but she bore him no ill will. She even wished that he was still with her, for she didn't like the idea of traveling alone with only a fish-gutting knife for protection. In the space of two days she had been robbed and violated. What will be next? she wondered, for everyone knew that trouble came in threes.

Eventually the rain started, and Melli led her horse on a route that promised as much protection as possible. She headed toward the most dense forest she could see, thankful for the trees' broad branches, as they prevented some of the rain from falling upon her. She sang a few songs to keep her spirits up and tried not to think too much about the future.

Tavalisk was eating one of his favorite delicacies: raw oysters. It was oyster season in Rorn, and their supply was plentiful. Tavalisk, however, would eat no common oyster. His were brought in fresh each day from the cold seas of Toolay. The expense of such an endeavor did not concern him; it would be borne by the church. After all, he thought, an archbishop deserves whatever meager pleasures life affords.

Tavalisk prised open another shell with an expert hand and sprinkled vinegar over the milky creature, noting with pleasure the faint shudder as vinegar touched oyster flesh. The shudder was a sign of a healthy, live oyster. He cupped the half shell up to his lips and savored with relish the sensation of oyster in his mouth. He was careful not to puncture the creature with his sharp teeth. He liked to swallow them alive and whole. With displeasure, he heard a knock on the door. Why must that fool Gamil always come while he was eating?

"Yes. What is it?" he asked, careful to keep his voice sounding bored and indulgent.

"I thought you might like to know what our friend the knight has been up to." Tavalisk ignored his aide while he opened another shell. He could tell straight away the oyster was bad: it had a grayish bloom to its skin.

"Would you care for an oyster, Gamil?" he said, proffering the unsavory creature to his aide. Gamil looked rather astounded; Tavalisk never offered him food. He was obliged to accept the morsel and swallowed it quickly, making an unpleasant slurping noise.

"Now, wasn't that delicious?" The archbishop smiled with benign indulgence. "I have them brought in from Toolay, you know." Gamil nodded in agreement. "You were saying about the knight?" Tavalisk opened yet another oyster.

"Yes, Your Eminence. The knight visited Frong Street yesterday and went into The Grapes, where he bought a long-knife."

"Very good, Gamil. Is he showing his circles?"

"No, the marks were concealed beneath his cloak."

"He is wise to keep them hidden; the people of Rorn have no love for the knights of Valdis." Tavalisk allowed himself the smallest of smiles, parting his lips just enough to reveal the glint of teeth. "I think I've made sure of that. Though their hatred needs little prompting at the moment. The knights paint themselves as religious fanatics, but what they're really after is trade, not conversions." He poured a clear, heavy liquid into his cup. "Anything else?"

"One more thing. The knight was asking about Larn."

Tavalisk, who had been about to drink from his cup, put it down quickly. "Larn. What was he asking about Larn for?"

"I can't say, Your Eminence."

"If I remember rightly, that old fool Bevlin has no love for Larn. He tried to put a stop to what went on there once. Of course, he failed miserably. Larn is not a place to suffer interference gladly." Tavalisk paused while he toyed with his cup. "Perhaps he's using the knight to mount a second offensive. He really should keep to his books and prophecies— he's far too old to be indulging in moral causes."

The archbishop turned to Gamil. "You may go now. You've made me lose my appetite with all this talk of Larn." Gamil obediently withdrew. As soon as the door was closed, Tavalisk immediately returned to his oysters, his eyes scanning them greedily for the biggest.

Tawl was out on the streets of Rorn again. When he returned to Megan the previous night, he had questioned her about the Seers of Larn, but she had never heard of them. Today he was determined to do two things: first, he wanted to build up the strength in his muscles by walking several leagues, and second, he was going to find someone to tell him about Larn.

The crowds were still out on the street, but there were not nearly as many as the day before. What people there were seemed pale and drawn, heavy drinking and overindulgence stealing the spring from their step.

Tawl was feeling a lot better. His arms and wrists were slowly recovering and his legs were feeling stronger. His training as a knight had left a legacy of physical resilience that even now, five years later, could still be drawn upon. With concentration, he could control the blood flow into his muscles, swelling the arteries, making the tissue supple and ready for action. Tawl found that this technique, taught to be used in preparation for battle, was helping his damaged muscles recover their strength more quickly.

His training seemed far behind him now. He was a different person than the young, idealistic boy who'd presented himself at the gates of Valdis so many years before. There was hope, then, and dreams and the thrill of achievement.

During his first year at Valdis, the emphasis had been on physical strength. Novices were set a series of tasks to test and develop their skills of endurance. Tawl was sent into the Great Divide with only a knife at his side. He was lucky; some before him were caught in blizzards and never came back. Two months it took him to reach the mountain shrine. Even now he could remember the terrible cold, his hair stiff with ice, the saliva freezing on his teeth. The shrine was set upon the second tallest peak in the Known Lands. It was a symbol, and to meditate in its barren chamber was essential for gaining the first circle.

When he returned to Valdis, flushed with pride at his success, they sent him out again, this time to search the length of the milk flats. Pride was not tolerated at Valdis.

The milk flats, which were located south of Leiss, were deceptively named. They were formed from white porous rock and were flat when viewed from a distance, but up close they were a maze of tunnels and sinkholes. The rock was as brittle as old bones: one wrong step, one sudden rain shower, or even the smallest of earth tremors, could lead to death. Tawl was ordered to bring back a knight who'd gone to the flats in search of Borc's sword. Nothing lived on the sterile rocks. Night and day were cruel masters: the sun was merciless and the moon cold-hearted. Close to starvation and madness, he eventually found the body. The knight had slit his own throat. Before he died, he etched the words *es nil hesrl* into the face of the rock. *I am not worthy.*

To a knight of Valdis the only thing that mattered was to be worthy. It was what all the training, all the learning, all the searching was for.

Tawl looked back on his time as a novice with mixed feelings. The first circle had brought him renown. He'd surpassed all others in the art of swordplay, though before his training he'd never even handled a sword. He'd gained the shrine in two months, when most took over three. And then there was the body, carried home from the milk flats on his back. Valdis liked to bury its own.

Renown brought resentment, and his first conferment had been marked by subtle tensions. He was called too young, too common, too favored.

The second circle brought derision. He had no learning; the only book he'd ever read was Marod. Yet after gaining his first circle, he was thrown into the company of men of culture. It was a struggle to master the classic texts, to learn the great histories, to speak in foreign tongues. He was constantly shown for what he was: a lowly boy from the marshlands. Most of the knights came from the nobility; they had manner and bearing and speech on their side, and they never once let him forget that he wasn't one of them.

Tawl had gone through a hundred different humiliations: he didn't know how to bow, how to dress, how to speak with great lords. It made him more determined than ever to learn their ways—not because he wanted to be what they were, but to prove that any man could be a knight. If it hadn't been for their taunting, he wouldn't have gained his second circle so fast—at least he had that to be thankful for.

He did have some friends, good men who'd been like brothers. Once he got his second circle and was free to go out in the world, they'd planned to go on a journey together, beyond the drylands in search of sacred treasures. But it all changed. Everything changed when he came home to visit his family. His life had been forever altered and now only the quest remained.

Tawl walked aimlessly through the streets of Rorn, searching out diversions. When his thoughts circled too closely around his family, he became desperate to change their path. Women, with their ability to give so tenderly of themselves, could usually lead his body to a place where his mind would follow. And if he'd been in a different city, he might have gone in search of some comfort. Megan was here in Rorn, though, and she'd done so much and asked so little that the least he owed her was fidelity.

Tawl chose streets that were bright with people, seeking

out distractions where he could. Eventually he found himself heading down to the harbor. The smell of the sea was sharp but not unpleasant. Tawl found his spirits reviving with each salty breath.

Rorn was the greatest trading city in the east: rare spices, exquisite silks, fabulous gemstones, and fresh seafood all found their way through the great port. Rorn's main source of income came from trade. The terrain to the north of the city was both rocky and barren, and Rorn grew no crops, or reared no livestock to speak of. The city owed its prosperity to the fortunate trade winds which gently drew ships from all the Known Lands to its safe harbors.

The harbor was large, spread over several leagues of seafront. Tawl enjoyed the brisk, salty air. It made a change from the smell of decay in the whoring quarter.

He walked for some time before deciding upon a likely looking tavern. THE ROSE AND CROWN, declared the old and peeling sign. Tawl slipped inside out of the wind.

The tavern appeared to be doing a fine business. Customers were talking loudly, there were people shouting for ale, a group of men were noisily proposing toasts to famous local beauties, and others were placing bets on times ships would come to harbor. There were those who sat around tables engaged in heated discussions and others who drank alone. It was a seafaring tavern, a place where sailors came to talk about the sea.

A large and comely woman approached Tawl. "What's your favor, sir?" she asked, smiling and thrusting her magnificent bosom out to its best advantage. Tawl, almost against his will, was drawn into the familiar cadence of flirtation. Exchanging smiles was enough to create the potential for a liaison. He was tempted to see the dance through, to feel the joy—no matter how visceral—of shared intimacy. The woman waited for a sign, confident of her attractions.

Tawl's gaze moved from her eyes to the floor. "All I'll take is a mug of ale, if you please."

She raised an eyebrow, surprised but not put off by his restraint. "Certainly, sir," she replied, her full lips curving slightly. "I hope the ale serves to warm your blood." She retreated slowly, giving Tawl plenty of time to regret the loss of her ample curves.

After a few minutes the woman returned. He watched as the eyes of many a man appreciated her generously proportioned form—she possessed an abundance of flesh that was sadly lacking in many women of the day. "There you are, sir. Be sure to let me know if you change your mind and take a fancy for something else." She acknowledged Tawl's rueful smile and then left with a saucy turn of her hips.

Tawl made himself comfortable and sampled his ale. It was really quite delicious: foamy and cool, with a pleasant nutty taste.

"The owner here brews his own." Tawl looked up to find an old, red-faced man standing over him. "Do you mind if I sit a while with you?"

"Please, feel free to do so, sir. It would be my honor."

The old man was clearly pleased with Tawl's courtesy. "You have a nice manner about you, young man, but you have a strange accent. I cannot quite place it."

"I'm originally from the Lowlands." Tawl did not want to say any more on the subject and the old man, sensing this, let the matter be.

"I'm known hereabouts as Jem." The old man smiled kindly. "Do you have a name you would share?"

"I am Tawl." His name sounded short to his ears without its normal title.

"I wish you joy of the day, Tawl." The man finished the last of his ale and placed his empty mug loudly on the counter. Tawl offered to buy him another. The man accepted graciously, and minutes later the two were sitting and supping.

"What is your trade, Jem?"

"Better to ask what *was* my trade." The old man sighed heavily and stared into his ale. "I was a seafarer. I've spent the best part of my life on the high seas. I'd be out there now if it wasn't for my bad leg—dry land is too still for my taste."

"So you have visited many places?" Tawl asked casually.

"Aye, that I have, on both coasts."

"Tell me, Jem, have you ever heard of a place called Larn?"

The old man sucked in his breath. He was silent for a while. When he finally spoke, his voice had changed its timbre. "Why would you wish to know of such a place?"

Tawl decided to take a chance. "I would visit with the seers there."

"I would not risk going there if I were you." Jem shook his head. "No, I would not, indeed."

"You know where it is?"

"How could I call myself a seafarer and not know, eh?" he responded sharply, but then continued more quietly. "Larn is not that far from where we stand. Only a couple of days sailing southeast. It's a tiny island, so small you will find it on no charts. But seafarers know it well. It is a death-trap to sailors. The sea for miles around is rocky and shallow. Woe betide the sailor who is blown off course to that damned isle."

"There must be a way to get there, though?" Tawl tried to disguise his eagerness by taking a long draft of ale.

"No captain who valued his ship would take you there. The best way would be to sail as far as was safe, and then row the rest of the way in a small boat."

"How far would one have to row?"

"A sane captain wouldn't sail any closer than twenty leagues."

"Yet people must journey there to consult with the seers?"

"No one in his right mind would want to consult with the Seers of Larn, boy," warned the old man.

"What have you heard of them?"

"Plenty." Jem sipped his ale. His eyes flicked around the room, and when he spoke again, his voice was a whisper. "I've heard plenty. Tales so horrifying that even an old man like myself doesn't like to repeat them."

"Why don't I buy you another drink and you can tell me what you know."

Jem considered the offer. "Very well, boy. You are getting a good bargain." Tawl called for more drinks; both young man and old waited in silence. The drinks came and neither man noticed the charms of the barmaid this time.

The old man spoke. "The Seers of Larn have existed for as long as anyone can remember. They were around long before the city of Rorn was founded. There is said to have been seers on Larn since the time of the great purge. What strange beliefs they have I don't know, what Gods they worship I cannot tell you. What I do know of is the terrible way the seers are created.

"The powers that be on Larn pick young children—boys who are rumored to have a little skill in foretelling. They pay the parents of these children one hundred gold pieces. The parents never set eyes upon their sons again. The boys are shipped to the dread isle, and they are kept in a darkened room for a full year to cleanse their souls and minds. They are fed nothing but bread and water, for they believe that all other foods interfere with the foretelling.

"After a year in the dark, the boys are measured. A huge stone weighing many tons is cut for each boy. The stones are then hauled into the Great Hall of Seeing and are laid flat on the ground. Each boy is then bound to his stone.

"They lay the boys out, limbs spread wide, and bind them to the stone with the strongest of ropes. They lash them as tight as they dare. The boys cannot move as much as a finger or a toe. All they can do is watch and breathe. They spend all of their lives so bound. Never able to move a limb. As the months pass, their limbs atrophy, becoming useless husks. All the better to think and foretell. It is the worst fate I can imagine for any man.

"The powers that be ensure that the seers are fed and cleansed. They claim the seers are closer to God. They say that the seers are allowed, through their sacrifice, to know the will of God. They spend their days contemplating the great pattern of life. They live and die bound to the stone. Lost in a world of hallucination and madness."

The old man grew silent. Tawl could hardly believe what he had been told. He shuddered at the fate of the seers and wondered how desperate a family would have to be to sell their sons into such a living hell.

Tawl could stand the silence no longer. "Old man, you

have told a story that has chilled my blood. I fear I owe you more than a drink."

The man spoke quickly, as if he had already prepared his answer. "You owe me nothing. Save a promise not to visit that cursed place."

"I can give you no such undertaking. For I fear I am fated to go there." The old man stood up to leave. Tawl caught his arm. "Tell me, what is the price for a foretelling?"

The old man walked away as he spoke. "The price is whatever they decide. Be careful they do not ask for your soul."

Tawl watched as Jem left. It was getting late. He wanted to get back to Megan. He needed to feel her warm arms around his body.

The queen was in the king's chamber, probably the most splendid room in the whole castle. She watched as the king was bathed by his manservant. He had not remembered her name this night. Baralis was right: he was getting weaker. Only last spring he could sit a horse, now he barely left his bed.

Ever since the hunting accident, she had lived with less than a man. At first the injury had not seemed so bad. The wound had healed normally, and although it had left an ugly scar, the physicians were not unduly concerned. However, as the weeks passed a deep fever had set in that seemed to rob him of his strength. Gradually, the weeks had turned to months. The physicians began to shake their heads; they blamed infection, fever on the brain, poison on the arrow. But they could do nothing to heal him.

First they tried hot poultices to draw out the infection. Next they had tried leeches to cleanse his blood of bad humors. The physicians had then attempted to expunge the malignant biles by piercing the king's stomach. They had shaved his head, pulled his teeth, and let his blood—all to no avail.

The queen had watched these horrific remedies and many more, and she saw that they only served to weaken her husband further. Finally, she had driven all the physicians away, preferring to tend to the king herself. She engaged the services of a wisewoman who knew the ways of herbs.

After the physicians left, the king's health actually improved. The wisewoman's remedies were a lot easier for the king to bear: mulled holk with a sprig of juniper, herb-laden vapors, and rubs with therapeutic oils. Unfortunately, the wisewoman's treatments seemed to slow down his decline, not stop it. Years passed and his strength lagged further and his mind grew clouded. The queen could not count the times she had lain alone in her bed crying through the night. She was a proud woman and would allow no one to see her private anguish.

The attendant wiped a speckle of drool from the king's chin. The sight of the small gesture wrenched at her heart. What had her husband come to? The once proud King Lesketh reduced to being spoonfed and nursed like a baby! He was not yet an old man; others his age were in their prime.

The queen thought on the audience she'd had with Baralis. He'd hinted that he had something in his possession that might help the king. No matter how much she loathed the chancellor, she would have to summon him back. She was desperate to try anything that might improve her husband's condition. She decided to see Baralis and find out what he wanted from her. She was no fool; she knew there would be a price to pay.

Six

Jack lay awake for some time before opening his eyes. He could smell the freshness of trees and ferns and the odor of wood smoke. Then he detected the smell of food, a savory stew or soup. Lastly, he smelled the delicious aroma of warm holk.

Tempted by such a beguiling array of odors, Jack opened his eyes. Soft, green light filtered through the trees and onto his face. He looked at his surroundings. He seemed to be in a sort of nest or den, which appeared to be woven out of leaves and branches. He was lying on a low pallet that rested upon a blanket of ferns and velvet mosses. He was alone.

Drawn to the smell of food, he caught sight of a small brick stove in the middle of the den. A gap had been left in the weave of trees to allow the smoke out. Jack tentatively put his foot on the floor and found to his surprise that the moss was warm to the touch. As he swung both his legs off the pallet a wave of nausea swept through his body. Jack felt dizzy and wondered whether he should just stay in his bed. The promise of hot food and holk proved too tempting to be put off by mere physical discomfort, and Jack rose from his bed.

Shakily, he approached the small stove. An open pot contained a rich, dark stew. Jack scanned the den, and found various cups and plates lying in wait on a low, wooden table. He ladled some of the fragrant mixture onto a plate, and poured himself a cup of mulled holk.

The stew was delicious; it contained mushrooms and rabbit meat, carrots and onions, all flavored with robust herbs and spices. He felt sure he could detect the subtle taste of apples and cider. He ate a hearty portion, and then another one—the last time he had eaten seemed to be a long time ago. It didn't occur to him to question where he was or how he'd gotten here. Food and warmth were quite enough to occupy him for the moment.

After his meal, he felt the need to relieve himself and he looked for a way to leave the den. He could not find one. He was not too worried, as he had noticed a chamberpot at the foot of his bed. After he had finished, he climbed back onto the pallet and immediately fell into a deep and restful sleep.

Some time later Jack was woken by the sound of movement in the den. He opened his eyes to find a tall, long-bearded man staring back at him. "I see you have eaten well, young man." He spoke in a curious lilting accent. Jack could only manage to nod his head; he was feeling a little guilty for eating what he had not been invited to. The man appeared to recognize Jack's concern.

"You did well to eat, 'twas meant for you. I hope you found it to your liking?"

Jack nodded enthusiastically. "It was delicious—the best stew I have ever tasted." He hesitated. "I thank you for it, sir." Jack took in the strange appearance of the man: he seemed neither young nor old and was dressed in skins and coarse weaves. His most remarkable feature was his magnificent, long, ash-colored beard.

"I am no sir, young man. I have not been a sir in many years, and I do not wish to be one now." A half-smile graced the man's lips.

"I am truly sorry if I have offended you." Jack felt the man was amusing himself at his expense.

"No matter, no matter. I suppose I will have to give you my name."

"If you would rather not, I will understand. My own name is Jack, though. You are welcome to it."

This speech seemed to please the man. "Well, Jack, you shame me. You would give freely of your name to a stranger who has not given his. There are many people who believe that if you know a person's name, you gain power over them. What do you say to that?"

It was a little difficult for Jack to follow what the man said, for his voice made speech sound like song. The man continued, "I will give you my name, Jack, but I can only give you half of it. I have lived without naming myself for many years. The trees do not ask my name, the birds would gain no benefit from it, the streams run and do not stop from want of knowing it. But I will give it to you, Jack, for man, unlike nature, has need of names. People do well to be wary of names—they have power. If I were to name a tree, I would make it mine, and no man should have such a claim over a tree, or a brook or a blade of grass." The man grew disheartened and breathed wearily.

Jack spoke to fill the silence. "If a bird does not ask your name, then neither will I. I refuse to know even half of it."

The man smiled and shook his head sadly. "My half name is Falk." Jack felt as if he was being let in on a great secret. He wanted to offer some comfort to the man, but found he could think of nothing to say.

Eventually the man spoke again. "You have been sick, Jack. You caught a wet fever, and you should rest for now and regain your strength. I must be off. I will bring you more food later. Before I go, I would have you take a sip of this medicine." Falk crossed the room and came back with a cup of pungent-smelling liquid. Jack obediently swallowed all of the concoction, not at all sure he liked the taste. He wondered what the medicine was made from. Jack gave the man a questioning look, and Falk smiled kindly. "I have given you half my name, would you know all my secrets, too?"

Jack felt suitably chastened and handed the cup back to the man. He watched as Falk walked toward the wall. With gentle hands, he pulled the weave of branch and twig apart, creating an opening. He then stepped out into the cool air. Once on the other side, Falk rewove the flexible branches which served to seal and conceal the entrance to the den.

*   *   *

Baralis could hardly contain his pleasure when the messenger arrived from the queen. She had not only taken the bait, she had swallowed it whole. She was on the hook now. All that remained was to reel her in.

All his other concerns were petty annoyances. The girl Melliandra he was still tracking; he would move in on her more carefully next time. She would not elude him twice. As for Jack, well, how far could a boy on foot get in a few days? He would find him soon.

Baralis took from his drawer a measure of the white powder that was his pain-killing drug. He was about to swallow the foul tasting crystals when he thought better of it. His head would need to be clear. He would have to endure the pain in his hands until after his audience with the queen. It was a small price to pay.

He once again dressed with care, ensuring he chose a different robe than the one he had worn for his last meeting. It suited him to go along with the customs of the court.

This time the queen did not keep him waiting outside the door. She beckoned him in the moment he knocked. Her tone was still as cold as ever, though. "Good day, Lord Baralis." She was dressed with exquisite care: her gown was embroidered with rubies and pearls, and matching gems sparkled at her throat and wrist.

"Joy of the day to Your Highness."

"I will not keep you long. I would rather get straight to the point, Lord Baralis." The queen smoothed her hair nervously; Baralis was gratified to note that her hand trembled as she did so.

"As you wish, Your Highness."

"You hinted during our last meeting that you had something in your possession that might help the king. Am I right to assume that was what you meant?"

"You are, Your Highness." Baralis decided to say little, preferring to let her talk.

"Then am I also right in assuming that you speak of some medicine or potion that will help the king's illness?"

"Yes, Your Highness." He watched the queen grow impatient with his short answers.

"Lord Baralis, what is the nature of this medicine, and how do I know it will work?"

"The answer to the first question is that I cannot divulge its nature. The answer to the second is that you cannot know it will work until you try it."

"What guarantee do I have that it is safe? How do I know it is not poison or worse?" The queen looked directly into his eyes, challenging him.

"I give Your Highness my gravest undertaking that it will do the king no harm."

"And what if I have no faith in that undertaking?"

"Your Highness, I have a proposition." Baralis dug into the fold of his cloak and brought out the small glass bottle containing the potion. He held the bottle up to the light, and the brownish fluid sparkled with promise. "This vial contains hope for the king." He handed it to the queen. "In it is ten days supply of medicine. Take it from me this day, and administer it to the king. If you see a noticeable improvement in his health, I will be willing to supply you with as much of the remedy as the king will ever need."

The queen regarded Baralis impassively. He suspected that beneath her serene exterior was a frenzy of emotions. "I repeat, Lord Baralis, how do I know this remedy is safe?"

Baralis remained calm. He had expected no less and was prepared for it. He approached the queen and noticed that she winced slightly as he did so. Slowly, for his hands were in pain and he was anxious not to betray that fact to the queen, he pulled the stopper from the bottle. He then raised the bottle to his lips and swallowed a quantity of the thick, brown liquid. Baralis resealed the bottle and held it out for the queen to take.

For what seemed to Baralis like an eternity, but was in fact only a few moments, he stood there offering the bottle to the queen. At last, she stepped forward and took it. Their fingers touched for the barest of seconds.

"If this works, what will you expect in return?"

"Your Highness, let us first see if you are willing to buy before we talk of the price."

The queen's face was as cold as stone. "You may go now, Lord Baralis."

He left obediently. Everything had gone perfectly. The medicine would appear to work well. It would improve the king's condition, as it was part antidote to the poison that had been on the king's arrow. Of course, the king would never be himself again, but the medicine would halt further decline, and might enable him to remember names and walk a little once more. Might even stop his constant drooling. Nothing too drastic, mused Baralis. Nothing that would interfere with his plans.

It would only be a matter of days before the queen would come to him, eager for more of the medicine. So eager, she would agree to anything he asked. He must remember to make the second batch much weaker. It wouldn't do to have the king too well.

As Baralis returned to his chamber, he had the vague feeling he was being watched. He turned around, and no one was there. He shook his head. He was probably imagining things; it might even be an aftereffect of the king's medicine. Baralis smiled to himself. A little paranoia would go unnoticed among the king's other ailments.

The assassin watched as Baralis returned to his chambers. He was careful not to approach the door too closely. He had seen markings like those before, and he knew they were wardings. Maybor had tried to make light of the man's powers, but *he* was no fool. He knew what the dangers were. In part that was why he'd accepted the commission. Baralis' murder would be his finest achievement, the crowning glory in his long dance with death. He was excited by the prospect of taking such a craftily guarded life.

Scarl had spent several days monitoring Baralis' movements. He suspected the king's chancellor had access to secret passageways, for the assassin had waited outside rooms, only to find that Baralis never left them, yet he would appear in a different part of the castle later. The assassin liked the idea of secret passages as much as the next man. He would make it his business to find out more about them.

He was, he admitted, a little afraid of Baralis. That the man possessed great power was highly evident, despite Maybor's attempts to deny it. The secret of murdering a sorcerer was to catch him unawares, to give him no chance for a defensive drawing. Scarl would have liked to kill Baralis whilst he slept, but it was impossible to gain access to his chambers—Crope and the wardings saw to that. He would have to find a time when the man's attentions were diverted by something just as compelling as sleep.

One moment off his guard and the knife would be his fate. Scarl had yet to meet a man who would not succumb to a blade. All died equally as fast when their windpipes were severed. That was how Scarl liked to do his job: one clean, deep sweep with a sharp knife. It had proved most successful in the past. It would do for Baralis, too.

There was a lot to be said for slitting the throat. It silenced the victim instantly, it was quick, there was never a struggle, one approached one's victim from behind, and lastly, if one was skillful, which Scarl was, one never got as much as a drop of blood on oneself.

Yes, mused Scarl, others might go in for the showier executions—the dagger in the eye, the blade in the heart— but nothing beat a good throat slitting.

Scarl knew he had to be careful to choose the right moment. The castle passageways were too public, guards or others could approach at any time and foil his plans. He would not rush into this. It was his nature to watch and wait. At some point Baralis would be vulnerable, and that would be the instant he felt the keen blade of Scarl's knife at his throat.

After Baralis left, the queen sat for a long while, turning the small bottle in her hand. She watched the tawny fluid move within the glass. On impulse she unstopped the cap and smelled the contents. She pulled away from its strong and unpleasant odor. She tipped one single glistening drop onto her fingertip and raised it to her lips—she would rather endanger herself than the king. The taste was bitter.

She waited for many hours, refusing food and drink, and could detect no harmful effects. It was true she had only sampled a drop, but she was satisfied nonetheless. She would take the medicine to the king.

As she walked to the king's chamber, she came across her son Kylock. Seeing him thus, she realized how very little she saw of him normally. He was a stranger to her. She didn't know what he did from day to day. His chambers were out of bounds; he had never once invited her past his door. Several months back, when she knew Kylock was off for the day on a hunt, the queen stole into his rooms. The act had been unworthy of her, but curiosity won over pride and she made her way to the east wing. She chose her time well and met no one on the way. Her first feeling on entering the chamber was relief. It was clean and orderly, every chest in its place, not a fold falling amiss. Then it occurred to her: it was too meticulous. The rugs were perfectly square, not a mote of dust on the sill, not a flake of ash in the fire. Too orderly by far for a boy of seventeen, it was as if he didn't live there at all. One particular rug drew her eye—the deep crimsons of its weave seemed strangely random. The queen crouched down and ran her fingers over the silk. Even before she raised her hand to her face, she knew what it was: blood. Sticky, nearly dry, less than a day old.

The most unsettling thing was not the blood itself as much as its presence in such a pristine setting. Like a beautiful maiden in the company of old dowagers, the blood seemed more striking by comparison.

The following day she'd passed Kylock in the stables. He'd asked how she was and then, just as she stepped away, he said, "So, Mother, what did you think of my rooms?" His tone was mocking. He didn't wait for a reply, merely smiling, then walking away.

She never felt easy in his presence. He was so unlike her or the king, and not just in appearance—though he was as dark as she and the King were fair. It was his whole bearing that was different. He was so secretive, so introverted. Even as a child he preferred to be alone, refusing to play with other children. Baralis was his only friend.

Kylock approached her now, lips curved in an ironic smile. "Good evening, Mother." His low, seductive tone reminded her of another's, but she could not remember whose.

"Good evening to you, Kylock." Her son looked at her, and she could think of nothing else to say to him.

"What have you there?" He motioned to the bottle she carried.

"It is medicine for your father."

"Really. Do you suppose it will do him any good?" The queen was troubled by his nonchalant tone.

"Lord Baralis has prepared it for him."

"Well, in that case it is bound to do *something*."

The queen could not make out what her son meant by the ambiguous comment. She regretted mentioning that the medicine was from Baralis. Her son had that effect on her: he either robbed her of speech entirely or impelled her to speak unwisely, as she had done now. She looked up to say something else, but he had gone.

She found herself wishing that she had never been queen—she had little joy in it. Of late, she had been king in everything but name. She would have liked to give it up, take her sick husband away to their castle in the Northlands and live a peaceful and quiet life. Something stopped her, though. It was partly her pride, but there was also something in her that balked at the idea of her son as king.

She had never loved him properly, not with a mother's true affection. She remembered the day he was born, when he was handed to her—pale and silent and smelling of cloves. There had been no surge of warmth in her breast, no pull of emotion. The midwife nodded her head wisely and told her love would come. And it had in a way, for she loved her son with an almost jealous frenzy, but she felt no tenderness, no affection.

It upset her to think of the many years she had been childless. The years of longing for a baby, the countless disappointments, the unceasing humiliations. She had been married to the king for ten long years before she had conceived.

For the first few years the king had been full of gentle encouragements and considerations. "No matter, my love," he would say as her blood flowed anew each month. "There is time aplenty. You are young and fertile; the Gods choose to make us wait until they are ready." He would smile and squeeze her hand and invite her to bed to try again.

The pressures of sovereignty had eventually taken their toll, and the king became desperate for a son—an heir was essential to the stability and continuity of the country. Sly whispers assailed the king's ears:

"A country without an heir is an invitation to war."

"It is your sacred duty to provide an heir for the kingdom."

"The queen is not fertile."

"Strike the marriage asunder."

"Replace the queen with a breeder."

The king had loved her dearly and could bear no talk of setting her aside. But the fulsome urgings of the court had their effect upon him. She could hardly blame him—they were right, the country did need an heir.

She had been desperate to conceive. She tried everything from scalding poultices to arcane ceremonies . . . all to no avail. Of course there was no mention that the king could be infertile. The very thought was preposterous. He was the king: symbol of life, renewal, and continuity. Even the queen dared not harbor that treasonous thought, and she resigned herself to her barrenness.

The king had not once spoken to her about annulling the marriage, even though he was legally entitled to do so as she had been proven barren. Instead he brought other women to his bed, hoping to father a child and later legitimize any issue resulting from the union. He'd tried to be discreet, but servants whispered and courtiers talked. The queen shuddered at the memory of the shame—surely no other queen in all the histories had ever had to bear such humiliation—to carry on at court each day as if nothing was wrong, to appear regal and composed while her husband dallied with numerous women.

The strange thing was that none of those women had borne him sons. The few women who did conceive gave birth to daughters, and a daughter was of no value in male-dominated Harvell. The king had sent the women and babes away, caring little for their fate.

Eventually, he gave up his attempts to conceive a son and they both became resigned to remaining childless.

Then, one chill winter month, nearly eighteen summers ago, her blood had failed to flow. She hardly dared hope: ten years without a child was proof beyond doubt that she was barren. A second month had passed and then a third; her body swelled and her breasts grew tender. She was with child. The king and court were jubilant. There were parades and dances and feasts in her honor, and she had duly given birth to a son.

She'd counted back nine months from her son's birth. Kylock had been conceived in mid-winter and the queen had no memory of the king visiting her bed at that time. Of course, she could not be certain, and she did remember one occasion when she'd drunk so unwisely that she had no memory of the night before. She recalled waking in the morning and feeling the familiar soreness of lovemaking. Her husband must have taken her while she was drunk. A disturbing thought.

The queen raised a finger to her lips and bit softly upon the fleshy tip. The sting of pain brought her back to the present and she was glad; there were too many unanswered questions in the past, too much sorrow, too much lost.

She made haste along the lofty corridors, eager to try the medicine upon the king.

people off Sharlett's bleak streets. There was a feeling of corruption in the very air, an atmosphere that held promise of ill deeds and decay.

It was to this place that Tawl was headed. He noticed the gradual changes that took place in his surroundings: fewer people on the streets, rats scurrying through the slop of human refuse, failing to observe the usual after-dark hours of their kind.

As he walked, picking a careful path through the filth, Tawl considered the tale the old man in the tavern had told him. He shuddered to think of the helpless seers leashed to the rock for the length of their lives. Tawl knew what it was to be bound. He'd felt the snag of rope upon his flesh. He wondered at the nature of the powers who would do such an inhuman thing. And he bitterly wished that he did not have need of their services.

To go to Larn and consult with the seers was condoning what was done there, when he, as a knight of Valdis, should be striving to free them from their captivity. The knights were founded upon one basic principle: to help their fellow men. For over four hundred years the order had striven to alleviate human suffering. Their greatest triumph was the campaign against slavery in the east. Thanks to their actions, cities such as Marls and Rorn could no longer trade in flesh from the far south. Even today the knights still manned the eastern harbors, checking the hulls of merchant ships.

Tawl uncovered the double circle on his arm. He had hoped, many winters ago, that he would gain the third and final ring. That was why Tyren had sent him to Bevlin in the first place. To attain the final circle and become a ranking knight, a novice was expected to go out in the world and not return until he had "achieved merit in the eyes of God."

The first circle was for physical excellence, the second for learning, and the third for achievement. What constituted merit in the eyes of God was hard to judge, and many knights spent many years in search of a glorious, but often elusive, cause. Most chose to go on missions. The year Tawl had been conferred, two knights went to the northwest to mediate in the dispute over the River Nestor; a few sailed down the Silbur in pursuit of river pirates; and his friends had traveled to the far south in search of lost treasures—Tawl didn't know what had become of them.

At the end of it all, when the knights thought they were ready, they presented themselves at Valdis to be judged. Four men heard the testimony and then acting upon their recommendation, the leader, Tyren, either conferred the knight with his final circle, or sent him out to begin again. It brought great shame to a knight if he presented himself and was found unworthy. To avoid this humiliation, many knights spent years, even decades, away from Valdis. Some never returned.

Tawl couldn't imagine a time when he'd be ready for judgment. He'd been set a nearly impossible task, and until it was completed he couldn't show his face at Valdis. It seemed many years since the head of the order had sent him on his way. He still remembered Tyren's words: "Go visit with the wiseman Bevlin. You will find him in the north. I have faith that you will do what he asks." It had been a difficult time; he'd come close to giving it all up. The feeling that he was needed, and—if he were honest—the promise of glory, was all that kept him going.

The reality was so much different than the dream. He had spent all save one of the last years in a fruitless search: he'd traveled through much of the Known Lands asking people if they knew of a boy who was different in some way from others.

He had been told of boys with six fingers, boys with yellow eyes, boys with madness eating away at their brains. These and countless others Tawl had sought out, only to know in his deepest soul that none of them were the one.

Eventually he had come to Rorn, his spirits low, his task appearing hopeless. He'd made the mistake of asking in the wrong place and had been picked up by the authorities. It was a risk one took being a knight of Valdis, for the knights were no longer in favor. They were used as scapegoats for any problem a particular city had—if crops failed in Lanholt, it was the knights who willed it; if trade was down in Rorn, it was the knights who slowed it. Tawl sighed heavily. He had heard all the rumors about how the knights were building up stockpiles of cash, of religious fanaticism and greed for political power. If the knights were corrupt, then so was their leader, and Tawl would hear nothing malicious said about Tyren.

He had many things for which to thank the head of the order. Tyren had been good to him. He was the one who had made it possible for him to join the order. He, a common boy from the marshlands, with no rich family to sponsor his training. Tyren had helped him through the worst time of his life. When everything seemed meaningless, and the burden of guilt was too new to be bearable, Tyren had sent him to Bevlin and given him reason to carry on.

The skitter of soft feet brought Tawl back to the present. He was being followed. Surreptitiously, he felt for his knife. His fingers closed around the cool blade, and its deadly smoothness was a reassurance. He was much stronger than he had been a week ago, and he was ready for an attack if one should come.

Tawl walked calmly on, careful not to speed his step and thereby give away the fact that he knew he was being followed. His ears strained to hear the soft patter of feet; his shadow must have shoes of cloth. Tawl managed a grim smile. He wouldn't enjoy walking these streets with only a thin stretch of fabric between him and the filth.

He was forced to slow down. He was not entirely sure if he was following Megan's instructions correctly. She'd directed him to what he thought was this alleyway, but she had told him it would branch off to the left. There was no such opening: the alleyway ran straight up without any turnings. He felt his skin prickle. There was a breath of air, a flash of blade, and the man was upon him.

He swung to meet his foe, drawing the long-knife with one graceful stroke. The man had a curved sword. Tawl had seen such blades before and knew that when handled well they were deadly. The man slashed at him, forcing him to move back. He slashed again, a wild and reckless attack. Tawl jumped out of the way of the blade. As his foe prepared for another onslaught, Tawl took the opportunity to strike with the long-knife. He caught the man's arm and blood welled quickly to the surface. Distracted for a fatal instant by the sight of his own blood, the man looked up to see Tawl knife him in the chest.

It was a clean strike. Tawl had no liking for those who sought to prolong a fight with cruel and intentionally torturous blows. The man fell to the ground, blood rushing from his wound. His curved blade fell by his side, clattering harshly upon the dull stone.

Tawl was feeling a little shaky. It had been a long time since he had last drawn a blade. He took no delight in his win, it was merely something that had to be done.

He considered the curved blade. It was sorely blunted: not the weapon of a man who was serious about murder. He had probably been a thief . . . and a desperate one at that. Tawl picked up the sword, noting with surprise its goodly weight. It would look better once polished and sharpened; maybe he would be able to sell it and gain some money for his passage. He tucked the sword in his belt, ensuring that it could not be seen by casual eyes.

Now he had to find the right alleyway. He decided to continue down the one he was in. He walked for a while, and found to his annoyance that it came to a dead end. He turned, resigned to walking the length of the treacherous street once more. As he wheeled around he felt a powerful blow to his head. He attempted to draw his long-knife, but another crippling blow to his skull made the world go black.

Jack was slowly recovering from his bout of wet fever. He could now walk around the den without feeling dizzy and light-headed.

His recovery was definitely aided by Falk's various arrays of medicines and ointments. Jack, however, lay most of the credit to the delicious food that Falk served up. Every day there was a savory stew, or a roasted rabbit, or turnips baked in rich meat juices. Jack had spent his whole life in the castle kitchens, but had never been allowed to eat food this tasty. The diet for a baker's boy was usually thin gruel and all the bread he could eat.

Jack felt almost guilty in the delight he took from eating. It didn't seem right. He was leagues away from home, supposedly on a grand adventure to find a new life, or the truth behind his mother's origins, or whatever seemed the best idea of the day, yet here he was comfortably settled in the warmth of the den eagerly awaiting his next meal.

Each day Falk would bring the makings of a fine meal into the den. He would carefully prepare the ingredients, chopping onions and slicing carrots, skinning rabbits and grinding spices. Jack could see Falk enjoyed his work and admired how content he was doing such ordinary tasks. There had been times at Castle Harvell when he too felt a similar joy, but as he grew older, dreams and dissatisfactions had conspired to take it away.

Jack did not like to be idle and had asked Falk if he could help. "No," Falk replied. "It is a blessing to me to handle the bounties of nature. I love to cook. I take only what I need, and I waste not a thing. The bones from a roast will be next day's soup, the scrape from the apple will be set to dry." Jack hadn't known how to reply to this and so had offered to bake bread for Falk.

"Boy, you are weak yet. Baking bread must wait. Besides, I have only a make-shift stove."

"I could make griddle cakes," said Jack, hoping that Falk would agree, for he did miss bread in his diet.

"Very well, Jack. I see you have a need to repay me. It would be ungracious of me if I did not let you do so." Falk had a way of saying things that left Jack at a loss for words.

So, this day Falk had returned with the flour and eggs that Jack had asked for and the boy set about making the batter for griddle cakes. As Jack mixed the ingredients, he felt that his old life as a baker's boy was far behind him. There would be times, like this, when he would bake bread, but there was no going back to the past. He could probably find a town far away in the east where he could take up a position as a baker's apprentice, only he wasn't sure if that was what he wanted anymore.

He knew he would have to move on soon, and although he had enjoyed his time with Falk, he needed to be on his own. He was worried about the future: Baralis was after him, he had no money in his pocket and nowhere to go. The time was fast approaching when decisions would need to be made—he could choose to forget about the incident with the loaves and live quietly as a baker, or he could change the course of his life and make himself anew.

As he thought, Jack made the batter, adding a combination of beer and water to thin the mix. He stirred it, seasoning the mixture with a touch of salt. He would let it sit for just long enough to enable the flour to soak up the water—if it were left too long, the yeast in the beer might cause the mix to rise. Master Frallit would beat a boy whose griddle cakes were anything less than flat.

Falk had just returned from one of his mysterious forays. Jack would have liked to ask what the man did on these outings, but could not find the right words to do so.

"So, you are indeed a baker," commented Falk, nodding toward the batter.

"I was never made a baker. I was a baker's apprentice."

"Words! Titles! If you can bake, surely you are a baker." Once again, Jack could think of nothing to say.

He checked the hot iron platter on the fire and greased it with a little pork fat. The grease smoked: the temperature was just right. He gave the mixture one final stir and then poured it in separate rounds onto the hot surface. The iron platter hissed and smoked but soon settled down, and minutes later the delicious aroma of griddle cakes filled the den. He had no wooden spatula to flip the cakes over with and had borrowed an old knife of Falk's to do the job.

Falk watched Jack with a certain skepticism at first, but then seemed genuinely interested in what he was doing. "Well, Jack, I am impressed," he said as Jack loaded a plate with the hot and fragrant griddle cakes.

After they had eaten their fill and were relaxing close to the warm stove, Falk made a simple request: "Tell me who you are."

The fire dimmed and the wind calmed, as if waiting for his reply. Time drifted away from him, and if asked later, Jack would never know how much had passed before he spoke.

"I don't know who I am. Only days ago I thought I knew, but now everything has changed." Jack waited a moment to see if Falk would speak. He didn't, and it was his silence that gave Jack the courage to carry on. He could trust this man.

"Over a week ago now, something happened to me— something evil. I burnt some loaves, then I felt a terrible pain in my head. When I looked again, they were barely browning." As he spoke, Jack felt relief. It was good to speak it out loud; it lost power by being shared.

"That's why you left the castle?"

"Yes." Jack was glad that Falk didn't seem shocked. "I couldn't risk anyone finding out what I'd done. They might have stoned me."

"People in the Known Lands are fools. Anything they don't understand they seek to destroy!" Falk shook his head in anger. "They call themselves *civilized,* but they have no idea about the way things are.

"Sorcery, for that is what it is—I'll make no bones about it—isn't a gift from the devil. Sorcery is neither good nor bad—it is the person who draws upon it who controls its nature."

"But everyone at the castle says it's evil, and only wicked people use it," said Jack.

"They are right and they are wrong. It is mostly drawn by people who are wicked, or rather greedy. But it wasn't always that way. At one time, many centuries ago, sorcery was common in the Known Lands. It came out of its making and was as ancient as the land itself. Gradually people in power came to resent the random spreading of sorcerous gifts—a common laborer was just as likely to be favored as a great lord. People in high places could not tolerate such a dangerously indiscriminate scattering of power. They acted swiftly, eradicating all who could practice. 'Tis easier to rule by sword than sorcery.

"Only a few practitioners survived the Great Purge. Today the art endures more by rumor than practice. Its time has nearly passed; this world is too modern for it to continue. Like most things old, its worth has long been forgotten.

"There are still a few places where it thrives. Places cut off from the changes of time, places where the land itself is as magical as the people who stand upon it. But they are ever decreasing, and fewer and fewer people can draw upon its source."

Jack's mind was in a turmoil. Could what Falk had said be true? All his life he'd been taught that sorcery was devilment, and now this man had turned everything around. "So I'm not evil?"

"There is dark and light in every man, as there is in every day." Falk shrugged. "I doubt whether you are evil. Though there is much you are not telling me." He looked Jack squarely in the face. "You never really told me who you are. What about your family? Where were they from?"

Anger flared within Jack. It was the same as ever, people asking casual questions, never realizing how hard it was for him to answer. "I'm a bastard! *Satisfied?* My mother was a whore and she didn't keep count of her customers!" He stood up and threw his cup in the fire.

"Where is your mother now?"

Was there no end to the man's probing? Jack watched as the wooden cup succumbed to the blaze. His anger left him as quickly as it came. He turned to face Falk as he said, "She died eight years ago. She had a growth in her breast and it ate away at her."

"How did you manage with her gone?" Falk's eyes were impossibly blue. There was such compassion in them that Jack felt free to say things he'd never admitted before.

"It was easy. In some ways, it was even a blessing. After her death the taunting stopped for a while, and I could pretend I was normal."

For the second time Jack expected condemnation for his words and received understanding instead. "It's not a sin to be ashamed of your parents. What *is* wrong, though, is to accept the words of others without questioning. Just because people called her a whore doesn't mean that she was."

Jack turned to face Falk. "But why—"

"Why do people belittle others? It's the same as with sorcery. If they didn't understand, if she was different in any way, they would hate her for it."

"She *was* different!" Jack felt an excitement growing in his breast. Falk had not only freed his thoughts, he was altering the very nature of them. "She was a foreigner. She came to the kingdoms when she was fully grown."

"Where was she from?"

Jack shook his head. "I don't know. She never said. I think she might have been afraid of someone or something in her past."

"Aah." Falk stroked his beard and thought for a while. Then he said, "Perhaps she was afraid for you more than herself. If she was just concerned with her own safety, then what would be the harm in taking you into her confidence? It seems to me that she might have kept her past a secret to protect you."

What was it about this man that he could so casually challenge beliefs Jack had held true for years? He cast his mind back to his childhood, to the mornings on the battlements. He remembered her words, "Keep your head low, Jack, you might be spotted." Spotted by whom? Jack's head was reeling with new ideas. Up until now, until this conversation with Falk, he felt as if he'd been looking at the world through a brewer's filter. Things had suddenly been thrown into sharp focus.

"As for being illegitimate, Jack, some of the most powerful men in the Known Lands had similar starts in life. Why, the archbishop of Rorn himself had no father to call his own—yet no one knows it." Falk stood up and put his arm on Jack's shoulder. "A word of advice. Don't hate the man who fathered you."

Jack moved away. "What makes you think I do?"

"I have experience with such feelings—I too was called a bastard. I made the mistake of letting it ruin my life. I managed well until I passed my twenty-third year. I had a wife and three children and land of my own. One night I overheard two people talking in a tavern. One man mentioned my name and said I was doing well. The other just sniggered and said, 'Once a bastard, always a bastard.' I went for the man's throat; it took four men to pull me off. He nearly died. I was sentenced to work a year in the slate quarries. Instead of spending the time wishing I was with my family, I festered in a pool of hate. I hated my father for making me an object of contempt. I blamed him for everything.

"Unlike you, I knew who he was. When my year was up, I tracked him down. It took many years before I finally found him. I was full of anger and ready for battle. He was an old man, stiff with rheumatism and pathetic to behold.

"I held my fist to his face and he begged for mercy. I am thankful to this day that I gave it.

"We sat and talked and supped a while. He told me that the reason he never married my mother was because she came from a good family and would be better off not wed, for he had no money to look after a mother and child. I don't know if I believed him—it doesn't really matter. The point is, he was just a man—not evil, not cunning, not deserving of punishment.

"I left him and returned home. My wife and family had moved away and left messages for me not to follow. The rest of my tale is too long to tell. I've seen much of life and men, traveled to scores of cities, talked with countless people and been known by many names. I ended up here, alone. What I say to you, Jack, is don't make the same mistake as me. Don't spend your time inventing fantasies of revenge. They will only destroy you in the end." Falk put down his cup and made his way out of the den, leaving Jack alone to contemplate his words.

Baralis had decided to make his move on the girl, and to this end he had called his mercenaries to him. Once again they were meeting outside the castle gates. A vague uneasiness of late had caused him to take Crope with him on any of his expeditions. Baralis found a certain reassurance in the huge bulk of his servant. There was one unexpected bonus to this arrangement—the mercenaries looked decidedly intimidated by Crope's presence.

"I want you to pick up the girl. I know her position. She is southeast of Harvell, four days hard ride." Baralis' gaze challenged anyone to doubt his knowledge.

"What about the boy?" asked the leader. Baralis had no intention of letting them know he had no idea where the boy was. He didn't like anyone to think he might not be infallible.

"I will personally see to the boy myself. He is not traveling with the girl anymore." Baralis watched with amusement as he saw that his mercenaries were wary of how he knew so much. One final twist of the knife, "When you pick up the girl this time, I strictly forbid you to lay one finger on her. I will not have her raped by mercenaries like a common tavern wench." Baralis saw the faces of the men register many emotions: amazement, guilt, hatred, and fear. He was not displeased. "Go now, and do not fail me again."

The men mounted and rode away. Baralis was wondering if he had left it too late. The girl would soon emerge from the forest and begin to encounter towns and villages. Still, he thought, as long as she is away from court there will be no betrothal. Once the girl was caught and in his haven, he could turn his full attention to finding Jack. The dove was weakening and would soon die. The baker's boy could be leagues away by now; a second bird might be unable to locate him. Baralis was not unduly concerned—a dove was not the only way to search the forest.

"Come, Crope. Let us get out of this bleak wind. There is much for me to do."

"Will there be anything for me to do, master?" asked Crope, his hand inside his tunic, doubtless holding his precious box. Baralis wondered what was in it—probably his dead mother's teeth.

"If there is not, I will find you something." The huge man smiled, and Baralis added, "Something tailored to your unique skills."

As they walked back to the castle walls, Baralis considered the queen. It was now common knowledge that the king's health had improved. It was only a matter of time before she would summon him again, and then they would strike a deal.

Baralis and Crope approached a remote section of the castle wall. Baralis' twisted hands felt carefully for the tiny protrusion in the stone. He caressed it gently and the wall swung open. The smell of dank earth met his nostrils. They stepped into the opening, Baralis closing it straight after, and headed into the dark depths of the castle.

* * *

The assassin watched as the wall sealed itself once more. Watch and wait. It always pays off in the end. Scarl had watched earlier as Baralis and his giant servant had discreetly left the castle. The assassin had been expecting them to return the way they had come. It was with growing interest that he watched master and servant as they veered off from the expected route and walked toward a seemingly unremarkable section of wall.

Scarl was not usually a man given to outward show of emotion, but when he saw Baralis uncover an opening in the wall, he permitted himself a satisfied smile. He sat back among the tall grass and, picking himself a long shoot to chew on, prepared to wait for a while.

After waiting what Scarl deemed to be an appropriate amount of time, he approached the wall. A thorough man, he checked to see he had exactly the right section. Yes, this was it. Two sets of footprints in the damp mud led into the wall: Baralis' light and, in Scarl's opinion, stealthy looking prints and Crope's large and heavy ones.

The assassin ran his fingers lightly over the smooth stone. Nothing. Undeterred, he attempted to repeat the gestures he had seen Baralis make earlier. To aid this ploy, Scarl cleverly placed his feet in Baralis' own footprints. Once again he ran his hands over the cool gray stone. Still nothing. The assassin was not alarmed; he was a patient man, well suited to his particular line of work. He tried again, this time scanning one stone at a time, his keen eyes searching for something unusual. He could find nothing.

The assassin moved away from the wall and considered his next move. He was sure that the entrance was not warded; he was able to smell out such things. No, there was some practical way to gain access, if he could just think of it. Scarl chewed on his blade of grass, finding its bitter taste pleasing, and regarded the wall.

He desperately wanted to gain access to the entrance; he was sure the castle would be riddled with secret passageways and rooms. All these old castles were built by people who knew the value of a discreet escape. Scarl's motives were more than just tracking his mark. Scarl loved secrets, underhanded dealing, deception, concealed motives—anything, in fact, that had the low whiff of subterfuge about it.

He had it! Why had he not thought of it sooner? Baralis was over a foot taller than he. He had his feet in the right place, but his hands had not been high enough. He then realized why it had not occurred to him sooner: the enormous Crope had the ability to make anyone appear small, when Baralis was in fact a tall man. Excitement grew in Scarl's stomach, registering only as a mere tightening of his thin lips.

He returned to the wall, feeling higher this time. The stone was smooth; his fingers trailed its length. There was something, a tiny inconsistency. His fingertips brushed over it, and then back once more. Scarl stepped aside as the wall sprang open.

The assassin stepped into the cavity. A smell old and damp assailed his senses. The darkness enveloped his unready eyes. He checked in his pocket and found flint and tallow—Scarl had been prepared for this event for some time now. With hands as steady as an assassin's must be, he lit the candle. The light it gave was feeble, barely enough. Scarl began to check the inside wall for a means to close the opening. Some time later, he detected a similar protrusion to that on the outside, and the wall moved back into place.

His eyes gradually became more accustomed to the blackness. Without his candle, he could not have seen anything. Scarl was faced with a choice: left or right. He chose the left. The passage took him downward and soon became a tunnel with rounded sides. The walls were dripping with damp, and pale mosses, of a kind that Scarl had never seen before. Impulsively, he reached out to touch some—it felt soft and springy and left a slight residue on his fingers. Scarl studied the sticky substance and then carefully wiped his fingers clean; one could not be too careful when dealing with strange moss. Although no expert on poison, Scarl was aware that certain mosses were often used in its manufacture.

The tunnel led downward for some time longer, and then there was another branching. Scarl decided to take it and soon came upon a flight of stone steps. He felt sure he must be under the castle by now. The stairway presented him with many options: it twisted around and upward and many passages led off on each new level. When the assassin had ascended enough for his liking, he took one of the passageways. It was long and straight with many doorways, some sealed. He was beginning to realize how vast and intricate the network of tunnels was.

The assassin was full of admiration for the men who must have designed and built it. He was also a little envious of Baralis' mastery of the system. He, too, yearned to know where all the doors and passages led. He was sure he had seen but a tiny fraction of the whole. Scarl was aware that the maze of tunnels promised access to many forbidden places: bedchambers, supply rooms, meeting areas. He knew well how such an extensive system could be put to great use. The assassin revised his estimation of his mark—Baralis was not only a man of great power, but also of great resources.

He looked ahead, wondering how he could gain access to the inside of the castle. He picked a doorway at random and found himself at a dead end. Knowing that a passage usually leads somewhere, he felt the end wall and, sure enough, his fingers alighted on the tiny lump that marked an opening. Scarl stood to one side as the heavy stone wall drew back without a sound.

He found himself in a part of the castle with which he was unfamiliar. Looking around, he was surprised to find that he was still underground. He had calculated he would be on the first or second floor of the castle. Instead he was in what looked to be an unused dungeon. His gaze took in the old torture devices. There was a rotting, wooden rack, a wheel, a press, and many others.

Scarl looked over the devices with professional interest—before he became an assassin, he had gained some experience in torture. His trained eye told him that the equipment had hardly been used. It was also badly out of date. He had been in Rorn some months ago and had been impressed by the new devices they had there. Rorn was a city which kept abreast of the times.

The assassin looked for a way out of the dungeon, vowing he would make it his business to become familiar with the secret passageways. He was sure they would prove to be useful to him.

Melli noticed that the trees were beginning to thin out. The forest had gradually become less dense: there were more glades and patches of open land. She had even seen the roof of a small cottage the day before. She had been tempted to approach the dwelling, but caution won over curiosity and she had moved on.

She'd been in the woods for ten days now and was surprised at how quickly she had adapted to the ways of the forest. She, Lady Melliandra of the Four Kingdoms, had actually enjoyed sleeping under the stars and drinking water from bubbling streams.

Melli was both excited and anxious about leaving the woods. The forest had in some ways protected her from the worries of the outside world. Things were simple for her: she walked, she ate, she slept. Now there would be other things to deal with: people and money and shelter. She had been lucky with the weather; although chill, it had not snowed, and the thick forest was a natural barrier to the wind. Melli knew snow would come soon, and she realized she would need warmer clothes when it did.

If only her purse had not been stolen! She could have bought a saddle and hastened her journey. As she was now, without her valuables, she did not know what she would do when her food ran out. There was always her horse, but she suspected she would only get a silver or two for him. Besides, she didn't like the idea of parting with him.

As she walked in the bright cold morning, Melli began to notice signs of human habitation: smoke spiraling upward in the distance, a patch of grass grazed short, a cleared ditch. She quickened her pace, and the forest began to give way to open land. A farmhouse appeared on the rise, and then another one. Melli spotted a dirt track and led her horse onto it.

By afternoon she had approached a small village. It boasted a tavern but no smithy. Melli's appearance garnered much attention from the village people: the women looked at her with mistrust and the men with speculation. It was apparent to her that she must present a strange sight to the hostile villagers. She still wore her sack over her dress, and instead of a cloak she wore a blanket. She thought her face was clean, for she splashed it with water when she could, but she suspected her hair was a wild tangle.

Noticing the inimical stares, she decided the village would not be a good place to stop. As she passed the last of the buildings, a woman's voice rang out, clear and shrill, "Good riddance to you. We don't want your sort here. Go to Duvitt—that's where your kind belong." Melli could hardly believe she was being addressed in such a way. All her life she had been spoken to with courtesy and respect. The cruel tone of the woman's voice caused her more distress than all the days she had been alone in the forest. Determined to be dignified, she did not look back, and she and her horse walked away from the village.

Melli walked through the afternoon, and the road she traveled became wider and better maintained. Eventually, as it began to grow dark, Melli saw in the distance the lights of a town. Not wanting to make the same mistake twice, she took off the woven sack and smoothed her hair as best she could. Sometime later, she entered the town of Duvitt.

Duvitt was enjoying a time of great prosperity. Situated between Harvell and the River Nestor it was in an ideal locale to exploit the war between the Four Kingdoms and Halcus. The past five years had seen a substantial increase in business, as the town catered to the hundreds of soldiers that passed through each week. Although Duvitt was firmly in Four Kingdoms' territory, the enterprising business owners were not above catering to the needs of the Halcus. And so Duvitt had become an unofficial neutral zone, where a weary soldier in any colors could find lodgings and a cup of cool, albeit rather expensive, ale.

There were of course drawbacks to this arrangement; drunken soldiers find it hard to remain neutral for long, and so there were many violent brawls. Minor property damage and a few dead men were considered a small price to pay for prosperity. The town now boasted more taverns than anywhere else in the Four Kingdoms, and many a tavern owner, in the privacy of his bed at night, prayed that the war would continue indefinitely.

Melli approached the town warily. There were many people in the streets, none of whom gave her more than a second look. She had little idea of what she was going to do. She would perhaps try to trade the few pots and pans Master Trout had included in her purchase. Duvitt seemed bigger to her than Harvell; it was certainly busier. She noticed that many of the people on the streets were soldiers, and this she took as a sign that she had not gone too far off track.

She slowed down, looking for a safe place to leave her horse, wishing that she'd had the sense to tie him to a remote tree or bush before she'd entered the town. Melli decided to risk tying her horse to a wooden fence in plain view of many people, hoping that no one would steal a horse so openly. She smiled a little at her own caution; her horse would hardly be a great prize for a thief.

She hailed a young boy who was passing. "Can you tell me where I might be able to sell some items?"

The boy was immediately interested. "What items?" he asked, feigning casualness.

"Two tin cups and a plate and a copper pot."

The boy's interest visibly waned. "You might try Master Huddle, two doors down." Melli was about to thank the boy, but he was off, looking for more profitable prospects.

She duly followed his advice and entered a small, dirty-looking shop crammed with all manner of wares. The shopkeeper looked at her as she entered, took in the poor condition of her clothes and then ostentatiously ignored her, turning his attention back to his other customer.

"Yes, Mistress Greal, I'll try and have your boots mended by this time tomorrow."

"See that you do, sir. And I want a good job, mind, no half stitches."

"I will personally ensure that my boy does full stitches."

"Very well. Good night, sir." The woman turned around and was about to leave when she caught sight of Melli. Her eyes narrowed and she looked Melli up and down. She watched as Melli approached the shopkeeper.

"What d'you want, girl?" demanded the man in an entirely different tone than the one he had just been using.

"I would sell some items," said Melli with dignity.

"What've you got?"

"Two tin cups and a plate and a copper pot."

"Not interested, girl. Now get out of here!" Melli's face flushed with anger and embarrassment. She stormed out of the shop and was about to head for her horse when she felt a tap on her arm. She swung around and saw it was the woman customer who had stopped her.

"What's the rush, deary?" said the woman. "Got no money, no place to stay?" Melli did not reply, and the woman continued, "I can see you're a pretty girl under all that dirt." Melli blushed further and tried to move around the woman, who was now blocking her path. The woman stepped ahead of her and spoke once more. "I'll give you hot food and a bed for the night."

"Why would you do that?" replied Melli, suspicious of the woman's intentions.

For the briefest instant, a look of cunning passed over the woman's face. "I have need of some pots and pans, of course."

Melli did not believe the woman, but the sound of hot food and a bed was very tempting to her. "Is there somewhere to stable my horse?"

"There most certainly is, my pretty. Follow me. I'll have a boy see to your horse."

Melli followed the woman to a large tavern. Seeing Melli's puzzled look the woman said, "Oh, I have my rooms upstairs. You'll be staying there with me." Melli was forced to walk through the tavern to reach the stairs at the back. As they passed one man, he shouted to her companion:

"Mistress Greal, I see you have a new girl." Mistress Greal did not look very happy at this outburst and hurried her along. Melli wondered what the man had meant by his comment, however she soon forgot about it when Mistress Greal showed her to her room.

"This will be yours, deary. I'll see about some food and hot water for a bath." With that she was gone. Melli looked around the small room—it contained a bed, a chest of drawers, and a washstand. The room made Melli feel a little caged in at first, for she had become used to the vast forest as her bedroom.

She started to feel better when Mistress Greal returned carrying a huge tray full of delicious smelling food. There was hot game pie, thick leek soup, a wedge of crumbly white cheese, and crusty bread lavished with butter. To her delight Mistress Greal left her to dine alone, and so she felt free to eat as much as she liked as fast as she liked. When she had eaten her fill, she wrapped the leftovers of pie and cheese in a piece of cloth and tucked them away with her other possessions. Then, as an afterthought, she rummaged in her blanket and found the cups and pot that formed her half of the bargain. She placed them on the chest of drawers: no one would say *she* did not pay her debts.

Melli drained the last of the tall mug of cider that Mistress Greal had provided with the meal. As a lady of court, she had only been permitted to drink watered wine, and the strong and heady cider of the region went straight to her head. She lay on the bed, noting that it was rather lumpy, and fell fast asleep.

Lord Maybor was not at all happy about what he had to do. He had asked the queen for an audience and she had granted him one. Ten days had passed since the betrothal was agreed upon, and now it seemed it was more unlikely to happen than ever. He paced his room. Damn Melliandra. The girl had made a mockery of his plans, and now he was forced into telling a dangerous lie to the queen.

He regarded his reflection in his shattered mirror. He did not feel his usual satisfaction at the sight of himself in fine robes. Nothing was going right—even the assassin was slow in slitting Baralis' treacherous throat. Scarl had been much faster the last time he'd commissioned his services. Lord Glayvin was seen to within three days.

Reluctantly Maybor proceeded to the meeting chamber, knocked on the door, and was bidden enter.

The queen held out the royal hand for him to kiss, a

warm smile gracing her lips. "Lord Maybor. I take it you are here to discuss the details of the betrothal?"

"I am, Your Highness. But I fear there may be a delay."

"Delay." Gone were the queen's pleasing tones. "What delay? I had hoped to announce the betrothal on Winter's Eve festival. It was to be a double celebration—the king's improved health and the announcement of the betrothal to the court. And now you speak to me of delay. I can brook no delay, Lord Maybor."

Maybor could understand the queen's nervousness; just last week news had come from Bren of the duke's advancement. This year alone he'd already conquered three towns to the southeast of the city. The man would soon style himself a king. "Your Highness, my daughter is not well." Maybor inwardly cursed his daughter once more.

"That is no problem. The marriage will not take place until spring. The betrothal ceremony is a brief one. Surely your daughter could make an effort to attend."

"Your Highness, Melliandra cannot leave her bed. She has a bad fever and is most seriously ill." Maybor watched as the queen's face became grave.

"Maybor, has she the pox? I can not risk marrying Kylock to a girl who has had the pox." It was well known the pox caused disfigurement and impotence.

"No, Your Highness, it is but a wet fever. She will be well in a few days. That is all I ask for: ten days."

"Ten days is more than a few, Lord Maybor." The queen paced the room. "Very well, I will delay it."

Maybor breathed a sigh of relief. "I have heard that the king's health has much improved, ma'am."

"Yes, Lord Baralis has made a medicine that seems to help him a little." Maybor grew cold. What mischief was Baralis up to now—trying to ingratiate himself with the queen?

"You may leave now, Lord Maybor. I trust I will see you at the Winter's Eve festival."

As Maybor made his way back to his chamber, he decided he would meet with the assassin on the morrow and order him to make haste with his task. Baralis was up to no good.

Eight

*T*awl was shaken awake. As he came to, someone splashed icy cold water on his face. "Come on, my friend, wake up." Tawl opened his eyes.

"Look, he's awake now. Leave off. The Old Man won't like it if you treat him too rough, Clem." Tawl was now being slapped hard on his cheeks.

"I don't think he's quite awake enough, Moth." Tawl felt another sharp blow.

"Clem, his eyes are open. Leave off." Tawl looked around. He was in a small dark room with two men looming over him. His hands were tied behind his back.

"Head hurtin' a bit?" The smaller of the two was speaking. "Sorry about that. Clem gets a bit carried away, if you know what I mean. Don't you, Clem?" The one called Clem nodded. The other man continued, "Nothing personal. The Old Man says bring him in, and we bring him in. Is that right, Clem?" Clem nodded once more. "Course, you'll have a few beauties on your head, but you know what Clem says?"

"What do I say, Moth?" asked Clem.

"You say, better a lump on your head than a lump in your bed. That's what you say."

"That's what I say, Moth," repeated Clem.

"Here, we'd better get a move on, can't keep the Old Man waiting. Will you do the honors, Clem?" The one called

Clem produced a huge and deadly-looking knife and cut the rope that tied Tawl's wrists together.

"Clem's sorry if he tied you up a bit tight. Aren't you, Clem?" Clem obediently nodded. "He's also sorry that he's going to have to 'fold you. Aren't you, Clem?" Tawl never got to see Clem's nod this time, as a thick black cloth was pulled over his eyes. He felt his arm being taken and he was guided out of the room.

"You look a bit stiff, friend. Don't worry, Clem won't lead you off a cliff. Will you, Clem?"

Tawl was guided down some stairs and on a journey through somewhere that smelled strongly of human excrement.

"Never mind the smell, friend. It won't do you any harm. Clem's spent his whole life down here and it didn't hurt him. Did it, Clem?"

"No, Moth. Should we go the usual route, or the fancy one?"

"I think the fancy one, don't you, Clem? I feel like a bit of sea air." Tawl was guided up some stairs and then into the sunlight. He immediately felt salty sea breezes.

"Weather's right nice today ain't it, Moth?"

"You've never spoken a truer word, Clem. Beautiful, balmy breezes for so late in the season."

"You should've been a minstrel, Moth."

"Alas, Clem, if a life of crime hadn't called, I might have been."

"It's minstreling's loss, Moth."

Tawl was led down another set of steps and the reek of the sewer returned stronger than ever. After a while their route led upward and the odor became less pervasive. He was then guided through a confusion of twists and turns and was finally brought to a standstill. The scent of fresh flowers assailed his senses.

"The Old Man likes things to smell sweet. Don't he, Clem? Could you stay with my friend a minute while I tell the Old Man we're here?"

"Should I take the 'fold off him, Moth?"

"Best wait until the Old Man gives the nod, Clem." Tawl and Clem waited in silence for a few minutes until Moth returned.

"Take the 'fold off now, Clem, if you would." Tawl blinked from the light. "Old Man says step inside." Tawl was pushed gently through a door.

He found himself in a room filled with flowers—a small, old man was sitting by a bright fire.

"Come in, young man. Would you like a cup of nettle tea?" The Old Man didn't wait for a reply. "Of course you would, eh. Nothing like nettle tea for a swelling of the head. Everyone I bring in swears by it. Of course, to my mind, the best thing to cure anything is the lacus, but you know all about that, young man, don't you?" The Old Man gave Tawl a shrewd look. Tawl decided his best policy was silence. He watched as the Old Man poured him a cup of greenish-looking tea and handed it to him.

Tawl made no motion to drink the tea. "Come, come, young man, you'll regret not taking the tea when those lumps swell to the size of your balls." Tawl reluctantly took the cup of unpleasant-looking liquid. "Sit down, Tawl. You don't mind if I call you by your name, do you? When you get to my age there's no time for formalities. I might drop dead at any second." Tawl secretly thought that he had never seen a healthier looking old man.

"Of course, I'm sorry about the way you were brought in, but I find it's the best method in the long run. No awkward questions, no unpleasantries. I'm sure you understand." There was a soft knock on the door and Moth stepped into the room.

"Sorry to interrupt you, Old Man, but Noad's just told me there's been a bit of trouble with Purtilan."

"You know what to do then, Moth." Moth nodded his head gravely and was about to leave when the Old Man spoke again. "Make it unpleasant, Moth. You and Clem do one of your specials. There's been far too much trouble in the Market District of late."

Moth left and the Old Man continued, "You are a man who attracts interest in high places. Do you know that the archbishop of Rorn is having you followed?" The Old Man did not wait for Tawl to answer. "Now whenever the venerable archbishop is interested in a person, I'm interested in that person, too. Especially when that person and I have a mutual friend." The Old Man was looking rather smug. "Bevlin, the wiseman, is an old, old friend of mine."

Tawl finally decided to speak. "And what if I have never heard of this Bevlin whom you speak of?"

"You disappoint me, Tawl. I would expect nothing but the truth from a knight of Valdis." The Old Man crossed the room and chose an orange-colored chrysanthemum from one of the many vases. He drew it to his nose and inhaled deeply. "When you were captured by Tavalisk's cronies, they found a skin of lacus on you. Now, I have a few resources myself and I managed to obtain that skin. As I suspected, it had Bevlin's mark upon it.

"Why did you think he gave it to you? Let me explain. Bevlin is no fool; he knew that the lacus skin was marked, and he hoped that his mark might at some time prove useful to you. He has many friends who would aid his causes. Unfortunately, Tavalisk also saw the mark, and that is why you spent a year in one of his dungeons." The old man replaced the flower in the vase, careful to maintain the arrangement.

"Now, I would help you. I owe many debts to Bevlin and I would pay one back."

Tawl considered all the Old Man had said, he made a decision and then spoke. "I need a fast ship to take me to Larn."

The Old Man's sharp gaze did not falter. "So be it. I will arrange it for you. Is there anything more?"

"I would repay a debt of my own."

"The girl Megan? I will see she is compensated for her troubles." Tawl tried to conceal his surprise—was there nothing this man did not know? He was pleased, however, that the Old Man had not questioned his reasons for heading to Larn.

As if reading his thoughts, the Old Man said, "I have no wish to know what you do on Bevlin's behalf. But I do have two warnings for you. First, I have many contacts throughout the Known Lands, and I know that the knights are no longer welcome in many places and hatred for your order grows. I say keep your circles well covered; they will only bring you trouble." The Old Man spotted Tawl's expression. "You're young and idealistic—you probably can't see what's going on."

"I know the knights are much maligned in Rorn."

"And rightly so. Tyren is leading them astray. He wants money and power and seeks to gain them while hiding behind a smoke screen of religious fanaticism."

Tawl stood up to leave. "A man should not be condemned by hearsay alone. Tyren was a friend to me when I needed one most." The Old Man waved him down.

"Sit down, sit down, I meant no offense. The knights are not my concern. If you choose to follow them, then I am not the man to block your path. You are full of dreams and think that gaining the final circle is all that matters. Let me tell you, I have known many knights and the third circle is just a beginning not an end." The Old Man gave Tawl a sharp look. "What do you think you'd do once you got it, eh? The sort of great deeds that guarantee your memory outlives your flesh?"

Tawl felt his face flush. It was so near the truth. He hadn't thought beyond the third circle, except for vague dreams of glory. The future was not for him—the present was the only currency he could safely deal in.

The Old Man smiled pleasantly. "Now where was I?"

"You had two warnings. I am yet to have the benefit of the second."

"Ah, yes. The second one is this: Larn is a treacherous isle, be wary of the price."

The Old Man took the cup of nettle from Tawl. "Moth will see to your needs. Unfortunately, he and Clem are out doing a little business at the moment. My boy Noad will escort you. Moth will contact you when it's all arranged." The Old Man spoke Noad's name softly, and a young boy came into the room. The boy led Tawl out, and the Old Man turned back to his fire.

Tawl underwent the same blindfolded, foul-smelling journey, this time without the benefit of sea breezes. The boy led him back to the small dark room, and from the top of a high shelf took Tawl's long-knife and the curved blade. These he handed to Tawl. "Old Man don't want you knocked out again." The boy replaced Tawl's blindfold and led him up some steps and outside. They walked for a short while and then the boy removed the blindfold.

"Here you go. Turn left at the top of the street and

you'll find yourself in the whoring quarter in no time." The boy was off, quickly slipping down a thin alleyway.

Tawl followed the boy's directions and soon found himself in an area he was familiar with. Deep in thought, he made his way back to Megan's.

Tavalisk was eating plums. He had a bowl full of the deep, purple fruit. He popped one between his pink lips, and as he chewed, its juice dribbled down his chin. He dabbed at it fastidiously with a silk napkin and then spat out the stone onto the floor.

"Enter." Gamil entered carrying a bowl of hazelnuts.

"Your Eminence's nuts," he said, placing them on his desk.

"So, Gamil, what news have you for me today?" Tavalisk selected a fat and shiny plum and placed it between his sharp teeth.

"Our knight has emerged from the Old Man's clutches."

"And what state is he in? Was he beaten?" Tavalisk spat out the plum stone in the direction of his sleeping dog.

"I don't think he was, Your Eminence."

"Oh, how very disappointing. I wonder what they're up to?" Tavalisk, having missed the dog with the stone, now shook the little dog awake.

"Well, I can't say for certain, Your Eminence. Not even you can tell what the Old Man is up to." Tavalisk was about to bite on another plum, but put it down untouched as he heard Gamil's words.

"It is not your place to tell me my limitations, Gamil. You would be a fool to think that you are my only source of intelligence."

Gamil, suitably contrite, bowed his head low. Tavalisk continued. "The Old Man only has power as long as I choose to let him. For the time being his activities undermine Gavelna's leadership. And it is in my interest to keep the first minister's authority suitably—" Tavalisk chose the plumpest plum "—contained. I must be the leading power in Rorn. The old duke lives like a hermit, shunning his rightful position as leader. Someone has to fill the void, and it suits me for the moment to let the Old Man and the first minister both think they have. While those two are busy at each other's throats, I have Rorn to myself."

The archbishop dabbed at the corner of his mouth with his silk napkin, removing the dribble of plum juice that had escaped his ravenous lips. "Our spy in Castle Harvell—I would have you communicate to him."

"Certainly, Your Eminence. What would you have me say?"

"I would know who Baralis' enemies are. That man is trying to wed Kylock to Catherine of Bren, and I need not tell you how little I like the thought of that alliance. Bren is already too powerful. With the kingdoms at its side, the duke would be set to dominate the north. Who knows where the alliance might lead? The two powers could conquer all the territories between. Halcus, Annis, Highwall—before we know it the good duke could be ruling virtually half the Known Lands."

Tavalisk was feeling quite agitated; he poured himself a cup of fortified wine. He winced as the liquor met his palate: not a good mix with plums. "Not to mention trade. The duke of Bren is up to something with those damned knights. They are looking to steal trade from under our feet. They seek to make Rorn look greedy by charging lower prices. The tactics of charlatans!"

"It is indeed an insidious evil, Your Eminence, to charge a fair price."

Tavalisk gave Gamil a shrewd look. He took a second sip of wine; it tasted no better than the first. "This situation is very serious indeed. I need to monitor events carefully, and I must have players in place. Baralis will have powerful enemies whom I can contact. Why do something yourself when you can get someone else to do it for you?" Tavalisk took a third sip; the wine, though still bitter, found acceptance on his tongue.

"I will discover who has reason to hate Lord Baralis, Your Eminence."

"Knowing Baralis as I do, I'm sure there will be more than a few people in Castle Harvell who would wish him ill."

Tavalisk took another gulp of wine. How could he have ever considered this nectar bitter?

"Is there anything more, Your Eminence?"

Tavalisk picked up his dog and handed it to his aide. "Take Comi for a walk in the gardens, Gamil. He hasn't been out all day and needs to relieve himself." Gamil flashed Tavalisk a look filled with malice. Tavalisk pretended not to notice.

Once Gamil had left, Tavalisk fetched the platter of nuts and, with a sly smile on his face, proceeded to crack them open.

Today was the day that Jack was going to leave Falk's den and head east. Jack would be sorry to leave, but he had his own life, and now, thanks to Falk, it appeared more hopeful than before. Life wasn't as simple as he'd thought, but it was rich with possibilities. His mind had been opened up to other points of view. He was beginning to see that there was more than one way of looking at things, and that beliefs he'd held for years demanded questioning. Falk had given him much to think about, and now he needed time alone to reach his own conclusions.

"Why did you help me that day when I was sick?" asked Jack. They were sitting by the fire, and ale had made them pensive. Falk sipped his drink and remained silent. Jack thought that he had overstepped the boundaries of their peculiar friendship by questioning his motives. He was about to apologize for asking when Falk finally spoke up.

"I cannot lie to you, Jack. I helped you because there was more to you than sight alone."

"You saw the thing in me that changed the loaves?"

Jack was surprised by Falk's answer. "No, I am no magician. Only they can spot the potential for sorcery in each other. I am a woodsman—I know the earth not the heavens."

Jack felt the hair on his neck bristle. He was afraid. "What did you see, then?"

"You are persistent," said Falk, "I'll give you that. I helped you the day you fell sick in the rain, because I felt a pulling in my blood. I saw the potential for . . ." Falk looked at the floor, flattening the leaves with his shoe ". . . I cannot say. Destiny escorts you, and given the opportunity, she would lead you to the dance."

Falk stood up quickly, clearly uncomfortable with the subject of conversation. "Seems you are on your way. I have gifts I would give you."

Destiny? It seemed to Jack his life had never been more confusing: sorcery, choices to make, and now some shadowy destiny accompanying him. He was a baker's boy, nothing more. Life had been a lot easier when his only concerns were baking, scribing, and courting.

He ran his hands through his hair, longer than ever now. Master Frallit would have wielded his knife at the sight of it. The kitchen girls had liked it long, though. Not that he was interested in them anymore; a man could hardly be expected to think of women when he had just recovered from a wet fever and was about to set out on a new life. Still, the image of one woman kept playing on his mind: the girl Melli. Even now he could see her perfect skin, almost feel the contours of her body.

He felt a little ashamed of the progress of his thoughts. Women, no matter how much he tried and how pressing his problems were, had a way of insinuating themselves into his thoughts. Why, only minutes ago Falk had told him something important—true, it was a little vague, but important no less—and here he was imaging how Melli would have looked in a low-cut dress!

He laughed out loud and Falk laughed with him. He wasn't to ask why Falk laughed along—he feared being told the woodsman could read his thoughts. Which only made him laugh more. It was good to laugh; it was hard to believe there was anything bad in the world that wouldn't retreat at the sound of laughter.

Falk walked to a corner of the den and knelt down, then lifted a bed of moss to reveal a small pit. He sorted through the contents, found what he wanted, and replaced the moss. Falk came and sat beside Jack once more and started to unwrap several items from their linen swaths.

"You came with nothing, and I cannot let you part that way. I did not save your life for it to be forfeit as soon as you leave." He handed Jack a small but heavy dagger. "You will need a knife." Falk unwrapped another item. "You will need a water flask." The final item was a thick and luxuriant cloak. "You will need warmth."

Jack was sobered by such generosity. "Falk, I don't know how to thank you." He was saved from saying more by Falk, who grunted in a dismissive manner.

" 'Tis nothing. Though I ask one thing in return."

"What?"

"Don't be bitter, Jack. You are young and life has set you a difficult path. Don't make it worse by blaming others for its course." The woodsman gave him a look filled with understanding. It was Jack who looked away first.

Satisfied, Falk busied himself with placing food onto a cloth. He then drew the cloth into a sling and tied the cord tightly. A few moments looking through a chest, and he pulled out a pair of boots. He looked at Jack's feet critically, shaking his head in disbelief. When Falk handed the boots over to him, Jack didn't know whether to smile or be ashamed. Lastly, Falk gave him a leather purse. "It's not much," he said, "a few golds, but it will help you once you clear the forest."

Jack tried to thank him again, but his words seemed stiff and formal. "I owe you much, Falk. I thank you for your kindness and promise to repay you."

"I want no thanks and I will have no man beholden to me. I absolve you of any debt or obligation." Jack tried to think of a suitable reply. Not finding one, he decided silence was his best course.

The two companions left the den, and stood side by side. Although Jack had seen the den from the outside several times before, he could not help but admire it once again. It appeared to be nothing more than a mass of dense bushes. Falk caught Jack looking at it. "I have few things to be proud of, my home is one of them."

They stood in silence for a few minutes, taking in the beauty of the forest.

Falk surprised Jack by coming forward and placing a light kiss upon his cheek. "I envy you, Jack. You are young and your life is ahead of you—*make an adventure of it!*" For the last time, Jack could find no words. The two men's eyes met, and Jack turned and walked away.

He did not look back. He headed into the deep forest, checking the position of the sun to ensure he was walking east. All the great cities lay to the east. It didn't matter where he ended up, what counted was the experience. Now that Falk had set his mind ablaze, he needed fuel to feed the flame.

Jack broke into a run. He enjoyed the sensation of cool air on his face, and when it began to rain, he counted it a blessing. Many leagues he traveled, his thoughts too joyful for contemplation. His life *would* be an adventure, and that was enough to sustain him through the day.

When night began to make its presence felt with cool breezes and a darkening sky, Jack slowed and looked for a place to sleep. He found a flat area of ground by a narrow stream and unpacked his bag. He was overwhelmed with the contents; there was a side of cured ham, a round of yellow cheese, salted venison, apples, nuts, dried fruits, and dried meats. Besides food there was a light woolen blanket and a flask. Jack drank from the flask and found it was filled with cider. Smiling, he cut himself a large wedge of cheese to complement the brew.

Jack opened the leather purse and found five gold pieces. To a boy who'd not owned a penny his entire life, five golds was a fortune.

He tucked in to a hearty meal, testing the blade of his dagger on the side of ham. As he ate, Jack wished he could have thanked Falk more eloquently for all he had done. He considered the strange character of his benefactor and realized the best thing he could do was simply to enjoy the bounty he had given. Jack raised his flask and made a toast: "To Falk, a man alone but at peace." Jack downed the remaining cider and belched appreciatively. It was a good brew.

Baralis was not pleased. His dove had died; the wretched bird had finally succumbed to starvation and cold. Now he had no way of ensuring his mercenaries would pick up the girl. He would have to send out another bird. He would do it tomorrow—he had a meeting with the queen later this day and he needed his wits about him. To add to his displeasure, he had just received a letter by courier from the chubby, scheming Tavalisk, asking for his library back. The corrupt and corpulent archbishop was up to no good, he could feel it in his blood. The man lived for intrigue, and he wouldn't let something as juicy as the marriage of Kylock go unquestioned. The map of the Known Lands would soon be changing, power would shift from the bloated south to the ravenous north. There was no place for a glutton in a world dominated by a lean and hungry empire.

Tavalisk would bear watching; he would not have his plans foiled by the archbishop's pudgy hand.

Baralis did have some reasons to be pleased: the queen had finally acquiesced and had requested an audience with him this night. She wanted more of the medicine. Winter's Eve festival was the following night, and he hoped to have the queen's seal of approval on his proposal by then.

As Baralis thought, he mixed a batch of poison. A new formula—one that he had not tried before. With hands made deft once more by his painkillers, he ground powders and measured liquids, careful to attain the exact proportions. Too much of the moss extract might overpower the other ingredients and the delicate balance would be disturbed. Making poison required a meticulous eye and a steady hand.

This poison was not meant to be consumed—this was more subtle. Baralis smiled grimly as he considered his handiwork; this was undoubtedly the most amusing poison he had ever made. It was designed to be poured onto the victim's robes. The poison was strong and would only need a few drops, preferably around the collar and shoulders. The victim would wear his cloak and be able to detect nothing amiss, for the potion was clear and had little odor. The victim would then proceed about his business unaware that he was breathing in the deadly fumes that the poison gave off. It would be a slow death, for the fumes would be slight and take many hours to work their deadly commission.

Baralis now reached the point in the manufacture where he was forced to don a mask—he did not want to take any chances himself. The death that the poison brought would not only be slow but also painful. The victim would find himself short of breath as the noxious substance burnt into the delicate flesh of throat and lung. The victim would assume he had indigestion or heartburn and would think nothing of it. Gradually the poison would eat away at the victim's lungs to such an extent that he would suffocate, desperately struggling for breath that could not come.

Baralis, having finished making the poison, cautiously tipped it into a glass jar upon which he placed a firm stopper. Tomorrow, when the attention of the castle was diverted by last-minute preparations for the festival, he would slip into Maybor's chamber. Baralis would douse Maybor's best robes in the poison. As there was to be a court dance that evening, the vain Lord Maybor would be sure to wear his most extravagant and expensive robes. Little would he suspect that the clothes he wore to impress the court would be the very instrument of his downfall.

Baralis was most satisfied with his plan. This time no unsuspecting servant would step in and save his master. Maybor had been lucky once; he would not be so again.

Maybor was waiting downwind of the middens once more. Impatiently, he stamped his feet on the hard ground. The assassin finally came, his diminutive figure emerging over the gentle rise. Maybor did not stand on ceremony. "Why have you not done what was agreed?"

The assassin did not appear to be concerned with Maybor's angry tone. "The time has not been right so far. I would not endanger myself by moving too soon and without due care."

Maybor was not happy with this answer. "It has been many days since we met last. I would have expected you to find a propitious moment before now."

"I have been carefully monitoring Lord Baralis' movements. He goes nowhere without his fool Crope."

"That is not my problem. I want him dead, and I want it done soon."

"You will not have to wait much longer, Lord Maybor. It is my intention to make my move soon."

"How soon?" pressured Maybor.

"Lord Maybor, I will not tell you the details. It is better that you do not know when and where. Let it come as a surprise—you will be better able to act your part that way."

Maybor knew that what the assassin said made sense. "Very well, so be it. I must have your word that it will be done soon though."

"You have it, Lord Maybor." The assassin was about to withdraw when a question occurred to Maybor.

"What have you found out about Baralis? Surely you must have seen some interesting things by following him around."

The assassin appeared to hesitate for a moment before speaking. "I have found out little about the man's secrets, he barely leaves his rooms."

Maybor suspected that the assassin was holding something back from him. He decided to press no further until the job was done; he could not risk aggravating the assassin before then. Once it was completed was another matter. In fact, once the deed was done, he might even arrange for Scarl himself to have an accident. Maybor dearly loved his apple orchards and was loathe to part with thirty acres of them. These thoughts cheered his spirits considerably.

"Very well, Scarl. I trust you will do as you say."

Scarl gave him a brief guarded look and said, "I will do my job, have no fear, Lord Maybor." With that, he withdrew leaving Maybor to the stench of the middens.

Maybor watched as the assassin walked away. He did not trust him; after all, what was he but a hired murderer? He would do his job, Maybor was sure of that. Once he had done it, however, he might find *himself* a victim of an assassin's knife.

Maybor waited a while and wondered how long it would be before his daughter was found. Twelve days now had passed since she bolted. He knew she would be alive and well: the girl had spirit and initiative—after all she *was* his daughter. Now he had his men riding into all the towns and villages that bordered on the great forest in case Melliandra turned up in one of them. He had even spread a discreet word about rewards that could be received, if information leading to his daughter's recovery was given. There was a risk with doing so, but he was running out of time. He was forced to take broader measures: he had to find Melliandra. She *would* be betrothed! He *would* be father to a queen.

Melli awoke and immediately felt sick. She hurried to the washstand, where she threw up, retching violently. She felt awful. She returned to sit on the bed, as she was feeling a little faint, and tried to think what to do next. She did not trust Mistress Greal. She would retrieve her horse and move on. Unfortunately, she was feeling so weak that the last thing she felt like was walking all day.

There was the briefest of knocks on her door and Mistress Greal sailed in. "My, my. What's happened to you?" She saw the mess in the washstand. "Oh, I see, not used to cider, eh? Well never mind, you'll live. A jug of cider's never killed anyone, save old Ma Crutly—she got hit over the head with one." The woman busied herself tidying the room.

"I thank you for your hospitality, but I will be on my way today. I have left the pots we agreed upon on top of the chest. I trust you will be happy with the payment." Melli indicated the plate and pots.

Mistress Greal's already small eyes narrowed further. "You don't look to be in any state to be off, deary. You'd best stay another day. Relax and have a nice bath. I drew one for you last night, but when I came to ready you, you were fast asleep."

The sound of a hot bath and a day relaxing was far too tempting, and Melli relented. "Very well, Mistress Greal, I will stay another day. But I warn you, I have nothing else to pay you."

"Don't worry about that, deary, that's nothing to me. I just want to help a fellow woman on her way. Now, I'll have a nice breakfast sent up and arrange to have another bath drawn. I also took the liberty of seeing about a new dress. You can't go having a nice bath and then put on those filthy clothes, can you?" The woman regarded Melli's dirty and disheveled clothes with distaste, making Melli feel ashamed.

"You are too good to me, Mistress Greal. But if you

could just have my clothes cleaned, I would not trouble you for new ones."

"Nonsense, that dress is badly torn. Besides, the clothes won't be new. They're very pretty, though—show you off to your best advantage." Mistress Greal left the room, and Melli had no chance to ask what she meant by showing her off to her best advantage. Melli had no desire to be shown off.

Her attentions were diverted by the arrival of a hot and delicious breakfast: crisp bacon, poached egg, grilled mushrooms, and plenty of bread and butter. She tucked in heartily. Whatever Mistress Greal's motives, Melli thanked her for providing such delicious food.

After she had eaten, a sallow-faced girl appeared and led Melli to a small room that contained a round, wooden bath. The water was steaming hot and Melli soaked for a long time, soothing the aches of her body. After a while she permitted the girl to scrub her back and wash her hair. She dried herself on a woolen towel: it felt so good to be clean. She looked at the bathwater and was horrified to see it was a murky brown color. She had obviously been a lot dirtier than she had thought.

Once dry, the girl handed Melli a deep, crimson-colored dress. It was not to Melli's taste, but as her own dress had been taken away, she was forced to put it on. The bodice was cut low and exposed much of Melli's breast. The girl then pulled the lacing so tight that Melli could hardly breathe, and her breasts were pushed up high toward her chin. There was no mirror so she could not see what she looked like, but she suspected she must look rather improper, not at all like a lady of the court. She asked the girl to loosen the lacings a little, but the girl refused.

"That's the way Mistress Greal likes 'em," she said.

A few moments later, as the girl was dressing her hair, Mistress Greal herself walked in. She seemed pleased at what she saw. She walked around Melli, making approving, clucking sounds. She finally spoke. "My, my. Who would have guessed you would have turned out so well? Of course, I have got a good eye for beauty, but I can see I've surpassed myself this time." She then spoke to the girl, "Keddi, leave her hair down. Such fine hair, it's a waste to tie it up." The girl obediently took the pins from Melli's hair. Mistress

Greal came toward Melli and smoothed her hand over Melli's face and bosom.

"My, my, you are a pretty one." She noticed Melli's distaste at being touched. "No need to be coy, girl. I would have thought such a pretty posy as you would be well used to being admired."

"Please, Mistress Greal, I find this all rather embarrassing. If you could ask your maid to hurry washing my dress, I would be most gratified. I fear that this one is not to my taste." Mistress Greal's expression turned cold as Melli spoke.

"Nonsense, this dress suits you fine. You should be grateful! That dirty thing you wore is not a patch on this one for quality." Melli had to bite her lip. Torn and dirty though her dress was, it was made from the finest lambswool and was by far the better quality of the two. However, Melli knew better than to speak of such things. She did not want Mistress Greal to know of her former position as a lady of the court.

Mistress Greal seemed to regret her sharp words, and when she spoke again it was in a more beguiling tone. "Perhaps you would care to join me for a sup of ale in the tavern?" Melli most definitely did not wish to do so.

"I would prefer to spend the day in my room. Of course, I would like to check on my horse first."

"There's no need to check on the horse," said the woman quickly. "It is well looked after, my boy has seen to that." Melli began to feel decidedly uneasy. She did not press the point further, but resolved to go and check on her horse later anyway.

"Why don't you join me for a sup? It would be a shame to waste such a pretty dress. Besides, you must be hungry and the tavern keeper does not serve midday meal in his private rooms." Mistress Greal shot a glance to the maid, warning her not to contradict what she said. Melli knew she was being forced; she also knew she couldn't now refuse.

"Very well, I will join you for a short while."

Mistress Greal was most pleased. "Very good, very good. We shall have a nice time."

She and Melli walked through the tavern and found a table at which to sit. The table was too public for Melli's liking, right in the center of the room. When Melli protested and asked to be seated somewhere more discreet, Mistress Greal spoke of the warmth from the fire and the fresh air from the door. To Melli the table appeared to be close to neither.

Melli sat quietly and drank little of the ale. Mistress Greal appeared to know everyone in the tavern: she nodded and waved at all of the men. In fact, their little party seemed to be the focus of attention in the room. Melli hoped that no one who knew her from Castle Harvell was there. On a brief scan around the room, she saw no one familiar.

After a little while, a man came up to them. He spoke to Mistress Greal, but his eyes were on Melli. "I wish you joy of the day, Mistress Greal," he said, his eyes lingering over Melli's exposed bosom.

"Joy to you, Edrad," replied Mistress Greal, noting with approval where the man's eyes looked.

"May I have the pleasure of being introduced to your lovely companion?"

"Why, certainly, sir. This is Melli. Where did you say you were from my dear?"

Melli had not said; she struggled to think of a suitable place. "I am from . . . Deepwood."

"Deepwood? Never heard of it. Where might that be?" asked the man.

"It's far south of here."

"It must be very far south if I have never heard of it," remarked Mistress Greal sharply.

Melli was thinking of a polite way to excuse herself when the man spoke to her companion: "Mistress Greal, I wonder if I might have a word with you in private?" The woman agreed, and the two withdrew beyond Melli's hearing distance. She watched as the man asked something and the woman shook her head. The man then asked something else and this time Mistress Greal nodded. The man departed, with one last look toward Melli, and Mistress Greal returned to the table.

She appeared to be most pleased. Her eyes checked the room, and seeing many of the men glance appreciatively at Melli, she smiled widely. "I think you've had enough excitement for one day, my dear. I can see you are tired. I will see if the tavern keeper will bring some food to your room after all." Melli was surprised at this sudden kindness.

"Why, thank you. I do rather feel like a short nap."

Mistress Greal smiled again. "Yes, deary, you get all the beauty sleep you need. Tomorrow you will need all your energies." Melli was instantly suspicious.

"What do you mean by that?"

"Why nothing, my dear," said Mistress Greal sweetly. "It's a local saying around here, that's all." As Melli stood up and prepared to walk away, her companion had one final thing to say: "Take the dress off before you sleep, Melli. I wouldn't want it wrinkled."

Baralis was on his way to his audience with the queen, a flutter of excitement in his stomach. He knocked on the door to the meeting chamber, and the queen beckoned him to enter.

Even to Baralis' dispassionate eye the queen looked regal and beautiful. Her heavy pale hair was piled high on her head, and her gown of burnished silk reflected a gentle, golden light onto her fine features. For a brief moment before she spoke, Baralis indulged himself in remembering a certain night, many years before, when he had partaken of her delights. The memory gave him a feeling of power and he suddenly felt more confident than he had been on entering the chamber.

"Lord Baralis. I bid you welcome." He watched as the queen decided whether or not to favor him with her hand. She decided against it.

"It is an honor to be in your presence, Your Highness." He bowed low.

"Lord Baralis, I trust you have heard that the king's health has improved somewhat?"

Baralis nodded. "I hope Your Highness is well satisfied with the medicine."

"I am indeed. The king had been getting much worse of late. Now I see him improving for the first time since his tragic accident."

"I am grateful to be the cause of such good news," said Baralis, bowing slightly as he reminded the queen of his role in the recovery. The queen did not miss the reminder.

"Yes, Lord Baralis, I am most thankful to you. You

know there is to be a great feast tomorrow evening to celebrate the king's health?"

"I will, of course, be in attendance, Your Highness." Baralis was in no rush to get to the point. He would let the queen be the first to speak of the deal.

"Lord Baralis, I think you know why I have asked you here this day."

He would not make it easier for her. "I would not so presume, Your Highness." With pleasure, Baralis noted a flicker of anger pass over the queen's features.

"I will not exchange small talk anymore, Lord Baralis. The point is this—I need more of your medicine for the king. What do you require in return for supplying it?"

Baralis concealed his delight. "Your Highness is most forthright. I would indeed expect a favor for a favor."

"Speak what you would have: lands, gold, appointments." The queen made a negligent gesture and turned away from Baralis.

"I would have a say in who Prince Kylock marries."

The queen spun around. "What trickery is this? You will have no influence over who my son will marry." The queen was now trembling with anger. In contrast, Baralis was very calm and even beginning to enjoy himself.

"There is no need for deception with me, Your Highness. I know of Lord Maybor's plans to marry his daughter to the prince." The queen hid her surprise well.

"How have you come to know this?" she demanded coldly.

"Lord Maybor has a tongue that loosens when wet." The queen regarded him with barely concealed malice. He knew, though, that she believed his excuse. Maybor was famous throughout the court as being a heavy drinker.

"Well, Lord Baralis, if you know of this planned betrothal, you must also know that it has been firmly decided. I will not rescind the agreement."

"Unfortunately, there are matters of which Your Highness knows little." Baralis spoke almost condescendingly.

"What matters?" hissed the queen.

"Matters concerning Lord Maybor's delightful daughter, Melliandra."

"If you are to tell me she is ill, I know that already,

Lord Baralis, and Lord Maybor assures me she does not have the pox."

"Regrettably, Lord Maybor has been lying to Your Highness." Baralis met the queen's eye and continued. "Lord Maybor's daughter has run away from the castle. She has been gone over ten days now. Lord Maybor informed you she was sick to prevent you from learning the truth." He could tell the queen was already beginning to doubt Maybor's word.

"What reason had the girl to run away?"

"I cannot say for certain, for with young girls who can tell what is in their hearts." Baralis managed an almost wistful sigh. "However, I have heard it said that Melliandra ran away because she could not bear the thought of marrying your son."

The queen's face paled with rage. "You say, you *heard* this foul rumor. Who else knows of it?"

"Half the court, Your Highness," lied Baralis.

"This is intolerable!" The queen fingered the embroidery on her dress in agitation.

"I sympathize with Your Highness' predicament," said Baralis humbly. His tone only served to annoy the queen further.

"I would discover for myself if these accusations are true. Before I have done so, I will not speak any further on this matter."

"As Your Highness wishes. However, I feel it my duty to point out that if we do not resolve the situation to both our satisfactions, I fear the king may lose what little ground he has gained. The medicine must be given regularly or its effects may be reversed."

The queen was obviously displeased with his sly pronouncement. "Lord Baralis, I do not take kindly to blackmail. Go now. I will summon you again at my leisure."

Baralis bowed and left. The queen would undoubtedly call him back soon. He smiled with satisfaction at the thought of Maybor's imminent downfall; too bad the man would be dead and unable to feel its sting.

Nine

*T*awl was sitting quietly in Megan's room when a loud knock startled him from his reverie. Cautiously, he went over to the door and asked who was there.

"It's me, Moth. Friend of the Old Man's." Tawl opened the door and let him in. "How are you, my friend?" said Moth, looking speculatively around the room. "I trust you're no worse for those knocks on the head? You know Clem, though. Takes a real pride in his work. Old Man says bring him in, quiet like, and Clem takes him on his word. Two knocks from Clem are enough to make anyone quiet for a while. *Three* knocks from Clem and you'll never talk again. Anyway, enough of this chatter. Let's get down to business."

Tawl was rather bemused by this outpouring, but managed to beckon Moth to sit down. "I take it you're here about the ship?"

"That's right, friend. Old Man says find a ship. I find a ship. A fast one, too, I'll have you know. Very nice. Wouldn't mind a life on the high seas myself if I had the time. Captain. That's what I'd be. Clem could be my first mate. Anyway, back to your particulars. The ship's called *The Fishy Few*. Kind of strange name, ain't it? So, I had a word with the good captain, and needless to say a few coins exchanged hands, but that's not for you to worry about, friend.

When the Old Man says he'll take care of something, he takes care of it. Now where was I?"

"You had a word with the good captain," prompted Tawl, amused by Moth's digressions.

"And so I did. I spoke to the good captain, told him that a friend of the Old Man's wants to head to Larn. Let me tell you, he didn't look too pleased. But I reminded him that the Old Man has great pull with the merchants of Rorn, could lead to a lot of business, I told him. Course, a few more coins exchanged hands. Larn ain't a cheap place to go, I can tell you that."

"What about a rowboat, so I can land on the island?" interrupted Tawl.

"No problem. The good captain said that a man who goes to Larn needs two things: first his head felt for malformations, and secondly a rowboat. So, the captain's got a boat you can use. He'll even provide a man to row you.

"The good captain *does* insist that you don't keep him waiting too long, though. Apparently, the seas around there are real rough. He says he can't wait for you longer than a full day. That'd better be enough time, friend, 'cos the good captain will be pulling up anchor and sailing off into the sunset before you know it. And from what I've heard of Larn, it ain't a place a man would care to be stuck on."

"When does the boat set sail?" Tawl was hoping he would have time to say good-bye to Megan.

"First light tomorrow. You'll have to be up with the lark. I wrote a song about a lark once—one of these days I'll get Clem to sing it for you, he's got a fine voice has Clem. Where was I?"

"The ship."

"Aye, the ship. *The Fishy Few* sets sail from the north harbor. It's a two-master, you'll find it all right. Captain's name is Quain. Captain Quain, he'll be expecting you."

"Send my thanks to the Old Man, Moth."

"It's as good as done, friend."

"I thank you, too, Moth." Tawl thought for a moment and then added, "And send my regards to Clem."

"Clem will be most gratified. And as for me, it was my pleasure. I got a nice walk down to the harbor out of it."

"Oh, one more thing, Moth. The Old Man mentioned helping my friend Megan."

"The Old Man does what he says. I'm glad you reminded me." Moth rooted into the depths of his cloak and handed Tawl a heavy purse. "The Old Man wouldn't have been pleased if I'd forgotten to give you that. He'd have me strung up . . . and Clem, too. We're a pair: I mess up, he pays for it. Clem wouldn't have it any other way, though.

"Oh, one more thing. The Old Man says you should take some gold for yourself. He hates to see a knight without a decent sword. No offense intended, but that knife you got ain't up to much. Course, I saw you put that thief away—real fast you were, but you could have done better with the right equipment. Pity you ain't here much longer. I could have got you something real nice in the way of weaponry. Never mind, there's always another time. I must be off, Clem's expecting me to help him with a little business. I bid you well, friend." With that Moth was off, letting himself out.

When he had gone, Tawl couldn't help but wonder what business Moth and Clem had to do. He decided he was best not knowing. He emptied the purse and found twenty gold pieces. Tawl replaced all save one of them.

A little while later, Megan let herself in. She had, as always, brought him some tasty morsels to eat and drink. She was about to lay a meal out when he stopped her, beckoning her to sit with him for a while. "Megan, I must leave you tomorrow."

Her pretty face grew grave. "I had not expected you to go so soon." Megan pulled away from him, stood up and, bowing her head, began to slice oranges.

Hair fell over her face, such a glorious mix of chestnut and gold. She was so young—Anna, the youngest of his sisters, would have been about the same age. There was something in the plane of her cheeks and the gold in her hair that reminded Tawl of his sisters. Such gentle girls, like Megan. Yet unlike her, they were so dependent upon him. His mind traveled back to the little cottage on the marshes. He was all they had, and he'd let them down so badly.

*　　*　　*

The midwife nodded her approval. Tawl remembered the blood on her apron: his mother's blood. "You made a wise decision," she said. "I'll open her now, while the cord still holds." As she turned to enter the cottage, he put a hand upon her arm.

"Let me see her first."

The midwife huffed her disapproval, but let him go ahead. His sisters greeted him, taking the fishes from his pack. Anna had just learned her numbers and slowly counted the fish on her chubby fingers. Sara, the eldest, had no patience with her and counted them loudly with a superior air. "There's one extra," she said, superiority giving way to excitement. "Is it for the baby?"

Tawl nodded and turned away. Tears prickled in his eyes and he swept them away before they could fall. He could hear his sisters behind him, busily picking out the biggest fish for the baby.

"Can he have this one?" cried Anna, a large fish in her lap.

"Yes," said Tawl, kneeling down and putting his arms around her shoulders. "The baby must have the biggest one of all." He kissed her cheek and put his arm out for Sara. She came to him as she always did, resting her head upon his shoulder. Tawl hugged her close and stroked Anna's golden hair. Such baby-fine texture, but then, what was she but a baby? Barely five years old. Too soon they would know the truth. He crushed his sisters to his chest, using his strength to express what he could never say with words.

The moment passed, leaving him calmer. Standing up, he left his sisters sitting on the floor amidst the fish, and opened the door to his mother's room. He would be the one to tell her, the news would come from her son, not the mouth of a stranger.

The smell was sickly. Flies buzzed around the bed and finding no hindrance landed on the drying blood. "Tawl, is that you?" His mother's voice was gentle. He could tell she was afraid.

"Yes, Mama, it's me." He came and sat on the stool by

her bedside, keeping his eyes low, so as not to look at the swell of her belly.

"How many fishes today?" It was strange how in this time of distress his mother chose to speak of everyday events. He played along, too young to see where she led.

"Nine, but they were slow to bite."

She sighed in sympathy. "Never mind, you may need fewer tomorrow."

So she knew. For an instant a weight was taken from his shoulders, but then, just as quickly, it returned, heavier than ever. "Mama, I'm sorry."

"Ssh, Tawl." She clasped his hand in hers. "Don't worry about me, it's your sisters who need you now. You must be strong for them." His mother's eyes held such strength of purpose, it was impossible to believe she was so weak. "You must promise me you'll look after them."

The pressure of her hand upon his was almost unbearable. "And the baby," he said, half statement, half question.

"And the baby, if it lives."

Megan took his hand. "Tawl, are you all right?" His legs buckled under him and he sat down on the floor. The mixture of present and past disoriented him—the images took longer than normal to leave. The baby had survived, and the midwife had known of a wet nurse. The pay was two fishes—his mother's portion. She'd been wrong, then, his mother: the catch had remained the same.

Megan handed him a cup filled with steaming liquid. Its sharp tang of oranges brought him to the present more forcefully than any words. Oranges were unheard of in the marshes.

"Forgive me, Megan," he said. "I am still a little weak."

"Are you sure you should be on your way, then? Stay a little longer. Not for my sake, but for your own."

He had to go. The quest was all there was, and he couldn't allow anything else to matter. He was destined to always leave like this: a soft good-bye with no chance of returning. "No, Megan. I must be on my way." He searched for the familiar words of parting, but they wouldn't come. By giving so much, Megan had taken something from him—he could not leave her with glib phrases. She deserved more than that. He took her face in his hands. "I'm afraid that if I stay any longer, I might never go. You would be better off with someone else. There is much about me you don't know."

"I know you're in pain." Megan's voice was tender. "Tawl, I can tell you're not happy. You make the mistake of thinking that once you finish your quest and find who you seek, everything will be all right. But you're wrong—it's love, not achievement, that will rid you of your demons."

Was he that transparent? Or was she just perceptive? He kissed her gently—it was his only reply.

Later, when passion had gone, leaving tenderness in its wake, Tawl handed Megan the heavy purse. "Take this, it will help you live a life of your own choosing."

Megan took the purse and opened it up. Seeing the many gold pieces, she handed it back to him. "I want no payment from you, Tawl, save your promise to keep yourself safe." Tawl gently pushed the purse back to her.

"This is no payment, this is a gift. I beg you to take it."

Megan picked up the purse. "Will I see you again?"

"I am a knight of Valdis, Megan, sworn to make no promise that can't be kept." Tawl found strength in the formality of his words. He knew he sounded cold, but he was a knight first and foremost, and it was time to do his duty. Megan drew away from him, just as he expected. It took all his willpower to stop himself from pulling her back.

Baralis slipped into the concealed passageway and headed for Maybor's chamber. On his way, he noted what he thought to be an entirely new moss clinging to the wet, stone walls. He made a mental note to come back another day with a specimen dish. Mosses were always a thing of great interest. A new one could mean interesting innovations in his poisoning skills.

He decided he would take a less direct route to Maybor's chamber than usual. He felt the need for great caution, but could not exactly say why. Finally, having taken a twisted path, he found himself outside the lord's bedchamber. He checked that the room was empty and then slipped quietly through.

Baralis knew little of such things, but even he could tell that Maybor's rooms were furnished with more money than taste. Hideous scarlet tapestries lined the walls, silver and crimson rugs covered the floor, even the bed was covered in lurid red silk. He had little time to amuse himself with Maybor's bad taste, however, and stole toward the small dressing room, which was just off the bedchamber.

Baralis allowed himself a thin smile as he took in the contents of Maybor's wardrobe. The man had more robes than most court ladies—in colors to outdazzle any peacock. He quickly decided that Maybor would wear one of two red-colored robes that evening. The queen was to be in attendance at the Winter's Eve dance and Maybor would surely use this chance to display himself in his richest. The two robes that Baralis picked out were by far the most ostentatious: gold embroidery, ruffles, and pearls. Baralis shuddered. He himself would wear a discreet black. He never liked to draw unnecessary attention upon himself.

With haste, he sprinkled the poison on the shoulders and neck of the robes. He then beat a quick retreat. He knew just how deadly the poison was and he had no intention of being in a small room with the lethal fumes for an instant longer than necessary.

Pleased that the task was done to his satisfaction, he slipped out of the chamber and returned to his own rooms by the same indirect route he had used coming.

The assassin was not unduly worried that he'd lost Lord Baralis when he slipped into the passageways. Baralis was probably spying on someone, or up to some other ill deed. That no longer concerned him. What did concern Scarl were his plans for this night.

Tonight he would make his move, carry out his commission. The assassin had thought long and hard over how best to do his job and had finally decided on carrying it out on the night of the Winter's Eve dance. The great banquet hall would be crowded with people, all drinking and eating. Baralis would not dare to bring his servant Crope to such a grand event.

The assassin had found, on his many explorations of the labyrinth, a passage that led to a small antechamber just off the banquet hall. It would be easy for him to slip into the hall, unnoticed amid all the drunken revelry and watch his mark.

The assassin knew Baralis' ways well: he was not a man who liked to keep in the forefront; eventually he would retire to a remote corner to better observe the foibles of his fellows. Then, as Baralis watched with studied boredom, the assassin would make his move. The great lord would barely feel the touch of the knife before he fell dead to the floor. Scarl would return to the passage before anyone noticed what had happened.

The assassin was beginning to feel the familiar knot of excitement in his stomach which always accompanied the time leading up to his task. He was eager that it be done, and anxious that it be done right. He did not doubt his own skills—he was the best with a knife in the Known Lands— but he did worry in case anything should go wrong. Still, he had never failed before and he had a fine plan.

It really was a most beautiful plan. To carry out a murder in a room full of people would actually be a lot easier than it seemed. He would wait until such a time when the crowd's reactions were dulled by drink; no one would notice a shadowy figure move about the room. In addition to the plan's other merits, Lord Maybor would be in full sight of the room, and so no guilt would fall upon him.

Scarl considered Lord Maybor—he did not trust him. It was true that Maybor had paid willingly in the past for his services, but the assassin had seen something in the lord's face when they had met last that boded no good. The assassin would be wary. He had taken a risk by not requesting his payment in gold—for if he had been paid in the traditional manner he would by now have half his fee in his keeping. As it was, he had nothing more than a promise from Lord Maybor to deed him some land after the job was done. He sincerely hoped that Maybor would not try and renege on his word . . . that would be most unfortunate—most unfortunate, indeed.

These matters the assassin put to the back of his mind; he would deal with such difficulties when and if they arose. For today and tonight he would need his complete concentration for the task in hand. Almost as a reflex, Scarl took his knife from his belt. He ran his finger lightly over the blade; the subtle motion drew blood. The assassin was well pleased at the sight: his blade had never been keener.

Jack was heading east through the forest. He was making a good pace; sometimes he even broke into a short run, his sack banging against his side. He had never felt more free in his life. It was a joy to him to be in the woods running at his own speed. All his life he had been at the beck and call of others: Master Frallit, the head cellarer, Lord Baralis. Now, for the first time he was experiencing what it was like to do things when he wanted, to eat when he was hungry and to sleep when he was tired.

He was light-headed with freedom. He owed so much to Falk. Thanks to him, he didn't feel that what he'd done to the loaves was evil. Now, with time and the goodness of nature to give perspective, Jack realized Falk was right: he hadn't intended to do anything bad. All he'd felt the morning of the loaves was worried. A worried man was not necessarily an evil one.

Still, he had done it. He couldn't hide from it. In fact, part of him didn't want to. It made him different, and he no longer felt the overpowering need to be the same as everyone else. A thought drifted through his mind, and when he realized its importance, he spoke out loud: "I might have inherited it." Whatever it was that he had—power, sorcery, magic—he could have got from his parents.

Falk had led him to believe that his mother had not been afraid for herself but for him. What if she'd been afraid for both of them? If she'd had any similar power, she would have needed to keep it hidden in order to continue living in Harvell. If only she'd taken him into her confidence. But had he really given her the chance? He had been too young, too keen to be out at play when all she wanted to do was sit by the fire and talk.

Jack wished Falk was with him; he would know if magic, like hazel eyes and large feet, could be passed down in the blood.

It was really quite unbelievable: he, a baker's boy—and, according to Frallit, not a particularly good one at that—had somehow managed to change the natural order of things. He felt no differently—perhaps a little wiser since his visit with Falk, but for the most part he was unchanged. He was still unsure what to do with his life; various ideas warred in his mind, and depending on his mood he either wanted to search for his mother's family, settle down to be a baker in an eastern town, or wander through the world finding adventures as they took him, ideas of revenge against his father, which Falk had so shrewdly guessed at, were not something he would let govern his life.

For today, though, he was content to be out in the forest. Decisions were for the future. The food was good, the ground was firm, and time, at last, was his own.

He began to feel a chill once more, and broke into another run to keep himself warm. He leapt over ditches and fallen logs, dodging trees and trampling the undergrowth. When he finally stopped, his feet were a little sore. The boots that Falk had given him were not a very good fit; he was grateful as they kept his feet warm and dry, but they pinched at his toes. He'd always had a problem with shoes and clothing, everything was always too small, and he'd become accustomed to tying his jerkins with string and cutting holes in his boots for his toes.

Breathless, Jack fell to the ground. Hungry as ever, he decided upon a bite to eat. He cut himself a slice of venison and chose an apple to round it off. He dreamt of where he would go: there was Annis, the jewel of the north, beautiful and proud; Highwall, austere and majestic; or Bren, powerful beyond measure. Jack took a hearty bite of his apple. There was only one choice that seemed right, one city where he felt he *needed* to go. He would head to Bren.

The noise was unclear at first, masked by the apple

crunching against his teeth. He swallowed quickly and concentrated. Jack's stomach churned with fear as he recognized the sound of horses galloping in the distance. Baralis had come for him! It had been so long, he'd thought himself safe. Quickly, he searched for somewhere to conceal himself. The surrounding land was flat and without bush—just the thin trunks of tall trees. Jack grabbed his sack and started to run.

The horses were drawing closer. He decided his best course would be to run toward a distant rise. He was already short of breath, but forced himself to run further. The horses were almost upon him and he dived to the ground, hoping the riders would not spot him. The cold earth echoed with the thunder of hooves. He was now able to see the riders as they raced through the trees: they were the same men he had last encountered, only this time there were more.

He thought he might go undetected, for he had managed to clear the riders' path, and they were obviously headed in a specific direction. However, the first rider shouted something and the troop slowed down. Jack tried to make his body as flat as possible against the ground. The first man had now dismounted and was examining the undergrowth. He bent down and picked something up and showed it to the others. At first Jack could not see what it was, then he realized the slice of venison and the apple had been left behind when he had fled. He cursed his stupidity—his brain was as addled as crumpets!

The mercenaries were now looking in his direction. Running, he had probably left tracks. Jack became weak with fear. Should he stay where he was or should he at least try to outrun the men? He didn't feel comfortable hiding—the need for action was upon him. Grabbing a tight hold on his sack, he jumped up and started to run. As he fled, he heard the shout of the armed men as they spied him in the distance. With speed born of desperation, Jack ran like the wind.

He led the men on a fine chase, heading for the most dense part of the forest, knowing that it would be his only chance of escape. As he ran, he heard the leader call to spread out. They were gaining on him. Jack hurled himself onward, trees and bushes becoming dim blurs. One thought consumed his mind: he must escape. One of the riders drew abreast of Jack and another was at his heels. He tried to swerve away, running for a narrow gap between two trees.

He felt the net descend upon him. The nearest rider had thrown a webbed rope over him, and his feet became tangled in it. He fell to the ground, still struggling forward, trying to free himself. Frantic, he worked to free his legs, pulling hard at the coarse rope. Just as he had managed to kick himself free, the armed men descended upon him. They had dismounted and were brandishing spear and sword.

"Don't move, boy," warned the leader, "or you'll feel a spear through your leg." Jack froze on the spot. "I can see you're a smart one. Bind him up, boys. I'm taking no chances this time." Two of the armed men approached Jack, one of them aiming a violent kick at his kidneys.

"Steady on, boys, we wouldn't want to do anything that would upset Lord Baralis." The men looked suitably cowed. "Besides, if we bring him back in good shape, we might get a bonus. Lord Baralis ain't expecting us to find the boy. I reckon it'll be extra gold all around." The leader surveyed his men. "So let's not blow it by roughing the lad up, all right?"

Jack was doubled up with pain; the kick had been well placed. The two men bound his wrists and ankles with leather strips, pulling the bindings so tight that Jack winced as they snagged his skin.

"Throw him over the back of the extra mare, and make sure he can't wriggle off. We've got a long ride ahead of us, and I don't want him going anywhere." Jack was slung over a large horse and bound to it with thick rope.

"Are we going to head back to the castle, Traff, or find the girl?" asked another of the men.

Traff, the leader, considered for a moment. "We go on and find the girl." The men mounted their horses, and with Jack as their captive, rode on into the forest heading southeast.

Maybor had just enjoyed a glass of lobanfern red as was his habit before dressing for a big occasion. He was a little worried as to why the queen had requested an audience with him the following day, but he told himself it was probably to establish a specific day for the betrothal. Time was becoming short. He must have his daughter found in the next day or so, or all would be lost.

The first effects of the sweet wine were beginning to make themselves felt and Maybor turned his thoughts to less worrying details. What would he wear? The queen and all the highest nobles would be in attendance at the dance, so he must look his most magnificent. His mind sorted through his wardrobe. It must be something red, he thought. But more than red, it must have gold embroidery and tassels and jewels. His wealth would be the envy of the court on this auspicious night.

"Crandle!" he shouted to his latest servant. The meek Crandle entered the room of the great lord.

"Yes, my lord."

"Fetch me my robe. I would dress for this evening."

"Which one, lord?"

"The red with the golden embroidery and the pearls. I would look like a king on this fair eve." Crandle went off to find the robe in question. Some minutes later, he returned with the requested robe in one hand and a dead rat in the other.

"What is this!" boomed Maybor, motioning to the rat.

"I'm sorry, sir. I don't know how it got into your wardrobe, but it seems to have died before it did any harm." Maybor was not at all pleased with the idea of a rat, dead or otherwise, in his precious wardrobe.

"You fool!" He searched his mind for a suitably threatening punishment. "If this happens again, I will have your ears torn off." His servant looked acceptably contrite, and Maybor regained some of his good humor. "Very well, Crandle, help me dress. I don't think I'll bother bathing—that sort of beautification is for dandies and priests."

The servant helped Maybor from his robes. "Be careful, you idiot!" cried Maybor as Crandle accidentally stepped on his foot. "Or I will have your toes pulled off as well as your ears."

*   *   *

Melli was once again being laced into the tight, red dress. She was not at all pleased when the sallow-faced Keddi gave the lacings one last strong pull, for it had the effect of pushing her breasts up so high she was sure if she as much as breathed deeply they would pop out.

"Keddi, what has become of my own dress?" she demanded.

"Mistress Greal said to throw it out, said as she didn't want you wearing no drab, cover-up dress while you were here."

"Keddi, I will not be here past today. I fully intend on leaving this town tomorrow and I will leave it wearing my own dress. Now run along and find it for me." The girl rushed out, and some minutes later Mistress Greal entered the room.

"Your old dress has been torn apart for rags. You've got no choice but to wear this one. If you're a good girl, I might see to buying you a new one at some point." The woman circled the indignant Melli. "I must say, though, I'd be inclined to get you another red. Shows your skin up just right. Men like nothing better than pale, creamy skin."

"Mistress Greal, I have no wish to cater to the taste of men. You are somewhat mistaken in your belief that I will be staying here. I must tell you now, I will be leaving in the morning." Mistress Greal did not seem concerned by Melli's outburst.

She moved close to Melli adjusting her hair and dress. "You could do with a little rouge, though, deary. Your cheeks are too pale." With that she pinched Melli's cheeks hard. "There, that'll do the job for now."

"How dare you pinch me!" Melli attempted to slap Mistress Greal, but she was not fast enough. The woman caught Melli's arm.

"Come, come, deary, there's no need for this. Let us adjourn for a sup, it'll calm your nerves. You're far too highly strung if you ask me."

"I will not go and sit in that wretched tavern again."

Mistress Greal showed her sharp, uneven teeth. "Come along, deary. You can't stay in your room. Keddi's got to clean it up." She guided the reluctant Melli out of the room, and practically forced her down to the tavern.

Once again Mistress Greal insisted they sit at the center table. It was early evening and the tavern was much busier than it had been when Melli was there the day before. It seemed to Melli that as they sat down, all eyes were upon her. Mistress Greal duly noted this and said: "See, these men appreciate a pretty girl when they see one." She waved and greeted many of the men. "I don't think we'll have to buy our own drinks this evening." Melli did not know what her companion meant by that remark, until a group of several men approached their table, one of whom she recognized as the man she had been introduced to the day before.

"Joy to you, Mistress Greal." Edrad bowed with exaggerated courtesy. "How are you and your lovely companion on this fine evening?" Melli tried hard not to breathe, for when she did so her breasts pushed out alarmingly.

"My dear girl and I are most agreeably well, Edrad," said Mistress Greal inclining her head graciously. "But we are a little dry."

Edrad was immediately penitent. "Oh, please forgive me, ladies. What a thoughtless creature I am!" Edrad called for drinks.

"My girl and I don't care for the rough stuff, Edrad, we want the reserve."

"The reserve it will be, then." Mistress Greal seemed well pleased. "Would you mind if my companions and I sat a while with you charming ladies?" Melli was alarmed to see Mistress Greal willingly agree.

"These are my two good friends, Larkin and Lester." The two men nodded at Mistress Greal and leered at Melli. Edrad then addressed his companions. "And this is the admirable Mistress Greal and her lovely companion Melli of Deepwood."

"Deepwood?" questioned the one called Larkin.

"Yes, Deepwood. It's far south of here, isn't it, Melli?" said Edrad mischievously.

"I've never heard of a Deepwood," persisted Larkin.

"Nonsense, it's just past Highwood." Edrad winked slyly at Melli.

Mistress Greal decided to move the conversation along. "Of course, you can tell my dear Melli isn't from these parts. Who around here has such pale coloring and perfect skin?"

"None that I've ever seen, Mistress Greal," replied Edrad, giving Melli's bosom an admiring look.

"Nor I," agreed Larkin. The one called Lester chose not to speak.

A short time later the drinks arrived, and Melli was glad to have something to divert attention away from herself. She took a deep and unladylike swig of ale. Mistress Greal gave her a warning glance.

"The reserve is strong stuff, Melli. Seeing as you're not used to ale, I would go easy." Melli found a small pleasure in deliberately ignoring the woman's words and taking another deep drink. The action may have displeased Mistress Greal, but it drew cries of pleasure from the men.

"There's a girl!" cried Edrad. "They obviously teach women how to drink like men in Deepwood." Melli could not help but smile. The strong ale was making her feel lightheaded, and she was beginning to wonder why she complained against coming to sit in such a pleasant place. Seeing Melli smile, the men smiled, and seeing the men smile, Mistress Greal smiled.

After a while, Melli began to feel decidedly merry. She laughed at the jokes made by Edrad and Larkin at Lester's expense, and downed more of the reserve. She caught Edrad and Mistress Greal exchanging glances and saw the woman's barely perceptible nod. "You know what you need, my dear?" she said.

"No, what do I need, Mistress Greal?" replied Melli.

"You need a little fresh air. A short walk to cool your face and clear your head." The idea of a walk in the cool, early evening was most appealing to Melli, who was feeling a little flushed and warm. She nodded enthusiastically.

"Will you accompany us, Edrad?" asked Mistress Greal casually.

"It would be my distinct honor." He bowed, and offered her and Melli an arm. The party of three walked to the door, to the great interest of the other tavern drinkers, and left.

The evening was refreshingly cool after the heat of the

tavern. Melli stumbled slightly, finding it difficult to walk straight. The strong arm of Edrad steadied her. After they had walked a short while, Mistress Greal spoke up, "If you two will excuse me, I must pop back to the tavern for my wrap. I seem to have forgotten it. I'll only be an instant." With that she was off.

Edrad took this opportunity to steer Melli toward the stables, and it seemed like a good idea to her. "I'll be able to check on my horse," she said. Edrad smiled and nodded, and guided her into the darkened interior. He then led Melli toward an even darker corner. "I don't think my horse is here," commented Melli, her speech slurring slightly.

"We'll see your horse later," said Edrad as he guided Melli against a wall. He began moving his hand up from her arm to her breast. He leaned forward and pressed his lips against hers. Melli was feeling confused and light-headed. She reluctantly agreed to the kiss, and soon found Edrad's tongue in her mouth. The next thing she felt was his hand squeezing her breast.

"Oh, you're such a lovely one," he murmured as he bent to kiss her breast. Melli was beginning to feel that this wasn't very nice, but her head was lazy with ale and her reactions seemed slow. She was backed up against the wall and Edrad was slavering over her breasts. She felt his warm hand reach under her skirt. Melli was beginning to feel a little panicky: kissing was one thing, but a hand under her skirt was quite another.

Fleetingly she remembered the armed men who had torn her dress. It occurred to her fuddled brain that Edrad was no better than those men. She felt his hand move toward her thigh. She decided she would tolerate this invasion no longer. With all the strength in her body, she raised her knee and violently slammed it into Edrad's groin. Edrad immediately fell back onto the floor murmuring cries of, "Bitch!" and clutching his vitals.

Melli had not expected her blow to be so effective. He seemed unable to retaliate in any way. Pleased with herself, but still confused by drink, she wondered what to do next. She had the distinct feeling Mistress Greal would not be too happy with her. Melli decided that since she was in the stable, she would get her horse and leave. She would even take a saddle—she had no intention of returning to the tavern, so they could keep her possessions as payment for it.

Melli walked past the groaning Edrad and wondered why he was still doubled up and obviously in great pain. Rather merrily she hurried on to find her horse.

After much fumbling in the dark, she located her horse. It seemed pleased to see her and whinnied softly. Melli searched, found rather a nice saddle, and placed it on her horse's back, not concerned too much with fit. She then led her horse out of the stable and, after a few tries, somehow managed to mount him, despite feeling rather dizzy.

She rode as quietly as she could out of town. Before long, however, both her head and her stomach began to feel very unsteady, and she realized she could go on no longer. She guided her horse off the track and managed to find a quiet glade out of sight of the road. Dismounting from her horse, she threw up in the bushes, and fell asleep on the cold ground.

Ten

The great banquet hall was aglow with the light of a thousand candles. The walls were strung with garlands of sweet-smelling winter flowers, and countless silk ribbons hung from the rafters.

Long tables were heavily laden with many foods: four whole suckling pigs, mouths stuffed with peaches; five roasted lambs; two sides of venison seasoned with rosemary and thyme; twenty silver salmon from the Farlands; and a score of lake trout from the east. There were platters of tender sheep's kidneys and plates full of steamed pheasant. There were a dozen varieties of cheeses and huge baskets filled with fresh fruits imported from the south.

There was a great selection of drinks to choose from: for the ladies' fancy, wines and sherries, sweet ciders and aromatic punches. For the men, potent ales and smooth stouts, strong ciders and pungent meads.

The room was full of exquisitely clothed women, wearing high-necked dresses of blue and green and gold, their hair piled high in elaborate curls, and their arms and necks bedecked in jewels which sparkled brilliantly in the candle-light. The men too wore their best, richly colored robes of scarlet and purple. They mingled with the women, bowing and giving gracious compliments, and flirting suggestively.

Servants were adorned in their best liveries, running

around the room, filling cups and plates and attending to the slightest wish of the court. If the guests had been more observant and less drunk they would have noticed many a serving boy slipping sides of salmon and wedges of cheese beneath his tunic.

Winter's Eve festival was only the second most important festival of the year; Mid Winter was usually the most anticipated. But this year, the court at Castle Harvell had much to celebrate: the war with the Halcus was rumored to be going well and, more importantly, the king's health had improved. There was a feeling of hope and excitement in the room. The future of the Four Kingdoms looked bright and the court was eager to celebrate.

The banquet hall was huge and filled to capacity. People had come from the four corners of the kingdoms. There were visitors from Annis and Highwall and envoys from Lanholt and Silbur. All had come to pay their respects and win favor with the queen. The men talked of the war whilst the women talked politics. All who counted were here; they were aware of their importance and basked in the glow of shared privilege.

The wine was strong and heady, and the ladies of court, who normally drank their wine watered, found themselves giggling and merry and ready to dance. The men, noticing this change, grew eager to please, fetching delicate morsels for them to eat, kissing their hands gallantly and escorting them onto the floor.

As the night progressed, the nature of the evening changed. Politics gave way to passion. The music of strings and flutes filled the air; its soft cadences vying with the sound of talk and laughter, enticing people to the dance. The music worked its magic in subtle ways, making the ladies flushed and excited, and tempting the men to make indiscreet suggestions and clandestine assignations.

Later there would be singing, the beautiful Hanella of Marls was to perform songs requested by the queen, songs telling of love and passion and intrigue. Harvell's own great tenor Tarivall would later perform, beguiling the women with his glorious voice and his magnificent bearing. There was said to be five breathtaking women from Isro who would perform the exotic dance of their distant land—dancing naked except for their golden bracelets.

It was to be the greatest and most splendid night of the year. Nothing had been spared: maids had spent months sewing dresses, cooks had spent weeks preparing foods, and servants had spent days hanging garlands. The banquet hall on Winter's Eve was a place of great excitement and captivating spectacle.

Baralis surveyed the room with a cynical eye, noting with distaste the excesses of the evening. Great ladies were acting like tavern wenches, lords were drinking and eating like gluttons, and the lowly gentry were trying to ingratiate themselves with anyone who would listen.

Baralis thought the whole evening was a waste of time and money. He looked at the brightly dressed women and saw vanity and frivolity. He looked at the drunken lords and saw greed and stupidity. The court of the Four Kingdoms was filled with fools!

He would be careful to play his part, though. He would have no one know what dark thoughts nestled in his heart. He caught the eye of one of the court beauties; he bowed gallantly and the absurd creature blushed and giggled. She was far too red of face and big of bosom for Baralis to find her attractive—he preferred young girls, slim of hip and breast. However, he knew he must go along with such charade, and so made it his business to bow and smile to any lady who crossed his path.

Baralis made sure that he spoke to the lords that counted: the ones with great holdings of land, the ones who wielded power at court, and the ones who had influence with the queen. They were all a little uneasy in his presence, but this served only to amuse him. He encouraged his companions to drink heavily, while careful to take only a few sips of wine himself.

He approached Lord Carvell; the man had financial interests in Bren and would prove a useful ally in the months to come. Carvell was in deep conversation with a nobleman from Annis. Fergil of Grallis was both cunning and wealthy.

He had a daughter of Kylock's age, by all accounts a sickly girl with eyes as large as mushrooms. Baralis spoke to Fergil, but his words were intended for Carvell: "Annis does well in keeping its distance from Bren," he said. "Though I doubt if it would fare so well, if it decided to ally with the kingdoms. Bren well likes its position as the mightiest power in the north and may balk at the joining of two of its rivals." Baralis shrugged. "Of course, it might not lead to war. But if it did, the first thing Bren would do would be to seize all foreign assets in the city."

There. That should be enough to put Carvell off listening to any proposals Fergil might make regarding his daughter and Kylock. Carvell might like to politic, but his financial interests would always come first. Sure that his words had hit the mark, Baralis bowed graciously and moved on. Fending off potential brides for Kylock was almost second nature to him. For nearly twenty years now, countless dukes and lords had tried to marry their daughters to the heir to the Four Kingdoms. Baralis counted it among his greatest achievements that none had found their match. As king's chancellor he was perfectly placed for diverting suitors away from the eyes and ears of the court, and if politics didn't work, poison or sorcery always did.

He greeted Lady Helliarna with a kiss to her hand. The old dowager simpered like a virgin. Besides the queen, she was the most powerful woman at court. As her beauty faded, her determination grew, and she had more influence with Arinalda than any other. She also had a son, an interesting boy, whose ambitions equalled her own—they would both be careful to choose the winning side if matters should come to a head.

Not that he had any intention of letting that happen. No, things would go smoothly, but it never hurt to tilt the land in case of rain.

Lord and Lady Hibray acknowledged him with all the aloofness of co-conspirators. It was partly due to them, many years before, that he was made a lord. The good lady had a problem holding her babies till term. Six had been born too soon—four of them sons. He'd helped her out, as only he could, in return for introductions in high places and a bequeathal of one of their many unused titles. It was a fair deal: they had three grown children now—two daughters and a son. Baralis was sure he could rely on their support for his choice of royal bride. If it wasn't given willingly, there was always blackmail to tip the scales.

Lord Vernal had come from the front to attend the celebrations—the battle would go worse for his absence. He was a sound military leader. Baralis made a point of raising his cup in the great man's direction. He might be a good friend of Maybor's, but he had sons and, much like Helliarna, would do what was necessary to secure their positions.

The two knights of Valdis were here. For five years they had traveled between the courts at Harvell and Helch, playing at peacemaking. Their efforts had waned over the past years, and Baralis suspected it was the desire for information not peace that kept them here. The knights were led by a dangerous fool. Tyren was close with the duke of Bren, and he was doubtless using his knights' presence in the kingdoms as a means to feed intelligence to the good duke. Let the knights act as spies; the duke of Bren would hear nothing save reports of stalemate about the war.

Baralis made a mental note to let Lord Vernal in on his suspicions about the knights. It was to his advantage to have the court wary of Bren's interest in the kingdoms. Fear of invasion had helped seal many an alliance.

Baralis managed to catch the eye of the queen and she gave him the most imperceptible of nods. He in return smiled graciously. He could well afford to be gracious; with Maybor and his daughter out of the way, the queen would soon submit to his proposal. He would then be able to influence who Prince Kylock would marry.

He scanned the room for Lord Maybor, but couldn't spot him at first, for the hall was crowded with people. He eventually spied the portly lord. Maybor had managed to surround himself with the pretty daughters of minor noblemen and was currently flirting outrageously and generally making a fool of himself. He was wearing the doctored robe. Baralis smiled, almost sadly. It would not be long before Maybor would begin to feel the sting of the poison at his throat. Maybor would collapse before the night was over, and people would nod and say it was due to immoderate drinking and a weak heart.

After a while, Baralis felt he'd had his fill of court pleasantries and he decided he would retire to a less crowded part of the banquet hall. He made his way to the back of the room where it was darker and there were few people around—save a few couples who were too overcome with passion or drink to notice his presence. It suited him well; he could watch the foibles of the court and not become involved with them.

The assassin was listening hard in the concealed passageway. The evening seemed to have reached the drunken fever pitch that was required for him to perform his task successfully. For the last time he checked his blade, more from habit than anxiety. And then, his face taut with concentration, he stepped out.

The assassin crept from the passageway. The only occupants of the small antechamber were an old man and a young girl, who were both so embarrassed to be caught in such a compromising position that they did not notice from whence the intruder came. The old man was about to speak—probably some excuse. Scarl drew a finger to his lips, halting any speech. He smiled understandingly and encouraged the man to continue with a small gesture of his arm. The old man, much relieved, returned to running his age-marked hands over the breasts of his adolescent companion.

The assassin slipped into the banquet hall. He was momentarily dazzled by the bright light and the noise. He checked carefully to make sure no one was looking his way, then slunk up against the wall. Feeling the brush of tapestries against his back, he made for the deepest shadows. The lords and ladies appeared not to notice the passage of his slight, unassuming figure against the dark recesses of the wall.

As he drew near the back of the hall, the assassin spotted his mark. Lord Baralis was there, dressed in fine, black robes, sipping from a golden cup and watching the revelry of the court with detachment.

Scarl reached the end of the room. Hanging from the

ceiling was a huge satin curtain which would provide cover until he was ready to make his move. With practiced stealth, the assassin crept to the back wall, lifted the rich curtain, and drew himself behind it. His body flat against the stone, he moved level with his mark. He was now a mere few feet directly behind Baralis.

Scarl checked through an opening in the curtain and was pleased to find that apart from two men in the corner—who were so inebriated they could barely stand—Lord Baralis was alone. The assassin's heart thrilled with anticipation. All was as he hoped.

The assassin drew his knife. He lifted the satin curtain. Blade poised in hand, he moved forward.

Lord Maybor realized that he was drunk. He was not just drunk, he was rip-roaring, out of his skull drunk. He was enjoying himself immensely.

Not only had everyone admired the magnificence of his robes, but he had also managed to attract all the young beauties of the court to his side. There is no one like a young girl for being impressed by great wealth and good looks, he thought. Who knew, he might even remarry! He fancied an attractive wife for a change. Of course, the catch was that the pretty ones never had any land—it was always the ugly girls who had the best dowries. Maybor decided that his next wife would be ugly, after all.

Who needed a comely wife when there were so many young poppets willing to jump into his bed and ask no more than a golden trinket or a new dress for the privilege?

Maybor tried to focus his bleary eyes. He was sure the queen had given him a most hostile glare earlier. Never mind, he would doubtless find out what the problem with Her Highness was in the morning, when he had his audience with her. The evening was far too stimulating to be worrying about the dour face of the queen.

He called loudly for more ale. As he did so, he detected a soreness to his throat. He hoped he wasn't coming down with a fever or the pox. He had noticed earlier that he had a certain shortness of breath, but dismissed this as an effect of the ale. The special brew was particularly potent and could easily be responsible for such symptoms.

Maybor had not spotted Baralis all evening. He hoped most fervently that his assassin would not wait much longer before murdering the demon! The thought of the man's imminent death cheered him and he downed more ale, feeling its liquid coolness most welcome on his burning throat. It was time to have some fun.

He picked the most becoming of his companions, a young woman with generous hips and gray eyes. He patted her rounded bottom. "You are indeed a pretty one, my poppet," he said, trying hard not to slur his words. The girl looked at him coldly, but Maybor was not to be discouraged and gently squeezed the curve of her breast.

"Lord Maybor! Please take control of yourself!" admonished the girl, scowling at him. Maybor was oblivious to this warning; he was more interested in feeling the wealth of flesh on her curvaceous posterior. He grinned at the girl and pressed his hand deep into the folds of her dress, grabbing one of her buttocks. The girl spun around angrily and dumped the contents of her cup all over Maybor's face.

"You bitch!" he shouted, looking wildly around for some sympathy. People were either staring at him coldly or openly laughing at him. He looked down at his precious robes, soaked in sickly fruit punch.

He had been humiliated in front of the entire court. He was a laughingstock. He would have to leave the celebration and get out of his sticky, sodden robes. The gray-eyed vixen had ruined them! He would never be able to wear them again. Maybor beat a hasty retreat from the hall, the crowds parting to make a path for the raging, drunken lord.

Baralis was aware there was an incident happening at the front of the hall, but could not make out what it was. Probably some drunken lord making a fool of himself, he thought with contempt.

He was about to bring his golden cup to his lips, when he heard the faint rustle of satin behind him. In that flutter of an instant, he knew what was happening.

Without another thought he wheeled around, unleashing the great forces of his power. He saw a man with a knife about to strike. The man's face filled with terror as the first waves of Baralis' discharge tore through him. He screamed in agony as his eyeballs were scorched by the fury. He dropped his blade and raised his hands to protect his head. It was too late: his face contorted grotesquely as his skin was burnt black by the heat. His clothes blazed into flame and his body became a torch.

The satin curtain caught light and the man staggered back, grasping at a face that was no more. Baralis had no control over the furious forces that he released. He watched grimly as the man's blackened body was consumed by flames.

He felt the backlash of power hit him, searing his skin and singeing his hair. He stepped backward to avoid further damage, and as he did so he was overcome by tremendous weakness. Never before had he released so much power. He tried to draw it back into himself, but it was too late. Trembling and exhausted, impelled only by the sheer force of his will, he staggered away from the blaze.

Bevlin was enjoying a late supper of greased duck when his bowels turned to water. He felt the wave that accompanied the drawing of great power. He dropped his knife, and a trail of grease streaked unnoticed down his chin. The hair on his arms and neck stood up and he shuddered, suddenly cold. He could not remember the last time he had felt the unleashing of such force.

Whoever had drawn power this night was mighty indeed. However, Bevlin perceived the power had failed to be drawn back; it had been allowed to continue and dissipate. The wiseman slowly shook his head: a man who drew such power and failed to repossess it would be so physically depleted, he would be in danger of collapse . . . or worse.

The wiseman suddenly felt very tired. He got up and closed the book he had been reading, then retired to his bed, the duck grease left to slowly congeal. He had lost his appetite.

*   *   *

Maybor was in his chamber. He had relieved himself of his wet and stained robes and was now lying on his bed. He was not feeling very well. Apart from being as drunk as a newt, his throat was burning and he was finding it difficult to breathe. He called feebly for his servant.

Crandle duly arrived. "Yes, Lord Maybor." The servant looked shocked at his master's appearance.

"Why are you looking at me that way, fool? Have I grown two heads?"

"No, sir. You just look a little flushed and there is a slight rash around your face and throat."

"What do you mean, slight rash?" Maybor was finding it harder to speak. "Get me some water, and bring me a sliver of the mirror so I might look on myself."

"Yes, sir." The obedient Crandle rushed off. Maybor brought his hand to his throat—it felt hot and fevered. When the servant returned with the shard of glass, Maybor snatched at it eagerly. He was horrified by what he saw. The skin around his nose and mouth and on his neck was red and inflamed.

"What is this?" he cried, bewildered and distressed by the sight. His servant brought over water, but seemed reluctant to get too close to his master.

"Maybe it's just the drink, sir," he said with little conviction. Maybor drank the cold water and it was like a balm on his painful throat.

"If this is the pox, Crandle, I will have your balls whipped off if you mention it to another living soul." The pox was one thing that everybody at court feared catching; the mere rumor of it was enough to have the unfortunate person ostracized. So whenever anyone did catch it, they kept the fact well concealed.

"I will not breathe a word, sir."

Maybor was beginning to struggle for breath. He motioned his servant to prop up the pillows, thinking that he would feel better if he were sat up. The reluctant Crandle was forced to drag Maybor's heavy body up toward the pillows. Once placed there, his breath came a little easier.

"I will have missed all of the goings-on in the banquet

hall," he complained. "I only had chance to down a jug or two of ale."

"Maybe it was just as well you retired early, sir. You wouldn't have wanted anyone to see you looking as you do." Crandle had not seen the stained robe and was unaware of the true reason for his master's hasty departure.

"Don't be so damned impertinent!" Maybor spoke with little fury as he was finding it difficult to breathe once more. He started coughing, his whole body shaking as he did so. With horror he saw that his undershirt was speckled with blood.

The sight of the tiny, scarlet drops filled Maybor with fear. What illness was this that stole upon one so fast? This very day he had been on his horse, riding over fields, feeling as healthy as ever. Now, only hours later, he was coughing up blood and short of breath. Frightened, Maybor settled down amongst his pillows and fell into a restless, wheezing sleep.

Crope heard a faint noise outside the door. He was in his master's chambers, as was his duty whenever Baralis was absent. He wondered whether to see what the noise was—no one could enter the chambers without Baralis' permission, so Crope was not worried about intruders. It could even be some castle children, the ones who liked to taunt him and follow him around. They might be outside the door, waiting for him to open it so they could throw sour milk at him, as they had done once before. Deciding that the faint noise had indeed been children, he ignored it and went back to looking at his books.

Crope could not read, but his favorite pastime was looking at pictures of flowers and animals. His master, noting the delight Crope took in this particular activity, had given him certain books to keep for his very own. These books, filled with beautifully rendered drawings of plants, insects, animals, and fish were Crope's most treasured possessions. He looked through them countless times, always careful to clean his hands before he touched the precious pages.

Tonight he was looking at his favorite, the one with all

the beautiful flowers in it. He immersed himself in his book, and it was some time before he heard another faint noise. This time it occurred to him that it was too late for children to be up, and so he opened the heavy wooden door. On the floor by his feet lay Baralis.

Crope wasted no time in scooping Baralis up in his arms. He hurried to the bedchamber and, with a gentleness surprising in such a huge man, laid his master down on the bed.

Crope wondered what to do next. He noticed that Baralis was trembling, and so he rushed off for extra blankets. He returned moments later and carefully laid them over his master's body. Next, he fetched water and a length of cloth and proceeded to dab his master's fevered brow with cool water. Crope saw that his master looked as if he was burnt: the skin on his face and hands looked red and sore.

He tried to remember what to do for burns. Baralis, he recalled, had special ointments for such things. Crope went off to look in the library where some such medicines were kept. He returned minutes later with what he hoped was the right ointment. He poured a little on his hand to check. It was some kind of oil and felt smooth and cool. With great care he applied the ointment to Baralis' burnt face and hands. It did appear to lessen the heat a little.

Finally, Crope poured a glass of rich, dark wine into a cup and, holding Baralis' head up a little, poured a small quantity of the liquid between his master's lips. Some of the wine dribbled down Baralis' chin, and Crope patiently dabbed the excess away with a soft cloth.

During all of this his master had not stirred. Crope was beginning to feel worried; he was convinced that there was more wrong with Baralis than burnt hands and face. There seemed little more that he could do. He went over and stoked the fire, and then sat by his master's bedside, once again wetting his brow. He would watch over Baralis through the night and hope his master became no worse.

Eleven

*T*awl made his way down to the harbor. It was chill in the burgeoning dawn and he drew his cloak close. As he rounded a corner, salty air blasted his face, and he sighted the deep gray sea that Rorn considered its own.

Tawl, having reached the waterfront, now made his way north. His route took him past rows of ships and boats; there were many humble fishing craft, a few mighty warships, some elaborate pleasure barges, and a great number of cargo ships. Tawl had never seen such a variety: boats from the south painted exotic colors with pictures of fantastic sea creatures or naked women on their hulls, vessels from Rorn with yellow sails, ships from Toolay beautifully varnished but unadorned.

He soon found himself at the north harbor and hurried down the line of ships, aware that he was late—first light had been some time back. He found the boat he was looking for: two masts, *The Fishy Few*. Men were at work uncoiling the huge docking ropes. *The Fishy Few* was preparing to set sail.

Tawl walked up the gangplank and was immediately met with a harsh cry. "Hey, you, what d'you think you're doing?" The voice belonged to a small, red-faced man with a head of hair to match.

"I'm here to sail to Larn. Captain Quain has already agreed to it."

"Borc's balls! So you're the mad devil who wants to go there." Tawl could only nod. "Come aboard then, quick about it." Tawl boarded the ship. The red-haired sailor looked him up and down critically. "You ain't gonna take to the sea. I can tell that just from looking at you."

"I've sailed before," said Tawl.

"When was that, eh? Dainty pleasure trip down the River Silbur." The man spat in disgust. "No, you're not a sailor. You're the type who'll be puking your guts up as soon as we've raised anchor." Tawl had in fact sailed several times before, and although not enjoying the experience, had never been seasick.

"What you called, then?" asked the man.

"Tawl."

The man spat again. "Tawl! I'd be ashamed to go to sea with a name like that." The man eyed him with mild disdain.

Tawl decided he would ask for the captain. He had no intention of standing here and being insulted any longer. "I'd like to speak to Captain Quain."

"Captain!" shouted the man in a voice so loud it set Tawl's ears ringing. Moments later another man appeared, also red haired.

"You're late." He looked Tawl up and down.

"I didn't realize the north harbor was as far as it was."

"Excuses! The sea doesn't care that for excuses." The captain spat to illustrate his point. "Tell the sea you're late." Quain's voice was scathing. "See if it'll make an exception and keep the tide in a little longer just for you." Tawl was wishing he'd never boarded *The Fishy Few*. The captain then shouted in a voice rivaling that of his crewman in loudness. "All hands on deck."

The ship became a flurry of activity—there were ten crewmen. The captain noticed Tawl counting them and said, "I'm a man short because of you." He was obviously waiting for Tawl to ask why, and so Tawl obliged.

"Why is that, Captain Quain?"

"I'll tell you why. Eleven crewsmen and me, plus you, would make thirteen. No man in his right mind would set sail with thirteen aboard. Sailing to Larn is lunacy itself. Sailing to Larn with thirteen would be suicide. And let me tell you now, boy, gold's not worth losing my ship over. First sign of danger and we'll be heading back to Rorn so fast the seagulls won't be able to shit on us." The good captain then turned on his heel, leaving Tawl to contemplate what had been said.

He decided the best thing he could do would be to go belowdeck. Seeing the man who had spoken to him when he boarded, he asked where he would find his cabin.

"Cabin! Listen to this, mates." The man was now shouting to the other sailors. "He wants to know where his cabin is. Not happy with makin' us sail to the godforsaken isle of Larn, now he wants a cabin. The next thing you know, he'll be asking us to bake him cake." Tawl decided he would take no more of this taunting, but before he could say a word another man chipped in:

"Let him be, Carver, anyone would think you're afraid to sail to Larn."

"I ain't afraid," said Carver defensively. "I've sailed to worse places than Larn in my day, I can tell you."

"Well, if you don't get on securing those ropes, we won't be sailing anywhere." Carver flashed the man a resentful look and moved on about his business. The man then turned to Tawl. "Good day, to you, friend. My name's Fyler. Don't worry none about Carver. He's got a harsh tongue, but nothing more."

"I wasn't worried in the least, Fyler. I was about to tell him I *did* fancy a bit of cake." Tawl grinned at the seaman, who promptly slapped him hard on the back.

"You're gonna do just fine aboard *The Fishy Few,* make no mistake about it. There are two things a sailor needs around here. First, he needs a sense of humor, and second, he needs to know how to swim." Fyler winked merrily at Tawl. "How are you at cooking?"

"I'm not too bad." Tawl wondered about the question.

"Good. We had to lose our cook to make way for you. You can do the honors. Course the good thing about being cook is that you get to sleep in the galley. Have it all to yourself, you can." Fyler smiled broadly, showing gaps among his large, yellow teeth. Tawl got the distinct feeling he had been successfully snared. "Why don't I show you to the galley. The men haven't eaten all day, and there's nothing like setting sail for increasing a man's appetite."

Fyler led Tawl belowdeck, down a narrow corridor and into a tiny room. "This is it, friend," he said. "You'll find the supplies under the table and in the larder. I'm off. Can't sail a ship without its navigator." Fyler left Tawl to the tiny cramped room. It didn't look like any kitchen he had been in. There was just a long, wooden table banded around the edges to keep the various pots and pans in their place and a curious-looking brick stove.

Tawl had no idea how to light the stove and could find no wood to fuel it. The crewmen, he decided, would have to eat a cold breakfast. He looked under the table and found sacks of vegetables in various stages of sprouting: old turnips, carrots and parsnips. Tawl could think of no worse things to be eaten raw. He smiled mischievously. He'd show the sailors of *The Fishy Few* a good breakfast!

Tavalisk was soaking his plump, short-toed feet in a bowl of water. His hands were occupied with cracking open the shell of a huge, live lobster. With a dainty silver hammer he pounded viciously on the shell, eager to get at the tender, translucent meat. He was most annoyed when a knock came at his door.

"Enter," cried the archbishop, venting his anger on the lobster by bashing its small legs off. His aide entered. "Yes, Gamil, what is it?" he demanded testily. The lobster apparently still had some life in it, as it snapped at Tavalisk's fingers with its huge claws. Tavalisk countered this indignity by smashing the lobster's head with all the might in his chubby body, sending flesh and shell flying.

"I thought you might wish to know what has become of the knight, Your Eminence."

"Say your piece, Gamil." Tavalisk noted with pleasure that his last blow had taken the fight out of the lobster: all it could do now was flail its one remaining leg.

"Well, Your Eminence, it appears that our knight has had an early start this morning."

"Yes, yes. Get to the point, Gamil." Tavalisk was now

looking around for the missing lobster legs; he wasn't about to have their succulent meat wasted.

"Well, Your Eminence, our knight has managed to commission a boat."

"A boat! What sort of boat?" Tavalisk decided that one last bash would split the shell open nicely and proceeded to hammer at the lobster once more.

"A small sailboat, two masts. Name of *The Fishy Few*."

"The Fishy Few!" Tavalisk now put down his hammer and with skilled hands prized open the lobster's shell, revealing the grayish, opalescent flesh.

"Yes, Your Eminence. I looked into it. Captain's name is Quain. Ship usually cargoes fish from Marls."

"Marls. How interesting, that's where my little friend here is from." Tavalisk motioned toward the ruined lobster, which was beginning to leak a greenish fluid onto the platter.

"Well, I'm not sure that the boat's heading to Marls this time, Your Eminence."

"You mean it's set sail? With the knight aboard?" Tavalisk was now cutting himself a sizable chunk of lobster flesh, careful to avoid its unpleasant discharges.

"Yes, Your Eminence. It set sail just after first light."

"Which way was it headed?" The lobster flesh was warm and salty. Tavalisk loved nothing better than freshly killed lobster. This one, however, was still alive: its leg continued to move slightly. The archbishop smiled and took up his hammer once more. It was most distracting to see one's meal hanging on grimly for its life.

"Well, Your Eminence, it's hard to tell which way it sailed, but I asked around, and the harbor workers said it was sailing to Larn."

"My, my, how interesting. Our knight has been most enterprising. How do you think he could afford to pay for such a charter?" Tavalisk saw with satisfaction that his last blow had finished the pathetic creature off. He could now settle down and enjoy its flesh.

"A captain would demand a high price to sail to Larn, Your Eminence."

"I'm sure you're right, Gamil." The archbishop now expertly gutted the lobster.

"I have a suspicion, Your Eminence, that the Old Man might have something to do with it."

"I think that would be a fair assumption, Gamil. But why would the Old Man want to help our knight?" Tavalisk cut into the succulent tail, mouth watering in anticipation. "It's probably that damned nuisance Bevlin again. He has no taste when it comes to friends. Probably asked the Old Man to keep an eye on his young knight."

Tavalisk felt something sharp bite into his tongue, followed by the distinct—but not unpleasant—taste of blood. It was a piece of shell. The cunning crustacean had got revenge from the grave! "Gamil, do we have any spies on Larn?" Tavalisk was now stuffing his mouth with lobster tail. His blood acted as a fair seasoning.

"No one has spies on Larn, Your Eminence."

"Oh, how disappointing," commented Tavalisk between mouthfuls of tail meat.

The archbishop drained a cup of light wine. "Tell me, Gamil, did you feel anything unusual last night?"

"What do you mean, Your Eminence?"

"I felt something. It woke me." Tavalisk now pulled the remaining leg off the lobster and sucked the flesh from it.

"What did you feel, Your Eminence?"

"I think it was the aftermath of a drawing. Must have been a damned powerful one. Only a few weeks back I felt something similar—may have come from the same man." Tavalisk was now using his teeth to pry out the remaining meat from the leg. "I'd like to find out who was responsible for it. The man capable of such forces would be a useful person to know. See to it, would you, Gamil?" Tavalisk surveyed the lobster for the presence of any meat he might have missed. Finding nothing left, he turned his attention to a bowl of cherries at his side.

"If you'll excuse me, Your Eminence, I will be off. I have much to attend to."

Tavalisk's eyes narrowed sharply. "Ah, before you go, Gamil, I wonder if I might trouble you to clear up this little mess I've made with the lobster. I know how you like to keep things clean and tidy."

*   *   *

Melli was shaken violently awake. Hands picked her off the ground and stood her up. The sound of Mistress Greal's voice rang through the air:

"Yes, Master Hulbit, that's the little thief." Mistress Greal then stepped forward and slapped Melli sharply on her cheek. Melli was prevented from retaliating by the firm hold of Master Hulbit, the tavern keeper. She realized that she was freezing: she had fallen asleep in the middle of a field wearing nothing but a flimsy dress. Master Hulbit twisted Melli's arm cruelly and guided her in the direction of the road. She was brought level with Mistress Greal, who gave her a venomous look. Melli ignored her and asked Master Hulbit where her horse was.

Before Master Hulbit could answer, Mistress Greal jumped in. "You haven't got no horse now, young lady. That horse has been confiscated by Master Hulbit to pay for the debts you incurred by staying in his tavern."

"I incurred no debts!" said Melli angrily. "I stayed at the tavern as your guest, Mistress Greal." Mistress Greal slapped her again.

"You little trollop!" she cried, and then, appealing to Master Hulbit. "Have you ever met such a bare-faced liar? My guest, indeed! You're in real trouble now, my girl, I can tell you that. Running away without paying your bill, blatantly taking one of my dresses and stealing a leather saddle. And to top it all off, you assaulted one of Master Hulbit's good customers."

Melli couldn't believe what she was hearing, all the lies that Mistress Greal was making up. Melli appealed to Master Hulbit: "It is Mistress Greal who is lying. She took my dress away and tore it up. She forced me to wear this. And as for that man last night, he assaulted me! I was only trying to stop him putting his hands all over me. Please, Master Hulbit, you must believe me." The tavern keeper seemed impervious to Melli's plea.

"I've known Mistress Greal for many years, girl. She's a friend of mine, helps considerable with my business, she does. If she tells me you're a liar and a thief, I believe her."

Melli watched as Mistress Greal threw the tavern keeper an approving look.

Melli was led to the roadside, where to her relief she spotted her horse. Mistress Greal's sharp eyes did not miss Melli's expression.

"I've told you, young lady, that horse is now the property of Master Hulbit. And what's more, not only do you owe me for that dress you've ruined, but you're going to have to answer to Edrad; it was his saddle you stole." Mistress Greal walked off, heading toward the village and leaving Melli to Master Hulbit.

Melli was shivering violently, chilled through. She wondered what could have possessed her to fall asleep in a field in winter. She was also feeling rather sick, and this time she recognized the symptoms of too much to drink the night before. Seeing her shivering in a thin dress, Master Hulbit gave her his horse blanket with which to cover herself. The kind gesture had the effect of making Melli want to cry—it seemed she had met with nothing but cruelty since leaving Castle Harvell.

Master Hulbit noticed the tears well up in her eyes and patted her shoulder lightly. "There, there, young'un. It's not that bad. I've taken your horse in payment, and if I do say so myself, I've got a bad deal. That's one sorry looking animal." Melli didn't know whether to be indignant or to laugh. It was true: her horse *was* old and worn out. "See, there's always something to smile about. I'll make sure Mistress Greal doesn't eat you up for dinner. You only took her for one dress. I'll let you work in the tavern to help pay it off. Of course, the saddle's another matter. It's a serious crime to steal a man's saddle, but I'm sure Edrad will deal kindly with you."

Melli thought it was most unlikely that Edrad would deal kindly with her. She had hurt him badly last night, she remembered. So badly that he couldn't even stand up. Not to mention the obvious blow to his pride at his advances being rejected. Melli dreaded having to face him again. She did not appear to have any choice in the matter; kind though Master Hulbit was, he obviously had no intention of letting her go.

Master Hulbit still had a tight hold of Melli's arm. He

took the reins of her horse and they walked the short distance back to the town of Duvitt. Melli was surprised at how near they were; she was sure she had ridden longer last night. She supposed the drink had clouded her senses. She counted the days since she'd left the castle, then wished she hadn't: thirteen wasn't a good sign.

Once they arrived at the town, Mistress Greal appeared and took over once more, guiding Melli into the tavern, where, to Melli's horror, she came face-to-face with Edrad.

"So you managed to find the little tart, Mistress Greal," he said, giving Melli the full benefit of his menacing stare.

"Farmer Trill spotted her horse this morning, Edrad," replied Mistress Greal. Melli noted there was someone else present, someone whom she had never seen before. The man spoke:

"Please if you would, Edrad, recount to me the events of the previous evening." Melli concluded from his rather pompous air that he must be Duvitt's magistrate.

"Certainly, sir. This young woman asked me to go with her for a walk. It was a fine evening so I foolishly agreed. She then lured me into the stables by promising me a kiss; the next thing I know she'd drawn out a knife. She threatened to stab me if I moved. I wasn't about to let a mere wisp of a girl get the better of me. But before I could make my escape, the little viper kicked me hard in the privates. Then she stole my saddle." Melli had to admit, Edrad sounded convincing.

"Are there any witnesses?" asked the magistrate, sweeping the room with his eyes.

"I was there when the little hussy asked Edrad for a walk. I also heard her promise him a kiss." Mistress Greal gave Edrad a conspiratorial glance.

"Well, as the young girl was found in possession of the saddle and did indeed leave without paying her bill, I can only presume her guilt." The magistrate was obviously pleased with the outcome. Melli could bear it no more.

"They are lying!" she cried. "It was Edrad who lured me to the stables. He kissed me against my will, that's why I kicked him."

"See!" shouted Mistress Greal. "The little hussy admits

it; she has no shame. If you don't mind me saying, sir, I think you should deal most harshly with the girl. Although young, she is obviously a practiced liar and a hardened thief."

Melli couldn't believe this was happening to her. How could the magistrate take their word against hers? She wondered with dread what her punishment would be.

The magistrate coughed loudly and spoke again, "I can see you speak the truth, Mistress Greal. The girl is obviously a bad seed. Master Hulbit has agreed to take her horse in payment for the tavern bill; however, I feel the girl must be punished. We must beat the evil from her. Not only must she pay a fine of five golds, she will also be flogged twenty times, in full public view in the town square." The magistrate looked to Mistress Greal and Edrad, both of whom looked satisfied with his pronouncement.

"It is a fair sentence, magistrate, very fair," said Edrad.

"Will she be flogged with a leather or a rope?" asked Mistress Greal.

"I think the rope will prove most unpleasant, don't you agree, Mistress Greal?"

"You are most wise, magistrate. The sting of the rope will certainly force the evil from the girl." Mistress Greal looked pleased. "Though may I be so bold as to make a suggestion?"

"Certainly, Mistress Greal, I value your judicious opinion in all matters."

"Perhaps the rope should be soaked in salted water first. We wouldn't want the girl's punishment to be a half-measure, would we?"

"Wise as ever, Mistress Greal," said the magistrate. "Now, I believe that Master Hulbit has said the girl can work in his tavern to pay off any fine?"

"He has indeed, magistrate," replied Mistress Greal, shooting a malicious glance in Melli's direction.

"Excellent. After the girl has recovered from the beating, she will be sent back here to work. This has turned out most neatly. She will be flogged at two hours past noon tomorrow. She will be kept in my custody until then." The magistrate turned to Melli. "Follow me, girl, and quick about it."

He led her out onto the street and through the town. Everyone on the streets was staring at Melli, and she hung her head in embarrassment. After a while they approached a stone building. "You'll be spending the night in the pit," said the magistrate. "Let it be a lesson to you."

Jack shifted against his bindings. Pain coursed through his arm and down his back. For the briefest instant, the pain crystallized into something tangible. The pit of his stomach contracted and pressure flared within his head. Even as Jack recognized what it was, it left him. The loaves. It was the same feeling he'd experienced before the loaves. Jack rested his head against the huge oak. There was no doubt now. The loaves hadn't been a lone occurrence. He'd felt power again, and its taste was sickeningly familiar.

He was suddenly afraid. It seemed to Jack as if his fate was now sealed. All his life, he'd lived in a world full of reason: dough rose because of yeast, the longer the rising the better the bread, the larger the loaf the fresher it kept: simple truths that never changed. Now he was in a world where nothing was certain; where burnt loaves turned to dough, where anger or pain could spark the flare of power, and where the future held no promise of peace.

Jack pulled against the rope—there was no give.

The mercenaries had bound him to a tree to stop him from fleeing. They'd ridden hard all morning, heading east in search of Melli, and were now resting their horses. Jack needed water. He had neither food nor fluid all day. And now more than ever, with the metallic tang of sorcery in his mouth, he was desperate for a drink. He called to the guards. One came sauntering over.

"What d'you want?"

"Water, please." Jack's throat was dry and sore. The mercenary kicked him hard on the shins.

"Bit uppity for a prisoner, ain't you." Just as he walked away, the leader, Traff, spoke up:

"Give him some water, Harl. After all, the boy did think

to bring us a few gifts. Right polite of him, if you ask me."
The rest of the men laughed heartily. Traff was referring to
Falk's sack of supplies, which the mercenaries had wasted
no time claiming as their own. It upset Jack to watch as they
greedily tore at the precious food, gnawing on joints of meat
and then flinging them away half-eaten. The dried fruits and
nuts were scattered over the cold ground—the men had no
interest in those.

"And find him half a loaf," said Traff. "If I remember
rightly, it was Winter's Eve last night, and we don't want to
be discourteous to our guest." More laughter followed this
remark. Jack was brought a cup of watered ale and a hunk of
bread.

Winter's Eve. Had he been gone from the castle that
long? Frallit would not be pleased at being a man short for
the second biggest festival of the year. There would have
been scores of fancy breads to be baked: honey cakes, gin-
gerbreads, malted fruit loaves. Normally at this time, Jack's
hands would be stained yellow with saffron. Rare spices
were sprinkled as liberally as salt on feast days. It was Jack's
job to cook the frumenty, which was cracked wheat mixed
with milk, eggs, and saffron. No festival was complete without a plentiful supply of that much-loved golden porridge.

Jack felt so alone. Feast days were the best time to be in
the kitchens: plenty of food and ale, everyone busy and
merry. There'd be joking and dancing and a few stolen
kisses. He missed it all so much. For the first time since leaving the castle, he realized what he'd lost: his friends, his life,
his mother's memory; they were all back at Harvell. He *had*
belonged there. It was his home.

Jack picked up the cup, turning it slowly in his hand.
Ale was dripping from its side. It took him a moment to spot
the hairline crack.

He might have belonged, but he never fitted in. Even
before the loaves he was an outsider. Everyone had something that set them apart: Master Frallit was as bald as a
berry, Willock the cellar steward had a club foot, even Findra
the table maid had to bear the shame of being caught in the
hayloft with the blacksmith. To them, being taunted was part

of being accepted; it was done in good humor and served to *include* rather than exclude the person in question.

For him it was different—the jokes were behind his back, not to his face. Jack took up the cup with his free arm. He noticed his hand was still trembling from what had happened earlier. Was this his fate, then? Always to be excluded, to be set apart, to be an outcast? He flung the cup from him. Let the flavor of sorcery stay in his mouth. It tasted of loneliness, and that was something he'd have to get used to.

"No, Bodger, just because you tumble a wench when it's raining doesn't mean that she won't get knocked up."

"But Master Trout swears by it. He says that it's a sure method to stop a girl from getting with child."

"The only reason Master Trout has never got a wench with child is that no sane woman would ever let him near her."

"He is a bit past it, Grift."

"Aye, Bodger, there's only one method to ensure a wench doesn't get knocked up and it ain't rollickin' her in the rain."

"What is it then, Grift?"

"The way to stop a girl getting knocked up is by making sure you never rollick her in the nude."

"What, the woman?"

"No, you fool, the man. Be sure to always keep your shirt on, Bodger, and you'll never be an unwilling father." Grift nodded sagely to Bodger, and Bodger nodded sagely back.

"It's terrible what happened last night in the banquet hall, Grift."

"Aye, Bodger. By all accounts the fire caused quite a panic. Lords and ladies scurrying like rats, they were."

"I took a look at the damage this morning, Grift. The whole back wall went up in flames."

"Aye, Bodger, I can't help wondering how it started."

"The queen's pronounced it an accident, Grift. Says it was fallen candles that did it."

"It's more than that, Bodger. I had a word with one of the lads who was serving the drinks. He said the whole room moved under everyone's feet, said something knocked people down where they stood, and all the metal cups were hot to the touch. If you ask me, something very nasty happened last night."

"Still, it was lucky that only one man was killed."

"You got a look at the body, didn't you, Bodger? Could they tell who it was?"

"Not a chance, Grift, the poor soul was burnt to a crisp . . . terrible death."

"So no one knows who died, Bodger?"

"No, no one's been reported missing, Grift. There was a drunken squire at the back of the hall when it happened, says he saw a man in black, but no one's paying his story much heed. The only clue is the dead man's dagger. It was found right next to him on the floor. Course the blade was ruined by the heat, but it was the only thing that was left—all his clothes had been burnt off his back. It was horrifying, Grift. I've never seen a worse sight in all my life than that charred and blackened body."

"What sort of knife was it, Bodger?"

"Well, that's the strange thing, Grift. It wasn't a man's eating knife. One of the lords said it was a curious kind of knife to take to a dance."

"There's a lot more going on here than meets the eye. The queen might have pronounced it an accident, Bodger, but I for one can't see anything *accidental* about the way that man died."

Lord Maybor was seriously ill; he had spent the night gasping desperately for each breath.

By the morning his condition was so bad that the physicians and priests were called. Maybor lay on his bed, barely conscious, struggling for air. He was coughing up much blood. The red rash looked much worse; his skin was now raised and puckered. Sores had formed around his nose and mouth, oozing blood and pus.

The doctors did not know what to make of the great

lord's illness. It was like nothing they had encountered before. They immediately ruled out the pox and water fever. It appeared to them that Maybor's windpipe and lungs were being burnt away from within. They shook their heads gravely, not holding out much hope. They prescribed filling the room with the smoke from fragrant woods to penetrate Maybor's lungs and drive out the malignant humors.

Maybor refused to let the physicians fill the room with smoke. Wheezing for breath, he ordered them away. The priests then stepped forward, with their precious oils and waters, sprinkling and chanting, preparing for death.

"Be gone, you damned clerics, I am not dead yet!" Maybor fell back amongst his pillows, coughing feebly, barely able to breathe, but still able to feel pleasure at the sight of the priests scurrying away like rats.

He asked for his sons, but his two youngest had headed off to the front to do battle with the Halcus. Such was the fate of younger sons—they either sought glory in battle or commiseration in the priesthood. Maybor was well pleased that he had raised no priests.

Kedrac entered the room, wrinkling his nose at the putrid smell of sickness. As he saw his father, he attempted, unsuccessfully, to conceal the horror that he felt. "Father, what has become of you?"

Maybor saw revulsion in his son's face and beckoned Crandle to bring the splinter of mirror. Kedrac took the mirror from the servant and would not let his father have it. Maybor had not the strength to protest.

"Father, I spoke with you only a day ago. What has happened since to cause this affliction?"

"I do not know, son." Maybor could only manage a rasped whisper.

"Could poison be the cause of this?"

"Any food or ale consumed by his lordship last night at the dance would have been sampled by many others. I have heard of no one else with any sickness," said Crandle. Both men turned to look as Maybor succumbed to a terrible fit of coughing. When he had finished, the sheets were speckled with blood.

"What do the doctors say?" Kedrac asked of Crandle.

"They do not know what ails his lordship. They advised smoke."

"Smoke! Are they out of their minds? The man can barely breathe as it is."

A soft knock was heard at the door, and the queen walked in. Her cold, haughty face changed when she saw the condition of Lord Maybor and she froze in mid-step. "Is it the pox?" she demanded of Kedrac.

"No, Your Highness," he said bowing. The queen breathed once more and approached the bed.

She saw the look of amazement on Kedrac's face and said in way of explanation, "Your father was requested to meet with me this morning. When he failed to come, I decided to seek him out for myself. I see he is most unwell. What ails him?" Maybor tried to speak for himself, but was overcome with coughing.

"The doctors do not know what afflicts him, Your Highness." Kedrac smoothed his hair and adjusted his clothes.

"Doctors! They are fools, they only made the king worse. I will send you my wisewoman—she is skilled in the lore of herbs. If anyone can help him she can." The queen looked with sympathy at Maybor. "I am well used to sickness, but this I cannot understand. Why, only last night I watched Lord Maybor. He was as healthy as a man can be. Was this caused by the fire?"

"No, Your Highness," offered Crandle humbly. "Lord Maybor left the hall just before the fire started."

The queen gently squeezed Maybor's arm. "I will go now, but I am glad I came. I will send my woman to you the moment I gain my chamber. Good day." She nodded to Kedrac and left the room. The moment she left, Maybor snatched the sliver of mirror from his son. With shaking hand he drew the mirror to his face. Seeing its hideous reflection, he dissolved into a fit of tortuous coughing.

Crope stood vigil as his master drifted in and out of consciousness. He had stayed awake all through the night, watching Baralis' limp form.

Later on, as dawn's first light stole into the room, Baralis had become restless, tossing and turning in his bed. Crope hurried to his side and saw that his master was drenched with sweat and shaking violently. He felt Baralis' brow and found it was hot to the touch. Quickly, he hurried for water to cool the burning, and with a gentle touch he wetted the brow.

Crope looked upon the burns that covered Baralis' face and hands—some of the skin was beginning to scar. Blisters and lesions could be seen, red and inflamed.

Baralis began to murmur words that Crope could not understand. He seemed filled with agitation and flailed restlessly in his bed. Crope felt great fear at seeing his powerful master so overcome. He worried that Baralis would wear himself out with his frenzied motions. So Crope tried to quiet his sleeping master, softly pressing Baralis' arms and legs flat against the bed and covering his body with sheets and heavy blankets.

He felt that his master needed to be able to sleep peacefully to better regain his strength. He could see that Baralis was getting no such peace—he was troubled by an inner turmoil that was allowing his body no rest. Crope decided he would administer a light sleeping draught to his master to help him fall into a more restful sleep. He walked to the library and searched among the various bottles—he'd watched many times as Baralis had taken the draught on late nights, when sleep refused to come. He found what he knew to be the right bottle, for it was marked with an owl on the stopper. Crope loved owls.

He returned to the bedroom and, with large and awkward hands, poured a small quantity of the liquid between Baralis' swollen lips. Crope then returned to his chair by the side of the bed and reached inside his tunic for his box. Just to look at it made him happy. It was beautiful, with tiny paintings of sea birds on the lid. He settled down, turning the little box in his hand, and prepared to watch over his master for as long as necessary.

Twelve

*T*awl was standing on the deck of *The Fishy Few,* staring out at the dark, sparkling ocean. Larn lay two days ahead, and he didn't know whether to be relieved or full of dread.

The harsh voice of Carver startled him from his thoughts. "Hey, you! What d'you think you were doing feeding us raw turnips yesterday. Had me pukin' my guts up all night."

"The turnips didn't make you sick, Carver," shouted Fyler, drawing near. "It's the sea that's finally gotten to you. Nobody born in the mountains makes a good sailor. It was only a matter of time before your true nature showed."

"I was not born in the mountains—it was the foothills." Carver's voice was suitably indignant. "And I was sailing before I was walking. Seasickness! Never had it once in my entire life. It's that boy's awful cookin' that set me off. Turned my guts to jelly." Carver turned his attention to Tawl. "You better watch it, boy. One more trick like turnip and parsnip salad and you'll be overboard before you know it."

"Well, I'm sorry the dinner wasn't to your liking, Carver. Perhaps if someone could show me how to get the stove lit and find me some wood to burn, I might be able to *cook* the turnips tonight."

"I don't want to see another turnip as long as I'm on

this boat. In fact, if I never saw a turnip for the rest of my life, I'd die a happy man. I want some decent food."

"Why don't you catch some fish, then, Carver?" said Tawl ingenuously.

"Can't stand fish." Tawl and Fyler laughed merrily at Carver's pronouncement. "What's a man doing at sea, on a boat name of *The Fishy Few,* who doesn't like fish?" Fyler was enjoying himself. "They must have been pretty high foothills, Carver. You're the only sailor I know who won't eat fish."

Carver was about to issue a scathing reply when another man turned up. He addressed Tawl: "Hey, you. Captain wants a word. Move sharpish—he's waiting in his quarters."

"Probably wants to give you a mouthful over those turnips," mumbled Carver as Tawl walked away.

Belowdeck in *The Fishy Few* was small and cramped. The rooms were so low that Tawl could not stand up straight, and he was forced to walk with his shoulders and neck bent. He knocked on the cabin door and was bidden to enter. He walked into a tiny, dim room lined with books and lit by one small oil lamp.

The captain looked at Tawl disapprovingly and told him to sit. When Tawl had done so, Captain Quain poured out two cups of rum. "Best rum in the known lands, this, boy," he said, handing it to Tawl. "Better be careful not to down it in one go. I don't want to have to answer to the Old Man if you fall overboard." Quain gave Tawl a scornful look.

"I believe you were well paid to carry out this charter, Captain Quain," said Tawl. "No man forced your hand. It was your choice to sail to Larn."

The captain appeared to ignore Tawl's words and took a slug of his rum, taking time to appreciate its flavor. "The test of a good rum is not how strong, but how mellow it is. Only the best rum has a taste so rich and smooth that it conceals its true potency. Go ahead, try it."

Quain beckoned Tawl to drink. He took a mouthful of the rum, wondering if the captain had heard what he'd said. Tawl's thoughts were diverted, however, when the heady liquid met his palate. He wondered how Quain could call this drink mellow; to Tawl it was fiery and strong.

The captain smiled, noting his companion's reaction. "The first taste is always a surprise. Take another sip, and no rushing this time—let the rum dance upon your tongue." Tawl took a second mouthful, pausing to appreciate the flavor before swallowing. He began to comprehend that the rum *was* in fact mellow; it was as smooth as late-summer honey. It warmed his mouth and his innards, and loosened the tension in his brow.

"Now you're getting the hang of it. Go easy, though, it's powerful potent." Tawl decided to heed the captain's advice and reluctantly put the cup down. "No self-respecting captain would dare set sail with less than four barrels of rum aboard. It's well known that a sailor can go months without a sight of land, weeks without fresh food, and days without fresh water, but stop that sailor's ration of rum for a day and you'll have a mutiny on your hands." Quain's eyes twinkled in the dim light. Tawl found it hard to tell if he was speaking the truth or joking.

The captain took another slug of rum and eyed Tawl speculatively. "You said before, I had a choice about sailing to Larn. I can tell from your words that you don't know Rorn very well." Quain poured himself more rum and then continued, "There are two people who count in Rorn. Forget the old duke and his nobles; even Gavelna, the first minister, is merely a figurehead. The people who really count are the archbishop and the Old Man. It doesn't do to cross either of them if you value your life.

"Now, when a crony of the Old Man's comes to me and asks me real nice, if I'd be so kind as to sail my boat to Larn, I'm not about to refuse. Sure, it's all amiable. They even see I'm well paid, say I'll be recommended to the right people. But what they and I both know is that I can't refuse. I can't afford to upset the plans of the Old Man. My business relies on word of mouth and, if I might say so, my own good reputation. If I was to refuse a favor to the Old Man, I might as well sail off into the sunset and never return." Quain drained his cup and looked Tawl straight in the eye.

Tawl was beginning to realize he had misjudged the man. "Captain Quain, I had no idea of the position you were in."

"Don't get me wrong, boy. I don't mind heading to

Larn. I've sailed this ship through waters more treacherous and shallow than any Larn has to offer. But Larn's more than just dangerous water. My crew has heard tales of Larn—tales to set your hair on end. Now I can't say if these tales are true, but what *is* real is the effect on my crew. They're all feeling a little edgy, though they won't admit it, and a nervous sailor is a bad sailor. That's what I'm worried about, boy, not the island itself." Quain downed more rum.

Tawl was beginning to feel a little guilty for feeding the crew raw turnips.

As if reading his thoughts, the captain said, "Here, boy, get someone to light the stove. I'll eat no more raw turnips. Ask Fyler to bring up some decent stuff from the hold and tell him Captain Quain says no hoarding. I'm sure he was *one* sailor who ate better than turnips yesterday." Quain motioned to Tawl to finish his cup of rum. "Don't rush it, boy. Rum's for savoring not for gulping."

Melli wished with all her heart that she was back at the castle. Surely marrying Prince Kylock could be no worse than this.

Following yesterday's trial, the magistrate had first led Melli into a small room, where he'd then insisted on searching her. Melli grew hot with anger as his hands lingered excessively over her legs and buttocks. It was obvious she was hiding nothing there! The magistrate had taken this particular duty very seriously, though, mumbling words to the effect that Melli might have a weapon concealed anywhere on her person.

When the magistate was satisfied that Melli had no hidden weapons on her, he led her back out onto the street. To Melli's surprise a small crowd had formed. As she walked down the street, people started shouting names at her. They called her a whore and a thief. One of them threw an egg at her, and then someone else threw a rotten cabbage.

Melli could bear no more, and so she spoke to the magistrate: "Unhandle me. I will no longer be treated as a common criminal. I am Lady Melliandra, daughter of Lord Maybor." She held her head high.

"Be quiet, you stupid girl. Do not make things worse for yourself with foolish lies. You are a common trollop, that much is obvious to me." The magistrate then twisted Melli's arm nastily and proceeded on.

Their destination was the town square. The crowd gathered round as the magistrate pronounced Melli's evildoings to the crowd: "This girl here, known as Melli of Deepwood, is guilty of the crimes of robbery, assault, prostitution, and deceit. She is sentenced to twenty lashes with the rope. The sentence will be duly carried out at two hours past noon on the morrow." The small crowd jeered at Melli. The magistrate then marched her a short distance, and with no warning pushed Melli into a deep pit.

Melli fell badly, landing hard on her shoulder and side. Pain burst through her shoulder and pelvis. She looked upward and was greeted by the sight of the crowd gathering round the top of the pit peering in. They seemed well pleased that she had taken a bad fall.

"Serves the dirty little thief right," called one woman.

"That'll teach her to go around stealing horses."

"A good whipping is just what her kind needs."

"It will show her we don't take kindly to filthy whores in our town."

Melli was almost positive the last voice belonged to Mistress Greal. Before she could confirm her suspicions, she was met with a barrage of rotting vegetables and meat. Most of the objects were smelly but soft, until someone started pelting her with turnips. Whoever it was had a good aim, and Melli was forced to shield her face from the barrage.

This action delighted the vicious crowd and only served to increase their enthusiasm. Someone dumped a large quantity of sour milk on her head, and then she was bombarded with crab apples. There was nothing Melli could do: she was trapped. She hung her head low and prayed that no one would start throwing rocks. After a while the crowd began to either lose interest or run out of things to throw. They slowly withdrew, with shouts of "whore!" and "thief!" on their tongues. Someone threw one last thing: a large melon. It landed right on her tender shoulder. Melli winced with pain.

She looked up to find the crowd had left. Tears welled

in her eyes. Her body was battered and bruised, and she was terrified at the thought of being beaten. Everyone had believed what Mistress Greal had said. They even seemed to believe more—she had not stolen a horse, or been a prostitute.

Melli tried to remove what she could of the rotten vegetables, brushing slimy cabbage leaves and moldy fruit from her dress. There was nothing she could do about the smell.

She looked around her grim surroundings. The pit was about two times the height of a tall man and barely wide enough for Melli to lie down. The walls were smoothed stone and the bottom was cold earth. Judging from the amount of vegetation in various stages of decay, the pit must have been used often. Melli tried to move her shoulder a little and pain shot through it. She managed to curl herself up in a ball and sobbed herself to sleep.

She was wakened several hours later by the shouts of men. Night had fallen while she slept.

"Hey there, missy! How's about flashing us your udders."

"Give us a look at your melons, or we'll throw our ale all over you." Melli could only stare wildly at the men.

"Little bitch! I expect she's only willing to do it for money."

"Dirty whore!" With that the men dumped the contents of their jug of ale over Melli's head. "Waste of good ale, if you ask me." Melli shivered as the ale soaked through her clothes.

The men obviously found the sight of Melli soaked hilarious and they laughed merrily. One of the men was carrying a lit candle, and as he held it over the pit, hot wax dripped on Melli's bare arms. The men were oblivious to this, and Melli felt it best not to speak out in case they decided it would be a good way to torture her further. The men, having run out of ale, soon moved away. Melli breathed a deep sigh of relief.

She was freezing, the night was cold, and she wore, thanks to Mistress Greal, the flimsiest of dresses. Now, to make matters worse, she was soaking wet. Every inch of her body ached: the turnips and crab apples had been thrown with cruel precision, and Melli's body was now a mass of bruises. Her most serious problem was her left shoulder. Tentatively she ran her fingers over the soreness. There was some swelling, but she could detect no broken bone.

As the night drew on Melli became colder, her body shivering. Eventually she fell into a fitful sleep, her body curled into a tight ball to keep warm.

In the morning she was wakened by someone pouring something foul over her head. Mistress Greal stood above her, carrying her now empty chamber pot. "That won't be the worst that happens to you this day, missy! You ungrateful little tart." Mistress Greal then turned on her heel and walked away.

Melli had spent the rest of the morning being cruelly insulted and having the remains of people's breakfasts thrown at her.

She knew she was due to be flogged this day, and her stomach fluttered with fear at the thought of the rope. She could think of no way out of it. She had attempted to tell the magistrate who she was, but in her current state not even her own father would recognize her. Melli suddenly wished very badly that she was with her father now. It was true he had slapped her and tried to force her into marrying someone she didn't want to, but he had loved her. She had been his precious daughter. He had bought her anything she wanted and delighted in seeing her dressed up and looking pretty. What a shock he would get today, she thought.

The time passed very slowly. Every minute seemed to drag on interminably. She was terribly thirsty, for she had not drunk anything in over a day. She was not hungry, though; the terrible, putrid smell of rotting vegetables kept her appetite in abeyance.

Melli noted with growing trepidation the angle of the sun in the sky. It was already noon: soon they would come and flog her.

Jack was thinking about Melli. He was worried that the soldiers who had caught him would soon capture her. Earlier, they had ridden through a small village. The horsemen had been met by hostile stares from the villagers. Traff, the leader, had asked one of the women if they had spotted a girl heading east, away from the forest. The woman's tongue had been successfully loosened by two silver coins.

"Yes, there was a girl, right odd-looking creature. Dark haired, like you said. Wearing a sack she was." The woman's eyes narrowed as she assessed the situation. "I felt sorry for the poor girl. I told the sweet thing she'd be better off in Duvitt."

"How many days back?"

"Oh, I can't be sure, maybe four or five days ago."

"How far is Duvitt?"

"Oh, about half a morning's ride east. Can't miss it, all roads lead to Duvitt around here."

They had sped from the village, riding much faster than before since they were now on open road. Jack did not get to see much of the change in territory from forest to farmland because of his position strapped over the horse's back. He *could* see that the road was wide and well maintained—a sign of large population and prosperity. The place they were headed for was obviously a wealthy town.

He fervently hoped that Melli had decided not to stay in Duvitt for any length of time. It seemed certain that if she were in town this day, she would be picked up by Baralis' men. They rode on toward Duvitt.

A rope was being lowered down to Melli. "Grab hold!" came a harsh voice. Melli found the idea of being dragged out of the pit by a rope very distressing. She didn't know if her shoulder could take the strain. A thought occurred to her: if she didn't grab hold of the rope, they wouldn't be able to haul her from the pit, and so they wouldn't be able to flog her. She refused to take the rope, shaking her head stubbornly.

"If you don't take hold of the rope, you little tart, I'll make sure your whoring days will be over for good." Melli still refused to take the rope. "Look, missy, I'll give you one last chance: take the rope or I'll get Master Hulbit to heat up some chicken fat, and I'll pour it all over your pretty face. Now move it!"

Melli grabbed for the rope. Pain coursed through her shoulder and hot tears prickled in her eyes. She took the rope and wound it around her waist, holding on tightly to the slack. She braced herself, gritting her teeth and then felt the pull. The skin of her arms scraped against the stone as she was pulled from the pit. The pain in her shoulder was unbearable. Once her head was level with the ground, two men grabbed her arms and hauled her out. Melli felt herself about to faint from the pain and she struggled to control herself. She had her father's pride and was determined not to give the crowd the satisfaction of seeing her swoon like a giddy maiden.

She looked around. There was a much larger gathering of people in the town square than the day before. The crowd hissed as Melli looked at them. The cries of "whore!" and "thief!" had little effect on her now and she ignored them. The crowd, seeing what they took to be arrogance, grew nasty. They hissed and shouted vile insults. One man, who called her "a pox-ridden trollop," she recognized as Edrad. Despite great discomfort, Melli could not help but smile at the irony. This, as far as the mob was concerned, was the worst thing she could have done.

"The brazen hussy!"

"The little bitch is pleased with herself." Melli was once again pelted with rotten fruit and vegetables. The men who held her shouted at the crowd to stop, for they themselves were being bombarded.

The two men led her into the middle of the town square. A wooden scaffold had been erected. One of the men pushed Melli forward so her back was to the crowd. He took hold of her arms, bringing them up level with her shoulders, and tied her wrists to the scaffold.

Melli was beginning to feel scared. She could no longer see the crowd but she could hear their taunts and jeers. As soon as the man backed away from the scaffold, the pelting started once again. Melli bit her lip in pain as hard objects were hurled at her back and legs. Her arms, spread out as they were, put great strain on her sore shoulder. Despite all of this, the worse thing to Melli was the wait.

No one seemed in any hurry to start the flogging. Melli

supposed that being tied to the scaffold at the mercy of the crowd was part of the punishment. The mob called to her, heckling and insulting. She could feel the excitement of the people: they wanted a good show, they wanted blood.

The crowd suddenly became silent. Melli strained her neck to look around. The magistrate had appeared, walking with a man who carried a rope whip. It was no delicate riding whip—it was thick, coarse and stiff, with a knotted end. Melli shuddered and the crowd cheered.

The magistrate began to speak, telling the people once more of Melli's various crimes. With a dramatic flair the magistrate listed each crime individually, allowing suitable time for the crowd to hiss between each one. The list seemed longer today; it now contained the charge of horse thief and swindler. By the time the magistrate had finished the list, the mob was in a frenzy:

"Whip the bitch!"

"Take the skin off her back."

"Show no mercy."

The magistrate then pronounced her sentence: "Thirty lashes with the rope!" The crowd erupted into a fit of cheering.

It had been twenty yesterday! Melli grew stiff with fear. The man with the rope whip was now showing it to the admiring crowds, holding it above his head so small children and those at the back could see. He then silenced the crowd by bringing the rope down to his waist, catching the knotted end in the palm of his hand.

He moved forward to the scaffold, his shadow falling over Melli's back. The crowd seemed to hold their breath. Melli tensed in preparation for the blow. The man drew the whip back, paused for the tiniest instant and then brought the rope down on Melli's back. She heard the crack before she felt the blow. Melli convulsed with shock and pain. The crowd *aah*'d in appreciation. The magistrate started the count:

"One."

The whip was drawn once more and brought down with terrible force upon Melli's back. The rope knocked the wind from her body and tore at the fabric of her flimsy dress.

"Two."

Tears of pain flowed down Melli's cheek. The man flexed the whip, bringing it high above his shoulders and lashed cruelly at her slender back. This time rope met flesh.

"Three."

The whip was up again, and down it came once more, welting Melli's tender skin. The first pinpoints of blood were drawn.

"Four."

The rope dug deep, raising skin and tearing flesh.

"Five."

Melli felt the sting of the rope and then the warm trickle of blood down her spine.

"Six."

Just as the whip was drawn again, a disturbance in the crowd distracted the man from his action. Melli was too weak to care.

The sound of hooves ringing on stone could be heard; the horsemen pushed through the crowd. The magistrate was livid about the interruption. "Who comes here?" he demanded. "Be off and do not disturb this flogging any longer."

"If you don't untie the girl this instant," came a cold, deadly voice, "I will order my men to slice these good people to ribbons."

"You wouldn't dare," said the magistrate with little conviction.

"Wesk, Harl," the voice called and two of the mounted men urged their horses forward. They were both wielding long swords. The crowd was now scared. None moved.

"Do as he says, untie the girl," murmured the magistrate.

The man tucked the whip in his belt and came forward, cutting the ties on Melli's wrist with a knife.

Released from the scaffolding, she could barely stand. She swooned and stumbled. She was weak with pain and her back was on fire. Dazed, she looked up and saw the leader of the armed men come forward. Melli recognized him as the man who had ripped her bodice in the woods. She was confused. He smiled grimly, grabbed her firmly in his strong arms, and scooped her up on his horse. Melli could hold out no longer; her world became black as she passed out.

Thirteen

*B*aralis lay in his bed. The past few days had been the worst of his life. He had come close to death. He was only now recovering a little of his strength. He had tossed and turned in his bed, sweating and weak. Unable to think clearly, he had been tormented by images and demons, and his body could find no rest.

He had been badly burned, but that was not the worst of his injuries. He had made a dreadful mistake. The moment he knew the assassin was upon him, he lashed out with all the power in his body—a reflex action of survival. There had been no calculation, no moderation; he had drawn his power with no thought except to obliterate the threat to his life. So furiously did the power flow through him, he could gain no control over its frenzy.

In the instant that he realized he had drawn too much from himself he tried to draw back, but it had been impossible. It was too much, too furious. It had a will of its own. Baralis could only watch the effects. He'd done something no master ever should: he lost control. Everything in him had been drawn forth. There had been nothing left, all his strength had been used in the drawing. He was left expended. If it had not been for the care of his servant, Crope, he might have died.

He'd made a mistake a novice would have been

ashamed of. All the years of training in his youth was under-lined by one basic principle: never outreach yourself. He could remember even now his teacher's hand upon his shoul-der: "Baralis, you have a gift and a curse," he said. "Your gift is your ability, your curse is your ambition. You draw too wildly. There is no temperance, and one day you will pay a high price for your boldness."

They always tried to hold him back, they were envious of his talents. Who were they but a few old fools who defied convention by setting up a school to teach sorcery? They wanted to bring people around to the idea that magic wasn't all bad and that Borc had been wrong to condemn it. The only reason they were allowed to go on for so long was that Leiss was a city that prided itself on its liberalism. Of course, all that had changed now.

So close to the Drylands, it took a farmer of genius to coax crops from its soil. Genius, and a little sorcery in his fa-ther's case. He'd come from a long line of successful farm-ers, their skills defying the thin soil that Leiss rested upon. Like savages, they married close: a half-sister, a distant cousin, a stepdaughter, it all served to thicken the mix. Sor-cery was instilled in their blood, and the poor simpletons hadn't even known it—they thought it was skill alone that nourished the grain.

His mother had known differently, though. Too clever by far for a farmer's wife, she had seen the truth behind the record crops. She had seen the potential in him, too, and had sent him to the one place in the Known Lands where he could be trained.

Yes, he'd been lucky to be born in that once liberal city. If it wasn't for his training, he wouldn't be here today, King's Chancellor. His teacher was wrong: ability *and* ambition were his gifts.

He'd traveled far and wide to learn all the skills that were now in his possession. In the Far South they'd taught him how to command animals and make them his own, from the herdsmen of the Great Plains he'd learnt his skills with potions, and beyond the Northern Ranges he'd discovered the art of leaving his body and joining with the heavens. Many cities had he visited, many people had he talked to, many manuscripts had he read: no one in the Known Lands could match him.

But Winter's Eve had proved he wasn't infallible. It would have been easy to eliminate the assassin with much less power, leaving himself with nothing more than a moderate fatigue. Instead he'd been unconscious for two long days before his mind returned to him. Sorcery took its power from the essence of a man: from his blood, his liver, his heart. To perform even the simplest of drawings made one weak for several hours. To perform a drawing of the scale he'd done on Winter's Eve could drive a lesser man to madness or oblivion.

Baralis could not help but wonder at the power he had drawn. True, it had been dangerous to himself, but the feeling of strength coursing through his body—fast and terrible—had filled him with elation. He had not known he had such potential in him. Once he was fully recovered, he would put his newfound abilities to good use. He would be careful, though, never to put himself at risk again.

He had much to do, much he needed to find out. He could not afford to let fatigue hinder his plans. He called for Crope.

"Yes, master." His servant entered the bedchamber.

"Crope, you have looked after me well and I thank you for your care."

Crope smiled, the many scars on his huge face pulling tight. "I did my best, master," he said, pleased that his efforts had been appreciated.

"Now, on to more important matters. How is the court taking the news of Lord Maybor's death?"

Crope looked puzzled at the question. "Lord Maybor isn't dead, master."

"Isn't dead! What devilry is this! Are you certain of what you say, you dim-witted fool?"

"Yes, master." Crope seemed pleased to be insulted. "Lord Maybor isn't dead. But he is powerful sick. People are saying that his face is covered in sores and he can't breathe very well. The priests were even called."

Baralis could not understand it. The poison had been lethal. He had tried it out on an old horse and it had killed the pathetic creature in a matter of hours. "When did Lord May-bor leave the dance?"

"Everybody's talking about that." Crope paused for a minute, struggling to remember the story. "He was said to have had punch poured all over him by a young girl. He was made a laughingstock and left before the fire started."

It seemed to Baralis that Maybor had the luck of Borc himself. He knew that the poison would have been rendered less potent by having liquid poured over it, and Maybor may have taken the robe off early because it was wet. *Damn him!* Baralis thought for a moment. "Is Lord Maybor's condition improving?"

"I can't say, master. The queen was said to have sent her wisewoman to look after him."

"The queen has visited him?" Surely the queen would want nothing to do with Maybor now that his lies had been uncovered.

"Yes, master. The queen's messenger came here the other day, said the queen wanted to see you as soon as possible."

"How did you reply?"

"I told the messenger that you had caught a slight fever while out riding."

"Good, Crope. You have done well." Baralis paused and then asked: "What are people saying about the fire on Winter's Eve?"

"They're saying it was caused by fallen candles, master."

"Good. Were there any witnesses?"

"One drunken squire said a man in black caused it, master."

"What is his name?"

"I don't know, master."

"Well, find out, then! And once you have found out, arrange for him to have an accident." Baralis' eyes met those of his servant. "Do you understand what I mean, Crope?" The servant nodded. "Good. Now go. I need to be alone to think."

Baralis watched as Crope lurched away. Once he had gone, Baralis rose from his bed. He was surprised at his own weakness; his legs were shaky and unused to his weight. He made his way slowly to his study. Once inside, he hunted among the many bottles and vials until he found what he was looking for. He lifted the stopper and drank the entire contents of the small bottle—he needed all the relief he could get from his pain.

He looked down at his hands, burnt by the aftermath of power. They were scarred, the skin shiny and taut. The curative oils had undoubtedly helped, and most of the scarring would heal. But it was the healing itself he was afraid of. The skin might permanently tighten, making it impossible to straighten his fingers. If that happened, he would be forced to slit the skin at his joints.

A drawing to quicken their healing was out of the question—he was too weak. There would be no sorcery for several days, which meant he would be unable to make contact with the second dove he'd sent to track Melliandra.

Maybor had a lot to answer for. Baralis was almost certain that he had been the one to arrange for the assassination attempt. He had many enemies at court, but none would like to see him dead as much as Maybor. The lord of the Eastlands was no fool; he would have wanted no blood on his hands and would have hired someone to do his dirty work for him.

Baralis had much to occupy his mind. He had to concentrate on bringing his plans to fruition. He must step carefully, for it seemed as if the queen was still sympathetic to Maybor despite his fabrications. He needed Maybor out of the way. He could not risk the queen becoming close with him.

Baralis decided he would not waste any more time trying to poison Maybor. The lord appeared to be almost charmed against such methods. He would arrange instead for his attentions to be diverted from the court. He knew the one thing that Maybor loved more than himself was his eastern lands. They were rich and fertile, planted with seasoned apple orchards from which the best cider in the Known Lands was produced. A curve of a smile stole across Baralis' face: he would arrange for Maybor's attention to be diverted eastward for a while.

* * *

Tawl squinted in the direction that Fyler indicated. "I can't see a thing," he said. Fyler had told him that Larn was on the horizon, but Tawl could spot no sign of it.

"You from the Lowlands, boy?" asked Fyler. Tawl nodded, amazed at how the seaman could know such a thing. The navigator winked and then explained, "People from the Lowlands are known for their bad eyesight. All those marsh gases affect the eyes. It was just as well you left home before they had a chance to do worse damage."

The two men were on the bow of the boat. All day the waters had been growing choppier. A strong easterly wind was blowing, whipping up the waves, causing them to crash mightily against the hull of the small boat. *The Fishy Few,* which for the first two days had seemed so sturdy to Tawl, was now at the mercy of the restless sea.

The crewmen, who had come to accept Tawl's presence, were now grave and silent. All hands were on deck. The sails needed to be constantly turned to accommodate the unruly wind.

Even as Tawl and Fyler stood on deck, conditions were worsening. The sky darkened ominously and the first spits of rain were felt. The wind blew hard and picked up the waves in its path, driving them high and rough. Tawl was forced to hold on tightly to the railing.

"How far before we reach Larn?" he asked. Fyler, who was much more used to the unstable sea than Tawl, stood with his arms folded.

"Well, I'm sure it was on the horizon, only it's gotten so damned dark and nasty that I can't see it no more. I'd say we're half a day away. Course in these sort of conditions it could take a lot longer. The wind is against us. And I don't fancy navigating low waters in a storm."

"How dangerous are the waters around Larn?" Tawl was now having to shout to make himself heard.

"Well, I've navigated worse waters, but Larn's are pretty bad. It's not just the shallows . . . though if you're not careful you could find yourself run aground." Fyler looked to the horizon. "No, the real problem is the rocks. The sea bounces off 'em and becomes unsettled. There's no telling which way the current runs, but one thing's for sure—if you're not careful, it'll run you onto the rocks."

"Captain Quain said he wouldn't take the ship too close."

"Aye, lad. Captain's no fool. Still, it won't be easy. You can see what's happening to the boat already." As if to illustrate this point, the sea swelled suddenly, causing the boat to roll beneath their feet.

"I thought it was just bad weather," shouted Tawl.

"There's always bad weather around Larn, boy. That's the problem. I can navigate shallows and rocks in a calm sea with my eyes closed. Larn's one of those godforsaken places that allows the sea no rest."

"Is is because of where Larn is?"

"No, it's because of *what* Larn is."

Tawl watched as Fyler walked away, marveling at the man's ability to walk so steadily with the boat heaving as it was. Tawl stayed at the bow, the wind and rain driving into his face. He looked ahead, trying to spot the island on the horizon. He could not see it. Something within Tawl knew that Larn was there: it called to his blood, beguiling and inviting. He looked ahead at the bleak gray of sky and sea, and he became afraid.

He did not know how long he stood, blasted by the elements. A sharp voice interrupted his thoughts: "You there! What d'you think you're doing? You'll catch your death there in this storm." Tawl looked round to see Carver. "Best get belowdeck, captain's askin' after you." Tawl realized that he was cold and his cloak was soaked through. The sky was growing darker, the waves higher, and the rain was now driving in sheets against the ship.

"See what trouble Larn brings," muttered Carver as Tawl made his way belowdeck.

The captain's cabin was warm and cozy and smelled of old leather and rum. "By Borc! You're soaked to the skin, lad. What have you been up to?" The captain swiftly poured Tawl a full cup of rum. "Take your cloak off. Here, wrap yourself in this." Quain handed Tawl a rough blanket.

"I was on deck. I didn't realize how long I was there."

"Lost in thought, eh?" The captain gave Trawl a questioning look.

"I was thinking about Larn."

"You're not the only one, boy. Larn's the sort of place that's hard to put from your mind."

"You've been there before?"

The captain nodded. "I came close as a lad and it's haunted me ever since."

"What purpose did you have with the island?"

"No purpose at all, it was my first job as navigator and I was as green as seaweed. We were bound for Toolay, but I was so nervous the ship veered off course." The captain took a deep draught of rum and was silent for so long that Tawl was surprised when he spoke again. "Can't say that I was sorry, though. To this day, I still hold that it was fate, not I, who steered the ship that cold and windy morn." Quain slammed his glass down on the table, effectively ending the subject.

"You'll be there tomorrow. Course if the seas don't calm you've no chance of landing. No one in their right minds would set a small rowboat on these waters. I'm beginning to think I've lost mine coming here with *The Fishy Few.*" Quain lifted his glass. "Come on, lad, drink up. That rum will warm you better than any fire." Tawl obliged the captain, finding his words to be true. The rum warmed him to his toes.

"Once you're on the island, you know I won't wait longer than a day for your return. The waters are just too treacherous. I'm sticking my neck out putting down anchor. If the waters don't calm by the morrow, no anchor will be able to hold her. That's not your concern, though, lad. I just want to make sure there's no misunderstanding. If you're not back within one day, then I'm off. And God help you; you could be stuck on Larn for many months." Quain gave Tawl a hard look.

"There is no misunderstanding, Captain. I've decided I'll go alone—you're one man short as it is. I can row myself." Quain grunted and poured them both another cup of rum.

"Pray for calm waters, boy."

* * *

Tavalisk was taking an afternoon stroll in the palace gardens. The gardens were famous throughout the east for their spectacular beauty. Tavalisk was more interested in what he was eating than the breathtaking surroundings. Walking a few steps behind the archbishop was a liveried servant holding a platter of delicacies.

"Boy, be careful no flies land on the chicken livers." Tavalisk beckoned the boy forward so he could pick what he would eat next. The brisk air had given him quite an appetite. Tavalisk decided on a large, juicy specimen and popped it in his mouth. It was just as he expected—rare and tender.

The archbishop sighed heavily as he noticed the approach of his aide, Gamil. "Come, boy," he said to the servant. "Let us make haste." Tavalisk hurried away in the opposite direction, his voluminous robes flapping in the breeze. "Do not drop the platter, boy," he warned as they turned into a hedged walk. Gamil's feet proved faster than Tavalisk's, and he eventually caught up with master and servant.

"Gamil, what are you doing here? I didn't see you approach. Did you see him approach, boy?" Tavalisk looked to his attendant; the boy obediently shook his head. The archbishop reached forward and took another liver from the tray. "Though I must admit you're difficult to miss in your splendid new robe. Silk, if I'm not mistaken. I didn't realize I paid you so well."

Gamil became a little red of face. "It's nothing, Your Eminence. I picked it up cheap in the Market District."

"Well I'm not at all sure I like my aides dressing better than I." The archbishop could not resist the exaggeration: his robes were by far the finest that could be bought in all of Rorn. "Now tell me why you're here." Tavalisk daintily spat out a piece of gristle.

"About the knight," said Gamil, brushing the offending piece of gristle from his robe. "My spies . . . "

Tavalisk cut him short. "Your spies, Gamil? *You* have no spies. *I* am the one who has spies." Tavalisk's small eyes took in the look of animosity on his aide's face. He pretended not to notice, though, and busied himself picking out another delicacy.

"Your spies have confirmed our suspicions, Your Eminence."

"What suspicions are those?" Tavalisk had now turned to admire a late-blooming flower.

"The Old Man paid for the boat that sails for Larn."

"This is indeed interesting. Do you think the Old Man knows I am having the knight followed?" Tavalisk picked the flower, smelled it, and then threw it away.

"I think he must, Your Eminence."

"His friendship with Bevlin aside, I wouldn't be surprised if the Old Man helped the knight merely to irk me, Gamil." Tavalisk now stepped on the flower, grinding its delicate petals into the ground. "He knows I have no love for the knighthood. Not that the Old Man is their greatest advocate, but he's not averse to doing a little business with them from time to time."

Tavalisk walked off, beckoning his servant to follow. As he had not been excused, his aide was forced to keep up with them. Tavalisk stopped a little later and chose another tasty morsel from the tray. "Oh, by the way, Gamil, what news have you of the drawing the other night?" Tavalisk threw a chicken liver into the air and nimbly caught it between his teeth.

"It appears, Your Eminence, that others felt the ripple of power several nights back. I have spoken with one who knows of these things, and she was certain that the aftermath came from the northwest."

"The northwest, indeed. If I am not mistaken, there is little else in the northwest beside the Four Kingdoms. They have that particularly fertile corner of the world all to themselves." Tavalisk began to feed the sweetmeats to the birds. "How soon can you question my spies about this matter?"

"If anything remarkable has happened in the Four Kingdoms, I will soon know of it, Your Eminence."

"If the incident of a few nights back was Lord Baralis' doing, then I will have to revise my estimation of him, Gamil. Great power was drawn that evening. Whoever is responsible bears watching closely. Power is seldom found in those without ambition." Tavalisk found it was more fun to throw the sweetmeats *at* the birds rather than *to* them. "It is all the more reason to track down his enemies."

"I will know who they are in a matter of days, Your Eminence."

"Good. Before you go, Gamil, may I be so bold as to offer you a piece of advice?"

"Certainly, Your Eminence."

"Red is a most unbecoming color for you. It shows up the pock marks on your cheeks most unpleasantly. I would try green next time, if I were you." Tavalisk smiled sweetly and began to walk back to the palace.

Lord Maybor was beginning to feel much improved. His breath still came in wheezes and his throat burned hot and sore, but he knew he was feeling better when the queen's wisewoman rubbed warm oils into his skin. The wisewoman was not a great beauty, and she had passed her prime some years back; however, when her skillful hands worked on Maybor's body, he began to find her most appealing.

With a firm touch she worked the fragrant oils into Maybor's flesh. She noticed the lord's reaction and smiled pleasantly, showing small, white teeth. "I see you will be up soon, Lord Maybor," she said softly. She leaned over him, her breast brushing against his face. He could not resist and squeezed the roundness gently. The wisewoman smiled on, moving her agile hands lower. Maybor drew more bold and squeezed the breast vigorously.

The woman laughed: a bright, pretty sound. "I do not think, Lord Maybor, that you are quite ready for a tumble yet. Maybe in a few days." Maybor was disheartened; the wisewoman was looking very attractive to him now. "It is a good sign though—when a man's urges return, his good health will soon follow." She stood up and smoothed her dress. "I must be off now. Be sure to drink your honey balm." She patted him lightly on the shoulder and left the room. *There is a lot to be said for older women*, thought Maybor regretfully.

When she had gone, Maybor called his servant, Crandle, to bring him his mirror. Maybor had always been very proud of his appearance; he considered himself to be strong boned and handsome. His greatest fear now was that the terrible sores that blighted his face would leave scars. He regarded his reflection carefully. There seemed to be a slight fading of the redness. His face was hideous; the sores had formed mostly around his nose and mouth. Some of the sores had started to heal, but some were still open and wet. The wisewoman had given him some herbal water, and it appeared to help a little.

He was still contemplating his reflection when Crandle rushed into the room and announced the queen. She followed directly after the servant, her beautiful face pale and unreadable.

"No, Lord Maybor, do not try to rise." She turned to Crandle and bid him leave. The servant scuttled away quietly.

"It is indeed an honor, Your Highness." Maybor was trying hard to keep his voice and breath steady. He did not like appearing ill to the queen.

"I have come this day because I have just spoken with my wisewoman, and she has advised me you are much improved."

"Your Highness was most gracious to send her to me." Maybor succumbed to a fit of coughing. He held his handkerchief up to his lips—he did not want the queen to see he was coughing up blood.

The queen waited until the coughing stopped before continuing, "My wisewoman is better than any physician. I am glad to see her remedies have helped you. You seem much better than when I looked upon you last. I am well pleased."

The queen moved away from Maybor and began to pace the room, her back rigid and her head high. "Lord Maybor, I must ask an unpleasant question and I require a straightforward answer."

Maybor began to feel a little apprehensive. "What would you ask, Your Highness?"

"I would know the truth about your daughter, Melliandra. I have heard say she has run away from the castle." The queen turned and looked Lord Maybor in the eye. "Is this true?"

Maybor instantly realized that if he lied and told her his daughter was in the castle, she would demand proof. He had no choice but to confess. Sick though he was, he rallied his wits about him. The queen was already sympathetic to him. His best defense would be to play on that sympathy. "Unfortunately, Your Highness is right. My daughter has run away. She has been gone seventeen days now."

"Has she run off with a lover?" The queen's voice was hard and unyielding.

"No, Your Highness. She has had no lovers. Melliandra is a virgin."

"Why did she run away, then? Was it because she didn't want to enter into the betrothal with Prince Kylock?"

Maybor thought quickly, glad that his affliction had not affected his sharpness of mind. "No, Your Highness, her fleeing had nothing to do with Prince Kylock. At the time she left, she knew nothing of the match . . . I thought it better not to mention the betrothal until the matter had been fully decided."

"So why then did your daughter flee, Lord Maybor?" The queen looked skeptical.

"Regrettably, Your Highness, I am to blame." Maybor hung his head low, coughed pathetically, and tried hard to bring a tear to his eye. "I have not treated my daughter as well as a father should." A single tear glistened forth. "I have been a bad father. All Melliandra ever wanted was my love and affection, for she is a sweet and lovely girl." The tear made its noble descent down Maybor's cheek. When the salty tear encountered one of his open sores, he winced in pain—a gesture easily mistaken for a shudder of remorse.

"Melliandra would come to me, begging for my attention, wanting to play me the latest tune she had learnt on her flute, or to show me how pretty she looked in her newest dress. I would send her away, unregarded. My sons were all my eyes could see. I am ashamed to say I neglected her badly." Maybor was warming to his theme: a second tear conveniently welled in his eye.

"It was I who drove her away. All she ever wanted was a father's love. I failed my daughter, Your Highness. I all but sent her away. She fled purely to gain my attention. I would give up my lands for just one chance to tell her that I love her. I would give up my life to have her back, safe within the castle." The second tear dropped, with perfect timing, off the end of Maybor's nose.

The queen came over to Maybor's bedside and placed her cool hand on his shoulder. She appeared deeply moved. "Lord Maybor, I am ashamed for having doubted you. We will find your poor daughter together. I myself will send the Royal Guard to look for her. I will not rest until she is brought safely back into your arms. Have no fear, the betrothal will go ahead as planned once she is found." The queen bent and kissed Maybor's forehead lightly before leaving.

After she left Maybor slumped back against his pillows. He smiled broadly, disregarding his painful sores. He would be father to a queen after all.

Jack watched as Traff laid Melli on the cold earth. He longed to be able to go and help her. He could see she was in a terrible state: she was hot and fevered, her face covered in a film of sweat. The worst thing was her back, where six welts were seared into her flesh. Two of the welts were scabbed with blood and badly swollen—a sure sign of infection.

The mercenaries had done nothing for her, save provide her with a blanket to draw around her torn dress. They appeared not to realize the seriousness of her condition. All Jack wanted to do was go to her. He hated to see anyone suffer, but to watch Melli's rapid descent into fever was almost more than he could stand. There was one point yesterday, when the mercenaries had laid her on the ground, heedlessly banging her shoulder against a hard stone, that he'd felt something building up inside him. Anger at her treatment became tension in his head. It was the same sensation that he'd felt two days earlier. He tried to hold onto it, knowing power was at its core: so close, he could feel the burn at his throat, so overwhelming that he nearly lost himself to it.

Traff had been the one who unwittingly brought him to his senses. The leader came over, holding out a cup of water. "Boy, see to the girl." And that was it. The power was gone more quickly than it came, leaving Jack with a sickening headache and a tangible sense of loss.

Since then, he'd had little chance to consider the importance of what had happened. His time was taken up with thoughts of Melli, not himself, which was probably a good thing, for Grift had warned him many times that "thinking leads to trouble." Armed men dragging him back to Castle Harvell was trouble enough for the moment.

They had traveled west three days now, and Jack expected they would reach the castle in a day or so. He was almost anxious to return, for Melli could then be looked after. It was obvious her wounds needed cleaning and tending.

Melli was in a weak, dazed state. She appeared to have little strength, and Traff had ridden with her leaning heavily at his back. This arrangement had forced the pace to be slowed, as Traff's horse was greatly burdened. Jack had managed to catch Melli's eye on one occasion; she seemed to recognize him, but could do no more than return his gaze.

They had stopped to eat and rest the horses. Traff, seemingly ignorant of Melli's worsening condition, placed the girl against a tree and left her to join his men. Jack was untied from his horse and was brought a cup of water and some drybread. He watched as Melli was given the same provisions. She was barely able to register their presence and made no move to drink. Jack was extremely worried about her; she was sweating and feverish and needed water. With his wrists and ankles tied he could not approach her, so he shouted to the mercenaries: "Help her! Can't you see she's sick with fever? She can't even drink her water."

The mercenaries looked around, astounded at his outburst. The one named Wesk came over to Jack and kicked him hard on his legs. "Hey, boy, don't tell us how to do our job. The girl will survive till we get to Harvell. After that we don't care." This statement was met with grunts of approval from his fellow mercenaries.

Traff, however, looked toward Melli and shouted, "Cut the boy's ties, Wesk. Let him tend to her. I for one don't fancy Lord Baralis holding me responsible for her death." Jack saw the treacherous look in Wesk's eye. "Go to it!" shouted Traff, and Wesk reluctantly cut the bonds.

Jack wasted no time relishing being cut free; he hobbled to where Melli lay. Raising the cup to her lips, he forced her to drink. Once she had enough to satisfy him, he tore off part of the lining from his cloak and soaked it in the remaining water. With great tenderness he cleaned the welts on Melli's back, washing away dried blood and dirt. With growing alarm, Jack noticed that underneath one of the welts the skin was soft and bloated: it was badly infected and needed to be drained.

"I need a clean knife," he shouted toward the mercenaries.

Traff sauntered over, pausing to spit out a wad of snatch. "What d'you need a knife for, boy?"

Jack was annoyed at the mercenary's casual manner and struggled to remain calm. "The wound on her back has become inflamed. It's full of pus and needs letting. *It must be done now.*" Jack gave Traff a hard look; he would not be hindered in this.

Jack saw something close to respect in Traff's face as he handed over his knife. "I hope you know what you're doing," said the mercenary, staying put, ready to watch the operation.

Tension that Jack had hardly been aware of made its presence felt by its retreat. His head was reeling as if from drink, and the bands of muscle around his stomach were as taut as a strung bow. The power had been upon him, and he'd hardly noticed its swell. He'd come close to losing control.

Jack had to make a conscious effort to focus on the present. Melli was what counted now. It was a relief to dismiss thoughts of what might have been if Traff had denied his request. With hands that wouldn't stop shaking, Jack cleaned the blade as best he could.

Thanks to Frallit's violent temper, Jack had a certain skill in tending wounds. He leaned over Melli and called her name gently. She did not respond. "I'll try not to hurt you," he said, more worried than ever. He felt her back, finding the spot where the inflammation was at its worst. He delicately sliced into the bloated flesh. Greenish-yellow liquid spewed forth from the incision. A fetid smell assailed Jack's nostrils.

He lightly pressed the skin, forcing all the remaining fluid from the wound. When he was sure that it had all been drained, he called for more water and was brought it quickly. He cleansed the wound and then patted it dry. He finished off by stripping the soft inner lining from his cloak. He made a makeshift bandage, tearing the fabric into long strips and bound it around Melli's back and chest.

Jack cooled Melli's brow with the remaining water. He looked up to find that he was being watched by all the men. Jack handed the knife back to Traff. "I think she should be allowed to rest for a while to give the wound a chance to scab over. If she were to ride now, it would take longer for the bleeding to stop." The men looked toward Traff for an answer.

"All right," he said roughly. "We'll make camp early, we'll ride no further this day."

Jack was relieved. He gathered the blanket around Melli. It was not enough to keep her warm, so he took off his cloak and laid it over her. He was pleased to see that she had fallen asleep—rest was the best thing for her. He regarded her pale, drawn features; they were glistening with sweat, and he knew the fever would get worse before it got better.

Brushing a strand of hair from Melli's face, he settled down beside her. Night was nearly upon them, and Jack closed his eyes, hoping for sleep. It didn't come. The moon made a slow arc across the sky as he tossed and turned, unable to find peace. Images of what might have been tormented him. Only hours earlier, he'd been on the point of lashing out wildly. There was such potential for destruction within him: he knew it as surely as bread needed salt. It took its strength from anger, and when he thought he wouldn't get his way with Traff, it nearly consumed him. Who could tell what might have happened? He was unpredictable—a coiled spring. He could have hurt Melli, and although the mercenaries were no friends of his, he didn't want their deaths on his hands. He was a baker's boy, not a murderer.

Jack turned on his back and faced the cold stare of the moon. He might not be evil, but he was dangerous, and it seemed that there wasn't much difference between the two.

Fourteen

*T*awl looked into the distance. The mists shifted and he received his first glimpse of Larn. He could see little except rocky, gray cliffs. Seagulls flew overhead, their haunting cries the only noise to disturb the deathly calm.

The sea, which had raged so the night before, was now still. It was early morning and a pale sun rose over Larn, its rays enfeebled by the low, restless mist. The sea was like liquid metal, heavy and slow, the color of silver. Tawl was filled with great apprehension.

The crewmen were lowering the small rowboat over the side. He would be on his way soon. Captain Quain approached him, and the two men stood silent, looking into the mists for some time.

When the captain finally spoke, his warm, gruff voice seemed to break through the spell of beguiling cast from the isle. "When you approach the island, head north around the cliffs. There is a rocky beach that you can land on."

"I've never seen a sea so calm," ventured Tawl.

"Aye, it sends the shivers down my spine. It's almost as if they know you're coming." Quain spoke the very words that Tawl himself was thinking. "I should be glad that the sea's calm. My ship's in no danger of running aground." The captain shook his head, speaking in a low voice as if he did not want to be overheard. "I know it's not right, though. A terrible storm like last night, and now, water as smooth as a maiden's belly. Take care. Lad, may Borc lend speed to your journey." Quain moved off, leaving Tawl alone once more.

After a while he was called over by Carver. The red-haired man put his arm around Tawl's shoulder. "Rowboat's all ready, lad. In it you'll find food and a bottle of rum, courtesy of the good captain." Carver hesitated while he looked toward the faint outline of Larn in the distance. "I understand, lad, I've something to thank you for."

"I don't know what you mean." Tawl was genuinely puzzled.

"I was the one who was due to go with you in the boat. Captain says as you insisted on going alone. Not that I was afraid to go, of course. It's just that my elbow's been playing up, and a couple of hours of rowing would've played havoc with it."

"Well, I'm glad not to be the cause of any further discomfort to you, Carver." Tawl spoke gravely, with no hint of mockery.

"Well, just thought I'd let you know," Carver said brusquely, moving away.

The mists parted for a brief instant and Tawl was given a clear look at the island—it was almost an invitation. He breathed deeply, rubbing his chin with his hand. It was time for him to be on his way.

He climbed down the knotted rope ladder and into the rowboat. Once he was steady, he looked up to the deck of *The Fishy Few*, where all the crewmen including Captain Quain were lined up. They were silent with grave faces as Tawl took up the oars.

He started to row, enjoying the feel of the smooth wood in his hands. He soon made his way from the ship and into the mist. Just before he lost sight of *The Fishy Few*, he heard the voice of the captain ringing out: "One day, lad. Back in one day."

Tawl was surprised at how much of his strength had returned in the few weeks since he had been released from Rorn's dungeons. His arms pulled the oars with powerful grace. He soon fell into a rhythm; it felt good to be doing something physical. Muscle and sinew stood out against the flesh of his arms. It was the first time since setting sail that he'd rolled up the sleeves of his shirt—he had taken the Old Man's advice about hiding his identity.

The sea was yielding and Tawl made good time; even the current was in his favor. He watched the cliffs of Larn loom near. After a while he altered his course north, as the captain had suggested. The banks of mist were lifting and sunlight was allowed to nuzzle the water once more. Tawl looked over his shoulder. Although the mists were clearing ahead, behind they were still thick—swirling and reeling, hiding *The Fishy Few* in their lair.

He rowed for some time and saw that the cliffs were lessening, gradually declining. He made his way around a rocky precipice and finally caught sight of the beach Quain had mentioned. Tawl rowed on, his arms growing tired, grateful that the tide was on its way in, bearing the boat forward in its push to the shore. As he approached the rocky beach, he could make out a solitary figure, black against the gray of rock and sky. Tawl knew the man waited for him.

Minutes later, his small rowboat landed on the shores of Larn. The figure in the dark cloak did not move forward to meet him. Tawl dragged the boat from the surf and tied its mooring to a sturdy outcropping. He made his way up the pebbled beach to the cloaked man.

"Greetings, friend," said Tawl. The man's face was hooded, casting his features in shadow. He said no word to Tawl. He beckoned him to follow by the briefest raising of his hand. Tawl trailed the stranger up the beach and onto a well-concealed path that led between huge slabs of granite. Part of the path had been hewn from the rock, enabling Tawl to see the many intricate layers within the stone.

The path began to steepen and bend as it headed upward into the cliffs. The path was cut entirely from the rock now, becoming a tunnel. Tawl was plunged into darkness. His guide did not seem concerned with the dark and led him further ahead. Light peeked through at irregular intervals and Tawl managed to follow. The path ended suddenly and he found himself in bright sunlight again.

He brought his hand up to shade his eyes and looked around. They were on top of the cliffs and the view out to sea was breathtaking. Tawl felt certain the shadowy object on the horizon was *The Fishy Few*. He turned his gaze inland. Ahead lay a large stone temple, stark and primitive, old beyond reckoning. Low and oppressive, it was built from huge slabs of granite, their edges rounded by the weathering of centuries, white with the droppings of countless generations of sea birds.

The cloaked man beckoned Tawl forth, and he followed him into the shadows of the temple.

What struck him first was the extreme cold. Outside the day was mild and pleasant, yet on entering the temple the air temperature dropped sharply. The interior was not at all gaudy and ostentatious like the temples he'd visited in Rorn and Marls; the walls were left bare and unadorned. Tawl had to admit there was an austere beauty to be found in the naked stone. They passed through several dark, low-ceilinged rooms. Low ceilings on *The Fishy Few* had not concerned Tawl, but these ceilings, formed by immense slabs of granite, caused him to feel a measure of foreboding.

He was led into a small room which contained nothing but a stone bench. His guide wordlessly motioned him to sit. He then withdrew, leaving Tawl to wait alone.

Tavalisk was toasting shrimp. He had by his side a large bowl of sea water, in it many live shrimp. With his little silver tongs he plucked a large and active shrimp from the water. He then impaled the shrimp upon a silver skewer. The specially sharpened point pierced the shrimp's shell with no effort. Tavalisk was pleased to see that the impaling had not killed the shrimp: the creature was still wriggling. The archbishop then lowered the unfortunate animal over a hot flame. The shell crackled nicely in the heat, blackening quickly, and the shrimp soon wriggled no more. Tavalisk then waited for the shrimp to cool a little before removing its shell and eating the tender crustacean within.

The archbishop heard the usual knocking that always seemed to occur when he was about to enjoy a light snack. "Enter, Gamil," Tavalisk breathed, his voice metered with boredom. His aide walked in. The archbishop did not miss the fact that Gamil was dressed in an old and decidedly green robe. "Gamil, you must forgive me."

"I do not understand what Your Eminence means. Forgive you for what?"

"For giving you bad advice." Tavalisk paused, enjoying the puzzled expression on his aide's face. "Do you not remember, Gamil? Last time we met I said you would look better in a green robe. Only now I find I was wrong. It appears that green becomes you even less than red. It makes you look decidedly bilious." Tavalisk turned back to his bowl of shrimp, so as not to betray his delight. "Maybe in future, Gamil, you should steer clear of the brighter colors altogether. Try brown; you may look no better, but at least you will draw little attention."

Tavalisk busied himself with picking out his next victim. "So, what have you to tell me today, Gamil?" He decided upon a small but lively shrimp: it was much more interesting to skewer an active one. Many of this batch seemed decidedly lethargic.

"I have received word from our spy of who Lord Baralis' enemies are."

"Go on." Tavalisk skewered his victim.

"Well, it appears that Your Eminence was correct in assuming that Lord Baralis has many enemies. The most powerful and influential one is named Maybor. He holds vast lands and has much sway at court."

"Hmm, Lord Maybor. I do not know of him. Gamil, I would like you to make contact with him. Be subtle, see if he would be interested in . . . keeping our friend Lord Baralis in his place." Tavalisk thrust the shrimp into the flames.

"I shall send the letter by fast courier, Your Eminence."

"No. Leave that to me, Gamil. I will use one of my creatures to hasten its delivery." This was an instance where it was worth using the debilitating art of sorcery. He had to find out what was going on in the Four Kingdoms. Tavalisk was becoming more and more uneasy about Baralis' doings of late. The man was intriguing on too large a scale. The duke of Bren was a dangerous person to be conspiring with; his greed for land, combined with his current association with the knights, made many people nervous. Baralis' plotting would further sour an already bitter mix.

The archbishop removed the skewer from the flame. "Use discretion when you write the letter, Gamil. Do not name me. These things have a habit of falling into the wrong hands and I would see if Lord Maybor takes the bait before risking my reputation." Tavalisk popped the hot shrimp onto the floor, where the little dog scooped it up. Burning its mouth, the dog howled and dropped the shrimp. The archbishop smiled—the sight of suffering never failed to delight him.

"If there's nothing further, Your Eminence, I will make haste to write the letter."

"One more thing before you go. I wonder if you'd be so kind as to take Comi and rub some oil into her mouth. The poor creature gave herself quite a burn." The archbishop watched as his aide struggled to pick up the dog. "I'd be careful of your fingers if I were you, Gamil. Comi has teeth like daggers." Tavalisk smiled sweetly, waving man and dog on.

Tawl was beginning to feel a little impatient. He had been kept waiting for some time now, and no one had come. He felt as if he was being made to wait on purpose, to make him feel uneasy. He noticed that his sleeves were still rolled up and his circles were showing. Tawl quickly concealed them under his sleeve; he wanted the people here to know as little about him as possible.

More time passed before someone finally came. An elderly man approached, his shadow preceding him. He, like the guide, was hooded, his face dark. The man led Tawl through a stone corridor and into a large, dimly lit room.

The room was dominated by a huge, low table formed from a single slab of granite. Four men sat, one on each side, around the rectangular stone. Tawl was relieved to see that these men had their hoods drawn back from their faces. Three of the men were old and graying. The fourth was much younger, with sharp but handsome features. The one who had led Tawl to the room silently departed.

Tawl was scrutinized by the four men for some time before any spoke. Finally, the oldest of the four addressed him, "Why have you come to Larn?" Tawl was surprised by the directness of the question. The four waited impassively for his reply.

"I have come because I was advised to do so." His voice seemed small and powerless, muffled by the heavy stone.

"You have failed to answer the question," said the younger of the four. Tawl did not care for his biting tone.

"I came because I need to find a boy."

The four men exchanged glances.

"What boy?" The younger's voice had the sound of one accustomed to having his questions answered promptly. Tawl defiantly waited a few minutes before replying.

"I cannot say. I will know him only when I find him."

"You hope our seers will point the way?" The elder spoke softly, in mild reproof of his younger companion.

"I have hope that they will."

The elder nodded. "Are you willing to pay the price?"

"What price?" Tawl was beginning to feel uneasy. "Name it."

"It is not as simple as that. The price can only be settled after the seeing has been given."

"What if the seeing fails?" Tawl felt he was being lured into a baited trap.

"That does not concern us. You will still be liable to pay the price." The younger of the four continued, "It is a risk you take. Leave now if you would not take it." The man's eyes challenged Tawl.

Tawl stood firm under the scrutiny of the four. "I am willing to pay the price."

The elder nodded once more. "So be it."

The younger stood up. "Follow me." He led Tawl out of the room and down a series of passageways. Tawl felt he was descending, and the walls grew damp, confirming his suspicion that he was being led belowground.

He began to hear a noise. At first he could not tell what it was—bats or wild animals, he thought, growing uneasy. As they drew closer to the source, he realized with horror that the sound was human cries. He grew cold as he listened to the desperate keening. He was led around a corner and suddenly found himself in a vast, natural cavern.

Tawl barely noticed the magnificent towering rock and the huge domed ceiling aglow with seams of crystal. He was transfixed by what he saw in the cavern. Rows of massive, granite blocks.

Bound to each stone was a man.

Tawl was horrified by the state of the men: their bodies were thin and emaciated, their hair wild and long. It was their limbs that were the most shocking: the muscle had atrophied and withered away, leaving only bone thinly coated by skin. The ropes were thick and coarse, and held the men motionless. Tawl wondered why the men were still kept bound, for they would surely never walk again.

It was the noise the seers made, even more than the sight of them, that chilled Tawl to the bone. Terrible, anguished howling, frantic screaming, each sound telling of the torment of their souls. The seers of Larn lived hell on earth. Tawl shuddered—the seers had been driven to madness.

He could not bear to look on their anguish. He turned his head, and by doing so locked eyes with the younger of the four. The man, seeing Tawl's distress, spoke: "The seers do God's work." His voice was without emotion. "Performing their task takes its toll. No one can look upon the face of God and remain unchanged."

"I thought God was good." Tawl found it hard to think with the tortured cries of the insane ringing in his ears.

"That is your mistake. Good or evil is not his concern. God exists. There is nothing more."

"Your God is not mine," Tawl said softly.

"All are one here."

"I cannot go ahead with the seeing. I will not be party to such inhuman cruelty."

"You knew what Larn was before you came." The younger stated the fact with the barest hint of malice.

"Yes, I was told, but I never realized it would be like this." Tawl motioned toward the rows of men, men destined to lie bound to the stone for life.

"It is too late to back out now. You have agreed to pay

the price. The seeing will go ahead." The man gestured
minutely with his hand and three hooded men stepped forward. "You will not leave Larn without paying your due."
The younger moved forward and Tawl was escorted behind
him by the hooded men.

As he walked down the rows of seers, they called to
him, wailing their terrible laments, their bodies jerking
gracelessly as they shifted against their bindings. Tawl was
escorted to the end of a row, near to the wall of the cavern.

The younger stopped and turned to him. "He is for you.
Ask and you shall be answered." With that, he and the
hooded men withdrew.

Tawl looked upon his seer. He saw with revulsion
where the man had been bound so tight for so long that his
skin had grown over the rope, its rough and knotted texture
clearly visible beneath the pale skin. Tawl realized that if the
seer were to be unbound it would tear open his flesh.

The seer was babbling frenzied words in a tongue Tawl
could not understand. He did not look at Tawl, he was lost in
his own torments. The seer urinated; he seemed unaware
when the liquid soaked his linen wrap and then formed a
pool around his hips.

Tawl wanted to be away from the place as quickly as
possible. He asked his question: "Where do I find the boy
whom I seek?"

He was not sure that the seer heard—his incoherent
rantings never stopped for an instant. Tawl could discern no
signs of comprehension from him. He waited, bitterly regret-
ting having come to Larn. He could not believe that God's
work was done here.

After a while the seer became visibly more agitated.
Spittle frothed at his mouth and his eyes rolled wildly in their
sockets. The babblings grew louder—strange, haunting
words, their meanings unknown to Tawl. The seer seemed to
be repeating the same phrase over and over again. He could
not understand it, and moved closer to the seer. He caught
the sharp smell of ammonia in his nostrils.

The seer was becoming frenzied, saliva dripped down
from his chin and onto his thin chest. Tawl strained for
meaning in his voice. He made out the word "king." The

phrase sounded like "for king on." Over and over the seer repeated it. Tawl puzzled at its meaning. The seer's speech became hysterical. Tawl looked closely at his wet lips. Suddenly the phrase took shape for Tawl. He realized the seer was not saying "for king on." The words were, "Four Kingdoms."

Tawl's blood ran cold. He became still, feeling a shifting within: the seer had spoken.

For some reason, he expected that the seer would stop, but he carried on, repeating the phrase with great agitation. A hooded man approached and drew Tawl away from the seer. He led him down the rows of bound men and toward the cavern entrance. Tawl looked back. The seer was oblivious to his departure: he still recited the same phrase over and over again, his dull eyes focused on the face of God.

Baralis did not bother to look up from his work when Crope entered the room. "Has our sharp-eyed squire met with an accident yet?" He continued his writing.

"He did that, master. A might unpleasant one, too. He mishandled a wheat scythe."

"How unfortunate for him. Disturb me no further, Crope. I have many matters to attend to. In the library you will find a book with a blue leather binding. It contains illustrations of sea creatures. It is yours. Take it and leave me alone." It was Baralis' way of thanking his servant for the care he had given him when he'd collapsed the night of Winter's Eve. Crope went off quickly, eager to look at the pictures in his new book.

When the man had left, Baralis stood up and began to pace the room. He had many matters on his mind. He had been disturbed by the sight of the Royal Guard riding out of the castle in the early morning; he needed to find out what mission they were on. The Royal Guard answered only to the queen. He had lost several days to exhaustion and he was anxious to waste no more time.

A knock came on the door of his chamber. Baralis opened the heavy door. "Yes?" he barked at the liveried steward, annoyed at being interrupted.

"Her Highness, the queen, requests your immediate

presence in the meeting hall." Baralis had been expecting such a summons.

"Very well, tell Her Highness I will be there directly." The servant withdrew. Baralis moved swiftly, preparing for the audience, donning the fine robes that were expected by the queen. He looked into his small hand mirror and saw that the burns on his face still showed a little. He would have to think of an excuse for them. He did not want the queen to suspect any connection between him and the Winter's Eve fire. He was soon ready and made his way to the meeting hall.

"Lord Baralis, I trust you are recovered from your bout of fever?" The queen greeted him coolly. She was dressed in magnificent splendor, wearing a gown of midnight blue, bedecked in pearls. She was no longer young, but age seemed to enhance her further, bringing grace and poise in exchange for the bloom of youth.

"I am feeling much better, Your Highness."

"Tell me, Lord Baralis. It must be an odd fever that would leave your face looking as if it were burnt." The queen drew her lips to a thin line.

"No, Your Highness, the burns I incurred in my chambers, when I was working on my medicines. I was careless with a flame, nothing more."

"I see." The queen turned and pretended to admire a painting. "Were you by any chance working on the medicine for the king?"

"I was indeed, Your Highness. I have prepared a fresh batch. I would presume by now that the initial dose has been used up?" Baralis was beginning to feel more confident. He could tell that the queen was trying to hide how desperately she wanted the medicine.

"There is none left. The king has been without it for two days now. I fear a relapse if he is without it much longer."

"Then Your Highness must be most anxious to have some more."

The queen wheeled around. "I can play your games no longer, Lord Baralis. I must have the medicine today." The queen was beginning to lose her composure. Baralis remained calm.

"Your Highness knows my price."

"I will not allow you to say who Prince Kylock will marry."

"He must marry *someone* and Lord Maybor's daughter is no longer a suitable choice. Even if she is found and brought back to the castle, Your Highness would not want the prince married to a girl who can not bear the sight of him."

"You are wrong, Lord Baralis. I have been told the truth of the matter by Lord Maybor himself. He has told me the true reason for his daughter's flight. I have much sympathy for him and have agreed to send the Royal Guard to search for Melliandra. When she is found, the betrothal will be carried out." Baralis could hardly believe what was being said. What lies had Maybor cooked up to fool the queen so effectively?

He hid his surprise. "And if the girl is not found?" The queen gave Baralis a sharp look. He continued, "Or if the girl is found but is no longer a virgin?"

"I have every confidence that Melliandra will be found, and that when she is, she will be untouched." The queen's eyes drew narrow and she spoke again, "Lord Baralis, I have a proposition for you."

"I am eager to hear it, Your Highness."

"If you agree to supply the king's medicine indefinitely, and the girl is not found within the month, I will agree to your terms."

"And if the girl is found within the month?"

"The betrothal will go ahead as planned, but you must still continue to supply the medicine, and do so until such a time as the king no longer has need of it."

"So you are offering me a wager."

"Are you a betting man, Lord Baralis?" The queen was now her serene self, poised and in control.

"I pride myself on taking risks. I accept the wager." Baralis bowed slightly and the queen smiled charmingly, showing her beautiful, white teeth.

"I warn you, Lord Baralis, the Royal Guard will find Maybor's daughter wherever she is."

"That remains to be seen, Your Highness. In the meantime I will arrange to have a portion of the medicine sent to the king's chamber." Baralis bowed once more and left.

Once out of the meeting hall, his step grew light. The queen was a most enjoyable adversary. He almost admired her. It was too bad that she would lose the wager.

Maybor was studying his reflection in the mirror. He was pleased to see that his good looks were returning. True, the sores marred his handsome features somewhat, but they would fade. The soreness in his throat was not of such importance to him, *that* he could live with. Today he would leave his bedchamber for the first time in days.

He rose from his bed, slapping the wisewoman's buttocks to awaken her. As she woke, Maybor could not resist pulling back the sheets to admire her nakedness. He had found to his surprise that being with an older woman had its advantages; she was much skilled in the art of lovemaking and was not subject to a young girl's modesty. Why, if she'd had land of her own, he might even have considered marrying her!

The wisewoman arose from the bed and proceeded to dress with slow provocation. Maybor looked on in appreciation. When she had dressed, she kissed him lightly on the cheek and left. That was another good thing about her, thought Maybor, she had asked for nothing in return for her favors. He wondered, for a brief instant, if the ailing king had ever partaken of her services. After all, even a sick man has desires.

Maybor did not bother to call for Crandle. He would dress himself this day. He strolled to his wardrobe, deciding he would buy himself a new mirror; he missed looking upon himself in full length.

He was feeling decidedly pleased with himself. He had managed to turn his circumstances round—he had gained the sympathy of the queen. Just this morning, she had sent out the Royal Guard to look for his daughter. Everything could not have worked out better. Now the only thing he needed to make his happiness complete was news of Baralis' death. He decided he would meet with his assassin one last time; the damned man was taking too long about his business. He would have Crandle arrange an assignation.

Maybor opened the door to his wardrobe and surveyed its contents, deciding which robe to wear. He remembered with regret that the red silk he had worn on Winter's Eve had to be discarded—the punch had not washed out. The gray-eyed vixen had ruined his best robe! Maybor's eye was caught by something in the corner—he looked closer and found it was a dead rat. This was most strange. If he remembered rightly, on the night of Winter's Eve, Crandle had come from his wardrobe carrying a dead rat. Rats were a constant nuisance in the castle, but it was unusual to find a dead one. Two dead rats were damned suspicious.

Maybor picked the stiff creature up by its tail. He held it at arm's length—it was well known they carried the plague. Maybor could see no obvious signs of the cause of the rat's demise. He brought the creature nearer. Now he could see that its nose was red and swollen. A thrill of revelation passed through Maybor. The rat had died of the same thing that had caused his affliction. There was something in the wardrobe that had killed the rat. Maybor thought back to Winter's Eve. He had been perfectly well; the illness overcame him only after he had dressed for the evening. His clothes had been poisoned!

Baralis had somehow managed to put poison onto his clothes. The fumes given off by the poison were what had caused his sickness. Everything fit into place: the reason he was not dead was that he had been forced to take off the doctored robe before it had finished its commission. The gray-eyed snippit had unwittingly saved his life.

Maybor stepped away from his wardrobe. What if all his clothes had been doused in poison? They would all have to be burned. Maybor was furious. He had spent years acquiring the most exquisite robes in all the Four Kingdoms; he had spent a fortune on them. Baralis would pay dearly for this, he vowed. It is one thing to poison a man's wine, but quite another to poison his robes!

* * * *

Tawl was led back into the room containing the large stone table. The four were waiting for him.

"You have your answer," said the elder, more a statement than a question. Tawl nodded. "The seers seldom fail. God is benevolent to them."

"It seems to me that God is more benevolent to *you*." Tawl could not stop his anger. It was a welcome release from the horror of the cavern. "You are the ones who reap the benefits of the atrocities performed on those men. You use them for your own gain. God has no hand in this!" Tawl was shaking. The four were unmoved by his fury.

"You know nothing of God. You know less of Larn." The elder was perfectly calm. "We do not use the seers, we are here to serve *them*. They are blessed by God and we are humbled by that blessing, we are their servants. Do not let the sight of them mislead you. They exist in God's own ecstasy. We can only guess at what joy is theirs."

"I am not fooled by your fine words. Where I have just come from is no place of God's; no heavenly ecstasy exists there. The seers are living closer to hell." The four looked upon Tawl as if he were a foolish child.

"The sight can be a little disturbing, but I can see you have no wish to understand. You did, however, use their services, and so now you must pay your due." The elder regarded Tawl with the slightest trace of contempt.

"What is my due?" said Tawl looking directly into the elder's eye.

"We require a service of you." The elder's voice became soft and seductive. "Nothing really, a mere trifle." Tawl felt his eyelids grow heavy. He struggled to keep his wits about him. The elder continued, his voice low and inviting, "The smallest of favors, the easiest of tasks." Tawl's eyes closed. "The tiniest of services, the most innocent of undertakings . . ."

Fifteen

*T*awl awoke and wondered where he was. As his head cleared he realized that he was still on Larn. He puzzled over how he had fallen asleep. He was in a small room, lying on a stone bench. As he rose, his aching back told him he had spent some time lying on the hard surface.

He had no memory of being brought to this place. He could recall nothing after leaving the cavern. Tawl felt alarmed. He could remember the seeing clearly, but nothing else. He realized he had to get back to the ship. Captain Quain had said he would sail after one day. Tawl had no way of knowing what time or what day it was. He had to leave immediately. As he made his way from the room, the youngest of the four entered.

"Greetings," he said. "I hope you are well rested."

"How did I come to be here?" demanded Tawl.

"It is a natural side effect of the seeing. The one who seeks answers is usually drained of all his strength. It is nothing to worry about. Seeing takes its toll on all of us. You became tired and we brought you here so you could sleep."

"How long have I slept?" Tawl did not believe a word the younger had said. He remembered feeling fine immediately after the seeing.

"You have slept for many hours. There is a new dawn."

"I must go. My ship is due to leave soon." Tawl remembered the earlier talk of price. "Tell me what due I must pay."

"Oh, that." The younger's tone was casual. "I think the price will not be high. I believe you will be asked merely to deliver some letters on our behalf in Rorn. You are sailing there, I take it?" There was something about the man's voice that made Tawl suspicious. He had been given the impression earlier that his due would be much greater than acting as a messenger.

"Is that all?" he asked.

"Why, of course. You should not believe all those fireside stories you hear about Larn. All we ever ask in return for a seeing is some small service. We looked upon you with benevolence and decided you should not pay too dearly. If you follow me, I will give you the letters." The man turned and walked from the room and Tawl followed.

He was given two letters, both sealed with wax. He was told where and to whom they should be delivered. He was then led by a hooded man down through the cliffside. As he walked, Tawl found he could not shake off his uneasiness. Something was not right. He could not believe the four were letting him off so easily—letters to deliver in a city he would be in anyway? The most disquieting thing to Tawl, though, was how he had managed to lose the greater part of a day and night.

Tawl was forced to focus on other matters as he approached the beach. He must row fast if he was to reach *The Fishy Few* before she set sail. The fresh air seemed to Tawl like a blessing after the stale atmosphere of temple and cavern. With every breath he took, he felt his mood growing lighter. Soon he would be free from this cursed place. He decided that when he eventually returned to Valdis he would talk to Tyren about the terrible plight of the Seers of Larn. He wanted to make sure that no more young men would ever be forced into such a life.

Tawl launched his rowboat into the surf, reveling in the cold water about his waist. He jumped into the boat and took up the oars, glad that his feet were no longer on the island. He was soon making good time. He put all his energy into pulling the oars. It helped him to put Larn out of his thoughts.

It was difficult for him to remember the location of *The Fishy Few*. Mists swirled at a convenient distance from the shores of Larn, hiding its presence from passing ships. Tawl tried to keep a heading southwest, hoping to eventually stumble upon the boat. After a few hours of rowing, he became anxious: surely he would have spotted the ship by now. He stopped rowing and started listening. He thought he heard a faint call. It came again: the sound of a fog horn. The crew of *The Fishy Few* were trying to help him by making their presence known. Tawl immediately became heartened and started rowing with renewed effort in the direction of the horn call.

Not much later, Tawl caught sight of the ship's high masts above the mist. His heart filled with joy at the sight. *The Fishy Few* had not abandoned him. He drew nearer and the mists parted; he was greeted by the sound of a cry, "Boat, ahoy!"

Tawl looked on as the crew of the ship gathered to watch his approach. He made out the form of Captain Quain, who raised his hand in greeting. Tawl heard the crew join in a loud cheer and then, as he drew alongside the ship, he heard the captain shout, "Break open a barrel, shipmates, our good friend has returned."

"No, Bodger, it ain't the miller's wife who'll tumble for a length of cloth and a spring chicken."

"That's what I heard, Grift."

"No, Bodger, there's no one better off than a miller's wife. No, it's the tallow maker's wife who'll tumble for goods. Everyone knows there's no profit to be made in tallow."

"The tallow maker's wife never looks short to me, Grift. She always wears the prettiest dresses."

"Exactly, Bodger! How can a woman whose husband barely makes one silver a month afford fine linen? She sets a good table, too, plenty of roasted chicken."

"Still, Grift, Master Gulch told me that he managed to

take a tumble with the miller's wife by giving her one length of cloth and a spring chicken."

"Master Gulch should have saved his money, Bodger. The miller's wife will take a tumble with just about anybody in breeches, and for no reason other than she's just plain randy."

"Do you think I'd have a chance with the miller's wife, then, Grift?"

"I'm not sure that you'd want to, Bodger."

"Why's that, Grift?"

"Unfortunately, Bodger, it appears that the miller's wife has been spreading her favors so far and wide that she's caught the ghones. And unless you fancy the idea of watching your balls slowly putrefying and then dropping off, I'd stay clear of her."

"I'm glad you warned me, Grift, you're a true friend."

"I consider it my duty to keep you informed of such matters, Bodger."

"What about Master Gulch, Grift? Did he catch the ghones?"

"Well, Bodger, all I can say is that judging by the way he's been walking recently, it won't be long before his plums hit the deck."

The two guards sat back against the wall and relaxed for a while, supping their ale.

"Hey, Grift, while I was up on the battlements this morning, I could have sworn I saw a group of horsemen in the forest."

"Whose colors were they wearing, Bodger?"

"Well, Grift, they were quite a distance away, but they looked like mercenaries to me."

"They'll be the ones in the pay of Lord Baralis, then. I wonder if they've found young Jack?"

"I didn't spot him, Grift."

"I hope he's got well away by now, Bodger. The boy's better off gone from the castle. He never fit in. Just like his mother, head in the clouds the pair of them."

"I heard say his mother was a witch."

"Aye, Bodger, the rumors abounded. Beautiful girl she was. Judging from her accent she came from the south, but whether she was a witch or not, I couldn't tell you. Though I did hear a few stories."

"What sort of stories did you hear, Grift?"

"It was said that she once turned an over-ardent suitor bald."

"Bald?"

"As a coot."

"It wasn't Master Frallit, was it, Grift? He's got a head as bald as your own."

"My lips are sealed, Bodger." Grift took a long draught of ale and said no more.

Maybor was beginning to wonder what had become of his assassin. He had sent Crandle to find the man, but his servant had been unable to locate him. The assassin had obviously not done his job, for Maybor had seen Lord Baralis with his own eyes that morning.

Maybor had been walking in the gardens, taking the air that the wisewoman had advised, when he had seen Baralis slithering around the castle walls, trailed by his lumbering idiot, Crope. It had suited Maybor that the man had not seen him; he had no wish to confront Baralis, he would rather stay in the background until his enemy was disposed of. Only now it seemed that the man commissioned to do that very job had disappeared.

Maybor did not even know if Scarl had been staying in the castle or the town; the assassin liked to keep his movements to himself. Perhaps the assassin decided that Baralis was so dangerous that he backed out. Maybor decided against that theory. He had dealt with Scarl before and knew him well. He was not a man to flee from danger.

Maybor was walking the length of his chamber wearing his servants' clothes. He had insisted that every robe in his wardrobe be burnt and now found himself in the humiliating circumstance of having nothing to wear. His sons were too slim to lend him any of their clothes, and so he had been forced to don the rather disgusting and none too clean clothes of his servant, Crandle. Maybor had commissioned the castle robemaker to fashion him some new robes, but they would not be ready for a week.

He, the great Lord Maybor, had been forced to walk in the castle gardens dressed like a common servant. Baralis had a lot to answer for!

Maybor was understandably beginning to develop a deep fear of being poisoned. What might Baralis try to poison next? His bedclothes? His shoes? Maybor had tried to force Crandle into testing his food and wine for him, but the thankless servant had adamantly refused. If Baralis was not out of the way soon, he would be forced to spend good money hiring a food taster and their services did not come cheap. It was, Maybor grudgingly supposed, a risky profession to be in.

He was not pleased with his assassin; he had waited too long to make his move. He decided that when Scarl finally did his job, he would have absolutely no qualms about having the man's throat slit. There was no way he was about to give up thirty acres of his orchards to a man who was so slow about his work.

Crandle entered the chamber with a brief knock.

"What do you want? Have you managed to locate the man named Scarl?"

"No, sir, it appears that no one knows where to find him."

"Where has that damned man disappeared to?" Maybor stamped his foot.

"Well, your lordship, a thought has occurred to me. Of course, I might be wrong."

"Get to it, man, do not dither." Maybor picked up his sliver of mirror and examined the sores on his face.

"You know, sir, that a fire occurred in the banquet hall after you left."

"Yes, yes." Maybor was becoming impatient.

"Well, there was one man killed in the fire. He was burned to death."

"What on earth has that to do with you not finding Scarl?" With great satisfaction Maybor squeezed a pus-filled boil.

"Not one person could identify the body, your lordship, and nobody came forward to report anyone missing."

Maybor grew still. He knew what Crandle was saying. He thought for a moment and then asked, "What state was the body in?"

"I heard the poor soul was burnt to a cinder, nothing of his face left."

"Was he found with anything on him?"

"I'm not sure. I heard his knife was the only thing that held up to the flames."

"His knife?"

"That's what I heard, sir. Right funny knife, too, by all accounts. Not your usual hand knife."

"Be gone!" Maybor spoke calmly, and watched as his servant left the room.

He had never seen Scarl's knife, but Maybor knew it would be something special: it was the only tool of an assassin's trade. He sat on his bed and pondered the implications of what Crandle had said. Maybor had last seen the assassin the day before Winter's Eve, he had not heard from him since, and Scarl had not carried out his commission.

Maybor shivered involuntarily. What if Scarl had attempted to murder Baralis and had failed? Baralis might in turn have killed the assassin and started the fire to cover up any evidence. Maybor had heard the strange rumors about the fire. Crandle had even said that a squire saw a man in black walk away from the flames. Baralis was known to be a man who liked to wear black. Maybor rang for Crandle. He could no longer call, his throat would not take the strain.

"Yes, sir," said Crandle, reappearing.

"I would speak with the squire you mentioned. The one who saw the fire start."

"Oh, you mean Squire Tollen. He met with a terrible accident just the other day."

"What happened to him?" Maybor grew chill.

"Well, it appears that he fell on a wheat scythe and ripped his guts open. He died instantly."

"Does it not seem strange to you, Crandle, that a man would fall on a scythe?"

"Now you mention it, it does seem rather odd. Squire Tollen was no farmer."

"Leave me now, Crandle. You have given me much to think on."

After his servant had left, Maybor paced his room. No one, farmer or otherwise, falls on a scythe. This was Baralis' doing, thought Maybor. He'd had the squire killed to avoid any possible link between himself and the fire. Baralis had somehow managed to kill his assassin. And Scarl was not just any fool with a knife; he had been the best in his profession. The assassin had been right to be wary of his mark. Baralis was becoming too ingenious. Maybor paced for a long time, thinking about how best to eliminate his problem.

Bringe surveyed the huge expanse of orchards. From his position on the hilltop he could see hundreds of acres of the low and leafless apple trees laid out in neat lines as far as the eye could see. Lord Maybor's orchards. Bringe smiled knowingly to himself and felt in his pocket for the letter. His rough hands curled around the smooth sheet and a tremor of anticipation ran through him.

Bringe knew the great wealth that the orchards represented: they were home to the finest apple trees in the Four Kingdoms. The best cider in the Known Lands was produced from these succulent and sharp-tasting apples. Cider that was exported to countless cities and towns where discerning drinkers were willing to pay the highest prices for a mug of the honey-colored brew.

The apple orchards were the most important industry in the east. If a man did not tend the apple trees, he brewed the cider, or crafted the barrels, or grew hops for the fermentation. Everyone from the youngest babe to the oldest woman in the town of Nestor helped pick the apples when they grew ripe on the tree. The elders held that the secret to fine-tasting cider was picking the apples when the color was just right: light yellow with just the beginning of a reddish blush. Too little red showing on the skin would yield a bitter brew, too much red would turn the brew too sweet.

Bringe drew forth the letter from his pocket and unfolded the document with elaborate care. He peered at the contents, unable to read a word that was written therein. When the dark rider arrived late the previous evening, delivering the letter, Bringe had been forced to take the humiliating step of having his wife read it for him. Of course, he had beaten the slovenly wretch senseless afterward, just in case she got any ideas about blabbing the contents to anyone in the village. As he brought his leather strap down upon her back, he felt he detected a glimpse of arrogance in her watery eye. Bringe hated the idea that his wife might think herself better than him just because she could read. Fueled by righteous indignation—for it was only proper that a man show his wife who was master in the home—Bringe looked around for something more brutal with which to hit her. His eyes alighted on a heavy iron pot, and with vicious enjoyment he beat his wife until she was bloody and senseless.

When he had finished with his wife he realized he was feeling aroused. His thoughts turned to his spouse's sibling, his young sister-in-law, Gerty. On Winter's Eve she had sat in his lap, her bottom heavy and warm, swaying suggestively against him. When his wife left the room to tend the stew, Bringe asked Gerty for a kiss. The girl willingly complied. It was no sister's kiss. Gerty had slipped her sharp tongue between his teeth, sending a thrill of excitement through his body.

Bringe's thoughts lingered over the abundant charms of his sister-in-law. It was, he thought, high time he took a new wife, and the young and full-thighed Gerty would do him nicely. There was, of course, the problem of his current wife to deal with. Indignation rose in Bringe's breast. That ungrateful sow had held him back too long. She did nothing but nag and harangue him, and now, because of the letter, she felt she had something on him. He'd show her.

Bringe raised the letter to the pale morning sky. He would be going up in the world soon. There would be gold aplenty, a move to a new town, and a new wife to bed. Bringe carefully placed the letter in his good pocket and strolled down the hill toward the village, a spring in his step and a glint in his eye.

*   *   *

The moment the door closed behind the guard, Jack rushed across the dark chamber to Melli. She was asleep, stretched out on her side on a low wooden bench. Jack tried not to wake her as he felt the texture of the skin on her back through the thin fabric of her dress. He could feel each individual welt, the skin still raised and puckered. He shuddered to think what would have become of her if the flogging had been allowed to continue. Melli had good reason to be thankful to the mercenaries.

Jack gently pressed the skin around the welts, testing for swelling and fluid beneath. Melli's skin felt much firmer and he drew in a sigh of relief. The infection which he'd drained some days back appeared to have abated: the skin was healing normally. Jack felt a wave of concern ripple over him. Melli would undoubtedly bear the scars of the rope for life. They would fade somewhat, but they would remain, unmistakable, indelible marks of shame. With great tenderness Jack brushed a lock of dark hair from Melli's face. Her beauty had been made only more poignant by her sickness. He dreaded to think what horrors she'd been through in Duvitt. Jack leant forward and placed a light kiss on her forehead.

Melli awoke. Her eyes first registered panic, followed by recognition and then annoyance. "What on earth are you doing hovering over me?" she said sitting up and rubbing her eyes.

Jack immediately felt like a fool—to be caught stealing a kiss! He hastily brushed his hair from his face in an attempt to smarten his appearance. "The guard has just left for a moment, so I thought I'd come and check on your . . . " Jack searched for a delicate word. "Condition." Melli looked at him with barely concealed hostility.

"I'm certain my condition is just fine, thank you, and I know it's no concern of yours." She drew her blanket around her shoulders.

"It's just that after your . . . er, after the incident in Duvitt, you took a fever." Jack met his companion's gaze and Melli was the first to look away.

"I will hear no further talk of Duvitt." Her tone was harsh, but she seemed to regret it immediately, for she spoke her next words in a softer voice. "Please, Jack, I cannot bear to think of that place."

"I won't mention it again," said Jack in what he hoped to be a gallant manner, bowing his head slightly. "We must talk of other matters while we can, though. The guard could return at any minute."

"Where are we?" Melli looked around the small, dark cell.

"We're about an hour's walk from Castle Harvell. When they brought us here dawn was just breaking. I caught a glimpse of the battlements."

"So we are in the town?"

"No, from what I could tell, we're in some kind of underground chamber. One minute we were walking in the forest, the next we were being led down a tunnel, horses and all. You were asleep the whole time. You've slept a lot these past days."

Jack paused for a second, took a deep breath, and then asked the question that had been on his mind for some time now. "Who are you, Melli?" His hazel eyes challenged her. "And what are you running away from?" Too late he realized he had laid himself open to interrogation.

"I might ask you the same question, Jack. What possible interest could a band of mercenaries have with you?" Melli spoke in the manner, and with the confidence, of a great lady. It was obvious to him that she was a noblewoman, used to giving orders and taking charge.

"I am, or rather was, a baker's boy at the castle. I did something that I shouldn't have and ran away to escape the consequences." Jack hung his head low, it was better that she thought him a thief.

"I too ran away from the castle." Melli's voice was surprisingly gentle. He looked up and saw that she was idling with the fabric of her dress. "I ran away because my father wanted me to marry someone whom I could not bear the thought of."

"So these men are in the pay of your father?"

"No, my father would never stoop to hiring mercenaries." There was more than a hint of pride in her voice. She spun around at him. "You must know who these men are paid by?" Before Jack could think of what answer to give, the door opened and in walked Baralis.

"I think you have your answer, my dear," he said in his low, alluring voice. Jack glanced toward Melli; she was managing to conceal her surprise well.

"Lord Baralis." She spoke graciously, inclining her head. "I trust you are here to see to my release." Jack could detect an edge of anxiety to her confident tone.

"If you would be so kind as to follow me, my lady, I will show you to more comfortable surroundings." Baralis made a slight gesture, indicating the sparse cell. Jack caught sight of the lord's hands. They had always been gnarled and twisted, but now they were horribly scarred. Baralis caught his glance; their eyes met. Jack felt fear as he looked into the cold, gray eyes. He looked away, unable to hold the gaze any longer.

Baralis turned his attention back to Melli. "Follow me."

"And what if I refuse?" Her head was high and her manner imperious.

"You have little choice, my lady." Baralis beckoned and two armed guards appeared, their swords drawn. Jack watched as Melli struggled to keep her composure.

"It appears you leave me *no* choice, Lord Baralis." Jack could not help but admire her calm aloofness. "I trust you will allow my man to accompany me." Jack did not know whether to be insulted at being called her servant or pleased that she had thought to include him.

"That unfortunately, my dear, is out of the question. Your man—" Baralis left a slight pause indicating to Melli that while he was aware of her lie, he was too much of a gentleman to contradict her "—will have to stay here. Now, please, come this way."

Melli stepped out of the room, flashing Jack one last look. Baralis waited until Melli was out of sight before turning to Jack, his voice no longer alluring. "I will speak with you later."

Melli's sharp ears picked up what Baralis said to Jack and she realized that her companion had not told her the whole truth. The king's chancellor would not be interested in talking to a castle thief or minor criminal. There was more to the baker's boy than met the eye.

Baralis led her down a long, stone corridor and Melli felt the chill dampness of being underground. Along the route she spied a pale, translucent moss clinging to the stone walls. On impulse she reached out to touch it.

"Don't do that," Baralis cautioned. She stopped, frightened by the warning in his voice. "One never knows with such growths, my lady, how deadly they might turn out to be." Melli drew her hand back. Baralis turned and continued walking.

After a while his course veered off to the right and he stopped beside a heavy, wooden door. Melli watched dispassionately as Baralis struggled to draw back the bolt with his crooked hands. Something about the sight of his disfigurement stirred up a wisp of memory—a memory from long ago in her childhood. She struggled for the recollection, but it eluded her.

Baralis pushed the door open, and he and Melli entered the chamber. It was brightly lit with many candles and surprisingly warm. There were rugs on the floor and a scattering of tables and chairs.

"I trust you will find this to your liking. My servant Crope brought these things from the castle. They are not much, I am afraid." Melli was aware that Baralis was playing the room down; he had obviously gone to a lot of trouble to provide her with comfort.

"I have also taken the liberty of having some food prepared for you." He indicated a low table where a tray of cold food was laid out. Melli's heart warmed at the sight. There was roast fowl, veal sausage, plover eggs, hearty red cheese, a round loaf, and a selection of hothouse fruits. She looked quickly away, determined to hide her keen interest in the food from her captor.

"It will do for now," she said icily, hoping he would leave her soon so that she could eat.

"You will probably wish for a bath and a change of clothes. I will arrange to have them brought to you." Baralis moved to leave, but Melli halted him.

"Why have you brought me here?" she demanded. Baralis paused for a moment, considering whether or not to answer. He looked at her and took a thin breath.

"Let me say this, my dear. We have a mutual interest."

Something in his voice struck a chord within Melli and his motives became clear to her. "You mean, Lord Baralis, that you do not wish me to marry Prince Kylock either?"

"You are indeed a bright girl, Melliandra." He smiled faintly. "So much brighter than your father." He issued the slightest of bows and then withdrew from the room. Melli heard the scrape of metal as the bolt was drawn on the other side.

She rushed over to the food, her mind racing. It was all falling into place. Baralis hated her father; he would not want Lord Maybor to be father-in-law of the future king and grandfather to a future heir. So he had captured her before her father could. She wondered what Baralis' plans for her were—she could not believe that he would harm her. He surely would not have provided her with such an agreeable chamber if he intended to kill her. Melli decided she would think on the subject no longer. The food looked too tempting and she did not care to ruin her appetite with apprehension.

She settled down upon a small footstool and poured herself a glass of light, red wine. Out of habit she reached for the water jug to dilute the wine—then stopped herself, deciding that she would take her wine whole. The customs of the fine ladies of court seemed trivial to her now. She raised the wine to her lips and drank deeply. It felt good to be flouting customs. Her eyes alighted on the delicate silver paring knife that had been so thoughtfully provided for her. She disregarded it and tore at the roast fowl with her bare hands, neatly twisting a drumstick off with a pleasant snapping of bone.

Baralis rubbed his hands together, massaging muscle and sinew. Since Winter's Eve he had been unable to open them completely; his fingers curled in toward his palms. Every day he rubbed therapeutic oils into the red, shiny flesh, hoping that their condition would improve and he would regain some flexibility. He was finding it more and more difficult to perform simple tasks: the mixing of compounds, the writing of letters, the drawing of a bolt.

Baralis turned from the door and walked a few steps down the passageway. Facing the blank stone, he brushed his thumb against a section of the wall. The wall slid noiselessly back. Crope stood up guiltily as he entered, his face reddening. Baralis looked to see the cause of his guilt. The dimwit had been petting a small rodent.

"Crope, I have told you before not to take my creatures from their cages; they are not pets to be stroked and fondled." It was his servant's responsibility to feed the animals that he kept for his various purposes. Crope, however, tended to get attached to the unfortunate creatures.

"I'm sorry, my lord," he muttered. "I'll take it back to the castle right away, see that it's locked up tight."

"The creature is of little importance to me now, you lumbering simpleton. I want you to heat up some water and bring it to our guest. Take those to her also." Baralis indicated a small heap of clothes and linens.

"Very well, master." Crope moved to leave, gathering up the delicate fabrics in his huge arms.

"One more thing, Crope."

"Yes, my lord."

"I do not wish to be disturbed for the rest of the day. Go back to my chambers and make yourself useful there once you have finished your task." Crope nodded. "And take that wretched rodent with you. I have no mind to sit here in the company of a large rat!" Baralis watched with growing impatience as Crope struggled to catch the creature while holding on to the linens. Finally his servant pocketed the sickly looking rodent. Baralis made a quick mental note of the state of the creature—the particular poison he'd been trying out on it obviously worked more slowly than he thought. He'd expected the animal to be already dead.

Once Crope had left, Baralis' attentions quickly turned to other matters. He was due to have an audience with the queen in the morning to deliver the new batch of the medicine for the king. He hoped that during the meeting he would be able to find out what progress the Royal Guard had made tracking the girl. It was important that they did not follow her trail back to him.

Baralis' thoughts lingered over the girl: such a tempting young morsel. True, she was a little worse for wear than when she had first run away, but he only found that more appealing. Perfection held little interest for Baralis. He had not decided what to do with her yet. There was no rush; her presence here could not be detected. The haven, as he liked to call it, was known to no one, although there *was* a tunnel running from it to the castle. Baralis surmised it had been built hundreds of years back as an escape route in times of siege and, like so many other things, had long been forgotten.

Baralis allowed himself to feel a little smug. Events were moving in his favor once more. Not only had his mercenaries found Maybor's daughter, they had also found the boy. Of course, the treacherous ingrates had insisted on a bonus for finding him. He decided he would let Jack sweat for a few days before he questioned him concerning the incident with the loaves. Two or three days left alone in a dark cell with only crust and water would serve to make the boy more compliant.

Baralis moved toward a faded tapestry on the far wall. He pushed the moth-eaten fabric aside. His gnarled hand resting upon the cool stone, he found what he was looking for—a small gap the size of a thumbnail chiseled out of the stone. Baralis leaned forward and pressed his face to the wall.

He could see every detail of Melli's chamber. He smiled to see the girl was heartily gulping down her food, biting lustily on a large sausage and swilling wine down her slender throat. The girl obviously had a piece of food stuck between her teeth, as she picked at it unashamedly with a thin pheasant bone. Having loosened the persistent morsel, she spat it out with gusto and then downed more wine.

Baralis could clearly hear the knock that drew her attention. He heard her bid enter, and watched as Crope lumbered into the room carrying a huge pail of boiling water. It amused Baralis to see the fear and revulsion in Melli's face as his servant crossed the room. With delight, he noticed her eyes alight on the open door, assessing her chance of escape as Crope filled the wooden tub with hot water. The girl casually stood up and inched toward the door. Crope turned around, his hands grasping the pail of hot water.

"I wouldn't do that, miss," he said so softly that Baralis had to strain to hear the words. Maybor's daughter was clearly surprised at his servant's gentle voice. She sat down again. Crope finished filling the tub. "Be careful, miss," he warned. "Be sure to put plenty of cold in before you take your bath. This water could scald the skin off your back." He left the room and returned seconds later with the clothes and linens. He placed them with great care on the bed. The servant then took his leave of the girl, bowing awkwardly.

Baralis watched as the girl looked over the clothes that had been brought; he could see her pleasure in what had been selected. Judging by the tatty red dress she was currently wearing, she had not known the pleasure of fine clothes for some time.

The girl crossed the room and tested the bath water, then quickly withdrew her finger. Satisfied that Crope had spoken the truth, she poured the contents of the cold pail into the bath. Baralis wetted his lips as the girl began to unlace her dress. He had seen many women disrobe in his time, but it was always more interesting when the person in question did not know she was being observed. A woman with a lover will preen and strut, holding in her stomach and thrusting out her chest. A woman alone has no need of such show; she will slouch and scratch and fart.

Melli quickly took off her skirt followed by her bodice. Baralis admired her high, white breasts. She turned to her bath and Baralis took a sharp intake of breath. On her back were six deep, red welts. They were obviously only a few days old, for dried blood was caked around two of them. What is this, he wondered? The mercenaries never mentioned a beating. Baralis could not tear his eyes from the sight; such perfection, such beautiful, creamy skin, such fine legs and buttocks, all thrown into magnificent relief by the presence of the vicious, red scars. Instead of detracting from her beauty they seemed, by their very hideousness, to magnify it. Baralis felt a stirring in his loins.

Melli gathered the soap, brush, and linen swab that she needed for her bath and gingerly lowered herself into the water. She soaked for a while, her head barely above water. Baralis looked on as she began to lather up her brush, she scrubbed her feet and her legs with the brush and then swapped to the cloth rag to clean her more tender areas. She then began to rub her back with the soapy cloth; she winced as it touched the welts. The girl put down the cloth and carefully felt the wounds on her back. She looked afraid of what she felt there. She stood up from the bath, water running in rivulets down her slender frame, and stepped out. She glanced quickly around the room. Baralis could guess what she was searching for: a looking glass. He was pleased that he had thought to provide her with one.

She rushed over to the mirror, her body scattering droplets of water onto the fine rug. She placed her back to the mirror and twisted her head and neck around so that she could see the cause of her distress. Baralis watched the girl's frightened face crumble into tears at the sight of her scarred back. She fell onto the floor, sobbing quietly.

Baralis moved away from the stone. He had seen enough for the time being. The sight of the girl crying had left him unmoved. He carefully replaced the tapestry and sat down in a comfortable chair, pouring himself a glass of wine.

He turned his attention to other matters, calculating if his letter to Bringe would have been delivered by now. He was anxious to go ahead with his plan to mutilate Maybor's orchards. Bringe, Baralis mused, was just the sort of man he liked—a greedy one.

Sixteen

*T*avalisk was down in the palace wine cellar testing the various vintages. "I will try a cup of this one," he said to the young boy who was shadowing him.

"If Your Eminence pleases, I am not allowed to touch the barrels. I will call for the master cellarer."

"You will do no such thing, boy, I cannot bear the sight of that sanctimonious toad. He knows nothing about wine." Tavalisk smiled pleasantly. "Come boy, a glass of the red." The boy reluctantly tapped the barrel, filled a cup, and handed it to the archbishop. "See, boy," he said, "you have already pleased me more than the cellarer ever did. He only pours me a mere quarter cup when I'm tasting." Tavalisk held the liquor up to the lamplight, admiring its rich color. A flicker of annoyance crossed his brow as he saw Gamil walking up to him.

"If Your Eminence would be so good as to forgive this intrusion?"

"What now, Gamil?" The archbishop swirled the wine around the glass.

"I have news for Your Eminence." Gamil eyed the young boy.

"There is no need for me to dismiss this young man, Gamil. I'm sure he can be trusted, and besides, he is being most helpful to me." Tavalisk favored the boy with another smile.

"I have delicate matters to speak of," persisted Gamil.

"Do not contradict me!" The archbishop's voice was icy cold. He turned to the boy, who was now red-faced, and said sweetly, "Fetch me a glass of the Marls white." The boy rushed off to another barrel. "Now, Gamil, tell me your news."

"Well, Your Eminence, I have confirmed that there was a fire at Castle Harvell the night of Winter's Eve—the same night you felt the drawing. I have heard reports of strange things happening at the time the fire started."

"Let me guess, Gamil. Metal objects warm to the touch? A wave of heat and force?" The boy had returned with another cup of wine and Tavalisk took a mouthful.

"Yes, Your Eminence." The archbishop savored the wine then spat it it out.

"Sorcery follows the same rules, whoever the practioner. It takes a strong aftermath to warm metals, though. Sounds to me like Baralis acted out of desperation, not cunning. He was trained at Leiss and should know the dangers of using such an indiscreet amount of force."

The archbishop paused to take a mouthful of wine. "This Marls white is quite delicious; here take a sip." Gamil lifted his arm to take the glass; Tavalisk ignored the gesture and handed the cup to the boy. "I'd be glad to hear your opinion of it." The archbishop averted his eyes so not to see the look of malice that momentarily passed over Gamil's features.

"Your Eminence has a wide knowledge of many subjects."

"I have a practical knowledge of sorcery, Gamil. As you know, I dabble from time to time; the odd ensorcelment here, the briefest of drawings there, but it is far too physical a pursuit to keep my interest long. Even simple things like the laying of a compulsion upon a dumb creature can make one weak for the day. Sorcery uses a man's strength as much as his mind, and can leave one's muscles as well as wits sorely strained."

Tavalisk beckoned the boy to bring him a glass from

another barrel. "People make the mistake of thinking magic comes from the land and the stars, but it comes from within, and when it is drawn out, it makes its loss felt—a man could hardly be expected to lose a quart of blood and then carry on as normal, could he? The same for sorcery." The archbishop took the fresh cup from the boy. "Sorcery is too debilitating for everyday use. I will use it when necessary, but on the whole I prefer to conserve my strength for the good of Rorn. Sorcery is a poor substitute for cunning."

Tavalisk grimaced, finding the wine harsh and sour. "Here, Gamil, try this," he said proffering his aide the cup. "Any news of our friend the knight?"

"He is back in Rorn, Your Eminence. The first thing he did on leaving his ship was to make his way to the whoring quarter." Gamil sipped cautiously at the wine.

"Probably looking for his own little whore. Come now, Gamil, drink it all up. It's a fine vintage." Tavalisk watched as his aide was forced to drink all of the bitter wine.

"Well, he won't find her, Your Eminence."

"Not much chance of that, considering where she is." Tavalisk took the cup from Gamil. "Of course, I do not want the girl harmed in any way."

"Of course, Your Eminence."

"I'm merely holding her on the off chance that she might prove a useful gambit to use on our knight at some point. I understand he was quite attached to her?"

"By all accounts he was indeed, Your Eminence."

"The whore will prove the least of our knight's worries before long."

"What does Your Eminence mean?"

"I mean, Gamil, that it's high time I took some action against his brethren. I'm considering expelling them from the city. The Knights of Valdis have irked me too long and I feel the need to chasten their movements. I'm sick of them manning our harbors and interfering with our trade. Ever since Tyren took over, they've stepped up their patrolling—looking for illegal slaves, indeed! Only last week they seized a cargo of spices, worth over a hundred golds it was. Said it was pirated stock!

"The situation is intolerable. They hide behind noble

motives when all they're after is trade. They undercut our prices merely to gain a foothold in the market. They have a near monopoly on the salt trade, and I need not tell you how dangerous that is to our deep sea fishermen—they depend upon salt to preserve the catch. I'm all for a man making a few golds, but let him not be a hypocrite when he does so." The archbishop thought his last words had a gratifying ring to them and ordered Gamil to write them down for the benefit of the masses.

"You may go now," said Tavalisk when Gamil had finished writing. He beckoned the servant. "Fill a flagon of the last wine for my aide, boy. I can tell that he enjoyed it enormously."

"There is no need to bother, Your Eminence."

"Nonsense, Gamil, it is my pleasure. Think of it as a reward for your scribing." The boy returned with a large pot of the sour wine and handed it to Gamil. "Be sure to drink it soon; it may lose its distinct flavor if left too long." Gamil withdrew, struggling to carry the large pot.

"Now, boy," said the archbishop, addressing the young servant, "let's move on to the next barrel."

After a few moments there was a soft patter of feet and a tall, thin man approached. "Ah, Master Cellarer, it is always a delight to see you. I was just telling your boy how much I value your opinion on wine."

Tawl picked his way around the filth on the streets. The stench of excrement and putrification was overpowering. The people of Rorn relied on the rains to wash the sewage from the streets, but the skies had not unburdened themselves for many weeks, leaving the city displaying its waste for all to see and smell.

He had taken his leave of *The Fishy Few* earlier that morning. He'd been sorry to bid farewell to the crew, for they had become his friends. Carver had told him he'd turned out to be a better cook than the one they'd left behind. Captain Quain had grasped his hand warmly and offered him help if he ever needed it. "Come down to the harbor any time," he'd said. "I'm usually here. 'Less I'm at sea o' course. You'll always find a measure of rum and a helping hand." Tawl did not doubt the offer for an instant, the captain was not one to promise his help lightly.

Tawl first made his way to the whoring quarter, hoping to see Megan one last time and perhaps stay with her overnight before leaving the city. He needed to talk to her. Ever since leaving Larn, her words had played upon his mind: *"It's love, not achievement, that will rid you of your demons."* How had she known so much? Achievement was all that mattered. It was all that he lived for, his personal curse. It was this longing for achievement—this need for fame and glory—that had marked him all his life. Searching for its elusive source had proven his downfall.

From the earliest he could remember he'd wanted to be a knight. Every day while fishing, his mind would soar eastward to Valdis. Knights were noble: they saved princesses from towers and fought long battles with demons.

To become a knight required money for training, and Tawl had started selling any surplus he caught. Four extra fish a day meant a copper penny a week. One morning he calculated it would take him fifteen years to make up the required sum. It made him more determined than ever.

He hid his stash at the bottom of the salt barrel. On many an occasion, when they were short of bread or tallow, he'd been tempted to hand it over. By the time his mother died, he had a cup full of coppers. Things were so bad for so long after her death, that he was eventually forced to spend it. Anna caught wet-fever, and the baby, by this time well over a year old, needed to be baptized. There was no choice but to use his savings. Oh, he'd been furious, taking his anger out on his sisters, storming and sulking and making everyone's life a misery. They didn't realize how important it was to him, and how, by giving up his stash, he was saying good-bye to more than money alone.

His sisters won him over with tenderness. Sara did the fishing for a week and Anna painted him bright pictures from her sick bed. Perhaps they *had* understood after all—he just didn't see it at the time.

It was so hard to see things clearly then. There was the family and nothing else. The responsibility was so great. He took whatever labor he could find: as a farmhand, a tavern boy, a peat cutter—there was always work for someone willing to take his pay in goods, not coinage. The hours were long and grueling. He'd go weeks without seeing the cottage by daylight.

The only time he had to himself was the early morning. His stash might have gone, but the dream still remained. He was strong; he'd known that for as long as he could remember. His fishing hole was precious and he'd defended it many times against newcomers. No one dared bother him anymore. The village cleric had told him that strength alone wasn't enough to be a knight. So each morning there'd be a book in his pocket as well as a knife. He could never manage to make much sense of old Marod, but if it was important that he could read, then read he would. Even after his coppers were gone, he still took his book along on his fishing trips. He'd tell himself it was force of habit, that the book was useful for securing his line, that old Marod would make a good weapon if he were attacked. The truth was something deeper: as long as he had the book, there was hope. If ever the chance to be a knight came along, and in his dreams it always did, he would be ready for it.

His memory of that time was marked with the sound of taunting. The village boys would never tackle him one-on-one but formed gangs, and when they spotted him going to market—sisters at his side, baby in a basket—they'd laugh and call him the "good housewife," and tell him to go home and suckle the baby. Sara and Anna would pull on his arm, begging him to come away. The fear in their voices was the one thing that stopped him from taking them on.

Only one day he came alone. He could still recall it now: the sky was blue and full of flies, the ground underfoot was firm. A leg of mutton was his downfall.

Summer Festival was approaching and he'd promised his sisters a treat. To girls who lived on fish and goose, a joint of meat seemed an unbelievable luxury, and no matter how much they annoyed him, Tawl loved to see them excited. He'd left Sara banking the fire in preparation for the joint. She was twelve now, and Anna was eight, the baby just turned three.

There was joy in his step that day. Not only would he buy a leg of mutton, there were extra coppers for ribbons and preserves. Sara and Anna had only rope to tie their hair. He'd seen the way they looked at the village girls with bright posies in their tresses; they longed to have them, yet never dared ask. Sara and Anna both knew there was no money to spare, and would not add to his burden by asking for things they couldn't afford. They were good girls, really. What they didn't know was that ever since the baby had been weaned and the wet nurse's services no longer needed, he had extra fishes to sell. It wasn't much, just enough for a little surprise on Summer's Eve.

Tawl bought the mutton; it was stringy and a little tough. He was a novice at haggling and paid the asking price.

He had a hard time with the flies on the way back. They buzzed and bothered, trying to land on the meat. Just as he left the town he heard a voice: "Hey, mother's boy, best hurry home and brown the joint!" Laughter accompanied the remark. Tawl didn't turn to look and carried on walking.

"Trouble with flies? They're attracted to the smell of girls!" A second voice. More laughter.

"You'll be sprouting breasts soon."

Tawl spun around. *"Say another word and I'll kill you!"* He had the satisfaction of seeing them flinch. Five of them. He knew them well. The leader smirked.

"What you gonna do, *housewife,* poison us with your cooking?"

Something snapped. Tawl lunged for the leader's throat. It was in his hands before he knew it. The boy's face turned red then purple. Someone at his back kicked him. Spinning round, he punched the attacker squarely in the face. Bone crushed beneath his fingers. A third jumped on his back. Tawl threw him off with such frenzy, the boy landed a horse's length away. A fourth boy hovered, clearly frightened; Tawl chased him and pulled him down. He kicked and kicked until the fury left him.

There was blood on the ground and on his clothes, the

leg of mutton lay in the dirt and there were four men down, one wisely fled.

Tawl was close to tears, not because of the fighting, but for the ribbons and the meat. All ruined. He hated the thought of disappointing his sisters. Picking up the joint, he tried his best to brush it free of dust. The ribbons were bloodied, but might wash clean.

He started to walk home, basket in hand, limping slightly from a blow to his leg. Seconds later Tawl heard footsteps behind. He readied himself to fight again.

"You're strong when angry, young man," came a voice. Tawl looked round. A man stood in his shadow, a foreigner from his coloring and accent. "That was a very impressive show you put on. You're vicious but badly in need of training."

"I asked for no opinion, stranger." Tawl studied the man. He was dark of hair and eyes. A sword was at his waist and a dagger at his breast, a deep blue cloak gave bearing, and well-oiled leathers suggested wealth.

"I am a man who likes to get what he wants. And I'll not dance around the maypole: I want you." The stranger spread his lips in something akin to a smile. He bowed. "I am Tyren, Knight of Valdis."

Tawl approached the whoring district. He was desperate to see Megan. More and more the past was catching up to him, and he needed her tenderness to help him forget.

He was bitterly disappointed when there was no answer at her door. Forcing his way into her room, he tore off a section of his deep green cloak as a message that he'd been there—Megan would be unable to read a written note.

He took a moment to look around. It was obvious that Megan had not been there for several days; rats scuttled across the floor, flies swarmed around a slice of rotting pie, and dust lay thick on table and chair. Megan was a girl who liked to keep things tidy. Puzzled, he searched around some more, noting that her few dresses and belongings were still there. He looked under the heavy hearth stone where Megan had kept her money; there was no sign of the gold coins. He sighed sadly. She'd taken the money and left. He could hardly blame her—he had urged her to go—it was just that he had not expected her to go so soon.

Tawl ran his fingers through his hair. It was better this way. He could only have stayed one night and they would have parted once more, bringing each other new pain. Tawl closed the splintered door behind him.

He walked for a while down the dirt-ridden streets, marveling at the warmth of the sun—at this time of year the marshlands would be bitingly cold. He took the two letters from his belt and shuddered to see that the wax seals they bore were embossed with an elaborately fashioned letter "L." He would rest a lot easier once they were out of his possession. Never having heard of the streets where they were to be delivered, he called to a young boy who was running past, "Hey, young fellow."

The boy looked surprised at being beckoned. "You mean me?" he said, stopping in his tracks.

"Yes, you. I wonder if you can help me. I need someone to direct me to a couple of streets."

"What's in it for me?" The boy looked squarely at him. Tawl could not help but smile at the boy's audacity.

"What do you want?" he asked.

"Two coppers," replied the boy, quick as a flash. Tawl regarded the boy: he was no more than eleven summers old, poorly dressed in a torn cotton tunic. He looked as if he had not eaten in several days.

"I will give you no money, young man, but I promise you a hot meal." Tawl could clearly see the boy sizing up his offer.

"How do I know you won't let me swing, once I've shown you to where you want to go?"

"You have my word."

"People round here say the word of a foreigner is as good as no word at all."

"So you think me a foreigner?"

"It's as obvious as my own left foot."

Tawl stifled a smile. "What would you say if I told you that I'm a knight, pledged to honor my word?" He bowed slightly and watched as the boy decided what to do.

"Very well, I'll take you where you need to go. Not that I'm impressed by you being a knight, not that I believe you either, mind. I'm only going with you because I've got nothing better to do at the moment and I quite feel like stretching my legs a bit. O' course I'll hold you to that hot meal."

"I'm grateful for your help. Now the places I need to find are called Mulberry Street and Tassock Lane."

The boy whistled. "You're getting quite a bargain."

"Why do you say that?"

"Because those streets are both on the other side of town. We've a long walk ahead, I can tell you. You must know someone in high places."

"Meaning?"

"Meaning Mulberry Street ain't for the likes of you and me. High and mighty that place is." The boy was obviously impressed.

"Let's get going then," urged Tawl. He was not interested in the people whom the letters were for, he just wished to finish his duty as messenger as soon as possible and be off.

"What's your name?" he asked as the boy led him down the street.

"You tell me yours first."

"Tawl."

"Is that all?" The boy was clearly disappointed. "I thought knights had long, fancy names like Culvin the Daring or Rodderick the Brave."

"We're only given the fancy bit once we've died a hero's death." Tawl's eyes twinkled merrily. The boy seemed pleased with his answer and was silent for a while as he led Tawl through a series of alleyways.

"A word of advice, Tawl, if I may be so bold." The boy spoke in the hushed tones of a conspirator. "If I were you, I wouldn't go around telling complete strangers I was a knight. Knights aren't the most popular people in Rorn these days, if you get my drift."

Had it come to this? Had the knights' reputation fallen so low that even street urchins warned him to hide his identity? But then what did he expect—Rorn and Valdis had long been at each others throats. Tawl wanted to believe it was rivalry, nothing more, that spurred the hate for his order. But it was getting harder for him to ignore the rumors. He knew Valdis would not answer its critics—that was not the knighthood's way—and although Tawl respected the silence, he also saw the harm it did. Indeed, *he* had been a victim of the silence: the archbishop had felt free to imprison and torture him for a year, because he knew full well that Valdis would do nothing to retaliate.

The boy spoke up, distracting him from his thoughts, "I'm known as Nabber, by the way."

"Well, Nabber, seems as you know so much about Rorn, what sort of food would you suggest I buy you for supper?"

"The best dish in all of Rorn is eel pie. I'll have a slice of that, some fried fish ends, and some leek soup—no carrots o' course."

"Of course," echoed Tawl absently, his thoughts far to the west in Valdis.

Maybor was in the process of being fitted for a new set of robes, when he was interrupted by the entrance of his servant. "What is it, Crandle?"

"A letter has just been delivered to you, my lord. A handler awaits your reply. Most excited he was, says it was flown by an eagle."

"Who is it from?" asked Maybor distractedly. He was trying on a particularly magnificent tunic and was admiring his reflection in his new mirror.

"I can't say, sir."

"Tell me, Crandle, do you think this tunic a little tight? My robemaker assures me it fits perfectly." Maybor casually slapped the unfortunate man. "Be careful with those pins, you sniveling dolt!"

"I think the tunic looks most becoming, sir."

"Well, Crandle, I'm inclined to think you are right, I do look rather . . . what's the word I'm looking for?"

"Regal," ventured Crandle.

"Yes, that's the one. Now tell me more about the letter." He turned to the robemaker. "You can go now. Remember I want more embroidery and jewels on all of them; they are far too plain at the moment." The man backed out of the room, taking his work with him. "Damn fool, he has no idea how to make fine robes. I'll have to send to Bren to get some decent attire and that will take nearly two months. If Baralis was here this moment, I would gladly squeeze the life out of his treacherous frame with my bare hands. Now, where were we?"

"The letter."

"Yes, yes, let me have a look at it, man. It must be something pressing to be sent on the leg of a bird." Crandle handed it to Maybor, who examined it carefully. "Go now!"

Maybor was beginning to feel a little excited. The letter had obviously come a great distance; the writing on its exterior was crafted in a style unfamiliar to him. He broke the seal and unraveled it. Maybor was not an accomplished reader and that, combined with the unusual handwriting, caused him some difficulty deciphering its contents. Once he was sure he understood what the letter said, he sat down on the side of his bed, rubbing his chin reflectively.

Maybor sat for some time, deep in thought. After a while there was a knock on his door. He was about to tell his servant to go away when in walked his eldest son, Kedrac.

"Father, you look pale, what is the matter?"

"Nothing is the matter, my boy. I am feeling quite well." Maybor looked down at the letter and then to his son. He made a decision. "I have just received an interesting proposal."

"From whom?" His son's tone conveyed studied disinterest.

"I'm not sure . . . I could hazard a guess, but I won't. Suffice to say I believe it to be from someone with great power and influence." Maybor watched his son's face become more attentive.

"And what does this person of power and influence propose, Father?"

"He proposes an alliance of sorts." Maybor picked his words carefully. "He suggests that we have mutual interests and that we would do well to combine our resources."

"You speak in riddles, Father."

"Baralis!" Maybor shouted angrily. "The man who sent this letter seeks to keep that foul upstart in his place."

"Surely, Father, we have no need of such an alliance. Can we not arrange for Baralis to be done away with ourselves? Say the word and I will slit his slippery throat myself."

"No," warned Maybor, his thoughts darting to the fate of the assassin. "I order you to stay clear of him." His tone invited no argument on the subject. The eyes of father and son met for a brief instant, and the son relinquished.

"So, Father, what will you do about the letter?"

"I will reply that I am interested in an alliance. I will be careful not to appear too eager and will insist that the sender names himself."

Kedrac nodded his approval. "How will you know where to send your reply?"

"There is a handler waiting upon it. I will pen it this very day."

"The person in question must be anxious to have used a pigeon."

"An eagle," corrected Maybor. Both men were silent for a moment. It was rumored that sorcery was the only thing that could compel an eagle to act as a messenger. Maybor thought it wise to change the subject:

"Tell me, is there any news of your accursed sister?"

"That is what I came to talk to you about. The search is not going well. She's been gone twenty-four days and her trail is cold. The Royal Guard have swept the forest and the nearby villages. They have found no sign of her."

"Melliandra cannot have vanished into thin air. She must be somewhere."

"There have been rumors."

"What rumors?"

"A girl fitting her description was said to have been whipped in Duvitt."

"Duvitt! Why, that treasonous town is five days hard ride from here; she would surely have not made it so far on foot."

"We already know she bought a horse in Harvell the first day she escaped."

"Still, Kedrac, no one would dare to whip a nobleman's daughter. It must be nonsense made up by idle minds." Maybor considered for a moment. "Look into it, anyway. Do not leave it to the Royal Guard, send one of your trusted men to

Duvitt to check out the rumor. Time is rushing on, she must be found."

"Very well, Father, I will see to it right away."

Maybor watched his son leave the room, and once the door was closed he read the letter once more. A ghost of a smile played at his lips, this was indeed a most interesting development. He sat down at his writing table and started the painstaking task of penning a reply.

Baralis was making his way from the meeting chamber; he'd just had an audience with the queen. He had given her the medicine for the king—much watered down, of course—and he was now feeling quite pleased. The queen had reluctantly admitted that the search for Melliandra was not going well; not only was there no trail leading back to him, there was no trail at all. He should have expected no less. All the Royal Guard was famous for was looking good in uniform!

It had been many days since he and the queen had struck the wager, and now all he had to do was hold the girl for a further few weeks to win the bet. And what a prize! His plans would at long last start to come together—he would force the queen to marry Kylock to Catherine of Bren, the duke of Bren's only child. It would be the greatest match in the history of the Known Lands. Kylock would rule over the two largest powers in the north. With the great military might of Bren and the Four Kingdoms combined, Kylock would be able to crush the other northern states. The Halcus were already weak—he had seen to that. Annis and Highwall, and as far east as Ness—they would all fall. Kylock would rule over the mightiest empire ever known. He, Baralis, son of a farmer, would be kingmaker, shaper of an empire.

Kylock was his creature. With more subtlety than a courtesan's smile, he'd drawn him in. A tantalizing conversation here, a glimpse of greatness there, a provocative use of power, and the boy was his. Kylock's mind, so like his own, craved intimate knowledge of those forces that could neither be seen nor touched. It had been so easy; the boy was set apart from birth—and he knew it—a loner, incapable of making friends, gradually retreating to a world of inner torment. Kylock was on the edge of madness. 'Twould be so easy to guide him along—*he was born to it!*

Baralis made his way into the castle courtyard. Once he was sure he was not being observed, he slipped into the concealed entrance of the passageway that led to the haven. Thinking about the future was one thing, making it happen was another. He would let no one, no matter how small and inconsequential, stay his path. It was time he questioned the boy.

Jack was sitting on the wooden bench, his legs drawn up to his chest for warmth. He had no cloak, as he had torn it up and used it to bandage Melli's back. There had been much time to think over the past days. He'd been entirely alone except for the occasional guard who came to taunt him.

So much had happened since that fateful morning with the loaves: it wasn't worth denying the incident; it *had* happened and he *was* responsible. What it made him varied according to who he spoke to. Tradition would call him a demon. Falk would call him a man capable of making his own choices for good or evil.

Too many times now for denial he'd felt the buildup of power within. It set him apart, but was there a purpose behind it? Or was it random, like a scattering of autumn leaves? There had always been a part of him that felt different from everyone else. For so long now he'd thought it was due to a lack of background in his life. With a mother full of secrets and a father unnamed, it was a form of escape to believe he was special. In his mind his father had been a spy, a knight, a king. His mother was a gypsy princess in hiding from her family. Such romances were his greatest conciliation as a child.

Yet one of them had given him this. Did his power come with some obligation? Was it meant to be used, or hidden?

Jack had worked as Baralis' scribe for several years and knew some of the powers the man possessed. Was his fate to be like Baralis? A man who concealed more than he showed, a man who frightened small children and provoked warding signs when his back was turned?

Jack looked up as the door creaked open. Standing on the threshold was Baralis. He was not surprised to see him, and in fact felt relieved that he had finally come. Jack had not enjoyed the waiting. It was time they sorted things out. He started to stand, Baralis raised his arm.

"No, Jack, do not rise." His voice was smooth and commanding. "You know why I am here?"

"You are here to question me." Jack stood up in defiance. He would not look up to his captor.

A flicker of annoyance registered on Baralis' face, but he remained unprovoked by Jack's action. "I am here to find out the truth." Baralis stepped forward, his shadow falling upon Jack. "What are you, Jack? Who do you work for?" His voice was almost a whisper. "What happened that morning in the kitchens?"

Jack shook his head. He was frightened, but nothing in the world would make him show that to Baralis.

"You refuse to tell me, boy?"

"I can't tell you what I do not know myself."

"Don't play games with me, boy. You will regret it if you do." Baralis continued, his voice menacingly low. "The loaves, Jack. You and I both know those loaves had been . . . altered. Tell me what happened. Were you practicing your skills of drawing and lost control?"

"I don't know." Jack struggled to keep his voice level. "If I made anything happen, it was not by intention." He'd spoken the truth, but it held no charm of protection. He was more afraid than ever.

Baralis thought for a moment, his gray eyes the color of blades. "Tell me, boy, has this happened to you before?"

"No."

"Come, come now." Baralis' voice was a silk sheath with a dagger at its center. "A trick to please the maidens? A prank to annoy Frallit? What have you done before?"

"Nothing. The loaves were an accident."

"*An accident!* Power is never drawn by accident."

Jack felt the stirring of something, the same pressure as before, only minutely different. It took a moment to realize it came from Baralis, not himself. Fear consumed Jack's consciousness, leaving barely enough space for thoughts of survival.

Baralis' voice became louder. Jack had never seen the man so riled. "Look at me, boy." The weight of Baralis' will pressed against him, and he looked into his eyes. "Tell me the truth. Where did your power come from?" Jack's head began to feel heavy, burdened with a force he could not name. He felt in danger of losing himself, of his mind being crushed by the strength of Baralis' will.

"I don't know."

The burden lifted a little. Jack felt his stomach heave with nausea. Baralis held him in his thrall. "Oh yes, you do, Jack. All the answers are there within you. If you choose not to tell me, I will be forced to pry them out."

Strangely, amidst the turmoil, Baralis' words stood out like glowing embers in the dark: was the man right, were the answers within him?

A sharp stab of pain followed by unbearable pressure stopped all thought of answers. It felt like a hundred tiny incisions were being made in his brain. Baralis was the surgeon.

"Who are you working for? *Tell me.*"

"I work for no one." Pain made Jack strong. *"Leave me alone!"* There was something growing, something of his own. Bile came to his throat. Such sickness it made him dizzy.

For an instant, Baralis backed away. A second later Jack was in agony. Pain coursed through his spine. His eyes were drawn into their sockets; he felt as if Baralis were wringing the power from him.

"I will have the answers from you," he said.

The man was in his mind, searching, burrowing deep within his being. The pain was all consuming; it blazed away, kindling his very soul. His thoughts collapsed downward to a place where they'd never been. Through suffering came peace. Everything was clear. He knew what he was and what he must do. His mother was there, her secrets revealed; she'd been so much cleverer—and braver—than he had ever known. The figure in the shade was his father. Jack strained to make him out. A spasm wracked his body, and he fought against it—he would not lose himself to the force of Baralis' mind.

The pain was so terrible it pushed the breath from his lungs. The visions fled with the light at their side, and left him to darkness. Alone, he struggled till he knew no more.

"Didn't I tell you Mulberry Street was grand?" Nabber looked to Tawl for confirmation.

"You did indeed." They were in a part of Rorn that Tawl had never seen before. Fine buildings lined the street, elegantly pillared, sided in marble and gleaming white stone. The road was tastefully thread with trees and bushes, not a piece of rotting vegetation in sight; even the air smelled fragrant. Tawl had just delivered the first of the letters from Larn. He was anxious to deliver the second one.

"The archbishop's palace is not a stone's throw away," said Nabber. Tawl had found the young street urchin to be a wealth of information regarding Rorn. Their journey to Mulberry Street had been marked by Nabber waving hellos at every dodgy-looking character they'd passed. "Now, if you think that place you delivered the letter was fancy, you should set your eyes on the palace. I could take you there next, if you like."

"Another time. Lead me on to Tassock Lane, Nabber." Tawl didn't know what it was that made him so eager to be free of his debt from Larn. It was as if as long as he held their letters, they had some claim upon him. "How far away is it?"

"Not far, but it's not as nice as this place." Tawl was glad to hear it; he had not liked the feel of Mulberry Street one little bit. It seemed to him that beneath all the splendor lay something rank and furtive.

Before long the district changed. People walked on the streets, vendors sold their wares, tempting passersby to purchase hot chestnuts or toasted onion cakes or rolls stuffed with fragrant lamb. Tawl could see that Nabber was hungry, and he admired the way that the boy ostentatiously ignored the food on display; he was determined to show Tawl that he would complete his part of the bargain before expecting the payment.

The two walked a little further, and then Nabber slipped down a little side street. "Tassock Lane," pronounced the boy. It was a dark street, the buildings blocking out what little light was left of the day. It was home to many traders: boot repair, sign painting, saddlers, none of whom appeared to be doing much business.

Tawl bid the boy wait and walked down the lane alone. The priest had told him to deliver the letter to a man who lived above a small bake shop. He was beginning to think the priest was mistaken. He had walked nearly the full distance of the street and had found no such place. He could see a dead end looming ahead, but as he drew nearer he saw that the last building was indeed a bakery. Tawl walked into the small shop; what few items it had on offer looked neither fresh nor appetizing.

The tired-looking woman behind the counter was openly hostile. "What d'you want?" she demanded. Tawl thought that it was rather an odd way for a shopkeeper to greet her customers.

"I have a letter for the man who lives upstairs."

"Oh, have you indeed? And who might this letter be off?"

"I'm afraid, madam, I cannot say." The woman snorted loudly and Tawl decided not to leave the letter with her. "If you please, I would be grateful if you could direct me upstairs." The woman snorted again, but stood up.

"Follow me." She led him through a doorway and up a narrow flight of stairs. There was a brief passageway with three doors leading from it. "You'll be wanting the second door," said the woman.

"How can you be sure who I want? I have not told you his name."

"You'll be wanting the second door," she repeated. "All people coming here delivering letters want the second door." She watched as Tawl knocked on the door.

A slight, wiry man answered. Tawl saw confusion and something more in the man's eyes. He spoke the name he had been given by the priest and the man nodded, shaking slightly.

"I have a letter for you." Tawl pulled it from his belt. Understanding dawned in the man's eyes. He grabbed at the letter and shut the door in Tawl's face. Tawl looked around for the woman, but she had withdrawn. He made his way down the stairs and out of the shop, his mind trying to grasp what expression he had seen flit across the man's features when he first set eyes upon him.

"I thought you'd skipped out on me," said Nabber as Tawl walked up to him. "You've been a fine time. A man could starve to death with waiting." Tawl smiled, knowing this was the boy's way of reminding him about his part of the bargain.

"Fish pie and eel ends it is, then." They both laughed heartily. Tawl was relieved to be free of his obligation to Larn.

Bringe drew his blade once more over the whetstone. The action produced a scraping noise which he found pleasing. He ran his thumb across the huge ax blade. Swords and knives were for weaklings. The ax was the weapon of a real man. No simpering lord had the balls to yield an ax. Bringe rolled his phlegm and spat in disgust. He dipped his rag into the pot of congealing pig fat and proceeded to work it into the blade; it would need to be well greased tonight. He scooped out a handful of the soft, yellow lard and wrapped it in the rag in case he had want of it later.

There was little need for him to be quiet as he left his house. His wife was drunk, and that, combined with a sound beating, had rendered her unconscious. As he passed the inert form of his spouse lying on the dirt floor, he aimed a passing kick at her chest. She groaned faintly in acknowledgment.

It was a fine night, thought Bringe as he walked down the hill balancing the weight of the massive ax on his shoulder. A crescent moon glowed weakly in the cold sky, providing just the right amount of light he needed. A full moon would have been too bright; sharp eyes could see on a full moon. His step was light and he hummed a tune to himself. A fine tune, with words that spoke of the delights of a certain young maiden. Bringe always thought of Gerty when he heard it. It was true that she had neither the golden hair nor perfect skin of the girl in the song, but she was warm and willing and he required no more in a woman. It would not be long before she would be his. With his wife out of the way and money in his pocket, he would take Gerty for his own.

After a short while he reached his destination: a secluded area of apple orchards. The portion of land lay in a gentle valley with the ground rising around it. Bringe knew the nearest farmhouse was way over the rise. He would be observed by no one. He was not a counting man, but he figured there were at least five score of trees in the valley. It would be hard work.

He rolled up his sleeves, the curve of his muscles catching the moonlight. He approached the tree nearest to him, a sturdy, low specimen with a thick trunk. Probably more than forty years growth, he reckoned. Bringe swung the huge ax above his head and brought it down with all the force in his body. The blade hacked viciously into the tree trunk, its cruel edge biting deep within the tree. Bringe swung again, bending his back low and setting the ax at a different angle. Two more blows and a large wedge of trunk fell from the tree, leaving it mutilated. The tender inner wood was now badly exposed. There would be rain and then frost in the coming days. The rain would permeate the trunk and the frost would cause the moisture to freeze and swell, damaging the integrity of the tree. Even if the tree did not wither and rot, it would be some years before it could once again bear a decent quantity of apples.

Bringe moved on to the next tree. He reckoned it would take him the greater part of the night to hack all the trees in the valley, and he had no time to waste.

Seventeen

*T*awl awoke with a start. He was aware of someone moving around the room, and as a reflex he went for his knife; it wasn't there.

"This what you're looking for?" The boy held it out for Tawl to take.

"By Borc! How did you get in here?" Tawl was annoyed at being caught off guard—and by a mere boy no less.

"Easy as can be," said Nabber. "After that excellent meal last night, when I took my leave of you, I got to thinking that I had no shelter for the evening, and I thought that you wouldn't be opposed to the idea of sharing your room. So I made my way up here. You were flat out, so I just made myself comfy and went out like a light."

"The door was locked."

"You're a bit green, ain't you?"

Tawl was at a loss for words. The boy was right; he had been foolish to trust a locked door. He had, however, always thought of himself as a light sleeper, yet the boy had not only broken into his room but also managed to steal his knife. "What time is it?" he asked testily.

"Dawn's just about to rise. Time for breakfast, I'd say."

"Buying you breakfast was not part of the bargain."

"Well, I'll buy *you* some, then." The boy pulled a gold

coin from his tunic and grinned. Tawl checked in his belt only to have his suspicions confirmed.

"That's mine, boy."

"Has it got your name on?" The boy scrutinized the coin. "I don't believe it has." Tawl whipped across the room and over to the boy, caught his arm and twisted it.

"Give it to me this instant, you little robber." The boy dropped the coin and it rolled onto the wooden floor. Tawl released the boy and picked up the coin. When he looked up, the boy was making a great show of rubbing his arm. "You can stop pretending I hurt you; all I did was squeeze you a little bit. You wouldn't want me to think you were a cry-baby."

"Didn't hurt one bit," said Nabber with exaggerated dignity. "I was just rubbing it to improve the circulation."

Tawl ignored the boy and made his way around the room. Gathering together his things, he checked in his bag to make sure the boy had not stolen anything else. Once satisfied that everything was in his possession, he made his way toward the door.

"Hey, wait a minute," said the boy, chasing after him.

"Leave me be, boy. I have much to do this morning and I have no need for company." Tawl descended the stairs of the small inn and walked into the dining area. A middle-aged woman approached him.

"What can I be bringing you, sir?" The woman smiled invitingly, adjusting the ruffle around her bosom. He had no time for a dalliance this morning. He was anxious to be on his way. Now that he'd paid for the seeing at Larn, it was time to act upon it. He needed to head for the Four Kingdoms and find the boy.

"I'll take some mulled holk and a plate of bacon and mushrooms." Tawl knew the cost would be high, but he would leave the city this day and this could be his last chance for a proper meal for some time.

"And for your son?" Tawl looked around to see Nabber standing behind him. The woman waited expectantly.

He relinquished. "The same for the boy. Half portion." The woman scuttled off. Tawl spoke to Nabber, "Sit down, boy, and enjoy your breakfast. It will be your last meal that I pay for."

Nabber sat down and began to tear at the warm bread the woman had brought. "While you were asleep, my friend," he said, "I took the liberty of casting my eyes upon your circles. Nothing personal, mind, just testing your credentials. Anyway, I couldn't make out what the scar in the middle was—sort of runs right through 'em."

Tawl took a deep draught of ale. "It's none of your business, boy." Nabber opened his mouth to speak and then thought better of it. They ate the rest of their meal in silence.

By the time the Nabber was mopping up the last traces of bacon fat, Tawl was beginning to feel he'd spoken too harshly. To make up for his bluntness, he offered the boy a chance to show off his knowledge of Rorn. "Tell me, Nabber, how much would an old nag set me back in this city?"

"Two gold pieces," said the boy in between mouthfuls of bread. Rorn was an expensive place.

"What could I get for . . . " Tawl made a quick calculation, " . . . ten silvers?"

"A sick mule."

Tawl could not help but smile. A mule was no use to him; he could move quicker on foot. He was beginning to wish he'd kept back more than one gold coin from Megan. The Four Kingdoms was a great distance away; it could take him over two months to get there on foot. Not to mention the mountains: the Great Divide, as they were called, ran the length of the Known Lands. Tawl realized for the first time that he would be forced to cross them in deep winter. He would need warmer clothes and supplies. He decided he would wait until he'd left Rorn to purchase them, not only because they would be cheaper elsewhere, but also because the climate in Rorn was warm and he would be forced to carry any clothing he did not wear. If he was to walk, then he must keep his belongings to a minimum.

Tawl briefly pondered the idea of asking the Old Man for more money; he was sure it would be freely given. He was proud, though, and liked little the idea of asking any man for help. He would have to rely on his own resources. He was not too worried; there were always ways for a man with a strong arm to earn some money. Still, he would have to be careful with what money was left once he had paid for his food and bed.

Tawl finished his meal and paid his bill. The woman bit on the coin to test its worth, then handed him twelve silvers in return—less than he had expected. "Where can I buy some dried goods and a water flask?" he asked Nabber. "And I need to find my way to the north gate."

"I'll show you, if you like."

"No, Nabber." Tawl was anxious to be free of the boy. "I'd rather you just tell me where to go." The boy nodded and described a place nearby.

Tawl clasped Nabber's arm in the knightly fashion and bid him farewell. The boy gave him an unreadable look and wished him "profit on the journey," an unusual saying, and one Tawl suspected was unique to money-hungry Rorn. He watched as the boy slipped down an alleyway. Tawl thought he detected a certain reluctance to his step, but paid it little heed. Nabber would soon be off finding more lucrative possibilities.

Quickly finding the place the boy had described, he made his purchases, and was pleased to see that they were not too expensive. He checked the position of the sun in the sky. It was time to be on his way.

It was a bright, gusty morning and the odors of salt and filth mixed on the breeze—it was a smell that summed up the city in one sharp whiff. Tawl approached the towering north gate of Rorn. He would not be sorry to leave. Too much had happened here: imprisonment, torture, the loss of a friend in Megan, and the comprehension of just how low the knights' reputation had fallen.

Even now, though, he had things to be thankful for: a chance meeting with a fortune-teller had led him to Larn. And Larn, in turn, pointed his way west.

Was that always the way things happened, he wondered, by chance? Fate he wasn't sure of, but chance seemed a familiar tune. Its arbitrary strains had accompanied him more than once in his life. It was playing brazenly the day he met Tyren: what were the chances of a man, whose sole objective at the time was to find new blood for the knights, being present the afternoon he'd been taunted into a fight by the village bullies?

Dragonflies courted in the shade. The breeze was warm on his skin, too warm to dry the sweat. His legs felt weak—not from the fight, but from the shock of learning that the man who stood before him came from Valdis.

Tyren looked at the leg of mutton. "Come back to the village with me and I'll buy you another—that one's too dirty for roasting."

Tawl was still out of breath. Pride prevented him from accepting the man's offer. He shook his head. "No, this will do. Sara can wipe it down."

"Who is Sara?" asked Tyren.

"My sister."

"I'm sure she won't mind waiting on the joint a little while longer. Come join me for a drink, and let me tell you about Valdis."

Tawl took a deep breath; he was still shaken from the fight. "Sir, I don't want to waste your time. I can't go to Valdis with you." There! he'd done it: put an end to the matter. What alternative did he have? He couldn't run off and leave his sisters.

Tyren seemed amused. "You mean to tell me, boy, that you'd turn your back on the chance of free training at Valdis?"

Free. Tawl could hardly believe it. The cleric had told him training cost a small fortune. It made his refusal even more difficult. "Sir, I have other obligations."

"What obligations? Are you an apprenticed baker, or a tied fieldhand?" Tyren's voice mocked him. "What possible obligations could you have to prevent you returning with me to Valdis?"

Blood dripped down Tawl's chin—one of the boys had landed a decent blow. It would be so easy to go with Tyren and never return home. But he couldn't do it: his sense of what was *right* prevented him. "I have two sisters and a baby to care for. My mother died three years back and they depend on me to live."

"Ah." Tyren rubbed his short, slick beard. "What about your father? Is he dead, too?"

"No. We don't see him very often. He spends his days drinking in Lanholt."

"So you do the honorable thing. It's a shame you're not free. We could do with more of your kind in the knights." Tyren smiled, showing his teeth. "Not to mention the fact that you fight like a demon." He shrugged. "So be it. Perhaps when your sisters are older . . ."

"Sara is twelve, the baby is three."

"Hmm. Well, give thought to my offer, and if you change your mind I'll be staying at the Bulrush in Greyving for a week." He bowed with grace, his dark cloak brushing the dust, and then began to walk back to the village.

Tawl raised his arm to halt him, but never said the words. The sight of the figure retreating into the distance was more than Tawl could bear. He turned away and began the journey home—down along the riverbank, across the drying mire. He grew bitter with every step. He hated his sisters. He hated his mother. He hated his father. The leg of mutton became a symbol of his duty, and raising it over his head, he threw it from him with all his strength. The ribbons he crushed beneath his feet.

His sisters were at the window, watching for his return. Disappointment at seeing he was empty-handed was quickly replaced with concern over his injuries. "You've been beaten," said Sara, dampening a cloth for the blood.

"No, not beaten," he said. "I put on a fair show."

"You won?" asked Anna, her voice sharp with excitement.

"It doesn't matter who won. Go and get me some ointment from the shelf." Sara turned to Tawl. "They called you names, didn't they?"

Her sympathy annoyed him. "So what if they did? I'm a grown man. I can fight if I choose."

"What happened to the meat? Did it get lost in the fight?"

"Yes," he lied.

"It doesn't matter, Tawl." Sara kissed him on the cheek.

"As long as you're all right, fish will be fine for Summer Festival."

Slowly, through their gentle, good humor, they brought him round. He didn't mention his meeting with Tyren, preferring to be alone with his loss. Three nights he lay awake, tossing and turning in his bed, his imagination tormenting him with visions of what could have been. He knew it was unfair to blame his sisters, and he made an effort not to be short tempered with them. It was easy. Sara and Anna were so pleased he was unharmed by the fight—and he suspected a little proud of his performance—that they spent the next few days spoiling him: kissing and hugging and making his favorite foods.

On the fourth day they had a visitor. Chance played its final part. Tawl returned from fishing about mid-morning. The door was ajar and a voice could be heard saying, "See, I know what my beauties like!" It was his father. Anger boiled in Tawl's breast. He marched into the room.

"Get lost, you old drunkard. We've nothing left for you to steal!"

There was complete silence for an instant. Tawl took in the scene. Sara and Anna were sitting at their father's feet. The man had two large sacks with him and was dressed like a king.

"Papa's not come to steal," said Anna. "He's brought us gifts." She held out a hand filled with brightly colored ribbons.

"Yes, Tawl," said Sara. "Father's had a spot of luck at the table." She looked a little guilty, like a crewman with thoughts of mutiny.

"You mean gambling." Tawl's voice was hard.

"Gambling, carding, call it what you will. Luck kissed me then made me her lover." His father's voice was surprisingly level. Though his breath still stunk of ale. "I won a small fortune. And I'll be putting it to good use."

"How?" Tawl didn't like the sound of this. He was jealous of the way his sisters were so excited—he'd saved for months to buy them ribbons, and now his father turned up and was treated like a hero.

"I've come home to stay. There's no need for you to do

everything anymore, Tawl. I'll be head of the family from now on."

Anna and Sara looked at him, silently pleading. They were so innocent; they had no idea what their father was really like. A proper family was the dream they were asking him to accept.

"You think you can just come here, after years of neglecting us, and just take over?" said Tawl. "Well, we don't want you here."

Anna spoke up. "Tawl, give Papa a chance. He promised us meat everyday and new dresses each month."

"Ssh, Anna," said Sara, looking directly at Tawl. "It's not meat or dresses that we want. It's Father home again." She gave him a sad look.

"See?" said his father. "My daughters want me home. It's my duty to be here. And here I'll stay."

That night Tawl made his way to the Bulrush at Greyving. Tyren came downstairs to meet him. "I'm free to come with you to Valdis," he said. "My obligation has been taken away."

Jack was aware of feeling sick. He lay for some time with his eyes closed, in the hazy state between sleep and waking. Eventually he opened his eyes. He was staring at the stone ceiling. Drops of water seeped in through the cracks and threatened to drip down. His eyesight seemed somehow clearer than he remembered. He could see the rainbow of colors in the tiny droplets, and the minutest detail of the stone. He rubbed his eyes and looked again. The effect had gone away; he must have imagined it.

He rose up from the bench—a little too quickly. As a wave of nausea hit him, he leaned forward and brought up the contents of his stomach. He wiped his mouth clean and began to feel a little better. His head felt strangely heavy, and when he turned it seemed to take a minute for his mind to settle back into place.

He strained to recall the events of the previous day: Baralis had come to him, questioning. He could remember neither the questions asked nor his own answers, if indeed he had given any answers at all. He did not believe he had any to give. A glimpse of a memory tantalized his mind. Something about his mother. He tried to grasp at it, almost made it out, and then it was gone. Was there some connection between the questioning and his mother? Or was it just that he was badly shaken by Baralis' probing and wasn't thinking straight?

He dismissed all thoughts of the day before and tried to stand up. Testing the strength in his legs, he found them a little shaky. He had a great thirst and he looked around the room. There was no water. Jack hammered on the solid wooden door, calling for water. As he waited for it to be brought to him, he made a decision: he had to try and escape—he had been weakly submitting for too long. What right had Baralis to capture him? He had done nothing wrong. One thing was clear: Baralis suspected him of being more than what he was. If he remained here, he would surely be subjected to more of whatever Baralis had done to him, or worse.

There was a noise on the other side of the door. Jack heard the bolt being drawn back. He looked around, desperately searching for something to use as a weapon. The room was bare, the wooden bench its sole contents. Quickly, Jack slipped to the side of the door. It swung open and Jack, who was now behind the door, heard a man step into the room. Before the man had the chance to take another step, Jack pushed the door back with all his strength. The heavy door slammed into the man, knocking him off his feet. The man started to cry out. Jack rushed forward; desperate to quiet the man, he kicked him violently in the head. Blood rushed from the guard's nose and mouth. The man tried to get to his feet, but Jack kicked him hard in the kidneys and he crumpled to the floor again.

Jack wavered for a second, wondering what to do. He caught sight of the guard's sword tucked under his belt. He grasped the hilt and pulled hard. The guard reached for his sword but he was too late; he grasped the blade not the hilt, and as Jack drew the sword the blade cut deeply into the soft flesh of the palm of the guard's hand. The sight of so much of his own blood frightened the guard and he began whimpering. Jack's heart was pounding excitedly: he had the sword. He stood over the guard, sword poised, and found he could not stab him—the guard looked too pathetic.

Jack knew he had little time; he could not be sure if the man's cries had been heard. He gave the guard one last kick to the head, hoping to knock him out. It didn't work; the man was still conscious. Jack carefully took the blade in his hand and swung the weighted hilt down on the head of the guard. He had intended to get the back of the man's head, but the guard looked around at the last moment and the hilt hit him full in the face. Jack drew back, horrified as the man's face turned into a bloody mess.

Jack fled from the sight, appalled at what had happened—a clean blade to the innards would have been a kindness compared to what he had done. He had intended to draw the guard's unconscious body into the room and close the door, hoping to give himself more time for escape, but the sight of the guard's ruined face sent him into a panic. He began to run. He paid no heed to where he was heading. Down stone passageways he fled, each one looking the same as the next.

After some time he grew short of breath. He slowed down, gulping for air. He listened to see if anyone was pursuing him, but the only sound he could hear was the blood pumping through his veins. He had not realized that he was being held in such a maze of tunnels. Forcing himself to think, he decided what to do next. He looked back in the direction he had come from; he would not return that way. By sheer luck, it seemed, he had managed to avoid the guard room.

Jack walked on a short way and was presented with a choice as the tunnel he was in branched off. The passage running straight ahead was long and dark, and was not lit by torchlight. Jack did not like the thought of walking where he could not see. He decided instead to take the second tunnel.

The path that Jack chose took a sharp turn and he found that it was no longer lit. He paused on the verge of darkness. Should he go on? His eyes strained against the blackness. He had no way of telling how long the tunnel was. He stepped forward into the dark.

* * *

Baralis was pacing his chamber. As he walked to and fro, he worked the curative oils into his hands; they were causing him great pain. The rains had come this morning and he felt the ensuing dampness working on his stiffening fingers. Baralis hoped that Bringe had managed to damage the orchard the previous night; it would be a shame if they missed the benefit of all the rain.

The oils were doing no good. He dried off his hands and went over to his desk where he kept his painkilling drug. He carefully measured a portion of the white powder and transferred it into his glass. He poured a little wine to wet the mix, raised the glass to his lips and drank it dry.

The interrogation of the boy yesterday had disturbed him deeply. It left him physically and mentally exhausted. He felt sure the boy had spoken the truth—he did after all have his own ways of ascertaining such things. There was more to this, though. There had been a point when Jack had nearly driven him from his mind. He, Baralis, forced back by a mere boy.

It meant something. The boy's mind was closed as surely as a locked chest. For a brief instant something was there—a vision, almost a message: a woman, and behind her a man. He'd tried to dig deeper but was repelled, meeting blankness once more. Baralis had searched the minds of hundreds of men to get where he was now, and not one had resisted him like the baker's boy.

Of course he was far too skilled for the encounter to have caused him any harm. The boy had obviously suffered badly from the incident, while he'd come out unscathed. Still, there was something disturbing about the episode. The boy had access to a great amount of power. He probably spoke the truth when he said the loaves were the first thing he'd ever done. Such untrained might was dangerous. *The boy turned back time in the oven!* Baralis shuddered, almost against his will. He'd never heard of such a thing being done before. It shouldn't be possible. To hold time in abeyance for even a second took the skill of a master. He himself could barely stay a tallow's flame. And yet this boy from nowhere had done more, so much more, than that.

Jack didn't realize the magnitude of what he'd done. He thought it was just a case of turning burnt loaves to dough. It was time he turned, not bread. Only last week Baralis had returned to the kitchens. The aftermath could still be felt. That fool Frallit had been forced to change the baking slabs. They were acting strangely and the dough took hours longer to bake. It was Jack's drawing that had done it. All sorcery left an aftermath of some sort: a trace of what had been. Only the most powerful kind still lingered weeks past its drawing.

The boy had set something in motion that might take years to pass. The cinders from the oven had been ground for soap. 'Twould be a lucky lady who brought that lather to her face. At worst it might help preserve her looks, at best it might make them more youthful. The baking slabs might end up dumped in the middens—Baralis couldn't imagine what the result of that would be.

The loaves themselves had been destroyed. He'd at least made sure of that.

He would have to think carefully on what to do about the boy. His plans were running smoothly at the moment; he wanted no spoiler, no wild card. He had a nagging feeling that Jack could turn out to be one. At a different time he would have kept the boy, experimented, dissected, made it his business to get to the bottom of the mystery. He had too much on his mind at the present, too much was at stake. He would have the boy killed.

He was disturbed from his thoughts by the arrival of his servant. "Ahh, Crope. Just the person I was thinking of. I have a little job for you."

"Yes, sir."

"Well, you know our two guests."

"Guests?"

"The prisoners, you empty-headed numbskull! I want you to dispose of the boy."

"He's gone."

"What do you mean he's gone? Of course he's not gone. I saw him with my own eyes yesterday. He's guarded by ten mercenaries, he cannot have just gone." Baralis was shaking.

"Well, sir, I was just down at the haven, bringing some

delicacies for the lady—she appreciates it when I bring her honey rolls and sweet wine."

"Get to the point, man!" roared Baralis.

"Well, Traff comes running up to me and says the boy has escaped. Says he did some terrible damage to one of his men."

Baralis was frantic. "The girl? She has not escaped?"

"No, sir, I saw her myself just a short while back. I made sure her door was firmly bolted."

"Do they know which way the boy headed in the woods?"

"Traff said that they think the boy headed for the passages. He says that they would have seen him if he'd made for the way out."

Baralis thought for a while. It was a good thing that the boy had not headed for the woods; he might still be found. "Come with me," he ordered, and the two men rushed from the room. Before long they were heading down the tunnel that linked the haven to the castle, Baralis drawing light to illuminate the way.

"Crope, go and tell that useless imbecile Traff to search all the tunnels and rooms. Have him put two men on the entrance, in case the boy doubles back." The first thing Baralis had to do on reaching the haven was to check on the girl. He had seen that Jack had grown attached to her, and if he was in the tunnels he might try and find her. The boy had no bearing on his plans, he was merely a dangerous distraction, but he could not risk losing Melliandra. If the girl escaped he would forfeit his wager with the queen. The bolt on her door was no longer enough. She would have to be transferred to a room that could be securely locked.

To her surprise Melli found that she liked Baralis' huge, hulking servant. He treated her as if she were a fragile butterfly, bringing extra blankets when she was cold and special foods to eat, even rose water to splash on her face.

Melli had to admit she was living in considerable comfort. She was, however, far from satisfied. She found herself thinking more and more about her time in the forest; she had been truly free then, no one to tell her what to do or how to do it. She supposed that at some point Baralis would have to let her go. He could not hold her indefinitely, and she could not believe that he would harm her in any way. He was, after all, the king's chancellor.

Melli popped a honey roll into her mouth, wondering what had become of Jack. She was startled when Baralis let himself into her room. She noticed that he seemed relieved at the sight of her. He caught her with her mouth full of food. She swallowed quickly and took a drink of water, slamming her glass down when finished.

"It appears, Lord Baralis, that your servant has better manners than you. At least he thinks to knock before entering a lady's room."

Baralis seemed to be agitated, and when he spoke his voice was lacking its usual mellifluous tones. "Does a lady usually run away from home and end up whoring in Duvitt?"

"Does a gentleman usually hold a woman against her will?"

"I don't believe, my dear Melliandra, that I ever styled myself a gentleman." There was something slightly different about Baralis this day: he appeared less controlled, less cultured than usual.

"To what do I owe this pleasure?"

"I'm afraid I have some bad news. You will have to forgo these pleasing surroundings."

"Why?" Melli demanded.

"That is no concern of yours."

"Where will you be taking me?" She was beginning to feel frightened.

"Not far. Follow me."

"What about my things?" she said lamely, trying to forestall him. Baralis came close to her—he was barely a foot away. She could smell him: a heady, enticing scent. His fragrance drew her to him, a pull upon a thread. She leaned toward him. Their eyes met and she inhaled sharply; it was *his* breath that filled her lungs . . . it was potent like a drug. He raised his arm and drew his hand down her back, his fingers searching for the scars beneath her dress. The caress thrilled and stung, and her lips parted, relinquishing his breath and preparing for his touch.

Baralis seemed to resist her compulsion and spoke, his words altering the texture of the moment. "All you will need for now, my pretty one, are the clothes on your back."

Melli stepped away from him. She felt unsteady on her feet and starved of air. Baralis held her gaze a moment longer and then turned on his heels. "Come now," he said, his voice an impatient hiss. He led Melli a short way and then to her surprise, he stopped by the solid stone wall and felt the stone with his fingertips. Melli jumped back, startled, as the whole section of wall began to move. Baralis ushered her through the gap and into a large room. Several candles burned low and Melli could see it had been used recently; there was a flagon of ale resting on the table. There were a few chairs, a desk with manuscripts laid out upon it, and on the wall was an old, faded tapestry. The wall slid back into place and Baralis made his way across the room, pausing to take a key from his belt and light an oil lamp.

There was a low, wooden door on the far wall and Baralis opened it with a turn of the key. "In here." He beckoned her and she came forward, trepidation growing inside of her. The room was small and cramped, lined with shelves, obviously intended as a storeroom.

Melli mustered her courage. "I refuse to step inside that place."

Baralis turned on her, gripping her wrist cruelly. The oil lamp swung dangerously. "You will go in there." Melli looked to the lamp—the flame was close to her dress. She stepped inside, tugging her wrist free from his grip. Baralis came in behind her and set the lamp down on a shelf, then turned around and left the room. Melli was tempted to shout out as she heard the lock turn, but her pride prevented it. She would not have that man believe her frightened.

Melli looked around the room, rubbing her arms. The place was cold and damp, water was running down the walls, and the floor was wet. There was no chair or pallet to rest on; she could not sit on the floor, so she was forced to stand.

Her heart was still pounding uncontrollably. She could hardly believe she had let Baralis caress her back, welcomed the touch of his fingers down her spine. She could still feel the subtle pressure of his breath in her lungs. She shook her head vigorously, seeking to dispel the sensation. She had actually wanted him to kiss her. Absently, she rubbed her fingers across her lips. Baralis was rumored to have unusual powers, perhaps he had used them upon her. Her fingers stole into her mouth and she sucked gently upon them. No, she knew there had been no artificial inducement. Nothing save the pull of attraction—him for her and she for him.

Her breast was rising up and down rapidly, she could not bear to think on the subject anymore.

She looked around the small, damp room. How long would she be kept here, confined like an animal? She glanced down at her wrist where he had gripped her: a red mark was forming. Melli felt the pressure of tears behind her eyes. She would not give into them. After all, had she not been in worse situations? This room was a palace compared to the pit in Duvitt. She managed a weak smile, willing herself not to succumb to despair.

She forced herself to think about more practical matters. She checked how much oil was in the lamp: it was less than half full. Melli turned it down; she had no wish to be plunged into darkness. She checked the shelves, looking for something she could use to keep warm. They were all empty save for a collection of dead and decaying insects, the unsuspecting victims of long-waiting spiders.

Melli stood, leaning against the wooden shelves, hands hovering above the lamp for warmth, and wondered what had caused Baralis to move her. Perhaps her father had found out where she was, but somehow she did not think so. Something was obviously worrying Baralis, worrying him enough to lock her in a storeroom. Maybe it had something to do with Jack.

Her mind dwelled on the baker's boy. He had been good to her, tending her wounds, giving his portion of water for her to drink. She didn't believe his story about running away from the castle. Jack did not strike her as a thief, and Lord Baralis did not strike her as the sort of man who would waste his time chasing one. What then was his interest in Jack?

*   *   *

Jack did not enjoy walking down the darkened tunnel; he had never been in a place so devoid of light. He had been forced to feel his way like a blind man. He'd walked for some time, only to find that the passage was a dead end. It seemed strange to him that a passage would lead to nowhere; he decided he must have missed an opening. He traced back his steps, all the time listening anxiously for the approach of guards.

This time Jack was careful to feel both sides of the tunnel, moving from one side to the other with every step. This method required some time and Jack was afraid he would be caught. Suddenly his hands ran over a different texture than of stone. Wood. Jack spread out his palms; it was a door. He could feel no handle, so he pushed gently. The door did not move. He fervently hoped that it was not locked in some manner. He pushed harder and this time the door gave way, creaking loudly.

Jack stepped into more blackness. His leg smashed against a sharp object and he tripped and fell forward. He landed on something soft. He rested on the floor for some minutes, rubbing his throbbing shin, glad to have some time to think. It seemed to him that all the actions he had taken this morning had been performed with little thought, relying more on instinct. He now needed to plan, to decide upon his own course of action, rather than let fate decide it for him.

He wondered how he could get above ground and out of this series of tunnels. There must be another exit other than past the guardroom.

As he was thinking, he heard a faint rumble in the distance, and a pale light began to creep under the doorway. Jack quickly jumped to his feet, he had to hide. He could see no detail of the room, the only thing he could feel was the soft material beneath his feet. He felt around the area he had been lying on, it was a mound of old clothes or curtains. He could now hear distinct footsteps. Scrambling beneath the heap of fabrics, he raced to cover his arms and legs.

The door swung open, Jack could make out light flooding the room. He heard a man's voice: "See, Kessit, I told you there was no need to bother looking in here. No one's been in this room for years. Look at all this stuff."

"Should we head back, then?" said another voice.

"No rush, Kessit, let's have a little rest, take a bit of snatch."

"Traff won't be pleased if we dawdle."

"Traff won't know if you don't tell him." The two men moved forward into the room. Jack could hear the sound of a tin being opened.

"Come on, make yourself comfortable. A man can't enjoy his snatch unless he's relaxed. Settle down on that pile of old rags for a bit, take the weight off those enormous feet of yours." To Jack's horror, one of the guards sat on the edge of his hiding place. His leg was only a few layers beneath the man. Jack tried to keep his breathing to a minimum.

"Course, all this to-do is Harl's fault. Fancy letting yourself be overpowered by a wisp of a boy."

"Well, poor Harl's paying the price for his mistake."

"Aye. Did you see his face? It was ruined."

"He won't be attracting any more ladies, that's for sure."

"Nice bit of snatch this."

"There's more going on here than Lord Baralis is letting on. Were you there yesterday after he'd finished questioning the boy?"

"No, I don't believe I was." Jack was trying desperately to suppress a cough—dust had got in his throat.

"Well, something happened to Baralis, let me tell you. He came stumbling out of there, white as a sheet."

"Oh, was he?"

"Aye, you should have seen him. He could barely stand. Had to call for Crope to carry him away."

The two men were quiet for a while, the only noise being the sound of them chewing on their snatch. After a while one of them spat. "Aah, that's better. He's moved the girl, too."

"Who has?"

"Lord Baralis, you fool. He's moved her to one of his special places. He thinks the boy might try to rescue her."

Jack's leg had now gone numb with the weight of the man resting on it.

"D'you know how he gets in 'em?"

"I couldn't say exactly. I've seen him fiddling around with the stone. Had a go myself, didn't get anywhere."

"I think we'd better get going. Traff ain't in a good mood today." To Jack's relief the man stood up.

"I wouldn't care to be in his place, I can tell you." With that the two men left the room, the light receding behind them.

Jack let out a sigh of relief and then coughed the dust from his lungs. He pushed the coverings off him and stood up, trying to work out the numbness in his leg. He felt fairly safe for the time being; he didn't think the guards would return again soon.

He was feeling hungry and thirsty. He wished he knew what time of day it was; he had no idea how long it had been since he had escaped from his cell. The memory of the guard's bloody face returned to him, and he shuddered involuntarily. The guard had been doing him a favor—bringing him water.

Jack felt ashamed of the fact that since he'd escaped he had not given a thought to Melli's plight. He had assumed that Baralis would have returned her to the castle. When Melli told him that she'd run away to prevent her marriage, he'd supposed that Baralis had brought her back to enable the marriage to go ahead. Now it appeared that she was still locked up. He knew he could not make his escape from the underground hideaway, knowing that she was still held prisoner. He had nursed Melli and tended her wounds; he could hardly leave her now when she could be in even greater danger.

He had to find out where she was being held. The first thing he would do, however, was find something to drink. He needed food and water and a light of some sort. He needed no weapon—for the first time in his life he possessed a real sword. He groped for the blade tucked into his belt, but felt little joy of possession.

Jack settled down to wait. The guards were obviously looking for him and it seemed wiser to bide his time for a while. His pursuers might become less watchful as the day wore on. He decided he would try the second route next time, since the first one he'd taken had proved to be a dead end.

Several hours later, Jack slipped from the room, carefully closing the door after him. He made his way down the passageway. It grew lighter ahead as he approached where it split off. He took the route to his right and was once more plunged into darkness.

He felt his way down the tunnel and soon realized that this passage was much longer than the one he had first taken. He wasted no time feeling for side openings but walked ahead, arms held out to feel for obstructions. It was deathly cold in the tunnel and Jack was beginning to wish that he had thought to bring some of the linens he'd lain under. He continued on down the passage, hoping that this one would not turn out to end in a stone wall.

After a while his eyes began to make out a glimmer of light in the distance; he rushed toward it. The light grew brighter and the tunnel came to an abrupt end. Jack found himself in a long, rectangular room which had several passages leading from it. Something on one of the stones forming the wall caught his attention and he went over to investigate. Elaborately carved in the stone was the letter "H" flanked by two serpents. Jack knew what it meant: he was somewhere deep within Castle Harvell.

Eighteen

The land outside of Rorn was good for little, the soil shallow and barren. Only a farmer of extraordinary skill and patience could coax bounty from the earth. Goats and sheep, however, found the tough, yellow grasses to their liking, and soft, pungent cheeses were produced from their milk. There were many villages to the north of Rorn, all depending to some degree on the city for their livelihood.

Tawl judged it was time for his noonday meal and looked around for a suitable spot. Not far off the road was a rocky hill dotted with grazing sheep. He decided to climb the hill. It was about time he had a proper look at who was following him.

As he climbed, he fished in his sack and brought out a slice of dried beef. He chewed it with little relish. There were few who enjoyed drymeat. He washed it down with some water from his flask and finished his meal off with dried apricots and sea biscuits. He smiled grimly. No wonder so few sailors had any teeth left; sea biscuits were as hard as the sea bed itself. The shopkeeper had assured him the biscuits would stay fresh until Borc's second coming. Tawl did not doubt it.

By the time he reached the top of the hill he had worked up a sweat and was sorely tempted to pour the remaining contents of his flask over his head. He stopped himself, for he could not be sure where the next fresh water would be. He had to content himself with turning his face to the cool breeze.

He was pleased to find the small hill gave him an excellent view of the land. He could see Rorn on the horizon, looking as it could only from a distance—white and gleaming. The sea sparkled like a dark jewel in the south, and to the north there was a suggestion of mountains. Tawl felt exhilarated, glad to be on his way, glad to be free of the city.

He scanned the surrounding land carefully, aware since last night that he was being followed. His eyes traveled over bush and rock searching for movement, but he could see nothing moving except the sheep. He was not unduly worried; there was someone out there and he would root them out. Tawl made a great show of bedding down for an afternoon nap, unrolling and shaking out his blanket, yawning and stretching. He lay down on a particularly uncomfortable rock and pretended to sleep.

Tawl waited. He waited for several hours, the sun arching slowly across the sky. Finally out of the corner of his eye he saw a movement down below. Tawl strained to make out any detail, but could not. He watched as the shape moved from behind a group of bushes and approached the foot of the hill. Tawl sprang up, knife in hand, and hurtled down the hillside. The figure started to run away, but Tawl had gravity on his side and gained quickly. He was directly above the figure and he leapt onto his back, forcing him to the ground. Only when his knife was poised to strike did Tawl recognize who it was.

"Don't kill me," squealed the boy. Tawl twisted Nabber's arm back and drove his face into the dirt.

"What are you doing following me?" he demanded.

"You're hurting me," pleaded the boy, struggling to free himself.

"I will hurt you more unless you speak up. Now tell me, why did you follow me?" Tawl increased the pressure on the boy's arm.

"Who's to say I followed you? It's a free country, a man can travel where he pleases." Tawl twisted the boy's arm as far as he could without breaking it. Nabber howled with pain. "I didn't mean anything by it. Just thought I'd follow you."

"People just don't follow someone unless they have good reason."

"There was no reason, I swear! I just thought I'd like to go on an adventure with a knight."

"Are you working for the archbishop of Rorn?" Tawl gave the boy's arm another twist.

"No, no. I don't know what you're talking about." The boy was close to tears. Tawl released his arm and let him go.

"So, Nabber, if I've got your story right, you're telling me that you just picked up and left the city on a whim to follow a knight." Tawl was skeptical.

"Yes, that's right." The boy brushed the dirt from his face and inspected his arm. "There's nothing in Rorn for me, thought I'd find myself a bit of excitement."

"What about your family?" Tawl noticed the red marks on Nabber's arm where he had held him—he had been harder than he thought on the boy.

The boy shrugged. "I ain't got none."

"So where will you go when you get back to the city?"

"I won't go back." The boy's eyes challenged Tawl.

"Well, you won't be following me any longer."

"Try and stop me." The boy raised his chin defiantly.

"What did you plan on doing about food and water?"

"Thought I'd pick 'em up on the way." Nabber shrugged his shoulders with a great show of nonchalance.

Tawl took a deep intake of breath. "Playing at adventuring is one thing, boy. You won't be able to survive much longer on your own."

"I did fine in Rorn."

"Where I'm headed is a lot more dangerous than Rorn."

"Let me travel with you, then." The boy looked eagerly at Tawl.

"I'm traveling on foot. You'd only slow me down."

"I've kept up with you so far."

"I only have food for one and little money to buy more."

"Getting money has never been a problem for me." The

boy smiled brightly. "I've always been quite resourceful where coinage is concerned. Quite resourceful indeed."

"Look, Nabber." Tawl decided to stop trading words with the boy. "You can't come with me. I've got a long, hard journey ahead. I won't have time to be worrying about you. Now go back to the city and practice your *resourcefulness* on the deserving people of Rorn." Tawl knew he was being hard on the boy, but it was the only way to get the message across. "Go on now. If you hurry, you'll be back in the city by dawn tomorrow." The boy flashed Tawl a look filled with animosity. "Here," said Tawl, pulling some drymeat from his bag. "Take this; you probably haven't eaten anything all day." The boy refused the offered food and walked away.

Tawl watched for a while, satisfying himself that Nabber was indeed heading back to Rorn. After some time Tawl turned north and set a fast pace; he wanted to cover a fair distance before it grew dark.

Maybor was checking his reflection in the mirror; he felt he might be getting a little portly. Just this morning the queen's wisewoman had teased him about it, insisting that she went on top, telling him she feared to be crushed if she were beneath. Maybor did not like the idea of women being on top—that was a man's place. The wisewoman was getting far too demanding. It was time he chose a new filly. He would pick a young one next; he had lost his taste for old flesh.

He was considering Lady Helliarna's chambermaid as a possible dalliance when his thoughts were interrupted by his son striding into the room.

"What is it, Kedrac?" snapped Maybor, a little annoyed at being disturbed from his contemplation of the chambermaid's ample backside.

"I have just found out something most unsettling, Father." Kedrac poured himself a glass of wine.

"What, what?" Maybor was beginning to get worried.

"Someone has sabotaged our orchards."

"What!" roared Maybor.

"Over five score of trees have been viciously muti-lated." Kedrac ran his hands through his dark hair.

"Which ones?"

"The trees in the little valley, just off the hunting track."

"When was this done?" Maybor paced furiously around the room.

"Two nights ago. The overseer sent word by pigeon."

"Does he have any idea of who did it? It must have been those damned Halcus. By Borc! How I wish this cursed war had never happened."

"I'm not sure that it was the Halcus. I was only up there last month, and their men had been driven way back beyond the river."

"It must have been them. Who else would do such a thing?"

"They have never done anything like it before, Father. Don't forget, the Halcus have their eyes on our orchards, too. I can't see why they would defile that which they hope will one day be their own."

"Five score trees! Our yield is already low. How badly are they damaged?" Maybor was genuinely distressed. He was proud of his orchards—they were his prime source of in-come. No cider fetched a higher price than that made from Nestor apples.

"I can't say, Father. However, the overseer is not a man to send a pigeon without good cause."

"The frost will be here once the rains have gone; it could destroy them. The trees in the small valley are amongst some of our oldest—they yield sweet, mellow apples." May-bor searched for something to destroy. "I swear I will kill the man responsible for this." He flung the jug of wine across the room, where it broke against the wall with a satisfying smash, spilling red wine over the priceless rug. "Is there any news of your foolhardy sister?"

"I have not sent a man to Duvitt to check out the ru-mors. I thought to go myself today."

"I will go too. I will ride to Duvitt and then on to my or-chards. I would see the damage that has been done first-hand."

"Are you sure you are fit to go, Father? You are not fully recovered from your illness."

"I am fine, boy," boomed Maybor, adding slyly, "do not count on getting your inheritance just yet, my son. I am a long walk from death's door."

"I will make preparation for your journey, Father."

"I want nothing fancy, Kedrac. I will not be slowed down by ceremony. If we ride quickly, we can be in Duvitt within five days."

Melli awoke with a start. She was in darkness; the lamp must have gone out while she slept. She had no idea what time it was nor how long she had been in the room. Her limbs felt stiff, and as she raised herself off the floor she realized her dress and underskirts were wet. She knew she should not have slept on the damp floor, but she'd had little choice.

Melli moved over to where she thought the lamp was and felt for its presence—the lamp was cold. It must have been dead for some time. She thought that Baralis would have returned before now with some food and water. She hoped she would not have to wait much longer. A terrible thought flashed through her mind: what if Baralis intended her to die here, holed up in this tiny room until she starved to death? She shuddered violently, suddenly afraid of what her fate might be.

She forced herself not to dwell on thoughts of doom; she had other matters to worry about. She badly needed to relieve herself. The room was bare, with not so much as a pot or bucket. She made her way to the corner of the room and lifted her skirts up; a little more dampness would do no harm.

Once finished, she moved near the door to see if she could hear anyone in the next room. There was either no one there, or the door was too thick to let sound through. Melli tried hard not to fall into despair. She hated being in the dark, being in a small space, being thirsty. She began to sing to keep her spirits up, but her voice sounded thin and frightened and she soon stopped.

A short time later, she heard the jangle of keys and the turn of lock. The door swung open. Melli found herself blinded by the light. She held her hand up to shield her eyes.

"I bid you good day, miss." It was Crope. Relief flooded over Melli; she greatly preferred the servant to the master. Her eyes grew accustomed to the light and she could make out Crope's substantial form in the doorway. "Why, miss, you are cold and wet," he said gently. His kindness was too much and large tears started to roll down her cheeks. "There, there, lady, no need to cry." He came over to her and patted her hair gently. "Come now, time for you to stretch your legs a bit." He led her out of the storeroom and into the adjoining chamber. "See, I made it nice for you."

Some of the things from her room had been transferred: a rug and her clothes. There was a tray of food and jugs of water and wine. There was even a basin full of water for her to bathe her face.

"Thank you, Crope. You have laid everything out beautifully." The huge servant blushed.

"All the food's fresh this day, miss. Eat up, you must be hungry."

Melli smiled weakly. "I think I should first change out of my damp clothes."

"Maybe you should do that later." Crope looked uncomfortable. "When you're back in your room."

"I am being allowed back to my former room?"

"No, lady." Crope didn't meet her eye. "Lord Baralis says that once you've finished eating and such, you must go back into the storeroom."

Melli's spirits dropped; she would have to endure another day locked up like a caged animal. Crope appeared to sense her disappointment. "I'll make it more comfortable." He thought for a moment. "I'll bring you a lamp and a chair and some blankets." Melli could only manage a half-hearted nod. This was enough for Crope, however, who busied himself carrying various items into the storeroom.

Melli splashed some water on her face and poured herself a glass of wine. She looked over the tray of food. Her appetite was gone, but she forced herself to take some bread,

washing it down with a large quantity of wine. Soon, the al-
cohol began to have an effect on Melli, warming her skin
and improving her spirits; the food began to look more
tempting.

Crope finished what he was doing and hovered nervously around her. "You'll have to be going back soon,
lady," he finally said. "Lord Baralis says that you're not to
be out for long."

"Tell me, Crope," said Melli, cutting a slice of cured
ham, "what caused Lord Baralis to lock me in the storeroom?"

"I can't tell you, miss."

"Nonsense!" Melli put on her most imperious voice.
"Why, Lord Baralis himself was about to tell me yesterday,
only he had to rush off." She watched as Crope took in this
information.

"Well, miss, seems as he was about to tell you himself,
there can't be any harm in me telling you, now can there?"
Crope smiled showing an interesting selection of gaps and
yellowing teeth.

"I think that Lord Baralis would be pleased that you finished off what he had started."

Crope nodded judiciously. "Well, miss, you know the
boy, Jack."

"The baker's boy," encouraged Melli.

"Yes, that's him. Course he worked for Lord Baralis,
too, just like me." Crope smiled proudly. "Well, the boy has
upped and escaped. The guards can't find him, looked everywhere they have."

"And what has this to do with me?" Melli already
thought she knew the answer.

"Well, Lord Baralis figures that Jack might come looking to rescue you. So he put you here, where no one can find
you."

After she had eaten, Melli allowed herself to be led
back into the storeroom. She was almost grateful when the
door closed behind her; she needed to think.

She could not help but smile at Crope's handiwork. He
had tried hard to transform the little room; there were some
fresh clothes, a chair and a small table. Discreetly placed on

a low shelf there was even a chamberpot. The rug that had been laid on the floor served to soak up the damp, and Crope had provided her with several blankets with which to keep warm.

Melli took off her damp clothes. She wondered what Jack had been doing working for Baralis: he had certainly not mentioned that to her. She was a little annoyed that he had not told her the truth. She wondered if he would indeed come and rescue her—it was a nice notion, like tales of knights of old—but she put herself in Jack's place and thought that if she were to escape from Baralis' clutches she would run as fast as she could and not look back.

"No, you're wrong there, Bodger."

"But Master Gullip told me that nobles were naturally more randy than us commoners."

"Well, he's sorely mistaken, Bodger."

"Master Gullip says he's got proof, Bodger."

"It wouldn't surprise me if he had, Bodger. Master Gullip's well known for being a Peeping Tom. He can't get no rollickin' of his own, so he sneaks around watching others taking a tumble."

"So he could be right then, Grift, about the nobles."

"That's where Master Gullip makes his mistake, Bodger."

"What mistake is that, Grift?"

"Well, he's right that nobles do have more quantity of rollickin', but us commoners have better quality."

"So nobles ain't as good with the wenches then, Grift?"

"Take it from me, Bodger, the commoner the man, the better he is at pleasuring the wenches. No one pleasures the wenches better than a pig handler."

"A pig handler?"

"Aye, the lowest of the low, but always sought after by the wenches."

"I thought the wenches sought after the pig handlers for the bacon, Grift."

"You've got much to learn, Bodger."

The two men reflected for a while, savoring their ale and stretching their legs out.

"Does the same go for the ladies, Grift? The commoner, the more pleasing?"

"Aye, Bodger. The lowest wenches in the castle are always attracting the eyes and codpieces of the nobles. Even old King Lesketh himself was known to dally with servants."

Jack looked back—he thought he had heard a noise behind him. Probably a rat. He moved quickly on; rats were one thing he didn't like to keep company with. He knew it was foolish to be afraid of them, he a grown man of nearly eighteen, but something about their heavy bodies and skinny legs made him shudder. Frallit had once locked him up in the grain store all night in an attempt to cure him of his fear. All it had done was make him more scared than ever. He'd spent the night alone in the dark, crouched down by the door, praying to Borc to keep the rats away.

Jack had spent over a day exploring the labyrinth of tunnels and passageways that snaked darkly beneath Castle Harvell. He was astonished that he could have lived his whole life in the castle and yet have had no idea of what lay under its stone floors.

On reaching the castle the day before, he took a torch from the wall and had proceeded to investigate the various passageways leading from the room. Jack felt the thrill of the explorer as he traveled through the tunnels, taking turnoffs at whim. He imagined the people who stepped before him: kings fleeing from assassins, thieves stealing away with crown jewels. It was relaxing for a while to let his imagination run its course. So many disturbing things had happened over the past weeks that it was nice not to think about them for a couple of hours. He let his feet go where they fancied, and his mind was soon to follow suit.

One little niggling thing—well, two if he counted rats—kept bringing him back to the present: there was something to remember about his mother. Jack was almost certain of it. The night Baralis had questioned him, he'd been on the brink of remembering. There'd been a light and two figures; one was his mother. She'd been trying to tell him something and then everything had gone blank. Each time Jack tried to grasp at its meaning, the memory seemed to become less solid. At first he'd thought it was a dream. But dreams didn't leave you feeling as if you'd understand everything if only they'd go on for a few moments more. At least none of his used to.

Jack had always slept soundly. Master Frallit had often said the only way to wake him was a good kick to the shins. Since leaving the castle, though, his dreams had given him no rest. They taunted him with glimpses of places he'd never been and people he'd never met. Images flashed in his mind like fat on a fire: men in torment, a city with high battlements, a man with golden hair. It didn't seem to mean anything, and when he awoke in the mornings he was more tired, more confused, more restless, than when he lay down his head the night before.

One minute he was just plain Jack the baker's boy, the next he was running for his life, being chased by guards and questioned about powers that he had no control over.

Judging from what he'd overheard the mercenaries say, the king's chancellor had not emerged from the questioning unscathed. What was in him that was strong enough to repel Baralis' will? For there had been a fight, Jack was certain of that, and somehow, although he hadn't emerged the victor, he had managed to keep the man at bay. Like a boar on the scent of truffles, Baralis had burrowed into his mind in search of the truth. He nearly found it, too. They both had.

There were answers inside him, and Baralis' probing had brought them tantalizingly close to the surface.

Walking through leagues of empty passageways had given Jack time to think. Despite all that had happened since leaving the castle, he realized that he wouldn't change a thing. If he hadn't burnt the loaves and left Harvell, he would never have met Falk and Melli. Falk had given him the gentle gift of understanding. He'd taught him to question his views on the world and introduced ideas that challenged a lifetime of beliefs.

As for Melli: well, she was proud and beautiful, and somehow managed never to be out of his thoughts. He'd known girls and had kisses aplenty, but no one had made him feel the peculiar mix of attraction and bewilderment that he felt in her presence. Jack was glad the mercenaries had caught him; Melli might have died without someone to tend her wounds. Capture seemed a fair exchange for her life.

Now all he had to do was free her. He'd read many books in Baralis' library where heroes saved beautiful damsels. If they could do it, so could he. Skill with a blade might be lacking, but lifting sacks of grain had made him strong, and dodging Frallit's blows had made him fast on his feet.

He knew it would be better to lie low for a few days before returning to the haven. Right now the mercenaries would be vigilant and anxious for revenge. The longer he waited, the more chance there was of catching them unawares. Jack was under no illusions; if he was going to free Melli, it would be by sneaking *past* the guards, not fighting his way through them. Bakers had to live by more practical rules than heroes.

For the moment, food and water were his priority. He needed to find a way up to the inhabited rooms of the castle.

One of the strange things that he found while searching for entry into the cellars was that many tunnels ended in stone walls. It didn't make sense to Jack that someone would build an elaborate tunnel only to deadend it. He thought back to the conversation between the two mercenaries; they had mentioned Baralis opening up walls with his hands. Jack attempted to find some sort of mechanism on the wall that formed part of one dead end—perhaps Melli was being kept behind the featureless stone. He found nothing and gave up. Why waste his time with secret openings when there was so much that was *not* concealed to explore?

Finally, after some time, Jack came across a narrow flight of stairs. He headed up them and found a low wooden door at the top. His heart beat heavily as he turned the handle and looked out. He could not see much as his way was blocked by a large object. There was something familiar to Jack about the shape blocking his view. He brought the torch forward and was able to see clearly what it was . . . a huge copper brewing vat. He was in the beer cellar.

Jack decided to leave the torch in the tunnel—it would only serve to draw unnecessary attention to him—so he quickly ran down the stairs and placed it in the wall bracket. Seconds later he crept through the door. He slipped down the side of the copper vat, careful to stay in the shadows. There appeared to be no one around. He realized that it must be sometime in the evening, maybe even in the middle of the night.

The smell of hops and yeast pervaded the air, reminding Jack of the good times he had spent there as a child, fetching ale for the castle guards—more often than not taking an illicit tipple of his own. His youth seemed a long distance behind him now, and he knew in his heart that he would never be a baker's boy or kitchen help again.

He made his way up the cellar stairs and into the castle kitchens. They were hooded in shadow, only an occasional candle burning. Jack knew he had to be careful. Even late at night there were people in the kitchen: scullery maids scouring the pots and damping fires, drunken guards looking for a bite to eat.

Jack heard whispering coming from the larder. He glanced around and was surprised to see that the door which was usually kept locked was open. Lying on the floor inside was a man with his britches pulled down around his knees with a girl open-legged beneath him. Jack recognized the man at once. He was about to withdraw when the man called out to him: "Who goes there?" Jack froze on the spot, hoping the shadow was deep enough to conceal him. The man pulled up his britches and the woman smoothed down her skirts. "I know there's someone there," said the man, moving forward.

Jack took a chance and stepped into the light. "Master Frallit, it's me, Jack."

"Jack, lad, what are you doing here? I thought you'd run away." Master Frallit came out of the shadows. He was short of breath and decidedly red in the face.

"I did." Jack hesitated. "It's a long story."

"Just a minute, lad." Frallit turned back to the girl and motioned for her to go. The master baker waited for her to be out of earshot before he spoke again. "I trust, Jack, that what you saw tonight won't go any further?"

"I would ask the same of you, Master Frallit." The two men nodded in understanding.

"Is there anything I can do for you, boy?" Frallit looked eager to be on his way.

"No, I don't think so, Master Frallit." There was no mistaking Frallit's sigh of relief. "However," continued Jack, "if I could just take a few things to eat from the larder?"

"Go ahead, boy, and be quick about it." Jack made his way forward into the larder. "Don't be taking any of the roast venison, though. The sharp eyes of the cook can notice missing venison a league away."

Jack quickly filled a cloth with cheese and pie and anything else he found appealing. "Hurry, boy," hissed the master baker. Once satisfied that he had enough food, Jack tied the ends of the cloth and stepped from the pantry. Frallit's eyes rested disapprovingly on the size of his bundle. "Be on your way, boy," he said, intent on locking the larder door. Jack thanked Frallit and made his way back toward the cellar, pausing to pick up some candles and a jug of water.

Once Jack was back in the passageways he lit one of the candles from his torch and laid himself out a feast of a meal. He munched on grouse pie and blood sausage, blue cheese and apple dumpling. Nothing, however, tasted as good to Jack as his one slice of cold roast venison.

Jack lay down for the night in a partly concealed recess off one of the tunnels. The torch had burnt out, and although he knew it was tempting discovery, Jack kept the candle burning while he slept. He realized that he should have brought a flint and decided he would obtain one the following evening. He would need some warm clothes, too.

He awoke the next day stiff and cold. He ate a light breakfast and spent the morning exploring the tunnels once more. Jack had no doubt that Baralis used the passages regularly—a few of them were even lit by torches, and those Jack stayed away from. He did not want to chance a meeting with the man or his mercenaries.

Baralis had decided it was time he had a word alone with Traff. The head of the mercenaries had let him down badly by allowing the boy to get away. The man had expected to be rewarded when he performed his job well; he must also expect to be punished when he did it badly.

He watched as Traff made his men leave the room, and was pleased to note that each of them had looked afraid at his arrival. Traff poured himself a mug of ale. Baralis felt nothing but contempt for men who sought strength in liquor.

"So, Traff," he began with misleading mildness, "have you any news on the boy, any sign of him?"

"No, nothing. If he's still here we'll find him, and if he's outside he won't have gone far in this weather." Traff took a large gulp of ale.

"I'm very disappointed. I thought ten men would be able to guard one boy."

"He caught my man off guard, surprised him—"

Baralis cut him short. "I hate excuses." He could see that Traff was getting nervous.

"Since I've been working for you, I've had two men killed and another's so messed up even his own wife wouldn't recognize him." Traff took another gulp of ale. "Let me tell you, I'm about ready to get the hell out of here." The mercenary started to get up.

"You aren't going anywhere." Baralis drew gently from his power. He watched the panic in Traff's face as the man realized he couldn't move.

Baralis looked around the room for something suitable, his eyes alighting on a wooden-handled knife. He casually picked it up and caressed the blade with his fingertips, drawing heat to it. In seconds the blade glowed red, and Baralis was amused to see Traff's expression turn from fear to horror. He brought the knife within a hair's breadth of the man's face and watched him wince as he felt the heat from the blade.

"Now, my friend." Baralis spoke with a voice smooth as oil. "I think you know I could hurt you quite considerably." He moved the knife a fraction, nearly touching Traff's skin. "Quite considerably, indeed. But I won't, because you and I both know you will come to your senses. You are not about to walk out on me . . . no, my good friend, nobody walks out on me."

Baralis shook his head lightly. "I know you'll do a better job in the future." He gently grazed the blade over Traff's cheek, the flesh reddening beneath. Baralis suddenly drew the knife down to Traff's bare arm and laid the red-hot blade against his skin. The skin reddened and warped and then turned black. Satisfied, Baralis removed the blade and drew back his power. Traff fell forward against the table and began to whimper, tears of pain coursing down his cheeks.

"Well, Traff," said Baralis briskly, "I trust you have a better understanding of matters now." He let the knife drop into the jug of ale, causing the beer to sizzle and steam. "I must be off now. I will, of course, expect the boy to be found within the next few days." Baralis paused a second by the doorway, contemplating the sight of Traff cradling his arm, and then was off, back to the castle.

Baralis made his way to his chambers through the underground tunnel and up into the castle. As he walked he noticed a torch was missing from one of the walls. He puzzled over it for a second, making a mental note to ask Crope if he had it.

Once in his rooms, Baralis rubbed his hands, soothing them—gripping the knife handle had been a strain upon them. The wet weather was having a direct effect on the joints in his fingers, causing them to swell and stiffen. He resisted the urge to take the drug; he would endure the pain rather than risk losing his sharpness of mind. He poured himself a glass of holk instead. The drink afforded him a little relief.

Crope entered the room, his clothes wet. He had obviously been out in the rain. "I expected you back before now. Is the girl safely locked up?"

"Yes, my lord."

"You must not get too attached to her, Crope," warned Baralis. He had a feeling his servant had a soft spot for the girl. "Tell me," he said, satisfied that he had made his point, "why are you soaked through?"

"I've been outside, my lord. I've found out from one of the stablehands that Lord Maybor has left on a journey."

"Oh, really." Baralis was suddenly interested. "And where is Lord Maybor journeying to?"

"First to Duvitt and then on to his eastern holdings. Stablehand says that there's been some sort of trouble on his lands."

Baralis smiled. He was well pleased. Maybor would be out of the way for a couple of weeks. By the time he returned the deadline the queen had agreed to would be up, and there would be nothing to be gained by finding his daughter.

Crope was about to leave when Baralis called him back. "Crope, did you remove the torch from the room leading off the tunnel?" His servant looked blank. "Think carefully."

"Whenever I take the torches down, my lord, I always replace them with new ones."

"Are you sure?" Crope nodded vigorously. "Very well, you may go now." Baralis' mouth tightened to a thin smile. *So,* he thought, *the boy is in the castle.*

Nineteen

Tavalisk read the edict on his desk, then dipped his quill in the inkpot and drew the loaded tip across the paper, signing his name with a flourish.

"Gamil!" he called. His aide had been waiting outside and came hurrying in.

"Yes, Your Eminence."

"I have signed the edict banning knights from entering the city of Rorn." Tavalisk indicated the document on his desk. He then turned his attention to the platter of sweetbreads at his side, scrutinizing them carefully and taking in their subtle aroma. They were cooked just the way he liked them, fried in a little oil, no spices or other embellishments to mask their delicate flavor.

"The edict will surely upset the city of Valdis."

"That is my intention, Gamil. I'm quite sick of them interfering with Rorn's trade. Only last week they seized one of our ships. Kept it at sea for two days while they searched it from top to bottom. The whole cargo of fish was ruined." Tavalisk busied himself with choosing a sweetbread.

"On top of that, the knights are making nuisances of themselves in the city, telling people I'm corrupt and that I've no dealings with God. Tyren is playing a dangerous game and it's high time he learnt the power of his opponents." Tavalisk squeezed a sweetbread between his fingers, letting its pale secretions dribble over his fingers. He shot Gamil an accusing glance when the juices spilled onto his robe.

"What if they retaliate, Your Eminence?"

"The Knights of Valdis retaliate! I doubt it, Gamil, they will hold meetings and assemblies and send us letters of condemnation. The Knights of Valdis are incapable of fast action. Why, it took them one hundred years to decide where to build their damn city in the first place." Tavalisk reached over and selected the largest of the sweetbreads. "No, Gamil, they will do nothing."

"Then why has Your Eminence signed the order?"

"I thought that would be obvious." The archbishop popped the sweetbread into his mouth. He first rolled it around on his tongue, enjoying its rubbery texture and then pierced it with his sharp teeth, letting the delectable juices run off his tongue and down his throat. "I am hoping to start a trend. Don't you see, Gamil, the knights are welcome in fewer and fewer places, no one in the south trusts them anymore. One minute they act like dangerous fanatics, the next they're stealing trade by undercutting prices. Rorn will be the first city with enough nerve to finally dispel those self-righteous hypocrites. Once Rorn has shown the lead, other cities will follow suit: Marls, Camlee, Toolay, they all will do likewise. Before long the Knights of Valdis will find their movements in the east severely restricted." Tavalisk threw the remaining sweetmeats into the fire.

"May I venture to ask Your Eminence why he is so opposed to the knighthood?"

Tavalisk dabbed daintily at the stain on his robe. "Really Gamil, your short-sightedness amazes me. Tyren wants to control the trade routes. The knights are no longer content with controlling land and river trade. They're after the sea trade as well."

"But I thought the knights were there merely to ensure that goods got through safely."

"Yes, yes. They used to provide armed escorts for cargoes—still do, only the price for protection has got so high, the goods end up going to market at a premium. That's where they're winning; goods they ship themselves are half the price. They've got people in the north believing that Rorn charges artificially high prices, whilst Valdis struggles to keep its prices low."

Tavalisk took an orange from the bowl of fruit by his side. "Tyren is up to no good. The man is too ambitious. He makes friends with the duke of Bren to gain sway in the north. He mustn't be allowed to find similar friends in the south."

"If the knights are expelled from all the eastern cities, Your Eminence, it could lead to war."

"That, Gamil," said the archbishop with a heavy sigh, "is an occasion we will have to deal with if and when it arises." Tavalisk tore the skin from the orange.

"Since we speak of the knighthood, Your Eminence, perhaps you would like to know the progress of our particular knight."

"Go ahead," urged the archbishop, teeth glinting as he bit on the orange.

"Well, the knight left the city nearly a week back. He's currently heading north on foot."

"Is he still being followed by the boy?"

"Apparently he is, Your Eminence."

Tavalisk studied the bowl of fruit, deciding which piece he would eat next. "You may go now, Gamil, but before you do could you perform one small favor."

"Certainly, Your Eminence."

The archbishop unpinned his robe. "Could you try and remove this grease stain for me? If you can't, be so good as to deduct the cost from your wages."

Tawl entered a small town: a few traders, a stable, a smithy, and a tavern. He had set a brisk pace over the last few days and was pleased with his progress. He was now quite a distance from Rorn and the scenery had changed: the towns were fewer and smaller, the road had deteriorated to a mere dirt track and there were fewer people traveling it. Mountains lay ahead, their pale peaks hazy in the distance.

He decided he would pay a visit to the local tavern. It was drawing close to midday and he was due for a brief respite. His throat was dry and the thought of ale instead of water cheered him considerably.

He walked into the small tavern and immediately regretted his whim: it was no warm and jovial wayside inn. The place was deserted except for two men sitting in the corner playing low hand. There was no fire burning in the grate, the straw matting was stained and dirty, and the smell of rank meat hung in the air. Tawl was about to leave when a woman emerged from behind the bar and blocked his exit.

Tawl felt obliged to have a drink. The woman winked provocatively at him and headed off to fetch his ale. She returned moments later with a foamy brew and placed it on the table, her fingers lingering over the mug. "So tell me where you're headed, golden boy?" Tawl could not deny the woman was attractive; she had a pleasing plumpness and a pretty snub nose. Her eyes, however, were cold despite her smile.

"Just heading north."

"Toolay is it? I've got a cousin in Toolay, says the only good thing about the city is the eatin'. Crabs and lobsters, she says, as big as her head. And let me tell you my cousin's got a big head." The woman laughed at her own wit, a shrill laugh, lacking in warmth.

"I've no plans to visit Toolay." Tawl had no intention of sharing his plans.

"Fancy a bite to eat, a slice of pie or a bowl of stew?" The girl leaned forward, exposing the deep cleft of her bosom.

"No."

"Coffers running a bit low are they?" The girl moved back, withdrawing her favor.

"No, I've already eaten."

"Travelin' alone are you?"

"Yes." Tawl noticed the woman's speculative look.

"You don't seem to have much stuff for a man who's travelin' past Toolay."

He knew the woman was fishing for information. When he made no answer to her last remark she walked back behind the bar. Tawl supped his ale and watched as a man came from the back and spoke with the tavern maid. Their voices were hushed and the woman looked Tawl's way a number of times. Tawl decided it was time he left. He drained his ale and made his way to the door. As he walked across the room he made a show of checking his long-knife—it was wise to avoid trouble whenever possible.

He was glad to be outside; the sun shone mildly and the air was fresh. The dirt road led the way out of town and he took it, heading north as always. He started whistling a tune he'd learnt from Carver during his time on *The Fishy Few*. A jolly song telling of the strength, bravery, handsomeness and sexual prowess of sailors. Tawl was no singer and so contented himself with whistling the melody.

He had walked from the town only a short distance when he was jumped. He was ready for it, his knife was drawn in an instant. There were three attackers: the men from the tavern. One of them tried to force him to the ground. Tawl swung round and slashed at his belly. He missed and felt the sting of a blade on his arm. Anger made Tawl lash out with his fist. He felt the soft flesh of the man's side and his foe stumbled backward but did not fall. Tawl turned his attention to the second man, urging him to try his luck with a strike. His attacker plunged his knife forward, leaving his chest exposed. Tawl dodged the knife and stabbed at the man's chest; he felt his blade slip between ribs and his foe fell back.

Tawl felt a powerful blow to the back of his knees and stumbled forward, struggling to stay upright. Turning around he saw the third man was wielding a huge club. The first man was moving in with his knife, and Tawl was forced to deal with him as he parried the man with the club. The third man brought his club down on Tawl's shoulder blade with great force and he fell to the ground. The two attackers closed in.

Suddenly, someone jumped on the first man's back—it was all Tawl needed. The one with the club was distracted for a mere second, but it was enough for Tawl to jump to his feet and land his knife in the man's gut. Tawl finished him off and quickly turned to the remaining assailant, who was attempting to strike the person who had jumped him. Tawl whipped his blade down the man's flank and then dispatched him with a clean strike to the heart.

The boy cheered, jumping with excitement.

Tawl had to struggle for breath before he could speak. "What in Borc's name are you doing here?" Tawl rubbed his shoulder blade. It was sore to the touch, but it didn't feel broken.

"That's easy. Saving your life, of course." Nabber grinned triumphantly. Tawl walked a short distance from the fight scene, still gasping for air.

"The first one got away, you know. I saw him crawling into the bushes." The boy looked to Tawl to reply. When no response was forthcoming, he continued, "Ain't you gonna finish him off?"

Tawl shook his head. He was badly out of breath and hunkered down on the roadside. "You're supposed to be back in Rorn."

"It's just as well for you I'm not." Tawl could not deny that Nabber's intervention may have saved his life.

"What did you think you were doing jumping on an armed man's back? You could have been killed." Tawl began to clean his knife, wiping the blood away with a handful of grass.

"Didn't give it a thought. I saw you were in trouble and made my move. I'm no coward. I've been in worse scraps in Rorn."

Tawl checked the length of the road. There was no one about and it was time to be off; he didn't want to risk being discovered with two dead bodies. He glanced toward the boy, deciding what he should do about him. He made his decision and headed off down the road.

"Come on, boy," he called. "We'd better be going."

"You go ahead," shouted Nabber. "I'll catch you up in a few minutes."

Some time later, the boy drew alongside Tawl. He was short of breath and had obviously been running.

"What kept you?"

"A little job to do, that's all."

"What little job?"

"A bit of prospecting." The boy shrugged.

"What exactly do you mean by prospecting?" Tawl spoke sharply, losing his patience.

"I did a quick search of the bodies, see if they had anything worth having on them." Seeing Tawl's disapproving look, the boy explained further. "Well, I know you're a knight and all; you're probably too honorable to do any frisking. Thought I'd take the initiative myself."

"Hand it over."

"I found it," protested Nabber.

"Hand it over!"

The boy brought a coin purse from his vest and gave it to Tawl. "Six silvers and one gold," he said proudly.

"Anything else?"

The boy's reply was guarded. "Nothing to speak of."

"No robbing dead men in future, boy, especially ones you didn't kill yourself."

"What are you going to do with the money?"

"I'm going to be keeping hold of it. I'll have need of more money with you tagging along." Tawl watched as the boy momentarily beamed with pleasure and then resumed his nonchalant manner.

"I told you before, Tawl, coinage is no problem while I'm around."

"Look, Nabber," Tawl became grave, "this is no grand adventure. There's hard journeying ahead, bad roads and bad weather, and then *no* roads at all. You saw today what can happen to innocent travelers. I can't guarantee my own safety, let alone that of a headstrong boy. It's true that I owe you a debt, and in part that's why I'm letting you come along, but I think you may live to regret my particular form of repayment."

The day was growing late. The sun grew red in the western sky and the first chill of evening could be felt on the breeze. Tawl decided they would travel late into the night. Not only did he have time to make up for, he also wanted to test the mettle of the boy.

Mistress Greal was preparing to go down to dinner. She coated her face heavily with powdered lead and then squashed cranberries between her fingers, rubbing the juices onto her cheeks. She might not be as young as she once was, she thought, but she was still a fine figure of a woman. She looked through her wardrobe, deciding which of her dresses to wear. She picked the plainest—the blue, thinking to herself that the night promised little opportunity. Her sister, who now lived in Bren, had scolded her many times for wasting good dresses on unprofitable evenings.

"Mistress Greal, Mistress Greal!" Her maid came rushing into the room.

"What is it, you wretched girl?"

"Oh, Mistress Greal, such news!" Keddi was flushed with excitement.

"If you do not tell me this minute, girl, I will have you flogged. Now calm down and speak."

"Lord Maybor is in town. He has his son and a small company of men with him."

"This is indeed good news, Keddi. You have done well to tell me." Mistress Greal's eyes narrowed with greed. Lord Maybor was well known to be the wealthiest man in the Four Kingdoms. He was also well known for his considerable appetites for women and drink. Mistress Greal considered it her responsibility to see the great man was liberally and expensively provided with both while he was in town.

Although his lands were not far east of Duvitt, Mistress Greal could not remember him ever having visited the town before. "Keddi, where is he staying?" Mistress Greal had an arrangement with the innkeepers in most of Duvitt's hostelries.

"He's staying here."

"Good, good. Come and help me out of this dress, Keddi. I will wear the green tonight, I find green is the color that suits me best."

Once she was dressed, she made Keddi brush out her best wig. "Be careful, girl!" she snapped. "You're not grooming a horse."

As soon as the wig was in place she ordered the servant to see to her two girls. "Run along, Keddi, and make sure you pull their laces tight. I want to see high bosoms and small waists. Keep Willa's hair down—it serves to hide that unsightly blemish on her neck. Oh, and one more thing, tell them to stay upstairs until bidden. I would first tempt Lord Maybor with descriptions of their charms. Anticipation has helped beget many a deal."

Once Keddi had left, Mistress Greal made her way down to the inn. It was a little early, but she was eager to secure the best table, the one a decent distance from the nearest lamp. Unfortunately her recent girls had need of a little shadow. Once in place she ordered the cheapest wine and prepared to wait.

She did not have to wait for long. There was a bustle of voices and the inn door opened and a group of men came in. They were cold and wet and called loudly for service. She could tell straightaway from their fine dress who they were. One man stuck out above the rest; he had the bearing that only came with great wealth and nobility. His robes were crimson and gold, and his cloak was lined with ermine. His voice boomed out loudly as he called for food and drink, but Mistress Greal's sharp ears caught the sound of his low wheezes.

Mistress Greal noted with approval that the party had ordered the best that the inn had to offer: roasted venison, smoked salmon, grilled pheasant, to say nothing of the barrel of lobanfern red that the innkeeper dragged from the cellar. Mistress Greal knew to the last copper the cost of the various libations the inn had for sale, and lobanfern red was by far the most expensive.

She watched as the group became more rowdy, the drink animating their conversations and flushing their faces. Mistress Greal decided it was time to make her move. She stood up, smoothing her skirts, and sauntered over to their table.

"I bid you gentlemen joy on this fine night." All the men turned and looked at her. "I hope you are enjoying your repast. I would let you gentlemen know there are more tasty morsels available than those on the menu." The party caught her drift and banged their cups on the table.

"What morsels have you to offer, woman?" shouted the one she knew to be Lord Maybor. "I trust they have not been sitting as long in the pot as you have." The men broke into hearty laughter. Mistress Greal was more than a little insulted but covered it well.

"Let me assure you, fine sir, my morsels are young and tender, plump and well spiced." The party cheered rowdily at her reply.

"You know well how to tempt a hungry man," said the lord.

"In my experience, sir, a hungry man needs little tempting." The men erupted into laughter once more and Mistress Greal knew she was close to reeling them in.

"Tell me, woman, where do you keep these tender morsels?"

"Morsels as tender as mine must be kept under lock and key, lest they be eaten before their time."

"A man's appetite reaches its fullest only after he *sees* what he will be eating."

The lord's words were accompanied by enthusiastic shouts of "Aye!" by his men.

Mistress Greal judged it was time to bring out her girls. She nodded to the tavernboy, who promptly ran up the stairs. She used the brief interval to discreetly blow out a number of the surrounding candles. She then turned her attention back to the men, perceiving it would be in her best interest to encourage them to drink more. "May I be so bold as to propose a toast, gentlemen?" she cried.

"It is forbidden for a lady to propose a toast," shouted one of the group.

"Then we will not be breaking any rules by letting *her* propose one." The men dissolved into fits of laughter. Mistress Greal laughed along with them, the only indication that she was not truly amused a slight narrowing of her eyes.

Seconds later her girls appeared at the bottom of the stairs. Mistress Greal's critical eye rested upon them. Keddi had done a good job. The small party noticed the girls and cheered loudly, calling them to come over and sup with them. The two girls looked toward Mistress Greal, who shook her head minutely and indicated, with a furrow of her brow, that the girls should sit at the table she had picked out earlier.

Once the men realized the girls were not about to join them, they booed and hissed and banged their cups.

"Bring the girls to our table, woman," ordered the lord.

"Me and my girls would prefer to sit a while on our own, sir. We would, however, be pleased to accept refreshments from you." The lord grunted and indicated that a jug be tapped from the barrel and sent to the girls. Mistress Greal's small heart thrilled with excitement—a whole jug of lobanfern red!

She retired to her table, where the girls were about to pour themselves a glass of the overpriced brew. "Don't you dare," she warned. "The tavernboy will do a switch in a minute and you two can drink from the jug he brings." Mistress Greal was not about to pass up the chance of a small profit for selling the lobanfern back to the innkeeper.

The party of men kept whistling and calling to the girls, raising their cups in toast and cheering when either of the girls smiled their way. Before long, Lord Maybor walked over to their table, carrying another jug of wine. "I thought you ladies might have need of more refreshment."

He sat down between the two girls, admiring their figures. "My, my, woman, these are indeed tempting morsels." He squeezed the thigh of one girl, while leering down the dress of the other. "Very tempting, indeed." Mistress Greal took the opportunity to gently knock over the jug of cheap wine.

"Oh, dear," she cried. "Silly me, what have I done, such fine wine!" She made a show of mopping the spilt wine with her handkerchief. The lord called out for another jug to be brought. Mistress Greal smiled broadly; this night was already proving to be most profitable.

More wine came and the remaining men in the party came over, drawing their chairs around the table. The men were drinking heavily. Mistress Greal shot her girls a warning glance, in case they did likewise. The lord surveyed the drinking party with a benign eye and then whispered a word in Mistress Greal's ear. The two discreetly left the table.

"So, woman, tell me your price."

"Well, sir, for both girls . . . " Mistress Greal paused as

she decided her price. She took a deep breath and said: "Five golds." The lord did not hesitate.

"Done!" He looked toward his companions. "My men have ridden hard for five days; it is a cheap price for such alluring distractions."

Mistress Greal sucked in her breath. *Cheap!* She cursed herself; she could have charged him more! The lord began to step back to the table. "Tell me, sir," she said, anxious to hold him longer while she thought of a plausible way to up her price, "what business does such a fine lord as yourself have in Duvitt?" The lord hesitated for a second, and then motioned her to sit down at a remote corner table. He settled himself in place close beside her, and when he spoke she could smell the wine on his breath.

"You seem to be a woman who would know a lot of people in this town." Mistress Greal nodded. "You would notice if anyone new came to town?"

"I would indeed, sir." She was ready to agree with anything the lord said.

"I am interested in finding a girl. Rumors have reached my ears that she may have passed through this place."

"Who might this girl be?"

"That is no concern of yours." The lord's voice was sharp. "She must be found."

"Give me a description of the girl." Mistress Greal's words were laden with understanding. She assumed from the lord's harsh tone that the mysterious girl had either stolen something from him or given him a bad dose of the ghones.

"She is approaching her eighteenth summer. She is tall for a girl, and she has long dark hair and deep blue eyes."

"Does she bear any marks—from birthing or the pox?" Mistress Greal's heart began to beat faster. The description of the girl sounded just like the one she had taken in and fed a few weeks back—the ungrateful slut, Melli.

"She has no marks. Her skin is smooth and fair."

"Is there a reward for information about the girl?" She was now positive the girl the lord sought was Melli of Deepwood.

"What do you know of her?" demanded the lord. Mis-

tress Greal thought he sounded like a man most eager to find
and punish.

"There was a girl fitting her description in town a couple of weeks back. I'm sorry to say I took the wretched girl
in. I spent good money on her, thought she'd be an asset to
my business. By Borc, was I wrong! She was a bad one. She
turned on me, stole my dresses, stole a horse, and assaulted a
good friend of mine. Of course we managed to catch up with
her. I personally saw to it that the little trollop was sentenced
to a good flogging."

She had barely finished speaking when the lord viciously grabbed her wrist. "What was the girl's name?" His
voice was charged with anger; Mistress Greal became afraid.

"Melli. The girl said she was called Melli." The lord
slammed her wrist against the table with such force that the
woman could hear her own bones cracking. Mistress Greal
desperately looked around for help. The innkeeper and tavern boy refused to meet her eye.

"What became of the girl?" The lord's voice was
charged with fury.

"I don't know, sir." Tears of pain welled in her eyes.
The lord slammed her wrist down again and pain coursed
through her arm. She could see where one of the broken
bones had pierced her skin. "In the middle of her flogging a
band of armed men came and took her away." Mistress Greal
was almost hysterical. "I've heard no more of her, I swear."

"Which direction did the men head in?" The lord
ground her broken wrist into the table.

"They rode toward the forest, heading west." Mistress
Greal looked on in horror as the lord took the huge jeweled
ring from his finger. He pressed it against her mouth. She felt
the cool kiss of the jewel. With one quick motion he punched
the ring forward with such force that her front teeth were
knocked out. She screamed hysterically and blood rushed
down her chin and onto her breasts. The lord turned and
walked out, beckoning his men to follow.

Mistress Greal slumped over the table, sobbing violently, her blood flowing onto the wood. Not a single person
in the tavern came forward to help her.

*   *   *

Jack heard someone approaching and slipped back into the shadows, holding his breath as the man passed. He could tell by the shadow cast that the man was Crope. He waited for several minutes, body pressed close against the damp stone, and then moved on. The past few days he had spent waiting, lying low in the cold, dark maze beneath the castle. He headed toward the tunnel. Tonight he was going to find out where Melli was being held.

Jack tucked his sword under his belt and made his way to the oblong room that marked the entrance to the tunnel. He peered down its length and in the distance he saw a faint light. He watched it grow dimmer. Crope, it seemed, was also heading to the haven. Jack entered the passageway and followed the light.

Some time later he emerged from the tunnel. There was no sign of Crope and he cautiously moved on. The ways were dark and twisting and he attempted to retrace his steps back toward the cell he'd first been held in. Each step he took thundered loudly in his ears and he feared detection at every turn of his path.

Eventually he came across a door that was bolted on the outside. He listened a moment for any sound within. Hearing nothing, he drew back the bolt and entered the room.

Once inside, he lit his candle and looked around. It was a comfortably furnished room, containing a bed, a bath, and an assortment of chairs and tables. Lying on the bed were various clothes: a woman's nightgown and dresses. On one of the tables was a bowl of rosewater. A pile of dirty looking rags in the corner caught Jack's eye and he went over to look at them more closely. He rummaged through them. His suspicions were confirmed when he pulled a soiled and ragged red dress from the pile—Melli's dress. Melli had been kept in this very room. Where was she now? he wondered. He prayed that she had not been murdered.

Jack investigated the room further, looking for any clues as to what had become of her. Finding nothing else he decided to move on. As he opened the door he was astonished to see Crope emerging from the tunnel wall, the very wall that he had walked past only minutes earlier. He quickly brought the door back, leaving only a tiny gap through which to look. As he watched, Crope appeared to feel for something in the stone and seconds later the wall drew back into place. The huge servant then made his way back down toward the tunnel.

Jack stepped from the room and reset the bolt in its place. He walked over to where Crope had stood and mimicked what he had seen the servant do. He placed his palms flat against the stone and moved them against its cold surface. Nothing. Jack became nervous: the longer he stood here, the more chance he had of being discovered. In his frustration he beat the wall with his fist—and felt a tiny something give way inside the stone. The wall to his side began to rumble back and an entrance appeared. He was tempted to dash right in, but instead he carefully felt the area of stone that he had pounded. He found what he was looking for: barely there, nothing more than a minute bump in the stone . . . the opening mechanism. Jack stepped through the gap.

He emerged into a large room. The first thing he needed to do was to close the wall so he could look around undisturbed. Jack took a guess as to what side the closing mechanism would be on and was rewarded when he felt the tiny jutting of stone. He pressed on it and the wall swung back into place.

Jack surveyed the room. It was well lit; several candles were still burning. There were a few chairs and a large table with various items resting upon it. He saw there was a door leading from the back of the room. He rushed over and put his ear to the wood. He could hear nothing. He saw a lock and guessed it would not open. He pushed it anyway, it did not give way. He thought he heard a movement on the other side. "Melli," he called softly.

"Who's out there?" came the faint reply. Jack was thrilled as he recognized her voice.

"Melli, it's me, Jack."

"Jack, is it really you?" Her voice was louder now.

"Yes, I've come to get you out of here. Do you know if the key is kept in the room?"

"No, I don't think so. Crope and Baralis keep their keys with them all the time."

Jack tested the door. It was solid and the lock appeared

strong. "Stand back, Melli." He kicked the door as hard as he could, horrified by the large noise he made. The door did not give way. He tried again and again, the door eventually began to weaken. One final kick resulted in the splintering of wood and the lock gave way.

Melli rushed forth and flung her arms around Jack. "You did it! You did it." After a moment she appeared to regain her composure and drew away from him. "I thought you would be leagues away from here by now."

"I couldn't leave knowing you were still locked up." Jack couldn't meet Melli's eyes. He felt foolish and brushed back his hair nervously. He was suddenly very aware of his appearance. What must he look like to her? He was dirty, his hair unkempt, his clothes stained with blood. Heroes in stories somehow managed to rescue maidens while looking like court dandies. Next time he went adventuring he'd remember to bring a comb.

Melli's scrutiny was making him uncomfortable. "We must make haste," he said, glad of the opportunity to turn away. "Crope could return at any moment." He moved quickly across the room and caused the wall to open. "Let's go." Melli grabbed a small fruit knife from the table and then followed him from the room.

Jack decided it was better not to risk heading toward the way out. It would be well guarded and they would have to walk past the guardroom. He led Melli toward the tunnel and Castle Harvell. Once they reached the tunnel, he was relieved to see there was no sign of light ahead. "Come on, let's hurry," he said, catching Melli's hand in his.

Lord Maybor raised his hand and then reined his horse to a stop. The men behind him slowed down and came to a halt. He turned to face his company, "We will make camp here for the night." The tone of his voice discouraged any argument and the men set about making camp.

Maybor dismounted his horse and walked off into the woods. Sometime later he heard the approach of another; he was about to tell whoever it was to leave him be when he heard the sound of his son's voice.

"Father." Kedrac drew near. "What happened at the inn? Why are we heading back to Harvell?" Maybor did not turn to look at his son; he stared into the blackness ahead.

"Kedrac, I will not speak of what passed between that woman and me. I *will* tell you that I have good reason to believe Melliandra was abducted by Baralis' men and, if she is still alive, is most probably being held somewhere not far from the castle."

"Father, what did the woman say to you? If it concerns my sister I demand to know."

"Leave me be, Kedrac!" Such was the force in Maybor's voice that his son withdrew instantly.

Maybor was surrounded by darkness. A cold wind blew through the trees and the sky was without a moon. He stood and thought of his daughter, how he had loved her. It was true he had forced the betrothal upon her, but he had never sought to harm her. And now, to hear from that foul woman's mouth that his daughter had been abused and flogged. He shook his head grimly and headed back to the camp. A heavy rain began to fall and he was glad of its discomfort.

"Where does this tunnel lead to?" hissed Melli. She was feeling a little afraid. She hated being in the dark.

"It leads toward the castle." Jack tugged on her arm, urging her forward. "Come on, hurry. We don't want to be caught in here. Look, in the distance—that light marks the end of the tunnel. Not much further now."

She waited for Jack to take her hand again, but he didn't. She hid her disappointment by breaking into a run.

It felt good to Melli to stretch her legs properly after days of being confined in a small space. Soon the tunnel gave way to a long rectangular room. Jack took her down one of the many passages that led from it. Melli was about to speak, but he stopped her, raising his finger to his lips. She would just have to trust that he knew where he was going.

The route they traveled seemed a maze of turnings and

staircases. Jack lit a candle and Melli was able to see a little of what she passed. It was not a pleasant sight: cold, wet stone with pale mosses sprouting forth from the cracks. Melli kept her distance from the strange growths; she shuddered at the idea of one of them brushing against her.

Eventually they reached a flight of stairs with a wooden door at the top and Jack bid her wait while he checked if the way ahead was clear. Moments later, to Melli's great relief, his head popped around the door and he beckoned her to join him. As she walked through the door and into the huge, low-ceilinged room, the smell of beer and hops assailed her nostrils. She was in the beer cellar.

Melli knew the beer cellar well. It had been a place that she had played in as a child, running and hiding behind the huge brewing vats, rolling the barrels of ale. If caught, she and her friends would taunt the master brewer and the cellarer—the men would never dare take action against the children of nobles and would content themselves with chasing them from the cellar. Melli remembered that being chased was the best thing of all: frightening and exhilarating at the same time—there was the peril of being caught, but also the reassuring knowledge that they were in no real danger. Melli sighed deeply; she wished she had a similar reassurance now.

Jack led her up another flight of stairs and into the kitchens. She knew that it would be dangerous to walk through the castle at night: guards would be on patrol. They stole through the kitchens, finding the shadows whenever they could. There were a group of people in the servants' dining hall, but they all appeared merry from drink and paid no attention to the passing of the two companions.

Once free of the kitchens, they picked up their pace. They dashed down a corridor that Melli was unfamiliar with, and then came to an abrupt stop by a small, low opening in the wall.

"Come on, we've got to crawl through here." Jack knelt down.

"I'm not doing that. That hole isn't big enough." Jack

ignored her comment and began to force himself through the opening, feetfirst. "Where does it lead to?"

"It leads to a storeroom where the firewood is kept." Jack paused as he shifted his body, allowing his shoulders to slip through. "I used to hide here when Master Frallit was after me."

Melli bent down and inspected the gap in the wall. She did not like the idea of going through it feetfirst. It would be undignified and Jack might see her legs and undergarments. She would go through headfirst. Melli lay on her belly and pushed with her arms and feet. It was a tight squeeze and she wondered how Jack had done it so effortlessly. She finally forced her way through and scrambled to her feet. Jack was looking at her with amusement. "Let's go, then," she said sharply.

Jack was just closing the door of the storeroom when someone called out: "Hey, you there!" Melli could see a castle guard approaching in the distance. She looked around judging their chances of escaping into the gardens. The guard was quickly approaching them.

"Jack, come here and don't say a word." Melli opened her arms. He was about to protest, but she cut him short, "Now!" He came into her arms and Melli raised her face to his and began to kiss him, slipping her wet tongue between his lips. She felt the pressure of Jack's body against hers and his hands encircled her waist. The guard drew close.

"What's all this?" he demanded. Melli forced Jack's face down into her shoulder with a push of her hand.

"I might ask you the same, my man." Melli's voice was regal and commanding. "Be on your way."

The guard hesitated, trying to get a look at Jack's face. Melli shot him an indignant glance. "I'm sorry to disturb you, lady," he said with a sly wink.

"You will be sorrier if you do it again! Now go at once." Melli breathed a sigh of relief as the guard withdrew. Her lips found Jack's once more and she began to kiss him again, keeping an eye on the guard until he was out of sight.

Melli pulled away from Jack. She could feel his reluctance to let her go. She was determined not to betray a similar reluctance on her part. Flushed and breathless, she turned from Jack and proceeded to walk off into the grounds. Before long she heard the sound of him running to catch up with her. "Where do we head for?" She could not risk looking at him.

"The woods," came his reply.

Twenty

*T*he terrain leading to Toolay was hilly and mountainous. Like Rorn, most people who visited the city did so by boat. Toolay was a city that lived off the sea; the cold clean waters that surrounded it were teeming with fish and crustaceans. It was said that once you tasted a fish from Toolay, you would never be satisfied with a fish from anywhere else the rest of your life.

Besides its fish, Toolay was known for its embroidery. While the men were off at sea for weeks at a time, their wives would gather together in groups and work their fabulous creations. Mythical creatures, ancient heroes, and legendary princesses were designed with astonishing detail, painstakingly embroidered over months and sometimes years. Rorn and Marls willingly paid a high price for such finery. The fishwives of Toolay also did less grand commissions: cushion slips embroidered with patterns, shawls stitched with flowers. It was these more humble works that were in greatest demand. Many a young maiden about to be wed would dream of one day owning a shawl from Toolay.

Tawl and Nabber crested a rise and caught their first sight of the city. Perched perilously near to the cliff's edge, Toolay looked as if it were about to fall into the very ocean that provided its livelihood. The city was much smaller than Rorn, the buildings less grand. No marble or spires, just low, modest buildings kept white by the constant blast of sea and sand.

Tawl had never been to Toolay before, and he felt the familiar excitement churn in the pit of his stomach. He always experienced a mixture of worry and wonder whenever he visited a city for the first time. "Come on, Nabber," he called, racing down the hillside. "If we rush we will make it before noon." Nabber was quick to catch up, and before long they found themselves struggling for breath at the bottom of the hill. Tawl felt like he needed a moment to catch his breath, but the boy was off, heading toward the next slope.

"Hey, Tawl!" he cried. "You're not going to let a young boy beat you to the city, are you?" Tawl had little choice but to run after him.

A few hours later, their muscles sore and aching, the two companions approached the city. As they drew near, the wind brought the odor of fish to their nostrils—the men of Toolay not only caught fish, they also smoked and dried it. Huge straw mats were spread with single layers of fish and left in the sun to dry. Tawl and the boy passed many of these mats, each one watched over by a small child or a guard goose.

The city itself was bustling with life: a huge open market entirely blocked the street. Stallholders stood beside their brightly colored tents and called their wares:

"Ribbons, posies, tokens for your lady love."

"Fish, fish, biggest lobsters ever to see land."

"Peppers, spices imported all the way from exotic Tyro."

"Apples, cheap apples, only slightly bruised. If your young uns don't like the look of 'em, they'll make a lovely pie."

Tawl watched and listened, admiring the goods, and deciding what food he would buy for the boy as a treat.

He had been constantly surprised by Nabber since he'd allowed the boy to join him. The boy had tireless energy; he was up before Tawl in the morning, he raced ahead of him all of the day, and wanted to talk through all of the night. Nabber wanted to know the stories of the great heroes, but only liked the tales where the adventurer found stashes of gold and jewels. The tales of the heroes who died penniless, and the ones who gave away their money to the poor, just caused Nabber to shake his head in bafflement.

Nabber had admitted taking more than money from the bodies by the roadside. From his pack he had produced a large, notched knife. Tawl had offered to teach the boy how to use it to defend himself. Nabber had declined the offer, assuring him that there wasn't much he didn't know about the blade. Seeing the look of disbelief on Tawl's face, the boy performed several tricks of precision and dexterity with the knife, effectively dispelling any doubts the knight had.

Tawl found one market stall that sold hot pastries filled with crabmeat. He purchased two of the delicious smelling items. The stallkeeper threw in a third for free. "You are most generous, madam." Tawl gave a slight bow.

"It's my pleasure, sir," replied the woman. "You are from out of town, that much is obvious by your golden hair, and the people of Toolay have ever welcomed travelers." The woman gave him a kindly smile. Tawl thanked her and left.

He turned about, ready to hand the pastry to Nabber, but the boy was nowhere in sight. He looked around for a while and found no sign of him. Tawl resigned himself to the fact that the boy must have decided to go his own way once he was in the city. It was probably for the best. The boy would be better off with people around him and there would be regular shelter and plenty of food. Tawl climbed on top of a broad wall and sat eating the pastries. He found he had no appetite for the third one and wrapped it in a cloth, saving it for later.

He was half dozing in the warm noon sun when he felt a sharp knock to his temple. He opened his eyes to find the boy grinning up at him, poised to throw another stone. "Caught you sleeping, didn't I?" Tawl jumped down off the wall and grabbed the boy by his ear.

"What do you think you were doing by wandering off on your own? You might never have found me again."

Nabber struggled free of the grip. "I kept an eye to you."

"What were you doing?"

"A little bit of this, a little bit of that. You know . . . prospecting."

"All right." Tawl sighed heavily. "What have you got?"

"Plenty, the pickings are rich in Toolay, I can tell you. People walking this market have got more money than's good for 'em. I just creamed a bit off the top—the surplus, like."

"How much?" demanded Tawl.

"I don't see that you're entitled to know that, my friend." The boy's smug smile quickly changed as Tawl grabbed the back of his hair.

"Look here, *friend,* as long as you are traveling with me I'm in charge."

"All right, all right, let go then." The boy made a digni-fied show of smoothing his hair back in place. "Seems as you're insisting, I'll show you." Nabber opened his pack and let Tawl peer into it; there were plenty of gold and silver coins and a few bracelets and rings.

Tawl groaned. "I hope you were careful, the penalty for pickpocketing in Toolay is castration." Tawl had no idea of the real penalty—he just wanted to come up with something that sounded painful enough to put the boy off.

"Telling me to be careful is like telling the fish how to swim. Besides, I *heard* the penalty was a swift lashing." The boy grinned. "Anyway, what do you propose we do with all this loot?"

"I propose we take a room for a night at a discreet inn, enjoy a simple midday meal, and then go and purchase two horses. We'll also need saddles and grain and some more dry food."

"Sounds good to me. Just one thing, though. I can't stand any more of those sea biscuits—I'm too young to lose my teeth."

"Very well, we'll buy some dried fish instead." It was the boy's turn to groan. Tawl continued, a twinkle in his eye. "No use protesting, Nabber, there isn't anything better for you than dried fish."

They made their way through the town. Tawl asked an old flower-seller the name of a decent inn. She looked rather affronted at the question. "Sir, all the inns of Toolay are decent. For the likes of travelers such as yourselves, the Shrimp Coddler will suffice."

"Ma'am, where is the Shrimp Coddler to be found?"

"Why, on the dock road of course, where all the inns are." She was off, toddling down the street before she could be asked where the dock road was.

"We'll have to find it on our own. Come on."

"Tawl, I was just wondering. Do you think we'll have enough money to buy two fine horses? I could always do a spot more prospecting."

"We won't need two fine horses, Nabber. One fine horse will be enough for me, and you can ride a pony."

"A pony! I haven't worked my fingers to the bone, putting myself at risk, for a pony."

"Have you ever ridden before?"

"Well, no, but . . ."

"You will ride a pony and that's final."

They eventually found the dock road. It was a hive of activity; men were gaming in the streets, prostitutes plied their trade, and dock workers carried large crates heavy with fish to warehouses. A distance up the road Tawl spied a brightly colored sign emblazoned with depictions of shrimp.

They went inside. Tawl was pleasantly surprised; the inn was clean and well appointed. The decor consisted of polished wood and brass, vying with pictures of shrimp and shrimping. A demurely dressed girl approached.

"How can I help you gentlemen?" She curtsied to Tawl and smiled at Nabber.

"I'd like a room for the night for me and my boy, and for now we'd like some food. What is good here?"

"Why, the coddled shrimp, of course. I'll bring you a bowl of them and some nice shrimp pie, too. Anything else?"

"Don't you do anything beside shrimp?" asked Nabber. Tawl swiftly kicked his shin.

"The shrimp will be fine. I'll take a mug of ale." Tawl smiled slyly. "Water for the boy."

Once they had finished their meal, they went off in search of a horse trader. They found one not far from the dock road. As they walked in a bell rang, and a man jumped up, obviously surprised.

"We need to buy a horse and a pony."

"Oh my, this is unexpected. Folks around here don't have much call for horses." The man peered closely at them, as if he were a little shortsighted.

"Have you any to sell?"

"Sell, why yes, of course. I am a horse dealer. Follow me." He led them to the stables at the back; most of the stalls were empty. "You'll be wanting a stallion, I presume, sir."

"I will take the best of what you have."

"I do have a fine stallion, sir, once owned by Lord Flay-harkel himself . . ." The man droned on but Tawl was not listening; he had spied a beautiful chestnut mare. He went over to get a better look at her. Her legs were lean and powerful, her flank amply muscled. Her coat needed some grooming but was not in bad condition. When the man realized Tawl's interest, he quickly moved in. "Oh, sir, I see you have a fine eye. A beautiful mare, once owned by the illustrious Lady Daranda." Tawl ignored what he was saying—horse traders were notorious liars.

"How much?"

"Ten golds." Tawl turned and walked away. "Eight golds," the man cried.

"Seven golds and throw in a pony for the boy."

"I couldn't possibly, I might as well give it away. I paid twice that for it."

"Take it or leave it." Tawl took a gamble. "You are not the only horse merchant in town."

"Very well, you have a deal, though you rob the food off my plate."

"Good. I will need two saddles and some grain. I will pay you when I pick them up in the morning. Good day, sir."

"Well, Grift, I have to admit there's more truth in what you say than I thought."

"What d'you mean, Bodger?"

"Well, remember what you were saying about high and mighty ladies liking a bit of rough?"

"Aye, Bodger."

"Well, I saw it with my own eyes. Just the other night I

was patrolling the grounds. I heard a bit of noise coming from the direction of the woodshed. Well, I goes over there to investigate, and what do I see."

"What did you see, Bodger?"

"Only a couple going at it."

"Rollickin'?"

"Just about. So, I moves closer and it's some fine lady with a right rough type. She tells me to hop along quickish."

"Who was the lady, Bodger?"

"Well, I couldn't be sure, Grift, but it looked like Lord Maybor's daughter, the Lady Melliandra."

"Well, I'll be damned! You know she's supposed to have run off." Bodger looked blank, so Grift continued, "Who do you think the Royal Guard have been looking for all this time? Of course the official version is that she's sick with a fever, but I don't believe that for a minute. Did you get a look at who she was with?"

"No, Grift, his head was buried in her shoulder the whole time."

"My, my, my." Grift took a deep drink from his cup. "I got lucky myself last night, Bodger."

"Oh, really, Grift. Who was the fortunate wench?"

"Old widow Harpit. She finally succumbed to my charms."

"I saw the Widow Harpit at dinner last night, Grift. She looked as drunk as a newt."

"Well, she sobered up considerably by the time I got through with her." The two men laughed raucously and downed more ale.

"Seems like quite a few people were a-tumblin last night, Grift. Even Prince Kylock was doing some courtin'."

"Oh, aye?"

"I saw him taking a young girl to his room. Way after midnight it was."

"Who was the girl, Bodger?"

"Findra the tablemaid."

Grift sucked in his breath. "I saw Findra this morning, Bodger. Her face is badly bruised and her right arm's been broken."

"That's funny, Grift. She looked fine to me last night."

Both men downed the rest of their ale in silence. They both knew better than to say any more.

Baralis was on his way to see the queen. He walked noiselessly down the castle corridors, leaving the dust undisturbed in his wake. His skin was pale and drawn, and beneath his cloak his hands curled up like those of an old women.

When he had first heard of the girl's escape he had been wild with fury, and Crope and the mercenaries were afraid to come near him. He had spent the whole night searching the tunnels and passageways, but the labyrinth beneath the castle was too complex and extensive for any one man to cover. Why, he himself could only guess where some of the passages led. He knew there were places that even he could not gain access to: dark, furtive passageways and slyly cloaked rooms, built for purposes long forgotten, their contents untouched for centuries.

Once it had become obvious they would find neither the girl nor the boy that night, Baralis gradually became calm. Rage was a useful but dangerous emotion—logic and cunning were lost to brute force.

Baralis began to think more clearly. There must be a way for him to locate the girl before the Royal Guard found her. There was some comfort to be gained in the fact that at least Maybor and his men were conveniently out of the way in the Eastlands.

He would still have to be more discreet, though; a band of mercenaries roaming the woods would surely catch the eye of the Royal Guard. He would order the mercenaries to keep a low profile. He would rely upon his own resources to hunt down the girl.

They would not have gone far, he thought. The weather had been particularly foul these past days and incessant rain and high winds were not the ideal conditions for travel. When he found the girl this time, he would take no chances that she escaped again.

Baralis reached the queen's chamber and was bid enter. The queen came forward, her jewels dazzling in the candlelight. She inclined her head graciously but made no move to offer her hand. "Ah, Lord Baralis, I am pleased you could come at such short notice." The queen tried to be more civil to him of late; however, she could never quite disguise her distaste.

"I am always at Your Highness' service." Baralis bowed, observing the rules of the game. The queen was silent and so he was forced to speak again. "Tell me, Your Highness, what is required of me. Surely the king has enough medicine for the time being?"

"You know to the exact drop how much medicine is left, Lord Baralis, since you mete it out with such meticulous precision." The queen elegantly arched her eyebrow. "I am no fool, sir. I have observed that the medicine you last gave me is weaker than the initial dose." Baralis raised his hand to protest, but the queen continued, "Nay, sir, do not deny it. That is not the reason why I brought you here."

"What exactly did you bring me here for, Your Highness?" There was a hint of impatience in Baralis' voice. He did not care for her tone of subtle reprimand.

"I wonder if you can help me, Lord Baralis." The queen spoke with studied innocence. "Something rather worrying has reached my ears. It appears that the Royal Guard have spotted mercenaries in the woods and the commander of the guard has asked if I desire the disposal of these men. I said to him that if the mercenaries were not gone by the morrow, then the guard could go ahead and dispatch them." The queen drew her lips back in the tiniest of smiles. "Tell me, Lord Baralis, did I do the right thing?"

"Your Highness is most wise." Baralis had little choice but to nod his approval. He was well aware that the queen's speech was to warn him to withdraw his men. "I trust Your Highness realizes that time is running out on our little wager?"

"Lord Baralis, you have no need to remind me. Our wager has been in my thoughts constantly. My confidence is high that the girl will be found within the next few days. For some strange reason I believe that she may be in the very woods that the mercenaries were searching this morning."

The queen gave him a meaningful glance and turned her back on him.

Baralis took his leave and made his way back to his chambers. He could not help but admire the queen's intelligence: she had deduced that because his men were in the woods they were in all likelihood looking for Maybor's daughter, which in turn meant that they knew something of her whereabouts. He would have to move fast; the queen would waste no time ordering the Royal Guard to step up their search in the forest.

As soon as he reached his chambers he ordered Crope to tell the mercenaries to halt their search.

Once he was alone, he let himself into his study and mixed the drug he needed. He ground lichen in a mortar and extracted juices from a moss that grew in the darkness underneath the castle. Other ingredients were added: powders and extractions. Swiftly he sliced open the skin on the tip of his finger. His blood was a bright bead upon the flesh. He squeezed the wound, allowing three drops only to fall into the cup.

Baralis drew power into the cup—a mere trace, a catalyst. The liquid swirled within, moved by an unseen hand. Baralis daubed a streak of the drug on his forehead. Immediately the skin around the smear erupted into tiny blisters. His whole body broke into a cold sweat. Baralis drew the cup to his face and breathed in the fumes; his body recoiled from the noxious vapors, but he forced himself to breathe deeply.

He could feel the burning of nostril and lung. He swayed as the drug worked its effect, stealing through tissue and sinew into his mind.

Since they had escaped things had not gone smoothly. The weather had been so bad that they had been unable to travel far, and they were both soaked to the skin. They had run out of food and had not eaten in two days. The nights had been the worst: they had to sleep out in the open on the wet earth, pressed close against each other to keep warm.

Jack was well aware that the mercenaries were out looking for them—the whole forest seemed riddled with men on horseback. They had managed to conceal themselves so far—whenever they heard guards approaching they hid in ditches or undergrowth. Jack knew, however, that it was only a matter of time before some sharp-eyed mercenary spotted them cowering among the dead leaves.

They pushed onward, the rain pelting against their faces and the wind robbing them of any chance of warmth. The forest floor was thick with damp, decomposing leaves. Their smell was not unpleasant—a rich, furtive scent that spoke of growth and renewal. Jack found he had more appreciation of the forest since his stay with Falk. He saw the grace of the bare trees and the modesty of the undergrowth—brush and bracken, destined always to live in the shadow of their more glorious relations.

After some time Melli came to an abrupt halt. "Over there," she said. Jack looked toward where she was indicating and could see nothing. "Behind that large oak tree." She dashed off and he was obliged to follow. He soon realized what he had seen: a wooden hut. It was almost totally concealed by trees and bushes, and ivy vines snaked against its walls.

They cautiously approached the hut. There was no sign of a path leading to the doorway and the ivy vines extended over the door itself. Jack looked to Melli, who nodded her head enthusiastically and pushed at the door. It was very stiff; years of rainfall had warped the wood and corroded the hinges. The door gave way a little and then could be budged no further. They managed to squeeze through the gap and into the hut.

The inside smelled musky and damp. Once Jack's eyes became accustomed to the dimness, he realized they had stumbled upon an old hunting lodge. Before King Lesketh became ill, he and his men would often spend many days in the forest tracking game; huts were built so the men would not have to return to the castle at nightfall. They afforded some shelter and provided a place to keep their kills and equipment until the hunt was over. Since the king's illness the huts had mostly lain unused and forgotten.

Jack forced the door closed, and he and Melli began to search the hut for items they could use. They found some

old, dusty horseblankets and wrapped themselves up in them
to keep warm. There was a selection of hunting implements:
chains, prodders, spears and hoods, and even a rather battered brass horn. There were two wooden benches and an old
table on top of which sat an empty oil lamp and the long-de-
cayed carcass of a fox. In the corner was an old painted
chest.

Jack pried the chest open with a spearpoint. Inside were
various men's clothes: breeches, waistcoats, and tunics.
Right at the bottom, buried beneath the blankets and oilskins,
was an ancient-looking book. Jack drew it forth from the
chest. Its bindings were loose and mold grew on its pages.
He opened it up, the paper thin and brittle between his fingers.

"What's that?" Melli came up behind him. "Here, give
it to me." Jack handed the book over to her and she turned to
the title page, elaborately decorated with depictions of the
stars in the heavens. *The Book of Words by Marod.* Oh,
how disappointing. I thought it might have been some juicy
revelations about the king's ancestors. Instead it's just boring
old Marod."

"Who is Marod?" asked Jack, who had never heard of
him.

"Oh, I thought everyone knew about Marod. As a girl I
had to learn the poems. Of course, it's mostly for the priests
and scholars—they read and study it. It's a load of old nonsense if you ask me." Melli flicked through the pages. "This
is a pretty bad copy . . . the paper has been used twice. You
can still see writing from the first script." Melli carelessly
dropped the book back into the chest. "Let's see if we can
find anything to eat."

She began to search the planked floor. "I remember one
year when I was very young, my father took me out on a
hunt—of course, it wasn't a real one, more a treat for my
brothers." Melli dropped to her hands and knees and started
knocking on the wooden boards. "Anyway, we came to a hut
like this. We were tired and hungry and Father surprised us
by lifting up some of the floorboards. Underneath was a
small store of food. Apparently food was kept underground
because it stayed fresher longer, and it kept any animals from

stealing away with it. Aha!" Melli excitedly pulled up a
length of wood. "What have we here?" She reached down
with her arm and pulled out a stoppered flask; she opened it.
"Wine." Jack took it from her. It was indeed wine; he poured
a little into his palms and then tasted. It was a little sour but
still drinkable.

Melli meanwhile had brought forth other items from the
hold; bags of oats and grain and several items wrapped in
linen cloths. "It would appear that the hunters of old cared
little about their own refreshment and more about their
horses. Oats and wheat are of no use to us." Jack ignored her
comments and checked around the hut. There was a primitive brick stove. He smiled. All he needed now was some
firewood and a pot. He found an iron cauldron thrown in
with the hunting equipment. There was not, however, any
firewood in sight.

"Why not burn that old book?" quipped Melli as she
busily opened the various packages.

"No." Working as Baralis' scribe, Jack had grown to
treasure books and didn't like the thought of burning one, especially one that looked so old. "I'll break up the chest, instead. That will burn well." He picked up the book and
flicked through its pages; as he did so a loose leaf fell onto
the floor. He crouched down and picked it up. It was a letter.
Melli came over and snatched it from him.

"It's signed with a wreathed 'L.' That's King Lesketh's
signature." She read the short note: *"My sweetest love, I can
see you at the lodge no more. The queen is with child, and
our meetings must end. Take the book, it is yours, I know
how much you loved reading it. Let it be a parting gift. L."*

Melli looked at him. He could tell from her face that she
felt the same way he did: ashamed. They had pried into
someone else's life. Jack took the letter from Melli and carefully replaced it in the book. Reading the letter wasn't right.
Its secrets were not meant to be shared. He put the book on a
shelf and began breaking the chest down for firewood.

It grew dark quickly and Jack began to feel safer; the
mercenaries would call off their search until the morning.
The fire burning in the stove warmed the little hut and the
smell of cooking filling the air. He prepared porridge, enrich-

ing its flavor by throwing in a length of dried meat. He wa.
not entirely sure if the drymeat was still edible, but decide
to take the chance. Melli turned up her nose at the porridge a
first, but hunger changed her mind. Once she had tasted it
she finished off the whole pot, eating far more than he did
She then curled up close to the stove and fell asleep.

Jack sat for a while, wondering what would be best t
do tomorrow. The idea of spending another day in the refug
of the hut was very tempting. Outside the wind howled an
the rain fell. He decided he would wait and see what th
morning would bring.

He soared high above the clouds, the firmament twin
kled with the cold brilliance of the millennium. Never had h
seen it so beautiful, so terrible: it taunted him with its near
ness. He was without body, without soul, a wisp of smoke, a
scattering of particles, borne upward by the strength of hi
own will.

It was time to descend; madness came to those wh
looked too long upon the heavens. He raced downward, leav
ing the stars and the blackness of space behind him. H
moved through the clouds and was untouched by their wet
ness. Down he went, the earth a vague darkness below.

He began to discern shapes and forms: the gray quad
rangle that formed the walls of the castle, the sprawl of th
town. He turned his gaze southward and spied his huntin
ground, the shadowy blackness of the forest.

Lower and lower. The canopy of the forest, which a
first had seemed without feature, began to take shape. H
perceived the patterns of the tree and bush and sapling. H
saw the glow of life moving within; from the largest stag
standing magnificent on a grassy rise, to the smallest earth
worm burrowing its way through the hard earth. The abun
dance of nature was laid out beneath him, teeming an
striving.

He moved inward, searching. Through the trees h
raced, bare branches caressing the air as he passed. He spie
the flicker of possibility and changed his course. He drev
close and recognized the work of man. It was a building o

some sort, almost hidden by a dense growth of trees. He floated downward and then slipped his tenuous form between the cracks in the wood.

His suspicions had been proven right. The boy and the girl lay sleeping by a low-burning stove. He passed over them, each in turn stirring but not waking.

Content that he had accomplished his task, he withdrew, willing his shadowy insubstance back to meet his body. Once more he sped across the skies, not pausing to admire their spectacle. His time was limited and he would not risk being stranded, bodiless, for all eternity.

He began his descent into the castle. Down he came through the many layers of stone, anxious to be reunited with flesh and blood once more. He floated above his body. How shallow his breaths were, how pale his skin. Down he came, joining himself, penetrating deep into the soft grayness. He knew such weakness, such fatigue, and then no more.

Twenty-one

Melli shifted her position; the wooden floor was hard and she was seeking to make herself comfortable. Through closed eyes, she was aware of the onset of dawn. She was reluctant to get up. She had been having such a pleasant dream and did not want to break the spell. She knew that getting up would mean another day of running and hiding, being chased by Baralis' mercenaries and her father's men. She would be cold, hungry, scared, and exhausted. It was pleasant just to lie here in the dying warmth of the stove and pretend that none of it existed.

Melli found that she could not pretend; images intruded into her peace, confusing and distressing her. Images of being flogged, images of being locked in a small, dark room and, most disturbing of all, the image of Baralis running his fingers down her spine. She shuddered, repulsed at the memory, but she knew she was not being honest with herself: for a brief instant she had wanted, even willed him to caress her. She had stood and let him touch her, and part of her had thrilled at that touch. Baralis was widely held to be a powerful and seductive man, but she had never thought she would succumb to his allure. It was better, Melli considered, to get far away from Castle Harvell and to put all pain and bewilderment behind her.

She gradually became aware of a vague murmuring.

She listened and it grew louder—the noise of horses at the gallop. She felt a bitter churning in her belly; they had come for her. She looked to Jack, who had been awakened by the noise. He sprang up and began to gather some food into a cloth bag.

"We haven't got time," cried Melli. "They are almost upon us." She rushed over to the door and began pulling on it. It would not budge. "Jack, hurry, help me with this!" Together they dragged the door open and forced their way through the narrow gap.

Outside, trees were lashing frantically in the wind, fallen leaves were whipped into a frenzy, and rain beat against their faces. The sound of horsemen was now an insistent rumbling and Melli could tell there were many. She grabbed Jack's hand and they plunged deep into the forest.

The wind was against them, seeming almost to force them back. The riders were gaining, and the sound of them, charging through the undergrowth, struck fear into Melli's heart. There would be no hiding this time. Jack dragged at her arm, pulling her to him with all his strength. The wind would not let them go. It held them in its thrall, lashing against them whenever they managed a step forward.

Cries could be heard; they had been spotted. The wind caught Melli's shawl and dragged it from her back. She tried to hold on, but it was too late—the shawl blew away. The rain soaked her dress, but she paid no heed. Her hair came unpinned, but it did not matter. All she could think of was getting away; she could not bear to be caught again. They pushed ahead, their pursuers fast approaching.

Melli looked back: the horsemen were in view now—spears poised, ready to strike. She glanced toward Jack. His grim expression confirmed her fears; the men were sent not to capture but to kill, to slaughter them like wild animals.

An arrow whirred past her cheek, missing by a finger's breadth. She stood, dazed with shock for an instant before Jack dragged her forward. With horror, she realized that he had been hit, a shaft was embedded in his shoulder. He did not cry out, but his face registered the pain of the blow. The horsemen charged forward. They desperately scrambled up a muddy hillock—Melli felt a sharp pain in her arm. She

screamed with panic as she saw the arrow sticking out of her
forearm. She felt the strength ebb from her body and willed
herself not to faint. Blood gushed forth, soaking her dress,
and tears prickled in her eyes. Jack, seeing what had happened to her, lifted her to the top of the rise. She leaned on
him for support, and to her amazement he turned and faced
the horsemen.

His face was ashen with pain and anger. Arrows shot
past them, Melli felt one graze her ear. She raised her arm to
check for blood, and as she did so she felt a shifting of the
air. Time seemed to slow down; the wind calmed for a fleeting moment; the mercenaries' horses reared in fear. The air
shimmered and thickened and blasted into the horsemen,
knocking them from their horses. Leaves took flight from the
forest floor, tender saplings were uprooted, and branches
snapped from trees.

The mercenaries were thrust back. One man's neck was
broken as he was flung against a tree trunk, another man was
impaled on his own spear. Melli looked on, as a horse fell on
one man; the creature tried frantically to stand once more and
in doing so kicked the man's skull in. She grabbed hold of
Jack's arm for comfort: his flesh was cold and rigid. She
pulled at him to come away, but he did not move. Frightened, she shook him. "Jack, come on, let's get away from
here." There was no response. He stood, staring ahead, his
face slick with sweat. "Jack, please, wake up." She shook
him with all her might, ignoring the pain in her arm.

He turned to look at her. Relief flooded through Melli.
"Come on, Jack, let's go." There was no comprehension in
his eyes, no sign that he recognized or even understood her.
She led him away, eager to be gone. She could not resist
looking back, though—men and horses lay dead or bleeding
on the ground below. One man was crawling away, his left
leg trailing after him, useless. The air was still now: no wind,
just the relentless pour of rain. Melli shivered, not wanting to
think about what had happened, or why she and Jack had remained unaffected.

Taking hold of Jack's arm, she began to guide him
down the side of the slope. By the time they reached the bottom, Jack's tunic was soaked with blood. Melli decided to

head toward the eastern road—they both needed help and shelter and would find neither in the forest. She knew it was a risk, but the road was their only chance of finding someone willing to aid them.

Tavalisk was dressing in his most dazzling robes. Expelling the knights had proven such a popular move that the city had organized a parade in his honor. The people of Rorn loved spectacle and expected their leaders to look magnificent on such occasions. Once, many years before, Vesney, the first minister at the time, had turned up for a parade wearing only a plain brown robe, no adornments, no jewelry, not even a hat. The people of Rorn took this as a grave insult. *They* had put on their best clothes. The fact that the first minister had not put on his showed how little he valued their approval. The crowd had turned into an indignant mob, pulling the unfortunate Vesney from his horse and beating him to death.

The irony was that Vesney had thought the people would appreciate his gesture. He thought he was showing them that he was a frugal man, who would not spend their taxes unwisely on the frivolous trappings of power. Tavalisk knew better. The people of Rorn required little else from their leaders: they needed to be dazzled by wealth and pageantry and then bask in reflected glory. Rorn was the richest city in the Known Lands: its people liked their leaders to be an embodiment of that fact.

The archbishop was being sewn into a tunic of bright yellow silk. He was amusing himself by looking down the dress of the seamstress as she stitched up the sides. There was a brief knock and Gamil entered.

"Ah, Gamil. I was just thinking about you. I was wondering when you will bring my little Comi to visit me." Tavalisk had recently acquired a cat. The sly creature had captured his interest and so he'd given his dog to Gamil—the archbishop only had room for one favorite. Now he had the strong suspicion that his aide had either killed the dog or set it out on the streets. His suspicions were confirmed by the guilty look on Gamil's face.

"I will bring him as soon as he has recovered from his illness, Your Eminence."

"See that you do, Gamil. I will remind you to do so in a few days." The archbishop smiled agreeably to his aide. "It warms my heart to think my dear Comi is with someone who I know will take good care of him." He turned to the seamstress. "Not so tight, girl. I do not wish to look like a sausage about to burst its skin. There will be a feast later and I will need room for digestion." Tavalisk gave his attention back to his aide. "So, Gamil, what news have you for me today?"

"Word has reached Marls about your expulsion of the knights."

"And how is that unfortunate city taking the news?"

"There have been demonstrations in the streets, Your Eminence. The people of Marls are calling on their authorities to follow your example. Marls has no love for the Knights of Valdis."

"Excellent, Gamil. Though the news is no surprise to me, it has long been rumored that the knights brought the plague to the city."

"Your Eminence demonstrated great forethought by starting that particular rumor."

"Yes, it is always a wise move to have one's rivals at each other's throats. I only wish I could claim the credit for starting the confounded plague in the first place."

"I will be expecting to hear reports on what Toolay thinks of your edict within a week. If I am not mistaken, they should have heard about the news by now."

"Toolay's reaction will be most interesting. They have long associations with the knighthood. However, they, like most cities today, live in fear: fear of invasion, fear of the plague, fear of losing trade. Yes, I will watch Toolay carefully." Tavalisk moved forward to pick at a pile of grapes, and doing so stepped on the hand of the seamstress who was hemming his cloak. "Talking of that delightful fishing port, any news of our knight?"

"Well, Your Eminence, he was last spotted some days ago approaching the city in the company of the small boy who had been following him."

The archbishop admired his reflection in the mirror. "Are we still holding the prostitute?"

"Yes, Your Eminence, but with all due respect it could be a long time before the knight returns to Rorn."

"Ah, Gamil, you have a woefully short memory. Only seconds ago you praised me for my forethought. I intend to keep the girl for as long as it takes: months, years, who knows? What I do know is that eventually she will be useful, and Rorn will not mourn the loss of one less whore in the meantime."

"If there is nothing more, I will take my leave, Your Eminence. I, too, must ready myself for the parade."

"I wouldn't bother to change if I were you, Gamil. You always look so becoming in brown."

Tawl awoke to the sound of shouting. He wiped the sleep from his eyes and went over to the window to investigate. In the street below there was a crowd of people chanting and waving banners. Tawl stood horrified as he realized what the people were crying.

"Ban the knights, expel them from our city."

He watched as a banner depicting the knights' symbol—a circle within a circle—was set afire. There was laughing and cheering at the sight. Gradually the crowd made its way down the street, heading toward the center of the city.

Tawl could hardly believe what he had seen and heard. For the first time he was forced to acknowledge the full extent of hostility toward his order. How had this happened? Hatred where there once was respect. What had caused people to turn against them so completely?

"Boy!" He shook Nabber awake. "I will breakfast alone. Do not move from this room until I have returned."

"What about me, what shall I eat?"

"Do not pester me now. I will be back before long." Tawl left the room and made his way down to the dining room. He was going to find out what had caused the demonstration.

The eating hall was busy with people eating and drinking. He picked a table that was already occupied. The stranger looked rather apprehensive as Tawl sat down and began to gather his things together.

"No, sir, please do not go on my account. I have no wish to disturb you." Hearing him speak, the man appeared to relax a little.

"Forgive me for my discourtesy, but looking as you do, you must not be surprised at my reaction."

"It is not always best to judge a man's intentions by his size. Even a small man can carry a long knife." Tawl quoted a well-known travelers' proverb. Tawl was a good head above most men in height and was well used to his size making men nervous.

"You have put me in my place, young man. I would buy you a drink." He called the tavern girl and ordered the traditional morning refreshment of Toolay: ale mixed with goat's milk.

"Did you happen to see the crowds that were gathered on the dock road?" Tawl winced as he drank from his cup—brought up in the marshlands, he had no love of goat's milk.

"Aye, that I did. It's a bad business." The man shook his head wearily. "It's that slippery archbishop's fault. He's only gone and expelled the knights from Rorn."

"When did he do that?" asked Tawl nonchalantly.

"Just got word of it today. There's people around who'd like to see the same thing happen here."

"The protesters?"

The stranger glanced nervously around the room. "More powerful people as well."

"I thought Toolay had long been on friendly terms with Valdis."

"No one in the south is friendly with Valdis since Tyren took over. The man wants to control all the trade routes to the north and east. He's using strongarm tactics one minute and calling us heretics the next." The man took a long draught. "Toolay owes a great debt to the knights. Almost a hundred years ago they helped us fight off an invasion from the barbarians who came from over the water. No one has forgotten that, but it comes down to priorities, lad. Toolay lives for trade. Threaten our trade and you threaten our livelihood. We export a fortune in embroidery and cold-water fish to Rorn. Upset Rorn and we stand to lose money. Valdis has little taste for fish or finery." The stranger looked at Tawl suspiciously. "Where are you from, boy?"

"I am originally from the Great Marshes." Tawl took a hearty swig of his ale and then looked the man squarely in the eye.

"Well, lad, I must be on my way. There are fish to be cleaned and salted—though even that's more expensive thanks to the knights. Bought up all the salt pans, they did." The stranger stood up, sighing heavily. "There's trouble simmering, but Valdis isn't the only one with a spoon in the pot. Rorn and Bren aren't above stirring the mix." He bowed politely. "I wish you joy of the day, and fish in fortune and famine." Tawl returned the blessing and watched him leave. Feeling restless, he decided to wander into town and see what the marchers were up to.

Toolay was a bright and busy place in the early morning. Facing easterly as it did, the city benefited from the sun's first tentative rays. Tawl made his way toward the marketplace and could soon hear the sound of chanting and shouting. He followed the noise and eventually came upon a crowd of people. The men whom he had seen from his window were there, and many more. There were also a small group of people who were for the knights; these unfortunate men were heckled and pelted with fish heads. The crowd was angry, crying out harshly:

"Down with the knights."

"The knights bring the plague."

"They steal our trade."

"Valdis is rotten to the core."

Tawl could take no more. Hanging his head low, he returned to the inn. It seemed that none of the people he'd met since being freed from Rorn's dungeons had a good word to say about Valdis. Tyren's name was on everyone's lips, and he was branded a charlatan with each breath. It had been so long since he was last at Valdis, could he really say with conviction that he knew what was going on there? It had been almost a reflex action to deny the rumors in Rorn. The city was corrupt, and the archbishop took care to create a strong antiknight sentiment amongst the people. But Toolay

406 / J. V. JONES

was different. Its people were pious and hard working, and as the stranger in the tavern had pointed out, it owed a great debt to Valdis.

For the first time, Tawl was forced to admit there must be some truth in the rumors. But Tyren? He couldn't believe it. Tyren had all but saved his life, and had certainly saved his soul. He was the one who first brought him to Valdis and acted as his protector when others called him too lowborn to be a knight. Tyren defended him, saying the knights needed the strength and vitality of new blood, peasant blood. Tawl admired him for the courage he'd shown. Challenging the very foundations of the knighthood hadn't been easy, but Tyren hadn't rested until the knights agreed to let any man regardless of birth, try out for the circles.

Two years into his training as a knight, Tyren was made head of the order. The last leader, Fallseth, had died a mysterious death, his body was found in a brothel on the outskirt of Valdis. After the humiliation of Fallseth's death, the knights wanted to choose someone of high moral character Tyren was chosen.

Tawl wondered what had happened in his absence When he'd first set out on his quest, he was proud to show his circles. Strangers let him into their homes on the strength of them. They had stood for honor and bravery and faith Now they were marks of shame, never to be shown in the presence of others.

Pushing up his sleeve, he brought his circles into view He would walk back to the inn with them on show. They were the only thing he lived for, and he would not see them condemned on the strength of a few ugly rumors. Walking with his head high, he felt ashamed of his doubts; the knight valued loyalty above anything else. And considering, even for a moment, that there might be truth behind the reports of corruption was disloyalty of the highest order.

No one challenged Tawl as he returned to the inn which was probably a blessing as he was eager for a fight. It would have been an unlucky man who chose to make an issue of his circles on this bright morning.

When he got to the inn, Tawl was surprised to find that Nabber had actually heeded his words for once and was wait ing obediently for him. "What took you so long?" the boy asked, but seeing the look on the knight's face, he became quiet and set about putting his belongings into his pack.

They made their way to the stables and picked up their mounts. When the mare was brought out into the full daylight Tawl was well satisfied with his choice—she was lithe and graceful. His mood lightened when he saw what Nabber would be riding. It was a stout and bad-tempered looking pony with a coarse, sandy-colored coat. He laughed outright when he saw the boy's indignant expression.

"I'm not riding that sorry-looking mule."

"I assure you, young man, that is no mule. It is a hill bred pony—a good little work horse." The horse merchant was most offended.

"The pony will do fine." Tawl handed the man seven gold pieces. "How much do I owe you for the saddles and grain?"

"Two more golds." The man was busily testing the coins he had been given. He scraped the top of them with his knife, checking there was no base metal beneath the gold. Tawl knew the merchant asked too much for the saddles, but he had no desire to bargain. He handed over the money and took his leave.

Tawl gently patted his horse's head, allowing the creature to become accustomed to him. Nabber took his example and did likewise. The pony turned quickly and bit him.

"You dumb mule." The boy rubbed his hand. "I'll get my own back." Nabber thought for a second, obviously considering what would be a suitable punishment for the pony. "I know, I'll give you a stupid name. I'll call you Smircher!"

"That doesn't sound like such a bad name." Tawl was busy checking his harness and saddle.

"You don't know much, do you? A smircher is what they call people who make their living out of searching for coins and stuff down amidst the sewage on the streets. Ain't no worse insult in Rorn than to be called a smircher. Lowest of the low they are."

"Well, I quite like the name. I'm sure it will make little difference to the pony." Tawl mounted his horse.

"What will you be calling yours?"

"Well, you appear to have a flair for names. What do you suggest?"

"Petal. I had a pet rabbit once, called her Petal because she liked to eat flowers, drove the flower-sellers up the wall."

"Petal it is, then. Come on, Nabber, let's get a move on. I want to get a good start on the day." As Tawl pulled on his reins, he noticed his circles were still showing. He resisted the urge to hide them. For today at least he would defy anyone to denounce the knights in his hearing.

Maybor stripped out of his wet clothing and stood shivering in front of the fire while his servant laid out new robes. He and his men had ridden hard through bad weather and Maybor was cold and tired. He called angrily to Crandle, urging him to hurry. He had things he must be doing.

As soon as he was dressed he made his way through the castle. It was high time he paid Baralis a visit; the man had toyed too long with him. He would squeeze the truth about his daughter from his scrawny frame. He would, of course, take no chances; he knew well the tricks Baralis had up his sleeve. No, he would not go alone. He would not give the king's chancellor a chance to burn *him* to a crisp.

He knocked on the door of Kedrac's chamber, and hearing no answer, walked straight in. His son was abed with a wench. "You have wasted no time, Kedrac. Why, it has been less than an hour since I took my leave." Maybor was pleased at finding his son wenching. Some of his own prowess had obviously been passed down in the blood.

"Father, what do you want?" Kedrac did not seem in the slightest bit ruffled by the interruption. His hand moved under the covers as he continued caressing the girl.

"I have decided to confront Baralis about your sister. He knows where she is. It is time we found out exactly what that snake is up to. Are you with me?" Kedrac leapt naked from the bed and rushed into his dressing room, eager to be on his way.

While his son was dressing, Maybor turned his attention to the girl in the bed. It was none other than Lady Helliarna's chambermaid. "What is your name, girl?" he asked. The girl looked both embarrassed and frightened and did not answer him. "Come, come, speak up."

"I am named Lilly." The girl spoke in a whisper.

"Well, Lilly, do you enjoy bedding my son?" Maybor was keeping an eye on the door lest his son return.

"Why, yes, sir, he has been good to me."

"Well, my sweet Lilly, if the son is good to you, think how much better the father will be."

Comprehension dawned on the girl's face and her demeanor became more alluring. "Why, sir, what are you proposing?" She spoke coquettishly, allowing the sheet to slip artfully from her breast. She made a pretty show of reclaiming her modesty, pulling the sheet up to her neck and blushing charmingly.

"Be at my chamber one hour past nightfall and I will give you the details of my proposal."

"Father," said Kedrac, bounding into the room, "I was thinking it would be wise to take some men along with us." Maybor quickly turned, pretending to admire the crossed swords on the wall. The girl slid deep beneath the covers.

"No, we will go alone. Take your weapon."

They left the chamber and headed up to Baralis' lair. They came to a halt by a door etched with strange markings. Maybor rapped loudly upon it with the hilt of his sword. After some time the door swung open and the two men fell under Crope's shadow.

"Where is your master? I demand to see him now." Maybor refused to be intimidated by any servant, no matter what his size.

"You cannot see Lord Baralis." The servant spoke like an idiot who had learned his lines but did not understand them.

"If he is in his chambers then I *will* see him."

"Lord Baralis is unwell and cannot receive visitors."

"He will see me!" Maybor tried to force his way past Crope, but it was like walking into a stone wall. "Let me pass."

"Let him pass, Crope." Baralis stood behind his servant. Maybor was shocked by his appearance; his servant had not lied when he said his master was ill. Baralis was white as a ghost. Kedrac moved toward the door. "No, Maybor," said Baralis, his voice thin and strained. "I will speak with you alone or not at all." Kedrac looked to his father, who nodded his head. It was not likely that Baralis could do him any damage in his present state.

Maybor had never been in Baralis' chambers before. Like everyone else he had heard wild tales about vials of blood, pickled brains, and skeletons, but he found none of these things. Instead he found a well-appointed room which was discreetly and, to Maybor's discerning eye, expensively furnished. There were deep blue handwoven silk rugs, intricately worked tapestries from Toolay, and furniture of the finest tropical woods.

"Can I offer you some refreshment?" Baralis indicated that he should sit down.

"I want no wine of yours." Maybor was beginning to feel like a fly in a spider's web.

"As you wish. You will forgive me if I take a glass. As you can see I am not well and I find a glass of red strengthens my blood."

"I think you know why I am here." Things were not going the way Maybor had planned. He felt he was allowing Baralis to take the lead.

"I'm afraid I cannot guess, Lord Maybor."

"What have you done with my daughter?" Maybor's voice was charged with anger.

Baralis remained calm, pouring himself a glass of wine. "I do not know where your daughter is."

"I have reason to believe that mercenaries in your pay took her from Duvitt."

"Come, come now, Lord Maybor. You know mercenaries—one week they work for one man, the next for another. I do not deny having used the services of mercenaries. I have matters of my own that require their particular skills, but I have neither the time nor the inclination to hunt down your errant daughter."

"You are lying to me, Baralis." Maybor could barely contain his rage and frustration. His sword itched in its sheath.

"*You*, Lord Maybor, are in no position to call me a liar." Baralis' voice had gained a hard edge. "Now I would prefer it if you leave."

Maybor stood and drew his sword. He had the satisfaction of seeing fear in Baralis' face. The blade flashed brilliantly in the candlelight. Crope sprang forward, but Maybor had already resheathed the sword.

"Do not make the mistake of underestimating me, Baralis." Their eyes met. The mutual loathing was unmistakable—it filled the space between them with the tension of a torturer's rack. Baralis was the first to look away. Maybor held his head high and walked from the room.

Kedrac was waiting outside for him. "Did you find out anything about Melliandra from him, Father?"

"No, but I discovered something more useful." Maybor slowly rubbed his chin with his hand.

"What is that?"

"Baralis is human; he can be scared by the edge of a blade just like any man." His son was unimpressed by this pronouncement, but *he* knew its true worth. Ever since the incident with the assassin, Maybor had feared that Baralis had supernatural powers, yet today he had tested them and none had been forthcoming. He had not been smitten down by a bolt of lightning nor blasted into purgatory. Maybor walked back to his room with a light step, suddenly more confident about the future.

It took Melli many hours before she reached the eastern road. She had dragged Jack through the forest in the driving rain. They were both soaked to the skin; she had lost her shawl and was chilled to the bone. Her arm had ceased to cause her pain some time back, now it just felt numb and strangely heavy. She had broken the arrow shaft from Jack's shoulder, but could not face the thought of removing the head. Instead she had pressed hard against the wound for some time until the bleeding had stopped. Unfortunately as soon as he began to walk again, the wound began to bleed once more, and the longer they walked the worse it became. Her own wound seemed quite clean. She could clearly see the outline of the arrowhead in her arm. It was lodged in muscle just beneath the skin. Her ear stung and had bled a little, but no real damage had been done.

Melli was bitterly disappointed when the road came into sight; there was no clearing of forest which usually marked the presence of farms or cottages. She had no way of knowing how far along from town and castle they were, and decided to continue heading east. She did not bother to leave the road for cover, for it would be some time before Baralis could get together more men to replace the ones he'd lost. As for her father's men, let them come if they would—she had almost forgotten the reason she'd run away in the first place.

Jack had still not spoken a word. Melli supposed he was in some kind of shock. She was worried about him and anxious that he get help. It was *his* need for care that kept her strong. She could not recall a single time in her whole life when someone had needed her help before. She had always been the weak one, the one who was protected and cared for. She found she liked her new role and was determined not to let Jack down.

After a time, Melli spotted a dirt track leading from the road. She followed the path, which led to a small but well-maintained farmhouse. She decided it was best if she approached on her own and guided Jack behind some bushes, where she bid him sit and wait. She could not tell if he heard her, but he made no effort to move. Melli straightened her hair and dress as best she could, wishing the wind had not taken her shawl, for it would have served to hide the wound on her arm. Satisfied she could do no more for her appearance, she headed toward the farmhouse.

Melli could tell by the smell in the air that it was a pig farm. There were many such farms around the castle: Harvell liked its pork. Local custom held that it was unlucky for a farmer to have a door at the front of the house, so Melli made for the side of the building. She banged loudly on the door and stood shivering while she waited for an answer. An old woman opened the door. "What d'you want?" she demanded in a voice surprisingly strong for one so old. "If you're a-beggin', I'll tell you now, you'll get nothin' from me. Be off with you."

Melli took a deep breath. "Please, I need help."

"Be off with you or I'll get my son." The woman made a shooing gesture with her hands.

"Please, I'm injured and—"

"Your troubles are not mine," interrupted the woman. "I'll get my son if you're not off my land in three seconds."

"If you could just—"

"If you don't remove yourself from my doorstep this instant, I'll have my son come after you with a carving knife."

"Get your son, then," cried Melli, angry at the woman's attitude and close to tears. "See if I care. He can't do any more harm than has already been done." The woman hesitated. Melli became slightly hysterical. "Go on, bring him out, make sure he's got his sharpest knife!" The old woman was looking afraid.

"You'd better come in," she said wearily.

"I have a friend who is wounded; he's in the bushes over there." Melli couldn't understand the woman's complete turn of face, but she was not about to question her luck. "If you wait a moment, I will bring him over." The woman nodded and Melli dashed off to get Jack.

She was relieved to find the door still open when she returned.

"He's in a bad way," commented the old woman looking at Jack. She led them into a warm and cozy kitchen: a fire burned brightly and there was stew on the boil. "Sit down. I will bring you something to dry yourselves off with."

Melli made Jack sit and then looked around the kitchen—something caught her eye. The table was set for one: one plate, one mug of ale, one knife. The woman came back with an armful of woolen blankets. "I thought we might have seen your son," said Melli, feigning casualness as she took the blankets from her and began to dry off Jack.

"He's gone to Harvell for the day." The woman turned her back on Melli and proceeded to stir the stew.

"I thought he was in the house." Melli winced as she dried her wounded arm.

"Well, he's not," said the woman flatly. "And I don't see that it's any of your business."

"You have no son, do you? You live alone here. Don't worry—I'm not about to tell anyone." Melli knew there were strict laws against women holding farms in the Four Kingdoms. A woman who was widowed had her farm confiscated by the authorities unless she had a son to pass it down to. Any woman who was caught in defiance of the laws faced severe beating and even hanging. The laws were not limited to farms—no woman could hold either land or property in the Four Kingdoms. Melli herself had not even owned the dresses and jewels that she had worn at court; they had all been the property of her father.

"I have worked this farm on my own for the past twenty years. No man could have done a better job." There was pride in the old woman's voice.

"What about going to market? How can you sell your pork?"

"I have an arrangement." The old woman ladled the rich, brown stew into bowls. "I pay dearly for it." She sighed heavily. "But I have little choice. He could go crying to the authorities at any time and then I'd have nothing. So he sucks me dry, little by little, leaving me just enough to get by on." The woman dropped a spoonful of pig lard into each bowl to enrich the stew. "Everyone in Harvell thinks the reason they don't see my son is because he's lame."

"I'm sorry."

"Don't be sorry for me, girl. I've got a better life than most widows. I have my own place, I have good food on my table, and no son-in-law to make my life miserable by constantly reminding me I live off his generosity." The woman shook her head. "No, girl, save your pity for one who deserves it. Come on now, eat up your stew before the fat melts."

Melli took a bowl to Jack, placing the spoon in his hand. To her surprise he took it up and began to eat.

"We'll have to see to your friend's wound. If it's left too long it will fester."

"So can we stay the night?"

"It would seem, girl, that we both have things to hide." She looked pointedly at Melli's arm and then to Jack. "I can see no harm in us hiding them together for one night."

Once they had finished eating, the woman boiled a kettle of hot water and then chose a thin-bladed knife from a high shelf. "This should do the job. It skins the pigs nice enough." She dipped it into the hot water for an instant and then wiped it clean. "Strip the lad's shirt off."

Melli was a little alarmed at the sight of the woman wielding the knife, but she had little choice. She herself knew nothing of surgery or doctoring; she would have to trust the woman. She was more than a little relieved, though, that the woman had chosen to attend to Jack first: she would watch her performance on him before committing her own arm into the old woman's care.

"Now don't be anxious, boy." The old woman washed the dried blood away with a clean rag. "This will hurt, I won't lie to you, but it's necessary." She turned to Melli. "Girl, bring the jug of spirits from the dresser." She peered closely at Jack's wound. "At least the point is not barbed." Melli handed the woman the jug. "Here, take a swig of this, lad, it will help to relax you." The old woman then took a mouthful of the liquor herself.

She cut deep into Jack's shoulder, ignoring the circular entrance wound, and slicing directly above where the arrowhead lay. Melli was horrified. "Couldn't you take it out the way it came in?"

"Hush, girl, you will ruin my concentration." The woman pulled back the skin and began to cut into the muscle. She ignored Jack's heavy bleeding, concentrating on freeing the arrowhead. She scraped the last of the muscle and sinew from around the point and then pulled it out with her fingers. "There. Got the little devil." She dropped it unceremoniously on the floor. "Hand me the twine and needle, girl. He'll bleed to death if we don't stitch him up."

The woman pinched Jack's skin together with one hand and drew the thread with another, making large irregular stitches. "Course I can't guarantee he'll look too pretty afterward. I'll be more careful with yours. Can't have such a pretty girl with a nasty scar on her arm. With men it doesn't matter; a few scars only serve to make a man more appealing to the ladies."

"How did you learn to do this?" Melli did not care for the subject of scars.

"The sows, of course. You can't be a pig farmer and not know how to tend creatures." The woman did not look up; she was intent on finishing her work. She cut the thread with her teeth and then turned her attention to the entrance wound. The woman drew the knife twice over the wound, forming a cross.

"What are you doing?" Melli was distraught. "You've made it worse." Fresh blood gushed forth.

"Girl, do you not know anything of surgery? The wound was round—a round wound will take forever to heal. Better to make it bigger and change the shape." The old woman took up needle and thread once more. "You mark my words, the cross will heal in half the time, and it will be a nice, clean scar. Round wounds heal messy."

"I'm sorry, I didn't know." Melli did not doubt the woman's words.

"No matter, girl." The woman finished stitching the wound. "Now help me get your silent friend to the pallet over there; he needs some rest. Then I'll see to your injuries." Melli did as she was asked, but dragged her feet as she did so. She little relished the idea of being cut and stitched.

Twenty-two

*T*awl was finding himself enjoying his journey—it was good to be on horseback again. He even liked the company of the boy, and it never failed to make him smile to look upon the way Nabber clung miserably to his pony. The boy was obviously not a born horseman. Tawl had tried to give him some advice on how to ride, but Nabber had ignored his pointers and continued to ride as though he were afraid he would fall off any second.

The mountains loomed nearer, but Tawl was sure that if they made their way to the western coast of the peninsula they could avoid most of them. The western coast missed the worst of the mountains, although the terrain was still rocky and hilly.

He calculated that their next main stopping point would be Ness. It occurred to Tawl for the first time that Bevlin was not far from that city—three days hard ride. He wondered if he should pay the wiseman a visit and tell him of his progress. There was, however, little to tell. What could he say—*there is a remote chance that the boy might be some-where in the Four Kingdoms?* No, he thought, better not to see the wiseman at all.

He tried to put Bevlin from his mind, but something nagged at him, something in the back of his mind. He felt as if he *did* have something to tell to the wiseman, only he could not remember what it was. He racked his memory—he had not discovered anything that Bevlin might be interested in, and the Old Man had given him no message. Maybe he should inform him that the knights had been expelled from Rorn. Tawl shook his head; Bevlin would probably already have heard about the knights. Wisemen had their own ways of acquiring information. The more he thought about Bevlin, the more certain he was that he should visit him—it felt right to do so. It would add but a few days to his journey.

They approached a small settlement, barely a village: a few run-down shacks and no inn.

"Why don't we stop and buy some fresh food?" Nabber had little taste for dried meat and hard biscuits. Tawl looked around the village. There was a woman on the road with three children; they were poorly dressed and thin.

"I don't think we'll find fresh food here." He could not remember passing any farms or herds recently, and he wondered how the people lived. "I think we will head on and try to reach the coast by nightfall." Tawl looked around and found to his annoyance that the boy had already dismounted his pony. He watched as Nabber spoke with the woman and then returned.

"Tawl, she says there is a small town just over the hill there. She said it would be worth a visit."

"Let's just be on our way." Tawl had a vague feeling of unease.

"It won't take long for us to reach the town, and if we did, we'd be sleeping on feather pillows tonight and eating hot food." The boy looked so eager that Tawl could not refuse him. He nodded and they headed off.

After about an hour's ride they finally crested the hill, and there was a fair-sized town nestled in the valley below. As they rode closer it was obvious something was wrong: there were no people on the streets. There were no signs of life; no smoke, no hens or goats, no cultivation. Tawl's hand rested upon the hilt of his knife as they rode into the town.

The deserted town had obviously once been prosperous. There were several inns—which were usually a sign of good trade—two blacksmiths, a wheelwright's shop—all deserted.

In the center of the town was a square which boasted a fine marble statue.

Tawl read the sign hanging above one of the inns: "The Water's Edge." He could not remember seeing any water and they were still some distance from the sea.

He heard footsteps approaching and turned to see an old man in rags. "Got any food to spare?" The man looked as if he would collapse at any moment.

"Here take these, friend." Nabber brought the sea biscuits from his pack and gave them to the man. Tawl suspected the boy's motives were less than charitable—Nabber hated the hard and tasteless sea biscuits. The man grabbed them from him and sniffed them apprehensively, then he proceeded to cram them into his mouth.

"Where is the water? Is there a lake or river nearby?" Tawl was thinking he could at least fill his water flasks. He waited as the man gobbled down the last of the biscuits.

"Ain't no water here anymore." The man smiled, showing blackened teeth.

"What happened to it? Did it run dry?"

"It's dry now, that's for sure." The man laughed as if he had made a joke. He then moved next to Nabber and tried to grab his pack from him. Nabber snatched it away, but gave him a length of drymeat.

"Was there a drought?" Tawl had heard of towns ruined by the cruel hand of drought.

"No, this was not nature's work. Come, follow me." The man scurried off with surprising speed. Tawl was reluctant to follow, but Nabber had already dashed after the man, leaving him little choice.

The man led them through the town and onto a sandy plain. "This was the lake, you're standing on it." Tawl and Nabber both stared at their feet: the ground was level. The man chuckled at their surprise. "Aye, it was the most beautiful lake on the peninsula. Not large by any man's reckoning, but breathtaking to behold. Famous it was for its therapeutic properties. People came from great distances to bathe in the clear waters. They were said to heal the sick and soothe the old."

The old man sighed wistfully. "You should have seen

the lake then. Just to look upon it filled a man with joy. Fishes, such fishes, the color of rainbows, so eager to be caught they'd leap straight into your net." He kicked the sand beneath his feet.

"It was a mighty wealthy town back then. All gone to dust now. Nothing to live off now the lake is dry. Everyone told me I was mad to stay. I think they were right, I am mad."

"What happened?"

"A man came to town to bathe in the waters. A rich and powerful man from a big city. Dressed like a king he was, bedecked in the finest silks. He went out on the lake trailing his fingers in the water. When he gets back to shore he finds his ring has slipped off his finger. He started to get angry, saying it was some official ring or something, and orders the lake to be searched. That's when we made our mistake. We told him he didn't have a chance of finding his ring. We told him to go and get another made, said it was his own fault for losing it.

"Well, the man turned nasty, said he couldn't replace the ring because it was hundreds of years old. He gave us one week to dredge the lake and find the ring. We did what we could, but the ring couldn't be found. For all we knew it could have been nestled in a fish's belly. The man came back a week later, and when we told him we hadn't found it he cursed the lake. He swore he would fill it in. Well, we just laughed at him—we never thought he'd do it.

"Seven days later, four score men come into town. They had mules with them pulling cartloads of sand from the coast. One whole year it took those men to fill in the lake. One year they worked, dragging and dumping, filling the lake with yellow sand. One year to destroy the livelihood of every person in this town. One year." The man knelt down and scooped a handful of sand, letting the wind gradually blow it from him.

"Why didn't anyone stop him?"

"No one dared to. We just watched like fools as the lake grew smaller and smaller."

"Who did this?" Tawl felt he already knew the answer.

"The archbishop of Rorn."

A sharp breeze picked up. It was time they were on their way. Tawl was eager to be gone from the abandoned town.

Tavalisk dipped his fingers into the sauce and brought them to his lips. Perfect—just a hint of garlic, the merest trace of herbs, exactly the right balance to best flatter the snail. Snails were not found in Rorn; the hard, thin earth could not support them. Like many things of luxury, rarity made them all the more sought after and Rorn supported a prosperous snail trade. High prices were paid for the succulent creatures and snails graced many a wealthy man's table.

Tavalisk picked up his little silver hook and set about extracting himself a snail from its shell. He finally hooked the flesh and drew it out. It was a fine specimen, plump and shiny. His delicious anticipation was ruined by the approach of Gamil.

"What do you want?" The archbishop chewed on the snail.

"Well, Your Eminence, a rather interesting letter has come into my hands."

"Is it a reply from that lord you wrote to on my behalf? What was his name . . . Maybor?"

"Oh, no, Your Eminence, I have not received his reply yet. This is more important."

"Go on." Tavalisk threw a snail to his cat and watched with amusement as the creature tried unsuccessfully to get at the morsel within the shell.

"Well, our spies in the north intercepted a letter from the duke of Bren to Lord Baralis. In the letter the duke of Bren asks what is causing the delay of the betrothal between his daughter and Prince Kylock."

"So, the marriage is definitely going to go ahead, then. I do not need to tell you, Gamil, how little I like the idea of those two places joining forces. Bren is already too powerful for its own good." Tavalisk paused in mid-snail. He spat the creature out, suddenly unable to eat. *When two mighty powers join as one.* It was Marod's prophecy coming true. How did the rest of it go? Something about a temple, something about the chosen one. *When men of honor trade in gold not grace.* It was the knights!—why had it never occurred to him before? The archbishop poured himself a glass of wine to steady his nerves. What else was there? *The dark empire will rise.* He didn't like the sound of a dark empire one bit. He preferred his world a shady gray—it was better for Rorn's trade.

Baralis was trying to make it happen! The fiend was trying to forge a huge northern empire!

Tavalisk stood up and, ignoring Gamil's look of amazement, actually stoked the fire himself. He was chilled to the bone. It all fit: the knights, Bren, the Four Kingdoms. He'd always known Baralis was dangerous, but the scale of this was unthinkable. Nowhere in the prophecy was it mentioned that the dark empire was purely a northern one! What if Baralis and the duke planned to take over the south as well? The combined might of the north was awe-inspiring. Were the knights positioning themselves, too? Tyren was certainly friendly with the duke of Bren. There were plots everywhere and he was party to none of them!

Tavalisk made a conscious effort to appear calm—he would not have Gamil think he was worried. He sat down again and took up his silver fork. "Anything else in the letter?"

"Nothing in the letter, Your Eminence, but last time I communicated with our spy at Castle Harvell, he had no knowledge of the match between Kylock and Catherine."

"So, Gamil, what are you getting at?"

"I believe that Baralis has arranged this marriage without the knowledge or permission of the king or queen."

This news did nothing to allay the archbishop's fears. "Hmm, that is interesting. Baralis has always been a sly one. Unfortunately, I'm sure that such a marriage will be looked upon most favorably by the queen." Tavalisk stabbed at the snails with his fork, not stopping until every shell on the tray was destroyed. "An alliance with Bren would be quite an achievement for her."

"There is good news, Your Eminence. Marls is seriously considering expelling the knights. A law has already been drafted."

"And what of Toolay?" Tavalisk ground the splinters of shell into the snails.

"There have been confrontations between those who are pro-knights and those who are against them. The largest crowd was reported to be those calling for their expulsion."

"Enough of this matter, Gamil." Tavalisk stood up. He was anxious to secure a copy of Marod's prophecy and study it further. "I would go for a walk in the gardens. This news of an alliance between Bren and the Four Kingdoms weighs heavily on my mind." The archbishop made his way toward the door. "If you would be so kind as to do me a favor?"

"Certainly, Your Eminence."

"Pluck the splinters of shell from the snails and feed them to my cat. I would hate for them to go to waste."

Baralis sat close to the fire. It was no use—the warmth he felt on his face could not penetrate the coldness in his bones. He sipped on his mulled holk, hoping that might relieve the pain a little. He was weary. It had been a mistake to draw himself from his body; he had expended too much energy and left himself with so little. The mind-altering drug was only supposed to be used for a short period of time; he had stretched for boundaries, gone too far, left his body too long. And now he was paying the price.

It had all been for nothing. They had managed to escape from him, and by all accounts what an escape! Four mercenaries had come back alive, one of them with a leg so badly broken he would never walk on it again. They told tales of a mighty whirlwind, a blast from heaven. Baralis had known something was wrong. Hours before they returned he'd felt the aftermath. It was the baker's boy once more. Baralis had the feeling he would live to regret not killing the boy when he'd had a chance.

Who was Jack? He'd come from nowhere and yet had powers at his command that defied reason. There was something more to this. The boy had secrets to reveal, Baralis had felt it the moment he entered Jack's mind. Things were concealed, shadowy figures protected him. Did he have some role to play in what was to come?

Baralis massaged his hands. The skin would need split-
ting. Why should a baker's boy have a capacity for such destruction? Jack had spoken the truth when he said he'd not
been taught. The drawing was crude—he used a bludgeon
when a paring knife would do. But such power! Baralis was
envious. Even now he could still feel the subtle pressure of
the aftermath, prickling the hairs on his neck.

There was, of course, a good side to this: Maybor's men
were not likely to capture Melliandra as long as she traveled
with Jack at her side. Perhaps destiny, in the shape of the
boy, was working for him. No. A spark of instinct deep
within Baralis always told him who his enemies were: the
baker's boy was his enemy. He was sure of it. They would
meet again, and next time he would destroy him.

Enemies were his stock in trade. Ambition bred them.
Even one-time allies had a tendency to turn. Maybor had
been an ally, without his help King Lesketh would never
have been disabled, but now the man was dangerously close
to feeling the full force of his wrath.

How he hated the man. He had actually drawn a blade
on him! Baralis cursed his frailty. He had been unable to do
anything. Maybor could have snuffed him out in an instant
and they both knew it. Baralis had shown humiliating weakness, and to one whom he despised above all others.

He counted the days off on his fingers: less than a week
before the deadline of the wager; at least then he would have
some satisfaction at Maybor's expense. Until then he would
concentrate on regaining his strength. Next time Maybor
came at him with a blade he would be ready.

He called for Crope. The servant came lumbering in, his
big hands wrapped around his beloved box.

"Go to the village and see if there are any mercenaries
hanging around the tavern. I will need more men. Tell them I
will pay them well."

"Yes, lord."

"Oh, and Crope, I am interested in finding out the name
of Lord Maybor's latest dalliance." Maybe he *would* extract
a small measure of revenge before the week was out. Maybor
was a notorious lecher. It would prove most distracting to
banish the heat from his loins.

*   *   *

Lilly was reeling her big fish in. She had thought herself lucky to be bedded by Kedrac, but now she had her eye on a grander prize: his father, Lord Maybor. The wealthiest man in the country desired her.

She knew well how to play the game; she had failed to turn up at his apartments when he asked—it did not do to appear too eager. The following day she had designed to cross his path in the gardens. The great lord had begged that she visit his chambers and had even slipped a silver bracelet upon her wrist. She'd said she would consider his proposal and mentioned her preference for gold.

She was ready to move up in the world once more. Lilly had started out as a milkmaid. Bedding with the master dairyman had ensured that she did not roughen her hands carrying straw for the cows to eat. Instead, she had spent her days forming freshly churned butter into pats, and the constant greasing of her palms left them as soft as velvet. Soft enough for her to be a lady's maid.

To be a lady's maid was her ambition. A lady's maid had the highest status of any female servant. They were allowed, and even expected, to wear pretty clothes and have their hair styled in ribbons. They accompanied their mistresses for walks in the grounds and were greatly admired by all the young men at court. Lilly knew that Lord Maybor had the power to make her one. He could force his daughter, or some other female relative, to take up her services. She flushed with excitement. She would not be a mere chambermaid much longer. Better things were in store for her now that she had managed to capture the eye of one so high and mighty.

She'd had her fair share of dalliances with minor lords—each one had seduced and gifted her, and one or two had even offered to keep her in a tavern at town. That was not what she wanted. She knew how fickle men's desires were; one day they could not live without you, the next you were an unwanted hindrance. No, she wanted more than to be kept. She knew she was close to getting it—a man was at his most generous when swayed by unfulfilled ardor, and

Lord Maybor was a man who could afford to be most generous.

Lilly spared little thought for his son. Kedrac, as an unlanded lord, did not enjoy high status at court, and he would not have been able to secure the position she wanted. Besides, she thought wickedly, he had been useless in bed. She hoped that his father would prove more skilled.

Lord Maybor! There would only have been one man she would have preferred more—the king's chancellor, Lord Baralis. Lilly shrugged. She might not have the most powerful man in court in her pocket, but she had the richest.

She pushed back the golden curls from her forehead and admired her reflection in Lady Helliarna's mirror. She looked perfect, her only complaint was that her waist was a little thick, but she knew many men regarded a plumpness in the belly as an extra curve, and so was not too worried. She dashed out of the chamber and down into the gardens; she expected Lord Maybor would be taking his afternoon walk.

She was not disappointed. She spotted him in the distance conferring with someone and hesitated for a moment before she approached, checking that the other man was not his son, Kedrac. As soon as he noticed her, he took leave of his companion and came toward her.

"My sweetest Lilly." He caught his breath for a moment. "I was sure that you would have visited me last evening. I was disappointed when you did not come." He took her hand and kissed it. As he let it go, he placed something cold and heavy into it. Lilly restrained her desire to see what it was and slipped the object, unseen, into her bodice.

"My lord, I cannot help but feel that I am unworthy of you." She bent her head low and fluttered her eyelashes in a way she knew to be most becoming. "I am only a chambermaid. I am not fit to dally with great lords."

"You dallied with my son." Lord Maybor seemed a little unsympathetic to her plea.

"Ah, but we both know you are far greater than he." She had said the right thing, for the lord nodded his head judiciously.

"What do you want from me, my pretty poppet? I would rather you speak out than be forced to bandy words with you." It was not quite what Lilly had hoped for, but she was not about to let such an offer pass her by.

"I feel I am good enough to be a lady's maid; my hands are soft and I am gently spoken." Lilly made her eyes as big as saucers and bit her full bottom lip with a becoming show of modesty.

"So that is what you are after, eh?" Maybor smiled with satisfaction. "And what if I were to attain such a position for you?"

"I would be most grateful to your lordship." She curtsied low, showing off her bosom to its best advantage.

"You are indeed a bewitching wench. I think we shall have a most pleasing time together." He laid a hand on her cheek. "Be waiting in my room at sundown one night hence. I will have secured you a position by then." He moved forward and kissed her full on the lips. "Until the morrow." Lilly pulled away, knowing full well that nothing fired desire in a man more than a show of virtue.

She watched as Lord Maybor walked away, his cloak flapping in the wind. Once he was out of sight she pulled the object he had given her from her breast. It was a stone: a beautiful honey-colored topaz. She laughed merrily and skipped her way back to the castle.

Jack awoke with a start. He had been having a bad dream. He sat up and looked around. He had no idea where he was. He was in a kitchen, there was something cooking on the fire, and bright copper pots hung from the rafters. An old woman came into the room.

"Well, it's about time you were awake, young man. You slept all night and the better part of a day. Here, let me look how your shoulder's doing." The woman bent over him and he pulled the blanket close around himself. "There's no need to be shy with me, boy. I'm too old to put up with such modesty." She pulled the blanket from him and looked at his shoulder. Jack tried to see what she was looking at, but it was too painful for him to move his neck. "They're both doing nicely. I did a good job, if I do say so myself." The woman made her way to the fire. "I suppose you'll be hungry. I'll fix you a spot of dumpling stew."

"Who are you?" Jack tried to recall how he had come to be here. He remembered being chased by Baralis' men and then he had seen Melli get shot. "Where's Melli?" He tried to stand up, but his legs were too weak.

"Calm down, lad. The girl has gone outside for a touch of air."

"How is she?" He vividly remembered seeing an arrow jutting out from Melli's arm.

"Oh, fine. She's doing a lot better than you are. The arrow came out nice and clean." The woman handed him a bowl of stew. "Here, lad, eat this. It will build your strength up."

Jack took the bowl and began to eat. He tried to remember what had happened after Melli was shot. He had been angry—angry about being chased, hurting from the sting of an arrow, furious when they shot Melli. His mind showed images of destruction, of men being flung from their horses, of saplings being uprooted. He dismissed them; they had been part of his nightmare. How had he come to be here? How had they escaped from the mercenaries?

"Hello, Jack." Melli walked in the door. "How are you?"

"What happened . . ." Jack realized he did not even know what day it was.

"During the hunting accident, you mean?" Melli looked relieved to hear his voice, but warned him with a flash of her eyes not to contradict her. "Well, I think you went into shock. You lost a lot of blood. We were too far away to take you home, but I managed to bring you here and this kind lady offered her help."

"Where are we?"

"Oh, we're just off the eastern road."

Jack could hardly believe what he had been told. When the men had attacked they had been leagues away from the road. How had Melli managed to bring him all this way? The old woman obviously decided to leave them alone to talk. She took her leave, muttering about pigs to feed.

"Tell me what happened, Melli." He looked at her and found she could not meet his eyes.

"I don't know what happened. One minute we were being chased, the next—" she made a small gesture with her hands "—there was chaos. It looked like a blast of air. It knocked everyone from their horses."

"And us. What happened to us?" Jack began to tremble as his nightmare solidified into reality. "Melli, what about us?"

"We weren't touched." She looked down at the floor.

The truth hung between them, unspoken. Both he and Melli knew what had happened. Both knew that he was responsible. Jack realized it was time to accept what he was. He was more than just a baker's boy; there was a force within him that set him apart. Although it was unasked for, he still had to learn to live with the consequences. Twice he had caused things to happen, twice he had changed the course of events. There was blood on his hands now.

"Jack, we'll get away," said Melli, as if reading his thoughts. "We'll go somewhere far from here, where Baralis will never be able to find us again." Melli paused for a moment, thinking. "We'll go to Bren. You can start a new life there."

"And what of you, Melli? You weren't born to travel rough, to live with no money, to make your own way. What would become of you in Bren?" Jack's voice was harsher than he intended; he could see that he had upset her.

"I could travel with you as far as Annis. My family has relatives there." Melli's voice was scathing. "They will take me in, which is just as well, as I am so useless on my own!"

"Who are your family, Melli?"

"My father is Lord Maybor." She looked at him coolly. Jack tried to hide his surprise. He had guessed Melli was a nobleman's daughter, but he'd never thought she would come from such a rich and influential family. Jack had heard it said many times that Lord Maybor was a favorite of the queen. Melli interrupted his thoughts: "Now, Jack, seems we are trading secrets, tell me the real reason why Baralis is after you." She lowered her voice and spoke with cold precision. "Or did I see the reason back in the woods two days ago?"

Jack could not reply and his silence answered for him. Melli's expression softened and she came and knelt by him. She took his hand and kissed it. "I'm sorry. Here am I losing my temper when you aren't well and need rest." She was so beautiful: her skin as pale as spring butter, her hair as dark as winter nights. Just to look at Melli, to have her hand in his, almost made everything worth it. Or it might have done, if he hadn't just learned he was a murderer. Falk had been so right when he said his life wouldn't be easy.

"You've been flustering the boy. Shame on you, girl." The old woman walked in and Jack wondered if she had been listening at the door.

"I am fine, really. Melli has not disturbed me. In fact, I think I might get up and stretch my legs." He squeezed Melli's hand and then released it.

"No, you don't. I've just rendered some fresh pig grease and it needs to be rubbed into your shoulder."

"I'll do it," volunteered Melli, an impish smile on her face.

"Oh, no you won't, girl. I watched you trying to roll dumplings this morning. I have little faith in you being able to soothe the boy's skin when you can't even roll a round dumpling." The old woman noticed Melli's blush. "If you want to make yourself useful, peel those turnips over there. We'll need them to thicken the broth."

The woman drew back Jack's blanket and bid him lean forward. She then dipped her hands in the pig fat and proceeded to rub it into his shoulder. The fat was still warm, and she worked it into his flesh, massaging the muscle beneath.

"This will keep your shoulder from stiffening. I saw a man once, his arm was slit open in a tavern brawl. The wound wasn't bad, more blood than flesh. It healed quickly and cleanly, barely a scar, but his arm stiffened. He could never straighten it up ever again. Course he tried all sorts of remedies; it was too late, though. He should never have let it stiffen in the first place." She finished her work. "There! That should be enough for now."

"Thank you," Jack found that he could now move his

neck and his shoulder did not ache as much. "Thank you for everything you have done."

"Nay, lad, do not thank me. I took you in out of fear for myself." The old woman noticed his baffled look. "So your friend has not told you, eh? I am alone on this farm. I have no husband or son."

Jack immediately understood. "You are afraid we would tell the authorities?"

"I was at first. Your friend has quite an insisting air about her, but now I feel a little safer. If I am to be honest, I quite enjoy having people to look after—the company of pigs can prove a little tedious at times." The woman smiled, showing large but even teeth. She moved toward the fire and began to stir the stew. "Their company can be tedious, but their meat never so." With that she threw a pig's trotter into the pot.

Melli, having ruined the turnips, turned toward the woman. "Do you know how far Br—"

"Bresketh is." Jack managed to interrupt her just in time. It was definitely not wise to let the woman know where they were headed. It was not that he did not trust her; it was more that it was an unnecessary burden to put on her. As soon as Baralis discovered they had stayed here—and Jack did not doubt that he would—the woman would be questioned. Better that she not know anything, else Baralis might extract what she knew at great cost.

"I've never heard of Bresketh. It mustn't be around here." The woman's brow creased in puzzlement.

"It's somewhere in the south," Melli said. Jack was pleased at how quickly she caught on. There was no such place as Bresketh.

"So you'll be heading south, then?"

"Yes, as soon as possible. We have no wish to burden you any longer than necessary."

" 'Tis no burden, lad. It's been a long time since company sat at my table. I had forgotten the joy of it. My husband died many years back and I haven't much longer to go myself. I have a good life, food, shelter, warmth, yet I realized today there is much I have missed. I have been without child or friend or neighbor—my circumstances have made contact with others all but impossible. No, lad, you are no burden." The old woman gave her attention back to the stew.

Jack and Melli exchanged glances, both touched by her words. Jack almost wished he could stay. It seemed he had been running for a long time and he could see little peace in his future. The old woman's kitchen was warm and restful— he would be sorry to leave. "We must go tomorrow." His voice was soft and low.

"Stay one more day past the morrow, lad. Give your wounds time to heal. If you leave too soon they might open and bleed. Besides, if you are going on a journey you will need clothes and food. They will take a few days to prepare." The woman smiled weakly and Jack relented.

"Very well, we will leave the day past the morrow."

Twenty-three

Baralis was a little worried. He had expected that the duke of Bren would have sent him a letter by now, if only to protest at the delay of the betrothal. He was concerned that the duke's silence might mean some kind of cooling off on his part. He could hardly blame the man; he had waited over six months for the betrothal to take place, and the duke of Bren was not the most patient of men.

He *was* however, the most ambitious. Baralis smiled thinly. The duke of Bren was just as eager for this match as he. There was no better choice of a husband for his daughter than Prince Kylock, heir to the Four Kingdoms. The unfortunate duke had been blessed with no sons of his own and so hoped to gain one in his daughter's husband. Because the duke had no male heir, he sought an alliance with the Four Kingdoms to stabilize his position—with a powerful prince as his daughter's husband, his adversaries would be less likely to challenge him. Once his daughter had provided him with a grandson, his sovereignty would be guaranteed. In the interim he sought to count on the help of the Four Kingdoms to maintain that sovereignty.

Marrying his daughter to a prince would bring the good duke one step closer to royalty, and royalty was something he was obsessed with. He wanted land, but he lusted after a crown. Oh, he could name himself a king today—he would not be the first man to have done so—but he would risk ridicule if his title was not backed up with the support of his lords. Bribery was how he gained their fealty, and land was the currency of kings.

Trade was a useful supplement. The knights now controlled the trade routes in the northeast, and Tyren and the duke reaped the benefits. It was a cozy little partnership; the duke allowed Tyren a near monopoly on certain goods in return for a cut of the profits. More and more these days, however, the duke was taking his payments from Valdis in manpower, not gold. And the knighthood was fast becoming a familiar sight on the battlefields of Bren.

The time was fast approaching when Baralis would be a party to the lucrative dealings in the northeast. The queen would lose her wager and she would be forced to agree to the marriage. He did not think she could object to the match; it would bring glory and honor to the court of Harvell. And, more importantly, it would turn a dangerous rival into a useful ally. Oh, the queen would make a show of protesting the match for no other reason than she hated him so much, and it would irk her to follow his advice.

He did hold one or two trumps in his hand that would serve to sway her to agreement. He quickly searched through the drawer of his desk. He soon found what he was looking for: a portrait . . . a miniature no bigger than a coin. It was a picture of a young girl, a girl of such beauty that even Baralis could not help but admire her: abundant, golden curls, the finest of brows, the smoothest of cheeks and the most perfectly small but full, pink lips. The very picture of innocence. He was looking at a likeness of the duke of Bren's daughter: Catherine.

Baralis knew that as soon as the queen looked upon the portrait her objections would cease. She would succumb to the girl's beauty. Who could gaze upon such an angelic face and not be moved by it? The queen might well query the authenticity of the likeness—many a portrait painter had overexaggerated the charms of his sitter. He, however, had a letter from the duke himself swearing upon his honor that it was indeed a true likeness of his daughter.

Baralis had, in turn, commissioned a likeness of Kylock. The only liberty the artist had taken with Kylock's portrait was to paint a smile upon his face. From the subsequent letter he had received from the duke, it appeared that Catherine had found him most attractive.

He decided he would write to the duke that day, assuring him that the betrothal would be finalized within the month. He would send the missive by fast rider; even then it would be three weeks before it was delivered.

He was disturbed from his calculations by the arrival of Crope. "What do you want, you dithering fool?"

"You are feeling better, master?"

"I have no time to exchange pleasantries with you, Crope. I have more important things to do. Now speak up and be gone."

"I have been to the tavern in town and I talked to some mercenaries there. They said they would see the color of your money before they agreed to anything."

"Yes, yes, I would expect no less from their kind. I will meet them tomorrow near the entrance of the haven. Arrange it."

"Yes, my lord. There is one other thing."

"What?"

"You asked me to find out about . . ." Crope paused, looking for the right word.

"About the latest slut that Maybor is sleeping with." Baralis supplied it for him. "Go on."

"Well, I followed him to the garden and I saw him talking to a lady."

"Hm, if I know Maybor's taste you are being a little generous in your description."

Baralis' humor was lost on Crope. "Well," he paused to think, "the lady agreed to be waiting in Lord Maybor's chambers at nightfall."

"Tonight?" Crope nodded. "Are you sure?" Crope nodded again. "Who is this woman?"

"Her name is Lilly. She is chambermaid to Lady Hel . . ." Crope struggled with the pronunciation.

"Lady Helliarna. I know the chambermaid you mean. The little vixen has given me the eye on more than one occasion." Baralis stood and thought for a while. Maybor needed to be taught a lesson for daring to draw a blade in his presence. In his experience the best lessons were visual ones. "Now think carefully, Crope, before you answer: did Lord Maybor say he would be waiting for her in his chamber?"

"No, my lord. Maybor told *her* to be waiting for him."

"Very well. Now this is what I want you to do. You know how to get to Maybor's chamber using the passageway, don't you?"

"Yes, my lord."

"Good. I want you to be there when the girl enters. Check carefully that Maybor is not around . . ."

Tavalisk murmured the appropriate words and made the expected gestures—he was blessing the sea of Rorn. Each year a bowl of seawater was drawn from the bay. It was then carried with great ceremony to the archbishop's palace where the water was blessed. This allowed the sacred spirit to infuse the water, enriching and sanctifying. The blessed water was then returned to the sea, where a chosen man emptied the contents of the bowl back into the dark waters.

The ritual of blessing the sea water had been practiced in Rorn for centuries. It was believed that the blessed water spread throughout the sea, bringing bountiful fish harvests and calm waters. Tavalisk rather doubted the effectiveness of the ceremony, but in his capacity as archbishop he was expected to perform the long list of religious rituals that the people of Rorn required.

He knew he was a lucky man. Since he had become archbishop, Rorn had experienced a great period of prosperity. The various troubles in the world, such as the plague in Marls and the Silbur running bad, had actually benefited the city, increasing trade and commerce. A man who wanted his money safe for the future was advised to invest that money in Rorn: it was the most stable and prosperous city in the south—a financial haven for the wealthy.

Naturally, he as archbishop had gained much of the praise for Rorn's prosperity. It was he who blessed the waters, he who blessed the merchant fleets, he who blessed everything from the money-lenders to the fish-gutters.

The people loved him; their gratitude knew no bounds. There was one tradition of which Tavalisk was particularly fond. If a trader or shopkeeper or merchant had a good year, besides paying the usual taxes and levies, they were expected to give hefty donations to the church. These donations were called the Archbishop's Purse and that was exactly where they ended up. The irony was that the people, while constantly complaining about taxes, were always happy to donate to the Archbishop's Purse. They felt it would bring them good luck and good business the following year.

Having finished blessing the water, he bowed to the attending priests and took his leave. He was anxious to return to his private chambers. He intended to spend some time studying the exact wording of Marod's prophecy.

On his way, Tavalisk walked through high-ceilinged corridors, lined with marble carvings of cherubs. He was admiring their beauty when he heard the sound of humble footsteps behind him.

"Gamil, is there nowhere I can hide from your disagreeable gaze."

"I am sorry to interrupt Your Eminence." Gamil had to hurry to keep up with the pace set by the archbishop.

"So, what news have you to bring me today?"

"Marls has banned the knights."

"Are they actively expelling them yet?" Rorn was currently expelling Knights of Valdis from the city. A reward of five silver pieces was given to anyone who informed the authorities of a knight's whereabouts. Mayhem had resulted as half of the city tried to inform on the other half. There was one particular practice that had made Tavalisk smile—unfortunate foreigners were hit over the head and knocked out, they were then branded with the mark of Valdis and taken to the authorities. Five pieces of silver was quite an incentive to the ingenious citizens of Rorn. Tavalisk cared little about these practices; the more knights expelled, genuine or otherwise, the more angry Valdis would be.

"No, Your Eminence, they have stopped them from entering the city, but expulsion has not begun yet."

"What of Toolay?"

"Toolay teeters on the brink."

"Toolay was ever a gutless city. Is there news of Camlee?"

"Camlee will be slow to act, Your Eminence. They may not take action at all; they live in the shadow of Valdis."

"I do not think Valdis casts as long a shadow as it once did, Gamil."

"You are right, Your Eminence. Valdis is not as powerful as it once was, but we would be unwise to underestimate it."

"Gamil, I make it my business never to underestimate anyone. I need no lessons in strategy from you." Tavalisk's thoughts kept returning to Marod's prophecy. What role the knights had to play in its fulfillment was unclear, but now more than ever it seemed that to expel them was the right thing to do.

Three dangerous men had their eyes on the territory and wealth of others: the duke of Bren was desperate for extra land; his population had grown twofold over the last decade, and his people needed farmland and pastures. He thought that by making Bren larger, he could name it a kingdom. Annis and Highwall, not to mention Ness and the Four Kingdoms, watched the duke's expansion with growing unease.

Not that the Four Kingdoms would have to worry much longer. They would soon be firmly allied with Bren. Baralis had seen to that. He was the second man, the son of a farmer from Leiss. Desire for power had made him king's chancellor, ambition made him want more. Sorcery and intrigue were his weapons—Tavalisk was only just beginning to guess at his strategies.

And lastly there was Tyren, head of the Knights of Valdis. Greed was his main vice. He was a shrewd profiteer, tying up trade routes in the north while managing to win the friendship of powerful people. Cities in the colder climes were easily fooled by a fleeting show of piety. Tyren's tactics had proven less successful in the south. He'd tried to gain a foothold in valuable commodities like silk and spices only to find himself rebuffed. The merchants of Rorn and Marls were wary of the knights. They'd heard all the rumors of corruption and intrigue, which the archbishop had so conscientiously propagated.

The Known Lands were becoming dangerously unstable. There was trouble ahead, and trade and ambition were at its core. Or money and power, if one were to name the motives plainly. Tavalisk smiled sweetly. "Ah, Gamil, there is nothing more exciting than the thrill of intrigue."

"Your Eminence's tactical skills are greatly admired."

"Indeed they are, Gamil. Who knows, the coming months may spread their fame even further." The archbishop was beginning to feel rather cheerful. He was looking forward to pitting his wits against the men of the north. He would prove more than a match for them!

"Any news about our knight?"

"He left Toolay some days back, Your Eminence. He and the boy have mounts now. They are still heading north."

"After he arrives in Ness, I would have him followed more carefully. Bevlin lurks not far from Ness. If our knight visits him I want to know about it."

"As Your Eminence wishes."

They arrived at the archbishop's chambers. Tavalisk opened the door but prevented Gamil from following him in. "You are excused now, Gamil."

"But Your Eminence there are more matters to discuss."

"Bore me with them another day, Gamil. I am about to eat and I intend to do so alone. If you want to make yourself useful, go back to the chapel. I think I left my gloves there." Tavalisk watched as his aide began to walk the long distance back to the chapel. Once he was out of sight, he pulled his gloves from beneath his belt and closed and locked the door.

Tawl had been giving a great deal of thought to the archbishop of Rorn of late. Why would such a powerful man have bothered to imprison and torture him? He was a knight, that was true. But why him? There were many other knights in Rorn: ones who monitored incoming ships for illegal trade, a few who acted as envoys and couriers, and some just passing through. So why choose to jail him? He had not been involved in any political intrigues, he was no spy, so why had he been followed? Tawl sighed deeply. And why was he still being followed?

He had noticed many times since leaving Rorn that he was being watched. He and the boy would ride through a village, and no matter how small, Tawl felt there was always someone amongst the villagers who was making note of their passing. In Toolay he had the distinct impression he had been followed once he'd arrived in the city.

"Tell me," he asked the boy, "what do you know about the archbishop of Rorn?"

"He's a slippery one and that's the truth." The boy wiped his nose in way of illustration. "Course he's well liked in the city. Everyone says that Rorn has never been richer since he came to office."

"What did he do before becoming archbishop?"

"That's a bit of a mystery by all accounts. Apparently he didn't go the normal route, you know, priesting and the like. He just sort of popped up overnight and took power. I don't know too much about it. After all, it happened before my time." The boy steered his pony around a group of rocks; his riding was improving. "I *can* tell you that he is rich beyond belief. Me and my friend slipped into his house once, near the place you delivered the first of those letters, d'you remember?" Tawl nodded.

"Well, we were doing a bit of staking out . . . I wasn't always a 'pocket; I used to work for a man who robbed houses. I'd go in first and make sure they had stuff worth robbing. Anyway, I slipped into this place, nice building, nothing that special. Once I was inside I couldn't believe my eyes: rooms packed with gold, silver, diamonds, and emeralds. Treasure, too—paintings, carved boxes, jewelry, tapestries, anything you could think of, piled to the rafters. It was one big warehouse full of loot.

"There's no need to tell you I was pretty excited. I sneaked out and gave my friend the nod. He was all set to do the robbing when a man arrives carried in one of those fancy litters. As soon as he stepped out into the street we could see it was the archbishop, there's no mistaking his chubby profile. Well, he let himself into the very place we were about to rob.

"As soon as my man realized whose place it was he

backed off the job. No one wants to mess around with the archbishop."

"So you think all the loot belonged to him?"

"I don't think it belonged to the litter carrier!" Nabber grinned knowingly. "Of course it was the archbishop's booty. He's been skimming the cream from Rorn since before I was born."

"Surely he has little need for money in the future. An archbishop is appointed for life." Tawl was trying to remember his history lessons.

"That's never stopped the people from getting rid of anyone they don't like. The people of Rorn are well known for their violent streak. They've run archbishops out of town before now, not to mention beheading their fair share."

"It seems to me that the archbishop is a vindictive man." Tawl thought of the old man kicking the sand beneath his feet. Sand where once had been a lake.

"You speak the truth there, Tawl. I heard that he had one of his servants and her family beaten to death just because the woman went around telling her friends that the archbishop was a glutton."

"So the archbishop has ways of finding out what is being said about him in the city?"

"Don't you know anything about Rorn?" Nabber tutted scornfully. "The city is crawling with Tavalisk's spies. They say if you're not spying *for* the archbishop, then you're being spied upon *by* the archbishop."

"How is it you know so much?"

"I listen and learn. People don't pay much attention to a young boy in a room; they talk as if I'm not there." The boy suddenly looked a little offended. "You don't think I'm a spy, do you?"

"It crossed my mind." Tawl turned and looked west to hide a smile.

"If you think I'm a spy then I'm heading straight back to Rorn." Nabber brought his pony to a less than graceful stop and said indignantly, "After all I did for you, saving your life and providing coinage, and you have the nerve to say I'm a spy."

"I never said you were one, I said the thought had

crossed my mind. I would have been lying if I had said otherwise. Now you can either return to Rorn or follow me. I have no time for argument." Tawl urged his horse forward, leaving Nabber behind him. After a few moments he heard Nabber's voice shouting out:

"Very well, I'll follow you." Then a moment later, "Wait for me."

They traveled a distance further, and then about midday they came across a fair-sized village. The place looked pleasant and well kept, so Tawl decided they would break the monotony of sea biscuits and drymeat by taking a meal at the inn.

The tavern was a small but clean place, with fresh rushes on the floor. A few local men stood in a group and one man sat alone at a table. A young girl was about to make her way to greet them when an older man stopped her. The girl went back into the kitchen and the man came to serve them instead.

"What can I be getting for you two?" The man's tone was not unpleasant, merely wary; strangers were notorious for bringing trouble.

"I will take a jug of ale and two helpings of whatever food you have to offer."

"I have roast leg of goat and goat's cheese." The man seemed to dare Tawl to object to the offered fare, and was surprised when he said:

"They both sound good, bring plenty."

As they waited for the food and ale to be brought, the man who was sitting alone began to hum a tune. He looked toward them, his bleary eyes taking time to focus. As the innkeeper brought the ale, the man burst into song. His voice was loud but the men standing in the group did not turn to look. Tawl murmured to Nabber to ignore the man, who was obviously drunk. Unfortunately the man had other plans; he stood up and stumbled toward their table.

He came and leaned against the table as he sang his song. The innkeeper hurried over with the food and asked in hushed tones if the man was disturbing them. Tawl shook his head. He wanted no trouble.

The drunk finished his song and then rested his eyes

upon the jug of ale. "How about a drink for another song?" His words were slurred.

"I will give you a drink if you promise not to sing again." Tawl shot a warning glance at Nabber, who was sniggering.

"Friend, you have a deal." The man sat down uninvited. He took the proffered cup and seemed to go into a drunken daze, staring at the ale. Tawl and Nabber ignored him and ate their food.

The roast goat was stringy and a little tough but the cheese was delicious, soft and pungent. They spread it onto warm bread and sprinkled freshly cut chives on top. They were happily eating when the drunk appeared to rouse himself. He put his hand out and went to grab the remainder of the roast goat. Tawl's arm shot out to prevent the man from taking the meat. He grabbed the man's wrist, not ungently. The drunk raised his eyes to Tawl's. He slowly focused and then looked deeply into Tawl's eyes. He seemed to recognize something he saw there.

He broke away from the hold and stood up, murmuring words that Tawl could not make out. The man tried to get away as fast as he could, but his drunken body could not properly form the moves. Tawl went after him and the man cried out wildly. "Leave me alone, you devil." The men standing in a group, obviously used to the man's drunken ravings, took no notice.

Tawl grabbed the man's arm. "Why do you run from me?" he demanded. The man struggled in vain.

"Let me go." Spittle foamed at the corners of his mouth. "I want to be gone from you," he said wildly, trying to free himself.

"Why?"

"Larn! You have the mark of Larn in your eyes."

Tawl let the drunk go and the man lurched uneasily away.

As Melli walked she felt the familiar soreness of breast and belly that marked the onset of her menses. She felt strangely pleased at this reminder of her womanhood; it brought a breath of normality and continuity into a life that was lacking in both. The menses seemed to be a symbol of hope and renewal for the future. Their predictable cycle was a comfort.

It was more than that. It reminded Melli that she was a woman, no longer a child, in charge of her own destiny. Now she was away from the castle she had the freedom to make her own choices, choose her own path, and set her own pace.

Melli turned and walked back toward the farm, drawing the blanket close around her. She would go as far as Annis with Jack and no further. Her destiny was her own. She knew that Jack had his own destiny and she was aware that his had a strong pull, and if she were not careful, she would lose her own and become part of his.

The sky was low and oppressive, bearing but not relinquishing rain. She could never go back to her old life in the castle. The past weeks had changed her in many ways. She was not the same girl as the one who used to sit and braid her hair, worrying over which ribbon would become her the most. She had endured much and survived. No, not merely survived, she thought, thrived and grown strong.

She lifted the rusty latch and let herself into the farmhouse. The old woman, whose name was neither asked for nor offered, was tending to Jack's wounds. He was naked from the waist up and the firelight shone upon his flesh. He looked strong and handsome. He, too, had changed, she thought. He was no longer the awkward boy who came to her aid by the roadside many weeks ago.

Melli suddenly shuddered despite the warmth of the kitchen; her skin became cold and the hair on her arms prickled. She saw with great clarity that Jack had an unsettling future ahead. She saw a temple and a city and a man with golden hair. Images crowded about her like beggars at a market. There was blood, war, death and birth. For an instant she even saw herself in the snarl. She forced herself back to the present, drunk with the heady wine of fate, yet scared by its aftertaste. To cover up her confusion she went over to Jack and took the blanket from her shoulders. "Here," she murmured, placing the blanket in his arms, "keep yourself warm." He noticed her troubled expression and caught hold of her hand.

"What is it Melli? What are you afraid of?"

"Better to ask who I am afraid *for*." She turned quickly, not wanting to look into his hazel eyes.

She joined the old woman by the fire and tried to warm her chilled body. The woman gave her a canny look. "Time for a drink of herb tea, my dear. It will warm and refresh you."

"I have no love of herbed tea."

"You have need, girl." The woman's voice was pitched low. "You are in your menses; it will take the cramp from your belly."

"Very well." Melli found herself feeling weak; she needed to sit down.

"Get yourself a seat, girl." The woman then turned to Jack. "Time you got a little fresh air, lad. Stay close to the farm." Jack put his tunic on and left the kitchen. The woman busied herself making the tea.

Melli lost count of the varieties of herbs that were put into the gauze. Some of the herbs she could not even name. With deft hands the old woman chopped or scored or de-leafed the herbs. Satisfied that she had the right selection, she gathered the gauze by its corners and tied it with a length of twine, forming a pouch. She then popped the pouch into the pot of boiling water. She let the water boil for a minute and then set the pot away from the heat. "It must be left to stand for a few minutes to ensure the greatest benefit." The woman then came and sat by Melli.

"My mother always said the best time for a tale is while the tea's brewin'." She fixed her light blue eyes firmly upon Melli's.

"I have no tale to tell." Melli looked down at the table. The woman appeared to have expected this reply.

"Then I shall tell you one," she said simply. "I had a sister once. Oh, she was nothing like me. She was beautiful and good-natured. Her laughter was the most heart-warming sound you could imagine.

"She came to her menses late, later than any other girl in the village. Once the cycle was upon her she changed. She became a different person. She was troubled and listless; she withdrew from us, even me, her own sister who loved her dearly. She began to have visions, terrible nightmares; she woke up screaming night after night, ranting about doom and destruction. She would fall into trances during the daytime. One minute she would be normal, the next she would be in a daze. When she awoke she would tell of what events would happen in the town. Things such as which girl would bear a child, whose sows would take the fever, when the rains were likely to fall. She even predicted our mother's death. The poor girl was in torment.

"We tried to keep her problems hidden from the people in town, but word soon got out. At first people begged her to make predictions for them, even offered her money though she never took it. It didn't take long for folks to turn nasty— there is always more bad news in the future than good—and the people blamed her for it. They began to hound her, saying she was a witch.

"Then one day as she walked home, a group of men from town jumped on her and beat her close to death." The old woman rubbed tears from her eyes. "Her beautiful face was battered and bruised, both her arms were broken and her ribs were crushed. Somehow she managed to make it back to my father's farm; how she did it I will never know. As soon as we saw her, I was sent to bring the wisewoman.

"By the time I arrived back with the wisewoman she was dead." The old woman took a deep breath and paused for a minute, looking carefully at Melli. "I suppose you are wondering what this tale has to do with you?"

"I didn't realize it had anything to do with me." Melli felt her voice sounded a little cold.

"Once the wisewoman saw there was nothing she could do to help my sister she came and comforted me. She told me never to think badly of my sister, despite what other people said. She said that all women when they come to their menses have a little foretelling in their blood, some more than others. My sister was an extreme example, but most women have experiences with it at some time or other. To some it comes as intuition, others it comes as a hunch or feeling of foreboding. Its potency is strongest when a woman is losing her blood. It is a natural part of being a woman; there is no need to be afraid of it."

Melli was saved from replying when the old woman stood up and began to pour the tea. She returned with a brew that was surprisingly fragrant. "Here," she said, handing a cup of the steaming liquid to Melli, "this will make you feel better." Melli took a sip; it tasted nothing like she expected. "Good, eh," prompted the woman.

"Very good. It is not at all like—" Melli was about to say "the tea they brew in the castle," but stopped herself. The old woman covered up the awkward silence.

"Girl, you should not worry if from time to time you have feelings of premonition." Melli was about to protest, but the woman waved her arms. "No, girl, don't deny it. I saw it on your face when you walked in. You saw something in the boy. Don't worry, I will not ask what."

They finished their tea in silence. Melli began to feel a little better; the cramps had gone and the strength returned to her legs. The old woman smiled, seeing that she had drunk the whole cup. "Come, girl," she said, "we have sewing and baking to do if you are to leave by the morrow."

Maybor was feeling very pleased with himself. He had just secured the position of lady's maid to Lady Belynda for the lovely Lilly. Of course the old crow Lady Belynda had given him a hard time, claiming she was most satisfied with the lady's maid she already had. Maybor had not been fooled; it had merely been a ploy on the old hag's part to squeeze him further. He had ended up settling a handsome pension upon the aristocratic but impoverished lady.

He hoped the tempting minx appreciated what he had done for her—it had cost him more to reel her in than his two former wives combined. She'd better be worth it! She was a charmer, just the sort he liked—a saucy vixen.

He could not prevent a smile from stealing across his face. Old Lady Belynda would be no indulgent mistress. The old crow would give the girl hell. There would be no parades around the garden in her best ribbons for Lilly. With Lady Belynda as her mistress, the girl would be much more likely to spend her entire day cooped up in the ladies' hall doing embroidery. And that, thought Maybor, suited him very well indeed.

He was no fool. He knew why the girl wanted to be a lady's maid. She wanted to show herself off in her finery until she attracted the eye of a minor nobleman. A nobleman who was either so stupid or so in love as to forgo his prestige by marrying a common servant. Maybor knew there were men who married for love or infatuation. He considered them to be unadulterated idiots—a man should only marry for social gain or land. A lord who married a commoner was beneath Maybor's contempt. Anyway, he thought, the avaricious little Lilly would find her plans sadly curtailed by her aged mistress.

Still, Lilly tempted him like no other woman had done in a long time. He always valued highest the objects for which he paid the most. He quickened his step. It was already dark and he was late, she would be waiting for him. He rubbed his hands together in expectation of her gratefulness.

He opened the door of his chamber and walked through the bedroom. The girl was there, waiting. She was actually in his bed, tucked beneath the covers for warmth, with only her head showing.

"I see you could resist me no longer." Maybor began unlacing his tunic. He was puzzled at first when she did not reply, but then decided she was feigning sleep or shyness. Maybor liked to play games as much as the next man and found his interest growing.

He took off his robe and tunic and then pulled off his leggings. He stood naked and erect. The girl kept her eyes firmly shut. "So you are too modest to look upon me, are you?" He strode toward the bed, his ardor swelling. "Then I must look upon *you!*" With that he tugged the covers off the bed.

He reeled back in horror, gorge rising in his stomach. The girl was skinned from the neck down. Her body was a mass of red flesh. "Oh my God, oh my God." Maybor's knees weakened beneath him. He fell to the floor and vomited, his whole body racked with spasms.

Twenty-four

Jack awoke and was eager to be up and on his way. Melli was still asleep, but the old woman had obviously been up for some time as the fire was well stoked and there was porridge cooking in the pot. She smiled her good morning and put finger to lip, urging him not to speak; she wanted Melli to sleep a little longer.

She ladled some porridge into a bowl and topped it with a spoonful of pig lard. Before she handed the bowl to him, she slipped something into his hand. Jack looked down to see one shiny gold coin. He immediately went to give it her back—a gold coin to the old woman probably represented five years of savings. She shook her head insistently and forced the coin back on him. Because they could not speak, Jack could neither protest nor thank her; he suspected that was the way she wanted it.

Jack enjoyed the pale warmth of the early morning kitchen. The banked fire and the smell of pork in the cauldron reminded him of life in the castle. He felt the need to be busy. He wanted to feel the soft touch of flour beneath his fingers and the familiar tang of yeast in his nostrils. He stood up and began to look around the kitchen for what he needed. His days at Castle Harvell were behind him now; at least by baking bread he could ensure they weren't forgotten.

"What you doing, boy?" whispered the old woman.

"I thought I'd bake you some loaves. It's the only thing I can repay you with."

"There's no oven for baking, I take my dough to the village."

"You have flour and yeast and plenty of pig fat?"

"That I do."

"Then I'll make pitchy bread."

The woman brought out the ingredients and Jack measured the flour into a bowl and set it to warm by the fire. He mixed milk and water, not adding the yeast until the liquid was warm to the touch. Master Frallit swore that the secret of good pitchy bread was not to combine the ingredients until they were as "warm as the blood of a lustful virgin." Once Jack had mixed in eggs and pig fat, he set the batter to rise. It would be two full hours before it was light enough to form the countless tiny holes that gave pitchy bread its unique texture.

Jack was surprised to find he had an audience. Melli was awake and quietly watching him. There was an unfamiliar expression on her pale face. She smiled gently. For one brief moment Jack let his thoughts arch upward. Was there something between them? Melli's expression was so tender; her eyes so dark and expressive as she looked upon his face. He began to feel self-conscious under her scrutiny: his arms were brushed with flour and there was grease beneath his fingertips. He resisted the urge to brush himself clean, to straighten his hair, to turn his back. He was a baker's boy and he would not pretend otherwise. Let her see him for what he was.

Melli was the first to look away. She stood up and poured herself a cup of buttermilk. Her hand was shaking as she put down the jug.

Determined not to rush, Jack picked up the cloth and began to wipe the lard from his fingers. He wondered what had happened between them yesterday. She had grown cold and afraid all of a sudden, as if she were looking beyond the present. He didn't want to think about the future. The past weeks had demonstrated to him that it was anything but set. Why, less than two months back he thought he would be a baker for life, and now he didn't even know where he'd be spending the next night.

As a baker he would have led a secure and stable life, food on his table, warmth and shelter, but Jack knew he wanted more now. The world of the castle kitchens seemed small and confining. It was true that he had been forced from it, but now he realized it had freed him to do what he wanted, to shape his own future. Never mind that Melli had seen bleakness ahead; nothing was preordained, he could change things for the better.

"Here you go, lad." The old woman handed him a new tunic and a cloak. "Try them on while the batter's rising, see if they fit. They were my husband's and unfortunately he was not as tall and broad as you are." Jack pulled the tunic on. It was a little tight. "Hmm, if you were only staying one more day I could alter it a bit more."

"It will do fine. I thank you for everything." Jack held the woman's gaze. He knew he would insult her if he mentioned the coin and so did not.

"Your turn, my girl." She held out a heavy wool dress, plain but beautifully colored. "This should fit you. I have taken the hem down." Melli looked a little reluctant to take her dress off, so Jack volunteered to step out for a while so she could change.

The day had begun clean and chill, no sign of rain—a good day for traveling. He walked down the dirt track to the road and looked east. Halcus, Annis, Bren—they all lay ahead, places of wonder and possibility. He almost wished he could walk away now, alone, so avid was he to begin his future. He wanted to be free from running and fear, to walk a path without having to look back.

Suddenly, the image of the terrified mercenaries being blasted from their horses flashed before his eyes. It was a warning—this was what he was capable of. He was unpredictable, a danger to those around him. Jack shuddered involuntarily, his mood of optimism gone in an instant. He headed back to the farm, feeling the need for company.

He entered the small door, bowing his head to get through. He was met by a beautiful sight: Melli had put on the deep blue dress; the color matched her eyes and complemented her dark hair. This, thought Jack, was Lord Maybor's daughter. How could he have thought, even for an instant, that a girl as high born and proud as Melli could be interested in him?

"Just in time for hot cakes," cried the old woman. She'd turned the batter onto the baking stone, and the pitchy bread was almost done. Catching Jack's look, she said, "Come now, lad, I'm too old to wait half a morning for a few extra holes." Her eyes twinkled brightly. "Besides, you'll be off soon, and I don't want you to spend your last hour baking when you should be resting." She piled the bread rounds onto a platter. "Eat up, you've a long day journeying ahead, and a full stomach is a traveler's best friend."

Jack and Melli sat down across the table and made a feast of piping hot pitchy bread smothered with butter and cheese. As they ate, the woman bustled about the room making bundles. "Jack," she said, "I noticed you have no blade." Jack realized he must have lost his sword at some point. "We all know there is trouble on the road, so I want you to take this." She handed him a long, nasty-looking knife. "I use this to slit the pig's throats with."

"How will you slaughter them without it?" asked Jack, swilling down the last of his food with a mug of ale.

"I'll have to club 'em to death." The woman smiled brightly and Jack couldn't tell if she was speaking the truth. "Now, in these packs," she indicated the two bundles on the table, "you will find hard cheese and as much salted pork as you can carry. I also put a few other things in there you might need."

Jack picked up the bundles, they were both surprisingly heavy. "You have been so kind to us."

"Yes," Melli interjected. "We owe you so much, how can we ever thank you?" The old woman's face crumpled up as she forced herself not to cry.

"It is I who must thank you. You have both brought me joy." She opened the door.

"There is something I must warn you about—" Jack was about to tell her to beware of people searching for them, but she interrupted him.

"Say nothing, lad. I am a woman who has outwitted the

world for many years; I must have a certain skill at deception by now." She was telling them, in her own way, that she would lie to protect them. Jack came forward and kissed her cheek.

"I will remember your kindness always." He turned to Melli, who was close to tears, and beckoned her forward. Together they walked away from the farmhouse and down the road.

"Tawl, are you all right?" Tawl flashed the boy a warning look, but it went unheeded. "It's just that you've been acting strange ever since we left that tavern yesterday." The boy waited for a reply. None was forthcoming, so he continued. "You shouldn't let the mad rantings of some old drunk get to you. He didn't know what he was talking about." Nabber hesitated an instant and then added, "What is Larn anyway?"

"Ssh, boy."

They were riding to the flank of tall, silvery peaks. The foothills provided a treacherous path: loose rocks and loose soil were a constant danger. The rocky slopes were ideal for Nabber's pony but a challenge to the mare. Tawl had to pick his trail carefully, less the horse misstep and lose her footing. The pony found its own path and seemed more content now that the weather was colder.

Tawl knew he was being unfair to the boy by ignoring him, but he couldn't get the man's words from his mind: *"Larn! You have the mark of Larn in your eyes."* Those were more than the rantings of a madman. The drunk had known he had been to Larn. What was it about that cursed place; why was he in some way marked?

He was three times marked now, he thought, glimpsing the circles upon his forearm and the scar running through them. Once for Valdis, once for his family, and now Larn. He could never remove the first and second marks; one told of what he was, the other told of what he had done. The two were bound as closely as the seers to their stones. They could never be separated: they were his fate and his past.

Now it seemed he had another mark. What did it mean,

had Larn altered him in some way? *"Beware the price,"* the Old Man had said. Maybe Larn had extracted a price he was not aware of. He felt the same, in excellent health if not spirits. Perhaps he bore the anguish of the seers in his eyes. Their torment had certainly left a mark on his soul. The more he thought about it, the more anxious he was to see Bevlin. The wiseman could help him; he would know the answers.

Impatient to make his way to Ness, he urged his horse faster. Ness was surely only a day or two away and from there, Bevlin was but a few days further.

"Tawl!" His thoughts were interrupted by the boy. "You're going too fast. Your horse is not used to the high ground."

"Don't presume to tell me how to ride, boy." He had not intended to sound as sharp as he did.

"What's the matter with you?" The boy sounded afraid and Tawl felt sorry for being short-tempered.

"Take no notice of me, Nabber. I mean nothing by my anger. My mind has had much to dwell on of late." He slowed his horse down. "Why don't we stop and take our midday meal? There is a snatch of grass ahead, enough to give the horses something to chew on." Tawl watched as relief flooded over the face of the boy. He was glad to be the source of it.

"I still have some roast goat and a pat of cheese left from yesterday," said Nabber, eager to please.

"Sounds good to me," cried Tawl, making an effort to be light-hearted. "I'll take the cheese—you can have the roast."

"Too late," said the boy stuffing the last of the goat cheese in his mouth.

"So, Nabber, you never told me about your life in Rorn." Tawl contented himself with chewing on a slice of roast goat. The flavor was little enhanced by being carried around in the boy's sack all day.

"What d'you want to know?" Nabber belched loudly.

"Well, how come you ended up in a life on the streets?"

"That's easy, Tawl. The streets are the only way for an enterprising boy with no trade or education to make a living. I started out as a grout."

"What's a grout?" Tawl stretched himself out on the grass, pulling his cloak around him; the weather was beginning to get cooler.

"Don't they teach you anything in the marshlands besides how to cut peat! A grout's a boy who works for a runner." The boy saw Tawl's perplexed look and explained further: "A runner is someone who collects dues for the Old Man. I take it you've heard of the Old Man?"

"What did you do for this runner?"

"You know . . . fetching payments, running errands, delivering notes, scattering sawdust on the blood . . . that sort of thing. Course I was young and didn't get paid much so I moved on, or rather I moved up."

"So what did you do next?" Tawl was wondering if the comment about the blood had been a joke. The boy had spoken it in such a matter-of-fact way that he doubted if any humor had been intended.

"Well, next I became a lookout. Not just any old lookout, mind. Lookout to the greatest thief Rorn has ever known." The boy waited expectantly.

"Who was this man?" Tawl asked the required question.

Nabber tapped his finger against the side of his nose. "Can't tell you his name, friend—that's why he's the greatest—he's the only one who's never been caught. He made me swear a vow of secrecy, told me I'd be smitten down with the ghones if I ever spoke his name. Taught me everything I know, he did. He was the one who gave me my name. He told me I was a boy of considerable talent and that I needed a name to match. Nabber, that's what he called me, and I've been known by it ever since." The boy spoke with great pride. "He was a honorable man and a fine thief."

"So how did you turn to pocketin'?"

"Well there's not much money to be made as a lookout. Oh, there's prestige all right, but no money. A good friend of mine suggested that I try my hand at pocketin' and I've never looked back." Nabber spread out on the grass, indicating the end of his tale by closing his eyes and settling down for a nap.

Tawl wondered how much the boy had left out—he did not doubt Nabber's words, but he felt that the boy was holding some things back. Tawl was a man who understood the need for privacy, so he asked no more questions and let the boy sleep.

Maybor spent the night in his daughter's bedroom. He was a man used to the gore of the battlefield; he had seen men's limbs pulled from their bodies, soldiers hacked into pieces, but the sight of the girl in his bed had been too much for him to bear. He had called for his servant, Crandle, who had dressed him and guided him away from his chambers while the body was dealt with.

Maybor found he could not stomach the thought of sleeping in the same bed in which the girl had lain, skinned. He had retired to Melliandra's chamber to await the questioning of the Royal Guard. The captain had arrived in due course and was thoughtful enough to bring a jug of fortified wine with him. Maybor was, of course, under no suspicion. He was a lord and the girl but a servant.

Maybor knew who had done the deed and why it had been done, but he mentioned neither to the guard: conflicts between lords were kept between lords. It was an unspoken code and Maybor had no desire to break it. This was between him and Baralis.

The king's chancellor was a proud man, and proud men do not like to show weakness. When he had drawn the sword upon Baralis, the man had flinched. The chambermaid Lilly had paid for that flinch with her life. Maybor cursed himself. He should have carved him up while he had the chance.

Maybor was tired. He had been unable to sleep, but it was more than that. He was tired of being beaten by Baralis, tired of looking for his daughter. He ran his fingers through his graying hair, contemplating how he should counter this latest move by the king's chancellor. It was appalling what the man had done. Of course he would not have performed the deed himself; Baralis was far too discerning to get blood on his hands. He would have sent his idiot Crope to do the job.

It seemed to Maybor that of late Baralis was always in the background scheming and contriving, sabotaging his plans with one hand and trying to poison him with the other. Maybor sat on the bed thinking deeply. He needed to become more calculating. He would have to match Baralis' cunning and wit if he were ever to get the better of the man. The king's chancellor favored intrigue and duplicity and it was time that he, Maybor, tried his hand at such methods. He smiled—a grim, bloodless smile. He would beat the master at his own game.

"My lord."

Maybor was surprised by the presence of his servant. "Yes, Crandle, what is it?" He sighed heavily.

"The queen commands you to her audience chamber."

"She wishes to see me now?" The servant nodded. "Go quickly to my chambers and bring my new red-and-gold robe. Hurry!" Maybor watched his servant dash away and then went over to the mirror and busied himself smoothing his hair and cleaning his teeth with a dry rag.

The servant returned minutes later with the robe and proceeded to dress his master. He brought fragrant oils to groom his hair and a sprig of rosemary to sweeten his breath. Once he was satisfied with his appearance, Maybor left his daughter's bedroom and made his way through the castle.

He walked the length of the ladies' chambers, and then down into the courtyard which divided the men's quarters from the women's. In the distance he spotted a familiar figure: it was his son Kedrac. Maybor was sure he had come to offer his help to revenge what had happened the night before. However, as Kedrac approached he saw the boy had a dark expression on his face. Maybor decided he had no time to deal with his son and hurried off in the direction of the queen's chamber.

"Father!" The cry was harsh and stopped Maybor in his tracks. Kedrac came level with him. "What is this, Father, running from your son?" His voice was cold, taunting.

"Kedrac, I have an audience with the queen. I will talk with you later."

"You will talk to me now, Father," hissed Kedrac. "The girl who was found skinned in your bed, she was the chambermaid, Lilly." Maybor made no reply. "Is that right, Father!"

"Yes, yes, she was the chambermaid Lilly. Surely it's of no consequence to you, son. She was nothing, a common slut, no reason to get angry over."

"Oh, I am not angry over the girl. You are right she *was* a slut. No, I'm not angry over the girl . . . I am angry at you, Father." Kedrac's voice was charged with contempt. "That you would steal a wench from my very bed. Are you that desperate, or is it just that you have something to prove?"

Maybor slapped his son's face. "How dare you speak to me that way?" Kedrac smiled unnervingly and touched his cheek, which now bore the mark of Maybor's hand upon it. He lingered a moment, meeting his father's gaze, and then turned and stormed off.

Maybor let out a sigh of relief. Kedrac was too head-strong, too proud. It was a grave mistake to let a woman, especially a common servant, come between men. He had to admit that he'd quite enjoyed slapping his son's face, though. The boy would recover; his pride had been wounded, nothing more. Maybor hurried ahead. He could keep the queen waiting no longer.

"Enter." The queen's voice rang out. Maybor walked into the sumptuous chamber and bowed low.

"I wish Your Highness joy of the day."

"Ah, Lord Maybor." The queen came over to greet him, smiling warmly and offering her hand. Maybor took it and brought it to his lips. "I was most distressed to hear about the girl found in your room." She gave him a querying look. "Tell me, Lord Maybor, have you any idea who was responsible for this . . . inhuman act?"

"I cannot begin to imagine who would do such a thing, Your Highness." Maybor suspected the queen knew there was more to the incident.

"It is certainly a tragedy. I have been informed that you did not sleep in your chambers last night." The queen poured them both a cup of wine and invited Maybor to sit.

"I slept . . . elsewhere." He didn't think it was a good time to mention his daughter's name.

"Yes, I can understand why you would not want to sleep in your own bed." The queen handed him the wine. "With that thought in mind I have a gift for you."

"A gift, Your Highness." Maybor had never seen the queen so gracious, pouring wine with her own hand and now a gift. He was beginning to feel wary. It was not usual for the queen to make such a show of hospitality: did she have bad news to break to him?

"I have arranged to have your bed taken from your chambers and burnt. In its place I will provide a new bed. A beautiful bed, carved by master craftsmen over two centuries ago. It was a gift from the city of Isro to my husband and me on our wedding day."

"Your Highness, I am overwhelmed with your generosity." Maybor knew of the bed of which she spoke. It was worth a fortune; inlaid with gold and precious jewels, carved from the finest darkwoods. His suspicions grew—why was the queen giving him such an extravagant gift?

"You will be sleeping in it this very night, Lord Maybor." She raised her arm in a silent toast. After she had drunk from her cup her face changed a little, and she got up and walked across the room. She came to rest by the window.

The queen stood and looked out on the courtyard for some minutes before speaking again. "Lord Maybor, I am afraid I have ill tidings for you." She did not turn to look at him. "I can no longer continue the search for your daughter. I have need of the Royal Guard for other matters."

"I understand, Your Highness." Maybor realized that the bed and the gracious reception were acts of contrition.

"You must also understand that we can no longer hope to find your daughter. The Guard have looked for her almost a month now. Tomorrow I will recall them from their search." The queen finally turned and faced him. "Maybor, even if Melliandra were found now, I could not sanction the betrothal. My son must be married to a girl beyond reproach. We have no way of knowing what your daughter has been through, who she has fallen in with. The woman who will be queen in my place must be impeccable. The betrothal between my son and your daughter will not take place." The queen bowed her head. "I am sorry, Lord Maybor, but I have made my decision."

"As Your Highness wishes," he said, struggling to keep

his voice level. "May I be permitted to know who you are considering in my daughter's place?"

"You will be the first to know when a suitable girl is found." There was an edge to her voice that Maybor could not understand. "There is, I hope, Lord Maybor, no need to tell you how much I value your continuing allegiance and support." It was as near to a plea as the queen could manage. She was asking him to accept her decision and remain loyal to her. She needed his support to maintain her position. He was not about to give her any such undertaking; they both knew his loyalty was worth more than a jeweled bed.

"I know well how much Your Highness *depends* upon my allegiance." He paused a moment so there was no mistaking the meaning of his words. "I can assure you that I will take no hasty actions." He bowed low, the silk of his robe rustling softly. "And now, if Your Highness will permit, I will take my leave."

As he made his way to the door he stole a glance back toward the queen. She looked like a woman greatly troubled.

Baralis was on his way to speak with the new mercenaries. Crope had arranged for him to meet with them close to the haven. There were only three of the first lot of mercenaries that were fit for duty. The leader, Traff, was the only one to have escaped completely unscathed. Baralis knew how much Traff hated him and wanted to be free of him, but Baralis had no intention of letting the man off the hook. Death would be the only discharge Traff could count on.

Baralis was feeling decidedly cheerful. The incident with Maybor and the chambermaid had gone off successfully; the whole castle was talking about it. The fact that the girl had also been bedding Maybor's son was an added bonus to be relished; it would surely cause some father-son tension. Perhaps he might even approach Kedrac at some point, nothing brash, just a subtle overture—a wronged son could prove to be a valuable asset against a father. He would wait and see. Having no family himself, it was difficult for him to gauge the pull of family loyalty.

Baralis almost felt sorry for Maybor. Finding the girl

must have been quite a nasty shock, and if he was not mistaken, he had been dealt another blow today. He knew the queen had summoned Maybor to an audience and strongly suspected that she had told him the betrothal would not go ahead. After all, the time was up. Two days. That was all that was left. Even if the wretched girl was found now she could probably not be brought back to the castle in time.

Poor Maybor, things were just not going his way! Baralis shook his head in mock commiseration. He had lost his daughter, his lover, his chance at kingmaking, and maybe even the loyalty of his oldest son. He would have to be monitored carefully. Maybor was a man who prized revenge as highly as Baralis himself did; he would undoubtedly retaliate in some way.

It was only a matter of days now before Baralis' plans were realized; the queen would reluctantly call him to her presence. They had business to settle. She had lost the wager and must pay the reckoning. He knew he had placed her in a difficult position—she had been forced to break her word to Maybor, and he was a man whose loyalty she relied upon to keep the lesser lords in their place. Maybor also contributed great sums of gold to the war against the Halcus, not to mention the use of his men and his lands.

The queen was probably feeling rather apprehensive at this moment, wondering how she could pay her debt yet keep Maybor's allegiance. Baralis did not doubt for one second her ability to do both; she was no novice in the art of statecraft. The truth was that she was far better at political maneuvering than her poor, sick husband had ever been.

Baralis had taken the precaution of walking to the haven through the woods. He did not want the men he was to meet to know anything about his hideaway unless they were firmly in his pay. He saw men waiting in the distance. He knew they would be watching his approach; they, like most people who passed through Harvell, would have heard tales about him. They would be a little afraid, a little wary, already intimidated by the sight of him drawing close in his black robes.

"Good day, gentlemen." He kept his voice low—let them strain to hear him!

"You are Lord Baralis?" spoke one of the number.

"I am he." Baralis made a point of meeting all the men's eyes.

"You are looking to hire some men?" The man spoke with a certain assurance.

"I am willing to pay well." The look of greed upon the men was unmistakable.

"I heard that the last men you hired were killed in the woods." The man was trying to raise the price.

"They were careless. It would not have happened if they had been better led." Baralis looked coolly at the leader.

"What have you in mind?"

"To start with I need two people tracked and found. After that I will require your services for other matters."

"How much?"

"Five golds apiece."

"Done!" cried the leader. He was a fool, thought Baralis. Traff had held out for eight.

"Here." He threw the leader a purse. "You start today."

"I will need a description of the two people."

"They are both young. The girl has long dark hair and pale skin; the boy is tall with brown hair. They will be traveling on foot. I believe they will be heading east. You can pick up their trail to the south of the castle near an unused hunting lodge. If you do not find them in a week, report back to me." Baralis began to walk away and then remembered something, "Do not approach the boy in full view. He must be taken off guard or better still when he is asleep."

"We will find them and bring them back."

"No, I don't want them brought back," murmured Baralis. "Kill them and then bury their bodies."

Twenty-five

The city of Ness nestled between graciously sloping hills, its backdrop formed by pale mountain peaks, their color a mere variance of the silvery gray sky. The hills surrounding the city were a patchwork of ploughed fields, meadows, and orchards. Ness was a farming town.

Tawl and Nabber arrived just as a late dawn was rising upon the city. The mountains to the east jealously guarded the sun's rays and daybreak always came later to Ness than elsewhere.

The city was old and weather-beaten, the buildings sturdy and unadorned, designed for practicality not for show. As the two companions made their way into the town they passed throngs of tradesmen: tanners, butchers, wheel-wrights. Ness was a town that survived on its sheep. Their fleeces were shorn every spring for wool, they were milked for cheesemaking, they were slaughtered and butchered for meat, their skins were tanned into parchment for writing upon, and their droppings used as fertilizer for spring planting.

The city was famous for its wool: the women of Ness had a light finger with the spinning wheel, and the wool they spun was fine and soft. Dyemakers excelled at making beautiful vivid colors, especially reds: bright hues of scarlet and crimson were favored by the men of the town for their cloaks and jerkins. The women were not allowed the privilege of wearing bright colors, and only wore dresses of muted browns and blues. Tawl did notice one or two brightly dressed women, however. They stuck out in the crowd, their gaudy colors proclaiming their particular trade for all to see.

The air was cold and sharp, and Tawl realized they would need to purchase extra clothing now they were in the north. He smiled looking at the market stalls piled high with sheepskins and bolts of wool—he had certainly come to the right place to buy warm clothes.

He kept a close eye on the boy; he had no intention of letting him go off prospecting in this town. They wandered around the market and Tawl had to keep a firm grip on Nabber's tunic on more than one occasion—the boy would catch sight of a portly merchant or a richly dressed woman and would gravitate in that direction.

"It's only a bit of pocketing; they'll never miss it." Nabber wiped his nose with his sleeve. He was not used to the colder climes of the north and had caught a cold.

"No, I won't have you getting us both into trouble."

"We need to make some purchases, don't we? There can't have been much coinage left after you paid the horse dealer in Toolay." Tawl checked his pack and found one gold and a handful of silvers.

"I thought we had more than that." He looked at the boy suspiciously, but Nabber just shrugged his shoulders.

"Looks like I'll be doing some prospecting after all, then." The boy linked the fingers of both his hands together and cracked all his knuckles simultaneously.

"Don't you be too long." Tawl watched as Nabber slipped away into the crowds. "And be careful." Tawl wandered over to a market stall that had various lengths of cloth for sale. He was looking for heavy wool; he could take the cold, but he could see it had been hard on the boy.

"Good day to you, sir." The cloth merchant had an unfamiliar accent; he looked at Tawl with undisguised speculation. "Come from the south, have you?" He didn't wait for Tawl's answer. "I can tell by the poor manner in which you are dressed. If you don't mind me saying, you could do with a new cloak. I have a beautiful length of wool here." He pulled out a bolt of scarlet fabric. "Feel it." Tawl dutifully ran his fingers over the cloth. It was certainly smoother than most wools he was used to.

"Do you have anything in a less noticeable color? A gray or a brown?" The cloth merchant looked at Tawl as if he were mad.

"Sir, those colors are for the women. A fine figure of a man such as yourself would look most pulchritudinous in a red robe." Tawl had no idea what *pulchritudinous* meant, and he was quite sure he did not want to look it.

"I insist on gray. How soon can you have two cloaks and tunics made ready?"

"Let me see." The cloth merchant scrutinized Tawl, obviously deciding how much he was good for. "I can have them made up by dawn tomorrow for the right price."

"And what is the right price?"

"Four golds." The man looked squarely at Tawl, defying him to challenge the price.

"Two," said Tawl with a slight raise of his brow.

"Sir, the cost of a seamstress alone will set me back two golds, not to mention the high quality of my cloth." The man waved his arms to illustrate his point. "I can do it for no less than three."

"Three it is, then." The price was still far too high, but Tawl had no love of bargaining. He told the cloth merchant what style he required and the approximate size of the boy, made the expected deposit and then left.

He decided to buy a bite to eat while he waited for Nabber to return. He was just choosing between a stuffed sheep's heart and blood pudding when he heard a female voice whisper in his ear, "If you follow me, I can show you where they serve the best food in Ness."

Tawl looked round to see an auburn-haired girl. She was wearing a brown dress and was therefore not a prostitute. There was something familiar about her. The girl saw his puzzled look. "You have just dealt with my father, the cloth merchant." She smiled and said flippantly, "You struck a bad deal, by the way." She had a light, pleasant voice with a trace of the same lilting accent as her father.

"What does it matter to you? Surely you will benefit from your father's skill at bargaining."

"He is quite rich enough as it is." The girl beckoned him away from the food stand.

"He was dressed poorly—or is that part of his ploy?" He followed the girl away from the crowds.

"Father has so many ploys I lose count of them. For one thing he will be paying no seamstress two golds. I will be making your cloaks."

Tawl could not help but smile. "Well, hadn't you better get started? I will need them by tomorrow."

"You are leaving Ness tomorrow?" The girl looked disappointed.

"What's it to you?" Tawl was always suspicious of people who asked about his movements. Unfortunately the question appeared to offend the girl.

"It's nothing to me," she said proudly. "I must be on my way. You wouldn't want your cloaks to be finished late." The girl began to walk off.

"Wait," cried Tawl. The girl spun around. "I am sorry if I offended you. I would be pleased if you would show me the best eating house."

"I never said it was an eating house," she said, returning to his side. "The best food in Ness is made in my own kitchen with my own hands."

He followed the girl through the market, down an alleyway and then into a wide, pleasant street. Tawl looked around to see if he could catch a glimpse of Nabber; there was no sign of the boy. He was not concerned. Nabber was most enterprising; he would find him somehow.

"Here we are," proclaimed the girl at the door of an old but well-kept townhouse. "Oh, don't worry. No one lives here but Father and me. He is far too thrifty to keep servants." She guided him in through the door and down the stairs into a warm and smoky kitchen.

"You do me a great honor by inviting me into your home." Tawl was familiar with the customs of the north and knew the appropriate words to say.

"You are not from around here, are you?" The girl busied herself around the kitchen.

"No. But if I am not mistaken neither are you. Your voice has a lilt to it that comes not from Ness." Tawl accepted the cup of ale he was handed.

"You have sharp ears. My father was originally from a place far to the west of here. After my mother died when I was but a child, we traveled east and eventually ended up here." The girl cut slices of warm, crusty bread and buttered them generously.

"What was the name of the place you came from?"

"The town of Harvell, in the heart of the Four Kingdoms."

"How long has it been since you left?" Tawl had never met anyone from the Four Kingdoms before, and now saw a chance of gathering some information before he got there.

"Ten years now. Of course my father goes back there every year or two to impress our relatives with his newly found wealth." The girl drew one of several pots from the fire. She took off the lid and a delicious aroma filled the kitchen. "Why are you so interested anyway?"

"I am heading west looking for work. I may head that way."

"I wouldn't go as far as the Four Kingdoms if I were you. They have warred with the Halcus for many years now and crops and livestock have suffered. There will be little work for an outsider."

"It is a war that does not seem to make much sense. Both sides deplete their strength and for little gain." Tawl tried to keep his tone casual; he didn't want to betray the full extent of his interest to the girl.

"Father says that there is something fishy about the whole thing. Each side appears to know the other's moves before it makes them." The girl ladled a large helping of stew into a bowl. It was thick with carrots, turnips, onions, and lamb.

"Such goings-on are usually a sign that someone in high places has an interest in keeping the war going."

"That's exactly what my father says. He says the king's chancellor—what's his name now?—Lord Baralis is behind it all."

"So this Lord Baralis is the power in the Four Kingdoms, then?"

"Ever since the king was shot by an arrow five years back, there have been a few men who would manipulate events in the kingdoms. The queen is supposedly strong, though—a better leader by all accounts than the sick king was in health. The best thing the king could do is die and let his son rule in his place. Maybe he can bring peace to the land."

The girl came and sat beside him and chewed on a slice of bread. Tawl watched her as she ate. She was a pretty girl with a sprinkling of tawny freckles across her nose and cheeks. He wondered why she had invited him to her house. As if reading his mind she said, "I'm not in the habit of asking men to dine at my table. I saw you at my father's stall and you looked . . ." She hesitated, a little embarrassed. "You looked in need of some home cooking." Tawl had the distinct feeling that she had been about to say something else but stopped herself.

"Surely there must be a lot of people who pass through the city?" He was not about to let her off the hook.

"Yes, but most of them are just smelly old fieldhands or pickpockets or worse." The girl stared into her bowl of stew. "You looked different, like you might be an adventurer or a prince in disguise or something."

"I am no prince." Tawl reached out and touched the girl's chin, tilting it upward so she was forced to meet his eye.

"I don't even know your name." The girl became suddenly nervous and started clearing away the bowls.

"I am Tawl." As always his name sounded short without the title Knight of Valdis behind it.

"I am Kendra, daughter of Filstus the cloth merchant."

"Well, Kendra, I must take my leave now. I have someone who will be waiting for me." Tawl had no wish to take advantage of a young and inexperienced girl. He bowed low in the courtly fashion. "Thank you for your hospitality." As he left the kitchen he saw the wish to call him back upon the girl's face, but he did not give her chance. He turned quickly and made his way up the stairs and out of the house.

Once back at the market, he attempted to find Nabber. After searching unsuccessfully for some time he decided the best thing he could do was wait in a noticeable place and let the ever resourceful boy find him.

Tavalisk was contemplating his archbishop's ring. When he had first been made archbishop, he'd been given the official ring bearing the seal of the City of Rorn. The ring was supposedly over a thousand years old, precious beyond telling. He admired its form in the sunlight. It really was quite good for a fake. Not that there was anything to compare it with, the real one being irretrievably lost at the bottom of a lake of sand.

Tavalisk had learned a valuable lesson from the fake ring—people believed what they saw. Of course it helped that he was an archbishop and therefore above repute, but he suspected the premise would also work at less auspicious levels than his.

Once he realized that the ring was accepted, he began to replace other items with fakes. He had started carefully to begin with: a priceless Tyro vase was replaced with an identical but worthless piece, sculpted by a brilliant, if not original, artisan of Rorn. Before long he expanded his enterprises, and now he could say with pride there was little left in the Archbishop's Palace that *was* real.

He had been careful, very careful, even to the point of having his copyists' throats cut and, when he deemed necessary, their families', too. As a result of his endeavors he now had a substantial stash of treasures concealed in a private residence not a stone's throw away from the palace. It was his nest egg. If the ungrateful and notoriously fickle people of Rorn ever decided to get rid of him, he could be assured of living well indefinitely. And Tavalisk was a man who valued living well almost as much as he did mischief-making.

His nest egg was on his mind more often of late. Events in the world were beginning to worry him. The ones that he initiated were in his control and so of no concern, but events in the north, particularly the proposed marriage between Catherine of Bren and Kylock of the Four Kingdoms, bore heavily on his mind: it was Marod's prophecy coming to life right before his eyes. He didn't know if anyone else saw it. The only thing he did know was that it was up to him to prevent it from happening. Rorn would not become a lackey to a northern empire. Tyren was after his trade, and the duke of Bren and Baralis were far too ambitious to let an empire rest in the north. It would all end in war.

Not that war was necessarily a bad thing. Tavalisk rubbed his chubby hands together. If he acted wisely, Rorn just might end up making a pretty profit out of the whole affair.

Gamil knocked on the door and let himself in. "The reply from Lord Maybor has finally arrived, Your Eminence." He handed over the letter to the archbishop, who studied the seal. It was unbroken: the letter M was clearly visible in the crimson wax. To one side of the initial was a miniature representation of a gray swan, to the other side was a double-edged sword.

"How appropriate," murmured Tavalisk. He broke the seal and opened the letter. He took some time deciphering its contents: the hand it was written in was crude and unfamiliar. Obviously Lord Maybor was no scholar, an observation which pleased the archbishop immensely. He always preferred to deal with men a little less clever than himself.

Gamil waited eagerly for him to finish reading the letter. Tavalisk deliberately took longer than necessary just to taunt him. "Pour me some wine. A little refreshment will aid my comprehension."

"What does Lord Maybor say, Your Eminence?" Gamil handed him a glass of wine.

"He wishes to know my identity. He says he is very interested in an alliance against—how does he put it?" Tavalisk read the letter. " '. . . against a certain black-hearted traitor known to us both.' " Tavalisk smiled. "He does have a certain primitive way with words, don't you think, Gamil?"

"So he is in agreement?"

"Oh, he is a most eager man. His hate for Baralis near leaps off the page. However he is most insistent that I name myself, though I do believe he has an inkling who I am."

"What makes you say that, Your Eminence?"

"He says, 'Be you lord or bishop, I am willing.' " The archbishop drank deeply of his wine, his spirits much improved.

"So you will name yourself to him, Your Eminence?"

"Yes, I believe I will. You must draft a reply at once. I would discover what he knows of Baralis' plan to wed Kylock to Catherine of Bren." Tavalisk smiled brightly. "Lord Maybor appears to be a man who bears a heavy grudge against Baralis. I feel sure his assistance will prove invaluable."

"I will pen a reply this day, Your Eminence. It will be a while before we can expect a reply."

"I am not too concerned about the time, Gamil. Even if the betrothal goes through, Kylock will not marry at once. He is a prince and will need a long betrothal. Besides, even without the possibility of an alliance between Bren and the Four Kingdoms I would still be interested in keeping a close eye on our friend Baralis. I have met the man but once, and let me tell you, Gamil, he is a dangerous man. He hungers for power and influence."

"I never realized Your Eminence had met Lord Baralis." Gamil was fishing for information.

"There are many things you don't know, Gamil." The archbishop was not about to give him any.

"Has Baralis always hailed from the Four Kingdoms?"

"I will answer no more questions, Gamil."

"If there is nothing further, Your Eminence, I will withdraw and script a reply."

"Very well, Gamil. I would see a copy before the letter s sent."

"If you are revealing yourself to him, will you be using our seal?"

"Don't be a fool. If that letter were to drop into the wrong hands and my seal was upon it I could be placed in a most uncomfortable position. No seal. Lord Maybor already knows who I am; he merely requires confirmation of his suspicions. Be subtle in your description of me—name me without naming me. Do you understand?"

"Yes, Your Eminence."

"Very good. By the way, Gamil, I've noticed a cooling

off on Toolay's part regarding the expulsion of knights. See to it the situation becomes more . . . heated."

"As you wish, Your Eminence. Is there anything else?"

"No, that will be all." Tavalisk waved his hand in dismissal, enjoying Gamil's surprise. It was best not to be too predictable; it kept one's servants on their toes.

Maybor was once more downwind of the middens. There was not much stench on this day, though. The dung must have frozen solid, he thought grimly, pulling his cloak about him.

A chance meeting in the woods two days before had led to this assignation. After his audience with the queen he decided to take his horse for a brief ride into the woods; he had wanted to get away from the castle and all his humiliations. He needed to be able to think clearly and decide upon his next moves. As providence would have it, he met a man while he was riding, a man who could prove most useful to him.

He had just decided to turn back when he spied a group of men in the distance. They were not in uniform, so he knew they were not the Royal Guard. He was about to draw closer to investigate when he saw an unmistakable figure approach the group. Cloaked in black, tall and striking: it was Baralis.

With growing interest, he watched the meeting. He was a distance away and could hear no words spoken, but he got the distinct impression Baralis was engaging their services. His suspicions were confirmed when he saw Baralis throw one of their number a purse. Obviously he was hiring yet more mercenaries.

He was about to withdraw, his curiosity satisfied, when he noticed a movement in the bushes to the left of the group—he was not the only one spying upon the meeting. He waited for the gathering to break up. Baralis headed back to the castle, and the men into the woods. He then urged his horse in the direction of the man concealed in the bush. Upon seeing him approach the man stood his ground. He was no fearful servant or petty poacher.

Maybor drew level with him. "What business have you in these woods?" he demanded.

The man looked at him insolently. "Last I heard they weren't your woods, Lord Maybor." The man was broad and well muscled. Maybor wondered where he had seen him before.

"Since you know my name, I would ask yours." Maybor noticed a thick bandage around the man's arm.

"I make no secret of who I am. My name is Traff." He spat out a wad of snatch.

"Perhaps you would care to tell me why you were spying on Lord Baralis?" Maybor watched the man as he considered his reply. He felt sure the man was a mercenary—his arrogant swagger and lack of respect were typical of their kind.

"What a man chooses to do in his spare time is his own business."

"Even when you choose to spy on the man who pays you?" guessed Maybor.

Traff sucked in his cheeks, contemplating his answer. "What's it to you?"

"You appear to be a man who is not happy with his current taskmaster."

"And if I'm not?" Traff spoke with studied disinterest.

"You could always change masters."

The mercenary's face remained expressionless. "There is always a risk when changing masters."

"But the rewards may be great." Maybor decided it was the right time to end the cat and mouse game—he'd left the cheese in full view. It was up to the rodent to make the next move. He pulled on the reins of his horse. "If you are interested in talking more, meet me downwind of the middens at this hour two days from now." He urged his horse forward and rode off.

So now he was waiting for Traff. He knew the mercenary would come; he had seen bitterness and loathing in the man's eyes. Maybor rubbed his hands together to keep them warm. There had been a sound frost overnight and the pinch of it could still be felt in the air. He was becoming decidedly impatient. Maybor was not a man used to being kept waiting.

A few minutes later a figure appeared from the chill mist. "You picked a fine place for a meeting," said Traff in greeting.

Maybor shrugged. "It has its advantages." He noticed that the mercenary was still wearing the bandage. "What happened to your arm?" He was just making small talk, gauging the man's temperament. However at the mention of his arm Traff's face visibly darkened and he made no answer. Maybor realized he must have touched upon a sensitive area.

"Tell me," he said, changing the subject, "did you hear anything to your advantage whilst you were in the bushes?"

"I heard some interesting things." Traff was guarded.

"Have you given any thought to what I said about changing masters?"

"How do I know you would make it worth my while?"

"I am the richest man in the Four Kingdoms," said Maybor simply. "Name your price." He could see that his offer had little effect on the man. He changed his tack, "Land, appointments, pensions, they could all be arranged."

"There is more than money at stake." Traff spat out his snatch and proceeded to grind the pulp into the frozen earth with the heel of his boot. Maybor was beginning to comprehend that Traff was not driven by greed but by another more basic emotion . . . fear.

Maybor spoke with calm deliberation: "Baralis is a very powerful man, but he is not invincible." He saw that his remark had sparked Traff's interest. "If his throat is slit, he will die like any other man. I myself have drawn a blade upon him and yet stand here to tell the tale." He conveniently pushed the memory of Scarl's failed assassination attempt to the back of his mind.

"If you want Baralis out of the way, I am not your man." Traff's voice was harsh and unyielding. "I value my life too highly."

"But I'm right in thinking you *would* like him out of the way?" Maybor saw from the look on Traff's face that was exactly what the man wanted. "You and I have similar goals my friend. We should join forces to achieve them." There His proposal was out in the open. He would give Traff chance to chew over the matter. Such negotiations were best not rushed. "I must go now, I have other business to attend to. If you are willing to come to some arrangement contact me in the next few days." Maybor gave the most imperceptible of bows. "I trust you will be discreet." He then headed off into the castle grounds.

The meeting had gone well. Traff was a man with little liking for his master; resentful retainers always prove fertile ground for treachery. Of course the mercenary was still wary of him. He would need a little more coaxing to come around, but he *would* come around. Maybor was not by nature a patient man and disliked the slow process of intrigue. Still, procuring a spy in Baralis' camp would be well worth the wait.

When Traff came to him next, he would begin to find out information from the man, discover exactly what Baralis had been up to. He suddenly stopped dead in his tracks—Traff was probably one of the mercenaries who had been sent to look for Melliandra. Maybor remembered Kedrac's words, *"I think they tried to rape her."* His blood turned cold. He stood and gazed into the depths of the swirling mist—what kind of man would he be to deal with one who had violated his daughter? His eyes narrowed and he saw the mist no more—it was all Baralis' doing. The king's chancellor had brought him to this, brought him so low that he now conspired with his daughter's rapist. Baralis must be dealt with at all cost. Honor and family pride would have to come later.

The day was darkening to dusk when the boy finally reappeared. Tawl was not happy; he had been waiting for many hours in the marketplace and his presence had aroused the suspicion of more than one of the local bailiffs. "Where have you been all day?" he demanded.

"I've been around, prospecting and the like." The boy shook his pack and coins jingled within. "Not a bad day's work." He smiled broadly, encouraging Tawl to forgive him.

"Come on, then. It's time we took a room for the night." Tawl had no wish to walk a great distance looking for the best inn and decided they would stay at the first one they came across.

As it happened, the first tavern they came to looked most comfortable—and expensive. The innkeeper boasted to Tawl it was a place where the wealthiest of traders stayed while they were in town. Tawl shot a quick glance at the boy and Nabber nodded vigorously. He had obviously collected more than enough money to pay the bill.

"We will take one of your smallest rooms for the night."

"No, I think we'll take two," interjected the boy. Tawl gave him a questioning look. "It's about time I had a good night's rest and the only way I can get one is to sleep on my own. You snore like a donkey!" Nabber and the innkeeper laughed companionably.

"We'll take one room," insisted Tawl.

"Sir, I can give you an extra room for your boy at only half the cost." The innkeeper was obviously eager to make any extra money he could. Tawl could not understand exactly what was going on, but he was sure Nabber was up to something. Both he and the innkeeper fixed him with pleading stares.

"Very well, two rooms, but make them small—put the boy in a cupboard if you will."

"You have made a wise decision, sir. You and your boy will wake more refreshed in the morning because of it." The innkeeper glowed with the knowledge of additional profit. "And now, would you care to partake of a spot of supper? We have boiled pheasant, pike in butter, roasted veal, and lamb, of course." From the drop in his voice at the end it was obvious that lamb was the cheapest item.

"We'll take the lamb." Tawl noticed disappointment on the innkeeper's face. "I'll also have a flagon of ale."

"The special brew?" asked the man hopefully.

"No, the plainest brew."

When he and Nabber were comfortably settled near the huge fireplace in the dining hall, he turned to the boy. "What's all this about two rooms?"

"I've got more than enough coinage to cover the additional cost." Nabber helped himself to a mug of ale.

"That's not what I asked." Tawl took the mug away

from the boy. "What have you been up to today besides prospecting?"

"I met up with someone." Nabber was defiant.

"Who?"

"A girl. That's all. A girl with red hair and freckles— pretty she was. She said she knew you and asked me to do her a favor."

"What favor?" Tawl's voice was deceptively calm.

"Well, she said she wanted to surprise you in your room." Nabber blushed. "She said she wanted to be alone with you and that I should take a separate room. Told me not to tell you. Gave me a kiss she did, for all my trouble."

Tawl leaned back against the wall. It was a ploy. The girl was in league with Tavalisk or Larn or Borc knows who else. She, or more probably, whoever she worked for, planned on either killing or taking him in the night. He was a little disappointed; he had thought she was just a nice girl. He was disgusted at his own naivete. He stood up.

"Where you going?" asked Nabber warily.

"It's about time I got myself a decent weapon."

A few hours later he was in his room oiling his new blade. The blacksmith he found had been most reluctant to fire up his forge so late. Tawl was not to be put off so easily and surprised the man by offering to buy the sword that was displayed upon the wall. The smith protested saying he could never sell it. He swore it was the first sword he'd made as an apprentice that had met up to his master's high standards.

Tawl could see it was a plain but sturdy sword, just the kind he favored—he had no love of embellishment in a weapon. He'd managed to persuade the man to part with the sword for the extortionate price of three gold pieces. The smith appeared somewhat remorseful at having charged such a high price, for as Tawl walked out of the building he ran up to him. "Here take this," he said, handing a soft pig-skin scabbard to Tawl. "My wife makes them. I'd like you to have it." The smithy then hurried back inside, his guilt suitably assuaged.

Tawl decided it was time to bed down for the night. He

pulled the covers over his fully dressed body. His new sword lay flat against his belly, the handle firmly in his grip. His knife was tucked in his belt. He blew out the candle and prepared to wait.

Some time later, when the moon drew long shadows across the room, Tawl heard the door creak open. A figure paused in the doorway and then crept toward him. Tawl's body tensed, ready to spring. The figure loomed over the bed. Tawl sprang up, sword in his hand. He grabbed the figure and flung it down against the bed, raising his blade to its throat.

"Stop! Please!" cried a female voice. So the girl had come herself!

"Who sent you?" he demanded, pressing the blade into her flesh.

"No one sent me. I came alone." The girl was almost hysterical. "Please let me go."

Tawl frisked the girl for weapons with one hand, holding the blade to her throat with the other. He found no dagger. He lit the candles with a flint so he could search the room—she must have dropped her weapon.

The light revealed the face of the girl to him. It was as he expected: the cloth merchant's daughter. Tears of terror coursed down her cheeks. She was a fine actress. "Don't move or I'll kill you," he hissed as he looked for her blade. He searched the room but could find nothing. He turned to the girl, who was cringing with fear on the bed.

"Where is your weapon?"

The girl looked confused. "I don't know what you mean." She was sobbing uncontrollably.

"You came here to kill me, don't deny it." A thought suddenly occurred to him and he flung open the door to his room; there was no one in sight. "Where are your accomplices?"

"Please, I don't know what you are talking about. I didn't come here to kill you."

"What did you come here for then?" Tawl's voice was cold and insistent.

"I came here to seduce you!" cried the girl, breaking into a new fit of sobbing. Tawl took a deep breath. The girl was either a consummate liar or telling the truth. He placed his sword in the scabbard.

"Why did you want to seduce me?" he asked brusquely, still skeptical.

"You seemed like a romantic stranger, almost like a knight with your golden hair and noble manner." The girl was now blushing and crying simultaneously. Tawl didn't know what to say to her. He was beginning to think he had made a mistake. He handed her a linen cloth to dry her tears. She snatched it from him and blew her nose vigorously.

"You seem a little young to be seducing strange men."

"I'm past seventeen summers." The girl smoothed down her skirts. "You have certainly put me off seducing any others."

"I'm glad to hear it," said Tawl with a grin.

"I thought you would be glad I came. Instead you jump on me and almost kill me." Kendra's spirit was returning. "I think you are quite mad! You are lucky I'm not calling the bailiffs."

"And how would you explain to the bailiffs your being in my room?" The expression of indignant rage on the girl's face made him want to laugh.

"I could tell them you lured me here."

Tawl went and reopened the door. "If you hurry, you might catch one before he retires for the night."

"You are insufferable! I don't know what I ever saw in you." She was angry but made no move to leave the room. Tawl closed the door.

"I'm sorry I startled you." He came and sat beside her on the bed.

"Are you always in the habit of trying to murder women who seduce you?"

"I thought . . . never mind." It seemed ridiculous that he had ever thought the girl was an assassin.

"Is someone trying to kill you?" Kendra was quite calm now and seemed excited at the prospect of being involved in danger and intrigue. "I knew you were an adventurer the moment I saw you. Are you working for the duke of Bren?"

"Why d'you say that?"

"Oh, everyone knows he has men all over the place up to no good."

"No, I don't work for the duke of Bren."

The girl looked a little disappointed. "But someone *is* trying to kill you, aren't they? That's why you attacked me—you thought I was the one." She eagerly awaited his reply.

"I mistook you for someone else, yes." Tawl suddenly felt very tired. "I think you had better go."

The girl moved over to him and kissed him on the lips—a gentle, tentative kiss. Tawl kissed her back, softly at first and then, as desire came upon him, his kiss became hard and unyielding, forcing her lips apart and searching out the succulence of her tongue. He placed his arms firmly around her waist and drew her to him. His fingers searched her body, feeling for the swell of breast and hip. He pulled at the strings of her bodice—they would not give, so he ripped the fabric. He slipped his hands under her skirt, seeking the smoothness of thigh. Kendra pulled away, her face flushed. Tawl let go of her and they sat for a moment staring at each other.

He stood up. The girl tried to stop him by catching his arm. He gently took her hand away and moved across the room. For the third time that night he opened the door. "Go now, Kendra, before I do something we'll both regret." There was a hard edge to his voice and she obediently got up and walked toward the door. As she left, she looked at Tawl with a mixture of fear and desire.

Twenty-six

Baralis was tired of waiting on a summons from the queen. The deadline for the wager had passed by two days now and yet she had still not called him. She was playing a game with him, forcing him to wait until she was ready, seeking to gain some small advantage in the battle of wills. It was high time he forced her hand. He had meticulously planned for years, and he was not about to be put off by simple delay tactics. "Bring me my robe," he called to Crope. "I am about to pay the king a visit."

Once he was suitably dressed, he picked up a small jar of oil and slipped it into the lining of his cloak; it was to be his prop. He made his way to the royal quarters, his silken robes rustling gently in his haste. The guards let him through unchallenged. He passed the queen's chambers and the guards there drew spears, indicating that the queen was in attendance and that he was not to enter. Baralis ignored them and walked on—he knew it would only be a matter of time before one of them reported to their mistress who they had seen walking the royal corridors.

Finally, he came to the most elaborate door in the entire castle. Molded from solid bronze it showed scenes from the history of the Four Kingdoms: Harvell, Reskor, Granwell, and many other ancient kings were all there—shown taller and more handsome than they ever were in real life. Lesketh's ancestors, thought Baralis dryly, were notoriously short and ugly men.

"Halt!" cried the guard. "No one is permitted to enter without the queen's permission."

"I suppose you know it is I who supply the new medicine for the king? The medicine that the queen values so highly." The guard nodded, it was a well-known fact around the castle. "Well," said Baralis softly, his voice gently coaxing, "I have a new oil that I have made, one that will bring motion back to the king's shoulder. I would first try it out to ensure that it works before I inform Her Highness about it. I would hate to build her hopes up only to disappoint her." The guard was nodding understandingly. "You would be doing both the king and the queen a great service by letting me through." Baralis altered the timber of his voice slightly; it was now low and compelling. "I will do His Majesty no harm. Why, you can even be in the room with me the whole time if you prefer."

"Where is this oil?" asked the guard. Baralis knew he had him. He whipped the jar from out of his cloak. The cut glass sparkled with convenient mystery. "Very well, Lord Baralis, you may enter, but no longer than a few minutes."

The heavy door swung back with noiseless ease, and Baralis entered the king's chambers. Lavish carpets and tapestries in vivid blues and golds dulled the sound of his footsteps. What a waste, mused Baralis, all this splendor for a bed-ridden king. The first room was merely a reception area, and he made his way across it and through to the bedroom.

Two people hovered around the king's bed: the queen's wisewoman and the Master of the Bath—rather a grand title, Baralis considered, for the man who was responsible for emptying the king's chamberpot. The two looked most surprised at his appearance. However, he was not about to give explanations to mere attendants.

"Lord Baralis this is most unexpected," said the Master of the Bath. The wisewoman knew her place too well to challenge his presence.

"Unexpected it may be, but most beneficial I hope." He pulled the lid from the jar, daring the man to question him further.

"Lord Baralis," said the wisewoman softly, "if you intend to use the contents of that jar upon the king, may I be permitted to see it first?"

"Wisewoman, go brew some herbs!" Baralis approached the sleeping king; drowsiness was a fortunate side effect of the medicine.

"Sir, I beg you not to disturb the king's sleep. He needs all the rest he can get." The Master of the Bath was beginning to look very nervous.

"Nonsense, man, the king has slept for too long, that is his problem." Baralis didn't really care what he said; he was just biding time before the inevitable arrival of the queen. To speed this eventuality he began to shake the king awake, and his action had the desired effect: the wisewoman rushed from the room, undoubtedly to inform the queen of his presence.

The king awakened, his slow gaze focusing upon Baralis. He mouthed some words, but no sound came from his lips, only spittle.

"Lord Baralis!" came the queen's voice, her words were charged with rage. "How dare you enter the king's chamber without permission?"

"Your Highness." Baralis bowed low, his back arching gracefully. The queen moved to the bedside and checked the condition of her husband.

"You have wakened him!" She turned on Baralis angrily. "Explain yourself."

"Your Highness pointed out that I had no permission," he said smoothly. "But may I ask who is qualified to grant such permission?" Baralis knew the queen would be aware of one specific written law of the Four Kingdoms. The law that stated a queen had absolutely no rights of sovereignty, even in the event of the king's disablement or death. Queen Arinalda was without any legal power, yet she ruled in the king's place. It was a law that had been conveniently forgotten by the court in the interest of unity and continuity.

"Lord Baralis, you are broaching a dangerous subject," warned the queen.

"Dangerous for whom, Your Highness?" Baralis' voice held a warning of its own.

"Why did you come here?" The queen backed away.

"I think Your Highness knows why. You are overdue on paying your debts."

"So you used the king to get my attention." Her voice was filled with loathing.

"It appears to have worked." Baralis permitted himself the briefest of smiles.

"I will speak with you no further this day, Lord Baralis." It was a dismissal.

"As Your Highness wishes, but I must insist upon an audience tomorrow."

"Insist! You forget who you are talking to, Lord Baralis." The queen looked as if she would strike him.

"My apologies, Your Highness, I meant of course that I hope for an audience." He could see the queen did not believe him, but it mattered not; she would see him now.

"Leave here at once," she said haughtily, turning her back. Baralis made a great show of bowing to the king and then left.

He sauntered back to his chambers at a leisurely pace. He was most pleased; the incident had gone as planned. Not only had he forced an audience, but he also had the chance to remind the queen just how vulnerable her position was.

Tawl cursed the snow; it would delay his arrival at Bevlin's for at least one more day. They had ridden from Ness two mornings ago and he'd known then that snow was on its way—the clouds had formed a gray blanket in the sky and the earth had softened a little underfoot.

He was glad of his new cloak and tunic. If Kendra had sewn it as she claimed she would, then she had done a fine job. The workmanship was flawless, the seams straight as reeds, the fabric beautifully cut. The cloth merchant had taken the liberty of having the cloak lined in the very color Tawl had refused. Nabber had taken a great liking to the vivid crimson and insisted on wearing his cloak inside out.

Tawl had been relieved when he picked up the clothes to find there was no sign of the girl. He found the idea of seeing her again unsettling. He had behaved badly to her. He had been ready in fact to force himself upon her. He'd had plenty of women in his time—but inexperienced ones were another matter and he usually stayed well clear of them. An inexperienced woman needed love and romance, needed wooing with care. They formed attachments quickly and were easily heartbroken. Tawl never stayed long in any place and he knew it would not be fair on such a woman to love her and leave her.

So he found his comforts with more seasoned women. Preferably older women, for not only were they more skilled in the arts of lovemaking, but they also felt the strong pull of physical desire that a young girl could only feign. Tawl liked his women to be willing and eager, and also worldly enough to understand when he moved on in the morning.

As a knight he was pledged never to marry. Valdis saw women as a threat; a rival claim on the loyalty of their knights. When the order was first founded marriage had been allowed, but following the Fifty Years War when nearly five thousand knights died, many of them leaving wives and children, the powers that be decided it was best in the future to avoid the tragedy of families left with no one to care for them. So marriage was forbidden. What began as a device to save wives and children from starvation eventually became a means of control. A knight was supposed to repress his natural desires and put the energy of his passions into serving Valdis.

Tawl, like so many other knights, found he couldn't live without the comfort of women. It seemed to him that Valdis, by disapproving of lovemaking, was in fact condemning women. They were looked upon as faithless distractions, who only served to dilute and divert the noble intentions of the knighthood. Tawl had known many women in many towns, and he knew in his heart that Valdis was wrong. Women had just the same capability for nobility as any man, and a greater potential for love and kindness. Valdis had made a mistake by stopping its knights from marrying; a man with a family cherishes and nurtures humanity. And wasn't that the founding precept of the knighthood: to protect the sanctity of human life?

Tawl drew his cloak about his chest. None of this excused his treatment of the cloth merchant's daughter. At very least, knights were expected to exercise self-restraint. The girl had obviously been a virgin, out more for adventure than seduction. He knew he shouldn't have kissed her, but the worst part was that he had been close to losing control. He had hardly known himself. If the embrace had continued a second longer, he would have been in danger of raping the girl. It little mattered that the girl was half-willing. She was young and hardly knew what she wanted. Tawl turned his face to catch the chill breath of the north wind. It was not like him to do such a thing. The girl had been too young. It was true that she had been about the same age as Megan, but Megan had been matured by her time on the streets and was schooled in the ways of passion.

Megan. Tawl wondered what had become of her. He trusted that she had built herself a better life. Maybe she was now a seamstress or a flowergirl—with nineteen gold coins in her purse she could afford not to work for a few years— even in an expensive city like Rorn. He hoped that she no longer walked the streets. The life of a prostitute was hard and often dangerous. It robbed a girl of her youth, her looks, and eventually her spirit. As long as she was anywhere but the streets he would be happy.

They were free of the foothills now, the land gently sloping before them. Fields and meadows were sprinkled with the first lowland snow of the winter. He was worried about the boy: his cold had not gone away, his cough had worsened, and there was a flush of fever on his brow. To Tawl it was one more reason to get to Bevlin as fast as possible—the wiseman would be able to cure the boy. One sip of the lacus would probably do it.

For the past few days Tawl had felt a vague tension growing within him, as if he carried a weight upon his shoulders, bearing him down, sapping at his spirit. He'd been short-tempered with Nabber and now the incident with the cloth merchant's daughter. He was filled with an impatience that he could not altogether understand. An impatience to see Bevlin. Being in the wiseman's presence seemed to offer the possibility of relief from his burdens. Bevlin would take him in and renew him, ready him to continue his task of finding the boy.

* * *

Tavalisk was at his bath. The large marble pool was being filled with warm water and perfumed essences. Servants were busy laying out what would be needed: fragrant oils for washing, pony hair brushes for scrubbing, linen wraps for drying. The archbishop himself sat in a robe of cauled silk, nodding distractedly at Gamil, who was muttering on about church policy whilst a young girl cut Tavalisk's toe nails. Apparently, He Who Is Most Holy had called upon his archbishops to urge leniency toward the knighthood. Leniency indeed! What did His Holiness know of world events, perched as he was in the very grand yet very distant city of Silbur? There was nothing he could do, he had no real sway: religious offices were only as powerful as the man who held them. And His Holiness had never been a great man.

"Careful with those scissors, girl," warned the archbishop, ignoring his aide and continuing to read his copy of Marod.

"Your Eminence has remarkable feet," commented Gamil. "Completely free of corn or bunion."

"Yes, I have, haven't I?" Tavalisk put down his book. "It comes from a life of studied repose. One cannot expect to have such perfect feet if one walks upon them all the time."

"Your Eminence is most fortunate to be in a position where walking is not often required." Tavalisk looked up sharply, but could see no sign of irony upon Gamil's face.

"The work of great men, Gamil, is done sitting. Lesser men such as yourself make their living while standing upon their feet." Tavalisk noticed the bath attendants were waiting in readiness. He stood up and one rushed forward to remove his robe. Gamil discreetly looked away as the pale and fleshly body of the archbishop was revealed.

Tavalisk slipped down the few steps and into the steaming water, his body reddened like a cooked lobster. The water was a little hotter than he normally preferred. Only when he was immersed up to his neck did Gamil see fit to look upon the archbishop again. "I have penned the reply to Lord Maybor, Your Eminence. I will have Hult bring you a copy of it later."

"Very good. It should be sent this day." Tavalisk daintily lifted his foot onto a raised shelf and one of the attendants oiled and rinsed it.

"I have received word from Valdis, Your Eminence."

"How are they taking the expulsion of their knights?" The archbishop raised his other foot to be cleaned.

"Tyren is most displeased. There is talk of issuing a letter of condemnation."

"A letter of condemnation! How very typical." Tavalisk was scathing. "Why I quake with fear at the very thought of it. Tyren is playing the pious bigot again."

"There have been riots in Toolay, Your Eminence."

"Riots, indeed. You *have* done well, Gamil." The archbishop looked up and noticed a certain smugness on the face of his aide.

"It was nothing, Your Eminence, merely a few well-placed actors; one pretended he was a knight and burnt Toolay's flag, the other incited the passions of the crowd."

"Burning Toolay's flag, indeed! I can see I'd better watch out, Gamil, lest you get too clever for your own good." Tavalisk lifted a plump arm to be washed.

"I was inspired by Your Eminence's own cunning." Gamil was now trying to flatter his way out of a sensitive situation.

"You would do well, Gamil, never to forget just how cunning I can be." He smiled benignly at his aide. "So, can we expect Toolay to pass a law banning the knights in the near future?"

"I would think so, Your Eminence."

"And what of our own knight?" The bath attendant was now rubbing oils into the archbishop's chubby shoulders.

"He left Ness several days back. I suppose he will be arriving at the wiseman's hut in the next day or so."

"Good. What about the girl we are keeping; are we treating her well, Gamil?"

"About as well as a prostitute deserves to be treated, Your Eminence."

"Now, now, Gamil, we all know damaged goods bring a poor price at market."

"I will try and ensure she is kept undamaged, Your Eminence. However, the dungeon she is kept in is small and damp and the air seeps up from the middens."

"Well, do your best." Tavalisk turned to the attendant. "More perfumed essences, girl."

"If Your Eminence will permit, I will be on my way. I have much to arrange."

"Before you go, Gamil, may I make a suggestion?"

"Certainly, Your Eminence."

"It would not be such a bad idea if you yourself took a bath once in a while. It is not fitting that an aide of mine goes around smelling like a week-old cuttlefish." Tavalisk watched with pleasure as Gamil blushed a particularly virulent shade of red and then beat a hasty retreat. As soon as his aide left, the archbishop picked up his copy of Marod. The page was well worn by now. He read it once more:

> *When men of honor trade in gold not grace*
> *When two mighty powers join as one*
> *The temples will fall*
> *The dark empire will rise*
> *And the world will come to ruin and waste*
>
> *One will come with neither father nor lover*
> *But promised to another*
> *Who will rid the land of its curse.*

Tavalisk smiled softly, the germ of an idea forming within his mind.

Maybor was waiting in the castle stables. Traff had called him to a meeting. The stables were large and spacious, but few horses graced the lines of stalls. Many young lords and squires were off warring with the Halcus, taking their men and horses with them. Maybor was thinking it was about time Kedrac joined the war—his other two sons had left ten days ago to join the fighting to the east of the River Nestor. It would do his eldest some good to get away from the court.

The past few days Kedrac had made a point of ignoring his father. When they had last met by chance in the dining hall, his son had made a point of cutting him dead, not even acknowledging his presence. It was a spectacle that had been seen by many at the court and had been a topic of much snide conversation ever since.

Yes, thought Maybor, it would do them both good if Kedrac left the court for a few months. It would give the boy a chance to cool down, and Maybor himself would be relieved from the strain of conflict that he felt whenever he saw his son. Kedrac was far too rash and strong-willed for his own good. Maybor remembered Kedrac's mother, his first wife. The woman had not only been deformed but had also been quite mad. Maybe that explained his son's temperament. Maybor preferred the company of his two younger sons and secretly wished that one of them would succeed him as lord. Unless Kedrac got killed at the front, that would probably never happen.

He was disturbed from his thoughts by the arrival of Traff. At his appearance Maybor felt a wave of loathing. He hated mercenaries—one minute they fought for the kingdoms, the next for the Halcus. Anyone willing to pay could be their master. He had fought in enough battles to know that mercenaries were first off the field at the sign of a rout and the first to rob the dead in victory. Any man who had fought honorably as a soldier hated mercenaries.

Traff made a point of checking the surrounding stalls. "Can't be too careful where Lord Baralis is concerned," he said by way of an explanation. "That man has means to get anywhere in the castle."

"Oh, has he?" Maybor deliberately kept a bored tone to his voice, though in reality he was most interested in finding out anything about his adversary.

"Yes, the whole castle is crisscrossed with tunnels. Baralis is the only one who knows how to use them."

"I know of the tunnels." Maybor knew that Harvell the Fierce was supposed to have built a few tunnels for purposes of seduction and escape, but he had no idea they were as extensive as Traff said. If Baralis had access to many rooms in the castle, he might even have entree to his own chamber;

that would certainly explain the two attempts on his life. "Have you been in these tunnels?" he asked casually.

"Maybe." Traff was still playing his hand close to his chest.

"I think it's time for some straight talking, my friend. I want to see Baralis put permanently out of the way and to do this I need some help. You can help me and help yourself at the same time."

"Seems as you're being direct, then so will I," said Traff. "I'll be willing to help you, but only if you agree to my conditions."

"Go ahead, speak them." This was what Maybor had been waiting for.

"First, I want two hundred gold pieces, up front in cash." Traff looked to Maybor, who nodded.

"I will agree to that."

"Secondly, I will not act as your assassin. I am willing to aid you in other ways: give you details of his plans, his secret hideouts, his special skills, and so on; but I am not fool enough to make an attempt on his life."

"Agreed." Maybor had expected such a condition. "Anything else?" Traff paused a minute, a calculating expression on his face. "Say it, man," urged Maybor, who was growing tired of the wait.

"I have a fancy for a wife." Traff paused again, and Maybor wondered where this was leading to.

"I will dower any girl you choose." Maybor assumed Traff was after more money in the guise of a dowry.

"You are bound to dower the girl I have in mind," said Traff.

Maybor grew very still. He could hardly believe what the man was saying—the only girl he was bound to dower was his daughter. Surely this mercenary was not suggesting that he marry Melliandra. His daughter! Why, the girl would have been queen had she not run away. How dare this man propose such an outrageous union. Melliandra was his and he would never give her up to such a contemptible swine. "Do you know what you are saying?" he demanded, dangerously close to losing his temper.

"I need a wife and your daughter fits the bill. She is a

comely girl, but I doubt she will find many lords willing to wed her now." Traff smirked a little. Maybor could not restrain himself; he slapped him hard across the face.

"How dare you speak of my daughter that way?"

"Come, come now, Lord Maybor." Traff was cool, even a little amused. "You must be aware that a girl who runs away from home and ends up being flogged in Duvitt as a whore is hardly a great prize. You should be glad to get her off your hands. She can never come back to court again, if she did she would only bring you shame."

Furious as he was, Maybor recognized there was a certain truth to the man's words. The whole court now knew Melliandra had run away from the castle. Traff was right, no lord interested in his prestige and position would marry her. There would be some who were willing, lesser lords and gentry, those who were interested in his money—the very men Maybor most despised. Melliandra had ruined her life by running away. She could have been the most elevated woman in the Kingdom, but now she had come so low that a common mercenary asked for her hand.

Maybor glanced at Traff, he was waiting upon an answer. One thing was certain, he would never let that man marry his daughter. Melliandra may have shamed and disobeyed him, but he still loved her, and the thought of Traff laying a hand upon her shocked him to his very soul. He would gladly murder him rather than let that happen. He felt like murdering him now, just for suggesting it. But where would that get him? If he were to find Melliandra, he would need Traff's help. He had no choice but to agree to his proposal. He took a deep breath, and as he did so he vowed solemnly that the man would never live to see his wedding day.

"So my daughter is still alive. When did you see her last?" Maybor found he couldn't bring himself to actually say: *you can marry my daughter;* the words burnt in his throat.

"You agree to my proposal?" Traff was suspicious. Maybor realized he would have to make a convincing effort.

He took a deep breath. "You are right, my friend, when you say no one will marry her. She is no good to me now, a millstone around my neck. You can have her if you find her. She is still my daughter, so you may rest assured that she will be adequately dowered." Maybor added one final flourish: "If when you are married I find you do not treat her well, I will make sure you wish you had never set eyes upon her. The girl may have shamed me, but she is ever my daughter and I will let no man abuse her." That appeared to do the job; the skepticism drained from Traff's face.

"It is agreed, then, when she is found I will wed her. How much dowry can I expect? I will of course require sufficient funds to keep your daughter in the manner to which she is accustomed." Maybor could hardly believe his ears. Was there no end to this man's audacity? He gritted his teeth.

"No daughter of mine shall be found wanting." Maybor struggled to retain his composure. "So, when did you see her last?"

"Lord Maybor, I said earlier I needed the cash up front before I entered into this agreement. I will be willing to tell you all I know, but I need the cash first . . . as security, you understand." Maybor could only nod. He was dumbstruck by the man's insolence. That a mercenary would not take his word on matters of cash was absurd.

"Bring the money here tomorrow at the same time. Take care to be discreet. Baralis has eyes everywhere." Traff walked off with an infuriating swagger to his step.

Maybor was sorely tempted to go to Baralis and tell him that one of his men had turned traitor. He was sure that Baralis would devise a suitably horrific punishment for the mercenary. And by Borc, the man deserved one!

As Maybor made his way back to the castle, he realized he was experiencing an unfamiliar emotion. There was something nestled beneath his anger and it took him a moment to realize what it was: he was ashamed. What sort of father was he? Not only had he conspired with his daughter's rapist, but he had promised her to him!

They were looking for a place to spend the night. It was still daylight, but experience had taught them that night came quickly to the forest in winter. Melli was in charge of finding suitable ground to sleep on and Jack was appointed as water finder.

For most of the time since leaving the old woman's farm, they had followed the eastern road, always careful to stay under cover of the trees. Sometimes it had proven difficult as either streams or ditches had blocked their path, and much time had been wasted as they circumvented these obstacles so they could remain with the road.

The weather had actually turned milder since their journey began, but Jack had been proven right when he'd predicted snow. The snow had started to fall early that morning and had persisted all day. It was in fact an advantage not to be traveling on the road, for with no roots to hold the earth in place, the road had quickly turned to mud. The few people they saw passing had great difficulty wheeling their carts and steering their animals in the quagmire.

The earth of the forest was kept firmly in place by the deep roots of trees, and although the earth was slippery underfoot, it was not nearly as treacherous as the road. The snow was not sticking; it was too light and the earth too warm. Water ran in rivulets down ditches and into the countless streams and brooks which laced through the forest.

Melli had actually found the past week peaceful. She liked being in the woods once more, enjoyed walking in the crisp air and watching the stark scenery that winter offered. After the experience of being locked up in a tiny storeroom for days, she found she truly appreciated the freedom of the forest, of setting her own pace and choosing her own road. As long as she was traveling she had only simple decisions to make: how much to eat, where to sleep, when to rest. It was only when her journey was over that she would have to worry about the real world once more.

Both she and Jack knew they were being followed, probably tracked by hounds and men. Only the day before they had heard the familiar rumble of hooves that marked the approach of a troop of riders. Jack had acted swiftly and pulled her down into a ditch, covering them both with a layer of wet leaves. The guard had passed by. Although neither of them had admitted it, they were both relieved that there had been no confrontation. Melli shuddered to think what might have happened if there had been.

Jack had not spoken about the incident at the hunter's lodge and Melli respected his silence and didn't mention it herself. She was certain he thought about it, though, for sometimes his face would grow pale and a blank expression enter his eye. One or two times he had cried out in his sleep, words of torment that Melli could not understand. She wanted to go to Jack to comfort him, to tell him everything would be all right, but he was changing, growing more distant by the day, and if she admitted the truth to herself, she was not sure *anything* would be all right ever again.

Yes, he had changed, thought Melli, as she watched him cut the wet bark from the firewood. He had become more mature, more self-assured. He no longer had the smooth brow of youth, and he bore the marks of worry upon his temples. She came and knelt beside him, spreading out her blanket on the damp earth. "It isn't a pleasant night to spend outside." She took the salted pork from her pack and began to slice it.

"That's why I thought we'd have a fire." He hacked at the bark, revealing the raw wood beneath. "This should burn now."

"Are you sure it's safe to have a fire? What if Baralis' men see the smoke?"

"If they're in the forest like us, they won't be able to see beyond the cover of the trees. I know it's a risk, but we're quite a way from the road, and you look in need of a little warmth." He smiled a little, his first that day.

"Please, don't light a fire on my account. I'm really quite warm. The dress the old woman gave me is thick and keeps out the cold."

"Melli, your nose and hands are blue with cold. Here," he handed her his blanket, "put this around you."

Melli accepted the blanket and watched as he built the fire. Eventually the flames took hold and the wood crackled pleasingly, giving off a pleasant aroma of smoke and forest. They both drew close, warming their hands and feet, Melli put the blanket over her head to keep off the falling snow. "What will you do once you get to Bren?" she asked.

"You mean what will I do *if* I get to Bren." Jack whittled away at a length of wood. He sighed deeply and then spoke again. "I don't know. I could become an apprentice baker I suppose, but I think I'm a little too old to be taken on as a new apprentice now." He sounded bitter.

"Surely there must be some other way you could make a living?" Melli thought quickly. "Once we reach Annis I could get money from my relatives there and you could use it to set yourself up as a farmer."

"I'm almost certain your relatives will not be prepared to give you money so you can loan it to a baker's boy." Jack threw the piece of wood on the fire. "Melli, my future is not your responsibility." His voice grew soft. "There is no need for you to worry about me. Better worry about yourself."

"What do you mean?"

"How long ago did you hear from your relatives? How do you know they will take you in? They might send you straight back to your father."

"These are not my father's relatives. My mother had a younger sister, Eleanor, I think her name was. She married a minor lord from Annis. I'm hoping she or some of her family will still be alive. We never received letters from her. I don't even know the name of the man she married, but I'm sure when I find her she'll take me in—my mother told me they loved each other deeply as children."

"Your mother is dead?" Jack spoke gently.

"She's been dead for over ten years. My father drove her to the grave. He only married her for her father's land. She had a miserable life; shut up in the castle, never loved, my father dallying with any woman who took his fancy. She was never a strong woman; the constant worrying just wore her out." Melli looked deep into the flames of the fire. "I would rather be here, freezing in this forest, penniless, than live the life that she did."

They were silent for some time, both caught up in their own thoughts. The snow stopped falling and the wind died down, leaving the smoke to tarry by the fire. "What about your family, Jack? Where are your parents?" At first she thought he hadn't heard her. Moments passed with no reply. Jack's face was turned to the fire, and his profile gave noth ing away. Just as she opened her mouth to repeat the question, he spoke:

"My mother has been dead for eight years. I have no father."

Melli waited, surely there was more? The fire crackled and brightened, throwing a halo of warmth into the cold of the night. She could hear Jack breathing, see the rise and fall of his chest. She followed his gaze to the stars.

"Somewhere under this sky lie the answers."

"The answers to what?"

Jack shook his head. "I don't know, Melli. There's so much I don't understand. It's as if I'm not allowed to know the things that everyone else takes for granted."

"What things?"

"Simple things," he said. "Like knowing where your mother was from." He stood up, suddenly agitated. "You'll never know what it's like not to have a father, to grow up with no background, to have no idea who you are. It's easy for you, Melli. You're so confident, so sure of yourself. When you meet people, you don't dread them asking about your family." Jack turned and faced her full on. "I do."

"I'm sorry . . ."

"What for? It's not your fault, you only asked the same thing as everyone else." He came over to her, crouching down by her side. She felt his hand searching for hers. "And now this with the mercenaries. What's inside of me, Melli? Why am I different?"

His hazel eyes held a simple appeal. But what could she say? She had no words of comfort, there were no answers to disclose. For some reason, Melli's mind returned to her premonitions of a week earlier. Squeezing his hand gently, she said, "Perhaps it's all for a purpose."

"If my life is meant for a purpose," said Jack, "then why have I no say in it?"

The wind picked up, drawing the flames from the fire. Melli was suddenly aware of the cold. Jack had answered his own question: fate never asked a man if he were willing to dance.

Twenty-seven

*T*he queen regarded her reflection in the mirror. She looked far more self-possessed than she felt, but she would have it no other way—show was an integral part of her position. She must appear calm, regal, and above all in control at all times. The queen had learned much about the importance of outward composure in the years following her husband's hunting accident. She had learned it was not just enough to *be* strong, one also had to *appear* strong. People set great store by appearances.

She had ruled in his place for five years now, and it was not self-flattery to say she had done well. She had managed to keep the various rival factions at court from each others' throats, although she had to admit the war with Halcus must take some of the credit: men will bicker less between themselves when there is a war to be fought. Despite the war she had kept good relations with other neighboring powers, tax revenues were up—except in the east—and her own popularity was high.

The queen had been aware for many years now of the need to consolidate her position and the position of her son. The Known Lands were becoming increasingly unstable. The Knights of Valdis were stirring up trouble in the south and the duke of Bren's avarice was causing apprehension in the north. Not only were there threats from outside to con tend with, but there were also those closer to home who sought to overthrow her. It had not been unknown in the Four Kingdoms for the throne to be usurped by a forceful challenger. The people considered the throne vulnerable without a strong king in power. So the queen had deliberately courted the most powerful lords in the country, the ones who had lands and men at their disposal and wealth enough to constitute a threat. She knew it was better to keep her enemies within the fold. The queen had played a delicate game and played it well—there had been no challengers to her rule, the kingdoms had remained stable, and her son's position as heir had seemed assured.

The final element to her plan was to have her son wed the daughter of the mightiest of these lords, Lord Maybor. However, things had gone awry. It was undeniably the fault of Maybor's headstrong daughter. The foolish girl had taken it into her head to run off, and in doing so wreaked havoc with the strategies of queen and country. If Maybor ever found the girl, she sincerely hoped he would give her a sound beating and then disinherit her—there was nothing worse than a disobedient daughter. The Lady Melliandra had a lot to answer for; because of her, the queen was forced to deal with a man she loathed above all others, Lord Baralis, King's Chancellor.

She had made a wager and lost. She had to pay up; her pride dictated that she would. In one sense she did not regret the wager—her husband needed Baralis' medicine, and nothing he had tried had improved his condition as much. It was in a way an equitable bet and one she had been sure of winning. Now, though, she realized it was naive of her to think that Baralis would play anything fairly. She strongly suspected that he had tipped the scales in his balance—and was sure he'd ordered his mercenaries to pick up the girl before the Royal Guard got to her. Unfortunately she could prove nothing and was therefore forced to concede defeat.

What price would she have to pay for her desire to cure her husband? What price for her gullibility?

She was expecting Baralis at any moment. She had called him to an audience and he would not keep her waiting. She smoothed her hair and looked upon her image. She could take comfort in the fact that she looked cool and self-assured. She would not give Baralis the satisfaction of seeing her anything less. Her steward walked in, bowed, and then announced: "Lord Baralis is awaiting Your Highness' pleasure in the audience chamber." She nodded and the servant left.

She had decided not to be present when Baralis arrived; she would let him sit and wait. There was only a small advantage to be gained by such a move, but she would take it nonetheless. The queen poured herself a quarter cup of wine and watered it heavily, she would need all her wits about her.

She sipped slowly at her drink, determined not to hurry. Once she gauged that sufficient time had elapsed to cause Baralis displeasure, she stood up and took one final look at her reflection—the queen had taken great care to dress most regally, and the crown jewels flashed brilliantly at her throat. She took a deep breath and went to meet her adversary.

She entered the audience chamber. Baralis was standing by the window. He rushed forward and bowed low. "Lord Baralis," she said with a slight incline of her head. She would offer no apologies for her lateness.

"Your Highness, it is indeed a pleasure. I hope I find you well?" The queen thought she detected a slight edge to his voice—he had not liked being kept waiting.

"I am well, Lord Baralis, unfortunately I cannot say the same thing for my husband. Your presence in his chamber was most disagreeable. I will not tolerate any other such infringements."

"You may rest assured, Your Highness, it will not happen again." He was so polished, so sure of himself. She was not about to make things easy for him. She turned her back on him and walked toward the window.

"I'm sure Your Highness is aware that the deadline for our little wager is past." There was a slight pause, and then he added, "Tell me, has the girl been found?"

The queen had to stop herself from whirling round in anger: *has the girl been found, indeed!*

"Come, come now, Lord Baralis, you know only too well that the girl has not been found." She kept her voice calm but loaded with warning. "Do not presume to play games with me, sir, for you will find it to your detriment i you do." He was about to reply, but the queen halted him by raising her arm. Her page walked forward and poured a glass of wine. She made no effort to water it. It suited her that Baralis believe she was drinking it unmixed—she had arranged that the wine be previously watered. She made no offer of refreshment to Baralis. She indicated that the page should leave and they both waited in silence for the door to close behind him.

"Since the girl has not been found, then I must claim payment of the wager. I know Your Highness to be a woman of great integrity, one who would not fail to honor her debts."

"Save your breath, Lord Baralis. I place little value on your flattery. I would rather get down to the meat of the business."

"You are most forthright."

"I would request the same from you." The queen noticed Baralis' hands. He tried to keep them behind his back or in his robe, but he could not hide them all of the time; they were gnarled and twisted. Strangely, she found herself drawing strength from the sight.

"Very well, Your Highness, I will speak candidly. Prince Kylock is at an age when he should marry. Lord Maybor's daughter, Melliandra, is no longer a suitable choice for his bride. I am sure you must agree with me so far?" Baralis looked to her for acknowledgment.

"Go on."

"I believe I am aware of your motives for wanting the match—you wished to strengthen your son's position by allying him with a powerful lord."

"And if I did?" The queen spoke sharply; she felt Baralis was attempting to manipulate her.

"It is a most commendable policy, and one which I wholeheartedly agree with. I applaud Your Highness' efforts at consolidation. I think, however, you may have set your sights a little low."

"What do you mean?" Her voice was cold as stone.

"I mean, Your Highness, that if you wish to secure your position and that of your son there are better ways of achieving those aims than by marrying Prince Kylock to the daughter of a mere local lord."

"Who would you marry him to, Baralis?" In her anger she dropped the pretense of courtesy.

"Catherine of Bren. The duke of Bren's only child." The queen was too stunned to say a word. Baralis capitalized on this and continued: "I need not tell you how powerful Bren is; the size of its armies are legendary. It is styled a dukedom, but it is richer and more populated than the Four Kingdoms. Such an alliance would be glorious for our country, and you, my queen, would be praised throughout history for bringing about such a fortuitous union."

Outwardly she remained calm, but inside the queen was reeling. An alliance with Bren. Such a possibility had never occurred to her; she had assumed Baralis had another lord's daughter in mind. Bren was so far away, so distant, foreign and unknown. She had heard Baralis' words and had registered his attempt to appeal to her personal ambitions: who did not want to be remembered throughout history? Oh, he had a clever tongue; he painted a dazzling picture, one that she had to admit held certain appeal.

"Have you approached the duke of Bren with such a notion?" She was careful to make her voice seem disinterested.

"I have taken that liberty, though only on a hypothetical basis." Baralis was lying, she was sure of it. He had probably planned this for months, even years.

"So, *hypothetically,* is the duke willing for such a match?"

"He is more than willing, Your Highness, he is eager. He too seeks consolidation. He has no son." Baralis paused dramatically. "If this union were to go through, *your* son would find himself heir to the two greatest powers in the north." The queen had never seen Baralis so animated. "Think of it, Your Highness: Bren and the Four Kingdoms . . . what an illustrious alliance they would make."

"The duke may be willing, but I cannot sanction a match for my son without seeing his proposed bride." The queen raised the first objection that came into her head. "My son must marry someone who is suitable in all ways. I know nothing about Catherine of Bren." To her amazement Baral smiled with delight. He dug into his robe and drew something out; he handed it to her with a flourish.

"Your Highness, I present Catherine of Bren."

She took it from him. It was a small portrait, no bigger than the palm of her hand: a painting of a young girl. A beautiful girl with the face of an angel, such sweetness in her pink lips, such innocence in her blue eyes, her golden curls almost a halo. "How do I know this is a true likeness?"

"I have letters of verification from the duke himself and his archbishop."

"How long since this was painted?"

"Six months at the latest. Catherine is approaching her eighteenth year."

"Is she willing for the match?"

"I took the liberty of sending a likeness of Prince Kylock to the duke. He assured me his daughter looks most favorably upon her proposed suitor."

"It would appear, Lord Baralis, that you have taken many liberties," reprimanded the queen.

"With all due respect, Your Highness, I *am* king's chancellor." He met her eye and they exchanged glances, each assessing the other.

"Lord Baralis," she said with great dignity, "you have stated your case in a most persuasive manner. I will, however, make no hasty decisions on a matter of such import. I must think long and hard upon the subject of who my son is to marry." The queen paused a moment. "I realize that I am under some obligation to you, but I think I am right to say that I only agreed to *consider* your choice. You have my word that I will do so." The queen was aware she was playing the terms of the wager down, however she knew that Baralis would not care to split hairs at this crucial point in his negotiations.

"Your Highness is most gracious," he said with a slight bow. "I could ask for no more."

"Very good, Lord Baralis. You may go now." She was still holding the portrait and assumed he would ask for it back. He did not. He bowed once more and took his leave.

Once he had gone, she breathed a sigh of relief and called for some unwatered wine. She sat down and looked upon the likeness of Catherine of Bren. The queen had never seen a more beautiful girl. She comprehended why he had not asked for her picture back: no one could look upon such a face and not be drawn to it. She laughed—a humorless sound. Baralis was undoubtedly a master of manipulation.

Although it had been five long years since he had last been on the northeastern plains, Tawl remembered them well: the gentle slope of the land, the open skies, the brisk winds and the bountiful earth. It was farm country and nature was generous with her gifts; the soil was rich and fertile and the waters ran clear and sparkling.

The sprinkling of snow that currently graced the plains only enhanced their beauty to Tawl. For the first time in days his mood was lightened. He had been brought up in the Great Marshes, where the land was often bogged down with water, and the soil no more than mud. When farmers actually managed to tease crops from the land, they were often blight ridden: the wet soil harbored diseases. Tawl, like most people who lived upon the marshes, had great appreciation for the blessing of fine soil, and the northeastern plains boasted some of the finest soil in the known lands.

He and Nabber rode on northward and eventually Tawl found himself recognizing specific landmarks: a grove of trees, the curve of a stream, the tilt of the land. He knew they were drawing close to Bevlin's cottage. They had not passed a village or a solitary farmhouse all day. The wiseman lived in moderate isolation, not shunning the world, merely keeping his distance.

As they drew nearer, Tawl felt tension coil within him. He could not understand why this visit was so important to him. It was true that Nabber needed help—the boy's condition had grown worse this past day and Tawl suspected we fever had set in. It was more than the boy, though. He had problems of his own. He hoped that Bevlin would be able to help *him*. Help erase whatever the drunk had seen in his eyes. Tawl had been haunted by the man's words ever since *Larn! You have the mark of Larn in your eyes.*

They headed into a sparse grouping of trees. As the

rode further the woods thickened and became dense: huge craggy oaks circled with ivy, their limbs heavy and low. Tawl knew this place—out on the other side lay the dwelling of Bevlin. He recalled one night five years back when he walked the same woods. He had been so vulnerable, so desperate for a cause. Tyren had promised him glory and the need was so strong it overwhelmed him.

A ghost of a smile crossed Tawl's lips. His desire for glory was nothing more than an attempt to make up for the past. For deserting his sisters and leaving them in the hands of a man whose only interest was his next drink. He had to succeed—failure meant that he'd abandoned his family for nothing. And that was a thought Tawl could not live with. The quest and the third circle had become the symbols of his success. Their attainment was the only thing that mattered. It was how he judged himself. He was beyond redemption, but at least he could do something, some small thing of value, that prevented his life from being in vain.

Megan's words came to him: *"It is love, not achievement, that will rid you of your demons."* She was wrong. Love was beyond him and demons would be forever at his back. The best he could hope for was to silence their accusations for a while.

The trees began to thin once more and Tawl spotted a clearing ahead. He urged his horse forward toward the break in the trees. As they emerged from the trees a small cottage came into sight; there was a vegetable garden at the front and a fenced paddock at the back. The roof was thatched and badly in need of repair. As the two companions approached, the door opened and an old man dressed in disheveled brown robes stood in the doorway. Bevlin wished them welcome.

"Come in, come in, it is good to see you again, Tawl, and I see you have brought a friend with you." He smiled brightly at Nabber. "You look like a man with a hankering for greased duck."

"Greased duck," said the boy skeptically.

"Ah, so you have never tried it, then? Well, you are in for a rare treat. As luck would have it, I just greased up a fresh one this morning. I had a feeling I might have visitors." Bevlin led them in through the low doorway and into the warm and crowded kitchen. As Tawl walked past him, the wiseman squeezed his hand. "It's fitting that you came, Tawl. I am pleased to see you again." He gave Tawl an inquiring look. "Are you well? You look a little pale."

"I am fine, Bevlin. It is the boy who has taken a fever. He is from Rorn and not used to the cold weather." Tawl turned away from the old man; he did not welcome the scrutiny.

"So you are from Rorn, boy. Most interesting. And what is your name?"

"Nabber." The boy had lost some of his natural exuberance to sickness.

"Well, Nabber," said Bevlin, "I can see you are a little fevered, but no matter, I expect Tawl has mentioned the lacus to you?" The boy shook his head. "Well, the lacus will make you better; however, it may make you a little sleepy once you've taken it. So I'm going to give you a bite to eat first, a little broth and a slice or two of duck, and then I'll give you the lacus. You'll be feeling as right as rain in a few days." Bevlin made himself busy clearing scrolls from the table and dusting chairs. "Sit, sit, it is a poor host who keeps his guests standing."

They sat at the large wooden table. Nabber was gazing around with unabashed curiosity at the strange array of items that crowded the shelves and every other available area of space in the kitchen. "You've got a lot of stuff," he said admiringly.

"Yes, I have. I just wish I knew what they were all for." Bevlin poured some broth into little pots and handed them both one.

"I can tell you what that one's for." Nabber pointed to a strange-looking device on the wall.

"Can you, indeed? I'd be most interested in knowing." He broke a loaf into hefty chunks and handed them round.

"It's what the smirchers use to search for coins amidst the filth of the streets. That end bit there is to grab coins with—stops them from having to put their hands in the—" The boy caught himself in time. "Course it doesn't work all that well and a master smircher wouldn't be caught dead with such a thing." Nabber smiled with the joy of one imparting knowledge.

"My dear boy, I do believe you are right. Your visit is proving to be most valuable to me." Bevlin brought another curious-looking implement forward. "You wouldn't happen to know what this is, would you, boy?"

"Sorry, I can't help you there, friend."

"That's too bad, Nabber." The wiseman sighed. "I've been trying to figure out what it is for years now. A man in Leiss gave it to me once. Ever been to Leiss, boy?"

Tawl ate his meal in silence. He had no desire to join in the conversation between the wiseman and the boy. He kept an eye on Bevlin as he ate. Now that he had got here it didn't seem like such a good idea to tell him about Larn and the drunken ramblings of an old man. The wiseman did not look like someone whom he could trust.

Bevlin caught Tawl looking at him, and their eyes met for an instant. "Come on, Nabber," said Bevlin, "time to take the lacus, then off to bed." He ignored the boy's protests and ushered him out of the room. As he closed the door, he flashed Tawl the briefest of glances—it promised he would return soon and they would be able to talk in confidence.

Tawl was relieved when the door closed and he was alone. He found he did not want to talk to Bevlin and began to wonder why he had ever thought the man could help him.

Maybor was once more in the stables. He personally would have preferred the middens, but apparently Traff didn't have the stomach for them. On the ground next to him was a heavy wooden box, and in it were two hundred gold coins of standard size. A fortune by any man's counting and one which Maybor was greatly adverse to parting with. He was a rich man, but like most men of wealth there was a streak of tightfistedness in him and he hated to pay for anything.

Maybor was feeling decidedly worried about certain events at court. He'd heard from one of the guards that the queen had called Baralis to an audience this very morning, and he had the unsettling feeling the king's chancellor was up to no good. To confound things further he had actually seen his own son talking to the man. How could Kedrac possibly talk to a man who had so badly wronged his whole family?

Maybor had discreetly taken his son's steward aside and asked him about the nature of the conversation. The steward, his palms sufficiently greased with ten silvers, had told him that Baralis had merely wished Kedrac a good day and asked him if he were well. A further ten silvers had assured that he would learn of any further meetings between his son and Baralis.

He knew what the man was up to: Baralis was finding out how strong the bonds of family were between him and Kedrac. Maybor was not too concerned. Baralis would find out they were stronger than he hoped. His son might have fallen out with him, but family loyalty ran deeper than any petty quarrel—Baralis was sadly mistaken if he thought he could lure Kedrac to his side. The thought that the man had miscalculated served to reassure Maybor. There were things that Baralis, as a man without family, could never hope to appreciate—he would never know how it felt to be secure about the loyalty of any man. He had to rely upon hired hands, and Maybor knew just how easily their loyalties could be shifted—the two hundred gold pieces on the ground beside him was proof of that.

Traff approached, well muscled and broad, with an annoying smirk on his face. How he detested the man. The mercenary thought he had struck a hard bargain and it rankled Maybor to think it would be quite some time before Traff realized how wrong he was.

"Good day to you, Maybor." The man checked the stalls for spies. "I see you have brought me a little gift." His eyes lingered over the box.

"It is what you asked for, no more." Maybor had not missed Traff's pointed lack of respect—the man failed to call him lord.

"If you would be so kind as to open it. Nothing personal, you understand. In my line of business you learn it' best to check everything." Traff watched greedily as Maybor opened the box. "Everything looks to be in order. I won't in sult you by counting them." Maybor could not stop himself from snorting indignantly. The man had already insulted him by insisting that the box be opened in the first place.

"Before I release this money into your possession, I demand to hear what you know about my daughter."

"Yes, the lovely Melli." Traff spoke with an air of proprietorship. "Well, Baralis hasn't got her any longer. Spirited girl, she has escaped from under everyone's noses. Course she had the boy to help her. That little bastard killed half a dozen of my men." Maybor could not take all this in. He attempted to clarify it.

"So, Baralis was holding Melliandra?"

"Right. We picked her up in Duvitt and brought her back here. Kept her in Baralis' hideaway in the woods."

"Hideaway?" Maybor was determined to hide his amazement at Traff's story. He had always suspected that Baralis was trying to find his daughter, but to be told the truth of the matter turned him cold. There was only one reason why the man would want to capture Melliandra and that was to stop the proposed betrothal from going through. Maybor now knew without a doubt where the blame lay—Baralis had thwarted his ambitions and stopped him from becoming father-in-law to the future king.

"There's a tunnel leading to it from the castle—it's underground. The place gives me the creeps."

"How long ago did she escape?" Maybor could hardly believe that his daughter had been so near to the castle.

"Over a week ago now, the boy helped her to escape. We caught up with them in the woods a couple of days later, but that boy's a devil and they managed to get away. They could be anywhere by now. Baralis has sent another crew out looking for them . . . I wouldn't want to be in their shoes, I can tell you."

"Why aren't you with them?"

"I was injured in the woods. Besides, Baralis has always got a few other things up his sleeve that need taking care of nearer home."

"Who is this boy you speak of?"

"Jack's the name—he was a baker's boy at the castle. We

captured him just before we got your daughter, brung 'em both back we did."

"What interest does Baralis have in a baker's boy?"

"Me and my men wondered just the same thing, if you know what I mean. I know differently now, though—that boy is trouble. First of all he mangled the face of one of my men, and then in the forest . . ." Traff shook his head savagely.

"What happened in the forest?"

"All hell broke loose, that's what happened. That boy caused havoc, stirred up the devil he did. Lost good men that day. Baralis never even bothered to warn us the boy could be trouble, just let us charge right in." Traff's expression was grim.

"And this boy is with Melliandra now?" Maybor knew better than to ask for specifics of what went on in the forest. He'd caught the whiff of sorcery and he had no desire for a tasting.

"As far as I know."

"What condition was she in when you last saw her?"

"Well, she'd had that flogging." Traff was guarded.

"Did she come to any harm in the forest?" persisted Maybor.

"The boy never harmed her, if that's what you mean."

"Your men, did they harm her in any way?" Maybor was not about to let Traff off the hook. The mercenary looked down at the ground.

"She might have taken a shot to her arm. Nothing much a mere skimming, heal in no time it would."

Maybor wanted to kill the man on the spot. He felt his sword as a heavy presence against his leg. It would be so easy to draw it and hack the man's head off. He had to suppress the urge to kill. If he was ever to get the better of Baralis, he must play by Baralis' rules: rules of deception and cunning. He forced himself to keep a dispassionate demeanor. "So, if Baralis finds Melliandra again he will bring her back to this hideaway in the woods?"

Traff hesitated a moment before answering. "I can't say that he will."

"What d'you mean?" demanded Maybor.

"Baralis told the new crew to kill Melli and the boy as soon as they found them. Kill them and bury 'em, that's what he said."

"She has not been found yet?" Maybor was surprised at how calm his voice sounded.

"I know the new lot, a blind donkey could track better than them. I'm sure they won't have found her. Besides, Baralis ordered them back within a week. By my reckoning they haven't got much time left."

"What will Baralis do when his men return?"

"Send 'em out again. Most probably he'll do one of his little tricks and tell them where they will find Melli and the boy." Traff saw Maybor's puzzled expression. "Baralis has a few crafty moves up his sleeve—with birds and the like. I think he gets them to talk to him."

"Don't be ridiculous, man." By refusing to hear about sorcery, Maybor was stubbornly attempting to deny its existence. He changed the subject swiftly. "When Baralis sends the men out, you must arrange to go with them. I have no intention of letting my daughter be murdered in cold blood."

"I'm ahead of you there, friend," said Traff smugly. "I wouldn't want my betrothed to be buried in a shallow grave in the woods. No, it's my intention to go along with the crew, help them find Melli and the boy, and then whisk your daughter off to safety."

"Can you be sure of succeeding in such a venture?"

"I've seen what that boy can do when he's cornered. He'll create such chaos that no one will notice me slipping away with the girl."

Maybor did not think much of Traff's plan, but could not come up with a better one himself. He wanted to question Traff further—there was much he needed to learn about Baralis and his future plans. However, a stablehand and two grooms walked in and broke up their meeting. The mercenary quickly lifted the wooden box and, ignoring the curious stares of the grooms, made a quick exit.

Maybor made his way across the courtyard. His meeting with Traff had proven most illuminating. He was just beginning to comprehend the true depth of Baralis' scheming. There was far more at stake than he had imagined. Baralis had gone to great lengths to make sure Melliandra would not marry Prince Kylock. Perhaps, thought Maybor, he had a candidate of his own whom he would see marry the prince. It would certainly explain his eagerness to get Melliandra out of the picture.

Bevlin laid his hand gently upon the boy's forehead: his fever was high. Sleep and the lacus would help to bring it down. He had stayed with Nabber for over an hour before the boy had finally dozed off, partly to reassure the boy and partly to give himself enough time to arrange his thoughts before speaking with Tawl.

The knight had changed so much since his last visit five years back. Bevlin knew a lot of that change was his responsibility. He had sent Tawl on an almost impossible task, and that undertaking had served to shape the man he had become. He wondered if he had been right to do such a thing, to rob a young man of his youth and his optimism. He supposed it would have happened eventually: no man could live in such a world as theirs and remain unchanged by it. Nevertheless, the wiseman had to question his own judgment in setting one so inexperienced to such a thankless task.

When Tawl had ridden up to his door earlier that day, Bevlin had seen disillusion on the knight's face, and something more . . . distrust. He took a deep breath and made his way to the kitchen, where he found Tawl sitting at the table as he had left him over an hour ago. The knight shot him a questioning glance and the wiseman found some relief in the fact that he was obviously concerned about the condition of the boy.

"He is asleep. Borc willing, he will be a little better when he wakes. He may sleep through the whole day tomorrow and into the next night. The lacus gives itself time to work."

"He is a long way from home." Tawl spoke quietly.

"So are you, my friend," stated Bevlin simply. He came and sat opposite Tawl and poured them both a mug of ale. "I brew it myself and I admit it's not very good, but I find bad ale warms a man just the same as good, though it may leave

him with a worse hangover in the morning." Bevlin saw
Tawl smile politely at his jest, though the smile did not reach
his eyes. The wiseman tried to maintain eye contact with the
knight, but Tawl looked down, guarding his eyes. "So, you
have come from Rorn?"

"I have not found the boy, if that's what you mean."
Tawl spoke with unnecessary sharpness. "Though I suppose
you know that already."

"Do you want to give up the search? Just say and it will
be so."

"You tell me this too late, wiseman!" Tawl slammed
down his mug. "There is only one honorable way out for me
and you know it. I would rather cut off my own arm than
admit defeat."

Bevlin could well understand bitterness—he was a
knight and would bring shame upon himself if he did not
achieve what he set out to do, or die in the attempt. But there
was more than that. It was not difficult to see that Tawl lived
for his quest. Why then was he suddenly so bitter?"

"We are not all dealt a fair hand, Tawl."

"I was not dealt blindly, wiseman. The cards were
stacked against me." He looked at Bevlin then looked
quickly away.

"Where have your travels taken you?"

"To the far south, to the Drylands, to Chelss and Leiss
and Silbur," he said harshly. "Do you want me to go on?"

"You know of the trouble between Rorn and Valdis,
then?"

"I know that Rorn had banned knights from entering the
city." Tawl gazed into the fire.

"It has expelled them, too, and Marls has followed suit.
The archbishop of Rorn is stirring up antiknight sentiment
throughout the southeast. He is seeking to bring about a confrontation. He wants to break the power of Valdis and the
knighthood."

"What has he against Valdis?" Tawl spoke with genuine
interest for the first time.

"Tavalisk is the first man in the south to realize that
dangerous forces are coming together in the north. Tyren has

placed himself as an ally to Bren, and Bren is about to join with the Four Kingdoms.

"Marod's prophecy is coming to pass: *When two houses join in wedlock and wealth.* The empire which he predicted could encompass the Known Lands. Those who shape will also corrupt. More than ever, Tawl, I need you to find the boy."

"I will find him, Bevlin."

"Yes, I believe you will. There is a link between you, and it is your destiny to help him fulfill his." As he spoke, Bevlin felt the disturbing ring of prophecy in his voice.

To break the spell he stood up and poured himself a second mug of ale. He drained the cup dry. With his heart still racing from the shock of foretelling, Bevlin made an attempt to lighten the mood of the conversation. "Tavalisk is at heart a mischief-maker. He is not happy unless he is at the center of events, scheming purely for the love of it."

"Why do *you* scheme, wiseman?" Tawl seemed to regret his words and he said with a sigh, "I am sorry, Bevlin. I don't know what has gotten into me. I looked forward to seeing you and now that I am here I find myself saying things that I don't mean." He rubbed his eyes tiredly. Bevlin was glad to hear Tawl speak more kindly.

"Where will you head to next?" he asked. "Bren, Annis Lairston?" Tawl's eye became hooded and Bevlin knew to expect a lie.

"Lairston. I'm heading further north."

"The air is bitingly cold so near to the northern ranges." Bevlin realized Tawl was not listening to him anymore; the knight had lost his concentration to the fire. He stared deep within the flames, and the wiseman wondered what torment he saw there. "Tawl," he said gently, placing his hand on the knight's arm. "Go to bed. You can sleep in my room—it is dry and warm."

Tawl looked up at him, and for the briefest moment Bevlin saw something in his eyes, something he could not name, but familiar nonetheless. The knight cast his eyes downward, almost in shame. "I am tired, Bevlin. I have ridden hard all day."

"Maybe a touch of the lacus would help you. You have

been long in the south yourself." Bevlin wanted to reach out and help him; he could tell the knight was in some kind of anguish. He instinctively knew that any offer of help would be unwelcome.

"No, save the lacus for those who need it. I am not suffering from anything a good night's rest won't cure." Tawl stood up. "So, Bevlin, how about showing me to my room?"

The wiseman led him to his room. He pulled the bedclothes back and removed the warming pan, took the knight's pack and laid it on the chest. Bevlin then went to bid Tawl good night. As he did so, Tawl lowered his head and the wiseman laid a kiss upon his brow. "Sleep well, friend," he said as he left the room.

Twenty-eight

*H*e awoke with the taste of salt on his lips. He tried to recapture the fleeting images of his dream: he remembered the sea, cold and unforgiving, the color of slate. He sat up and was disappointed to feel the sound earth beneath his feet. He walked to the window and opened the wooden shutter. There was solace to be found in the sky; it was not unlike the sea. They bore the same color and neither could be bound by man. Earth was the weak link; it allowed itself to be divided and possessed and consumed.

The pale moon lowered as he watched. It was time to move on, time to pay his debt.

With the grace of a ghost he moved across the room. He dressed with great care . . . it seemed fitting. He pulled on his soft leather shoes and buckled his hard leather belt.

He wanted to look upon himself, but there was no mirror. With anxious hands he felt for what he needed. His fingers enclosed the cool metal, warming. He was ready. The prospect of unburdening was a salve upon his heart; it lured him forth with promises of peace.

The door opened noiselessly—he knew it would. He slipped into the room. The lazy fire cast him a long shadow. He moved forward discovering his perspective, deciding his course.

The man was there as he expected, lost in sleep, snoring

with gentle determination. The knife was warm now; it grew large in his hand, shifting its position. He drew near. He felt the thrill of anticipation and the pain of regret. He watched the man, unafraid he might wake. He was old and not unready for death.

He raised the knife, a beautiful move, well mimicked by his shadow. He paused for a single instant and then brought it down. Cleave of bone and through to the heart. The man's eyes opened—confusion and then understanding—they closed.

He freed the knife and dark blood flowed forth. He raised it once more and thrust again. Again and again. Blood spattered his face and he welcomed its cooling touch.

He was finished; the man moved no more. His debt was paid.

With great care he cleaned his knife, spitting to bring off the last of the blood. He returned to his room and undressed. He stood naked in the moonlight, receiving benediction. He slipped between the smooth sheets and slept the sleep of the innocent.

"No, Bodger, there's only one cure for the ghones and it ain't soaking your privates in boiling water."

"Master Frallit swears it's the only way, Grift."

"Well, there's little doubt that Master Frallit has need of cure, Bodger. I'm pretty sure he hasn't tried boiling his privates, though. If he had we'd be calling him Mistress Frallit by now."

"So what's the proper cure then, Grift?"

"The only way for a man to rid himself of the ghones is for him to rub his privates with virgin's water ever'day for a week."

"Virgin's water, Grift?"

"Aye, Bodger, of course the difficult bit is actually finding a virgin."

"I would have thought getting the virgin to piss for you would be more difficult, Grift." Bodger smiled ruefully at his companion and the two men drank heartily. Once they had finished supping, they leaned back against the wall, both belching loudly.

"Lord Maybor and Lord Baralis are both trying to double-cross each other, eh, Grift?"

"What d'you mean, Bodger?"

"Well, Lord Maybor's talking to Baralis' mercenary and Lord Baralis is talking to Maybor's son."

"I wouldn't care to place bets on which side's going to win, Bodger."

"I'd bet on Baralis, myself, Grift."

"I think you're right, Bodger. I'd bet on Baralis, too."

"Course there's something big going to go down in the next few days, Grift."

"Why d'you say that, Bodger?"

"Well, I was passing the storerooms this morning, you know the ones where they keep all the regalia, and the servants were bringing out the carpets and dusting down banners."

"Sounds like someone is planning a ceremony, Bodger."

"Let's hope it's a celebration, Grift. I've a yearning for some special brew."

"I wouldn't build my hopes up if I were you, Bodger. I would take nothing short of a royal marriage to make that old tightpurse, Willock, break open a barrel."

Baralis awoke with a feeling of great contentment. His audience with the queen yesterday had gone extremely well. Oh, she had played it cool, she was good at that, but she could not hide the interest in her eyes—and when he gave her the portrait there was no mistaking her attraction. He had, of course, left it with her; it was a far better persuader than he.

Baralis knew, however, that the portrait would not be inducement enough. The queen was fearful of the ambition of the duke of Bren—everyone in the north was. This was her chance to neutralize the threat by means of a judicious alliance. And, perhaps more importantly than anything else, the queen wanted power: for herself, her son and her descen dants. A union with Bren would bring such power and she would see herself participating in its wielding—she was an ambitious woman, and that fact would seal her fate.

Yesterday had indeed been most fruitful. After he left the queen's chamber, he had the good fortune to run into Maybor's son, the arrogant and conceited Kedrac. Baralis had simply offered his greetings and Kedrac had offered his back. It was a start, no more, but it would do for now. Families were sensitive and required delicate handling.

Baralis warmed himself some holk and sat and drank it by the fire. Sometimes he thought that the heat of the cup in his hands did more than the actual liquid it contained. Whichever it was it eased the pain a little, making it more bearable. He thought of his mother for the first time in years. She would always warm him some holk whenever he had a chill or an ache, and sometimes for no more reason than it was cold outside and she wanted to show her love.

Baralis was disturbed from his memories by the appearance of Crope. "What is it, man?" He spoke harshly, annoyed at the interruption.

"My lord, the queen's steward has called you to a meeting."

"Why would the queen's steward want to meet with me?"

"No, master, it's the queen who wants to meet with you."

"An audience! Why didn't you say so in the first place, you fool?" Baralis' mind raced forward—could she possibly have made her decision so quickly? "Bring me my finest robe, Crope." He thought for a moment. "And fetch me my chancellor's chain—I would look the part on this auspicious day."

Crope dashed off and Baralis stood up and went over to the window. He unlatched the shutters and looked out. Cold air blasted his face: a heavy snow had fallen in the night and the earth was pristine and white. A glorious day. His servant came forth and placed the robe and chain upon the bed. Baralis took one last mouthful of the now cool holk and then readied himself for the queen.

Minutes later he made his way to the royal apartments.

The armed guards let him pass and he fancied he saw greater respect in their faces than before. He was surprised to find the queen ready to greet him; he had thought she would have made him wait as she had the day before.

"Good day, Lord Baralis." She inclined her head slightly. "I see you have come in your official capacity today." She indicated his heavy chain.

"I hope to honor Your Highness with this mark of my respect." He bowed once more, emphasizing the compliment. He was pleased to note the queen had taken similar care with her appearance: her gown was edged in ermine and a golden diadem sparkled in her hair.

"I have called you here to inform you of my decision concerning the proposed betrothal of my son Prince Kylock and Catherine of Bren." She favored him with a cold but tantalizing smile.

"I am pleased that Your Highness has made such a fast decision." Baralis resisted the urge to bow once more; it wouldn't do to appear too eager.

"Mistake me not, Lord Baralis, I have the will and the means to make any decision I choose." It was a simple statement of her power, and he acknowledged it with the slightest of nods. The queen, satisfied that her meaning had been understood, continued, "I have thought long on the matter we discussed, and now that I have come to my decision, I see no reason that you should wait upon its telling."

"As Your Highness wishes."

"Lord Baralis, I must admit there was much merit in your words and I am not a person to let past animosities blur my judgment." She paused taking a deep breath. "I can see that a joining with Bren would be most beneficial to my son's future and that of the Four Kingdoms, and that understanding has laid the basis for my decision." She positioned herself by the light of the window, knowing it would serve to adorn her. She drew herself up to her full height, her diadem glittered brilliantly. "I will sanction the betrothal of Kylock and Catherine of Bren." She looked Baralis full in the face. "Make your arrangements, Chancellor."

"Your Highness has made a wise decision." He w

careful to keep a note of humility in his voice—now was not the time for self-congratulation.

"I would move on this matter with great alacrity. I daresay the duke of Bren has been long awaiting." She gave Baralis a knowing look.

"He is most anxious for this match, Your Highness."

"Then I would keep him waiting no longer. An envoy must be sent to Bren."

"Your Highness will not go herself?"

"No, my place is here with the king. My son will also stay here until the match is finalized. I will not have him risk humiliation by wooing the girl before the matter is settled. I will send him to Bren only when it is official." Baralis could not help but admire the queen's caution, even as he knew there was no cause for it.

"I hope that I might be able to serve Your Highness in the capacity of envoy." Baralis noticed a trace of cunning on the face of the queen.

"I will require two envoys, Lord Baralis. One to represent Prince Kylock and his interest as heir, and one to represent the Crown." She smiled graciously. "You will be Prince Kylock's envoy. I have great faith in your abilities to strike a most favorable contract for my son."

"And the second envoy? Who will represent the Crown?" Baralis was beginning to feel a little nervous; it should be *he*, king's chancellor, who represented the Crown.

"I have not made my decision as to that particular appointment yet. I will, of course, advise you in due time."

"As Your Highness wishes." He was careful not to let his misgivings show. "How soon should I move on this matter?"

"As soon as possible. It will take many weeks to travel Bren in this inclement weather. It would be best if we uld send the delegation as soon as it is arranged. Within n days."

"Ten days will be sufficient." Baralis was pleased the een wanted to move quickly.

"There will be much to arrange, Lord Baralis. You will ed an armed escort, at least five score of men. There will gifts to be sent and contracts to be drawn up."

"I will dispatch a letter this day informing the duke of your decision and my imminent arrival."

"There is no need, Lord Baralis." The queen smiled slyly. "I have already done so."

"Your Highness is indeed a woman given to fast action." Baralis could not keep the edge of annoyance from his voice. She had deliberately bypassed him.

"There is little point in keeping this matter secret. Things like this have a way of slipping out. It will be all over the castle before the day is through, so I have decided to make an official announcement. I will gather the court together later this day and tell them of my plans." The queen said the word *my* with much relish. "I will, of course, stress the fact that this matter has not been finalized and can only be celebrated once the official contracts have been signed."

"Very well, Your Highness." Baralis had to concede what the queen said was true, much as he would have preferred to keep the betrothal secret.

"Now, I am sure you have business to attend to, so I will grant you leave to do so. I will call you to me in the next couple of days—we must discuss certain stipulations that will require in the betrothal contract. Good day, Lord Baralis. I trust you will send the next batch of medicine promptly." She dismissed him with little ceremony, merely turn of the cheek.

Baralis left and walked back to his chambers. He was stunned by how quickly the queen had reached her decision. What cause had she for such urgency? he wondered. Or did she do it merely to baffle and confound him? He would not put it past her.

He was not entirely pleased with the turn events had taken. The queen was trying to distance him from his own plans. She would not succeed, though. He was not about to give up his position in the forefront now that those plans had come to fruition. Now more than ever he needed to move events in his favor, guide them to his intended conclusions.

Tavalisk was feeling a little under the weather. His cook had prepared the most tempting of delicacies for him, but found he had no appetite for them. The smell of highly spiced offal assailed his nostrils and served only to make him feel bilious. He pushed the plate aside and his gimlet-eyed cat jumped onto the table and began picking at the meat.

There had been yet another dull ceremony to perform earlier that morning. It was the Day of Forgiving and tradition dictated that he, as archbishop, should absolve twelve men of their sins. The twelve men were all convicted criminals who were given pardon by the first minister. However, the men were not considered completely free from their crimes until the archbishop had given them God's grace and granted absolution.

To this end, Tavalisk had to let all twelve men kiss his ring and then lay his hand upon their foreheads. The criminals were an unsavory, decidedly unclean bunch, and in Tavalisk's opinion not one of them deserved to go free. He went through with the ceremony nonetheless, and even managed to add a certain dramatic flourish to the proceedings by squeezing a few salty tears from his eye—the gathered crowd had appreciated that: their beloved archbishop reduced to tears by the act of forgiveness. What benevolence, they would say, what humanity, what humility!

The people of Rorn loved him, he knew, but it never hurt to tip the balance in one's favor by the use of a little stagecraft now and then. The first minister, on the other hand, had handled the proceeding with a decided lack of interest. He had picked a singularly dreary group of criminals—pickpockets, thieves, and swindlers—and the crowds had been disappointed. They would have preferred famous murderers, dashing pirates, and brazen madams; the first minister had no sense of the dramatic.

Tavalisk shooed the cat away from the offal and it hissed viciously at him. He went to kick the creature, but it leapt out of the way and he missed. He heard a noise behind him and was annoyed to see that Gamil had entered. "I did not hear you knock."

"My apologies, Your Eminence. The door was open and I presumed—"

"It is not your place to presume, Gamil," interrupted

Tavalisk. "You must always knock before entering my private apartments, is that clear?"

"Quite clear, Your Eminence."

"Good. Would you care for any offal?"

"No, thank you, Your Eminence. I have already eaten."

Tavalisk poured himself a glass of wine in the hope that it would settle his stomach. He noticed his aide was reading the title of the book on his desk. "Marod is such a dreary scholar," he said with an illustrating yawn. "Some foolish woman gave me it as a gift for blessing her spinning wheel." The archbishop wasn't ready to let Gamil in on his suspicions about Marod's prophecies. "So, what news do you bring me this day?"

"Toolay has decided to ban the knights. It would seem that the last spate of violent protest was just too much for the authorities."

"Good, I knew Toolay would follow our example."

"Nine knights were slain on the streets of Marls last week. They were pulled from hiding and dragged into the street. They were hacked to death by the crowd. They used anything they could lay their hands on: blades, knives, shears."

"How unpleasant. I suppose this incident will speed the sending of the dreaded Letter of Condemnation." Tavalisk shuddered with mock fright.

"I think it has upset many people, Your Eminence."

"Marls was ever a foolish city. No matter, as long as no one lays the blame at our door." Tavalisk yawned widely. "Is there anything else?"

"I do have some news Your Eminence might be interested in."

"What is that, Gamil?"

"A certain Lord Cravin entered the city last night."

"And who pray tell is he?" Tavalisk poured honey into his wine.

"Lord Cravin is a very powerful man in Bren."

"Is he really?" The archbishop licked his fingers clean of honey. "What's he doing in Rorn?"

"Trade, I think. He has many business interests in the south."

"How very interesting. I think I would like to meet this man. I am looking to make the acquaintance of someone from the fine city of Bren."

"I will arrange a meeting, Your Eminence."

"Good. Any news on our knight?"

"I think he must be nearing Bevlin's home by now, Your Eminence."

"Hmm. The knight is up to something. People like the Old Man and Bevlin don't deal with trivialities. I must give the matter some deliberation. I can't help thinking that it's all connected somehow."

"What's all connected?"

"Our knight and his brethren, Bevlin, Baralis—" the archbishop raised his arms expansively "—everyone."

"It is the first sign of derangement, Your Eminence, when one begins to see plots all around one."

"Gamil, you will never realize the dangers and responsibilities that accompany the bearing of great power. There *are* plots all around, and the fact that I'm aware of them is a measure of my astuteness." The archbishop drained his cup of honeyed wine. "You may go now, Gamil. I am not feeling too well and would like to be left alone. I think I caught something from those damned criminals this morning."

"How very unfortunate."

Tavalisk looked up, detecting a note of sarcasm in his aide's voice, but Gamil had already turned his back and was walking from the room. The archbishop considered calling him back, and then, as his stomach began to rumble unpleasantly, decided against it. There would be other days to pay the man back for his impertinence.

Maybor was chilled to the bone. He had called another meeting with Traff and the man was late. Snow lay thick on the ground and he had to admit he'd never seen the middens looking so good. He drew his cloak close and stamped his feet to keep warm. He was beginning to wonder if the mercenary had just taken the money and run when he came into sight. Traff did not look very pleased.

"You picked a foul day to be outside." Traff was ill-dressed for the cold, wearing the thinnest of cloaks.

"The stables are too risky. I will not meet there again."

"What d'you want? I thought we'd agreed on the plan yesterday."

"Yesterday we agreed what to do about my daughter. That is only part of what concerns me." Maybor was short-tempered.

"I've already told you I won't act as your assassin as far as Baralis is concerned."

"You have made that very clear. I need information from you. I didn't pay you two hundred golds just so you could marry my daughter."

"I gave you information," snapped Traff.

"You told me about what Baralis *has* done. I want to know what he is *planning* to do. He is up to more than tracking down Melliandra. He has schemes afoot and I would know of them."

"I've told you all I know. Baralis is not the sort to take hired hands into his confidence."

"Do not lie to me. You know more. Need I remind you that Baralis is not a man to take treachery lightly. Who knows what he would do if he found out one of his men had been meeting with his enemy." Maybor was pleased to note a change in Traff's expression. The man obviously had good reason to be scared of Baralis.

"Look, I said I don't know what he's up to." Traff hesitated. "But I have seen some things you might be interested in."

"Go on."

"Well, I know he's been sending letters to Bren, to the duke there. I saw him give one to a messenger only last week."

"Anything else?" Maybor wondered what business Baralis could have with the duke of Bren.

"Well, I think he's planning a journey." Traff's nose was running unpleasantly and he wiped it on the corner of his cloak.

"Why d'you say that?"

"Well, just before noon this morning, I heard him telling Crope to get things ready for a little trip."

"Where can he be going? He has no lands to speak of."

"I can't say, but it must be somewhere important to make a man travel in this weather." Traff had a point; no sane man would journey with snow on the ground and more threatening to come.

"I want to be told the moment you know anything further." Maybor decided to let the mercenary go; it was obvious he was going to get no more information out of him. He was beginning to regret the deal he had struck. The man was not nearly as useful as he hoped. There was, however, some consolation to be found in the fact that Traff would not be around to collect on the second half of the payment.

Maybor waited until Traff was out of sight and then made his way back to the castle. As he walked across the grounds he was interested to see activity in the great hall: servants seemed to be preparing it for some event. As he drew close he noticed the Royal Guard were in their ceremonial uniforms, musicians were carrying their instruments into the hall, and a small crowd had gathered. Maybor puzzled over the occasion. He had not been aware of any official ceremony. He caught the arm of a servant girl. "What is going on here?"

"I'm not sure, sir. The queen ordered us to make it ready. She has some kind of announcement to make."

"When will this happen?" Maybor considered the girl for a moment. She was not unattractive, though her teeth were a little crooked. She was pleasingly awestruck at being addressed by him.

"Soon, I think, sir. The steward told us to make haste." The girl seemed torn between dashing off and wanting to stay.

"What is your name, girl?" She would be worth a bedding, nothing more.

"Bonnie, sir."

"Well, Bonnie, why don't you come to my chambers after dark tonight? I am a lonely man in need of company." The girl was suitably flattered. She nodded coquettishly and then ran off to do her duties.

Maybor strolled toward the hall. He would ensure himself a good place to hear whatever the queen had to announce.

He watched as the hall was prepared for ceremony: banners were unfurled and hung, carpet was rolled out, candles were lit, and wood was polished to a fine gloss. Before long other courtiers started to arrive; they were dressed in their finest clothes, the rustle of silk competing with the murmur of voices. They split off into small groups and spoke in hushed tones about the queen's intent. He spotted Baralis entering the hall. Something flashed at his throat and Maybor realized the man was wearing his chain of office. *What mischief is this?* he wondered.

Finally the horns sounded and the herald proclaimed the entrance of the queen. The crowd hushed and watched as the queen made her way through the hall. She was dressed finely in crimson silk, a golden diadem upon her head. Maybor caught her eye and she sent him a look he did not understand. Prince Kylock followed his mother. The boy was dark and handsome, dressed in raven black.

The horns quieted and the queen turned to face the gathered nobles. She stood and waited, letting the tension of the crowd grow. The room was silent. The voice of the queen rang out. "I have brought you here today to share my good news." She paused for dramatic effect. "King Lesketh and I have made plans to arrange the betrothal of our son, Prince Kylock." The crowd murmured with anticipation. Maybor could hardly believe what he was hearing. Betrothal so soon after his daughter had been rejected?

The queen continued: "We have arranged a historic match for our son, one that will serve to increase the prestige of our beloved country. Prince Kylock will wed Catherine of Bren." The crowd erupted in excitement, preventing the queen from speaking any further.

Bren, thought Maybor. The second time that day he'd heard its name. There was not coincidence; Baralis was behind this. With the noise of the crowd sounding in his ear, Maybor realized the extent of Baralis' cunning. It had all been for this—the attempted poisonings, abducting Melliadra—all so Kylock would marry his choice for bride. Baral had wasted little time moving in on the queen. What seductive words had he used to persuade her to agree to this . . . or had he blackmailed her?

The queen was speaking again, but Maybor was not listening. What a fool he had been; he'd let Baralis steal the jewel of kingship from under his very nose. It should have been his daughter who was proclaimed this day as bride, *he* who stood poised to take his place as father to king and country. He had lost everything.

He thought the queen owed him more than this. It was a slap in his face for her to accede to Baralis' choice. She had not even kept her promise to inform him first—he was hearing it along with the court and the servants.

Why Bren? he wondered. Surely it was madness to join with a power as mighty as Bren. The Four Kingdoms would undoubtedly come off worse in any alliance with that dukedom, or did Baralis think himself clever enough to manipulate their politics as well?

Maybor shifted his concentration back to the queen: "And finally I would like to announce that Prince Kylock's envoy to the court of Bren will be King's Chancellor, Lord Baralis." Maybor flinched at her words. Was there no escape from the man?

The queen and Prince Kylock withdrew to great cheering from the crowd. Maybor doubted how genuine the acclaim was. As the queen passed by, she put her arm out to him. "Tomorrow in my chambers," she whispered softly, and then was gone.

Twenty-nine

Tawl awoke refreshed—sunlight shone down upon his face. The shutters were ajar; he could not remember opening them. The room was freezing and he jumped out of bed to shut them. He stole a quick look outside. It was a day of rare beauty: the sun shone from a bright blue sky and dazzled the resting snow.

He felt strangely at peace. It had been the right thing to do—visit Bevlin. He felt as if a great burden had been lifted from his shoulders. The days which had stretched out bleakly before him now seemed to offer hope and promise. Tawl felt full of confidence, all things seemed possible—he would find the boy.

He remembered, a little guiltily, his lie to the wiseman. Today he would tell the truth about where he was heading and why. Larn seemed to have lost the power to intimidate him. It would be good to tell Bevlin about his trip there, and maybe together they could come up with a way to stop the atrocities that occurred on the island.

Tawl lathered up his soap stone and shaved. There was no mirror so he trusted to the feel of his hands. Once finished he splashed his face with water and laughed at the shock of its coldness. He went to his pack and picked out his new tunic to wear. He would honor his host by wearing his best.

It was still quite early. If he were lucky he could snea

quietly into the kitchen and make breakfast before Bevlin and the boy were awake—he had a vivid memory of the wiseman's cooking and decided it was best if he prepared the food the remaining time they were there. Besides, he fancied something a little more appetizing than greased duck.

Tawl opened the door and winced at the loud creak it made—so much for his plan of a surprise breakfast. He walked into the kitchen. Bevlin was not up. With disappointment, he realized the fire was out and would have to be lit anew before any cooking could take place. There was a stack of firewood in the corner of the room. As he made his way over to it he saw something out of the corner of his eye. He turned and looked.

Blood: dark and congealed. Tawl grew very still. Bevlin lay on the wooden bench, his robes stained with blood. Tawl forced himself forward, dread surging within him. He laid his hands on the wiseman: he was cold and stiff. Long dead. *No,* mouthed Tawl. *No.*

The scent of blood was heavy in the air. He gathered the dead man in his arms and drew him to his chest, desperately trying to warm the cold flesh. Bevlin was so light, so frail. Tawl hugged the wiseman's body close like a baby and rocked him back and forth. Tears coursed down his cheeks and onto the wiseman's back. *No, No, No,* he murmured his body racked with sobs. Tawl knew only one thing: *he had done this.* It was a certainty that suffered no questioning. His demons dragged him down into oblivion, the weight of his guilt speeding the descent.

It was a beautiful day in the marshlands. The rushes were green and in season and butterflies danced in the air. Tawl was glad to be coming home. Three years he'd been gone. Three years and two circles. His arm still throbbed from the branding. He knew it was foolish not to bandage the wound, but pride wouldn't allow it. He wanted everyone to know he was a knight of Valdis, newly honored with the second circle.

Soon he would go to the far south in search of treasures. If he were lucky, he'd find gold. If he were blessed, he'd find

merit in the eyes of God. The future was his and he was
eager to be started.

His horse topped a rise and he saw his old village ahead
of him. Excitement not anticipated stirred within his blood:
he was coming home. Nothing had changed: old Hawker's
barn was still threatening to collapse, the village green was
unkempt as ever. Boys continued to hang around the edge of
the village, looking for a fight or a girl.

Tawl spurred his horse forward, women turned to look
at him—not many people had horses in the marshes. He acknowledged their glances with a gracious incline of his
head—just like he'd been taught at Valdis. His fine cloak
drew glances and the villagers could see their reflections in
the shine of his boots. No one seemed particularly friendly.
Perhaps they didn't recognize him.

Picking a careful path through the bog, he made his way
home. His heart was light with joy. He had such presents for
his sisters: a dress of silk for Sarah and a bracelet of beads
for Anna. For the youngest there was a toy boat that actually
sailed. He could imagine their faces. There would be surprise
then delight. A hundred sweet kisses would be his. Tawl
smiled, suddenly feeling a tightness in his throat—he'd been
away too long.

Strange, the lay of the land seemed different. The cottage should be in view by now. Tawl galloped forward, mud
splashing on his boots. Something black caught his eye. He
pulled at the reins. The ground was burnt. There were the
charred remains of rafters and walls. A stone fireplace was
all that was left standing.

Tawl felt his stomach churn with horror. It was his cottage. The remains looked long burnt. He turned the horse and
raced back into the village. He stopped the first woman he
saw. "What happened to the cottage by the bog?"

The woman patted her lips, a sign of warding in the
marshlands. "Burned to the ground it did. The blaze took
three of them. Poor mites, all alone."

Tawl's world shifted out of focus. He wrapped the rein
around his fist. "Who died?"

The woman looked at his hands—the strain of the
leather had drawn blood. "You all right, young man?"

"Who died?"

"Two sisters, and a young'un," said the woman. "Beautiful girls they were. The eldest brother deserted them, left them to fend for themselves." She gave Tawl a hard look. "You're him, ain't you? Same golden hair." She shook her head sadly.

Tawl's throat was so tight he could barely speak. "I left them with their father," he said quietly, more to himself than the woman.

"Oh, that good-for-nothing scoundrel. He hung around town for a couple of weeks after you left. Then he was off, back to Lanholt. Never seen him since." The woman held a hand out to Tawl. "Nay, lad, don't take on. I'm sorry I spoke sharply."

"How did it happen?"

"Nobody's quite sure, but the magistrate thought it was caused by one of the girls, probably the youngest, putting a skin filled with goose fat on the fire. Seems they had no money for fuel and had taken to burning whatever they could find for heat. Course the thing flared up on them." The woman motioned to Tawl's hands. The blood now dripped over the horse. "Put the reins down, lad."

"When did it happen?" His voice was barely a whisper.

"Nearly three years back now, only a month or two after you left. I remember now, you ran off to be a knight."

Nearly three years back! All the time he'd been at Valdis, imagining his sisters were safe in the marshes, they'd been dead. The pain was unbearable: Sara and Anna dead. And for what? Two circles, one newly branded.

He looked at his circles. Only hours before they were everything to him. Now, before his eyes, they turned into marks of shame. Their price was the lives of his sisters.

Tawl unsheathed his sword. The woman made a second warding gesture and quickly moved away. Handling the sword in his left hand, he raised it high above his shoulders. Tears stung at his eyes. With one swift gesture he brought the blade down upon his arm—it sliced through both circles. The pain felt right. It was his and he would bear it. Throwing the sword as far as he could, he took up the reins and rode like a demon into the night.

*　*　*

Maybor awoke and felt the warmth of a body next to his. The servant girl Bonnie. She was fast asleep and looked better for it, lips firmly closed over her crooked teeth. He found he had little appetite for lovemaking and shook the girl awake. "Be off, girl, and quick about it." She looked startled but obeyed his orders, hurriedly pulling her clothes on. Maybor, who normally liked to watch a woman dress, turned away with disinterest. When she had finished dressing, the girl coughed to get his attention, undoubtedly wanting some trinket or the promise of a further assignation. Maybor had no desire to see her again; she had been witness to his lack of performance and was therefore to be despised. He threw her a gold coin and watched with distaste as she scrambled eagerly for it.

He stood up and went to his mirror, as he did most mornings since Winter's Eve. He checked the skin on his face: the sores had nearly disappeared now and only a slight redness remained. Although the outward signs of the poisoning had all but gone, Maybor knew his throat and lungs would never fully recover. He wheezed now when he breathed—an unpleasant sound, like an old man.

Crandle came into the bedchamber bearing his breakfast: warm buttered rolls and smoked herring. It was his favorite and he judged his servant had brought it as a small act of consolation: Crandle had been aware of his plans to betroth Melliandra to Prince Kylock. Maybor was glad that his intentions for the most part had remained secret—it would have caused him great humiliation if all the court had known about his failed attempt to marry his daughter to the heir.

"Her Highness has sent word for you to be in her chambers within the hour, my lord."

"Very good." The queen appeared most eager to see him; it was barely after sunup. He knew what she would try and do: she would be charming, maybe even flirt a little, asking how comfortable he found his new bed, and then she would implore him to remain loyal and support her. Maybor squashed a herring against the bread, releasing its smoky aroma. She would find him no doting lackey. He had no intention of guaranteeing his support. Let the woman fret and worry, he would no longer be at her beck and call. "Cran-dle," he cried, "bring me more herring and fill me a bath."

"But, my lord, there isn't any time. The queen awaits."

"Then she will have to wait a little longer." Maybor's tone brooked no further argument and the servant dashed off obediently.

Sometime later, when the lord was well fed and washed, he made his unhurried way to the queen's chamber. He had taken great care with his appearance—the day before Baralis had worn his chancellor's chain, Maybor had no such sign of office, but he did have the most fabulous collection of gold and jewels in the kingdoms. He wore a golden torc around his neck with two matching sapphires at each end, huge stones the color of midnight. There was no mistaking their value: one such stone would be worth great riches, but two, perfectly matched, was such a rarity as to set their value beyond guessing. It was well known that the queen loved sapphires more than any other stone, and they would not go unnoticed.

"Lord Maybor, I am pleased that you could come." She held out her hand to be kissed with no sign of annoyance at being kept waiting. He took her hand but failed to bring it to his lips. Their eyes met and the queen was the first to look away. She walked a short distance from him and then spoke again. "I'm sure you were a little disappointed at hearing my announcement yesterday." She waited, giving him a chance to deny the charge. Maybor did not speak and she was forced to continue. "I am sorry that you heard of the betrothal in such a public manner."

"I believe you promised me I would be the first to know." There was accusation in his voice.

"You are right, I did," she demurred. "I can only say in my defense that events have moved swiftly."

"You certainly wasted no time finding a replacement for my daughter." He cared little if he sounded bitter. There was nothing to be gained by courtly manners now.

"Lord Maybor, I think you forget that your own daughter brought this misfortune down upon you. If she had not taken it upon herself to run away, then matters would be looking very different for both of us today."

"It was Lord Baralis' idea, was it not," said Maybor, deliberately ignoring her words, "to betroth Kylock to Catherine of Bren?" The queen looked down at her hands; it was all the answer he needed. "Tell me, is he forcing you into this?"

"No, Lord Maybor." The queen spoke with harsh dignity. "Lord Baralis may have suggested it, but it is my decision. No one forced my hand."

Maybor did not doubt the queen *thought* she spoke the truth, but he knew Baralis had a way of compelling people to do what he wanted by making them believe it was best for them. What insidious words of persuasion had he whispered in her ear?

"I did not call you here for you to question my decision, Lord Maybor," reprimanded the queen mildly.

Maybor had little desire to mince words. "What did you bring me here for? To secure my allegiance? My support? Maybe to try and buy them—with another jeweled bed, perhaps?"

"Lord Maybor, I undertand your acrimony, but I think it best if you hear me out before making accusations." She looked at him levelly. "You were there when I announced that Baralis was to be envoy for Kylock in Bren." Maybor nodded and she continued. "I want you to be the second envoy. The Crown's envoy, representing myself and the king. I want you to travel to Bren and oversee the arrangements for the betrothal. I need not tell you I have little trust in Baralis. I would feel happier knowing that you were keeping an eye on him." The queen paused, allowing Maybor to take stock of the offer. He was careful to show no emotion. "Of course, as Crown's envoy your position in Bren would be superior to Lord Baralis'." A tiny smile graced the queen's pale lips.

This was certainly unexpected, thought Maybor. The queen was turning out to be a most ingenious woman. In one simple offer she was seeking to retain his loyalty, monito Baralis, and very probably have Baralis monitor *him*. It wa tempting, though; to go to Bren, to be at the forefront of suc a historic event and at the same time be a source of provoca tion and annoyance to Baralis—the man would detest hi being in Bren and loathe his superior rank.

The queen took his silence for misgiving. "Lord Maybor, I must stress the fact that I cannot let you represent the Crown in Bren unless you can assure me that you will not allow personal enmity to cloud your judgment. I am most anxious for this match to go through and will tolerate no attempts at interference."

"Your Highness does me great honor with this proposal." Maybor spoke plaintively, hoping to ease the queen's doubts.

"What do you say then, Maybor?" She dropped his title in an attempt at rakishness.

"I will be pleased to serve as Crown's Envoy in Bren." He bowed slightly and the queen rushed over and kissed him affectionately on his cheek.

"Good. I am glad you agreed." There was unmistakable relief on the queen's face; she had successfully brought him back into the fold. "Here," she said, handing him a small object. "Look upon the future queen of the Four Kingdoms." He took it from her. It was a miniature portrait showing a picture of a golden-haired girl. She was undeniably beautiful, but a little insipid when compared to his own daughter.

He could not bring himself to praise the girl. "When do we set off for Bren?" he asked, handing the portrait back.

"Within ten days. Baralis has already started making the arrangments."

"It will be a hard journey. The weather is bad and there's the Halcus to attend to." Maybor's mind was already racing ahead. He would have the queen agree to allow him to take some of his own men with him. He would feel safer at night knowing loyal men were around him.

"You will have an escort of five score Royal Guard."

"I would feel happier if I could take a score of my own men."

"Done!" The queen smiled widely, showing her small, white teeth. She moved over to a low table where a flagon of wine was waiting with two glasses. Had she been that sure of him? She saw Maybor comprehend the significance of the two glasses. "You cannot blame a woman for hoping," she said by way of an explanation as she poured the wine.

She handed him a glass and took the other for herself.

"To Bren," she said, raising the glass. "May it prove to be a most advantageous partner."

"To Bren," echoed Maybor.

Jack had not slept well since the incident at the hunting lodge, but over the past two nights things had gotten worse. He had been plagued by unsettling nightmares. They were unusually vivid. He had dreams of one man stabbing another in the moonlight. Even now, in daylight, with a pale sun glimmering, he shuddered to think of the images.

They had been on the eastern road for many days. Jack was beginning to think that their pursuers had given up on them, for they had seen no signs of them in the past days and the only people that traveled the road were farmers, tinkers, and tradesmen. The road itself was now in better condition, packed snow lay firmly atop the mud, and Jack and Melli had taken to walking it now that the threat of pursuit had lessened. They still dived into the nearest ditch or bush whenever they heard a rider approaching, though.

Jack decided that the snow was probably making them harder to track—their footsteps were covered over and if the men were using dogs it would be difficult for them to follow a scent buried beneath deep snow.

Unfortunately the snow was making it increasingly difficult for them to find places to spend the night. They risked frostbite and exposure by sleeping on the ground under such conditions. Last night they'd sneaked into a dairy farmer's barn and slept amongst the cows and hay. Melli had awakened early and found the farmer's store of winter cheeses. The large, red wheels had looked incredibly tempting to them. Jack had not wanted to take any, but Melli had insisted, telling him that she was already a convicted horse thief and one round of cheese would make little difference. He could find no argument with that and consequently his pack was now heavier than it had been in some time.

Yesterday they had passed close to a small village. They saw the turn-off and then later the smoke above the treetops. Jack had considered slipping into the town to buy some badly needed food, but Melli had pleaded with him no to go. She was afraid, but Jack suspected it wasn't for herself, but for him. He could understand why: she didn't want to risk another incident. What happened to the mercenaries had shocked Melli badly. Every now and then Jack would catch her looking at him, and there was wariness on her face.

What must she think of him? Was she scared of him? He doubted that. Melli was not the type of girl to be afraid of a mere baker's boy. But he was more than that now; she knew it, and ever since the mercenaries' attack, she'd treated him differently. Almost with respect.

The kind of respect he'd seen hunters use on trapped bears. Jack smiled. Is that what his powers had made of him—a dangerous animal? Still, he had to admit, it was rather nice to have Melli treat him with more regard. In fact, things weren't really that bad: he was off on an adventure to find a new life, perhaps learning something about his mother on the way, he was free from Master Frallit's temper tantrums, and there was a beautiful girl at his side.

Jack laughed out loud: he sounded just like a hero from one of Baralis' books. Some men might even consider him lucky.

Melli came running back at the sound of his laughter. She'd been fetching water from a stream. "What's the matter?"

"I'll be the only hero who knows how to roll shortening." Melli appeared so worried that he might have lost his mind, he forced himself to stop laughing. "I'm all right. I was just considering how lucky I was."

Melli gave him a withering look. "Next time you're considering yourself lucky, I'd appreciate it if you didn't do it so loudly. You made me spill the water." She peered into the flask, and smiling sweetly at him, she said, "At least it was only your portion that was lost."

Brushing the snow from a fallen log, Melli sat down. "How far before we're in Halcus territory?" she asked, munching on a wedge of cheese.

"The River Nestor is still about two days' walk, I think." Jack had little idea himself, but he was determined not to let Melli know that. "Once we cross that we'll have to watch out."

"We're southeast of Harvell, aren't we?" Jack nodded. "Well, last I heard most of the fighting was in the northeast."

"Your father has lands around here?" Everybody at court knew of Maybor's extensive land holdings.

"It wouldn't surprise me, Jack, if we're walking through his lands as we speak. Most people only think my father owns the land next to the river, and he did at one time, but he's been secretly buying up land in the east for years now. Not just apple orchards, either—forest, meadow, fields." Melli waved her arms expansively. Jack noted a touch of pride in her voice.

"Your father's a very rich man."

"The richest," she stated simply.

"Do you regret leaving Harvell behind? You've lost so much. It's different for me—I never had anything to start with."

Melli sighed deeply. "I don't know, Jack. I had much, if you mean fine gowns and fancy food; I had little, if you mean freedom. I couldn't even walk in the garden unchaperoned." She gave him a bittersweet smile. He decided it was time to ask her a question that had been on his mind for some time.

"Who were you to be wed to?" He watched as Melli considered whether or not to answer the question.

Finally after some time she said in a low voice, "Prince Kylock." She looked down, drawing circles in the snow with her fingers. "That's why Baralis wanted to capture me."

"To force you to marry him?"

"No." Melli shook her head and laughed. "To *prevent* me from marrying him." She saw Jack's confusion and explained further. "Baralis hates my father. He would do anything to stop him from getting nearer to the throne."

"You could have been queen." Jack could hardly believe it. The dark-haired girl sitting next to him on the snowladen log looked anything but royal.

"Well, I won't be now." Her voice was matter-of-fact. "And I can't say that I'm sorry. Kylock was not my idea of an ideal husband. Oh, he is handsome and clever and good with a sword, and doubtless some woman will find him irresistible. I always thought he was lacking in something." She thought for a moment. "Something basic like kindness or h

manity. He was always perfectly polite but I felt as if . . ."
She shook her head, unable to find the right words.

"I think I know what you mean."

Melli looked up surprised. "You saw him around the castle?"

"Yes, sometimes he visited Baralis' chambers."

"Baralis friends with Kylock. That's hard to believe."
Melli's hand stole to her face. "Or is it? There's something very similar about those two."

Jack considered what she said for a moment. "You're right. They're both . . ." He struggled to find the right word. ". . . Secretive."

"I wouldn't know about that. I was thinking more of their appearances. Both tall and dark." She shrugged. "So, what business did Kylock have in Baralis' chambers?"

"He was interested in Baralis' animals." Jack put his head down. He knew Melli wanted to hear more, but he wasn't sure if he should go on. Sometimes he would arrive early for scribing and catch Kylock and Baralis together. The things he'd seen Kylock doing to Baralis' creatures were sickening. Kylock liked to discover just how much he could torture an animal before it finally died on him. He would delicately stab a dove countless times, or slowly crush a mouse in the palm of his hand. Jack shuddered. The most disturbing thing of all was that Baralis just looked on, nodding his head like an indulgent father.

It was good to be free of the castle.

Melli, almost as if she guessed at the nature of Kylock's action, said: "So you don't blame me for running away?" She seemed to be looking for reassurance.

"No." He placed his hand on her arm. "I would have done the same thing in your place."

Melli smiled gently and stood up. "It's time we were on our way. I'm just going to fill the skin up with water." She dashed off into the trees, a small figure in a dark cloak.

Jack collected his pack together and swung it over his shoulder. Pain shot through his body. He had forgotten about his injury. He sat down for a minute to recover himself, glad that Melli was gone—he didn't want her knowing how bad it still was. Her own wounds had healed quickly and she assumed that his had done the same. Jack's wound was more serious: the arrow had lodged deep within his muscle, grazing the bone. He tentatively felt his shoulder. At least there was no blood—the old woman had done a good job with the needle. He stood up once more and held his pack on his other side.

He made his way along the eastern road, wondering what lay ahead. Danger for one thing: the Halcus would kill them if they realized they were from the Four Kingdoms. They'd have to keep their mouths closed; the accent of the Halcus was entirely different from their own and to speak would be to give themselves away. There was even greater danger for Melli if they found out who she was—Lord Maybor was a hated figure amongst the Halcus, and they would take cruel delight in torturing his daughter and then ransoming what remained of her.

Even if they made it through Halcus, there was no guarantee they would get as far as Bren. Jack had little idea of what lay beyond the River Nestor; he only knew Bren was an impossibly long distance away, especially for two people on foot in winter. Then there were the mountains, the Great Divide—they ran the length of the Known Lands. He had heard that they were not as steep around Bren and there were many passes, but everyone knew passes were treacherous in winter.

Melli came bounding out from the trees, her waterskin full. Jack suddenly remembered she was not going as far as Bren—her journey ended at Annis. He would be crossing the mountains alone. She came and linked his arm, and they walked eastward together.

Nabber woke up feeling much better. He could tell by the light stealing in from under the shutters that the morning was well gone. He sat up and found his head felt clearer than it had in days—the wiseman's medicine had worked its cure. Nabber liked Bevlin. He liked his house and all the interesting things in his kitchen—he hadn't liked the greased duck much, but he supposed that a man with as few teeth as Bevlin needed food that would slide down without much chewing.

Nabber considered it was the best thing he'd ever done, linking up with Tawl. He was getting to see the world, go adventuring, meet strange people, and make a handsome profit on the side. He felt a little guilty about keeping some of his stash back from Tawl, but what was a boy to do? Who could tell when he might have need?

A good friend of his named Swift, the same one who had introduced him to the lucrative world of pocketing, had taught him a word once: *contingency*. "It means," he had explained, "keeping a little back just for yourself." Swift himself held a healthy contingency back from his gaffer, not to mention his wife and family. Nabber had immediately embraced the idea of contingency and always made a point of having one. Since being with Tawl his contingency had grown considerably and had now become rather difficult to conceal.

Nabber got out of bed and dressed. He was worried about Tawl. His friend had been acting strangely ever since the drunk in the tavern had accosted him. He was short-tempered and moody. Nabber hoped that the wiseman might be able to help him; Tawl had certainly been eager to see him.

He looked at the cold water in the wash bowl and decided against it. Being clean was not a priority with him. He did, however, make an effort to comb his hair. Swift had told him that being a guest carried certain responsibilities, one of which was to look reasonably neat for your host, "else you won't get invited back." Nabber wanted to make sure Bevlin invited *him* back.

As soon as he was ready he burst in on the kitchen, eager for some hot food and company. He knew something was wrong the second he entered: the fire was out and the room was bone cold. He heard a noise—the sound of floorboards creaking—and he moved around the huge table. Tawl was there, covered in blood, crouched down holding Bevlin his arms, rocking him back and forth like a baby. The wiseman was dead.

Nabber had lived in the worst part of Rorn amidst cutthroats and murderers. He had seen prostitutes with their wrists cut, swindlers with knives in their belly—he was no stranger to blood.

He knew the first thing he had to do was get Tawl away from the body and get something hot inside him. Nabber went and knelt beside Tawl. He put his arm around his shoulders. "Come on, Tawl," he said gently. "Time to get up." Tawl looked up at him and Nabber saw no recognition in his face. The boy tried to pull Bevlin's body away from Tawl. The knight fought it at first, trying to keep hold of the dead man, but Nabber's words seemed to soothe him. "Come on, Tawl, time to let go, time to let Bevlin go." Tawl released his hold on the wiseman and Nabber laid the old man on the floor.

He gripped Tawl's arm and urged him to stand up, all the time gently coaxing. He looked around for somewhere to sit Tawl. The bench wouldn't do—it was covered in blood. He led him to a chair by the fire and made him sit. His body was blue with cold and Nabber wondered how long he had been crouching there in the kitchen. He ran into the bedroom and pulled out a heavy woolen blanket and covered Tawl with it. The knight looked tired and dazed and seemed willing to stay put.

Nabber built a hasty fire and put several pots to boil. Tawl needed something hot to drink. He decided he would deal with Bevlin's body later—the dead benefited little from haste. He tried not to wonder what had happened. He had learned early on in life not to ask too many questions, but he could not help noticing the thickness of blood around Bevlin's chest—the man had been stabbed in the heart.

He searched the wiseman's larder for suitable fare; he found eggs, milk, butter, and ducks. A waterskin caught his eye—the lacus. It had cured him; it probably wouldn't do Tawl any harm. He poured a measure of the pale, milky substance into a pot and warmed it a little before giving it to Tawl. The knight took the offered bowl and held it close to his face, breathing in the pungent vapors. After a while he brought the bowl to his lips and drank. Nabber heaved a sigh of relief and put more logs on the fire.

He was feeling rather hungry himself, but he didn't think it was very respectful to eat with a dead man in the room, and he was sure Swift wouldn't approve. So Nabber bided his time, cleaning the blood from bench and floor and keeping an eye on Tawl. He scrubbed away, trying not to look at Bevlin, but the face of the old man seemed to draw his eye. It was not an upsetting sight. The wiseman looked as if he was in a deep sleep, a little pale perhaps, but at peace.

Blood, Nabber considered, was not an easy thing to clean off. He tried his best, but it just seemed to make everything worse, causing ugly red smears over the floor. He looked at his hands and they were covered in bloody water; he felt a tension in his throat and found he had to stop. He stood up and glanced over to Tawl. The knight was sitting motionless with his eyes closed.

Nabber knew he was getting upset, but fought it, Swift would be ashamed of him—stoicism was highly valued amongst 'pockets. He clamped his lips together tightly and moved away from the body, talking himself round. "Come on now, Nabber," he murmured. "You're no baby, seen worse than this in your time."

He had to get the blood from his hands. It was the sight of *them*, he decided, that was upsetting him. He needed some fresh water to wash them in. He'd just slip back into his bedroom for a minute, where there was clean water and a cloth. He looked over to Tawl, checking that the knight would be all right for a few minutes. He seemed to be asleep. Satisfied that he wouldn't be missed, Nabber went into the bedroom, shutting the door after him.

Once there Nabber gave in to the tension. He sat on the bed and his body shook; he told himself the room was cold, that was all. Tears welled in his eyes and he quickly brushed them away: Swift would laugh at him. Willing himself to remain calm, he went over to the wash bowl and splashed cold water on his face. What had been so undesirable only an hour before, he now welcomed readily. The sting of cold revived his spirits. He scrubbed mercilessly at his hands, removing the last traces of blood.

By the time Nabber had dried himself off he was feeling much better. Composed and ready to return to the kitchen, he straightened his clothes and went into the next room.

Tawl had gone. The chair was empty. The door was open. Nabber cursed himself; he should never have left him. He went over to the window. Tawl's horse, which had been tethered to the gate, was gone. Nabber dashed out of the house and into the garden. In the distance, heading to the west, he spied Tawl. The knight was riding fast and furious and was soon out of sight.

Nabber stood for a while, watching the horizon over which Tawl disappeared. Clouds passed over the sun and it grew dark and chill. Reluctantly, he returned to the cottage.

He checked in Tawl's room and was relieved to see his pack had gone; the knight would at least have food and blankets.

Nabber made himself something to eat: a little porridge and some duck. He took it into the bedroom so he could eat without looking at Bevlin's body. He thought about what to do next. He could return to Rorn—Swift would take him back as a 'pocket, no questions asked; the prospecting in Ness had been fruitful—he could set up on his own there; he could even sit out the winter here in the wiseman's cottage— there was plenty of food.

Nothing seemed as appealing as it should. He was in a good position, his contingency had never been bigger, he could go where he pleased and do what he wanted. Nabber knew what he wanted to do and knew it was foolish to consider it. He wanted to go after Tawl, to find his friend and travel with him once more. *It's madness,* he told himself. He didn't know the country, it was the middle of winter, and he didn't know where Tawl was headed and couldn't even be sure the knight would welcome him if he found him.

Tawl was his friend, though. They had adventured together. He had saved the knight's life once; it might need saving again. He would do it. He would follow Tawl west. When Bevlin had given him the lacus, Nabber had asked what cities lay nearest to his cottage. The wiseman had said Lairston was to the north, Ness to the east, and Bren to the west. Bren, that would be where Tawl was headed.

He would head west, then, following Tawl's trail. Nabber had heard tell that Bren was a rich city, there was bound to be good prospecting there. First though, he had to sort out things here. He would have to bury Bevlin—Swift would have thought it fitting to do so. He would also tidy and s

cure the cottage. He would head for Bren in the morning—
there was much to do this day.

Tavalisk was eating gruel. His stomach complaint was
getting no better and the only food he could keep down was
thin porridge. The physicians had come that morning. How
he hated them with their proddings and whisperings and
damn-fool remedies. They had told him he had malevolent
humors in his stomach and suggested that they put a poultice
of hot mustard seed on his belly to draw them out. When he
had refused the poultice, they suggested bloodletting followed by a medicinal enema. Were they trying to kill him?

He had thrown them out and would heal himself. His
latest cook from the far south had ways with herbs and had
sprinkled some atop his gruel. It would not be long before he
was feeling better. The archbishop had of course suspected
poison, a man in his position could expect such things, but
Tavalisk made a point of making his various aides eat whatever he was having and they were all fine. Maybe it was all
the spicy food he had been eating lately—he would have to
change his diet.

Tavalisk heard a loud knock. Ever since he had reprimanded his aide, Gamil had taken to knocking with ostenta-
ious vigor. "Come."

"Your Eminence is feeling a little better, I trust?"

"Just a little, Gamil, no thanks to the physicians."
Tavalisk finished his gruel. "I would have you spread a little
rumor, Gamil."

"What rumor, Your Eminence?"

"The truth, really. I would have the people of Rorn
now I am ill."

"But Your Eminence is recovering?"

"Yes, but I would have them worry over my condition
for a little longer. People value things more when they think
they are about to lose them." The archbishop noticed
Gamil's expression. "There is nothing like a serious illness
increase one's popularity."

"But Your Eminence is already well loved by the peo-
e."

"Exactly, and I intend to keep it that way. Be sure to let the people know I refused the help of physicians—the common people can't afford their services and therefore resent them. Personally I think that's why the common people live longer than the wealthy; they are allowed to die in their own time and not prematurely physicianed into the grave."

"I will do as Your Eminence wishes."

"See that you do. Now, have you any news for me? What about our knight?"

"It will be some time before our spies are able to report back, Your Eminence. I did hear that while he was in Ness he spent some time with a cloth merchant's daughter."

"Really, Gamil, I thought you were above such tittle tattle. Who the knight beds is of little interest to me."

"The girl and her father were originally from the Four Kingdoms, Your Eminence. I believe he questioned the girl about her former country."

"It seems as if a lot of people are interested in the Four Kingdoms at the moment." Tavalisk poured himself a little sheep's milk and honey. "By the way, Gamil, did you arrange a meeting with the lord from Bren . . . what is his name?"

"Lord Cravin." Gamil seemed reluctant to continue.

"Go on, man," urged the archbishop.

"Well, Your Eminence, I myself approached the illustrious lord on your behalf. I told him who I represented and informed him that Your Eminence requested the pleasure of meeting with him."

"And?"

Gamil fingered the material of his robe. "Well, Lord Cravin saw fit to decline the offer. He said he was far too busy to waste time meeting with churchfolk and told me not to bother him again."

"*Churchfolk!*" exclaimed Tavalisk. "*Churchfolk!* Does the man know who he is dealing with?"

"He was a most arrogant man, Your Eminence."

"He is also a foolish one to decline a meeting with me. I have never been so insulted. Churchfolk!" The archbishop rubbed his chubby hands together in agitation. "I can see that the people of Bren are lacking in both intelligence and good manners."

"It is a well-known fact that all the people in the north are barbarians, Your Eminence," said Gamil soothingly. "And that the people of Bren are the most barbaric of all."

"That I can well believe." Tavalisk sipped his milk and honey and regained his composure, a smile playing at the corner of his mouth. "If they are so barbaric, it will be interesting to see how successfully Baralis can pull off his plans with them. By attempting to wed Kylock to Catherine of Bren he just might have bitten off more than he can chew." Tavalisk was now smiling broadly, showing his little, sharp teeth. The course of Marod's prophecy might not run that smoothly after all. And, if he were right about its meaning, it could be *his* responsibility to prevent it from coming to pass. All this talk of chewing has made me hungry, Gamil. Go and fetch me some real food, something with a bite to it. I am sick of gruel."

Kylock was washing his hands. Using a boar's bristle brush, he cleaned beneath his fingernails. After a while, he held his hands up to the light. They were still not clean enough. He poured more boiling water into the basin and rubbed them once more.

It was the smell that he could never remove. No matter what he did he could never quite rid himself of the stench of the womb. It was on him even now, nearly eighteen years later. Many skins had he shed, every particle renewed a hundred times, but it still remained. The smell of his mother clung to him like a vine to an oak, and it would destroy him if it could.

It worked his mother's purpose, reeking of her adultery, seeking to corrupt. He would not succumb. Catherine would help him. He would bathe in her purity and emerge forever cleansed of the taint of his mother's corruption.

Kylock dried his hands on a soft cloth. The portrait was where his mother had left it. He took it up. Hundreds of leagues it had traveled and it was still fragrant with the smell of innocence. Opening his fist to the light from the candle, he looked upon the likeness of Catherine of Bren. She took his breath away. Perfection. An angel, pure and virginal, untouched by the hand of man or time. Catherine was his, and she alone would save him.

Baralis poured himself a glass of deep red wine. He held it against the firelight better to admire its color and clarity. He was normally a fastidious person not given to excesses of food or drink, and in fact despised people who were, but today he had cause for celebration and would finish off a glass or two. Yesterday the queen had announced to the whole court her plans to betroth her son to the duke of Bren's daughter. There was no going back for her now. She was fully committed to the marriage and his plans were therefore secure. The world turned in his favor and his dreams were one step nearer realization.

He liked not the thought of the long trip to Bren, but it was something that would have to be endured, a mere inconvenience. He wondered with idle curiosity which fool the queen would pick out for Crown's Envoy. Probably some lily-livered nobody who was well under Her Highness' finely manicured thumb. It was of little consequence. Bren was his affair and he would brook no interference from an vacuous nobleman.

There were a few loose ends he would prefer tied up before he departed from Bren, but it did not appear he would be able to do so in the time left. His latest mercenaries had proved useless. They had returned today saying they had seen no sign of the girl and boy. It was true that Melliand was no longer in the running as Kylock's bride, but it would cause an uncomfortable scandal if she returned to court telling the story of how she had been held captive by the king's chancellor. He could not afford to risk such accusations and the girl must be permanently prevented from making them.

As for the boy, he too must be found and killed. The incident at the hunting lodge had proven just how dangerous he could be. He wanted him out of the way. Jack represented uncertainty . . . he was a dark horse, a spoiler. Whenever

Baralis thought of him he was filled with apprehension. The baker's boy was trouble.

He sipped on his wine, considering what he would need to take with him to Bren. He heard heavy footsteps and then Crope loomed above him. As always the fool was carrying his painted box. "I told you I was not to be disturbed."

"Lord Maybor is asking to see you."

"Maybor, what does he want?" Baralis had no desire to see *him*. He had too vivid a recollection of what happened last time; the maniac had drawn a sword.

"He says he wants to talk to you, says he's unarmed."

"What is his demeanor?" What could Maybor want? Baralis wondered. Had he come to vent his rage over losing out on the betrothal?

"He seems happy, smiling he is."

"Let him come in." The man was probably drunk. If he tried to draw a sword this time, he would find things turned out a little differently than when they'd last met. Crope went off and a minute later Maybor stepped into the room.

"Ah, Lord Baralis. I'm so pleased you agreed to see me this late hour, but then, as I'm sure you'll appreciate, we have much to plan." Maybor smiled broadly.

"We have nothing to plan that I am aware of, Maybor."

"Oh, but we have, Baralis. We have our trip to Bren to plan." Maybor helped himself to a glass of wine. "I trust this won't be poisoned?" he said pleasantly.

"You are not going to Bren." Baralis' voice was soothing. "You are obviously drunk."

"Well, I do admit to having a few mugs of ale, but I can assure you, Baralis, I am far from drunk." He gulped down the wine with little finesse. "I will, of course, be taking some of my own men to Bren. I don't feel five score is enough, do you? The queen agrees with me."

"The queen?" Baralis was beginning to feel nervous.

"Yes, Her Highness said I could bring a further score of my own. While I was with her she showed me the portrait of Catherine. A lovely girl, I can't wait to meet her in person. Of course, as Crown's Envoy I suppose I will have the honor of meeting her before you do. After all, Crown takes precedence over Prince, does it not?"

"The queen has appointed you Crown's Envoy?"

"Yes, didn't you know?" said Maybor slyly. "Here, let me fill your cup." He refilled both glasses. "May I propose a toast?" He didn't wait for an answer. "To Bren, a city that holds great promise for the future." He drained his glass and stood up. "You look a little pale, Baralis. We'll plan our journey another day."